READER'S DIGEST
CONDENSED BOOKS

www.readersdigest.co.uk

The Reader's Digest Association
Limited 11 Westferry Circus
Canary Wharf London E14 4HE

For information as to ownership of
copyright in the material of this
book, and acknowledgments, see
last page.

Printed in France
ISBN 0 276 42674-6

READER'S DIGEST
CONDENSED BOOKS

*Selected and edited
by Reader's Digest*

CONDENSED BOOKS DIVISION

THE READER'S DIGEST ASSOCIATION LIMITED, LONDON

CONTENTS

Den Donovan, the Metropolitan Police's most wanted criminal, is about to pull off a multi-million-pound drugs deal when his personal life goes haywire. His wife goes missing, his young son's fed up with him, and he's being chased by Colombian drug dealers who think he's double-crossed them. With the Met on his tail as well, Den is fighting a losing corner. Can there be any way out for London's number one hard man?

PUBLISHED BY HODDER & STOUGHTON

Sailing the oceans of the world as a rich man's personal trainer seemed to Jim Leighton like the opportunity of a lifetime. But in mid-voyage he and his employer, Will Spark, are attacked by the crew of another boat and the whole enterprise begins to look decidedly sinister. Who is chasing Will and what do they want? And why is the old man so secretive? Superb high-seas adventure and suspense that grips to the last page.

PUBLISHED BY WILLIAM MORROW, USA

JULIE AND ROMEO page 295
Jeanne Ray

For as long as anyone can remember, there's been a bitter feud between the Cacciamani and Roseman families—though no one can fathom why. It's only when widowed florist Romeo Cacciamani meets divorcée Julie Roseman, and romance blossoms, that both families are forced to confront their long-held prejudices. A delightfully funny and perceptive story which proves that heady passion is not something solely for the young.

PUBLISHED BY SIMON & SCHUSTER

DEAD SLEEP page 397
Greg Iles

More than a year after her twin sister Jane's disappearance, photojournalist Jordan Glass has almost given up hope of ever seeing her again. Then, amazingly, in a Hong Kong art gallery, she stumbles across a painting of Jane depicted as asleep—or dead. The artist is unknown, but that doesn't stop Jordan. Assisted by FBI agent John Kaiser, she travels to New York, Grand Cayman, and finally to New Orleans to discover her sister's fate.

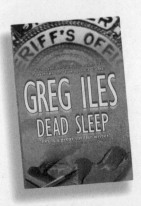

PUBLISHED BY HODDER & STOUGHTON

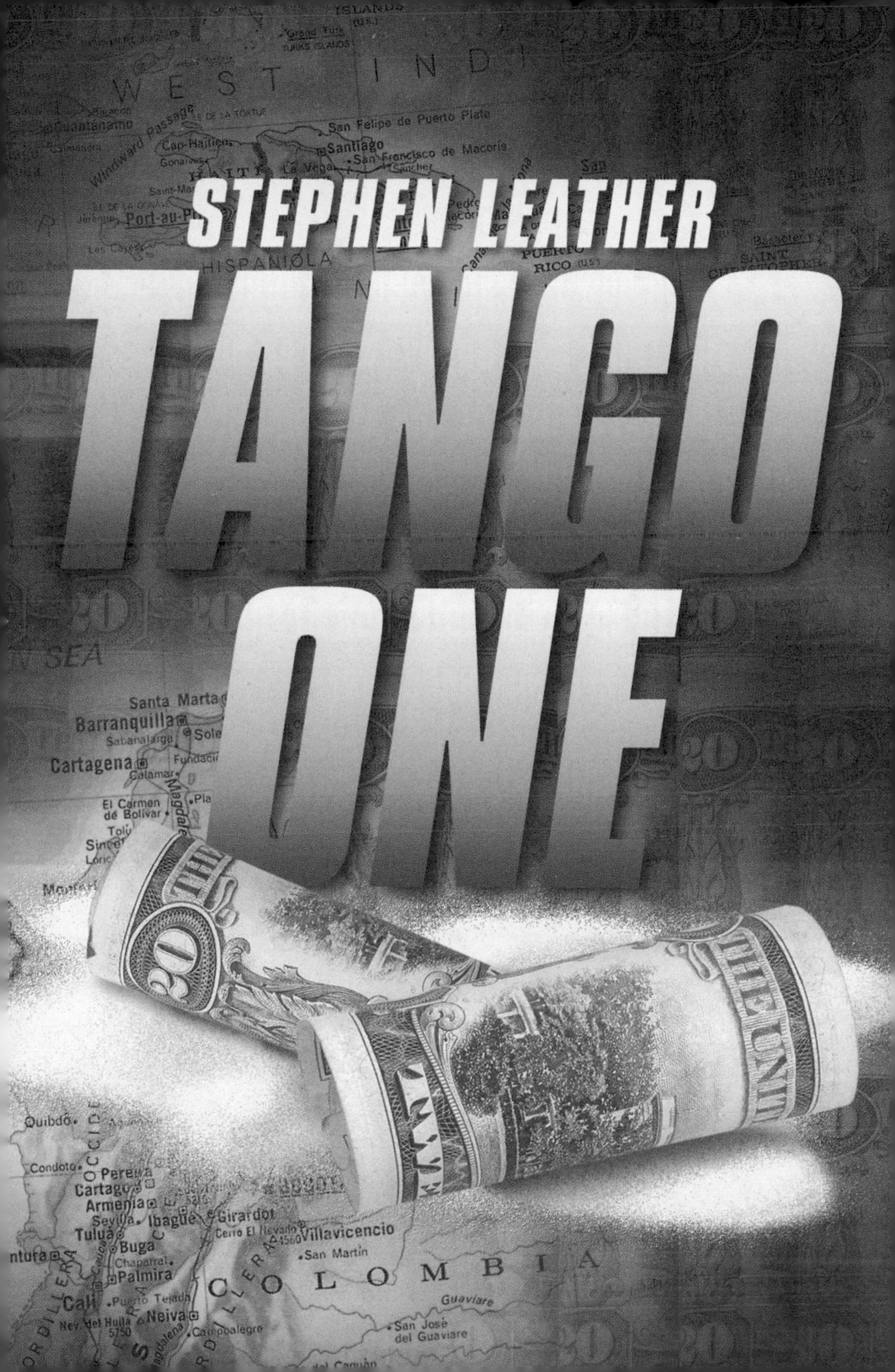
STEPHEN LEATHER
TANGO
ONE

When new recruits Jamie Fullerton, Tina Leigh and 'Bunny' Warren begin their training for the Metropolitan Police, they find they've been chosen to join a very special team, dedicated to covert penetration of the criminal underworld.

And the unit's first mission? To catch the elusive and cunning Den Donovan——Tango One, as the Met call their most wanted target.

The man had been tied to the chair for so long that he'd lost all feeling in his hands and feet. His captors had used strips of insulation tape to bind him to the wooden chair and slapped another piece across his mouth, even though he was in a basement and there was no one within earshot who'd care whether he lived or died.

The three men who'd brought him hadn't said a word as they'd dragged him out of the back of the Mercedes and across the flagstones into the pink-walled villa.

He looked round the room where he was being kept prisoner. No windows. A door that had been bolted when the three men left. Bare stone walls. A concrete floor. A fluorescent strip light above his head. One wall had been shelved with slabs of rough local timber and there was a scattering of tinned goods at head level—Heinz baked beans, Batchelor's peas, bottles of HP sauce and boxes of Kellogg's cornflakes and PG Tips. The cravings of an Englishman abroad.

In front of the man was a digital video camera on a tripod, its lens staring at him. He racked his brains, trying to think where he'd gone wrong. Had someone recognised him? Had he said something to give himself away, some stupid slip which they'd picked up on?

He knew two of the men who'd brought him down to the basement. One was Scottish, the other Brazilian. He'd known them for almost two years. He'd drunk with them, whored with them, on occasion almost felt they were friends. But when they'd picked him up on the pavement outside the hotel, their eyes had been hard and he'd known even before they'd grabbed him that he was in trouble.

The third man, the one who'd driven, was a stranger. But like the other two he hadn't said a word during the drive to the villa.

Initially the man had tried to bluff it out, to make a joke of it, then he'd faked anger, saying they had no right to treat him that way, then he'd threatened them. They'd said nothing. The Scotsman had jabbed the barrel of an automatic into the man's ribs and kept his finger on the trigger. Eventually the man had fallen silent.

He heard footsteps on the steps that led down to the basement, and the door opened. He recognised the man who stood in the door-way. He was a shade over six foot tall with chestnut-brown hair that was unfashionably long, pale green eyes and a sprinkling of freckles over a nose that had been broken at least twice. Dennis Donovan.

'Don't get up, Andy,' said Donovan, and laughed harshly.

The Brazilian appeared at Donovan's shoulder, and the two of them walked in and closed the door. Donovan was wearing a red short-sleeved polo shirt and khaki chinos and in his hand was a sharp kitchen knife. The Brazilian was holding a large plastic bag.

The man said nothing. There was nothing he could say. Donovan had used his real name, which meant that he knew everything.

'You've been a naughty boy, Andy,' said Donovan. 'A very naughty boy.' From the back pocket of his chinos he took a black ski mask and slipped it on his head.

He bent over the video camera, pressed a button, then nodded at the Brazilian, who had also put on a ski mask. Donovan tossed the knife to him in a gentle arc and the Brazilian caught it deftly.

The Brazilian advanced towards the man in the chair and went to work with the knife.

PETER LATHAM stabbed at the lift button, shrugged his shoulders inside his grey suit jacket and adjusted his blue and yellow striped tie. It had been a long time since Latham had worn plain clothes during the day and he was surprised at how much he missed his uniform.

The lift doors opened and Latham stepped inside. He pressed the button for the fifth floor. The hotel was in an area of London that Latham rarely frequented, just east of the City, and he'd travelled by black cab instead of using his regular driver. Strictly speaking, as an assistant commissioner with the Metropolitan Police, Latham was higher in rank than the man he was coming to see, but the man was an old friend and the manner and urgency of the request for the meeting was such that Latham was prepared to put rank aside.

The room was at the end of a long corridor. Latham knocked and the door was opened by a man in his early fifties, a few inches shorter than Latham's six foot and several stones heavier.

'Peter, thanks for coming,' said the man, offering his hand.

Latham shook it. 'We're getting a bit old for cloak and dagger, aren't we, Ray?' he said.

Raymond Mackie pulled an apologetic face and stepped aside to allow Latham into the room. Two single beds, a dressing table and wardrobe, and a small table with two armchairs, and a sofa. There was a bottle of whisky and two glasses on the table and Mackie waddled over to it, poured two large measures and handed one to Latham. They clinked glasses and drank. Mackie's official title was Head of Drugs Operations.

A combined TV and video recorder stood on the dressing table. Mackie picked up a video cassette. 'This arrived at Custom House yesterday,' he said.

'I hope you haven't brought me all this way to watch a blue movie,' said Latham, dropping into one of the armchairs.

'I warn you, it's not pretty,' said Mackie, slotting the cassette into the recorder and pressing the PLAY button. He shuffled over to the sofa and eased himself onto it, then took a long slug of whisky as the screen flickered to life.

It was several seconds before Latham realised that what he was seeing was the brutal torture of a fellow human being. 'Sweet Jesus,' he whispered.

'Andy Middleton,' said Mackie. 'One of our undercover agents. He went missing on Anguilla two weeks ago. This came via Miami. Middleton was trying to get close to Dennis Donovan. Donovan's been active in the Caribbean for the past six months, meeting with Colombians and a Dutch shipper.'

A second masked figure stepped into the frame holding a plastic bag. He stood for a second or two looking directly at the camera.

'We think this is Donovan,' said Mackie. 'Same build. There's no way of knowing for sure, though.'

The man walked behind Middleton and pulled the plastic bag over his head, twisting it round his neck. The undercover Customs agent shuddered in the chair. It was a minute before his head slumped down against his chest but the man behind him kept the bag tight round his neck for a further minute to make sure he was dead.

The recording ended and Mackie switched off the television. 'Middleton is the third agent we've lost in the Caribbean. Like

Middleton, the first two were hoping to bring Donovan down.'

'Were they killed on tape?' asked Latham.

Mackie shook his head.

'So why this time? What was special about Middleton?'

'It's a warning,' said Mackie. 'He's telling us what he'll do to anyone we send against him. I guess we've become a thorn in his side and this is his way of saying enough is enough.'

'And is it? From your perspective?'

Mackie looked at the assistant commissioner with unblinking grey eyes. 'I knew all three of them, Peter. I worked with Andy way back when. Checking cars at Dover, believe it or not. I'm not going to send any more men into the lion's den.'

'So he's won?'

'Not exactly.' Mackie fell silent and stared at a painting of a vase of flowers above one of the beds.

'Spit it out, Ray,' said Latham eventually.

'The problem is, no matter how good our agents are, and Andy Middleton was one of the best, an operator like Donovan can still spot them. No matter how good they are they're still playing a role.'

Latham nodded but didn't say anything.

'We put our guys through the most intense training imaginable, same as you do with your SO10 people. We teach them surveillance and countersurveillance, how to act, how to think like a criminal. And up against low-level operators they pass muster. But it probably isn't good enough for a man like Donovan. He treats all strangers with suspicion. And he has an instinct for undercover agents. Apart from the three who've died, I've had half a dozen bail out of their own accord, convinced that Donovan was on to them.'

'I get the picture, Ray. But what do you want from me? From the Met?'

Mackie took a deep breath and turned to look at the assistant commissioner. 'Virgins,' he said, quietly. 'We need virgins.'

JAMIE FULLERTON pounded along the pavement on the last leg of his two-mile run. He was barely sweating and knew he had the stamina to run for at least another hour, but he had nothing to prove. If it had been the weekend he might have pushed himself harder, but it was Monday, the start of a new week. The start of a new life. He looked left and right and dashed across the King's Road, heading for his basement flat.

He increased the pace as he turned into Oakley Street and sprinted the last hundred yards, then went down the metal steps to his front door and let himself in.

He walked through the flat to the bathroom and showered before going into the bedroom with a towel wrapped round his waist. On the back of the bedroom door was a dark blue uniform with silver buttons on a wire hanger. He grinned at the uniform. 'A bloody cop,' he chuckled to himself. 'Who'd've believed it?'

His doorbell rang, and he rushed down the hallway to the front door. He opened it, and was faced with a man wearing a dark blue blazer and grey slacks.

'James Fullerton?' asked the man.

'Yes?' said Fullerton hesitantly.

'There's been a change of venue,' said the man.

'And you are?'

'The man who's been sent to take you to the new venue.'

'Look, I'm supposed to be at Hendon at eight thirty,' said Fullerton. 'The police college.'

'I know what Hendon is, sir,' said the man in the blazer. 'You're to come with me instead.'

'Do you have a letter or something?'

'No,' said the man coldly. 'No letter.'

Fullerton looked at the man. The man returned his look with total impassivity. It was clear that the man wasn't going to divulge any further information. 'Right,' said Fullerton. 'Let me get dressed.'

'The uniform won't be necessary, sir.'

Fullerton stood in the hallway wondering what the hell was going on. His application to join the Metropolitan Police had been accepted three months earlier and the letter telling him when to report to Hendon had arrived shortly afterwards. The sudden change of plan could only be bad news.

CLIFF 'BUNNY' WARREN poured milk over his Shredded Wheat, dumped on two spoonfuls of sugar and carried the bowl over to the Formica table in the corner of his kitchen. He wrapped his dressing gown round himself, propped a textbook against the wall and read as he ate. *Reforming Social Services*. The content of the book was as dry as the cereal straight from the packet, but it was required reading. Warren was already behind in his Open University reading and had a stack of videos still to watch.

The doorbell rang, three sharp blasts. Warren put down his spoon and walked down the hallway. He put the chain on the door before opening it. The part of Harlesden he lived in was home to an assortment of drug addicts and thieves who wouldn't think twice about kicking down a door, beating him senseless and taking what few possessions he had.

A white man in a dark blue blazer smiled through the gap. 'Clifford Warren?'

'Who wants to know?'

'I've a car waiting for you, sir.'

Warren opened the door further. Parked in the street was a brand-new Vauxhall Vectra that was already attracting the attention of two West Indian teenagers.

'Does every new recruit get this treatment?' asked Warren.

'You're a special case, sir,' said the man. 'I've been told to tell you uniform won't be necessary.'

'Am I in some sort of trouble?' asked Warren, concerned.

'Not that I'm aware of, sir. But then they don't tell me much, me being a driver and all.' The man looked at his watch. 'Best not be late, sir.'

Warren nodded. 'OK, OK,' he said and closed the door.

He walked into his bedroom and took off his dressing gown. His police uniform was hanging from the wardrobe door. He stroked the blue serge. Warren had thought long and hard before applying to join the Metropolitan Police. He'd had a few minor convictions when he was a teenager, mainly joy-riding and stealing from cars, and he'd been up-front about his past during the interviews. But a slump in recruitment had forced the Met to drop its requirement that applicants had a trouble-free past. They were especially keen on Warren as he was West Indian, and they were bending over backwards to increase their intake of ethnic minorities. But the man in the blazer standing outside his front door suggested that his entry into the ranks of the Metropolitan Police wasn't going to go as smoothly as he'd hoped.

TINA LEIGH LIT her first cigarette of the morning, inhaled deeply, then spent a good thirty seconds coughing as she walked slowly towards the kitchen, wrapping her robe round her. 'Tomorrow I'm giving up,' she promised herself for the thousandth time.

She switched on the kettle and heaped two spoons of coffee into a white mug. As she took a second pull on her cigarette she frowned at the clock above the refrigerator. 'Eight o'clock?' she muttered. 'How the hell can it be eight o'clock already?' She hurried back into the bedroom and took her blue uniform out of the wardrobe and laid it on the bed. Her hat was hanging on a hook on the back of the door. She picked it up and sat it on her head, then adjusted the angle. Try as she might, it didn't look right and she wondered whether day one at Hendon would involve teaching recruits how to wear the bloody things. The doorbell rang and she jumped.

She rushed to the door of her flat and flung it open. A grey-haired man in his early fifties smiled down at her. He was wearing a dark blue blazer and grey trousers.

'Whatever you're selling, I really don't have the time,' she said. She took a quick pull on her cigarette. 'Or the money.'

'Didn't anyone tell you that smoking in uniform is grounds for dismissal?' said the man in a soft Northumbrian accent.

'What?' said Tina, then realised she was still wearing the police hat. She grabbed it and held it behind her back.

'I'm not a cop yet,' she said. 'A police officer, I mean.' She stabbed the cigarette into an ashtray on the hall table. 'What do you want?'

The man smiled at her. 'Christina Leigh?'

'Yes?' said Tina hesitantly.

'Your chariot awaits.'

'My what?'

'I'm here to drive you, Miss Leigh.'

'To Hendon?'

'To an alternative venue.'

'I'm supposed to report to Hendon at eight thirty.'

'Your itinerary has been changed, Miss Leigh. You won't be needing the uniform, either. Plain clothes.'

'Am I in trouble?' Tina asked, suddenly serious.

The man shrugged. 'They treat me like a mushroom, miss. Keep me in the dark and—'

'I know, I know,' Tina interrupted. 'It's just that I had the course work, I've read all the stuff, and I was up all night polishing shoes. Now you're telling me it's off.'

'Just a change in your itinerary, miss. That's all. If you were in any sort of trouble, I doubt they'd send me.'

Tina nodded slowly. 'OK. Give me a minute.' She closed the door.

The arrival of the grey-haired stranger on her doorstep could only be bad news. The day she'd learned the Metropolitan Police had accepted her as a probationary constable had been one of the happiest in her life. Now she had a horrible feeling that her dreams of a new life were all going to come crashing down around her.

THE DRIVER SAID not one word during the forty-minute drive from Chelsea to the Isle of Dogs. Jamie Fullerton knew there was no point in asking any of the dozen or so questions that were buzzing round his brain. He stared out of the window of the Vectra and tried to calm his thumping heart.

When he saw the towering edifice of Canary Wharf, Fullerton frowned. So far as he knew, none of the Metropolitan Police bureaucracy was based out in the East End.

The Vectra slowed in front of a nondescript glass and steel block, then turned into an underground car park. The driver showed an ID card to a uniformed security guard and the barrier was raised. They parked close to a lift and Fullerton waited for the driver to walk round and open the door for him. It was a silly, pointless victory, but the man's sullen insolence had annoyed Fullerton.

The driver slammed the door shut and walked over to the lift. To the right of the metal door was a keypad and he tapped out a four-digit code. The door rattled open.

'Tenth floor, sir,' said the driver, almost spitting out the honorific. 'You'll be met.' He turned and headed back to the car.

Fullerton walked into the lift and stabbed at the button for the tenth floor. The door clattered shut.

The floor indicator lights flicked slowly to ten. The lift whispered to a halt and the door opened. Fullerton stepped out of the lift and stood in the lobby, looking left and right. At one end of the corridor was a pair of frosted glass doors. Fullerton adjusted the cuffs of his white shirt and shrugged the shoulders of his dark blue silk and wool Lanvin suit, then headed towards the glass doors. He had just raised his right hand to push his way through when a blurry figure on the other side beat him to it and pulled the door open.

Fullerton flinched, but recovered quickly when he saw that the man holding the door open was wearing the uniform and peaked cap of a senior officer of the Metropolitan Police.

'Didn't mean to startle you, Fullerton,' said the man.

'I wasn't startled, sir,' said Fullerton. He recognised the man from his frequent TV appearances. Assistant Commissioner Peter Latham. The articulate face of British policing.

'This way,' said Latham, letting the door swing back. Fullerton caught it and followed the assistant commissioner down a corridor to a teak veneer door with four screw holes where a plaque had been. Latham pushed the door open. The office was the size of a badminton court with floor-to-ceiling windows at one end. The walls were totally bare except for a large clock, though there were brighter patches of clean paint where pictures had once hung and screw holes where things had been removed. The only furniture was a cheap pine desk and two plastic chairs.

Latham sat down on one of the chairs so that his back was to the window. He took off his peaked cap and placed it on the table in front of him, then motioned for Fullerton to sit. Fullerton did so.

'You know who I am, Fullerton?' said the assistant commissioner. Fullerton nodded. 'Sir,' he said.

'No need for introductions then,' said the senior police officer. He tapped the fingers of his right hand on the desktop. 'Tell me why you wanted to join the force, Fullerton.'

Fullerton frowned. His application to join the Metropolitan Police had been accepted after more than twenty hours of interviews, a battery of psychological and physical tests, and a thorough background check. He'd been asked his reasons for wanting to join more than a dozen times and he doubted Latham expected to hear anything new or original. 'It's the career I've always wanted, sir,' he said. 'A chance to do something for the community. To make a difference.'

Latham studied him with unsmiling brown eyes.

'I'm not totally altruistic, obviously,' Fullerton continued, lifting his hands and showing his palms, using the body language of someone who was open and honest, with nothing to hide. 'I don't want an office job, I don't want to sell people life insurance they don't want, or spend my life with a phone stuck to my ear. I want to be out and about, dealing with people, solving problems.'

Latham's fingers continued to drum softly on the desktop. 'How did you feel when you weren't accepted onto the accelerated promotion scheme?'

'A little disappointed. But I figured that if I joined as an ordinary entrant, my talents would soon be realised. It might take me longer to reach the top, but I'll still get there.'

'Those talents being?'

Fullerton leaned forward and looked Latham in the eye, meeting his cold stare. 'The talents that were recognised by the interview board, for one,' he said. 'The talents that got me in the top five per cent of my university year. At Oxford.' He knew that the assistant commissioner had only managed a second-class degree from Leeds.

'What about your other talents,' said Latham quietly. 'Lying. Cheating. Blackmail?'

Fullerton sat back in his chair, stunned. 'What?' he gasped.

'Did you think we wouldn't find out about your drug use, Fullerton? Do you think we're stupid?'

'I don't know what it is you think I've done, sir, but I can assure you someone has been lying to you.'

'Are you denying you are a regular cocaine user?' asked Latham.

'Emphatically,' said Fullerton.

'And that you smoke cannabis?'

'I don't even smoke cigarettes, sir. I gave a urine sample as part of the medical, didn't I? Presumably that was tested for drug use.'

'Indeed it was.'

'And?'

'And the sample you gave was pure as the driven snow.'

'So there you are. That proves something, doesn't it?'

'Are you denying you were caught dealing at university? Caught with three ounces of cannabis resin at an end-of-term concert?'

'If that had been the case, sir, I'd have been sent down.'

'Unless your tutor also happened to be a customer. Unless you threatened to expose him if he didn't get the matter swept under the carpet. Might also explain how you managed to graduate with a first.'

'I got my degree on merit,' said Fullerton quickly. 'There's no proof of any of this. It's all hearsay.'

'Hearsay's all we need,' said Latham. 'This isn't a court, there's no jury to convince.'

'Is that what this is all about? A conviction for possession that wouldn't even merit a caution?'

'Do you think I'd be here if that was all that was involved, Fullerton? Don't you think I'd have better things to do than interview someone who thinks it's clever to get high now and again? I'm not interested in slapping the wrist of a recreational drug user, Fullerton. But I am interested in knowing if you're serious about wanting to be a police officer.'

'Yes, sir. I am.'

Latham nodded slowly. 'Very well. From this moment on I want absolute truth from you. Do you understand?'

Fullerton licked his lips. 'Agreed, sir.'

'Thank you,' said Latham. 'Exactly what drugs do you use?'

'Cocaine, sir. Occasionally. Cannabis. Ecstasy on occasions.'

'Heroin?'

'In the past, sir. Only inhaling. Never injecting.'

'And you switched urine samples?'

'I gave a friend fifty quid for a bottle of his piss.'

'Do you still deal?'

'That depends on your definition of dealing, sir.'

'Selling for profit.'

'I sell to friends, and it'd be stupid to make a loss on the deal, wouldn't it? I mean, you wouldn't expect me to sell at a loss.'

'That would make you a dealer,' said Latham.

'What's this about, sir?' Fullerton asked. 'I assume there's no way I'm going to be allowed to join the force. Not in view of . . . this.'

For the first time, Latham smiled with something approaching warmth. 'Actually, Fullerton, you'd be surprised.'

'DON'T YOU THINK it's going to be tough for you in the Met, being a nigger?' said Assistant Commissioner Latham.

At first Cliff Warren thought he'd misheard. 'I'm not sure I understand the question, sir.'

'The question, Warren, is don't you think that being black is going to hold you back? Haven't you heard? We're institutionally racist?'

Warren frowned. This didn't make any sense. The drive to the Isle of Dogs. The empty office, empty except for a desk and two chairs and a senior police officer who was using racist language that could lose him his job if it were made public.

'I thought the Met wanted to widen its minority base,' he said.

'And you were eager to take up the challenge, were you?'

'I wanted the job, yes.'

Latham studied Warren with unblinking eyes. 'You're not angered by what I've just said?' he said eventually.

'I've heard worse, sir.'

'And you're always so relaxed about it?'

'What makes you think I'm relaxed, sir?'

Latham nodded slowly, accepting Warren's point.

'That was a test, was it, sir?'

'In a way, Warren.'

Warren smiled without warmth. 'Because it wasn't really a fair test. I'm hoping to become an officer in the force in which you're a commander. I'm hardly likely to lose control, am I?'

'I suppose not.'

'See, if you weren't an assistant commissioner . . .' Warren leaned forward, his eyes never leaving Latham's face. 'I'd be kicking your lily-white arse to within an inch of your lily-white life. Sir.' Warren smiled. 'No offence intended.'

Latham smiled back. There was an amused glint in his eyes and

Warren knew he'd passed the test. 'None taken,' said the assistant commissioner. 'How do you feel about your criminal record?'

Warren shrugged. 'I was just an angry teenager out looking for kicks, who didn't know how close he was to ruining his whole life. I was lucky not to be sent down, and if it wasn't for the fact I was assigned one of the few social workers who actually appeared to care about her work, I'd probably be behind bars right now.'

'Suppose you hadn't been turned round by the social worker. Suppose you'd continued along the road you'd started on. Petty crime. Stealing. Where do you think it would have led to?'

Warren shrugged. 'Drugs, I guess. Dealing.'

'And what sort of drug dealer do you think you'd make?'

'Probably quite a good one. Because I've a knowledge of criminal law and police procedure that most villains don't have. And to be quite honest, I consider I'm a hell of a lot smarter than most police officers I've come across . . . I'm not going to Hendon, am I?'

'Not today, no,' said Latham. 'But this isn't about stopping you becoming a police officer, Warren, I can promise you that. You scored highly on all counts during the selection procedure; you're exactly the sort of material we want. The question is, how would you be able to serve us best?'

Warren frowned, but didn't say anything.

'You see, Warren, putting you in a uniform and having you walk a beat might make for good public relations, but it's going to make precious little difference to the crime figures. We'd like you to consider becoming an undercover agent for us. Deep undercover.'

'You're asking me to pretend to be a criminal?'

'No, I'm asking you to become a criminal. To cross the line.'

'For how long?'

'For as long as you can take it. Hopefully years.'

'If I'm not going to Hendon, how would I be trained?'

'You wouldn't,' said Latham. 'At present undercover operatives are drawn from the ranks. We spend years training them to be policemen, then we send them undercover. It doesn't work. No matter how long they grow their hair or how they try to blend, they're still policemen acting as criminals. We don't want you to put on an act, Warren. We want you to become a criminal. You already have the perfect cover—a criminal record. We want you to build on that.'

'I can break the law? Is that what you're saying?'

For the first time, Latham looked uncomfortable. 'That's not a conversation we should be having,' he said. 'That'll come later with your handler. I'm here to ask you to take on this assignment.'

'And if I refuse?'

'As I've said, you'll be an asset to the force. You can start at Hendon tomorrow. I'm sure you'll have an exemplary career, but what I'm offering you is a chance to make a real difference.'

'YOU SHOULDN'T HAVE LIED, Tina. Did you seriously believe we wouldn't find out?' said Assistant Commissioner Latham.

'It was a long time ago,' said Tina, looking over the senior policeman's shoulder at the tower block opposite. 'A lifetime ago.'

'And you didn't think that your criminal record would stop you becoming a police officer?'

'I don't have a criminal record,' Tina spat. 'I was cautioned for soliciting. Under a different name. I wasn't even charged.'

'You were a prostitute for more than a year, Tina,' said Latham. 'You were known to Vice. You were known on the streets.'

'I did what I did to survive. I did what I had to do.'

'I understand that.'

'Do you?' said Tina. 'I doubt it. Do you know what it's like to have to fend for yourself when you're still a kid? To have to leave home because your stepfather spends his time trying to get into your knickers and your mum's so drunk she can't stop him. Do you know what it's like to arrive in London with nowhere to stay and a couple of quid in your pocket? I don't bloody think so.'

'Your past precludes you from joining the Metropolitan Police as a normal entrant,' Latham said. 'Suppose you had to arrest someone who knew you from your previous life? Suppose your past became public knowledge? Every case you'd ever worked on would be compromised. It wouldn't matter how good a police officer you were. All that would matter is that you used to be a prostitute. It would also leave you open to blackmail.'

'I know,' sighed Tina. 'I just hoped it would remain a secret.'

Latham smiled thinly. 'Why did you apply to join the police, Tina? Why not the army? The civil service? Nursing?'

'Because I want to help people.'

'So why didn't you become a social worker?'

'I want to make a difference. I want to help put away the bastards who break the rules. Who think it's OK to molest kids or steal from old ladies. Why all these questions? You've already said that I can't join the police.'

'That's not what I said,' said Latham. 'I said you couldn't join as a

21

uniformed constable. But there are other opportunities available to you within the force.'

Tina frowned and tilted her head on one side.

Latham continued. 'It's been obvious for some time that our under-cover operations are being compromised. The reason is simple—villains, the good ones, can always spot a police officer, no matter how good their cover. Police officers all undergo the same training, and have much the same experiences on the job. It's that shared experience that binds them together, but it also gives them a standard way of behaving, common mannerisms. They become a type.'

Tina nodded. 'We could always spot Vice on the streets,' she said. 'Stuck out like sore thumbs.'

'Exactly. So what we want to do is to set up a unit of police officers who haven't been through the standard Hendon training. We need a special sort of undercover officer—people who have enough strength of character to work virtually alone, enough life experience to cope with whatever gets thrown at them. And with a background that isn't manufactured, that will stand up to any scrutiny.'

'Like a former prostitute?'

'While your background precludes you from serving as a regular officer, it's perfect for an undercover operative,' said Latham. 'The very same contacts that would damage you as a regular officer will be a major advantage in your role undercover.'

'Because no one would ever believe that the Met would hire a former prostitute?'

Latham nodded.

Tina groped for her handbag on the floor and fumbled for her packet of cigarettes. She toyed with it and took a deep breath. 'OK,' she said. 'I'm in.'

Latham beamed. 'Good. That's very good, Tina.'

'What happens now?' she asked.

'You go home. Someone will be in touch.'

ASSISTANT COMMISSIONER LATHAM paced up and down in front of the window. 'I'm still not convinced that we're doing the right thing here,' he said.

Gregg Hathaway unhooked the clock from the wall and placed it on the table. 'Morally, you mean?' Hathaway was wearing a dark brown leather jacket, blue jeans and scuffed brown Timberland boots. He had a slight limp, favouring his left leg when he walked.

'I was referring to their training and handling,' Latham said.

Hathaway shrugged. 'It's not my place to query operational decisions,' he said. 'I leave that up to my masters.' He was a short man, thought Latham, well below the Met's height requirements. The intelligence services clearly had different criteria when it came to recruiting and there was no doubting Hathaway's intelligence.

'They applied to join the police, not MI6,' said Latham.

Hathaway went back to the wall and pulled out a length of wire that had been connected to the small camera in the centre of the clock. The wire led through the wall and the ceiling to the video monitor on the floor above, where Hathaway had watched all three interviews. But there was no video-recording equipment, no record of what had gone on in the office, either on tape or paper. Officially, the three interviews hadn't taken place. Hathaway put the clock and the wire into a briefcase and shut the lid. 'Right, that's me then.' He swung the briefcase off the table.

'Take care of them,' said Latham. 'I know they're not my responsibility, but that doesn't mean I'm washing my hands of them.'

Hathaway nodded and limped out of the room.

Latham looked out of the window. He had a nagging feeling that he'd betrayed the three individuals who'd been brought to see him. He'd lied to them, there was no doubt about that, but did it matter in the grand scheme of things? Or did the end justify the means?

WARREN HEARD THE WAIL of an ambulance siren as he got out of the Vectra and headed down Craven Park towards his house. He didn't want his neighbours to see the car or the driver. The noise barely registered with Warren as he walked. Sirens were an all too regular occurrence in Harlesden. He turned left and saw that the side street had been closed off midway with lines of blue and white tape. Three police cars had been parked haphazardly, their doors open and blue lights flashing.

In the middle of the road a man and a woman dressed in white overalls were studying a red smear, and a man in a sheepskin jacket was drawing chalk circles around several cartridge cases.

Three Jamaican teenagers were huddled outside a newsagent's, wrapped up in gunmetal-grey Puffa jackets. Warren nodded at the tallest of the youths. 'What's the story, PM?'

PM shrugged carelessly. His real name was Tony Blair and he'd been given the nickname the day his namesake was elected to Number 10. 'Jimmy T took a couple of slugs in the back. Should have seen him run, Bunny. Almost made it.'

Warren shook his head sadly. Jimmy T was a fifteen-year-old runner for one of the area's crack cocaine gangs.

'He OK?'

'He look dead as dead can be.'

'Shit.'

'Shit happens,' said PM. 'Specially to short-changers.'

'That what he did?'

'Word is.'

Warren gestured at the police. 'You told the Feds?'

PM guffawed. 'Sure, man. Told 'em who killed Stephen Lawrence while I was at it.'

All three youths laughed and Warren nodded glumly. Shootings were a regular occurrence in Harlesden, but witnesses were rarer.

'You saw who did it?'

'Got eyes.'

Warren looked expectantly at PM.

The teenager laughed out loud but his eyes were unsmiling. 'Shit, man, I could tell you but then I'd have to kill you.'

Warren wondered how much PM would have told him if he'd been standing there in a police constable's uniform.

'You look wound up, Bunny-man. You want some puff?'

'Nah, I'm sorted. Gotta get back to the house.'

THE MAN WHO'D RUNG Fullerton's bell was almost a head shorter than him with thinning brown hair, a squarish chin and thin, unsmiling lips. 'Jamie Fullerton?' he said. He was carrying a laptop computer in a black shoulder bag.

'Maybe,' said Fullerton.

'Gregg Hathaway. You're expecting me.'

'Come in,' said Fullerton. He stepped to the side as Hathaway walked by. There was something awkward about his right leg, as if it was an effort for Hathaway to move it.

'You don't mind showing me some form of ID, do you?' asked Fullerton as he closed the front door and followed Hathaway into the sitting room.

Hathaway put his laptop case on the coffee table and turned to look at Fullerton. 'Your name is James Robert Fullerton, you were born on April 15 twenty-six years ago, your parents are Eric and Sylvia, your father committed suicide after he lost the bulk of your family's assets in a series of badly advised stock market investments and your mother is confined to a mental hospital outside Edinburgh.'

Fullerton swallowed, but his throat had gone so dry that his tongue felt twice its normal size and he started to cough.

'Is that enough, or shall I go on?'

Fullerton nodded. 'You don't look like you're in the job.'

'Neither do you. That's the point. Black with two sugars.'

Fullerton frowned. 'Sorry?'

'You were going to offer me a coffee, right? Black with two sugars.'

It was only when he was filling the kettle that Fullerton realised how quickly Hathaway had taken control of the situation. The man was smaller than Fullerton, maybe a decade older, with none of the bearing or presence that Latham had shown, but there was a toughness that suggested he was used to being obeyed.

When Fullerton returned to the sitting room with two mugs of coffee, Hathaway had powered up his laptop and was sitting on the sofa, tapping on the keyboard. He'd run a cable from the computer to the phone socket by the window.

'You're the handler, right?' said Fullerton.

'Handler suggests physical contact,' said Hathaway. 'Ideally we won't meet again after today.' He gestured at the laptop. 'This is a safer way of keeping in touch.'

THERE WAS a document pouch on the side of the laptop case. Hathaway opened it. He took out a large glossy colour photograph. 'Meet Dennis Donovan. Tango One.'

Cliff Warren studied the photograph. It was the face of a man in his mid-thirties. He had a square face with a strong chin, pale green eyes and a broken nose. The man's dark brown hair was brushed carelessly across his forehead. 'Tango?' he said.

'Tango is how we designate our targets,' explained Hathaway. 'Dennis Donovan is Tango One. Our most wanted target. One of the country's biggest importers of marijuana and cocaine. Virtually untouchable by conventional methods. He never deals with anyone he doesn't know.'

'And you expect me to get close to him?' said Warren. 'In case you haven't noticed, I'm black. Donovan's white. It's not like we went to the same school, is it? Why's he gonna let me get close to him?'

'We don't expect it to happen overnight,' said Hathaway. 'Donovan is a long-term project. I'll supply you with details of his associates and as you go deeper you keep an eye out for them. You build up contacts with his associates, and use them to put you next to Donovan.'

Warren studied the photograph again. Donovan looked more like a footballer reaching the end of his career than a hardened criminal.

'He's thirty-four, married with a six-year-old son. Wife is Vicky. She's twenty-seven. They've got a house in Kensington but Donovan spends most of his time in the Caribbean.'

'Are they separated?' asked Warren.

'No, it's just easier for him to operate out there. He was under round-the-clock surveillance here—Customs, police, the tax man. His kid's settled in school and his wife likes shopping, so they've resisted moving out there. Donovan's over here every month or so and they spend all their holidays in the sun, so it seems to be working out OK.'

'And just how do I get to him?'

'You start dealing.' Hathaway nodded at the window. 'Most of the crack cocaine sold in the streets out there can be traced back to Donovan if you go back far enough.'

'If you know that, why don't you arrest him?'

'Knowing and proving are two very different things, Cliff.'

'So the idea is for me to work my way up the supply chain until I get to Donovan?'

'That's the plan.'

TINA LEIGH RAN both hands through her hair, brushing the strands behind her ears. 'I'm not a criminal. Why's Donovan going to be interested in me?'

Hathaway looked away, awkwardly.

'I'm his type, is that it?'

'You're a very sexy girl, Tina.'

Tina glared at him. 'Go screw yourself.'

'Give me a chance to explain, Tina. Please.'

'You don't need to explain. I used to be a hooker, but that's all behind me now, Hathaway. I ain't going back.' She stood up.

'That's not what I said, and not what I meant.'

'I know exactly what you meant. I can't join the Met because I worked the streets, but I'm being given official approval to sleep with a gangster. How hypocritical is that?'

'I didn't say you had to sleep with him, Tina.' He waved at her chair. 'Please hear me out.'

Tina brought her temper under control. 'OK,' she said. She sat down, lit a cigarette and waited for Hathaway to continue.

'There are a number of clubs that Donovan frequents when he's in London. We'd like you to apply for a job. Once employed, we'd want you to keep your ears open, pass on anything you hear. And if you get near Donovan, that'll be the icing on the cake.'

'These clubs? What sort of clubs are they?'

'They're sort of executive entertainment bars . . .' He tailed off as Tina's face hardened.

'Lap-dancing clubs?' she hissed. 'You want me to be a lap-dancer?'

'Lap dancing isn't prostitution,' said Hathaway. 'Students do it to work their way through college, single mothers, it's totally legal.'

Tina took a long pull on her cigarette. 'It's not much of a plan, is it? Putting me undercover in a lap-dancing bar in the hope that Donovan wanders in and spills his guts.'

'This is long term, Tina. You might not meet Donovan for years. But the pool he swims in isn't that big and I have no doubt you'll come across his associates if not the man himself. And they're going to open up to you because you're a pretty girl.' He held up a hand. 'I'm stating that as a fact, Tina, not trying to soft-soap you. Put guys together with booze and pretty girls and tongues start to loosen. These guys work under such secrecy that often they're bursting to tell someone. To boast. To show what big men they are.'

'Let's suppose I agree to do this. What happens to the money?'

Hathaway looked confused. 'What money?'

'I'll be a police officer, right? On standard pay and conditions?'

Hathaway nodded.

'But if I'm working in a, what was it you called it—an executive entertainment bar? If I'm working there, I'll get wages. And tips.'

'Yours to keep.'

Tina smiled. 'Do you know how much those girls earn?' she asked.

'Sixty, seventy grand. Sometimes more.'

'And I get to keep it, yeah?'

'Every penny.'

JAMIE FULLERTON'S JAW dropped. 'Let me get this straight,' he said. 'Any money I make from illegal activities is mine to keep?'

'Believe me, the powers that be aren't happy with the idea,' said Hathaway, 'but we don't have any choice. If someone puts your bank accounts under the microscope, how's it going to look if you're making regular payments to the Met?'

'And I won't ever be asked to pay the money back?'

'I don't see how that could ever happen.'

Fullerton stood up and paced around the sitting room. 'And you're going to set me up in this new life. Make me look like a criminal?'

'Initially. Hopefully you'll become self-funding quite quickly.'
Hathaway waved at the section of bookshelves devoted to art. 'You
studied art history at university. Got a first, right?'

Fullerton nodded.

'So we'll build on that. Set you up in a gallery. Give you some
works of art to get you started. Put some stolen works your way to
add authenticity.'

Fullerton's eyes widened in astonishment. 'You're going to give me
stolen paintings? To sell? And I get to keep the money?'

Hathaway looked uncomfortable. 'We will be establishing your
cover, Jamie. This isn't a game. If Donovan, or anyone else for that
matter, discovers who you are or what you're doing, your life will be
on the line.'

Fullerton nodded. 'I understand. But how does me being an art
dealer get me close to Donovan?'

'He's an art freak. A bit of a collector. What we're suggesting is
that you establish the art gallery, then start moving into the drug
business. You presumably have your own suppliers?'

'Sure.'

'So start with them. Start increasing the quantities you buy from
them, then move up the chain towards Donovan.'

'Have you ever done it?' Fullerton asked. 'Gone undercover?'

Hathaway nodded. 'Several times. But never long term.'

'What's it like?'

'It means living a lie. It means developing a second personality that
has to become more real than your own. Everything you say and do
has to be filtered through the person you're pretending to be. It means
never being able to relax, never being able to let your guard down.'

'That's what I thought.'

'But you'll be in a slightly different position. When I was undercover, I was pretending to be a villain. You'll be the real thing.'

HATHAWAY REACHED OVER to his jacket and took out a wallet. From
it he removed a business card. He handed it to Cliff Warren. Printed
in the middle was a single London telephone number. 'You can call
this number at any time of the day or night. No matter what trouble
you're in, we'll have you out of it within minutes. Memorise the
number. Then destroy the card.'

He turned round the laptop so Warren could see the screen.

'The same goes for what I'm going to show you on the computer.
Memorise the procedures and passwords. Never write anything down.'

TINA WATCHED as Hathaway tapped away at the keyboard. 'So I'll be emailing you reports, is that it?' she asked.

'It's the safest way,' he said. 'No meetings that can be watched, no phone conversations that can be tapped.'

She pointed at the laptop. 'Do I get to use this?'

Hathaway shook his head. 'Absolutely not. Under no circumstances must you ever use your own machine. Everything you do will be stored somewhere on your hard disk. Someone who knows what they're doing will be able to find it. I'll use this to show you what to do, but you should use public machines. There are Internet cafés all over the place these days.'

He sat back from the laptop. On screen was a web page. 'This is SafeWeb,' he said. 'You can use it to move around the web without being traced. That goes for web sites or email.'

'Does that mean you think someone will be watching me?'

'If you get close to Donovan, there'll be all sorts of agencies crawling over you, Tina. The Drugs Squad, Customs and Excise, law-enforcement agencies right across the world will put you under the microscope. They can all open your mail, listen in on your phone calls and intercept your email. If any of them were to discover you were an undercover agent, your life would be on the line.'

'Even though they're the good guys?'

'Someone at Donovan's level can't operate without inside help.'

'Bent cops?'

'Bent cops, bent agents, bent politicians,' said Hathaway. 'There is so much money in the drugs trade that they can buy almost anyone. Everyone has their price.'

'What about you, Gregg? What's your price?'

'I don't do this for the money, Tina.'

'You're on some sort of crusade, are you?'

'My motivation isn't the issue.' He turned the laptop towards her. 'Once you've logged onto SafeWeb, type in this URL.' His fingers played across the keyboard. The new web page loaded.

She looked at the graphics and wording on the screen. It appeared to be an online store selling toiletries. There was a 'Feedback' section where emails could be sent to the company.

'That's where I send my stuff?' she asked.

'That's it. You'll need a password. Something you'll never forget. A number, a word. Anything up to eight characters.'

Tina gave him a password. He tapped it in and gestured at the screen. 'Right, this is you logged on. If there's a message for you, there'll be an envelope signal here. If you want to send me a message, you click here.' Hathaway clicked on a letter icon. 'When you've finished, click on SEND and you're done.'

'And am I supposed to be in contact with you every day?'

'Once a week would be enough. But you want to avoid making it a routine. If you sit down at a computer every Saturday morning, it's going to be noticed.'

CLIFF WARREN looked at Hathaway. 'Where do I get my cash from?'

'I'll be supplying funds. At least in the early stages. And drugs.'

At first Warren thought he'd misheard, then the implications of what Hathaway had said sank in. 'What? The police are going to be giving me heroin?'

Hathaway winced. 'I was thinking cannabis,' he said. 'Just to get you started. You ever taken drugs, Cliff?'

Warren shook his head. 'Saw what they did to my folks.' Warren's mother had died of a heroin overdose when he was twelve. His father had ended up in prison for killing a dealer in North London. Warren had been passed from relative to relative until he'd been old enough to take care of himself, and every household he stayed in was tainted by drugs. He had steadfastly refused to touch so much as a joint. 'I don't see that's a problem, though. Plenty of dealers don't use.'

'Absolutely. But you're going to have to know good gear when you see it.'

'I've got people can show me. The stuff you're going to give me. Where's it coming from?'

'Drugs we've seized in previous operations,' said Hathaway. 'They're destroyed if they're no longer needed as evidence. We'll just divert some your way.'

 **Three years later**

Robbie Donovan picked up his sports bag as soon as the bell started to ring, but dropped it by his desk after Mr Inverdale gave him a baleful look. Mr Inverdale finished outlining the homework, then turned his back on the class. There was a scramble for the door and Robbie hurried out into the corridor. He pulled his mobile from his bag and switched it on. He had one text message waiting. Robbie's heart began to pound. Elaine was the prettiest girl in his year, bar none. He pressed the button and the message flashed up. I'M BACK. COME HOME NOW—DAD.

Robbie grinned and pumped his fist in the air. 'Yes!' he said. It had been more than two months since Robbie had seen his father.

He stuffed the phone back into the sports bag and headed for the school gates. He looked round nervously, but there were no teachers in the playground. It was lunch break and everyone was rushing towards the refectory. Robbie walked purposefully through the gates and broke into a run.

He was out of breath by the time he reached his house. His mother's silver Range Rover was parked in the driveway. Next to it was a dark green Jaguar. Robbie walked down the side of the house and through the kitchen door. There were two mugs by the kettle. 'Dad?' There was no answer.

Robbie put his sports bag on the kitchen table and went into the hall. 'Dad?'

Robbie went upstairs. He could hear voices coming from his parents' bedroom. Robbie broke into a run and pushed open the bedroom door, grinning excitedly. He froze when he saw the two figures on the bed. Two naked figures. His mother turned to look at him, a look of horror on her face. 'Robbie?' she gasped.

Robbie recognised the man on the bed. It was Uncle Stewart, but he wasn't really an uncle, he was a friend of his father's. Stewart Sharkey. His father always looked serious when Uncle Stewart came round to the house, and they'd lock themselves in the study while they talked. 'That's my mum!' Robbie shouted.

Robbie's mother wrapped the duvet round herself and twisted round to face him. 'Robbie, this isn't—'

'*It is!*' he screamed. 'I know what it is! I can see what you're doing! I'm not stupid.'

Robbie's mother stood up. She took a step towards Robbie. Robbie moved backwards, holding his hands up as if to ward her off. '*Don't come near me!*' he yelled.

'Robbie, I'm sorry.'

'Dad's going to kill you. He's going to kill both of you!'

'Vicky, for God's sake, do something!' hissed the man.

Robbie backed out of the bedroom and rushed downstairs. His mother hurried after him. 'Robbie! Robbie, come back here!' But Robbie was too quick for her. He pulled the front door open, slipped out and slammed it behind him. Vicky scrabbled at the lock, but by the time she got the door open Robbie was already sprinting along the pavement. The strength drained from Vicky's legs and she slumped to the floor, tears streaming down her cheeks.

Sharkey walked slowly down the stairs, buttoning the cuffs of his shirt. 'Shit,' he said quietly. 'What are we going to do now?'

THE WIND BLOWING off the Caribbean Sea tugged at Den Donovan's hair and flicked it across his eyes. He brushed it away and shaded his eyes with the flat of his hand. The waves of the turquoise sea were flecked with white. 'Thought I might get a boat, Carlos,' Donovan mused, staring out across the water. 'What do you think?'

Carlos Rodriguez shrugged. 'I get seasick,' he said.

'I was thinking a big boat. Stabilisers and that. Save me flying between the islands. I could travel with style.'

'I still get sick,' said Rodriguez.

Donovan started walking down the beach. Rodriguez hurried after him. Donovan looked across at the road to his right. Barry Doyle was leaning against Donovan's silver-grey Mercedes, his arms folded across his massive chest. Doyle gave Donovan the merest nod, letting him know that everything was clear on the road.

A small jet banked overhead and turned towards Bradshaw Airport. Well-heeled tourists, thought Donovan; booked into a suite at one of the resorts on the neighbouring island of Nevis. St Kitts wasn't one of Donovan's favourite places, but it was an ideal setting for a meeting with one of Colombia's biggest cocaine suppliers.

'How's everything?' Donovan said, keeping his voice low.

'The freighter is leaving Mexico this evening,' said Rodriguez.

'And the consignment?'

'The fuel tanks of the yellow ones.'

'Every yellow one?' asked Donovan.

Rodriguez nodded. 'Every one.'

'Isn't that a bit . . . predictable?'

Rodriguez grinned. 'Less risk of confusion. You'd prefer we used engine or chassis numbers? You want to go down on your hands and knees with a flashlight?'

Donovan chuckled. The cocaine Rodriguez was supplying had been transported from Colombia into Mexico. Mexico had a factory manufacturing Volkswagen Beetles. Up to four hundred Beetles a day rolled off the production line and many went overseas. Rodriguez had bought a consignment of sixty of the cars and arranged to ship them to the UK.

'Don't worry, Den,' said Rodriguez. 'Palms have been well greased at both ends. Yellow, green or rainbow-coloured, no one is going near those cars.'

'Sweet,' said Donovan. 'I'll put the first payment in this afternoon.'

'And the rest on arrival?' said Rodriguez.

'Soon as we've got the gear out.' Donovan slapped the Colombian on the back. 'Come on, Carlos, have I ever let you down?'

'Not yet, my friend. But a little bird tells me you have been talking to Russians.'

'Carlos, I talk to a lot of people.'

'Russian pilots. With transport planes. Staying at a hotel in Anguilla. Not far from your villa, in fact.'

'I've no interest in their cocaine, Carlos. I'm talking to them about some business on the other side of the world. Poppy business.'

Donovan heard his name being called from the direction of road. It was Doyle, waving a mobile phone and walking across the sand in their direction. It was Donovan's phone but he never carried it himself. And he never discussed business on it. He was too aware of how easily the authorities could listen in to cellphones.

Donovan strode towards Doyle. 'What the hell are you playing at?' he yelled. 'I told you to stay on the road.'

'It's Robbie,' said Doyle, so quietly his Scottish burr was almost lost in the wind. 'He sounds hysterical. Something about Vicky.'

'Oh, Christ,' said Donovan. He grabbed the phone out of Doyle's hand and slammed it to his ear. 'Robbie, what's wrong?'

Robbie explained what had happened. Donovan told him not to worry, that everything would be all right, that he'd take care of it.

'Dad, you have to come home. Now.'

'I will, Robbie. I promise. A day or two. I've got to get a flight and stuff. Where are you?'

'I'm near school. I ran away. But I don't know where to go.'

'Call your Auntie Laura. Right now. She'll pick you up.'

'I don't want to go home, Dad.'

'You don't have to. You can stay with your aunt until I get there.'

DONOVAN CALLED HIS SISTER from a call box close to a beachfront café. Doyle stood by the car looking uncomfortable. Laura answered on the fifth ring. 'Den, thank God. I can't believe this,' she said.

'Have you got Robbie there yet?'

'He's watching TV with my kids,' she said.

'Thanks, Laura.'

'Anything I can do, Den, you know that.'

'Can you go round to the house? Robbie's passport's in the safe in the study. You got a pen?' Donovan gave her the combination of the safe. 'Get the passport, and there's cash there, too. And a manila envelope, a biggish one. In fact, clear everything out, will you?'

'What if she's there, Den?'

'It's my house. And Robbie's my son. I don't want her doing a runner with him. Are you OK looking after him for a while?'

'You don't have to ask, Den. You know that.'

Donovan cut the connection and dialled again. A man answered. Donovan didn't identify himself, but told the man to get to a clean phone and call him back. Donovan gave him the St Kitts number. The man began to complain that he didn't have enough coins to make an international call from a box. 'Buy a bloody phone card, you cheap bastard,' said Donovan, and hung up.

LAURA'S HUSBAND, Mark, drove her over to Donovan's house. She'd asked a neighbour to sit in with the children.

'We've met this Sharkey guy, haven't we?' asked Mark, accelerating through the evening traffic.

'Yeah. That barbecue last time Den was over. He's an accountant or something.'

They drove the rest of the way in silence. Mark parked outside Donovan's house. Vicky's Range Rover was parked outside.

'She's still home,' said Laura.

'Maybe not,' said Mark. 'She might have left in his car.'

Laura took the house keys from her bag and climbed out of the car. She opened the front door. She had the combination of the burglar alarm, but there was no bleeping from the console so she figured Vicky hadn't set it. She was about to step inside when Mark put a hand on her shoulder. 'Best let me go in first,' he said. 'Just to be on the safe side.'

Laura smiled at him gratefully and moved to let him go inside.

Mark walked down the hall, checked the two reception rooms and the kitchen, then came back into the hallway, shaking his head. 'No one here,' he said. He looked up the stairs. 'Vicky?' he shouted.

They went upstairs to the master bedroom. Laura opened the doors to the fitted wardrobes. There were clothes hanging there but there were also more than two dozen empty hangers. 'Can you get some clothes from Robbie's room?' asked Laura. 'There's something Den wants me to do.'

As Mark went along the hallway to Robbie's bedroom, Laura headed downstairs. She opened the door to the study, walked over to a large oil painting of yachts hanging behind an oak desk and pulled the right-hand side away from the wall. Behind was a safe with a circular numbered dial in the centre. She'd written the combination on the back of a receipt, but it took her several goes before she could get the door open. The safe was empty.

CHIEF SUPERINTENDENT Richard Underwood buttoned his coat and walked out of Paddington Green Police Station. He walked past the first two phone boxes. The third was about half a mile from the station. Underwood tapped in the pin number of his phone card, then tapped out the number in St Kitts. Donovan answered.

'You'd better be quick, Den, there's only twenty quid on this card.'

'Yeah, put it on the tab, you tight bastard,' said Donovan. 'Look, I need to know what my position is back in the UK.'

'Bloody precarious, as usual.'

'I'm serious, Dicko. I'm going to have to come back.' He told Underwood what had happened.

'Hell, Den, I'm sorry.' Underwood had known Donovan for almost twenty years, and Vicky Donovan was the last person he'd have expected to betray her husband.

'Yeah, well I need to know where I stand.'

'You're Tango One. So far as I know, that's not changed. They'll be all over you like a rash if you come back.'

'Check it out, will you?'

'If that's what you want, Den, sure.'

'One more thing. I want you to get Vicky and that bastard Sharkey red-flagged. They leave the country, I want to know.'

DONOVAN WALKED OVER to the convertible Mercedes. 'Where to, boss?' asked Doyle.

Donovan tried to collect his thoughts. He turned to stare at Doyle, but there was a faraway look in his eyes as if he were having trouble focusing. 'I need a computer. Now.'

'The Resort, yeah?'

Donovan nodded. The Jack Tar Resort Hotel had a fully equipped business centre. Doyle started the car and blipped the engine.

The mobile phone rang. Doyle had it on the console by the gear stick and he grabbed it. 'Yeah?' He handed it to Donovan. 'It's Laura.'

Donovan listened in silence as his sister told him that the safe had been emptied. He cursed. 'OK. Laura, I think you'd best keep Robbie away from school until I get back. If she's got his passport she might try to get him out of the country. Just tell the school he's sick or something.'

'Will do, Den.'

'And you know what to do if she turns up at your house?'

'She'll get a piece of my mind if she does, I can tell you.'

'Do me another favour, Laura. Call Banhams. Get them to change the locks and reset the alarm with a new code. Any of the paintings missing?'

'I didn't see any missing, no.'

Donovan considered asking his sister to put the paintings into storage, but figured they'd be safe enough once the house was secured. He'd had them valued five years earlier, and they'd been worth close to a million pounds. The art market had been buoyant recently and Donovan figured they'd probably doubled in value since then. 'I'll call you later, Laura. And thanks. Tell Robbie I love him, yeah?' Donovan cut the connection.

Doyle drove into the hotel resort and pulled up in front of reception. Donovan walked through to the hotel's business centre.

A pretty black girl flashed him a smile and asked him for his room number. Donovan slipped her a hundred-dollar bill. He sat down at a computer terminal in the corner of the room and said a silent prayer before keying in the URL of a small bank in Switzerland. He was asked for an account number and an eight-digit personal identification number.

Donovan took a deep breath and prepared himself for the worst as he waited for his account to be accessed. The screen went blank for a second and then a spreadsheet appeared, listing all transactions over the past quarter. Donovan sagged in the leather armchair. There was just two thousand dollars left in the account.

Ten minutes later Donovan had visited half a dozen financial institutions in areas renowned for their secrecy and security. His total deposits amounted to a little over eighty thousand dollars. Sixty million dollars was missing.

ROBBIE WAS SNORING softly. Laura carried him upstairs. Seven-year-old Jenny was fast asleep on the top bunk of her bed. Jenny had shared a room with her sister until Julie had declared that she was too old to be sharing and had insisted on a room of her own. At the time Julie had been all of four years old and Jenny had been three.

Laura eased Robbie into the lower bunk and pulled the duvet up around him. As she straightened up, the phone rang. There was an extension in the master bedroom, but Laura headed downstairs, knowing Mark would pick it up. As she walked into the sitting room, he had the receiver to his ear.

Mark shook his head. 'You'd better speak to Laura,' he said into the receiver, then held it out to her. 'It's Vicky,' he said.

Laura took the phone. 'You've got a damn cheek, calling here,' she said coldly.

'Is Robbie there, Laura? I've been trying his mobile but it's off.'

'He's asleep.'

'For Christ's sake, Laura, I just want to talk to him.'

'I don't think that's a good idea.'

'You've spoken to Den, haven't you? What did he say?'

'What do you think he said?' asked Laura.

'He's coming back, isn't he?'

'Of course he's coming back. Like a bat out of hell.'

DONOVAN CHARTERED a small plane to fly him and Doyle back to Anguilla. Donovan went into the charter firm's offices and made arrangements for another flight later that day. Then he walked over to the terminal building, where he made three calls from a payphone while Doyle went to pick up the car. The first was to a German who had access to genuine passports and travel documents from around the world. The German gave Donovan a name and Donovan memorised it. The second call was to the agent who made most of Donovan's travel arrangements. Donovan explained what he wanted and gave him the name he'd memorised. The third call was to Spain, but it wasn't answered. An answering machine kicked in and Donovan said just ten words in Spanish and hung up.

Doyle arrived in the Mercedes and Donovan climbed in and sat in silence during the drive to his villa. The Drug Enforcement Agency (DEA), British Customs and whatever other agencies were operating in the millionaires' paradise weren't above planting a surveillance device in the vehicle while it had been parked at the airport. Until it had been swept, the Mercedes was as insecure as a mobile phone.

Doyle stayed in the car while Donovan went into the villa and packed a Samsonite suitcase and a black leather holdall. From the wall safe in the study, Donovan took a bundle of US dollars and stuffed them into the holdall. On the way out he picked up a Panama hat and shoved it into the holdall.

He threw the bags into the back of the car, then got into the front with Doyle. 'The Russians first,' he said. 'Then the German.'

Doyle drove to a five-star hotel about a mile from Donovan's villa. They found the Russians sitting by the pool. Gregov was the bigger of the two, broad-shouldered and well muscled. His grey hair was close-cropped and his face was flecked with broken blood vessels. He looked in his early fifties but he was only thirty-five.

Gregov stood up and pumped Donovan's hand. 'Champagne, huh?' he asked, gesturing to a bottle of Dom Pérignon.

'No can do,' said Donovan. 'I've got to get back to the UK.'

'Who are we going to party with?' said Gregov's partner, Peter, who stayed sprawled on his lounger. Peter was the younger of the two men, a six-footer with a wiry frame. Like Gregov, his hair was cut close to his skull. His face was red from sunburn and his legs and arms tanned, but his chest remained a pasty white.

'From what I've seen, you don't need me to help you two party,' laughed Donovan.

'But we can do business, yes?' asked Peter.

'Definitely,' said Donovan. 'I've got a personal matter to take care of back in London, but then I'll get back to you and we'll do a deal.' He clapped Gregov on the back. 'Look, your bill's taken care of. Anything you want, it's on me. I've got your UK office number. They'll be able to get in touch with you?'

Gregov nodded. 'We are backwards and forwards between the UK and Turkey three times a week, but we check in every day. The earthquake relief charities are paying us thirty thousand dollars a flight. Not quite as profitable as your business, but a good living, yes.'

'You've done well, you and Peter. The Russian army's loss, yeah?'

'Yes, their loss, our gain. Screw communism, yes?'

'Definitely,' said Donovan. 'Capitalism rules.'

The two Russians laughed, then took it in turns to hug Donovan and Doyle.

After they'd said their goodbyes to the Russians, Doyle drove Donovan to the east of the island where the German lived. They were checked out by closed circuit TV cameras and then the twin metal gates clunked open.

Helmut Zimmerman greeted Donovan at the front door. 'Next time I could do with more notice, Dennis,' he said.

'This isn't by choice, Helmut.'

Zimmerman took Donovan along a marble-floored hallway to a windowless room with white walls, a huge desk and decorative chairs. Behind the desk was a bank of monitors linked to CCTV cameras inside and outside the villa. On one of the monitors Donovan could see Doyle sitting in the Mercedes.

Zimmerman pulled open one of the desk drawers and took out three passports. 'One UK, one Irish, one Spanish. As requested.'

Donovan's picture was in all three passports, though each had a different name and date of birth. The passports were genuine and would pass any border checks. Zimmerman had a network of aides across Europe who made a living approaching homeless people and paying them to apply for passports they'd never use. The passports were then sent to Anguilla, where Zimmerman replaced the photographs with pictures of his paying customers.

'Excellent, Helmut, as always.' Donovan took an envelope from his jacket pocket and slid it across the desk. Thirty-six thousand dollars.

Zimmerman put the envelope into the drawer and shut it. Donovan put the passports into his jacket pocket, and the two men shook hands before Zimmerman showed Donovan out of the villa.

Doyle already had the door of the Mercedes open. They drove in silence to the airport. Doyle parked in the short-term car park and they walked together into the terminal building. There was a brown envelope waiting for Donovan at the information desk. Inside was the return segment of a charter flight ticket from Jamaica to Stansted Airport in the name he'd given the travel agent—the name that was in the UK passport—and a Ryanair ticket from Stansted to Dublin. It too was in the UK passport name.

'OK, boss?' asked Doyle.

'Sure,' said Donovan. 'You know how I hate small planes.' It wasn't flying that was worrying Donovan, it was what Carlos Rodriguez would do when he discovered that his money hadn't been paid into his account. Doyle would bear the brunt of Rodriguez's fury, but if Donovan told Doyle to make himself scarce it would be a sure sign of guilt. Doyle would have to stay and face the music.

The pilot was warming up the engines by the time they reached the Cessna. Doyle took Donovan's luggage from the boot of the Mercedes and the owner of the charter company came out to help load it into the plane. Donovan shook hands with Doyle, then hugged the man and patted him on the back. 'You take care, you hear,' said Donovan.

'Sure, boss,' said Doyle, confused by the sudden show of affection.

Donovan climbed into the plane. The copilot closed the door and two minutes later they were in the air. Donovan peered out of the window. Far below he could see the Mercedes heading back to the villa. Donovan flashed the car a thumbs up. 'Be lucky, Barry,' he whispered. He settled back in the plush leather seat. It was a two-hour flight to Jamaica.

DONOVAN SPENT the night at the Hilton Hotel in Kingston. He checked in wearing a Lacoste polo shirt and slacks, but when he checked out in the morning he was wearing baggy jeans, a T-shirt he'd bought in a gift shop in Rasta colours with I LOVE JAMAICA spelt out in spliffs, and a woollen Rasta hat.

Donovan knew he looked ridiculous, but so did most Brits returning home after two weeks in Jamaica. The worst that would happen is that he'd get a pull by Customs at Stansted, but they'd be looking for ganja, not an international drugs baron.

He settled his account with dollars and took a taxi to the airport. He put on a pair of sunglasses and joined the check-in queue for the charter flight. There was a sprinkling of Rasta hats and lots of T-shirts with drugs references, so he blended right in.

It took an hour to reach the front of the queue. He handed over the passport and ticket. The Jamaican girl checked the passport against the name on the ticket. Donovan's travel agent had worked wonders to get him a seat on the charter flight. A scheduled flight would have been easier, but there'd be more scrutiny at Heathrow. Holidaymakers returning to Stansted would barely merit a second look. The agent must have had a pre-dated return ticket issued in the UK and then Fed-Exed it out to Kingston. The unused Stansted–Jamaica leg section of the ticket had already been discarded. It was that sort of creativity that merited the high prices the agent charged. The check-in girl ran him off a boarding card and handed it back to him with the passport.

VICKY DONOVAN shook her head. 'I can't do this, Stewart.'

They had checked into one of the airport hotels to wait for their flight. Sharkey reached over and massaged the back of her neck. 'We don't have any choice, Vicky. You know what he's capable of.'

'But running isn't going to solve anything, is it? He'll come after us.' She looked across at Sharkey, her lower lip trembling. 'I can't leave Robbie. I can't go without him.'

'It's temporary.'

'Den won't let us take him, Stewart.'

'He'll calm down eventually,' Sharkey said soothingly, even though he knew it would be a cold day in hell before Den Donovan would forgive or forget. 'I'll get a lawyer to talk to him. We'll come to an arrangement. Divorce. Custody of Robbie. It'll be OK, I promise.'

Sharkey stroked Vicky's soft blonde hair and kissed her on the forehead. She wasn't wearing make-up and her eyes were red from crying, but she was still model pretty. High cheekbones, almond-shaped eyes with irises so blue that people thought she was wearing tinted contact lenses, and flawless skin that took a good five years off her age. She would be thirty-one on her next birthday.

'We shouldn't have taken the money, Stewart.'

'We needed a bargaining chip. Plus if we're going to hide, that's going to cost.'

'You'll give it back, won't you?'

'Once we've sorted it out, of course I will.' He smiled and corrected himself. 'We will, Vicky. We're in this together, you and me. I couldn't have moved the money without your authorisation. And I'm the one who knew where it was. And where to put it.'

Sharkey pulled her towards him and kissed her on the mouth. She tried to pull away, but Sharkey kept her lips pressed against his until she surrendered to the kiss. Only then did Sharkey release her and she sat back, breathing heavily.

'Christ, I want you,' said Sharkey, placing his hand on her thigh. 'We've time. We don't have to check in for our flight for three hours.'

'Stewart . . .' said Vicky, but he could hear the uncertainty in her voice and he knew he'd won. He pulled her close and kissed her again, and this time she made no attempt to pull away.

DONOVAN STAYED AIRSIDE when he arrived at Stansted. He collected his luggage and went through Customs without incident, still wearing his sunglasses and Rasta hat. Like most UK airports, Stansted had installed a video recognition system during the late nineties. Cameras scanned passengers departing and arriving, cross-checking faces against a massive database. Donovan knew that his photograph was in the database. The technology was ninety-five per cent accurate, but it could still be fooled by dark glasses and hats.

There were only two uniformed officers in the 'Nothing to Declare' channel and they didn't seem interested in the charter-flight passengers. Donovan knew that the lack of interest was deceptive— the area was monitored by several hidden cameras and Customs officers behind the scenes would be looking for passengers who fitted the profile of drugs traffickers. Donovan's Rasta hat and druggie

T-shirt would work in his favour—it would mark him out as a user, but no major drug smuggler would be wearing such outlandish garb.

Donovan passed through without incident. He shaved and washed in the airport toilets and changed into a grey polo-neck sweater and black jeans. He kept his sunglasses on and carried a black linen jacket. He dumped the Rasta hat and T-shirt in a bin.

His Ryanair flight to Dublin took just under an hour. There were no immigration controls between the UK and Ireland so there was no need for Donovan to show his passport.

He collected his Samsonite suitcase, walked through the unmanned blue Customs channel and caught a taxi to the city centre. The taxi dropped Donovan at the top of Grafton Street. He carried his suitcase and holdall into the Allied Irish Bank, showed an identification card to a uniformed guard and went down a spiral staircase to the safety-deposit-box vault.

'Mr Wilson, haven't seen you for some time,' said a young man in a grey suit. He handed a clipboard to Donovan, who put down his suitcase and holdall and signed in as Jeremy Wilson.

'Overseas,' said Donovan. 'The States.'

'Welcome back,' said the young man. He went over to one of the larger safety deposit boxes, inserted his master key into one of the locks and gave it a twist. 'I'll leave you alone, Mr Wilson. Give me a call when you're done.'

Donovan waited until he was alone in the room before putting his personal key into the second lock and turning it. He opened the steel door, slid out his box and hefted it onto a desk with partitions either side to give him a modicum of privacy.

There was a CCTV camera in the vault but it was behind Donovan, so no one could see what was in the box. He lifted the lid. More than a dozen brick-sized bundles of British fifty-pound notes were stacked neatly on the bottom of the box. On top of the banknotes were four gold Rolex watches, four UK passports and two Czechoslovakian Sparbuch account books, one with a million dollars, and the other containing half a million.

Donovan placed his holdall next to the metal box and packed the money into it, then put the passbooks and passports into his jacket pocket. He put the UK passport that he'd used to fly from Jamaica into the box, then replaced the box in its slot and locked the metal door. He pressed a small white buzzer on the desk and the young man came back with his master key. Donovan thanked him and carried his suitcase and holdall upstairs.

Donovan walked to St Stephen's Green and along to the taxi rank in front of the Shelbourne Hotel. A porter in a black uniform with purple trim took the suitcase from him and loaded it into the boot of the lead taxi. Donovan gave him a ten-pound note and kept the holdall with him as he slid into the rear seat.

'Airport?' asked the driver hopefully.

'I want to go to Belfast,' said Donovan. 'You up for it?'

The driver grimaced. 'That's a long drive and my wife'll have the dinner on at six.'

'Use the meter and I'll treble it. I've got a plane to catch.'

The taxi pulled into the afternoon traffic.

STEWART SHARKEY nodded towards the bar. 'Do you want a drink?' he asked Vicky. Their flight hadn't been called and the boarding gate was only a short walk away.

Vicky shook her head. 'I'm going to use the bathroom. Go and get your drink. I'll see you in a couple of minutes.' She walked away quickly, her skirt flicking from side to side.

AT BELFAST AIRPORT Donovan walked into the terminal building and bought a business-class ticket to London at the British Airways desk. Before checking in he took his holdall and suitcase into the toilets and pulled them into a large cubicle designed for wheelchair access. He put most of the money into the suitcase, since it was less likely to be noticed than the holdall. He wasn't committing an offence by flying from Belfast to London with bundles of fifty-pound notes, but he didn't want to attract attention to himself. He kept one of the UK passports in his jacket pocket and hid the rest in a secret compartment in his wash bag.

He put his dark glasses back on and took the Panama hat from his holdall and put it on his head at a jaunty angle. He checked in for the flight, bought a telephone card and called the Spaniard from a pay-phone. This time the Spaniard answered.

'Damn it, Juan, where the hell have you been?'

'*Hola*, Den. I have only just got back from'—the Spaniard chuckled—'wherever I was. So what can I do for my old friend?'

'Same old, same old,' said Donovan. 'I'd like a face-to-face.'

'Where?' Juan Rojas asked.

'Remember the last time we met in the UK? The park. Tomorrow. Same time as before, plus two, OK?' Nine o'clock at night. Dark.

'I will be there, *amigo*.'

VICKY WALKED OUT of the Ladies. To her left was a rank of public phones. She stopped and stared at them. No calls, Stewart had said. Calls could be traced, and he'd insisted they throw away their mobiles before leaving for the airport. She fumbled in her handbag and pulled out her purse. She had a British Telecom card that still had several pounds on it. She picked up the receiver of the phone in the middle of the row and slotted in the card, then tapped out the number of Robbie's mobile. It rang through immediately to his message bank and she cursed.

She was about to hang up, but then she changed her mind. 'Robbie, it's Mum. I just called to say hello. You know I love you, don't you? I am so sorry about what happened, love, I really am. If I could turn back the clock . . .' She felt tears well up in her eyes and she blinked them back. 'I'm going away for a few days, Robbie. Not far, I promise. But I'm going to see you again soon, I miss you so much—' The answering service buzzed and the line went dead.

DEN DONOVAN was less than a hundred yards away, collecting his suitcase from the carousel in Heathrow's Terminal One. Even though he was wearing his Panama hat and sunglasses, he kept his head down until he was out of the terminal building. He joined the queue for a black cab and forty-five minutes later was being driven down the Edgware Road. He told the driver to drop him in front of a small, run-down hotel in Sussex Gardens. The reception desk was manned by an East European girl, who told Donovan they had a room available and that she'd need to see a credit card.

Donovan told her his credit cards had been stolen while he was on holiday, but he had a passport and was happy to leave a cash deposit. Donovan never used credit cards if he could help it—they left a clear trail that could be followed. He gave her six fifty-pound notes and checked in under the name of one of his UK passports.

ONCE IN HIS ROOM, Donovan took a reefer jacket and an old base-ball cap from his suitcase and put them on. He peeled off several hundred pounds in fifties from one of the bricks of banknotes in his suitcase, and shoved them into his wallet. Then he put his sunglasses on, locked his door and went out with the door key in his pocket.

He walked down the Edgware Road to an electrical retailer's and bought eight Pay As You Go mobile phones—two One2One, two Vodafone, two BT, and two Orange—and two dozen Sim cards. A CCTV camera covered the cash register, but Donovan kept his head down and the peak of the baseball cap hid his face as he handed over the cash.

Donovan walked back to the hotel. He stopped off at a newsagent on the way and bought five twenty-pound phone cards. There were four power points in the room and Donovan put four of the phones on charge before heading for the shower.

Half an hour later, he was walking back towards the pedestrian underpass on the corner of the Edgware Road and Harrow Road. Most people used the pedestrian crossings at the traffic lights, but Donovan walked down the sloping walkway.

There were half a dozen exits. Donovan loitered for a while until he was satisfied that no one had followed him down, and then he walked quickly up the stairs that led to the Harrow Road exit, close to Paddington Green Police Station.

He headed towards Maida Vale and stopped at the Church of St Mary. Just along from the churchyard was a park, with two phone boxes at its entrance. Donovan sat on a bench in the graveyard and took out a mobile phone. He'd only been able to charge it for half an hour, but that would be enough for what he wanted. He tapped out the number of Richard Underwood's direct line, dialling 141 first so his number wouldn't show up on Underwood's phone.

The chief superintendent answered with a long groan before saying, 'Yes?'

'What's up, Dicko? Piles giving you jip?'

'The perfect end to the perfect day. Where are you?'

'You know the churchyard on the Harrow Road?'

'Yes,' said Underwood, suspiciously.

'Fifteen minutes. I'll call the one on the right.'

'Why don't I call you?'

'Because I don't want this phone ringing, that's why. Fifteen minutes, yeah?'

Donovan cut the connection, walked round the churchyard a couple of times, then went and stood behind a clump of trees. A few minutes later, Underwood came walking briskly from the direction of the police station, a look of discomfort on his face. He was a big man, with a large gut that strained over the top of his trouser belt. He reached the two phone boxes and stamped his feet impatiently.

Donovan took out his mobile phone and dialled a number. A second later and the phone in the box on the right started to ring. Underwood looked round, then pulled open the door to the box and picked up the phone.

'You're breathing heavily, Dicko, you out of condition?' said Donovan.

'It's a long bloody walk and you know it. Whereabouts are you?'

'Behind you.'

Underwood turned round and his jaw dropped as he saw Donovan striding across the grass towards him. 'What the hell are you doing here?' he exploded.

Donovan laughed and put his mobile phone away. Underwood stood with the phone still pressed against his ear, his mouth open in surprise. Donovan pulled the door open for him. 'Put the phone down and let's have a chat, yeah?'

Underwood squeezed out of the phone box and they walked down the Harrow Road towards the canal.

'You shouldn't be here, Den.'

'You can say that again. But that bitch'll get my boy if I don't do something.'

'You think you'll get custody?'

'I'm his bloody father.'

'Yeah, but . . .'

'There's no buts, Dicko. I'm his dad and his mum was caught naked with my accountant. What's my situation?'

'Same as it's always been. Still Tango One.'

'Hopefully I'll get Robbie and be out of here before anyone knows where I am. What have they got on me that's current?'

'So far, nothing,' said Underwood.

Ahead of them was a pub. The Paddington Stop. The two men nodded at each other and headed towards it.

Donovan waited until he had a Jack Daniels and soda in front of him and there was no one within earshot before speaking. 'How close have they got to me?' he asked, and sipped his drink.

Underwood toyed with his pint of lager. 'Strictly surveillance.'

'No one up close and personal?'

'Give me a break, Den. What do you think, I can just wander up to SO10 and ask what undercover agents they've got in play?'

'You're NCS liaison, aren't you? National Crime Squad would have a vested interest.'

'Which would have been sparked off by what? Do you want me to tell them you're back? Because if you're out in the sunny Caribbean, why would the Met or the NCS give a rat's arse what you're up to?'

'If they've sent anyone against me, I need to know.'

'And I've got another ten years of a career ahead of me.'

'You could retire tomorrow.'

Underwood grinned. 'Not officially.' He had a little under a million pounds secreted away in various offshore accounts, but he had to be careful. He and Donovan went back a long way. But friendship alone didn't warrant the risk of spending ten years behind bars.

'Just find out what you can, Dicko, yeah?'

'Sure.'

'You know I'll see you right.'

'Yeah, I know,' said Underwood. Virtually every penny of the million pounds that he had salted away had come from Donovan. And at least two of his promotions had been a direct result of spectacular arrests following up on information provided by Donovan. Sure, Donovan always had his own agenda, either settling a score or putting a competitor out of business. He drained his glass. 'I better be going.' He nodded at Donovan's mobile. 'Can I call you on that?'

Donovan flashed him a sarcastic smile. 'I'll bell you.' Underwood shook his head sadly. 'Just because I'm paranoid doesn't mean they're not listening in, Dicko,' said Donovan. 'I'll be ditching the number today. What about Vicky?'

'It's bad news, Den. They left two days ago.'

'To where?'

'Spain. Malaga.'

'No way.'

'Booked on a British Airways flight out of Heathrow. Sharkey left his car in the long-term car park. Left a deposit on his credit card.'

'No way they'd go to Spain. I know too many faces out there. And the car is too obvious. He wanted it found.' Donovan sat shaking his head, then leaned forward, eyes narrowed. 'Luggage? They check in any luggage?'

'Hell, Den, how would I know that?'

'You ask. You say, did they check in, and if they did, did they have any luggage? It's the oldest trick in the book. Done it myself with Vicky a couple of times. You check in for an international flight. Tickets, passports and all. But you have another ticket for somewhere where they don't check passports. Dublin, Glasgow. The Channel Islands. You pass through Immigration, then you go and check in for your real flight. Tell them you didn't have time to check in at the other side. Providing you haven't checked in any luggage, the flight you didn't get on will depart, and they won't even take you off the manifest. Once in Jersey you get the Hovercraft to France. Or from Dublin you fly anywhere.'

DONOVAN GOT TO HAMPSTEAD an hour before he was due to meet the Spaniard. He walked through the village, doubling back several times and keeping an eye on reflections in the windows until he was sure he hadn't been followed. He walked out onto the Heath, hands in the pockets of his leather bomber jacket.

He went to the place he'd arranged to meet Rojas, and lingered in a copse until he saw the Spaniard walking purposefully down one of the many paths that crisscrossed the Heath. Rojas looked like a young Sacha Distel: soft brown eyes, glossy black hair and a perfect suntan. His looks were a disadvantage in his line of work—he could never get close to his quarry because heads always turned when he was around. That was why Rojas always killed at a distance. A rifle. A bomb. Poison. A third party.

Donovan waited until he was sure Rojas was alone before whistling softly to attract his attention. Rojas walked over to the copse and gave Donovan a bear hug. 'Dennis, good to see you again.'

They walked round the copse. Donovan told Rojas about his wife and his accountant and their departure through Heathrow. The Spaniard listened in silence, nodding thoughtfully from time to time.

'I want them found, Juan.' Donovan handed Rojas an envelope. 'There's their passport details, credit cards, phone numbers. They know I'll be looking for them and they'll be hiding.'

'I understand.'

'When you've found them, I need to talk to them.'

'You mean you want to be there when I . . .' Rojas left the sentence unfinished.

'I need some time alone with them. That's all.' Donovan wasn't prepared to tell the Spaniard about the sixty million dollars. 'You can finish up after I've gone.'

'Both of them?' asked Rojas, his face creased into a frown. 'She is your wife.'

'Both of them,' repeated Donovan.

They shook hands, then Rojas walked away across the grass and back to the path. Donovan watched him go until he was lost in the night, then he turned and went in search of a taxi.

IT WAS JUST after eleven o'clock when Mark Gardner got home. He dropped his briefcase by the front door and tossed his coat onto a rack by the hall table. 'Don't ask!' he said, holding up a hand to silence Laura. 'But if Julie or Jenny ever express any interest in entering the advertising industry, take them out and shoot them, will you?'

Laura handed him a gin and tonic and went into the kitchen. Mark walked through the archway that led to a conservatory. He flopped down on one of the sofas and looked out of the French windows. Scattered around the garden were knee-high mushroom-shaped concrete structures in which were embedded small lights.

Mark took a sip of gin and tonic and sighed.

Something moved in the garden, something dark, something that was striding towards the French windows. A man. Mark jumped up, his glass shattering on the tiled floor of the conservatory.

'Are you OK?' Laura shouted from the kitchen.

'Stay where you are, Laura—there's someone in the garden.'

As usual, his wife did the exact opposite of what he asked and came running from the kitchen. Mark looked round for something to use as a weapon and grabbed at a heavy brass vase they'd bought while on holiday in Tunisia.

The man walked up to the window, his hand raised. He was wearing a leather bomber jacket and had a baseball cap pulled low over his eyes. Mark feared he was going to be shot, but the man's gesture turned into a wave, and when he pressed his face against the glass, Mark sighed with relief.

'It's Den!' said Laura.

Mark grinned sheepishly. He put the brass vase back on its table and went to unlock the French windows.

Donovan stepped into the conservatory and shook Mark's hand, then rushed over to hug his sister. Mark knelt down and started picking up pieces of broken glass.

Donovan moved to help him put the glass splinters on a copy of *The Economist*. 'Didn't mean to spook you, Mark. Sorry.'

'I wasn't spooked. You caught me by surprise, that's all.' Mark lifted the magazine and carried it to the kitchen.

'When did you get back?' Laura asked.

'Yesterday. How is he?'

'He's OK. Cried his eyes out the first night, now he's sort of numb. Shock.'

Donovan shook his head, his lips tight. 'OK if I see him?'

'Sure.'

Laura took Donovan upstairs. She pushed open the bedroom door and stood aside. Robbie was lying on his front, head twisted away from the door so that all Donovan could see was a mop of unruly brown hair on the pillow. He tiptoed over to the bunk bed and knelt down, then gently ruffled his son's hair. 'Don't worry,

Robbie, I'm here now,' he whispered. He felt a sudden flare of anger at Vicky and what she'd done.

He straightened up and slipped out of the bedroom. They went back downstairs and into the conservatory.

'What do you want to drink?' asked Mark.

'JD and soda.'

Mark disappeared into the sitting room and returned with the drinks. He sat down on the sofa and leaned forwards, cupping his gin and tonic. 'No offence, Den, but how much trouble are you in?'

Donovan smiled thinly. A very angry Colombian on his trail and sixty million dollars missing from his bank accounts. Quite a lot, really. 'I'll be OK,' he said, then asked Laura if she'd had the locks changed. She went into the sitting room and came back with a set of new keys and a piece of paper on which she'd written the new code for the burglar alarm system. Donovan took them, drained his glass, then gave his sister a big hug. 'I'm off,' he said. 'I'm really grateful for what you and Mark are doing for Robbie. I'll drop by and see him tomorrow, yeah? And don't tell him I was here tonight, OK?' He shook hands with Mark, then left through the French windows, keeping in the shadows as he headed back down the garden.

DONOVAN FLAGGED DOWN a black cab and had it drop him a quarter of a mile from his house. He kept his head down as he walked along on the opposite pavement, scanning left and right under the peak of the baseball cap. There were no occupied cars, and no vans that could have concealed watchers. A couple were leaning against a gatepost but they were way too young to be police.

Donovan checked out the houses opposite his own. There was nothing obvious, but if the surveillance was good then there wouldn't be. He walked on. At the end of the road he turned right. Donovan's house was in a block that formed one side of a square. All the houses backed onto a large communal garden. It could be entered from the back doors of the houses, but there was a side entrance. One of the keys on the ring that Laura had given him opened the gate that led to the garden. Donovan stopped to tie his shoelaces, taking a quick look over his shoulder. The street was deserted. Donovan opened the gate and slipped inside.

He stood for a minute listening to his own breathing as his eyes got used to the gloom. There were lights on in several of the houses, but most of the garden was in darkness. Donovan walked across the grass, looking from side to side to check no one else was taking a late evening stroll. He was alone. He walked quickly to his house, and as he crossed the flagstoned patio a halogen security light came on automatically. He unlocked the back door and the alarm system began to bleep. He closed the door and walked to the cupboard under the stairs and tapped out the four-digit number Laura had given him. The alarm stopped bleeping. He left the lights off in case the house was under surveillance.

Donovan went into the study and checked the safe, even though Laura had told him it was empty. He stared at the bare metal shelves and cursed. Would Vicky have realised the significance of the Sparbuch passbooks in the manila envelope? Donovan doubted it, but Sharkey certainly would have known what they were, and what they were worth. Donovan slammed the safe door shut and put the painting back in place. He ran his fingers along the gilded frame and smiled to himself. Luckily Sharkey was as ignorant of art as Vicky. The oil painting of two yachts was more than a hundred years old, and together with its partner on the opposite wall was worth close to half a million dollars. They were by James Edward Buttersworth, an American painter.

Donovan walked round the house and satisfied himself that none of the works of art had been taken. Then he reset the alarm and let himself out through the back door. The security light came on. Donovan hurried off across the grass.

He unlocked the gate leading out of the garden, checked that there was no one around, then slipped through and relocked it. He put his head down and walked briskly along the pavement.

As he walked by a dark saloon he heard a car door open. Donovan tensed. He'd been so deep in thought he hadn't noticed anyone in any of the parked cars. He took a quick look over his shoulder. A man in an overcoat was walking round to the boot of his car.

Donovan turned away and walked faster. Two men were walking along the pavement towards him. They were big men, too, as big as the man who was opening the car boot behind him. Donovan stepped off the pavement but they were too quick for him. One grabbed him by the arm with shovel-like hands and the other pulled out something from his coat pocket, raised his arm and brought it crashing down on the side of Donovan's head.

DONOVAN SLOWLY REGAINED consciousness. His head throbbed and he was having trouble breathing. The room was spinning round him and Donovan blinked several times, trying to clear his vision. Then he realised it wasn't the room that was spinning. It was him.

He had been suspended by his feet from a metal girder with a rope and his hands had been tied behind him. His nose felt blocked and his eyes were hurting and he had a piercing headache. He'd obviously been hanging upside-down for a long time.

Two pairs of legs spun into view. Brown shoes. Grey trousers. Black coats. Then they were gone. Machinery. A dark saloon car. Welding cylinders. A jack. A workbench. Then the legs again. Donovan craned his neck but couldn't see their faces.

One of the men said something in Spanish. Donovan didn't catch what it was. He knew who they were, though. Colombians.

He heard footsteps and a third pair of legs walked up. '*Hola, hombre,*' said a voice. '*Qué pasa?*' Donovan twisted round, trying to get a look at the man who'd spoken. A short, thickset man in his mid-twenties. A goatee beard. It was Jesus Rodriguez, Carlos Rodriguez's nephew. Donovan had seen him in Carlos Rodriguez's entourage but had never spoken to the man. He'd heard the rumours, though. Ears cut off. Prostitutes scarred for life. Bodies dumped at sea, still alive and attached to anchors.

'Oh, just hanging around,' said Donovan, trying to sound confident even though he knew that the fact Doyle hadn't called to warn him about the Colombians meant he probably wasn't able to.

'Where's my uncle's money, Donovan?' said Rodriguez.

'Somebody borrowed it,' said Donovan.

'Well, *amigo*, I hope they're paying you a good rate of interest, because that loan is going to cost you your life.'

Donovan heard scraping, then sloshing. Then something being unscrewed. Then a strong smell of petrol. Then the three pairs of legs swung into view. One of the men was holding a petrol can. Donovan's insides lurched. 'Look, Jesus, I haven't got your money. I've been ripped off. By my accountant.'

'Where is he?'

'I don't know.'

'Wrong answer.'

The man with the can started splashing petrol over Donovan's legs. It dripped down his chest and dribbled into his nose, stinging so badly his eyes watered.

'I'm looking for him. For God's sake, Jesus, he's ripped off sixty million dollars.'

'Of which ten million is my uncle's.'

'If I had the money, I'd have given it to him. You think I don't know what happens to people who don't pay your uncle?'

The man with the can poured the last of the petrol down Donovan's back. It trickled down the back of his neck and dribbled through his hair. The fumes made him gag.

'You thought you'd be safe in London, did you?' asked Rodriguez.

'No. I thought I might get the money back.'

Rodriguez reached into his coat pocket and took out a gold cigarette lighter. Petrol was pooling on the floor below Donovan's head.

Donovan panicked. 'For God's sake, Jesus, I've got money. I can pay you some of it.'

'How much?'

'I've got two Sparbuch passbooks. That's a million and a half bucks.'

Rodriguez frowned. 'What's a Sparbuch?'

'It's a bank account,' said Donovan. 'They're for accounts in Czechoslovakia. The ones I've got are in US dollars.'

'Fine. So transfer the money.'

'It's not as easy as that. They're bearer passbooks. Whoever has the passbooks and the passwords has the account. You have to show the passbook to get the money. They won't do electronic transfers.'

'That sounds like bullshit,' said Rodriguez. He flicked the lighter. 'It's barbecue time.'

'Look, talk to your uncle!' said Donovan hurriedly.

Rodriguez studied Donovan with emotionless brown eyes, then nodded slowly. He took a mobile phone from his jacket pocket and dialled a number. He kept staring at Donovan, then said something in Spanish. Donovan kept hearing the word '*capullo*'. Prick. Rodriguez listened, then nodded, then spoke some more. Donovan's Spanish was good but not fluent.

Rodriguez walked over to Donovan. 'He wants to talk to you.'

Rodriguez thrust the phone against the side of Donovan's head.

'What's this about Sparbuch accounts?' asked Carlos Rodriguez.

'Everyone uses them in Europe, Carlos. It's clean money, it's in the bank for God's sake.'

'But if I want the cash, I have to go to Czechoslovakia?'

'It's a three-hour flight, no big deal. But they're better than cash. You owe someone, you give them the passbook and the password.'

'That still leaves you eight and a half million dollars short.'

'I have paintings in the house. Three million dollars worth.'

'I'm not an art dealer, *amigo*.'

'Bloody hell, Carlos, work with me on this, will you? With the paintings and the passbooks, I've got almost five million dollars.'

'What about when the consignment arrives?' said Rodriguez. 'How were you expecting to pay the second tranche?'

'What can I say, Carlos? I haven't got the first ten mill let alone the second.'

'The people who are taking on the cocaine, they have paid you half, yes?'

'Yes.'

'I presume they are not yet aware of your financial situation,' said Rodriguez.

'If I can deliver the gear, they'll pay me another eighteen mill,' said Donovan. 'You can have all that. The eighteen plus the passbooks plus the paintings is more than twenty mill. You get your money, they get their gear. Everyone wins.'

'But why do I need you in this equation, *amigo*?' asked Rodriguez. 'It's my deal.'

'It *was* your deal,' he said. 'Who is taking delivery of the cars?'

'You can't do this to me, Carlos.'

'*Amigo*, I can tell my nephew to turn you into a kebab and do what the hell I want with the cars. Don't tell me what I can and cannot do.'

'It's being split between Rick Jordan and Charlie Macfadyen.'

'Jordan I have heard of,' said Rodriguez. 'But who is this Macfadyen?'

'He's a big fish in Edinburgh. They both are. This is their first big deal but I know them from way back. Look, let me run with this, Carlos. You'll get your money. All of it.'

'I don't think so, *amigo*. I will deal with Jordan and Macfadyen myself.'

'You bastard!'

Jesus Rodriguez took the phone away from Donovan's ear and slapped him across the face. 'Talk to my uncle with respect, *capullo*.' He put the phone back to Donovan's ear.

'Sorry about that, Carlos,' said Donovan. 'Your nephew wanted a word.'

'He's a good boy. Very enthusiastic. Now what were you saying? Questioning the marital status of my parents, I seem to remember.'

Jesus started to click his lighter again. 'OK, OK!' shouted Donovan. 'It's yours! The deal's yours!'

'Good call,' said Carlos Rodriguez. 'Let me talk to my nephew.'

Donovan tried to smile up at Jesus. 'He wants to talk to you.'

Jesus walked up and down as he listened to his uncle. Eventually he put the phone away and walked back to Donovan.

'You are one lucky *capullo*,' he said. 'I'm staying at the Intercontinental. Tell Jordan and Macfadyen to contact me there. I will explain the new arrangement to them.'

'OK,' said Donovan wearily.

'How long will it take to sell your paintings?' asked Rodriguez.

'Oh, come on. You'll get your money for the gear, Jesus.'

'My uncle says you owe interest, *capullo*. I will take the passbooks and the money from the paintings.' He held out the lighter. 'Or we end this now.'

The fight went out of Donovan. 'I should be able to sell the pictures within a few days,' he said.

'I will be in London for three days. Bring the money and the passbooks to me at the hotel.' He walked away.

'Jesus!'

Rodriguez turned and raised an eyebrow expectantly.

'Cut me down, yeah?'

Rodriguez nodded at his men. One of them took a penknife from his coat pocket and walked behind Donovan. Donovan felt the rope being cut from around his wrists and his ankles. He hit the ground hard, jarring his shoulder. He lay on the concrete floor, gasping for breath. He heard the doors of the car open and slam shut, then the engine revving. The car drove out and he was alone.

DEN DONOVAN woke up with a splitting headache. He wasn't sure if it was the petrol fumes or the clip on the side of the head that had done the damage, but either way his head throbbed every time he moved it. He found a plastic kettle and sachets of coffee, creamer and sugar on a table next to the wardrobe and he made himself a coffee. He picked up one of the unused mobile phones and dialled Macfadyen's number. The answering service kicked in. Charlie Macfadyen was a religious screener of calls, so Donovan wasn't surprised when he picked up the call before he'd finished speaking.

'How's it going, you old bastard?' asked Macfadyen.

'I've had better weeks,' said Donovan. 'Where are you?'

'London. There isn't a problem, is there?'

'Not for you, mate,' said Donovan. 'But from now on you're dealing with the man direct.'

'Screw that, I don't know him. I do know you.'

'Can't you just do as you're told?' said Donovan angrily.

'Look, mate, you've got a stack of my bread. How do I know your guy's gonna honour that? *Caveat emptor*, right? How do I know it's not gonna be guns blazing when I go to see him?'

'Your imagination's in overdrive,' said Donovan. 'Take a Prozac.'

'I'm serious, Den,' said Macfadyen. 'I need more than this or you can give me back my bread and we'll call it quits.'

'You know the Paddington Stop, yeah?'

'Little Venice?'

'See you on the terrace in one, yeah?'

'I'm bringing Ricky, with me.' It was a statement, not a question.

The phone went dead. Donovan pulled the battery off the back of the phone and removed the Sim card. He dropped it into the toilet bowl in the bathroom and flushed, then put a replacement Sim card into the phone. He got the two Sparbuchs out of his suitcase, put on his jacket and headed out.

DONOVAN WALKED down Sussex Gardens to Hyde Park. He had his baseball cap and sunglasses on.

Two young women were riding chestnut horses along the bridle path. Donovan watched them go by, then scanned the park, looking for familiar figures. He'd been checking reflections in windows and car mirrors all the way down Sussex Gardens and he'd knelt down to tie his shoelaces before entering the park and he was reasonably sure he hadn't been followed.

Half an hour later he was on the towpath opposite the Paddington Stop. He leaned against the railings and waited. There was a terrace between the pub and the canal with half a dozen tables, most of which were occupied by midday drinkers.

Donovan saw Jordan and Macfadyen arrive in a bright red Ferrari. They drove into the car park behind the pub and a couple of minutes later walked out onto the terrace. Donovan stayed where he was and watched as the two men checked out the occupants of all the tables. Jordan shook his head and Macfadyen looked at his watch. Eventually Macfadyen spotted Donovan and said something to Jordan. Both men looked at him across the canal. Donovan pointed to the footbridge and motioned for them to come over.

He walked back along the towpath as Macfadyen and Jordan walked over the bridge. 'What's up, Den?' teased Jordan in his nasal Liverpudlian whine. 'Thought we'd be here mob-handed?' Jordan was average build with a beaked nose and a cleft chin and ears that stuck out like cup handles. He was dressed in black Armani and had a chunky gold ring on his right hand. Macfadyen sported a black Valentino leather jacket and had a thick gold bracelet on his wrist.

He was balding and had shaved what hair he had left close to his skull, showing off a curved scar above his left ear. Both men, like Donovan, were wearing sunglasses. Jordan's were Armani.

Den smiled and shrugged. The bridge was an excellent way of making sure he knew exactly who he'd be meeting. If they'd turned up with reinforcements he'd have been able to beat a hasty retreat back under the A40 and disappear into the Bayswater shopping crowds. 'Just being careful.' He hugged Jordan and patted him on the back. He felt Jordan's hands run down his back, the fingers probing under Donovan's jacket. 'For Christ's sake, Ricky,' he protested. 'What are you looking for?'

Macfadyen was watching, an amused look on his face. 'Yeah, well you gotta expect us to be careful, too,' he said. 'You've got to admit, this isn't the gospel according to Den, is it?'

Donovan turned and started walking towards a children's playground. Jordan and Macfadyen followed.

'Who is he?' asked Macfadyen in his thick Scottish brogue.

'Carlos Rodriguez. He's Colombian. He's big, Charlie. No way's he going to rip you off.'

'He's the supplier?'

Donovan nodded.

'And you're giving him to us?'

'I think Carlos sees it the other way round,' said Donovan.

'He's cutting you out?' said Jordan.

'Are you two just gonna keep staring this gift horse down the throat?' said Donovan. 'If I was you I'd be biting my hand off.'

'We don't know him, Den,' said Jordan. 'We do know you.'

'Which is why they want to meet you.'

'He's here?' asked Macfadyen.

'His nephew. Jesus.'

Jordan fiddled with his ring. 'And Carlos has got our money, right?'

'Sort of.'

'Sort of?' repeated Macfadyen incredulously. 'How can he sort of have eighteen million dollars?'

'He's happy to proceed with the deal. When the consignment arrives you pay him the balance.'

'You can see why we're nervous, Den,' said Macfadyen. 'What happens if we turn up and this Colombian says he never saw our money? They're mad bastards, Colombians. Shoot first and to hell with the questions, right?'

'Carlos ain't like that,' said Donovan. He thought that Jesus might well be, but figured it better not to let them know that.

'Even so . . .' said Macfadyen.

'What do you want, Charlie? Spit it out.' Donovan already knew what Macfadyen was going to suggest. It's what he would have insisted on had the roles been reversed.

'You come with us to the meet,' said Macfadyen.

'That's not a good idea and you know it. You, me and the Colombian together in one place. Too many bloody cooks, Charlie.'

Macfadyen looked at Jordan and something unspoken passed between them. Jordan nodded. 'You're there or we walk away here and now,' said Macfadyen quietly.

'Look, if it makes you feel any better, I'll introduce you,' said Donovan. 'But once you've shaken hands, I'm outta there. OK?'

Macfadyen and Jordan exchanged another look. This time it was Macfadyen who nodded. 'OK,' said Macfadyen. 'When?'

'Let me make a call.' Donovan took out one of his mobile phones.

DEN DONOVAN walked along the Serpentine. Macfadyen and Jordan were several hundred yards away, walking together, though they kept looking across at him. Donovan had insisted on walking to the park, but Macfadyen and Jordan had wanted to drive. They'd parked the Ferrari in the underground car park in Park Lane and were keeping their distance until they'd seen Donovan with the Colombian.

Jesus Rodriguez was standing on the bank of the Serpentine wearing a cream suit with a white silk shirt buttoned at the neck.

Donovan hated having to meet Rodriguez out in the open, because it made it harder to spot any surveillance, but Macfadyen and Jordan hadn't wanted a meeting indoors. They hung back as Donovan walked up to Rodriguez.

'Is that them?' asked the Colombian, nodding at Macfadyen and Jordan.

'Yeah. They're jittery. So am I.'

'We're just having a walk in the park, my friend.'

'A Colombian drugs lord, two of the main suppliers of Class A drugs in Scotland, and Tango One. The fact that we're in one place is just about grounds for a conspiracy charge.'

The Colombian started walking alongside the Serpentine and Donovan went with him. He took the Sparbuchs from his inside pocket and handed them to the Colombian.

Rodriguez nodded and put the passbooks into his jacket pocket. Donovan handed him a slip of paper with two passwords written on it. Rodriguez put it in his wallet. 'And you will have the money from the paintings before I leave London?'

'I hope so,' said Donovan.

'Just remember that we have another can of petrol,' Rodriguez said. 'Now, these two men in black, they know the score?'

Donovan nodded. 'They'll pay you on delivery. Eighteen mill.'

'How much do they know about me?'

'Your name. And that you're the supplier. They're worried it might be a set-up. That's why they want me here.'

Rodriguez grinned. 'So you can protect them?'

'So that if the shit hits the fan, I'll get hit, too.'

'Do you think they're satisfied yet?'

'I'll ask them.' Donovan beckoned at Macfadyen and Jordan. The two men looked at each other, then walked cautiously over.

Rodriguez nodded at Donovan. 'Perhaps you should do the honours.'

'This is Charlie Macfadyen. Edinburgh's finest. Charlie, this is Jesus Rodriguez.'

The two men shook hands.

'And this is Ricky Jordan.'

'From Liverpool,' said Rodriguez. 'Birthplace of the Beatles.' He shook hands with Jordan. 'I've heard of you, Ricky. You were in Miami two years ago doing business with Roberto Galardo.'

Jordan narrowed his eyes and Rodriguez laughed. 'Don't worry, Ricky, I'm not DEA. Roberto is an old friend.' The Colombian put his arm round Jordan's shoulder and hugged him. 'So, let's talk business, shall we?' He looked across at Donovan. 'Call me at the hotel about the other thing, OK? Two days.'

Donovan nodded. 'You OK now?' he asked Macfadyen.

'Yeah. I guess.'

'I'll leave you to it. Be lucky, yeah?' Donovan walked away.

THE GLASS DOOR to the gallery was locked and a discreet brass plate told visitors they should ring the bell if they wanted to be admitted. A brunette with close-cropped hair was sitting at a white oak reception desk.

When Donovan pressed the bell she stood up and walked over to the glass door.

'I'm here to see Maury,' said Donovan.

'Is he expecting you?'

'Just tell him Den Donovan's here, will you.'

She pushed a button on her side of the door. The locking mechanism buzzed and Donovan pushed the door open.

The woman walked away. Donovan turned his attention to the paintings on the walls. They were modern and mindless. Donovan wandered around, shaking his head scornfully.

'Den!' Maury Goldman strode across the gallery, hand outstretched. His mane of grey hair was swept back as if he'd been riding a scooter without a helmet. Not that there'd be a scooter on the roads capable of bearing Goldman's weight. He was a fat man and his Savile Row suits demanded at least three times the cloth of a regular fitting.

Goldman pumped Donovan's hand, and then hugged him. 'When did you get back?' he asked.

'Day or two. I need a favour, Maury,' said Donovan quietly.

'Come upstairs, we can have a chat there.' Goldman led Donovan through a door that led to a stairway. He was panting as he reached the top of the stairs and pushed open the door to his private office.

The paintings on the office walls were a world apart from the canvases downstairs and Donovan wandered around, relishing the art. Goldman eased himself down onto a massive leather swivel chair behind a dark oak desk.

'This is good,' said Donovan, looking at a small black chalk and lithographic crayon drawing of an old woman. 'It's a Goya, right?'

'None other,' said Goldman.

'Where the hell did you get it from?'

Goldman tapped the side of his nose. 'Trade secret.'

'It must be worth seven fifty, right?'

'Closer to a mill. But I could do you a deal, Dennis.'

'It's the other way round,' said Donovan, rubbing his chin as he scrutinised the painting. 'I need to sell what I've got.'

Goldman lit a cigar. 'You sure? Rock-solid investments. It's quality you've got there, Den.'

'I'm not doing this by choice, Maury, believe me.'

Donovan walked over to a green leather armchair opposite Goldman's desk and sat on one of the arms. He took out an envelope and dropped it onto the desk. Goldman opened it and took out a sheet of paper on which Donovan had written down an inventory of the paintings he wanted to sell.

Goldman took out a pair of gold-framed reading glasses and perched them on the end of his nose. He nodded appreciatively as he ran his eyes down the list. 'We must be talking two mill, Den. You know any bank would lend against these, don't you? Shove them in a vault and take out a loan. You'd pay six per cent, maybe seven.'

'I'd only get half the value. Maybe seventy-five per cent if I was lucky. I need all of it, Maury, and I need it now.'

'Now?'

'Tomorrow.'

Goldman's eyes widened. 'Are you in trouble, Den?'

'Not if you sell those paintings PDQ. Can you buy them off me?'

'Two million's out of my league, Den. You need a private buyer.'

'Do you know anyone?'

Goldman shook his head. 'No one who'd buy the lot, Den. It's a great collection you've got, but it's your taste, right? You've got a mixed bag. Quality, but mixed. We'd have to split the collection up, find buyers for them individually.'

'Can you do that?'

'I can try, Den.'

Donovan nodded glumly. He could tell from Goldman's voice that the dealer wasn't optimistic.

'I tell you what, I'd be happy to take the Van Dyck sketches off your hands. A hundred and fifty grand?' Donovan smiled tightly and Goldman sighed. 'You're a hard man, Dennis. Two hundred?'

'Two hundred it is, Maury. Cash tomorrow, yeah?'

Goldman nodded. 'I'll get on the phone right away about the rest of your collection. OK if I come to the house tomorrow morning?'

Donovan nodded.

Goldman continued to scrutinise the list. 'I know someone who might help,' he said.

'In what way? A buyer?'

'A dealer. Young guy, he's been making a bit of a name for himself. Bit of a chancer, it has to be said, but he turns over some good stuff. Sails a bit close to the wind when it comes to provenance, but he has cash buyers. Buyers a bit like yourself, if you get my drift.'

'You trust him? This is personal business, Maury. I mean, the paintings are kosher but there's going to be a money trail. I don't have time to do any laundry.'

'He's never let me down, Den. And he knows the faces. God forbid I should put you in touch with my competition, but if you're in a bind he might be able to help.'

Donovan nodded. 'OK, then. What's his name?'

Goldman blew a cloud of smoke across the desk, then waved it away with his hand. 'Fullerton. Jamie Fullerton.'

ROBBIE'S THUMBS were getting numb, but he didn't want to stop playing with the Gameboy, not while he was so close to beating his personal best. His mobile phone started to ring on the grass beside him. He put the Gameboy down, picked up his mobile and pressed the green button. 'Yes . . .' he said.

'Cheer up, you look like you've got the weight of the world on your shoulders.'

'Dad!' Robbie shouted. He stood up and looked round the garden, the phone still glued to his ear. 'Where are you?'

Donovan stepped out of the kitchen, waving at his son.

'Dad!' Robbie screamed, running towards him. He threw himself at Donovan, who picked him up and swung him round. Robbie put his arms round his father's neck and hugged him tight. 'I knew you'd come back. Are we going home?'

Donovan put his son back on the ground and ruffled his hair. 'We can talk about that later,' he said. 'There's something we've got to do first. You want a Big Mac?'

'Burger King's better."

Laura came out of the kitchen. 'Are you staying for dinner, Den?'

'Father and son time,' laughed Donovan. 'Junk food's a-calling.'

They caught a black cab to Queensway and Donovan took his son into Whiteleys shopping centre. Donovan headed towards a photograph machine on the ground floor.

'What are we doing, Dad?' asked Robbie.

'Passport pictures,' said Donovan, helping him into the booth. He gave him two one-pound coins and showed him how to raise the seat.

'I've already got a passport,' said Robbie.

'Your mum took it,' said Donovan.

'Why?'

'I don't know. You'll have to ask her.'

'Why do I need a passport?'

'For God's sake, Robbie, just do as you're told,' Donovan snapped. Robbie's face fell and he pulled the curtain shut.

Donovan leaned against the machine. 'Robbie, I'm sorry.'

Robbie didn't say anything. There were four flashes and then Robbie got out of the booth. He didn't look at Donovan. Donovan ruffled his son's hair. 'I'm having a bad day, Robbie. I'm sorry.'

'Will you get divorced?'

Donovan's jaw dropped. 'After what she's done, she can't come back, Robbie.'

'Yeah, I know. I won't have to stay with her, will I?'

Donovan knelt down so that his face was level with Robbie's. 'Of course not.'

'Most of my friends, when their parents split up, they have to live with their mums.'

'Yeah, but this is different.'

'I know. But it's the judge who decides, right?'

Donovan shook his head. 'After what she did, no judge is going to let her take you away from me. That's as long as you want to stay with me. You do want to stay with me, right?'

'Sure!' said Robbie quickly.

'So that's sorted.' Donovan gently banged Robbie's chin with his fist. 'You and me, OK?'

'OK, Dad.'

The strip of photographs slid out of the machine. Robbie picked it up and studied it. 'I look like a geek.'

Donovan took it off him. 'You look great.' He put the photographs in his pocket and smiled at Robbie. 'Burger King, yeah?'

Robbie grinned and nodded. 'Great.'

STEWART SHARKEY carried the two glasses of champagne out onto the terrace and handed one to Vicky. She stared out across the azure Mediterranean with unseeing eyes.

'Cheers,' said Sharkey, and touched his glass against hers.

The bay was dotted with massive white yachts.

'We could get a boat,' said Sharkey. 'Sail away.'

'Den always talked about getting one,' said Vicky, her voice flat and emotionless. 'But where would we go? He'll find us eventually.'

'Not here. He has never been to the South of France. Hates the French, you know that. He's no friends here. No contacts.'

Vicky turned to look at him. 'So that's the great plan? We stay in Nice for the rest of our lives.'

'This is temporary, Vicky. Just until we get things sorted.'

Vicky shook her head. 'This isn't getting things sorted. This is hiding.'

A helicopter buzzed towards one of the yachts in the bay.

'I miss Robbie,' she said quietly.

'I know you do.'

'I don't think you do,' she said. 'You don't have children. Den'll take Robbie to the Caribbean and I'll never see him again.'

'You took his passport, Den can't take him anywhere.'

Vicky scowled. 'That's not going to stop him. Den's got half a dozen passports. He can just as easily get one for Robbie.'

'Look, there are things I can do. I'll talk to a lawyer. Get some sort of injunction stopping Den taking Robbie out of the country.'

'You said we couldn't talk to anyone back in the UK.'

'I'll find a way. And things are going to get hot for Den—he won't be able to hang around London for long.'

Vicky shaded her eyes with her hand. 'What do you mean?'

'Den's got problems, you know that. Customs and the cops will be waiting for him to put a foot wrong. He'll have to go back to the Caribbean. And if I talk to a lawyer he won't be able to take Robbie with him. Once he's gone, we can go back to the UK.'

'Den won't run away with his tail between his legs.'

'No, but he won't risk twenty years in prison. He's got stuff on the go, and he's going to have to take care of business. He can't do that in London. Den's as mad as hell just now, but he'll calm down. He'll negotiate. He'll have to.'

'Because he wants his money back?'

'Exactly.'

'How much did you take, Stewart?'

Sharkey looked away. 'Enough for him to know that he can't push us around. A few million.'

'How much is a few?'

'Oh come on, Vicky. This was never about money. You know I love you. The money's just a way of keeping Den in check. As soon as he's calmed down, we'll give it back. I've got more than enough to take care of you.'

'You promise?'

'What? That I've got enough money?'

'That you'll pay Den back? Once we've sorted out Robbie and everything.'

Sharkey nodded. 'I promise.'

'I mean it, Stewart. It's one thing to walk out on him. It's another to steal from him.'

'You're not stealing. You're entitled. You had signing rights to all those accounts.'

Vicky shook her head. 'That was just to keep the money safe. He never gave me the money, it was just in my name.'

THE TAXI PULLED UP in front of Laura's house. Robbie gave his father a black look. 'I don't want to stay here.'

'Just a few days, OK?'

Robbie brushed tears from his eyes. Donovan put his arm round his son. Robbie tried to shake him away, but Donovan hugged him tightly. Robbie sniffed. 'Then we can go home?'

'Maybe.'

Robbie looked at Den, accusingly. 'What do you mean maybe?'

'Wouldn't you prefer to go to Anguilla?' asked Donovan.

'No!' said Robbie quickly. 'No way!'

Donovan was surprised by the vehemence in his son's voice. 'I thought you liked the Caribbean?' he said.

'For holidays, yeah. I don't want to *live* there.'

'Come on, Robbie. It's got the sun, the beach.'

'My friends are here. My school's here.'

'Robbie—'

'No!' Robbie shouted. 'I'm staying here! You're not taking me with you!' He fumbled for the door handle and rushed out of the taxi.

Donovan watched his son run up to the front door of Laura's house. He started to go after him, but then told the driver to go to Sussex Gardens and settled back in the seat.

DONOVAN ARRIVED at his house just after nine thirty the next morning. He let himself in through the back door and tapped in the burglar alarm code.

He walked through to his study, sat down at his desk and took out one of the mobiles he hadn't used. He dialled the UK number that Gregov had given him. It was answered by a woman with a Russian accent who said that she'd go and get Gregov.

He came on the line. 'Den, good to hear from you.'

'Hiya, Gregov. Wasn't sure if I'd catch you.'

'We're flying out tomorrow. Loading up the last of the supplies now. Forty thousand kilos of food and medicine. I love earthquakes, Den. My bread and butter.'

'When are you flying back?' asked Donovan.

'Next week. Are we in business, then?'

'Maybe. I'll try to get the finances sorted then I'll get back to you. Eight thousand keys, right? At three thousand a key?'

'That's right. Twenty-four total, call it twenty-five with expenses.'

Donovan raised his eyebrows. Twenty-five million US dollars. The deal Gregov was offering was so sweet it could be the answer to all his prayers. 'That seems cheap, Gregov.'

'Sure, they're friends of mine. Army buddies. I got them out of a few scrapes in Afghanistan; they sort of owe me. Their processing plant is in the middle of nowhere—once it gets anywhere near a big city the price doubles. Out of Turkey it goes up tenfold. It's cheap because I get it at the source. You have the bank account number?'

Donovan said he had.

'When you're ready to move, call Maya at the number you have. She'll get through to me, even if I'm in the air.'

'Sure,' said Donovan.

The doorbell rang as Donovan cut the connection, and he went and opened the front door. Maury Goldman stood there with a tall, blond-haired man in his late twenties, smartly dressed in a dark blue suit and grey shirt. The man looked fit, as if he worked out.

'Den, this is Jamie Fullerton,' said Goldman.

Fullerton stuck out his hand and Donovan shook it. It was a firm, strong grip, and Fullerton held Donovan's look as he squeezed. It wasn't quite a trial of strength, but Donovan felt that Fullerton had something to prove. Donovan continued to apply pressure on the handshake, and Fullerton matched it, then Fullerton nodded almost imperceptibly. 'Good to meet you, Mr Donovan.'

'Mr Donovan was my dear old dad and he's well dead. I'm Den,' said Donovan, waving them into the house. He closed the door. 'Do you want coffee?'

'Coffee would be good,' said Fullerton.

Goldman nodded. Donovan took them into the kitchen and made three mugs of coffee. Goldman and Fullerton sat down at the kitchen table.

'Maury told you what I need?' asked Donovan.

'You want to sell your collection ASAP,' said Fullerton.

'I showed Jamie your inventory,' said Goldman. 'He's spoken to several potential buyers already.'

'I hope you don't mind, Mr Donovan,' said Fullerton. 'Den,' he said, correcting himself with an embarrassed smile. 'I thought that with the time pressure, you'd want me to hit the ground running.'

'No sweat,' said Donovan. 'Have you had any feedback?'

'Some of them I can sell for you today. But the others I'm going to have to show. Can I bring people around here to see them?'

'I'd rather not,' said Donovan. 'With respect to your clients, I don't want strangers traipsing around my house. Plus, I'd rather not have people know where they've come from.'

Fullerton smiled. 'I understand, but the alternative is to let me walk out of here with two million quid's worth of fine art . . .'

Donovan looked at Fullerton, trying to get the measure of the

man. He had an air of confidence that bordered on arrogance and
there was something about his smile that reminded Donovan of a
shark. He was a good-looking guy and Donovan was sure Jamie
Fullerton had broken his fair share of hearts.

'How about we move them to my gallery?' asked Goldman.
'Anyone interested can come and see them there.'

Donovan nodded. 'That sounds good, Maury. Thanks.' He raised
his coffee mug in salute then looked at Fullerton. 'I want banker's
drafts. Tomorrow.'

'That's tight,' said Fullerton.

'That's the way it's got to be,' said Donovan.

'Made out to you?'

'Made out to cash.'

'Banks aren't over-happy about making drafts out to cash,' said
Fullerton. 'It might slow things up.'

'OK,' said Donovan. 'Get the drafts made out to Carlos
Rodriguez.' He spelt out the surname. 'Talk to me once you've got
them, right?'

Fullerton stood up. 'OK if I start loading the smaller paintings
into Maury's car?'

'Sure, I'll give you a hand.'

'We'll send a van for the larger works,' said Goldman.

'Can you get the van here this morning?' asked Donovan.

Goldman winked, pulled a mobile from his jacket pocket and
tapped in a number.

'Come and look at the Rembrandt,' Donovan said to Fullerton.

Fullerton followed Donovan upstairs. The Rembrandt drawing
was of a child reaching for an apple. Fullerton whistled softly. 'Nice,'
he said. 'Quill and reed pen with a brown ink. A similar drawing went
for almost three hundred grand at Sotheby's in New York a couple of
years ago. That was an old man—kids always fetch higher prices.'

'You're as much a Philistine as Maury,' laughed Donovan.

'I'm not saying it's not a great work, I'm just saying it's a very
saleable piece. I don't think I'll have a problem placing it.'

Donovan took the Rembrandt off the wall and placed it on the
bed. He went into the bathroom and pulled a towel off the rail and
tossed it to Fullerton. Fullerton carefully wrapped the drawing in
the towel. 'Can I see the Buttersworths?'

'Sure.' Donovan took him to the study.

Fullerton studied the painting that covered the wall safe.
'Brilliant,' he said.

'You know about Buttersworth?' said Donovan.

'Did a thesis on nineteenth-century American painters and I always had a penchant for maritime artists. Look at the detail in those clouds. And you use it to hide a safe. Who's the Philistine now?'

Donovan's jaw dropped. 'How the hell did you know that?'

Fullerton grinned and walked over to the frame. He pointed to the wall to the left of the gilded frame. 'See the indentations there?'

There was a line of small marks where the frame had been pressing against the wall when it was swung away from the safe. 'You've got a good eye,' said Donovan.

'A thief's eye,' laughed Fullerton. 'But don't worry, Den, your secret's safe with me.'

'Bloody thing's empty anyway,' said Donovan.

Fullerton went over to look at the second Buttersworth. 'I think I know just the man to buy these. A corporate finance chap over at Citibank.' He grinned confidently. 'This is going to be a piece of cake, Den.'

JAMIE FULLERTON drove his black Porsche into the underground car park. He was grinning as he stepped into the lift and pressed the button for the penthouse. Three years he'd been waiting to meet Donovan, and he'd finally been handed the man on a plate. He couldn't believe his luck. No, it hadn't been luck. He'd put a lot of time and effort into cultivating Maury Goldman, once he'd found out Goldman had been Donovan's art dealer. And it had worked. He'd been in the man's house. Shaken hands with him. Hell, Den Donovan had actually made him coffee.

Fullerton unlocked his front door and walked through to the kitchen. He opened the fridge and took out a bottle of Bollinger. He picked up a fluted glass and went out onto his terrace, which overlooked the Thames. He popped the cork and filled the glass. 'Onwards and upwards,' he said, then drank deeply. He was in.

Fullerton went back inside. He walked to his study and sat down in front of his computer. While it booted up he sipped his champagne. He logged on to the SafeWeb site and then switched through to the web site that Hathaway had assigned him three years earlier. Hathaway had warned Fullerton about using his own computer, but Fullerton had grown tired of using Internet cafés to file his reports. He'd made the decision to use his own machine though he religiously deleted all incriminating files after each session. Fullerton grinned and started typing.

GREGG HATHAWAY'S OFFICE was just five miles away from Fullerton's penthouse apartment, in the hi-tech cream and green headquarters of MI6, the Secret Intelligence Service, at Vauxhall Bridge on the south bank of the Thames.

Hathaway scrolled through Fullerton's report with a growing feeling of excitement. Over the years Fullerton had supplied intelligence that helped put more than a dozen top London criminals behind bars. But what Hathaway read on his screen was pure gold, and it made his pulse race. Dennis Donovan was back in the UK. And involved with Carlos Rodriguez. Rodriguez was a familiar name, a major Colombian player. If they could tie Donovan and Rodriguez together, Donovan could be sent down for a long time.

DONOVAN HAD TO WAIT almost two hours in the Passport Office before his number flashed up. He went to the booth indicated, where a bored Asian woman flashed him a cold smile.

'I need a replacement passport for my son,' said Donovan. He slipped a completed application form under the window.

The woman picked up the application form and flicked through it. 'You say replacement? What happened to the original?'

'He lost it,' said Donovan.

The woman looked at the photographs Donovan had clipped to the application form. 'If it's missing, you'll have to supply your son's birth certificate. And have the photographs signed by his doctor. Or your minister.'

DONOVAN LAY ON HIS BED, staring at the ceiling. He'd tried to get a new birth certificate for Robbie, but had been told it would be at least seventy-two hours. There was no way he was going to leave without his son, so he had no choice. He had to wait it out in London. There was nothing to stop him moving back into the house with Robbie. The police and Customs would put him under the microscope as soon as they discovered he was back, but Donovan wasn't planning on doing anything in the least bit criminal.

One of his mobiles rang. Donovan pressed the phone to his ear.

'Good news, Den,' said Fullerton. 'That Citibank guy loved the Buttersworths. I got him to go to seven hundred and fifty.'

Donovan sat up. 'That's good going, Jamie.'

'That's just the start,' said Fullerton. 'The Rembrandt. Guess what I got for the Rembrandt? Eight hundred grand.'

'Dollars?'

'Pounds, Den. Frigging pounds.'

'Bloody hell.' That was well above what Donovan had been hoping for. He ran through the numbers. Eight hundred thousand for the Rembrandt. Seven hundred and fifty thousand dollars was about half a million quid. Goldman had promised two hundred thousand pounds for the Van Dycks. So far he had one and a half million pounds. He sighed with relief. He was close to getting the Colombian off his back. 'That's brilliant work, Jamie. Thanks.'

'I'm pretty close to selling a couple of others, too. Should I bring you the drafts tomorrow?'

Donovan didn't want to see Rodriguez again, but the drafts had to be hand-delivered. Fullerton had done a great job selling the paintings so quickly, and Goldman had said he could be trusted. 'Can you do me a favour, Jamie?'

'Sure,' said Fullerton. 'Anything.'

'I need the drafts delivered. There's a guy called Jesus Rodriguez staying at the Intercontinental near Hyde Park. He's the nephew of the guy the money's to go to. Can you give them to him in person? Don't just leave them at reception, yeah? In his hand.'

Fullerton laughed. 'I should ask him for a receipt?'

'Yeah, and count your fingers after you shake hands with him,' said Donovan. 'Seriously, Jamie. Jesus Rodriguez is a tough son of a bitch. Don't take any liberties with him.'

'Understood.'

'Second thing. He's expecting two million quid. There's the two hundred grand that Goldman's paying me for the sketches, so I need one point eight mill from you. Anything above that keep for me, OK?'

'No problem. Pleasure doing business with you, Den. I mean that. If there's anything else you need, don't hesitate, OK?'

Donovan thanked him and cut the connection. Jamie Fullerton was proving to be a godsend.

JAMIE FULLERTON pounded down the pavement towards his apartment block. He'd run a seven-mile circuit but he'd barely worked up a sweat. He was so pumped up with adrenaline he felt as if he could run another circuit, but he had work to do.

He jogged into the reception area of the block and into the lift and ran on the spot as it climbed up to the top floor.

The message light on his answering machine was winking. He hit the PLAY button and did press-ups as he listened to the message. It was a property developer in Hampstead who had seen four of

Donovan's paintings the previous evening. He had decided to buy them and wanted Fullerton to call round to pick up a bank draft for half a million pounds. Fullerton punched the air in triumph.

In the space of eighteen hours, Donovan had raised two million pounds, a reflection of the quality of the collection. Donovan was clearly attached to his art and Fullerton couldn't work out why he was desperate to sell. According to Goldman, Donovan was worth tens of millions of dollars. Then there was the fact that the drafts had to be made out to the mysterious Mr Rodriguez. Fullerton had asked Hathaway for information on Rodriguez, but so far none had been forthcoming.

Fullerton called the Intercontinental and asked to be put through to Jesus Rodriguez's room. A man with a South American accent said that Mr Rodriguez was busy, but when Fullerton explained why he was calling a hand was put over the mouthpiece and Fullerton heard muffled Spanish. Then Rodriguez was on the line, saying he'd see Fullerton in his suite at one o'clock.

He went through to his bathroom and showered, then dressed in a Lanvin suit and Gucci shoes. He drove his Porsche to Hampstead and picked up the draft. The drive from Hampstead to the Intercontinental took almost an hour but he was still ten minutes early so he sat in reception until exactly one o'clock before phoning up to Rodriguez's suite.

Two large men in black suits were waiting for him on the seventh floor. They patted him down professionally without speaking, then one of them motioned for Fullerton to follow him.

Rodriguez was standing in front of a window offering a panoramic view of Hyde Park. He turned and smiled as Fullerton walked into the room. He was a short man but very muscular, dressed in a cream suit and chocolate shirt. He held out his hand to shake and Fullerton saw a ridged scar on the back of his right hand.

'So you are Donovan's money man?' he asked, gripping Fullerton's hand and squeezing hard.

'He apologises for not coming in person,' Fullerton said. He took his hand away and resisted the urge to massage his aching fingers.

Rodriguez laughed harshly. 'I quite understand.'

Fullerton took the drafts from the inside pocket of his jacket and handed them to Rodriguez. Rodriguez looked through them. 'Good,' he said. 'At least on this occasion he has kept his word.'

'Was there a problem before?' asked Fullerton. Rodriguez stiffened and Fullerton realised he'd made a mistake. 'I know Den was very keen that this transaction would go ahead smoothly.'

Rodriguez stared at Fullerton. He was still smiling but his eyes were as cold and hard as pebbles. 'How long have you worked for him?' he asked.

Fullerton tried to smile confidently. 'I'm not really an employee,' he said quickly. 'I'm an art dealer. He needed some works of art placing and I was able to help.'

Rodriguez visibly relaxed. 'You should come and see me some time in Bogotá. I too have an interest in art.'

'Do you have a card?'

Rodriguez chuckled. 'A card?' He looked across at his two body-guards and said something in Spanish. They started laughing and Rodriguez slapped Fullerton on the back. 'Just ask anyone in Bogotá. They'll tell you where to find me.'

'I will do, Mr Rodriguez.'

DONOVAN LEFT Laura's house just before 10.00pm. He walked along the path to the pavement, then turned and looked back at the house. The bedroom where Robbie was staying was on the first floor. Donovan looked up at the window. The curtain twitched. Donovan raised his hand and gave a small wave. The curtain moved to the side and Robbie appeared. He waved down at Donovan. Donovan blew his son a kiss. Robbie moved away from the window and the curtain fell back into place.

'Dennis Donovan?'

Donovan whirled round. A small, balding man was walking towards him, his right hand moving inside his raincoat. Donovan reacted immediately, stepping forward to meet the man, his left hand pushing him off balance so he couldn't pull out whatever was concealed underneath the coat. The man started to protest, but Donovan carried on moving forward. He grabbed the man's wrist and twisted it hard, then stamped down on the man's shin.

The man yelped and fell back. Donovan kicked his feet from underneath him and he slammed into the pavement. Donovan followed the man down, dropping on top of him, his knees pinning the man's arms to the ground. Donovan pulled back his right fist, ready to smash it into the man's face.

'Who the hell are you?' asked Donovan.

The man was confused, shaking his head, his eyes glazed.

'Who sent you!' shouted Donovan.

'Your wife . . .' spluttered the man.

'Bitch!' shouted Donovan. 'How much did she pay you?'

'Our standard fee. One hundred and twenty pounds plus expenses.'

'What?' Donovan was confused. The going rate for a hit in London was fifteen thousand, minimum.

The front door opened. 'Den? What's happening?' shouted Mark.

'Who the hell are you?' asked Donovan.

'I'm a solicitor's clerk,' said the man, gasping for breath. 'I serve writs in the evenings, for the overtime.'

Mark rushed up behind Donovan. 'What's going on?' he asked.

Donovan ignored him. 'You've got a writ for me?'

The man tried to nod towards his chest. 'Inside pocket.'

Donovan shoved his hand inside the man's coat. His fingers found an envelope and he pulled it out. His name was typed on it. In the top left-hand corner was the name and address of a firm of City solicitors.

'How did you know where to find me?' Donovan asked.

'I had a list of addresses. This was the third I tried.'

Donovan helped the solicitor's clerk to his feet and brushed down his raincoat. He took out his wallet and thrust a handful of fifty-pound notes into the man's hands, then pushed him away. The man walked unsteadily down the street.

'What the hell was all that about?' Mark asked.

'An injunction,' said Donovan. He ripped open the envelope and scanned the legal papers. 'Shit,' he said.

Laura hurried down the path. 'What's going on?' she asked.

'It says I can't take Robbie out of the country. Bitch!' Donovan screwed up the papers and threw them into the gutter.

Laura picked up the papers and straightened them out. 'You're going to have to show these to a lawyer, Den.'

Donovan snatched them from her and stormed off down the street. Upstairs, the curtain twitched at Robbie's bedroom window.

LAURENCE PATTERSON kept Donovan waiting in reception for fifteen minutes, but had the grace to come hurrying out apologising profusely. He pumped Donovan's hand and ushered him into his office.

'Got a client just been pulled in on a robbery charge, he's screaming blue murder. Sorry.'

'Business is good, yeah?' asked Donovan, dropping onto a sofa. There was a huge desk dominating one end of the palatial office, but Patterson preferred to talk to his clients on the sofas by the window, with its expansive view of the City.

'Busy,' said Patterson. 'Can I get you a drink?'

Donovan shook his head. He handed Patterson the writ that the solicitor's clerk had given him. Patterson read through it quickly. He had a sharp mind, a photographic memory and the ear of the best barristers in London. Patterson had helped get charges dropped against members of Donovan's team on several occasions.

Patterson rubbed the bridge of his nose. 'Cards on the table, Den, it's not really my field. This domestic stuff is a specialised area. Would you mind if I pass you to one of my colleagues?'

Donovan shifted uncomfortably on the sofa. 'I'd prefer you to handle it, Laurence.'

'We can do it that way, Den. But all that would happen is that you'd talk to me, I'd run it by her, then I'd tell you what she told me.'

'She?'

'Julia Lau. There's nothing she doesn't know about family law.'

'Lau? Chinese?'

'That's right. And you'd be better off having her arguing your case than me, Den. How's it going to look if you've got a criminal lawyer by your side in a custody fight? I keep people out of prison, Den. I don't discuss the finer points of parental control.'

Donovan nodded. 'And she's dead safe, yeah?'

'Anything you tell her is privileged, Den. Like talking to a priest.'

'OK, when do I meet her?'

'I'll get her down now. I'll sit in on the initial briefing, yeah?'

'Cheers, Laurence.'

Patterson went over to his desk, picked up his phone and spoke, then replaced the receiver and walked back to the sofas.

A few minutes later, there was a knock on the door. It opened and Julia Lau walked in. She was overweight and her thighs rubbed together in a dark green trouser suit as she waddled over to the sofas. She had a face that was almost circular, with thick-lensed spectacles perched on the end of a bulbous nose. 'Mr Donovan, so happy to meet you,' she said, extending a hand. Her accent was pure English public school.

Donovan shook hands with her. She had pudgy, sausage-like fingers. She lowered herself onto the sofa. It creaked under her weight and Donovan found himself sliding along the black leather towards her. He pushed himself away from her to the far end of the sofa.

Patterson handed Lau the injunction and she read it.

'Your wife says she believes that you intend to take your son to Anguilla. Is that true?'

'I have a house there.'

'But your matrimonial home is here in London?'

'If you can call it that,' said Donovan bitterly. 'It didn't stop her screwing my accountant there.'

'Your primary residence is here in the UK, though?'

'It's complicated.'

Lau flashed him a cold smile. 'Try to enlighten me, Mr Donovan. I'll do my best to keep up.'

Donovan nodded, accepting he had been patronising. 'I'm sorry. Yes, the family home is in London but for various reasons I don't spend much time in the country. I have a home in Anguilla; Robbie and his mother have stayed with me for weeks at a time. I don't see why he shouldn't be allowed to go there now.' He pointed at the injunction. 'We can get that overturned, right?'

'We can fight this. But I must counsel you that this is probably the first shot in what will develop into a salvo. I would expect your wife very shortly to move to get custody of your son.'

'No way!' said Donovan sharply.

Lau held up a hand to quieten him. 'If you have sole custody, that injunction simply cannot stand. If I was advising your wife I would have told her to rush through this injunction, but then to apply for sole custody on the basis that you are an unsuitable parental figure.'

'Bollocks!'

Lau looked at him steadily. 'Please don't take offence, I am sure you are a commendable father, but your wife is going to portray you in the worst light possible. Nevertheless, in view of your wife's infidelity, we can make a good case for you being granted sole custody of Robbie. However, that doesn't necessarily mean you will be allowed to take Robbie overseas.'

'Why not?' interrupted Donovan.

'Because even if you are granted sole custody, your wife would still have visitation rights, and those rights would be compromised if your son was living outside the country.'

'But she's the one who left,' protested Donovan.

'Do you know where she is?'

'I've got people looking.'

'If we could show that she is herself resident overseas, I think there might be less of a problem convincing a court that you be allowed to take Robbie abroad.'

'We'll see,' said Donovan. If he did find out where his errant wife was, custody wouldn't be an issue.

DONOVAN GOT BACK to the hotel and told the manager he'd be checking out. He went up to his room and packed. One of his mobile phones had received a voice message from Jamie Fullerton, saying he had the rest of the money from the sale of the paintings. Three hundred and fifty thousand pounds.

Donovan phoned Fullerton and arranged to meet him at Donovan's house later, then went and paid his bill in cash.

He caught a black cab to the house, let himself in, showered and changed into chinos and a polo shirt. The doorbell rang. It was Jamie Fullerton, carrying two holdalls. 'How's it going, Den?' he asked.

'Fine, Jamie. Come on in.'

Donovan took him through to the kitchen. Fullerton heaved the bulging holdalls onto the kitchen table.

'Beer?' asked Donovan. He took two bottles out of the fridge and uncapped them. He gave one to Fullerton and they clinked bottles.

'To crime,' said Fullerton.

Donovan froze, his bottle halfway towards his mouth. 'What?'

Fullerton took a mouthful of beer and wiped his mouth with the back of his hand. 'It was a crime, the way I ramped those paintings. Way over the odds they paid.' He nodded at the holdalls. 'There's your cash. A cool three hundred and fifty, on top of the one point eight I gave the Colombian.'

Donovan put his bottle on the table and unzipped one of the holdalls. It was full of wads of fifty-pound notes.

'It's spotless, Den. You could put that on a church plate with a clean conscience.'

Donovan put a wad of notes into his jacket pocket and zipped up the holdall. He raised his bottle in salute. 'Good job, Jamie. Thanks.'

'You want a line? To celebrate?'

Donovan's face hardened. 'You brought drugs into my house?'

Fullerton grimaced.

'You know I'm under surveillance, right? I'm Tango One, I am.'

'Tango One?'

'That's what the filth call their most wanted. T stands for target and it's T Tango. Tango One, Target One. And I'm it. And you brought drugs into my house? How stupid is that?'

'Shit. I'm sorry. It's only for personal use. Couple of grams.'

Donovan shook his head. 'Don't carry gear when you're anywhere near me. They're going to be looking for any excuse to put me away.'

'Understood, Den.' Fullerton picked up his lager and drained the bottle. 'You want to go out and celebrate?'

'What did you have in mind?' asked Donovan.

'Bottle of shampoo. Pretty girls. On me.'

Donovan thought about Fullerton's offer. He had things to do if he was to get the house ready for Robbie, but it had been a while since he'd let his hair down. A few drinks wouldn't do him any harm. 'OK. But no drugs.'

Fullerton made a Boy Scout salute. 'Dib, dib, dib,' he said.

Fullerton's black Porsche was parked a few doors down from Donovan's house. Fullerton drove quickly, weaving through the evening traffic. They'd been driving for only five minutes when Donovan pointed at a phone box.

'Pull up here, Jamie. I've got to make a call.'

Fullerton groped into his pocket and held out a mobile. 'Use this.' He pulled up at the side of the road.

Donovan took the mobile off him. 'Let me tell you about mobiles, Jamie. Everything you say near this, they can listen in to.'

'They?'

'The Feds. Customs. Spooks.'

'Den, no one but me has ever touched that phone. No way have they put a bug in it. On my life.'

Donovan shook his head. 'They don't have to. Once they know the number they can listen in to every call. Worse, they can tell where you are to within a few feet. They can look into your Sim card and get all the data off it. Your address book, every call you made and every call you received. They can see it all.'

Fullerton stared at the mobile in Donovan's hand. 'Shit.'

'OK, so long as they don't know you, you can carry on in your own sweet way, but I'm Tango One and any mobile I go near is a potential threat.' He tossed the phone back to Fullerton. 'And once they've seen you with me, your phone becomes a threat, too.' He gestured at the phone box. 'That's why anything sensitive, you use a public land line.'

Donovan climbed out of the car. He took a twenty-pound phone card from his wallet and used it to call Juan Rojas in Spain. The machine kicked in. Donovan dictated the name and address of the firm of solicitors that Vicky was using, then went back to the car.

'OK?' asked Fullerton.

'We'll see,' said Donovan. He knew people in London who'd be capable of getting the information he needed from Vicky's solicitor, but by using Rojas he'd keep himself one step removed.

'Problem?' asked Fullerton.

'Nah. Come on, let's get drunk.' He twisted round in his seat.

'We being followed?' asked Fullerton.

'Probably,' said Donovan.

Fullerton stamped on the accelerator and the Porsche roared through a traffic light that was about to turn red. Then he slowed so they could see if any other vehicles went through the red light. None did. Fullerton took the next left and then swung the Porsche down a side street on the right.

'Just don't get done for speeding,' Donovan warned.

Fullerton slowed down. Ten minutes later they pulled up in a car park at the side of what looked like a windowless industrial building. Three men in black suits stood guard at an entrance above which was a neon sign that spelled out LAPLAND. 'My local,' said Fullerton.

Donovan looked sideways at Fullerton. 'You know Terry, yeah?'

Terry Greene was the owner of the lap-dancing club. He was an old friend of Donovan's, though it had been more than three years since Donovan had been in the club.

'Terry? Sure. He's in Spain, I think. You know him?'

'Used to be my local, too. Way back when.' They climbed out of the Porsche and Fullerton locked it. 'Small world,' said Donovan.

The three doormen greeted Fullerton by name, clapping him on the back. They were all in their mid-twenties and selected for their bulk rather than their intelligence. Donovan didn't recognise any of them, and from the blank-faced nods they gave him it was clear they didn't know who he was. Donovan preferred it that way.

He followed Fullerton inside. The decor had changed since Donovan had last visited the club. The black walls and ultraviolet lights had been replaced with plush red flock wallpaper and antique brass light fittings. The music didn't appear to have changed, though. Raunchy and loud.

There were two raised dancing areas where seminaked girls gyrated round chrome poles. Sweating men in suits clustered around the podiums, drinking spirits and shoving ten- and twenty-pound notes into G-strings. A waitress in a microskirt and bikini top tottered over on impossibly high heels and kissed Fullerton on the cheek. Fullerton introduced her to Donovan. Her name was Sabrina.

She took them over to a table in a roped-off section with a clear view of both dancing podiums. Fullerton ordered Dom Pérignon and Sabrina tottered off to get it.

'See anything you like, Den?' Fullerton asked, gesturing at the dancing girls.

Donovan checked out the dancers. Two brunettes, two blondes, an oriental and a black girl. The blondes could have been sisters: they were both tall with long hair almost down to their waists, full breasts and tiny waists.

Fullerton nodded at the oriental girl. 'Mimi's my dish of the day.'

Sabrina returned with their champagne in an ice bucket. She poured the Dom Pérignon, then left them to it. Fullerton sighed and settled back. He put his feet up on the table and sipped his champagne. 'Do you want a lap dance?' he asked.

'Maybe later,' said Donovan. He frowned as he saw someone he recognised walking into the club. Ricky Jordan. Jordan waved and walked over.

'Den, didn't know this was one of your haunts,' he said. Donovan stood up and the two men hugged. Donovan introduced him to Fullerton. They shook hands. Jordan motioned for Sabrina to bring another bottle of champagne.

'How did it go with Jesus?'

'Sweet,' said Jordan. 'Volkswagen Beetles, huh. This one could run and run, Den.'

'Yeah,' said Donovan. Sabrina arrived with champagne and a glass for Jordan.

'Takes me and Charlie to the next level.'

'Yeah, well just remember who helped you on the way, yeah?'

Jordan clinked his glass against Donovan's. 'Cheers, mate.'

'Yeah,' said Donovan ruefully. 'Cheers.'

Fullerton banged his glass against Donovan's. 'Down the hatch,' he said. 'What's this about VWs? If you want a car, I can get you a deal on a Porsche.'

Jordan threw back his head and laughed. 'Bloody hell, Den. Where did you get him from?'

Donovan threw a warning glance at him.

'How's it going, boys?'

The three men looked up. It was one of the blondes. Jordan leered up at her. 'Getting better by the minute,' he said. 'Go on then, darling, do your stuff.'

The other blonde who'd been dancing on the podium walked over. 'I'm Angie,' she said. She slipped her arm round the other girl's waist. 'She's Kris.'

'With a K,' said Kris.

Fullerton leaned over. 'I know you, don't I?' he asked Kris.

Kris put her head on one side. 'Don't think so.'

'How long have you worked here?' Fullerton asked.

'A week. I was at one of Terry's other clubs. He asked me to move here for a bit.'

'Which club?'

'Angels. Marble Arch.'

'Didn't know Angels was Terry's.'

'Yeah, it was his first club,' said Donovan. 'I used to drink there all the time.' He held out his hand. 'Come and give me a dance, Kris.'

'Give?' she said, tossing her long blonde hair. 'Nothing here's for free, you know.'

Kris started to dance, a slow sinuous grind, her green eyes fixed on Donovan's. She had full lips and white, even teeth and she smelt of fresh flowers.

She put her lips close to his ear. 'What's your name?' she whispered.

'Mr Mysterious,' said Donovan.

Kris wrinkled her nose. 'I know who you are. You're Den Donovan.'

Donovan frowned. 'How do you know that?'

'One of the girls told me.'

'Which girl?' asked Donovan suspiciously.

'Elizabeth.' She jerked a thumb towards the podium. 'The black girl. She's been here for years. Knows everyone. Remembers you. Said you were a big tipper and you liked blondes.'

Donovan relaxed. 'That sounds about right.'

Kris was an accomplished dancer, totally at ease with her body. She brushed her lips against Donovan's and he moved to kiss her but she pulled away. She wagged a finger at him. 'No touching,' she said.

'What about later?'

'I'm a dancer. Not a hooker.'

'I wasn't thinking of paying,' said Donovan. 'I've never paid for it.'

'It?' she said, with an amused look on her face. 'You old romantic, you.'

The track came to an end and Donovan reached for his wallet. Kris shook her head. 'First one's on me, Den.'

Den took a fifty-pound note from his wallet and handed it to her. 'You're working,' he said. 'And I'm a punter. Take it.'

Kris looked like she was going to argue but then she smiled and took the money. 'Thanks.'

'Pleasure was all mine.'

'Another?'

'Later, yeah?'

A waitress was waving at Kris and miming she had a phone call.

Kris hurried to the bar, where a barman was holding the phone up.

Fullerton leaned over to Jordan and winked conspiratorially. 'Hey, Ricky. Fancy a line?'

'Dead right,' said Jordan.

'Den?' said Fullerton, and he tapped the side of his nose.

Donovan glared at Fullerton. 'For God's sake, Jamie. Didn't you hear what I said to you before? I don't go near gear.'

'Leave him be, Den,' said Jordan.

'Yeah, well you can say that when we're all behind bars.'

'We're among friends here,' said Jordan. 'Ain't that right, Jamie?'

Jamie gave Jordan a thumbs up.

'Come on, Den,' said Jordan. 'Lighten up.'

Jordan and Fullerton stood up and headed for the bathrooms. Donovan followed them, shaking his head.

Kris was still on the phone and she was pacing up and down as she talked. Donovan went over to her.

'You should call the police,' she said into the phone. 'You can't let him get away with shit like that, Louise. Next time he might have a knife.' She flashed Donovan a tight smile and pointed at the receiver. 'Friend of mine's got a problem,' she mouthed.

'Anything I can do?' whispered Donovan.

'No, it's OK, Den,' said Kris, then she held up her hand to silence him as she listened to whoever it was she was talking to. Kris sighed. 'Den Donovan, he's an old pal of Terry's.'

'Not that old, thanks,' said Donovan.

Kris shook her head and turned her back on him. Then she looked at her watch. 'OK, I'll come. Of course I will.' She listened again, and then she turned round to look at Donovan. 'Yeah, I'll ask him.' Kris nodded. 'I know, I'll see what he says.' She handed the phone back to the barman. 'Louise is a friend of mine; we worked together at Angels. A customer has just followed her home and tried to rape her. He's not there now but she's scared stiff that he might come back. I don't suppose you'd . . .'

'Of course,' said Donovan without hesitation. 'Knight in shining armour, me.'

'Really? I don't want to spoil your evening.'

'Come on. What's the choice? Drinking champagne with a couple of cokeheads or rescuing a damsel in distress?'

Kris grinned. 'Thanks. She sounded really desperate. Thing is, we're not allowed to leave with customers. You know the car park round the back?'

Donovan nodded. That was where Fullerton had parked his Porsche.

'Give me five minutes and I'll meet you there. Blue MGB.' She hurried off.

Fullerton was ordering a new bottle of champagne when Donovan got back to the table. Mimi was draped on his arm. Angie was giving Jordan a dance. Donovan sat down and sipped his champagne. After five minutes he put down his glass and patted Fullerton on the shoulder. 'I'm off,' he said.

'I'll come with you,' said Fullerton. He tried to stand up but Donovan pushed him back down.

'You enjoy yourself,' he said. 'I'll get a black cab. Catch you later. And thanks again for the paintings. You saved my life.'

Before Fullerton could say anything, Mimi leaned over and clamped her mouth over his. Donovan waved at Jordan, gave him a thumbs up and headed for the door.

Kris had the engine running. She had changed into tight blue jeans and a light blue long-sleeved woollen top that showed off her washboard-flat midriff. As soon as Donovan had closed the car door she put her foot down and shot out of the car park. She stamped on the accelerator and shot through a traffic light that was turning red.

Donovan reached over and put a hand on her leg. 'Take it easy, it's not gonna help her if you get pulled over.'

Kris nodded and eased back on the accelerator. 'If he's hurt her, I'll kill him.'

'Does it happen a lot? Punters giving you grief?'

'Not to me, but to some of the girls, yeah. You can't let them get too close, you know. They've got to know it's just business.'

'What about you? Is it always business to you?'

'You mean, why are you sitting in the car with me?'

'Well, you haven't known me for long, have you?'

'I know of you, Den Donovan. Your reputation precedes you. Besides, I'm using you as weight, not inviting you into my bed.'

'Is that right?' he asked.

She grinned. 'We'll see.'

'And that's how you see me? Weight?'

'Again, your reputation precedes you.'

She swung the MGB over to the kerb and was out of the car before Donovan even had the belt off. He hurried after her.

Kris pressed one of six doorbells to the left of the front door. The intercom crackled.

'Louise, it's me. Come on, let us in.'

The door buzzed and Kris pushed it open. Donovan followed her inside. The hallway was shabby with a threadbare carpet and fading wallpaper. Kris rushed up a flight of steep stairs.

Louise's flat was on the first floor and she had the door open with a security chain on. She unclipped the chain and opened the door wide for Kris. Kris hugged her. From the stairway Donovan could see a girl in her early twenties with a tear-stained face. She had black hair, cut in a bob that was slightly longer at the front than the back. Even with the tearful eyes, thought Donovan, she was gorgeous.

'This is Den,' said Kris, nodding at Donovan. 'Come on, let's sit.' Kris shepherded Louise into the flat. Donovan followed them and closed the door. Kris took Louise over to a sofa and sat down next to her. She pointed at a kitchenette and mouthed 'tea' to Donovan.

Donovan walked into the kitchenette. He switched on a kettle and went through cupboards until he found tea bags.

When he carried a tray with three steaming mugs back into the sitting room, Kris was sitting with her arm around Louise's shoulder and Louise was dabbing at her eyes with a large handkerchief. Donovan put the tray down on the coffee table in front of the girls. 'What happened?' he asked Louise.

'He pushed his way in and threatened to kill her,' said Kris.

Den went over and gently moved the handkerchief away from her face. Her left cheek was red and there were angry marks on her throat. 'He hit you?'

'He slapped me. Then he grabbed my throat and pushed me against the wall.' She smiled. 'I kneed him in the nuts and managed to lock myself in the bathroom with my mobile. Told him I was calling the cops.'

'You didn't, did you?' asked Donovan.

Louise shook her head. 'Fat lot of use they'd be. I called Kris.' Louise wiped her eyes with the handkerchief, then held out her hand to Donovan. 'Nice to meet you, anyway.'

'Pleasure,' said Donovan, shaking her hand. 'How did this guy find out where you lived?'

'He must have followed me back from the club. He used to send me letters. Tonight was the first time he turned up on my doorstep.'

'Do you know where he lives?'

Louise nodded. 'He wrote his address on the letters.'

'Can I see the letters?' Donovan asked Louise.

She frowned at him. 'Why?'

'Just want to see what sort of nutter you're dealing with,' said Donovan. 'Thing is, if he's not told the error of his ways he might come back. And next time you might not get the chance to lock yourself in the bathroom.'

Louise went over to a sideboard, took out a sheaf of papers and handed them to Donovan. He flicked through them.

'How old is he, this guy?'

'Mid-forties, I guess.'

Donovan nodded. At the top of each letter was the man's address. He'd signed the letters 'Nick'.

'What's his name?' asked Donovan.

'Nick Parker,' she replied.

'What does he do?' he asked.

'Stockbroker or something. To be honest, Den, I hardly listened to him. He was a punter. I danced for him, he tipped me and bought me drinks. I didn't lead him on.' She nodded at the letters. 'Not that way, anyway. I never led him to believe it was anything other than dancing. You know?'

Donovan handed the letters back to her. 'Yeah, I know.' He looked across at Kris. 'You've met this freak, yeah?'

'Yeah. Like Louise says, he seemed OK at first.'

'OK.' He finished his tea, then stood up. 'Do you want to give me a lift?' he asked Kris.

'Where to?'

Donovan gave her a tight smile.

She knew where he wanted to go.

'OK,' she said.

NICK PARKER'S HOUSE was a two-storey cottage in one of the prettier roads in Notting Hill. Expensive, thought Donovan, as he climbed out of Kris's MGB.

Kris got out of the car and stood next to Donovan as he looked up at bedroom windows. 'What are you going to do, Den?' she asked.

'I'm going to teach him a lesson,' he said.

'And I'm here because . . . ?'

'Because I wouldn't want to teach the wrong guy a lesson.'

'I'm not sure about this,' she said hesitantly.

Donovan turned to look at her. 'Take it from me, if you let him get away with slapping a girl once, he'll keep on doing it.'

Kris frowned. 'That sounds like the voice of experience,' she said.

'My stepdad used to hit my mum. I was too young to do anything at the time. I was only ten. By the time I was old enough to punch his lights out, she had died of cancer and I was in care. You've got to stand up to bullies, Kris.' He walked towards the front door. It was painted a rich dark green with a brass knocker. Donovan rapped with the knocker. Kris joined him on the doorstep.

The door opened. Nick Parker was middle-aged and slightly overweight. 'Yes?' he said.

'Is this him?' Donovan asked Kris. Kris nodded.

'What do you want?' Parker asked.

Donovan punched him in the face. Parker staggered back and Donovan followed him into the hallway, where there was a huge gilt-framed mirror. Donovan grabbed Parker's collar and flung him against the mirror. The glass cracked and pieces tinkled to the floor.

Donovan kept a grip on Parker's collar and dragged him along the hallway. Parker scrambled along on all fours, choking. Donovan pulled him into the sitting room, then kicked him in the side. Parker fell on his back, gasping for breath.

Donovan looked round the room. The windows overlooked the street but there were net curtains so no one could see in. There was a large Victorian black metal fireplace. Donovan pulled a brass poker off its stand.

'My wallet's in the bedroom,' said Parker. 'Take what you want.'

'This isn't about money,' said Donovan. 'You know Louise, yeah? From Angels?'

'Who are you? Her boyfriend?'

Donovan leaned down and put his face close up to Parker's. 'No, I'm not her boyfriend. She doesn't want a boyfriend. She wants to be left alone. Do you understand?'

'I love her,' said Parker.

'You don't love her,' said Donovan. 'You're obsessed with her. You've built some sad little fantasy round her, that's all. She doesn't love you. She doesn't even like you. She's scared of you.'

'If I could just talk to her . . .' said Parker.

'No, you're never going to talk to her again. You're not going anywhere near her again.' Donovan raised the poker above his head.

'Den, no!' shouted Kris.

'Go into the hall, Kris,' said Donovan, without looking at her.

He knelt down and banged Parker's head against the carpeted floor. 'Listen to me, and listen good!' Donovan hissed. 'You go near her again, and I'll kill you. Do you hear me?'

'I hear you,' said Parker, his voice trembling.

'I hope you believe me, Nick. Because I can and will do it. And this is just a taste of what it'll be like.' Donovan brought the poker smashing down onto Parker's right knee. Parker screamed. Donovan clamped a hand over the man's mouth, and hit him again, whacking the left knee. Parker's eyes rolled upwards and he passed out.

Donovan stood up. He pulled out Parker's shirt-tail and used it to wipe the handle of the poker and put it back in its holder.

Kris was standing by the front door, hugging herself. She looked at him, then quickly looked away. Donovan gently held her chin between his thumb and first finger and turned her face towards him. She looked into his eyes. 'You saw the marks on Louise's face. He hit her,' said Donovan.

'I know,' she said.

'This way he won't do it again.'

Kris put her hands on his shoulders and kissed him on the cheek. 'You don't have to explain, Den.'

KRIS PULLED THE MGB over at the kerb but kept the engine running. She looked out of the window at Donovan's house.

'Nice,' she said.

'Yeah. Do you wanna buy it?' said Donovan, deadpan.

'Oh, yeah, like I can afford a place like that. How much is it worth?'

'I dunno. Three mill, maybe.'

Kris whistled softly. 'You live there alone?'

'Yeah, well, I'm in a transitional stage. My wife has left me. My son's staying with my sister until I get things sorted. I don't know if I'm cut out to be a single parent.'

'You're his dad. That's all that matters.'

'I guess,' said Donovan.

Kris looked at her watch. 'I'd better be getting back to Louise. Check that she's OK. I said I'd stay the night with her.'

'She's a nice kid.'

'You interested? I could put in a good word for you.'

Donovan grinned. 'My life's probably complicated enough as it is, but thanks for the offer.'

'Not your type?'

'Where are we, the playground? She's a stunner, OK. Happy now?'

'I'll tell her,' said Kris. 'Seriously, Den. Thanks for tonight.'

'Happy to have been a help,' said Donovan. He climbed out of the sports car and waved as she drove away.

TINA LEIGH SAT DOWN in front of the computer and sipped her cappuccino. She was using an Internet café in Selfridges in Oxford Street. She'd walked from her flat. It was almost a mile but she'd wanted to get her thoughts in order. She'd met Den Donovan. Tango One. After three years of working in lap-dancing bars, of being pawed, ogled and propositioned, she'd finally met him.

She wondered how Hathaway would react when he got her email. She'd given him a wealth of intelligence over the years and at least half a dozen criminals were behind bars as a result of information she'd picked up in the clubs. She had long stopped being surprised at how hardened criminals who could withstand hours of police interrogation would open up like shucked oysters as soon as they'd had a couple of bottles of champagne and a look at her tits.

Tina sat with her fingers poised over the keyboard. She knew what she was going to write. What she didn't know was what Hathaway would ask her to do next. She'd met Den Donovan. She'd spoken to him. But she knew Hathaway would want more. He'd want her to get up close and personal. The question was—how close and how personal? She began to type.

DONOVAN WOKE with a hangover. He shaved and showered, then padded downstairs in his towelling robe, made himself a coffee and carried it through to the sitting room.

He unplugged the four mobiles that had been on charge overnight and connected another four. He sat down on the sofa, then called Robbie's mobile, using the same phone he'd used last time he'd called his son. Robbie answered almost immediately.

'Dad!'

'Hiya, kid. What are you doing?'

'Nothing much.'

'Yeah, well, change of plan. As of today, it's school. OK?'

'So we're staying? In London?'

'For a bit, yeah. Happy now?'

'Yeah. Thanks, Dad.'

'So school. Today. Let me talk to Auntie Laura, will you?'

Robbie called out his aunt's name and seconds later she was on the line. 'What have you said to him? He's grinning like the cat that got the cream.'

'I'm staying for a while.'

'Good decision, brother-of-mine.'

'Yeah, well, I don't have much choice at the moment. My lawyer says I can't take him out of the country, and if I'm going to get custody I'll have to play at happy families for a while.'

'Den!'

Donovan grinned. 'You know what I mean. I want to be with him, of course I do. But not here. Not in London. He's to go to school from now on. I'll pick him up tonight and we'll be at the house from now on. Thanks for everything. For letting him stay.'

'Not a problem, Den. You know that.'

Donovan thanked her again and cut the connection.

The keys to Vicky's Range Rover were hanging on a hook in the kitchen. Donovan drove to Chelsea, found a parking space, then walked to the offices of Alex Knight Security. Knight's entrance was a simple black door between an antiques shop and a hairdresser. Donovan pressed the bell button and a woman's voice asked who he was over the intercom.

'Den Donovan for Alex,' said Donovan. The door buzzed and he pushed it open. He went up a narrow flight of stairs, at the top of which a striking brunette had the door already open for him.

'Mr Donovan, good to see you again,' she said.

'Sarah, you're looking good,' said Donovan. 'How's the boy looking after you?'

'Boy? I'm twenty-bloody-eight,' said Alex Knight, striding out of his office. He was tall and gangly with black square-framed spectacles perched high on his nose.

The two men shook hands. 'Yeah, well you don't look a day over sixteen,' said Donovan. 'Whatever you're taking, I want some of it.'

'Clean living and early to bed,' said Knight. 'You should try it some time. Come on through.'

Knight's office was about twenty feet square but looked smaller because every inch of wall space had been lined with metal shelving filled with electrical equipment and technical manuals. His desk was a huge metal table that was also piled high with technical gear.

'So, you old reprobate, what can I do for you?'

'I'm going to be in the UK for a while, and I'm going to be under the microscope,' said Donovan. 'Cops, Customs, spooks. I need to be able to sweep my house and car, and to check if anyone who comes near me is wired. I want to do it myself.'

'No sweat,' said Knight. 'But I'd advise you to let me go over the house once. Show you the ropes, yeah?'

Donovan nodded.

'So far as sweeping goes, I've a state-of-the-art scanner from

Taiwan that'll do the job. Just run it round all suspect surfaces. You can use it on the car, too. And how about I fix up an acoustic noise generator for you in the house? You're going to be able to sweep for bugs, but everyone's using laser or microwave reflectors these days, picking up vibrations from windows. Bloody hard to detect. But switch on the noise generator and they'll just pick up static.'

'Excellent,' said Donovan.

THE MOBILE PHONE on the table bleeped and Stewart Sharkey grabbed for the receiver.

'Stewart? It's David.'

David Hoyle, a West London lawyer. Sharkey had known him for years, but this was the first time he'd used him professionally.

'Hiya, David. I trust you're using a call box?'

'I am, Stewart. But is this really necessary?'

'You don't know Vicky's husband, David.' Hoyle had never done any work for Den Donovan, or anyone like him. He was a family lawyer who specialised in divorce work and had never been within a mile of a criminal court. 'How can I help you?'

'We've heard from his lawyers. He is applying for sole custody. And of course he will try to have the injunction lifted.'

Sharkey grunted. They had expected that. So far as Sharkey was concerned, he would be quite happy for Donovan to get what he wanted. But he had to keep Vicky happy, for a while at least, and that meant going through the motions.

'I assume that Victoria still wishes to apply for custody?' asked Hoyle.

'Absolutely,' said Sharkey.

'I'll get the papers drawn up, Stewart. I'll be in touch.'

Sharkey cut the connection, walked over to a drinks cabinet and poured himself a brandy. 'Was that the phone?' asked Vicky, walking in from the terrace.

'The lawyer. He's on the case.'

'He served the injunction?'

Sharkey nodded. 'And Den's fighting it.'

'What about custody?'

'The lawyer's doing the paperwork now.' He raised the glass. 'Do you want one?'

'No, thanks. I thought I'd go out for a walk. Go to the beach maybe. Do you want to come?'

Sharkey sat down. 'Not right now. Don't forget . . .'

'I know,' she said. 'Dark glasses. Sunhat. Don't talk to anyone.'

'Just in case,' said Sharkey. 'You never know who you might bump into.'

'How long's it going to be like this, Stewart?'

'Not much longer.'

Vicky walked into the bedroom to change. Sharkey sipped his brandy. He was already bored with Vicky. Her dark moods, her insecurities, her constant whining. In a perfect world he'd just leave her, but it wasn't a perfect world so long as Den Donovan was in it. Hopefully the Colombians would soon catch up with him and when that happened then Sharkey's world truly would be perfect. With Donovan out of the way, he could walk out on Vicky without worrying about the repercussions. He'd be free and clear and in sole possession of sixty million dollars.

THE DOOR to the phone box was thrown open with a bang. Two men stood there. Men with hard faces and crew cuts, big shoulders and tight smiles. One of them pointed a finger at Hoyle. 'Out,' he said.

A third man appeared behind them. He was wearing an overcoat and looked like a younger version of Sacha Distel. But, when the man spoke, his accent was Spanish, not French. 'Mr Hoyle, I presume?' he said.

'Who are you?' asked Hoyle.

'That doesn't really matter,' said the man. 'What is more important is what I want and what I will do to you if you don't cooperate.'

ON THE WAY HOME, Donovan stopped at a call box and phoned Underwood. 'Dicko, call me back, yeah?' He gave the detective the number of the call box and then replaced the receiver. Underwood phoned back fifteen minutes later.

'Now what?' asked the detective.

'I need you to check someone out for me. Have you got a pen?'

'Bloody hell, Den, you can't keep using the Police National Computer as your own personal database. Checks leave traces.'

'I just want to know who he is, Dicko. He doesn't seem wrong but I just want to be sure.'

'OK, but let's not make a habit of this. A sergeant over at Elephant and Castle got sacked last week for doing a vehicle registration check for a journalist. Lost his job and his pension for a fifty-quid backhander.'

Donovan was going to point out that he paid Underwood a lot

more than fifty pounds, but he bit his tongue, not wanting to antagonise the detective. He gave him Fullerton's name and car registration number, and arranged to call him the following day.

HATHAWAY READ through Tina's report for the third time. Putting her in as a lap dancer had always been a long shot, and he still couldn't believe that it had worked. There was no mistake, however. Not only had she met the man, but it had quickly become personal. If Tina played it right, she could build on the connection.

He sent her a congratulatory email and told her to play it safe, that she mustn't do anything to scare him off. As he sent the email to Tina, he received notification that he had new email waiting. He clicked on the envelope icon and opened an email from Jamie Fullerton. Hathaway scrolled through Fullerton's report with a growing sense of elation. Donovan was letting Fullerton get close enough to do real damage.

Hathaway now had a connection between Donovan, Carlos Rodriguez and Ricky Jordan, a major distributor of hard drugs in Scotland. And whatever they were bringing in had something to do with VW Beetles. After a few minutes on the Internet, Hathaway discovered that there was only one place where VW Beetles were still manufactured. Mexico. Carlos Rodriguez ran most of his drugs through Mexico. Hathaway smiled to himself. Beetles packed with cocaine. And with Rodriguez involved, it had to be a huge shipment.

It took Hathaway less than an hour to ascertain that a shipment of sixty brand-new VW Beetles was on its way to Felixstowe. He reread Fullerton's report. Whatever was going down, it seemed that Donovan was taking a back seat. Jordan was dealing directly with the Rodriguez cartel, though Fullerton had the impression that it was Donovan who'd set up the deal. Plus there was the two million pounds that Fullerton had paid to Jesus Rodriguez.

The jumbled pieces of the mystery started to come together in Hathaway's mind. Donovan had screwed up, somehow. Maybe he'd failed to come up with the money for the consignment. Rodriguez had taken the two million pounds as a penalty payment, and taken over the deal with Jordan. Donovan was short of money, that's why he had to sell the paintings. His money had gone. Stewart Sharkey had screwed Donovan's wife and he'd cleared out the bank accounts. Hathaway grinned. Donovan would move heaven and earth to get his money back, and while he was focused on that, he'd be less likely to realise what was going on around him.

It was time to increase the stakes. Hathaway didn't want to run the operation through Customs or the police. They'd both be tempted to let the drugs run to see where they went in an attempt to blow apart the entire network. That was the last thing Hathaway wanted. There was only one option. It was time to call in the Increment.

THE ALARM BUZZED and Donovan groped for the button on top of the alarm and hit it with the flat of his hand. He squinted at the digital read-out. Seven thirty.

He padded across the bedroom, put on his robe and opened the bedroom door. 'Robbie, are you up?' There was no answer so he walked along the landing.

Robbie was curled round his pillow, snoring softly. Donovan shook him. 'Come on, it's time to get up.'

Donovan opened the curtains wide and went downstairs. He switched the kettle on and poured two glasses of orange juice.

The doorbell rang and Donovan went to answer it. It was Alex Knight carrying a moulded black plastic suitcase.

'Bloody hell, Alex, what time do you call this?'

'The early worm catches the bird,' said Knight, carrying the case in to the hallway. 'I'll start in the study, yeah?'

Donovan showed him through. Knight swung the suitcase onto Donovan's desk and unlocked the lid. It was full of equipment.

As Donovan came out of the study, Robbie came rushing downstairs. He frowned at Donovan's robe. 'You're not driving me to school in that, are you?'

Donovan gestured with his thumb at Knight, who was taking apart the telephone on the desk. 'I'm sort of busy here, Robbie.'

'Typical,' sneered Robbie. He went into the kitchen, picked up one of the glasses of orange juice and drained it in one go.

'I'll call you a minicab,' said Donovan.

'I'm not going to school in a minicab.' Robbie picked up his backpack. 'I'll walk.' He ran down the hall and slammed the front door behind him.

Donovan cursed and picked up one of his mobiles. He took the phone into the garden and called Underwood at the number where the detective had said he'd be. It was a phone box about half a mile from Underwood's flat. Underwood answered immediately.

'What did you find out?' asked Donovan.

'He's an art dealer, thought to be receiving, but never been proved. He's got a legitimate business that makes money. I think he just dabbles with stolen stuff. There's a couple of drugs busts, but both were small amounts of cannabis and he was warned both times.'

'No chance that he's one of yours?'

'He's not a registered informer, and they're all registered these days. No registration, no case, you know that.'

'Cheers, Dicko.'

'What's the story on this guy?' asked the detective.

'He's sold some paintings for me, that's all. I had him around the house and I just wanted to be sure he was clean.'

Donovan thanked the detective and ended the call. He took the back off the mobile phone and took out the Sim card, then went upstairs and flushed it down the toilet before shaving and showering. When he went back downstairs he was wearing black jeans and a Ralph Lauren blue denim shirt, the sleeves rolled up to his elbows.

Knight was in the sitting room working on the phone there. 'Do you want me to show you the portable MRF detector?'

'Sure.'

Knight went over to his suitcase and took out a blue and white box. He opened it and slid out a white polystyrene moulding inside which was a grey plastic box the size of a beeper, with a belt clip on one side. There were three jack points on one end. Knight removed a rechargeable battery from the polystyrene and tossed it to Donovan. 'Charge it up overnight. Charger's in the box.' Knight took a second battery out of his jacket pocket and inserted it into the back of the detector. He went over to Donovan and clipped it onto his belt, then took a length of cable with a jack plug on one end and a thin Velcro strap on the other. He told Donovan to thread the strap through his shirt sleeve and run it under the band of his Rolex. While Donovan ran the wire down his sleeve, Knight slotted the jack plug into the detector.

He went over to his suitcase, took out a small tape recorder and switched it on. He motioned for Donovan to come closer.

Donovan walked forward. When he was two paces away from Knight, the box on his belt began to vibrate. 'Yeah, there it goes.' He took a step back. The vibration stopped. He moved forward and it started again. 'Excellent.'

'It's even more sensitive to listening devices,' said Knight. He clicked the tape recorder off and put it back in the suitcase. He took out a black box the size of a telephone directory, and two small speakers. He placed the box and speakers on the coffee table and ran a power lead to the nearest socket. 'Acoustic noise generator. Switch it on, sit close to it, keep your voice down and the white noise will swamp what you're saying.'

The phone rang. Donovan picked up the receiver. It was Robbie. Donovan expected him to apologise for running out of the house, but Robbie had something else on his mind—he'd left his sports kit behind and was supposed to be playing soccer that afternoon. Donovan said he'd take the kit to school for him and arranged to meet Robbie outside the gates at half past twelve.

THEY CALLED IT the Almighty. Major Allan Gannon wasn't sure who had named the secure satellite phone system, or when, but now it was never referred to by any other name. The briefcase containing the Almighty sat on a table adjacent to Gannon's desk when he was in his office at the Duke of York Barracks in London, a short walk from Sloane Square, and went everywhere with him.

Gannon was standing by the window, peering through the bomb-proof blinds at the empty parade ground, when the Almighty bleeped. It was an authoritative, urgent sound. Not that Gannon needed to be told the urgency of calls that came through the Almighty. The only people who had access to the Almighty were the Prime Minister, the Cabinet Office, and the chiefs of MI5 and MI6.

Gannon strode over to the satellite phone and picked up the receiver. 'Increment,' he said curtly. 'Major Gannon speaking.'

The head of MI6 identified herself, and began relaying instructions to Gannon. Gannon repeated the information he'd been given, and replaced the receiver. The major's SAS staff sergeant looked up from his copy of the *Evening Standard*.

'Game on,' said Gannon. 'Freighter heading for Felixstowe. Interception as soon as it's in our waters. Possible drugs consignment.'

DONOVAN FOUND Robbie's sports bag by his bed. He put it on the passenger seat of the Range Rover and was about to get in when a car pulled up in the road outside. Donovan saw it was Louise, at the wheel of a BMW. She waved and climbed out of the sports car. Donovan wondered what it was about girls who worked in lap-dancing bars. They all seemed to want to drive powerful cars.

'I hope you don't mind me popping in on you like this,' she said. She was wearing a sheepskin flying jacket and blue jeans that seemed to have been sprayed onto her, and impenetrable black sunglasses. 'Kris told me where you lived.'

'No problem,' said Donovan. 'But I'm just on my way out.'

Louise's face fell. 'Oh. OK. I just wanted to say thanks. Buy you a coffee, maybe.'

'Tell you what, why don't you give me a lift to my boy's school? I've got to drop off his soccer kit. Then you can take me for coffee.'

Louise smiled. It was, thought Donovan, a very pretty smile. He'd only seen tears and a trembling lower lip when he'd been round at her flat. She turned and went back to the roadster and Donovan found himself unable to tear his eyes from her backside as she walked. He could see why she was able to afford a car like the BMW.

Donovan got into the passenger seat and gave Louise directions to Robbie's school.

'Kris told me what you did,' she said. 'Thanks.'

'It was nothing.'

She flashed him a sideways look. 'It was one hell of a thing, Den. You took a risk doing that.'

'Nah, he was out of condition. A middle-class wanker.'

'That's not what I meant. You weren't scared of . . . repercussions. You went right ahead and did what you did. For me.'

'Repercussions? Like him wanting to get his own back? Don't worry about that. His type are cowards. That's why they hit women in the first place, to make themselves feel big.'

Louise reached over and switched on her cassette. Oasis. 'I mean the police. The cops could have been called. But you weren't worried. You just went right on in.'

Something vibrated on Donovan's hip. He reached into his pocket, figuring it must be one of his mobile phones. Then he remembered that device Knight had given him and he stiffened.

'What's wrong?' asked Louise, looking at him sideways.

'Cramp,' lied Donovan. It was the detector. He was talking about beating a man and the car was bloody well bugged. She was setting him up. Louise was leading him on, getting him to talk about it, getting him to confess. He made a play of rubbing his side. What had he said? Had he given them enough evidence already?

The Oasis track ended. Louise kept looking across at him. 'Are you all right? Do you want me to pull over?'

Donovan shook his head. The next track started. Suddenly realisation dawned. He reached out and switched the tape off. The detector stopped vibrating immediately.

'Not an Oasis fan, huh? Thought you would be, both being from Manchester.'

'How do you know that?' asked Donovan.

'Oh, give me a break, Den,' she laughed. 'That's hardly an Oxbridge accent you've got there.'

'Sorry,' Donovan said. 'I'm jumping at shadows at the moment.'

They arrived at the school. Robbie was outside the gates. 'Won't be long,' said Donovan, climbing out of the car with Robbie's bag.

Robbie frowned as he saw Donovan getting out of the BMW. 'Who's that?' he said, looking through the windscreen.

'A friend,' said Donovan, holding out the sports bag.

Robbie took the bag. 'A girlfriend?'

'She's just a friend. OK? I helped her and she came round to the house to say thank you. Then she said she'd give me a lift to drop your gear off. You know I hate driving in the city.'

'You're a terrible driver,' Robbie mumbled.

'I'm a great driver,' Donovan protested.

'You lose your temper too easily. You keep hitting the horn. And you don't use the mirrors enough.'

'I'll pick you up tonight, yeah?' said Donovan.

Robbie nodded. 'OK. Thanks for bringing my bag.'

'You give them hell. Score lots of goals.'

'I'm a defender, Dad.'

'Defenders can score. Don't go letting them put you in a box. You see an opportunity to go for the goal, you take it, right?'

'It's a team game, Dad,' laughed Robbie, and he ran off.

Donovan climbed back into the car.

'Everything OK?' asked Louise.

'He thinks you're my new girlfriend.'

'Ah,' said Louise, putting the BMW into gear. 'Starbucks OK?'

'My favourite coffee.'

Louise drove to South Kensington. She was a good driver, thought Donovan. Maybe Robbie was right. Maybe he didn't use the mirrors enough.

'Penny for them?' asked Louise.

'Robbie says I'm a crap driver.'

'And are you?'

'I don't think so. But what guy does, right?'

'Quickest way to end a relationship,' laughed Louise. 'Tell a guy he's lousy in bed or that he's crap behind the wheel of a car.'

'You in a relationship right now?' asked Donovan. Immediately the words left his mouth he regretted them. It was a soppy question.

Louise didn't seem bothered by his probing. She shrugged. 'Difficult to have a regular relationship, doing what I do,' she said.

'Great way to meet guys, though,' said Donovan.

Louise sighed. 'Yeah, right. I'd really want to go out with the sort of guy who thinks shoving twenty-pound notes down a girl's G-string is a sensible way to spend an evening.'

'Beats sitting in front of the TV,' said Donovan with a smile.

'And would I want to go out with a guy who knows what I do for a living? What does that say about him?'

'You mean, if a guy really cared for you, he wouldn't want you to do what you do?'

'Exactly.'

'Maybe he'd think it better you have a career. My soon-to-be-ex-wife never did a day's work in her life. She went from her father's house to mine. From one provider to another.'

'Soon-to-be-ex-wife? You're getting divorced?'

'Something more permanent, hopefully,' said Donovan. Then he shook his head. 'Joke.'

'Didn't sound like a joke,' said Louise.

'I'm still a bit raw,' said Donovan.

'You'll heal. Here we are.' She parked the car at a meter and jumped out. She fed the meter, locked the car and went into the coffee shop with Donovan. He reached for his wallet but she slapped his hand away. 'No way. My treat, remember? Cappuccino OK?'

Donovan got a table by the window while Louise fetched their coffees. She sat down opposite him and slid over a foaming mug. She clinked her mug against his.

'Thanks. For what you did. I am really grateful, Den. You barely know me but you were there when I needed someone. Friends, yeah?'

Donovan nodded enthusiastically. He picked up his mug and clinked it against hers. 'Definitely,' he said.

STEWART SHARKEY'S mobile phone trilled. He picked up the phone and pressed the green button.

'Stewart, it's me, David.'

'Yes, David.' Hoyle sounded stressed. 'Is there a problem?'

'No, no problem,' said Hoyle. 'Everything's going as planned. I've some forms for Victoria to sign. For the custody application.'

'Can't you sign them on her behalf?'

'No can do, Stewart. Sorry. It has to be her.'

'What about faxed copies? Would that do?'

'Has to be originals, I'm afraid. Is there any possibility of you both coming to the office in the next few days?'

'Absolutely none,' said Sharkey. 'You'll have to have them couriered out here.'

There was a pause as if Hoyle had taken the phone away from his mouth, then he coughed. 'Fine. Where shall I send them?'

'Have you got a pen?' asked Sharkey.

THE DHL COURIER walked into the lobby and up to the reception desk. 'I have a delivery for Monsieur Stewart Sharkey,' he said in fluent French. The receptionist nodded at a man sitting at the far end of the reception area, sitting on a sofa and reading *Le Monde*.

The courier walked across. 'Monsieur Sharkey?'

The man lowered his paper. '*Oui?*'

'I have a package for you from London. Can you sign here please?' said the courier in accented English.

The man stood up and took the clipboard. He scrawled a signature and handed the clipboard back to the courier. The courier held out the package, an A4-size manila envelope, then frowned. He checked the serial number of the label stuck to the envelope against the clipboard and cursed.

'I am sorry, Mr Sharkey. I have the wrong envelope. I will have to get it from the van.'

'No problem,' said the man.

'Would you come with me? It would save time.'

'I'm not sure . . .' the man began, but the courier had already walked away, so he followed him. The DHL van was parked about fifty feet from the entrance to the hotel. The courier opened the rear door of the van and poked his head inside.

The man walked up behind him. 'Have you got it?' he asked.

The courier whirled round and pressed the twin prongs of a stun gun against the man's throat. He pressed a switch on the gun and the man slumped forward. The courier caught him and pushed him into the back of the van. Hands grabbed the man's jacket and hauled him inside. The door slammed shut as the courier walked round to the driver's door.

IT WAS JUST before midday when Donovan's doorbell rang. Then someone knocked on the door, hard. Donovan opened the door. It was Ricky Jordan and Charlie Macfadyen and they looked mad as hell. Donovan knew something was wrong and he tried to close the door. He was too slow—Macfadyen put his shoulder against the door and barged through, Jordan following close behind.

'You bastard!' shouted Macfadyen, slamming Donovan against the wall.

Jordan kicked the door closed and pulled a gun from inside his jacket. He thrust the barrel under Donovan's chin. 'You got cut out of the deal so you screwed it up for us,' shouted Jordan.

Donovan glared at the gun. 'You going to pop me and then walk out of here. Earth to Planet Jordan: you wouldn't get fifty feet.'

Jordan frowned. 'Why not?'

'Because I'm Tango frigging One, that's why,' said Donovan. 'Every man and his dog are watching me.'

'No one stopped us coming in, did they?' said Jordan.

'Well, you haven't shot me yet, have you?' said Donovan. 'Pull the trigger and see what happens.'

Jordan looked at Macfadyen, who shrugged.

Donovan smiled, trying to put them at ease. 'While you're deciding what to do, how about we have a beer?'

'Are you taking the piss, Den?' asked Macfadyen.

'I'm just trying to be civilised,' said Donovan. 'Go on, Charlie, get the beers. Ricky and I'll carry on the conversation in the sitting room.' Donovan grinned at Jordan. 'If it makes you feel any happier, Ricky, you can keep on pointing it at me.'

Jordan looked across at Macfadyen and nodded. 'Yeah, why not?'

Macfadyen went down the hall to the kitchen. Jordan slowly took the gun away from Donovan's neck. 'No tricks, yeah?' he said.

Donovan walked into the sitting room. He put his finger against his lips and then made a cut-throat gesture with his right hand. Jordan frowned and opened his mouth to speak. Donovan hissed and put his fingers against his lips again. He went over to the sideboard and picked up the acoustic noise generator that Alex had left. He put it on the coffee table, plugged it in and switched it on. The room was filled with static.

'What the hell's that?' asked Macfadyen, walking in with three cans of lager. He tossed one to Donovan and put one down on the coffee table for Jordan.

Donovan sat down on the sofa and motioned for Jordan to sit down next to him. 'It masks the sound of our voices.'

Macfadyen looked around nervously.

'I swept the place this morning,' said Donovan. 'And I've got the phones monitored. This is just to be on the safe side. And keep your voices down, yeah? Now what the hell is going on?'

Macfadyen took a copy of the early edition of the *Evening*

Standard from his jacket pocket and tossed it onto the coffee table. Donovan read the headline and cursed. 'SAS SWOOP ON £100 MILLION COCAINE HAUL.' The SAS had swooped on a freighter carrying VW Beetles from Mexico. Cocaine had been packed into the cars.

'That's bollocks, a hundred million,' he said, and Macfadyen nodded. The authorities always overestimated because it made them look good. But whatever the value, the drugs had been intercepted and Jordan and Macfadyen were looking for someone to blame.

'It wasn't me, lads,' said Donovan. 'Hand on heart.'

'Then who?' asked Jordan. 'If not you, who?'

'Who knows? Maybe you've been under surveillance yourself. You can't wear Armani suits and drive around in flash cars and not get noticed.'

'It wasn't us,' said Jordan, defensively.

'Fine. It wasn't you and it wasn't me. Which means it was either someone working for Rodriguez or someone on the outside. Maybe enough palms weren't greased in Mexico. We all know there's a million and one things can go wrong with every deal. Something else— why are you here giving me grief and not sitting in a cell? Don't you think if I were trying to stitch you up I'd have done it properly?'

'We're down millions on this deal,' said Jordan.

'That's the rules of the game and you both know it,' said Donovan. 'You budget for losing one in four consignments. You build it into your costs. You did that, right?'

'Sort of,' said Macfadyen. 'Not all the money was ours. We got three mill off a Yardie gang in Harlesden.'

'Smart move,' Donovan said, his voice loaded with sarcasm. 'I thought you didn't do business with the Yardies.'

'This guy's cool.'

'Yeah, well, if he's cool, why are you worried?'

'Because it was the first deal he'd done with us. He's going to think we ripped him off.'

'So explain it to him. Anyway, that's your problem, not mine.'

'We've lost a lot of money, Den. A shedload.'

'Nothing compared to what I'm down,' said Donovan.

'What do you mean?' asked Macfadyen.

Donovan closed his eyes. 'Forget it,' he said. 'It doesn't matter.'

Jordan jabbed the gun into Donovan's ribs. 'It matters,' he said.

Donovan opened his eyes. 'My accountant ripped me off for sixty million dollars. A big chunk of that was on its way to Rodriguez.'

Macfadyen pounced. 'Including our money, yeah?'

Donovan nodded.

'So that's why Rodriguez wanted to deal with us direct?'

Donovan nodded again.

'So our money never got to Rodriguez? You've still got it.'

Donovan sighed. 'I can see where you're going, Charlie, but you're wasting your time. I haven't got your money.'

'No, but neither had Rodriguez. So that wasn't our consignment.' He grinned. 'We haven't lost shit.'

'Your deal was with the Colombians. Not me.'

'You never gave them our money. So the buck stops with you.'

'You're not listening to me, Charlie. I haven't got a penny.'

'You've got this house.'

'It's in a trust. For my boy. Can't be touched.'

'What do we do?' asked Macfadyen. He gestured at Jordan's gun, which was still levelled at Donovan's midriff. 'Put it away, Ricky.'

Jordan looked as if he was going to argue, then he nodded and slipped the automatic inside his jacket.

'I can offer you a way of making your money back.'

'What?' asked Macfadyen.

'Heroin. From Afghanistan.'

'How much?'

'For you guys, ten grand a key.'

Macfadyen looked at Jordan and raised an eyebrow. Jordan nodded. Then Macfadyen's eyes narrowed. 'Yeah, but delivery where? It's no good to me in Amsterdam.'

'In the UK, mate. South of London, but if you want I'll get someone to drive it up north to you.'

'You can get Afghan heroin into the UK for ten grand a key?' said Jordan in disbelief.

'How do we know we won't be throwing good money after bad?' asked Macfadyen.

'Because this is my deal, Charlie. Me and a couple of guys who've come up with a sure-fire way of getting the gear in under the noses of Customs. As much gear as you can buy. I've got everything riding on this one, so I'm gonna make damn sure it works out OK.'

Jordan nodded. 'I say go for it. Let's go in for five hundred keys.'

Macfadyen nodded. 'Yeah, OK. How about I bring O'Brien in on this? Dublin prices are up, he'd be in for five hundred keys.'

'OK,' agreed Donovan. 'But get him to pay twelve a key.'

'What about the Yardies?' asked Macfadyen.

'Screw the Yardies. They're big boys.'

'The guy's a vicious bastard. He's going to want answers.'

'A minute ago you said he was cool.'

'Yeah, well, that was before we lost three million quid of his. You're going to have to talk to him.'

'Me? Why me?'

'Because he's not going to believe a word I tell him from now on. But you're Den Donovan. He knows about you.'

'Because you told him, right? For Christ's sake, Charlie, can't you ever keep your big mouth shut?'

'He already knew who you were,' said Macfadyen quickly. 'That was one of the reasons he was so keen to do the deal. All I said was that you were involved. I didn't say from where, I didn't say how, I didn't say when. Hell, Den, it was only when we met that Jesus guy we heard about the Beetles. The Yardies don't even know about that.'

'So you want me to tell him his three million's gone? And how do you think he'll react to that?'

'I dunno, Den. How do you think he'll react if I told him that his three million never got to the Colombians?'

Macfadyen stared at Donovan. Donovan met his gaze with unblinking eyes. The threat hung in the air between them.

Donovan nodded slowly. 'OK,' he said. 'What's his name?'

'PM,' said Macfadyen. 'His sidekick's the brains of the outfit, though. Doesn't say much but you can see the wheels are always turning. Watch out for him. His name's Bunny.'

JUAN ROJAS walked into the warehouse, rubbing his gloved hands together. 'Everything go to plan?' he asked.

A man was stripping off the uniform of a DHL courier. 'Like a lamb to the slaughter,' he said. The French accent had vanished.

'Excellent,' said Rojas.

He walked to the middle of the warehouse where a man sat on a straight-backed wooden chair. Thick strips of insulation tape bound his arms and legs to the chair and another strip had been plastered across his mouth.

Rojas cursed. 'This isn't Sharkey,' he said, ripping off the strip of insulation tape. The man gasped.

'I've a message from him,' said the man. 'He said Donovan can go screw himself.' He smiled.

Rojas's lips tightened. 'Where is he?'

'I don't know. He's not here in Paris, that's for sure. I only spoke to him on the phone.'

Rojas cursed.

'He said you're to phone him. You have his mobile number, right?'

Rojas nodded. 'Right. Did he tell you what I'd do to you, when I found out that you'd set me up?' He took out a small automatic.

The man smiled. 'He said you'd be professional. And he said he'd transfer a quarter of a million dollars to any account you nominate. I'm to give him the account number in person.'

Rojas looked at the man. A smile slowly spread across his face and he put the gun away. 'He is a good judge of character,' he said. 'Luckily for you.'

DONOVAN PUT ON a brown leather jacket, picked up three fully charged mobile phones and slotted them into various pockets. He got the keys to the Range Rover, secured the house, and drove to Marble Arch. He parked in an underground car park, then walked to Marble Arch underground station.

He went to a bank of public phones and shoved in his BT phone card. He called the Yardie that Macfadyen had brought in on the Colombian coke deal. The man answered. 'Yo?'

'PM?'

'Who wants to know?'

'I'm a friend of Macfadyen's. He wanted me to talk to you.'

'So talk.'

'Face to face.'

'Screw that.'

'He thought I should explain why the deal he cut you in on has gone belly up.'

'Say what?'

'Can you read, PM? Buy the *Standard*. Front-page story. When you've read it, call me back.' Donovan gave him the number of one of the mobiles he was carrying, then hung up.

He used another of his mobiles to phone Underwood. The detective wasn't pleased to hear from him, but Donovan cut his protests short and told him to call him back as soon as possible.

Donovan's next call was to Jamie Fullerton. He arranged to meet him at his gallery later that afternoon. Finally he called Louise. She'd given him her number after their cappuccino at Starbucks.

DONOVAN SAT on a bench in Trafalgar Square. One of the mobiles rang. Donovan pressed the green button. It was PM.

'What the hell's going on, man?' asked PM.

'Your phone clean?'

'Only had it two days and after this the Sim card goes in the trash.'

'You don't know me, PM, but you know of me. I put Macfadyen onto the deal. He wants me to talk through what happened.'

'Where and when?'

'This evening. Say seven.'

'Where?'

'You choose.'

PM gave him the address of a house in Harlesden, then cut the connection.

Louise arrived at two o'clock, walking up the steps of the National Gallery and standing at its entrance. She was wearing sunglasses and a long, dark blue woollen coat with the collar turned up. Donovan watched her from the square until he was sure she hadn't been followed.

She waved as she saw him walking towards her. He hugged her and gave her a kiss on the cheek. 'Thanks for coming,' he said.

'It's all very mysterious,' she said.

'Yeah, sorry. Had to be. Come on in.' Donovan ushered her inside.

'So what is it with you and art galleries?' she asked.

Donovan shrugged. 'Ran into one to hide from the cops. I was fourteen and should have been at school. Two beat bobbies were heading my way so I nipped into the Whitworth Gallery.'

'Where's that?'

'Manchester. Huge building, awesome art, but I didn't know that when I went in. I walked through a couple of the galleries, just to get away from the entrance, and then I got to a gallery where a guide was giving a talk about this painting. Two cavaliers with feathered hats facing each other with a pretty girl watching them. I'll never forget the way she talked about it. She understood what the artist was trying to say. The story he was trying to tell. The painting was about the two guys arguing over the girl, of course, but it was way more than that. There were political references, historical stuff, things you just wouldn't see unless someone drew your attention to it. She talked for almost thirty minutes. By the end I was sitting cross-legged on the floor with my mouth wide open.'

Donovan smiled. 'It opened my eyes. A photograph is totally real, it's what you'd see if you were there. But a painting is the artist's interpretation, which means that everything that's in the painting is in for a reason. Each one is like a mystery to be solved.'

'Can I ask you something?' said Louise.

'Sure.'

'Your wife left you, right?'

Donovan nodded.

'And you didn't see it coming?'

'I suppose I was too busy doing other things. I was away a lot.'

'Do you miss her?'

'Do I miss her?' said Donovan. 'She screwed my accountant. In my bed.' His face was contorted with anger and she took a step away from him. 'I'm sorry,' he said. 'Touchy subject.'

'I can see.'

Donovan took a deep breath. 'And you're right. I should have seen the signs. It must have been going on for a while.'

'And there weren't any signs?'

'Like I said, I was away a lot.'

'Which is a sign in itself,' she said. 'I mean, if everything was hunky-dory, you'd have spent more time with her, right?'

'There were other considerations,' said Donovan.

'For instance?'

'This is getting to be like an interrogation,' he said.

'I just want to know who I'm getting involved with, that's all.'

'Is that what you're doing? Getting involved?'

She turned and walked away, then looked back at him over her shoulder. 'Maybe,' she said.

Donovan caught up with her. 'I do appreciate you coming, Louise,' he said.

'I owe you, Den. Whatever it is you need, I'm here for you.'

Donovan nodded. 'How much do you know about what I do?'

'Enough, I guess. Kris said you had a reputation.'

'Probably right. I've got a problem. Some guys think I've double-crossed them and they're going to be after my blood. I haven't, but in my business it's often perceptions that count. I need someone to take care of Robbie until I get it sorted.'

Louise frowned. 'You want him to stay with me?'

'Is that a problem?'

'No, it's just . . . well, he doesn't know me.'

'That's the point. I could put him with my sister, but that's the first place they'll look if he's not at home. No one knows I know you.'

'Exactly,' said Louise. 'You've no idea who I am, yet you're putting me in charge of your son.'

'If it's too much trouble, forget I asked.'

'No, it's not that,' she said earnestly. 'I'm happy to help, believe me, but I'm looking at it from your point of view. With the best will in the world, Den, I'm a complete stranger to you.'

Donovan grinned. 'I know where you live and where you work. I know the registration number of your car and I know that you work for Terry Greene and Terry's a mate from way back.'

Louise nodded slowly. 'OK, but there's another thing to bear in mind. I'm not a mum, Den. I've never taken care of a kid before.'

'He's nine. He doesn't need much looking after. Feed him, make sure he cleans his teeth and give him the TV remote. He'll be fine. And it'll only be for a few days. Just until I get things sorted.'

Louise folded her arms. 'I can't believe you trust me that much.'

'Are you saying I can't?'

She shook her head. 'No, I'm just . . . surprised. Touched.'

'I'll pay you.' Donovan reached for his wallet.

'No!' said Louise quickly. 'I don't want your money, Den. I'm happy to do this for you.'

'I'll collect him from school and bring him straight round. It'll mean you not going to work.'

'That's OK. I was going to stay off until my eye healed anyway.'

Donovan hugged her. 'Thanks, Louise. I was starting to run out of people I can trust.'

ONE OF THE MOBILES in Donovan's leather jacket burst into a tune. It was the theme from *The Simpsons*. Louise grinned. 'Fan of the show are you?' she asked. They were walking across Trafalgar Square towards the underground station.

'Robbie's been playing with the mobiles,' said Donovan. He pressed the green button. It was Underwood. 'Hang on, Dicko.' He put his hand over the receiver. 'Louise, I'm gonna have to talk to this guy. Sorry. Do you want to go on ahead? I'll bring Robbie at about five thirty. OK?'

'Sure,' said Louise. She kissed him on the cheek and walked away.

Donovan turned his back on her and put the phone to his ear. 'Dicko, sorry about that. I need a check on two Yardies out Harlesden way. One's called Tony Blair, goes by the nickname PM. The other's Bunny. Don't know his real name.'

'At least I don't have to phone a friend on this one,' said the detective. 'The file's been across my desk several times. They're big players in Northwest London. Crack and heroin. Some legit businesses for cleaning the cash. Drinking dens in tough neighbourhoods. What's your interest?'

'Need to know, Dicko. Sorry. If you know about them how come they're still up and running?'

'How long have you been Tango One? Just because they're targeted doesn't mean they get put away.'

'Do they have someone on the inside? Are they getting tipped off?'

'I don't think so. I think they're just smarter than the average black gang-banger, that's all. In particular, this Bunny character has his head screwed on. PM was just a small-time teenage dealer until Bunny hooked up with him. Now he's a sort of . . . what's that thing that Robert Duval did for Marlon Brando in *The Godfather*?'

'*Consigliore?*'

'What's that mean?'

'It's an adviser.'

'Yeah. That's what Bunny does for PM.'

DONOVAN SPENT AN HOUR going in and out of department stores in Oxford Street until he was satisfied he wasn't being tailed, then walked to Fullerton's gallery in Wardour Street. He pressed a button and was buzzed in.

Fullerton came striding over from a modern beech and chrome desk, hand outstretched. There was no one else in the gallery.

'Den, good to see you,' said Jamie. 'Everything OK?'

'Not really,' said Donovan. 'Did you read about that big cocaine bust? The one where the SAS went in?'

'Shit, that was yours?'

'Sort of,' said Donovan. 'I set it up but then it got taken over by that guy we met in the club. Ricky. Now they're looking for the leak.'

'Anything I can do to help?'

'Maybe. It depends on how much you want to get involved.'

'Den, so long as it's safe and I make a profit, I'm your man.'

Donovan nodded. 'Maury said you know people with money, guys with lots of cash, not necessarily legal.'

'Good old Maury.'

'Is he right?'

'Sure. The art business is a great place to hide cash. Moveable assets. And when you sell you get an auction-house cheque.'

'OK, here's the scoop. I have a very sweet deal that I'm setting up, and I'm looking for guys who can market heroin. Top-grade heroin from Afghanistan. I can get it way, way cheaper than any wholesaler can supply it in this country, or anywhere in Europe.'

'How cheap?' asked Fullerton.

'Delivered to the UK, ten thousand a kilo. That's about a third of the regular dealer price. Almost a tenth of the street price.'

'I'm sure I could get some interest, Den. How much are we talking about?'

'As much as you want,' said Donovan. 'I'm going to be bringing in eight thousand keys.'

'No way!'

Donovan grinned. 'Like I said, it's a sweet deal. See what interest there is, but be bloody careful. I'm going to want money up-front, and I'll arrange for it to be delivered anywhere in the UK.'

'They're going to want to know how you're getting it into the country.'

'No can do, Jamie.'

'But you can tell me, right?'

Donovan pulled a face. 'Maybe later. But at the moment, all anyone needs to know is that the gear will be in the UK soon. Providing we get the down payment together.'

DONOVAN BEEPED the horn of the Range Rover when he saw Robbie walk out of the school gates. Robbie ran over, climbed into the front passenger seat and threw his backpack into the rear.

Donovan kept checking his mirror as he drove away from the school. They reached a roundabout and he drove round it twice before shooting towards an exit without indicating.

'Dad, you're driving like a nutter,' said Robbie. 'And this isn't the way home either.'

'There's been a change of plan,' said Donovan.

'What do you mean?'

'I need you to take a few days off school. Something's happened. Until I get it sorted, I need you to stay with someone.'

'What are you talking about, Dad?'

Donovan checked his rearview mirror. There was no one on his tail. 'I've got a bit of a problem about the house. We can't stay there for a while.'

'So I'm going to stay at Auntie Laura's?'

'No. You remember that lady who gave me the lift to school with your soccer kit?'

'Why can't I stay with Auntie Laura?' asked Robbie.

'Because I say you can't. You'll like Louise. She's OK.'

'I'm not staying with your girlfriend.'

'She's not my girlfriend. And you'll do what I bloody well tell you.'

'You can't make me.'

Donovan glared at his son. 'What do you mean, I can't make you? You're nine years old.'

Robbie sat staring out of the window. They came to a red light and Donovan brought the car to a halt.

'OK, look, I'll be honest with you. I've upset some people, Robbie. Over a business deal. These people aren't very nice and I'd feel safer if you stayed somewhere else. And didn't go to school. Normally I'd say stay with Auntie Laura and Uncle Mark, but these people might know where they live, too. That's all.'

'How long do I have to stay with her?'

'A few days. I'll be there most of the time.'

'Has she got Sky?'

Donovan shrugged. 'I think so.'

'OK then. I don't want to miss *The Simpsons*.'

JAMIE FULLERTON paced up and down his gallery. Den Donovan was planning to bring eight thousand kilos of heroin into the UK, and Fullerton had the inside track.

Fullerton knew he should tell Hathaway. But something was holding Fullerton back. Was it that he felt guilty about betraying a man who was close to becoming a friend? Or was it because Donovan was offering Fullerton a chance to make a lot of money? Easy money. In the three years since Hathaway had set Fullerton up with the gallery, Fullerton had stashed away almost a million pounds dealing in works of art, legal and otherwise. He could put that cash into Donovan's deal and treble it. It would mean crossing a line, but over the years that Fullerton had been undercover, that line had blurred to such an extent he was no longer sure which side of it he was on.

DONOVAN PRESSED the bell to Louise's flat and the front door lock clicked open. She had the door to her flat open as they got to the landing. She'd changed into a sweatshirt and jeans and clipped back her hair with two bright pink clips.

'You must be Robbie,' she said, holding out her hand.

'Yeah,' said Robbie. 'You've got Sky, right?'

'Sure.'

Robbie shook hands with her.

Donovan held up a small suitcase. 'I've packed some of his things.'

'Are you going right away? I've got shepherd's pie in the oven.'

'No, I can stay,' said Donovan.

Louise showed Donovan and Robbie into the sitting room. She pointed down the hallway. 'Robbie, your bedroom's on the right. There's a bathroom opposite.'

'Are you staying here as well?' Robbie asked his father.

Louise looked at Donovan, raised an expectant eyebrow.

'I'll be popping in and out,' he said.

'Your dad can sleep on the sofa, if he decides to stay,' said Louise.

Donovan handed the suitcase to his son. Robbie took his case to his room while Louise busied herself in the kitchenette.

Donovan went over to a sideboard, took his mobile phones out of his jacket pocket and lined them up. There were four of them.

'Expecting a call?' asked Louise.

'Different people have different numbers,' said Donovan.

'Which number do I have?'

Donovan picked up one of the Nokias and waggled it. 'Only you've got this number,' he said.

'I'm flattered.'

One of the mobile phones on the sideboard burst into the theme from *The Simpsons*. It was the Spaniard.

'He's not in Paris, *amigo*. He had someone else pick up the papers.'

'Bastard!' hissed Donovan. 'But you're still on the case?'

'Of course. I have a number for him.' Rojas gave him the number.

'That's a UK mobile, yeah?' asked Donovan.

'Yes. A roaming GSM.'

'Can we find him through the number?'

Rojas whistled through his teeth. 'Locating the handset would require a warrant and would have to be done at a senior police level or by one of the intelligence agencies. Even in Spain it's unlikely I'd be able to do it. In France . . .' He left the sentence unfinished.

'OK, Juan. Thanks anyway. Onwards and upwards, yeah?'

Donovan cut the connection.

AFTER DINNER, Robbie gathered up their plates and took them to the kitchenette.

'Do you want a coffee?' asked Louise.

Donovan looked at his watch. 'I've got to be somewhere. I'm sorry.'

'You're not going out?' Robbie called from the kitchenette.

'Business,' said Donovan.

'It's OK, Robbie, we can watch TV,' said Louise. She tossed Donovan a door key. 'In case you get back late,' she said. 'Save you waking me up.'

Donovan scooped the mobiles off the sideboard, put them into the pockets of his jacket and went outside in search of a black cab.

The address PM had given him was in a terrace in Harlesden. Donovan could feel the pounding beat of reggae music through the seat of the cab long before they reached the house. The driver twisted round in his seat. 'You sure about this?' he asked. 'It looks a bit ethnic out there.'

Donovan could see what the man meant. Half a dozen burly men in long black coats were standing guard at the open door to the house, four with shaved heads glistening in the amber streetlights, two with dreadlocks. A dozen young black men and women were waiting to be admitted. It was the sort of street the police never patrolled. If they turned up at all it would be mob-handed with riot shields and mace. Parked both sides of the street were BMWs and four-wheel drives, most of them brand-new.

'Yeah, this is it,' said Donovan, handing the driver a twenty-pound note. 'Keep the change, yeah?'

'Thanks, guv,' said the driver. 'Good luck.'

Donovan got out of the cab and the driver drove off quickly.

Donovan walked to the head of the line of people waiting to go in. He nodded at the biggest of the bouncers, who was wearing an earpiece and a small radio microphone that bobbed around close to his lips. 'I'm here to see PM,' said Donovan.

The man nodded. 'He expecting you. Third floor.'

Donovan pushed his way through the crowd and found the stairs. The air was thick with the smell of marijuana. Teenagers sitting on the stairs drinking beer from the bottle looked up at him curiously as he walked up to the second floor.

One of the second-floor bedrooms had been converted into a bar. There were tin baths filled with ice and loaded with bottled beer, and a table of spirits and mixers. Two black guys with turtle-shell abdomens and red and white checked bandanas were passing out bottles and shoving banknotes into a metal box without handing back change. Donovan went up to the third floor. At the top of the stairs, two young guys wearing headsets moved aside without speaking to Donovan. The big man must have told them he was on his way up.

Donovan knocked and the door partially opened. A pair of wraparound sunglasses reflected Donovan's image back at him in stereo.

'Den Donovan,' said Donovan.

The man opened the door fully. Donovan walked into the room. Half a dozen West Indians were sitting round the room on sofas, most smoking spliffs and drinking beer. Sitting behind a desk was a young black man with close-cropped hair wearing what looked like a Versace silk shirt. Around his neck was a thick gold chain and on his left wrist he wore a solid gold Rolex studded with diamonds.

'PM?'

The man at the desk nodded.

'Den Donovan.'

'What happened to my money, Den?' asked PM. Standing behind PM was a black man well over six foot tall dressed in a black suit and grey T-shirt. He had shoulder-length dreadlocks and a goatee beard.

'Your money paid for the coke and the coke is sitting in one of the Queen's warehouses,' said Donovan. He walked over to a sofa and sat down. 'A percentage of deals go wrong. You have to live with that. Build it into your price.'

PM slammed his hand onto the desk. 'I want my money back.' He reached into a drawer and pulled out a massive handgun. Donovan recognised the weapon. It was a Mac-10 machine gun. A spray-and-pray weapon. Spray the bullets around and pray you hit something. 'PM, you pull the trigger on that and there's gonna be bullets flying all round the room.'

'Yeah, but the first one's gonna be in your gut.'

The man with dreadlocks took a step forward. He fixed Donovan with a cold stare. 'You got any suggestion as to how we can get our money back?' he asked. The fact that he was the only one other than PM to open his mouth meant he was probably the one called Bunny, PM's adviser.

'I can cut you in on another deal. Heroin.'

'Price?'

'Ten thousand a key.'

PM drank beer as Bunny rattled off quick-fire questions.

'Source?'

'Afghan. Pure.'

'Delivered where?'

'UK. South of England.'

'Specifically?'

'An airfield.'

Bunny leaned forward and whispered into PM's ear.

'How much?' asked PM, when Bunny had finished whispering.

'Up to you.'

'We'll go eight a key. And we'll take two hundred.'

'Eight? I said ten.'

'Yeah, but you owe us one for the coke deal.'

'I'd be cutting my throat at eight, PM. Nine.'

'Eight five.'

Donovan hesitated, then nodded. 'Eight five it is. I'll get Charlie to arrange the money with you.' Donovan stood up.

The man with wraparound sunglasses opened the door and the pounding music billowed into the room.

'You drive here?' asked Bunny.

'Cab,' said Donovan. 'Worried about losing the CD player.'

Bunny laughed. 'I'll walk you down, fix you up with a ride.'

Donovan nodded his thanks. Bunny followed him down the stairs and out onto the street.

They walked slowly down the road, talking in quiet voices.

'This gear, where's it coming from?' asked Bunny. 'Ain't no way you're flying it out of Afghanistan. There's opium there, but the processing is done outside. Pakistan. Or Turkey maybe.'

'My contacts are in Turkey.'

'When do you tell us where we collect?' asked Bunny.

'Day of delivery.'

'Which will be when?'

'Assuming all the money is in play within the next twenty-four hours, probably three days. Charlie'll get the details to you.'

Bunny shook his head. 'We deal with you on this. No discussion.'

'OK,' said Donovan. 'Call me when you've got the money. It's going to be electronic transfer. No used notes in suitcases.'

'Not a problem. We have money in the system.'

Donovan gave him the number of one of his mobiles. 'Call this from a land line. Don't identify yourself, just give me the number but transpose the last two digits. I'll call you back from a call box.'

There was a squeal of brakes. Donovan whirled round. A large Mercedes had pulled up opposite them. The front passenger window was open and something was thrust through the opening. Donovan cursed. It was a gun. He'd been so involved in the conversation with Bunny that he hadn't been aware of the car driving down the street. The gun jerked and there was a series of muffled bangs. Bullets thwacked into the house behind Donovan. He felt himself being pulled down. 'Get down,' Bunny yelled.

Bullets were hitting the pavement all round Donovan. Bunny grabbed Donovan's jacket collar and hauled him behind a black Wrangler Jeep, then crouched over him.

Bullets whizzed around them. Donovan looked back at the house they'd just left. Two West Indians had pulled handguns from their coats and were blasting away at the Mercedes. The Mercedes leapt forward and then braked again. Now the gunman had a clear shot at Bunny and Donovan round the side of the Jeep.

'Bunny, watch out!' Donovan yelled.

Bunny whirled around just as the machine gun burst into life. Bullets slammed into Bunny's chest and he fell back onto Donovan. The Mercedes sped off.

Donovan crawled out from under Bunny, expecting to see his chest a bloody pulp. Instead Bunny was rubbing his chest and scowling.

Donovan got to his feet and helped Bunny up.

'Why aren't you . . .?' asked Donovan, his whole body shaking.

'Dead?' asked Bunny. He lifted up his shirt and showed Donovan a Kevlar bulletproof vest. 'Pretty much compulsory in Harlesden.'

Donovan clapped Bunny on the shoulder. 'I owe you, mate.'

'We're not home free yet,' said Bunny. In the distance they could hear sirens. 'The Operation Trident boys'll be on their way. They move fast on black-on-black shootings. We've got to move. Come on.' He headed down the street, away from the house.

Donovan followed. He knew Bunny was wrong about it being a black-on-black attack. As the car had been driven away, Donovan had seen a face he recognised in the back seat. Jesus Rodriguez.

'WANT A BEER?' asked Bunny, opening the door to a small fridge.

'Yeah, cheers,' said Donovan.

The two men were in a room five minutes' walk away from the shooting, above a minicab office. They'd hurried through the office, with Bunny nodding a greeting to a big Jamaican who was talking into a microphone, then up a flight of stairs and through a door marked MANAGEMENT ONLY. There was worn lino on the floor and a bare minimum of furniture: a desk, two chairs and a filing cabinet.

Bunny tossed Donovan a can of lager and sat behind the desk. 'We'll hang out here for a while, till things quieten down.' He unbuttoned his shirt and examined his Kevlar vest.

'You were lucky,' said Donovan. 'The way they were spraying bullets, you could have got hit in the head.'

'Firing from a car, they were lucky to hit anything. They've been watching too many movies.'

Donovan took a long gulp of beer. 'The taxi firm is yours?'

'None of it's mine. PM's the top man.'

'How long have you been with PM?'

'Three years, thereabouts.'

'Not thought about setting up on your own? Or joining a bigger operation?'

'Why? You recruiting?'

'You've got your head screwed on. You'd make more money working for yourself than helping PM up the slippery pole.'

'I'm happy with the way things are, Den. But if you were to make me an offer . . .' Bunny left the sentence hanging.

'You'd be an asset, that's for sure. I've not met many who throw themselves in front of a bullet for me.'

Bunny laughed. 'That's not the way it went down, and you know it. I practically fell on top of you.'

'Whatever,' said Donovan. 'The fact is that if it wasn't for you, I'd be lying on the street in a pool of blood. Seriously, Bunny, if I was going to be in this for the long haul I'd make you an offer, but after this Turkish deal, I'm out of the game.'

'For good?'

Donovan grinned. 'For as long as the money holds out. I've got a nine-year-old boy needs looking after. His mum's done a runner so I'm going to be a single parent for a while. What about you, Bunny? You see a future in the drugs game?'

'Long term, the only future's prison, right? You've got to quit while you're ahead. Make your stash, get it in legit businesses, then leave the dirty stuff behind. In a hundred years' time, drugs money will be old money and no one will care.'

'So long as we don't get caught.'

Bunny raised his can of beer. 'Here's to not getting caught.'

Donovan grinned, and clinked his can against Bunny's.

DONOVAN STAYED in the office with Bunny for the best part of an hour, then Bunny arranged for a minicab to run Donovan home to Kensington. He had the cab drop him half a mile from the house and went in through the communal gardens and the back door.

He showered and had a whisky, and then put his mobiles on charge on the bedside table before diving under the quilt. He was asleep within minutes.

When he woke, a pop song was playing. He rolled over and groped for whichever mobile phone was ringing.

As he picked up the phone, he realised it was his son's. Robbie must have put it on the sideboard in Louise's flat next to Donovan's phone and he'd picked it up by mistake. Whoever was calling had blocked their ID. Donovan pressed the green button and held the phone to his ear.

For several seconds there was silence. Then a voice. 'Robbie?' It was Vicky. She sounded close to tears. 'Robbie, talk to me.'

Donovan wanted to cut the connection, but couldn't bring himself to. He looked at the clock on the bedside table. It was seven in the morning. 'He's asleep,' said Donovan.

'Den. Oh God. I'm sorry, Den. I didn't mean it to be this way. I was lonely. You left me on my own too long.'

Donovan pressed the red button but instantly regretted it. He stared at the phone's read-out, hoping she'd call back, but she didn't. He began to flick idly through the phone's menu. He flicked through the message section. Robbie had a stack of saved messages. Donovan grinned as he read them. Probably girlfriends. Idle chit-chat. Childish jibes at teachers. Stupid jokes. Then Donovan froze. I'M BACK. COME HOME NOW—DAD. The message had been sent when Donovan had been in St Kitts. That was why Robbie had gone rushing home from school and found Vicky in bed with Sharkey.

The message had been sent from a UK mobile. It was the number that the Spaniard had given him. Donovan cursed. It had been Sharkey who'd sent the text message to Robbie. He'd wanted to be caught in bed with Vicky. It had all been planned.

Another phone rang. The land line. Donovan picked up the receiver. 'We have to meet,' said a voice. A man. English.

'Who is this?' asked Donovan.

'It's about Stewart Sharkey,' said the voice.

'What about him?'

'Do you want your money back, or not?'

Donovan hesitated for a few seconds, then sighed. 'Where?'

'Camden Market. In four hours.'

'You've got to be joking.' Camden Market on a Saturday morning had to be one of the most crowded places on the planet.

'Safety in numbers,' said the man. 'You are being watched. A bedroom across the street. And a British Telecom van. I wouldn't want you bringing any strangers to the party.'

'I'll make sure I'm clean,' said Donovan. 'How will I find you?'

'I'll find you,' said the man. The line went dead.

DONOVAN CAUGHT a black cab to Oxford Street and spent fifteen minutes in the Virgin Megastore looking for tails. He spotted two definites and a possible.

He left the store, dived into another black cab and had it drop him on the south side of the Regents Canal opposite the Paddington Stop, the place where he'd watched for the arrival of Macfadyen and Jordan. He paid the driver, dashed across the footbridge and ran along Blomfield Road to Jason's, a restaurant that had a sideline running narrowboat trips along the canal. The route terminated at Camden Market. Donovan had timed it so he arrived just as a boat was preparing to leave. He bought a ticket and climbed aboard. He adjusted the Velcro collar under his wristwatch. He was wearing the detector and already had it switched on.

They arrived at Camden and Donovan walked through the market. It was packed with tourists and teenagers. Then suddenly there was a man standing in front of him. A short man with thinning, brownish hair and a cocksure smile on his face.

'Long time, no see, Donovan,' said the man.

'Gregg Hathaway,' said Donovan, shaking his head. 'Can't say this is a pleasant surprise.' He moved his left hand forward, closer to Hathaway, but the detector on his belt stayed quiet. Hathaway's own left hand also moved and Donovan glanced down. He saw a thin strip of Velcro under the man's watchband and smiled.

Hathaway smiled, too. 'State of the art,' he said. 'The difference is, the taxpayer paid for mine.'

'Still with Customs then?' asked Donovan. If Hathaway hadn't come wired, then what did he want? A chat about old times? It had been more than ten years since Donovan had seen him.

Hathaway patted his right knee. 'Not much of a future for me in Customs and Excise after you put a bullet in my leg.'

'Sorry to hear that,' said Donovan. 'What's this about?'

'Let's walk.' Hathaway led Donovan through a shop-lined courtyard to a small coffee shop with outside tables. Two American tourists were just leaving and Donovan and Hathaway grabbed their table. Hathaway ordered two coffees from a waitress.

'Who are you with, then, if it's not Customs?' asked Donovan.

'A different bunch,' said Hathaway. 'People who don't mind so much I can't run the hundred metres in twelve seconds any more.'

'What do you want, an apology? You should be grateful, mate. I've done a lot worse.'

'I know. I mean, I lost my job and my wife but at least you didn't tie me to a chair and cut me to bits while you videotaped it.'

Their coffees arrived and the two men sat in silence until the waitress moved away again.

'You've never cared about the rights and wrongs of drugs, have you?' asked Hathaway, keeping his voice low.

Donovan couldn't see where this conversation was going. 'You said you had information about Sharkey. Or was that just to get me here?' He started to get to his feet, but Hathaway held up his hand.

'I want you to understand what it is you taught me when you put that bullet in my leg all those years ago. You taught me that it's just a game. It doesn't matter which side you're on, all that matters is how you play the game. And for that, I want to shake your hand.'

Hathaway reached out his right hand. Donovan slowly put out his own hand and shook. As their hands made contact he felt something hard in Hathaway's palm. He realised it was a folded piece of paper. He tried to pull his hand away but Hathaway tightened his grip.

'You're trying to set me up,' hissed Donovan. That's what this had all been about. Hathaway was planting drugs on him. Donovan looked around frantically, expecting to see police closing in on him.

'Don't be stupid, Donovan,' soothed Hathaway. 'Why would I plant a two-quid wrap on you? You deal in thousands of kilos. It's going to be all or nothing.' He eased his grip. Donovan felt the paper pressing against his own palm. 'Take it,' said Hathaway.

Donovan pulled his hand away. He opened the piece of paper. Typed on it was an address in the South of France.

'Sharkey's there,' said Hathaway softly.

'How do you know that?'

'Tracked his phone. Easy peasy when you work for the good guys.'

'And what do you want? A drink?'

Hathaway looked scornfully at Donovan. 'How much would you give me? A few grand? This isn't about a few grand. Besides, you seem to have forgotten you're pretty much broke at the moment.'

'If it's not about a bung, then what is it about?'

Hathaway grinned and tapped the side of his nose. 'Need to know, Donovan. At the moment, just don't look this gift horse in the mouth. You go and get your money, then we'll talk again.' He stood up, grunting as he put weight on his right leg, then turned and walked away, dragging his right leg slightly. He edged into the shopping crowd and within seconds Donovan had lost sight of him.

STEWART SHARKEY pulled the brim of his hat low over his eyes and waved at the waiter. He ordered an omelette and a caffè latte and a bottle of good wine in fluent French, then settled back and scanned the front page of *Le Monde*.

Sharkey heard chair legs scrape against the flagstones and he lowered his paper. A man in his thirties grunted and lowered himself into a chair at the table next to Sharkey's. The man ordered a coffee and lit a small cigar. Sharkey went back to reading the paper.

'Checking the currency rates?' said a voice. Sharkey lowered his paper again. The man at the next table tapped ash into a glass ashtray and nodded at the paper. 'Seeing how many francs you get to the pound.' The man spoke English but with an accent. Not French.

Sharkey formed his face into a pained frown, trying to make it clear that he wasn't looking for a conversation. 'I'm sorry, I don't speak English,' he said in his perfect French.

'Is it better to hold the pound, do you think, or dollars?'

'I'm sorry, I have no interest in the currency markets,' said Sharkey in French, raising the paper and flicking it to make a cracking sound.

The man leaned forward and blew smoke over the top of the newspaper. 'Are you sure about that, Mr Sharkey? I would have thought that with sixty million stolen dollars, you'd be very interested.'

There was another scraping sound behind Sharkey and he looked over his shoulder. Two men sat down at the table behind him. Big men with black sunglasses and flashy gold rings on their fingers.

Sharkey put down his paper. 'Who are you?' He glanced left and right, praying silently that there would be a gendarme close by.

'You don't know me, Mr Sharkey. And please don't bother looking round for help.' He reached into his pocket and brought out a small stun gun. 'There are two ways we can handle this. I can press this against your neck and give you twenty thousand volts. You go down, I announce that I am a doctor and my two friends behind you offer to transport you to hospital in their Mercedes-Benz. You wake up in about ten minutes with a very bad headache.'

Sharkey sighed. 'And the alternative?'

'I pay your bill and mine. We smile and walk to the car together. Which is it to be, Mr Sharkey?'

'Whatever he is paying you, I will pay you ten times as much.'

The man shook his head. 'Please do not embarrass yourself, Mr Sharkey. We are all professionals here.'

As Vicky turned off the shower she heard the door to the apartment open and close. 'Stewart? Is that you?' she called, then shook her head in annoyance. Of course it was him. Who else would be letting themselves in with a key? She opened the bathroom door, then jumped as she saw the man standing there, arm outstretched to grab the handle. She took a deep breath, ready to scream, but before a sound left her throat a second man stepped from the side of the door and clamped a cloth over her mouth. Her nostrils were filled with a sickly-sweet odour and then the room started to swim. She felt the strength drain from her legs and everything went black.

LOUISE COOKED LASAGNE and opened a bottle of red wine. Donovan sat down at the dining table as she heaped the pasta onto three plates. 'Robbie, there's salad in the fridge. Can you get it for me?'

'Sure,' said Robbie, dashing off to the kitchen.

'He's a good kid,' said Louise.

'He likes you,' said Donovan, pouring wine into their glasses.

'It's mutual,' said Louise, sitting down next to him.

Robbie returned with the salad. One of Donovan's phones started ringing. Donovan pressed the green button. It was the Spaniard. 'Hang on, Juan,' said Donovan, standing up. 'I'll go outside.' He left the apartment and hurried downstairs and out of the front door. 'Yeah, sorry about that, Juan. How did it go?'

'Your money is back in your account,' said the Spaniard.

'Juan, you are a star!'

'Yes, I know.'

'You took your fee out first, right?'

'Of course I did, *amigo*. And my expenses.'

'Whatever it cost, you are worth it, you dago bastard.'

'I couldn't have done it without knowing where he was.'

'How was Sharkey?'

'Cooperative. Eventually.'

'Make sure he's never found, Juan.'

'Thy will be done. And your wife, *amigo*?'

'Did she see what you did to Sharkey?'

'No, but she was in the other room. She heard everything.'

'Let me speak to her.'

The phone went quiet. Then Vicky was on the line. 'Den . . .' she said. 'I'm sorry. I didn't know how much he'd taken, I swear to God. He told me he was just taking some of it, so you'd have to talk to us.'

'He cleaned me out, Vicky. And a big chunk of the money didn't belong to me. It was promised to some Colombian guys.'

Donovan looked up at the house. Robbie was at one of the windows, looking down. Robbie waved and Donovan waved back.

'Sharkey wanted me dead, Vicky. He knew I owed that money to the Colombians, and he knew what they'd do to me when they didn't get it. There's something else you don't know. Sharkey wanted Robbie to find you in bed with him.'

'No . . .' sobbed Vicky.

'It's true, Vicky. He sent him a text message. Pretended it was from me. He wanted to be caught. He wanted you to have to run away with him. He used you, Vicky. From day one.'

'I'm sorry, Den. I swear to God, I'm so sorry. Please don't tell Robbie about the money. And about this. Just tell him I went away.' Then all Donovan could hear were sobs.

'Look, Vicky, don't cry. OK? Just stop crying.'

'I do love you. And I love Robbie.'

'Vicky, stop. Please. Nothing's going to happen to you. I promise.'

Vicky sniffed. 'You're going to let me go?'

Donovan hesitated, wondering if he was doing the right thing. 'Yes,' he said eventually.

'Oh, thank you, Den. Thank you. I'll never hurt you again, I promise. I'll never let you down again.'

Donovan took a deep breath. 'You're not going to get the chance, Vicky. You're not to come near me again. Not within twenty miles. I'm not going to stop you coming back to England, because that's where your family are, but you don't come near me. Or Robbie.'

'Den . . . please. Robbie's my son. You're my family.'

'The time for thinking about that was before you let him catch you in bed with Starkey. We're not your family any more. You walked out on us. But I will let you see Robbie. On his birthday. On your birthday. Christmas. Mother's Day. When he's twelve he can decide how much time he spends with you. Do you understand?'

'OK.' She sniffed again. 'OK. If that's how it has to be.'

'One other thing. You drop the injunction.'

'Yes. I'll do what you say. And Den . . .'

'Yeah?'

'I really am sorry.'

'Put the Spaniard back on.'

More muffled voices, then Rojas. 'OK, *amigo*?'

'Dispose of Sharkey, then let her go.'

'That's a good decision, *amigo*.'

'I hope so.' Donovan cut the connection, put the phone back in his pocket and went back to the house.

Louise and Robbie looked up as he walked back into the flat.

'Is something wrong, Dad?' asked Robbie.

'No, everything's fine,' said Donovan, 'but I'm going to have to go out for a while.' He nodded at Louise. 'Can I borrow your car?'

'Sure,' said Louise. She stood up and picked up the keys from the sideboard. 'Can I help?'

'I've just got to do something online, that's all.'

Louise kissed him on the cheek.

Donovan winked at Robbie. 'Look after her, OK?'

'Will do, Dad.'

Donovan went downstairs and climbed into Louise's BMW. He used one of the mobiles to call Fullerton. 'Jamie? I need a favour. You've got a computer, yeah?'

'Sure, Den. Come round. We need to talk anyway.'

Fullerton gave Donovan the address of his flat. Donovan drove to Docklands and parked the BMW on a meter.

Fullerton met him at the lift and led him to his computer. It was already connected to the Internet. Donovan logged on to the site of the Swiss bank into which Rojas had put the money he'd taken from Sharkey. Donovan grinned as he saw there was just under fifty-five million dollars in the account. 'Yes!' he said.

'Good news?' asked Fullerton.

'I'm back in the black,' he said. 'To the tune of fifty-five million dollars. If you've got any of that shampoo around, now might be a good time to crack open a bottle.'

Fullerton went off to the kitchen. Donovan transferred ten million dollars to Carlos Rodriguez's account. Legally and morally he figured he didn't owe the Colombian a penny, but after the attempted hit last night it was clear that legality and morality didn't form part of Rodriguez's vocabulary.

Fullerton came back with an opened bottle of Krug champagne and two glasses. He poured champagne for the two of them and they clinked glasses. 'To crime,' said Fullerton.

Donovan laughed and sipped his champagne. 'How much have you got so far, Jamie?' he asked.

'Five million, definite. Three from dealers, two from guys in the City who'll want the gear selling on.'

'That's not a problem. You've got the cash in your account, yeah?'

Fullerton nodded. 'Offshore. It's well clean.'

Donovan picked up a pen and started writing numbers down on a notepad. Five million pounds from Fullerton. O'Brien in Dublin was in for five hundred kilos at twelve grand a kilo. He'd already sent six million pounds through to Donovan's account. Five million pounds had already come from Macfadyen and Jordan, and PM had sent through one point seven million. That made a total of just under eighteen million pounds. Almost twenty-six million dollars.

'We're home and dry, Jamie,' he said. 'We're over budget. Even without what I've got in my account. It's a done deal.'

They clinked glasses again.

'How much have we got?'

'Twenty-six million US. Depends on the exchange rate.'

'And for that we get how much?'

Donovan tapped his nose. 'That's for me to know.'

'Oh come on, Den. If you can't trust me by now . . .'

'It's a lot, Jamie.'

'Bastard!' Fullerton said, only half joking.

Donovan took a long drink of champagne. 'OK, don't sulk,' he said. 'My guys are bringing in eight thousand kilos. For the money we've taken in, we've got to hand over about two thousand. I'm gonna have to see the six thousand off to someone with a distribution network and in the UK that means the Turks. If I'm lucky I'll get six grand a kilo.'

'Six grand a kilo, six thousand kilos, that's still thirty-six million quid.' Fullerton raised his glass to Donovan. 'I salute you, Den.'

Donovan toasted Fullerton. 'Back to you, Jamie. And a chunk of that money is for you. Couldn't have done it without you.'

'Nah,' said Fullerton. 'You could have funded it yourself.'

'Wasn't sure I'd be getting that money back, Jamie. That's an added bonus. Right, let's get that money transferred into my pal's account, then we're off and running.'

AFTER HE LEFT Fullerton's flat, Donovan used an international calling card to phone Carlos Rodriguez in Colombia.

'I want you to call Jesus off,' said Donovan. 'I've just transferred ten million dollars into your account.'

'If what you say is true, I will talk to my nephew.'

'Thank you, Carlos.'

Donovan hung up. His next call was to a Turkish businessman who lived in a twelve-bedroom mansion overlooking Wimbledon Common. A while later he caught a cab to Wimbledon and spent the best part of three hours with the man.

DONOVAN GOT BACK to Louise's flat just after midnight. He found her asleep on the sofa, curled up round a cushion. He went over to her and brushed her cheek, then blew gently in her ear.

'Wake up, sleepyhead.'

She opened her eyes and squinted up at him. 'Oh, hi, Den. I was waiting up for you.' She sat up and rubbed her eyes sleepily.

'You didn't have to, but thanks. How's Robbie?'

'He went to bed at ten,' she said. 'What time is it?'

'Late. Go on, you go off to bed and I'll make up the sofa.'

She stood up, then lost her balance and fell against him. He caught her, his hands instinctively slipping round her waist. She looked up at him, her mouth only inches from his, and before he knew what he was doing Donovan was kissing her. She responded, then pushed him away, gasping for breath.

'I'm sorry,' said Donovan. 'That was stupid. After what you went through with that guy, the last thing you want is some man mauling you.'

'It's not that, Den. Honest. And you're not just some man.' She slid her hand round his neck and kissed him again, softly on the lips. 'It's just that with Robbie next door, and everything else. Now's just not the time. It wouldn't feel right. You know what I mean?'

Donovan smiled. 'I know exactly what you mean. Now off to bed, I'm knackered.'

'Everything's OK?'

Donovan nodded. 'Everything's just fine. Couldn't be better.'

THE SHOWER WAS RUNNING when Tina got up, so she made toast and coffee and had the table set by the time Donovan came into the room.

'Robbie up yet?' he asked.

Tina shook her head. Donovan knocked on his son's bedroom door and shouted for him to get out of bed. He sat down at the table and bit into a piece of dry toast.

'Do you want to do something today?' he asked. 'Go to the zoo? Get Robbie out of the house?'

Tina shook her head. 'I have to go out for a while. Shopping. Women's stuff. I won't be long. But in the afternoon, sure.' She sat down at the table. 'How did it go yesterday?'

'Better than I'd hoped.' Donovan drank some coffee. 'I got the money back. The money my wife cleared out of my bank accounts.'

'Den, that's great news. That's brilliant.'

'It's better than a kick in the head. I've paid off the guys who were after me, so I'm almost free and clear.'

'Almost?'

'Just one more deal.'

'Can't you stop now? You've got your money back.'

'I've got to see this one thing through, Louise. Too many people will lose their money if I pull out now.'

Tina reached across the table and held his hand. 'Den . . .'

The bedroom door opened and Tina pulled back her hand. Robbie walked out, dressed in T-shirt and jeans. 'Hey, just because it's Sunday doesn't mean you don't shower,' said Donovan.

'Can't I have breakfast first?'

Donovan waved at him to sit at the table.

'Do you want me to cook?' asked Tina. 'I've got bacon.'

'I'll do it,' said Donovan. 'You go get your stuff.'

Tina picked up her bag and left. She walked to the main road and caught a black cab to an Internet café. She kept glancing over her shoulder but knew that there was no reason for anyone to be following her. Donovan trusted her completely. Trusted her with his only son. She paid the driver and went inside the café.

TINA SAT AT THE COMPUTER terminal. Two schoolgirls at the next terminal were giggling as they sent messages to a chat room. A waitress brought over a cappuccino and put it down next to Tina.

'Thanks,' said Tina. She waited until the waitress had gone before logging on to Hathaway's web site. Over the past few days she'd heard enough one-sided telephone conversations to get a rough idea of what was going on. Donovan was putting together a major deal and it was going to happen the following day. Tina wasn't sure where, though she'd heard Donovan say 'airfield' several times, so she'd assumed it was coming in by plane.

Tina began to type, then she hesitated. For the first time in three years undercover she felt guilty about what she was doing. She took no pleasure in betraying Den Donovan.

DONOVAN AND ROBBIE were watching television when Louise arrived home. 'Get everything you wanted?' asked Donovan.

Louise held up a Safeway carrier bag. 'Do you still want to go out?' she asked.

'Dad said we could go to the Trocadero and play video games if it's OK with you,' said Robbie excitedly.

'Fine by me,' said Louise. 'Let me put this stuff away and we're out of here.'

They drove to Central London in the BMW and spent two hours in the Trocadero, with Robbie rushing from machine to machine.

'I wouldn't mind kissing you again,' said Donovan. 'Some time.'

Louise looked at him. 'Where did that come from?'

Donovan shrugged. 'I just wanted you to know, that's all. Maybe in a few days, when everything's sorted . . .'

'Maybe what?'

'Bloody hell, Louise. Don't make me beg. I'm only asking for a date.'

Louise laughed. 'We'll see.'

'I'm serious.'

'So am I,' said Louise. She shook her head.

'What?' asked Donovan.

'I just wish we'd met under different circumstances.'

'We met, and that's all that matters.'

Louise looked as if she wanted to say something else but then she turned away and went over to stand behind Robbie. Donovan could see that something was troubling her, but he didn't want to press her. She'd tell him eventually.

DONOVAN WALKED into Tina's sitting room, his hair still wet from the shower. Tina was in the kitchenette, frying sausages. 'Good morning,' she said. 'You want breakfast?'

'Just coffee,' said Donovan.

The land line rang and Tina answered it. She listened and frowned, then handed the phone to Donovan. 'It's for you,' she said.

'No one knows I'm here,' said Donovan.

'It's a man. He asked for you.'

Donovan took the phone. 'Who is it?' he snapped.

'That's no way to talk to an old friend,' said a voice.

'How did you get this number?'

Hathaway chuckled. 'We need to meet.'

'I'm busy.'

'I know you're busy, Donovan. That's what we need to talk about. You've got the money back from Sharkey, right? Now I've got more information for you. Information that you're going to want.'

Donovan looked at his watch. It was nine o'clock. He had to be at the airfield at four, and it was a two-hour drive from London. He had time. 'You know Blomfield Road? Little Venice?'

'I know it. But since when have you been setting the venues?'

'I'm not going to Camden again. There's a bridge over the canal, opposite a pub called the Paddington Stop. I'll see you there at one o'clock. I can't get there any earlier, I've got things to do.'

'One o'clock is fine.'

The line went dead. Donovan finished his coffee and went into the kitchenette. 'I'm going to have to go out.'

'When will you be back?' asked Tina.

'I'm not sure. Late.'

'Don't go, Den. Please.'

Donovan put his hands on her shoulders and looked into her eyes. 'What do you think's going on, Louise?' he asked.

She shrugged his hands away. 'I've heard you on the phones, Den. I know what you're doing. You're bringing gear in and today's the bloody day.'

'Have you been spying on me?'

'Don't be stupid, Den. This is a small flat and your phones have been ringing red-hot for the last twenty-four hours.'

'I have to go.'

Tina shook her head. 'No, you don't. You can walk away. Walk away from it all.' Tears welled up in her eyes.

'Louise, I'm sorry, I have to go.'

'Damn you, Donovan!'

Donovan took a step back, surprised at the intensity of her reaction. 'I don't have time for this now, Louise. We'll talk about it later.'

'And what if there isn't a later, Den?'

Donovan pressed a finger against her lips, then he leaned over, kissed her on the forehead, and hurried from the flat. Tina rushed after him, but he closed the door without looking back.

She leaned against the door, her eyes filled with tears. She'd wanted to say more, but she couldn't. She couldn't tell him, because the truth was she was betraying him. She was helping to set him up.

And who was the man who'd phoned? There had been something familiar about his voice, but for the life of her Tina couldn't place it. Whoever it was, he'd unnerved Donovan.

DONOVAN WAITED on the bridge, whistling softly to himself. Jordan and Macfadyen had left for the airfield. Donovan had called PM and told him where the plane was landing and what time to get there. And he'd arranged to meet Fullerton at Hyde Park Corner so they could drive to the airfield together.

Donovan saw Hathaway walking down Formosa Street. He had a laptop computer case hanging from one shoulder. He walked to the middle of the bridge. 'Lovely day for it,' he said.

The detector on Donovan's belt remained still. Hathaway wasn't wearing a recording device or transmitter. 'What do you want?'

Hathaway smiled without warmth. 'You didn't think twice before putting that bullet in my leg, did you?'

'I thought about killing you.'

'Have you any idea how that bullet changed my life?'

'Got you a better job, didn't I?'

'I loved being in Customs, Den. Loved working undercover. I was bloody good at it.'

Donovan flashed Hathaway a sarcastic smile. 'Clearly you weren't. If you'd been any good, I wouldn't have made you.'

'Someone grassed me. One of your informers.'

Donovan shook his head. 'You gave yourself away. Some story you told. You told it wrong. Told it like you'd memorised it.'

'Bullshit!'

'Why would I lie? To hurt you?' Donovan chuckled. 'We're beyond that, aren't we?'

'It was the job I'd always wanted. I was one of the good guys, fast-track. Then you shot me and I'm in hospital for three months. And three months after that I'm sitting in human resources being told there is no place for me in the leaner, meaner Customs and Excise.'

'You got a pension, right? Disability?'

'Peanuts. Wife didn't like the idea of my being thrown on the scrapheap at twenty-four, so she went off in search of pastures new. You changed my life, Den. Now I'm going to do the same to you.'

'You're going to put me behind bars, is that it?'

'I want the money you got back from Sharkey.'

'You're out of your mind.'

'I know about the plane, Donovan. I know about the heroin. I know about Macfadyen and Jordan. I know about the airfield. You are screwed. You have one way out. Give me the money and I'll let you go ahead with the Turkish deal.'

Donovan shook his head. 'Why would I give you the money?'

'Because if you don't, you're going to prison. Possibly for the rest of your life. Eight thousand kilos of heroin, Donovan. Plus there's the Mexican deal. The Beetles. Mexico is next door to the States and Rodriguez has been shoving cocaine over the border like there's no tomorrow. I link you to Rodriguez and the Americans will want a piece of you.'

'I walk away from the deal and you've got nothing.'

Hathaway smiled. 'Conspiracy doesn't depend on you taking delivery, Donovan. You put the deal together. That I can prove.'

'Bollocks.'

'I have people undercover. Close to you.'

'Now I know you're lying.'

'Your infallible sense of smell? You can always spot an undercover cop? You always took pride in that particular skill, didn't you? Well, I got people in under your radar, Donovan. Up close and personal.'

Donovan stared at Hathaway. Is that how he knew about the plane? But who was the traitor? Jordan and Macfadyen? Had they been turned when the Mexican deal went belly up? It had always struck Donovan as suspicious that Customs hadn't let the consignment run. Now he knew why. He turned to go.

'It isn't Ricky Jordan. And it isn't Charlie Macfadyen,' said Hathaway quietly.

Donovan stopped. 'Why should I believe you?'

Hathaway patted the laptop computer case. 'Because I have proof.'

'What sort of proof?'

Hathaway looked at his watch again. 'We're going to have to start the ball rolling, Donovan. That plane is getting closer. You got sixty million dollars from Sharkey. I want it.'

'I don't have sixty million.'

'Why don't you just tell me how much is left. And don't bother lying, because I can find out.'

'Forty-five mill,' said Donovan.

'That's what I want, then. That's the price of your freedom.'

'So I give you forty-five million and you tell me who the undercover agent is?'

'Agents. Plural.'

'And how do I give you the money? Used notes?'

Hathaway tapped the case again. 'We do it online. You transfer five million. I show you proof. You transfer more money. I show you more proof. At any point you can stop.'

'And what then?'

'I walk away.'

'And the agents?'

'You do what you have to do, Donovan.'

'You know what that will be,' said Donovan coldly.

'It's a game, Donovan. That's what you taught me. There are winners and losers. I'm doing what I have to do to be a winner.'

'You're a callous bastard, Hathaway.'

'Well, gosh, Donovan. Sticks and stones. Are we going to do this or are you going to prison for twenty years?'

Donovan nodded slowly. 'OK,' he said. 'Let's see what you have.'

THE LAPTOP FLICKERED to life. Hathaway nodded at the bench. 'Take a pew, Donovan.' Hathaway had set the computer up on one of the trestle tables on the terrace outside the Paddington Stop. 'Tell you what, get us a couple of beers, yeah? We should celebrate.'

Donovan went into the pub, bought two pints and carried them outside. Hathaway had placed his mobile phone next to the laptop and was connecting to the Internet through the computer's infrared link. Donovan put the glasses on the table and sat down.

Hathaway turned the laptop towards Donovan, then handed him a piece of paper on which was written the details of a numbered Swiss account. 'Five million,' he said.

Donovan put his hands on the keyboard, then paused. What if he was being conned? But what choice did he have? If Hathaway did have undercover agents in play, then he was facing life behind bars. He made the transfer. When Hathaway was satisfied the money had been transferred, he opened a pocket on the side of the laptop case and took out an envelope. He handed it to Donovan.

Donovan opened the envelope. Inside was an application to join the Metropolitan Police. Clifford Warren. Twenty-nine years old. An address in Harlesden. Donovan frowned. He didn't know anyone called Clifford Warren. There was something else in the envelope. A photograph and another sheet of paper, folded in half. Donovan slid them out. The photograph was of Bunny. Donovan cursed.

He unfolded the sheet of paper. It was a print-out of an email message to Hathaway detailing when and where the flight from Turkey was due to arrive in the UK.

Hathaway patted the computer case. 'For the next one, I'm going to need another fifteen million.'

Donovan hesitated, but his fingers stayed on the keyboard.

'Getting rid of one is no good,' whispered Hathaway. 'It's all or nothing, Donovan.'

Donovan knew Hathaway was right. He input the instructions to transfer the fifteen million dollars as Hathaway watched. When he had finished, Hathaway handed him a second envelope. It contained another Metropolitan Police application and a photograph. James Robert Fullerton. 'No bloody way,' said Donovan. 'I've seen him take drugs. He handles stolen gear.'

'Deep cover,' said Hathaway. 'Deep, deep cover.'

There was another sheet of paper inside the envelope. It was a print-out of an email Fullerton had sent Hathaway, packed with details about the shipment of VW Beetles from Mexico.

'Funnily enough, I didn't hear a peep from him about the Turkish flight,' said Hathaway. 'He's either playing his cards very close to his chest or he's going over to your side.'

Donovan stared at the photograph of Jamie Fullerton. 'I trusted him,' he said quietly.

'And last but not least . . .' said Hathaway. 'Twenty-five million dollars and you get the third and final name.'

Donovan made the transfer and Hathaway slid a third envelope across the table. 'And with that, I'll say goodbye,' said Hathaway.

'What are you going to do now?'

'I'm going to retire. Do the things I've always wanted to do. I already have several identities fixed up. That's the beauty of working for the good guys. All I have to do is to slot myself into a new life. A life where I have forty-five million dollars.' He closed the laptop and put it in its case, then turned and walked away.

Donovan waited until Hathaway had turned the corner before opening the envelope. He slid out the by-now familiar application to join the Metropolitan Police. Christina Louise Leigh. The girl in the photograph had long blonde hair instead of a short black bob but there was no doubt who she was.

Donovan stood up. Louise? He'd trusted Louise with his child. He'd let her into his life, shared his innermost thoughts with her. And she was a cop. Everything she had told him had been a lie.

He walked back across the bridge and along the towpath. A narrowboat was moored opposite the Paddington Stop.

Donovan climbed on board and tapped twice on the wooden door. A woman opened it, then moved to the side to allow Donovan in.

Alex Knight was sitting in front of a rack of CCTV monitors. He took off a pair of headphones and grinned at Donovan.

'Did you get it?' asked Donovan.

Knight had half a dozen long-range directional microphones and as many video cameras targeting the area. He had placed two men posing as anglers on the canal side, a man and woman inside the pub, two men in a flat overlooking the canal and two teams on tower blocks close by. There was also a camera and a directional microphone in a British Telecom van parked in Blomfield Road and two small radio-controlled cameras mounted on streetlights close to the bridge.

'Every word,' said Alex. 'Sound and vision. I'll get it edited and boost the sound where necessary. Should have it done this evening.'

'Tomorrow morning should be OK,' said Donovan. 'First thing.'

'IS THAT IT?' asked Fullerton, his head on one side. Off in the distance was a faint throbbing sound.

'Maybe,' said Donovan. 'Relax, Jamie. It'll be here when it's here.'

Bunny and PM stood some distance away, deep in conversation.

'What do you think they're talking about?' asked Fullerton.

'Probably discussing when they should pull out their guns and blow us away so they can keep all the gear for themselves.'

Fullerton's eyes widened and Donovan slapped him on the back. 'Joke, Jamie. Jordan and Macfadyen have given everybody a going over with a metal detector; there's nobody here carrying so much as a pocket knife.'

It was just after seven in the evening and dusk was settling in. The airfield was a former RAF base that had been declared surplus to requirements during the early nineties. Until a more permanent use could be found for the facility, the government had leased the property to a group of EU charities. Along one side of the runway ran a line of metal sheds in which several charities and emergency aid groups stored equipment and supplies. Various logos were painted on the sliding doors of the sheds, including the insignia of the charity that was chartering the Russian plane.

Donovan and Fullerton were standing in front of the charity's shed next to half a dozen rented Transit vans, each with its own driver. Jordan and Macfadyen had supplied the drivers.

Bunny and PM had brought five of their own men and two large trucks with the name of a laundry company on the sides. The backs of the trucks were already open in anticipation of the plane's arrival.

One of Donovan's phones buzzed. He pulled it out of his pocket. He'd been sent a text message. He scrolled through it. DEN—IT'S A TRAP. RUN. LOUISE. He smiled to himself, deleted it and put the phone back in his pocket.

Everybody was now staring up at the sky and pointing. The plane was at about five thousand feet. The engine noise was louder now. The undercarriage and nose-heel dropped and the flaps lowered. The plane came in straight to land. It slowed visibly, the nose came up and the wheels hit the concrete with a squeal and puffs of black smoke. Then the plane was rolling by them.

Fullerton began to jump up and down. He punched the air, then turned and hugged Donovan. 'Bloody hell, Den, we did it.'

Donovan patted Fullerton on the shoulder. 'Yeah,' he said quietly. 'We did, didn't we?'

The plane turned towards them. It slowed and stopped, about a hundred yards away from where they were standing. The engines shut down one by one.

The engines of the Transit vans burst into life and Bunny motioned for his drivers to get into the laundry trucks. That was when all hell broke loose.

Three helicopters came in from the west, swooping over the perimeter fence. One hovered close to the tower building and six men in black, holding automatic weapons, jumped out. A second helicopter disgorged more armed men on the far side of the plane and they ran to surround it. The third helicopter landed at the end of the line of sheds. Another six armed men piled out and started running towards Donovan and his crew, guns at the ready.

'What the hell's this?' hissed Fullerton.

Donovan said nothing. He slowly raised his hands in the air.

An armoured Land-Rover crashed through the gate in the perimeter fence and then turned sharply to the left, allowing a dozen faster vehicles to speed by. Half were police cars, blue lights flashing, and half were dark saloons filled with big men in black jackets.

Two of the Transit vans roared off, but a burst of automatic fire ripped out the tyres of one and the other was rammed against the wall of one of the sheds by a police car. Jordan and Macfadyen made a run for it, but they were both rugby-tackled to the ground by police officers. PM slowly followed Donovan's example and raised his arms above his head. Bunny did the same.

The armed men in black surrounded Donovan and his men, swinging their weapons from side to side, their faces hidden behind respirators. They wore black body armour over black uniforms.

'Fuck me, it's the SAS,' whispered Fullerton.

Men in black jackets with CUSTOMS written on the back in bright yellow capital letters were piling out of their saloon cars and walking towards the plane. SAS troopers were waving at the pilots to open the door at the front of the fuselage.

Hands started patting down Donovan. He looked to his left. It was a burly, unsmiling police sergeant. 'It's OK, I'm not armed,' said Donovan. 'None of us is.'

The ramp at the back of the plane began to open. The sergeant nodded at two young constables. 'Take him over there, lads,' said the sergeant. 'Someone wants a word with him.' The two police officers escorted Donovan to the back of the ramp where an obese man wearing a black Customs jacket was waiting for him.

'Den Donovan,' said the man, barely able to contain his glee.

'You've no idea what a pleasure it is finally to meet you. Raymond Mackie, Head of Drugs Operations, Customs and Excise. Come on, I can't wait to see what eight thousand kilos of heroin looks like.'

Mackie strode up the ramp, breathing heavily, flanked by Customs officers. Donovan followed them up the ramp into the interior of the plane. Two men in their twenties wearing stained khaki jumpsuits were sitting on two seats fixed to the fuselage. Other than the two men, the plane was empty.

One of the men waved at Mackie. 'We want claim political asylum.' Mackie's jaw dropped. 'What?'

The other man punched his colleague on the shoulder. 'He make joke,' he said to Mackie. 'My friend has big mouth. Make big joke.'

Mackie looked round the vast space, his mouth still open in astonishment. The other Customs officers were equally surprised. 'What the hell's going on?' spluttered Mackie.

A door opened at the end of the cargo area and Gregov stepped out carrying a carrier bag. He walked through the hold. Two SAS troopers followed him. Gregov opened the carrier bag and took out two cartons of Marlboro cigarettes. He held them out to Mackie.

'I was going to declare them,' he said. 'Honest I was.'

JAMIE FULLERTON stared at the screen and for the hundredth time checked to see if he had email. There were no new messages for him. Fullerton had sent a full report on what had happened at the airfield to Hathaway and had expected an immediate reply.

Hathaway must have known about the abortive raid at the airfield and must have realised by now that Fullerton had been there. Fullerton had said in his email that Donovan had only told him about the flight at the last minute and that there hadn't been time to get a message to Hathaway.

Fullerton had been held in a cell for an hour, interrogated by two plain-clothes detectives whose hearts clearly weren't in it, and then released. No laws had been broken, not least because of Donovan's insistence that nobody carry a gun. They were all guests of the Russian aviation company, and the Ilyushin transporter plane had filed a valid flight plan. It was suspicious, there was no getting away from that, two dozen men and a convoy of vans all waiting for an empty plane, but there was nothing illegal about it.

Fullerton had tried calling Donovan's mobile several times but it was switched off.

The door intercom buzzed and Fullerton looked at the CCTV

monitor. It was Charlie Macfadyen. Fullerton buzzed him up and switched off the computer. He had the door open for Macfadyen by the time the elevator reached his floor.

'What's up, Charlie?' asked Fullerton.

'Not much,' said Macfadyen, walking into Fullerton's flat. He reached behind his back, pulled an automatic from a holster clipped to his belt and thrust the gun against Fullerton's chest.

As SOON AS HE'D BEEN released, Bunny had got a cab home. When the doorbell rang he hurried over to open it, but not before making sure the security chain was on.

It was Jordan. Bunny wondered why Jordan had turned up on his doorstep. 'You here for a reason, or is this social?'

Jordan leaned forward. 'We think we know who the rotten apple is,' he whispered. 'You'll never guess.'

Bunny unhitched the security chain and opened the door.

'Who is it?' asked Bunny.

Jordan pushed Bunny in the chest with the flat of his hand. Bunny staggered back, falling over a coffee table and crashed to the floor. Jordan reached inside his jacket and pulled out a gun. 'It's you!' roared Jordan, pointing the gun at Bunny's surprised face.

ROBBIE WALKED OUT of the spare bedroom, rubbing his eyes sleepily. Tina was lying on the sofa, wrapped in a bathrobe. 'Why aren't you in bed?' he asked.

'I was waiting for your dad,' she said, sitting up.

'He always stays out late,' said Robbie, sitting on the sofa next to her. 'Sometimes all night. It used to drive Mum crazy.'

'What about you? Didn't you worry?'

Robbie shrugged. 'He always comes back eventually.' He looked up at her. 'Is something wrong?'

Tina shook her head. 'No, everything's fine.' She picked up her mobile and called Donovan's number again. No answer. No message service. She had no way of knowing if the phone was even working, or if he'd received the text message she'd sent.

'He always has it switched off,' said Robbie. 'Don't worry.'

They both heard the knock at the door. Robbie stood up and ran over to it. 'Robbie, check first,' shouted Tina. 'And use the chain.'

There was the sound of a key being inserted in the lock and Tina opened her mouth to scream, but then Donovan opened the door.

'Den! It's you!' said Tina.

Donovan closed the door. He pushed Robbie towards the spare room. 'Get ready for school.' He grinned at Tina. 'Get your glad rags on, kid, let's go out and celebrate.'

'Celebrate?'

'We did it, Louise. Wasn't as smooth as I'd hoped, but we did it.' He took her in his arms and hugged her. 'We'll drop Robbie off at school and then there's some people I want you to meet.'

'Den . . .'

Donovan put a finger against her lips. 'We can talk later,' he said.

He pushed her towards the bedroom. She closed the door then leaned against it, her heart pounding. She was sure he knew. Something had gone wrong and now he was going to make her pay.

Her mobile phone was on the dressing table and she fumbled for it. With trembling fingers she tapped out the number that Gregg Hathaway had given her three years earlier. Her lifeline.

She pressed the phone to her ear and listened as it rang. No one answered it. No answering service kicked in. Something must have gone wrong, but what? Tina went into her bathroom and turned on the cold tap. She called up directory enquiries and asked for the main switchboard for the Metropolitan Police. The number was answered by a brisk female voice.

'I want to speak to Assistant Commissioner Peter Latham,' Tina said.

'He's no longer with the Metropolitan Police,' said the woman. 'Can anyone else help?'

Tina suddenly felt dizzy and she held on to the basin for support. 'No, it has to be him. How can I get hold of him?'

'Assistant Commissioner Latham retired two years ago on the grounds of ill health,' said the woman.

'But where is he now? This is urgent. Life or death.'

'I'm afraid he passed away six months after he retired,' said the woman. 'Can I put you through to his successor's office?'

There was a knock at the door. 'Louise?' asked Donovan. 'You OK in there?'

Tina switched off the phone. 'Yes, just going into the shower,' she said, trying to stop her voice from shaking. She showered and dried herself, then tried Hathaway's number again. Still no answer.

She threw on a dress, put on lipstick and mascara, then gave her hair a quick brush. She stared at her reflection. She looked as guilty as hell. She tried to smile but it was the smile of a terrified dog. 'It's OK,' she whispered to herself. 'It's going to be OK.' She took a deep breath. 'It's OK,' she said more confidently. 'You can deal with this.' Another deep breath.

'Are you OK?' Donovan shouted.

She opened the bedroom door. Donovan nodded appreciatively. 'Looking good,' he said.

'Thank you.'

Robbie was putting his books into his backpack. He'd changed into his school uniform. 'I don't see why I have to go to school,' he moaned. 'First I'm not to go, then you say I'm to go, then you pull me out, now you tell me I've got to go back. It's hardly consistent.'

'It's an inconsistent world,' said Donovan. 'Isn't it, Louise?'

Tina nodded.

They drove Robbie to school in the BMW, then drove across London to St John's Wood. Donovan told Tina where to park and they climbed out of the car.

'TANGO ONE is out of the vehicle,' said the detective into his handset. 'On foot. Repeat on foot.'

'Go after him, Alpha Seven,' crackled the speaker.

The detective nodded at the driver. 'Let's go.'

The two plain-clothes policemen got out of the saloon and walked quickly in the direction Donovan and the girl were heading. They saw the girl's back disappearing down an alley.

'Oh shit, I know what he's doing.' The detective put his transceiver to his mouth. 'Alpha Seven, he's going to cross the canal on foot. We need cover on the south side of the canal. We're going to lose him.'

The transceiver crackled. 'Affirmative, Alpha Seven.'

The two men hurried down the alley. It led to the canal towpath. A metal footbridge ran across the canal. Donovan and the girl were already dashing down the steps on the far side. A car was waiting at the side of the road, its engine running.

The detective grabbed the driver's arm and pulled him back. There was nothing they could do on foot and there was no point showing themselves. 'Tango One is getting into a blue saloon. Possibly a Vauxhall. Registration number unknown. We've lost him. Repeat, we have lost Tango One.'

'WHAT'S GOING ON, Den?' asked Tina as the blue saloon accelerated away from the kerb.

Donovan flashed her a smile. 'Gate-crashers,' said Donovan. 'Can't be too careful.' He leaned forward and patted his driver, Kim

Fletcher, on the shoulder. 'Nice one, Kim,' he said. 'Did you get the other thing?'

Fletcher popped open the glove compartment and handed Donovan a video cassette. 'He said something about the early worm catching the bird.'

'What is it?' asked Tina.

'The entertainment,' said Donovan, patting her on the leg. 'Come on, Louise, cheer up. You're behaving like a right wet blanket.'

Tina forced herself to smile.

'That's better,' said Donovan.

He and Tina sat in silence as Fletcher drove. He kept checking his mirrors and twice did a series of left turns to make sure he wasn't being followed, then drove east towards Docklands.

Tina stared out of the window with unseeing eyes, wondering where Donovan was taking her. And why. Did he know who she was? Or did he just suspect, and want to interrogate her?

Fletcher used a remote control unit to open a set of metal gates and the car bobbed into an underground car park. They parked close to an elevator. A balding man with a curved scar above his left ear and a black leather jacket was standing by the elevator door.

Donovan hugged the man. 'Everything OK, Charlie?'

The man nodded. Donovan introduced him to Tina. 'Charlie Macfadyen,' he said. 'One of the best.'

'Pleased to meet you,' said Tina.

'Everybody here?' Donovan asked Macfadyen.

'Just waiting for the guest of honour,' said Macfadyen. He punched the elevator button and the door rattled open. The three men stepped aside to allow Tina to walk in first. She felt her legs trembling but kept her head up and her lips pressed tightly together. She walked into the lift, then turned to face them.

Macfadyen pressed the button for the top floor. The penthouse. The door rattled shut. Donovan hummed as the lift rode upwards.

Macfadyen winked at Tina. 'All right, love?' he asked. 'Not scared of heights, are you?'

Tina shook her head.

The lift doors opened into a hallway. Another man was waiting outside a door. He pushed the door open and grinned at Donovan. 'OK, Den?'

'Perfect, Ricky,' said Donovan. 'I don't think you've met my date, have you? Louise, this is Ricky. Ricky Jordan.'

Jordan stuck out his hand and Tina shook it.

'In you go, Louise,' said Macfadyen.

Tina walked into the apartment. It was a large loft-style space with exposed brickwork and girders, and floor-to-ceiling windows that looked out onto the river. Two men were tied to chairs, strips of insulation tape across their mouths. One of the men was black, the other white. Next to them was a third chair. Donovan gestured at it. 'Take a seat, Louise.'

'What's this about, Den?' she asked.

'You know what this is about,' he said. 'Now sit down or I'll have the boys tie you down.'

Donovan stood in front of the white man. He held out a sheet of paper. 'James Robert Fullerton,' said Donovan. He dropped the sheet onto Fullerton's lap, then stepped across to stand in front of the black man. 'Clifford Warren.' Donovan held another sheet of paper in front of Warren's face, then placed it on Warren's lap. He held out a third sheet in front of Tina. It was her application to join the Met.

'Den . . .' she said, but Donovan put a finger against her lips.

'Don't speak,' he said. 'If you say anything. I'll have them gag you, OK?'

Tina nodded.

'Good girl,' he said. 'Christina Louise Leigh.' He held out the sheet. Tina took it but didn't look at it.

Donovan took a few steps back, then slowly began to clap. 'You all fooled me. I wouldn't have made any one of you as a narc. But then you're like no other narcs, are you? You're not in any under-cover unit with the Met or NCIS and your handler was a spook.' He smiled at the look of confusion on their faces. 'Didn't you know, Gregg Hathaway's a spook? MI6? You were being run by the Secret Intelligence Service.'

'No, that's not right,' protested Tina, but Donovan silenced her with a cold look.

Donovan took the video cassette out of his jacket pocket and walked over to a big-screen TV. He slotted the cassette into the video recorder. 'You were all playing yourselves, that's why I was fooled. You were real. But you were being used. Whatever you thought you were doing, whatever noble cause you thought you were serving, Hathaway had his own agenda.' Donovan pressed PLAY. Alex Knight had done a great job with the sound and he'd used close-ups wherever possible. There was no doubt who the two men on the bridge were, or what they were saying.

When the tape came to an end, Donovan switched off the TV.

Fullerton's face had gone a deep crimson. Donovan walked over and ripped the insulation tape off his mouth. Fullerton gasped. Warren had slumped in his chair. Donovan pulled the tape off his lips.

'Bit of a surprise that, hey, Bunny?' asked Donovan. 'In case anyone didn't quite get what was going on there, Gregg Hathaway slung me for forty-five million dollars. In return I got you. He sold you out. And as you saw on the tape, he was quite happy for me to kill all three of you.' He stood in front of the TV, grinning savagely. 'Any thoughts?'

'The heroin,' said Fullerton. 'What happened to the heroin?'

'It's exactly where it's supposed to be,' said Donovan. 'Five hundred kilos is being driven up to Scotland. Another thousand kilos should be on the ferry heading for Dublin. PM's got his, the Turks have got theirs.'

'But the plane was empty,' said Warren.

'Of course it was,' said Donovan. 'The Russians' job is to get supplies into places where there aren't mile-long runways. How do you think they do that, Bunny?'

'Parachutes,' whispered Fullerton. 'They dropped the gear.'

'They dropped three chutes about fifty miles east of the airfield,' said Donovan.

'You bastard,' said Fullerton. 'You set us all up.'

'I wanted to see what Hathaway would do,' said Donovan. 'The deal was that he gave me you and let me bring the gear in. Seems like he thought he could have it both ways: get to keep my money and put me behind bars for twenty years. And have you three killed into the bargain. He'd be free and clear.'

Jordan walked over. 'Are we going to do it, Den? Are we going to off them?'

'You can't kill us,' said Fullerton. 'We're cops.'

'That's the thing, Jamie,' said Donovan. 'Are you really cops? Or are you grasses? There's a difference.'

'We're on the Met's payroll,' said Fullerton. 'We get a salary. Promotions. Shit, we even get overtime.'

'Let's off 'em,' said Jordan. 'They screwed up the Mexico deal, didn't they?'

'Jamie, did, yeah. Bunny didn't know about it, nor did Louise.' Donovan nodded at Tina. 'Or is it Tina? Which do you prefer?'

'Either,' said Tina. 'My mother calls me Louise.'

'Tina, Louise, who gives a shit,' said Jordan. 'They're grasses. Let's do them.'

'A couple of weeks ago I'd have agreed with you, Ricky. But now I'm not so sure. We've got the gear, we're in the clear, and maybe they've seen the light.'

'What do you mean?' said Macfadyen.

'They can't give evidence against us. They're all compromised. Any case based on their evidence is going to be laughed out of court. And after what Hathaway's done to them, I don't think they're going to continue their careers as undercover cops or whatever it is they are. They're no threat to us.'

'They cost us a bundle on that Mexican deal.'

'Agreed, but they all played their part in putting together the Turkish thing. Couldn't have put the financing together so quickly without Jamie's help, and Bunny saved my life, for God's sake. And Louise, well that's personal. But all three of them made a difference. Maybe not the difference they were planning to make, but all's well that ends well, yeah? Killing them doesn't do anything for us.'

'It'd make me feel better,' said Jordan.

'Yeah, well that's something you're going to have to deal with, Ricky. You don't take someone's life just to make yourself feel good. You do it because it serves a purpose, and I don't think that killing these three is going to make a blind bit of difference to our lives. But letting them live might.'

'What are you talking about?' Jordan asked.

Donovan nodded at Fullerton. 'Jamie here didn't grass up the Turkish deal. Why not, Jamie?'

Fullerton shook his head. 'I don't know.'

'Yes, you do. You wanted the deal to succeed, didn't you? You didn't want Hathaway to know about it because you wanted it to go ahead.'

Fullerton nodded.

'Because of the money?'

'It wasn't just the money. I don't know what it was.'

'I do. For the kick. You wanted to see if you could do it. And you did, Jamie. You played the game and you won. We won. We made them look stupid and we made millions. How did that feel?'

'Yeah, it felt good. When that plane landed, it was better than a coke rush.'

'See what I mean?' Donovan said to Macfadyen and Jordan. 'You should use him. He's got a taste for it.' Donovan grinned at Fullerton. 'What about it, Jamie? They stitched you up, why not show them what you can do on the other side of the fence. You're a natural.'

Fullerton nodded slowly. 'Work with you, you mean?'

'Nah, I'm retiring, Jamie. I've got things to do.' He jerked a thumb at Macfadyen and Jordan. 'But Charlie and Ricky could do with your help. With me out of the game they'll need someone to hold their hands.'

Donovan walked to stand in front of Warren. Warren stared up at him defiantly.

'And you, Bunny, what the hell were you thinking of?'

Warren shrugged. 'They said I could make a difference.'

'Damn it, Bunny, being an undercover cop isn't going to get drugs off the street. You want to do that, be a social worker and make people's lives better so they don't want drugs. Be a businessman and create jobs so people have a reason to get up in the morning. But don't kid yourself that playing cops and robbers is going to make a blind bit of difference to the drugs trade. It's here to stay, and everyone knows that. Hasn't the way Hathaway behaved shown you how corrupt the whole business is?'

Warren looked up defiantly. 'What is it you want me to say, Den? That I've been fucked over? Well I have. I can see that.'

'I want to know what you're going to do about it, Bunny.'

'I'm dead on the streets now. PM'll be after my blood.'

Donovan nodded. 'Maybe he doesn't know.'

'Too many people know. Everyone in this room, for a start. It's not gonna stay a secret. I lied to him, man. Big time. He's never gonna forgive that.'

Donovan shrugged. 'You might be surprised what people will forgive, Bunny. Besides, PM got his gear at a rock-bottom price. It's pushed him a lot higher up the food chain and he's gonna need you to keep him on the straight and narrow.'

Warren shook his head. 'Nah.' He nodded with his chin at Fullerton. 'I ain't like him. I don't get no buzz from what I did. Drugs kill people. And it ain't no good just saying if it wasn't you it'd be someone else. It's got to stop somewhere. It might as well be you.'

'So you've got what you wanted, Bunny. As of today, I'm out of it. But you know what, it won't make a shred of difference.'

'You're really quitting?' asked Macfadyen.

'I've got all the money I need, Charlie,' said Donovan. 'Even with what Hathaway took. It's all offshore, I'll get it well laundered and put into something legit.'

'And what about me, Den?' asked Tina.

Donovan folded his arms. 'What about you, Louise?'

'I'm sorry, Den. There's nothing I can say, is there?'

Donovan shook his head, his lips forming a tight line.

Tina crossed her legs and her arms and sat staring at the floor.

'I saw the look on your face this morning. When you opened the door and I was there. You were relieved, weren't you?' said Donovan quietly. 'You thought I'd been pulled, and when you saw I hadn't been you were pleased.'

Tina nodded but still didn't look up.

'And yesterday, when I was leaving, you tried to stop me going.'

Tina nodded again. 'I wanted to tell you, Den. But I couldn't.'

'Because you're a cop.'

Tina sighed. 'Yes.'

'Being a cop didn't stop you sending me that text message, did it?'

'I didn't think you'd got it,' said Tina.

'I got it,' said Donovan.

'I didn't want you to go to prison,' said Tina. 'I didn't want Robbie to be without his dad, I didn't want . . .'

'What?' asked Donovan.

Tina wiped her eyes with the back of her hands. 'Nothing.'

Donovan stepped forward and put a hand on her shoulder. She rubbed the side of her head against his hand. 'They used you, Tina. They treated you like a whore. They were worse than pimps because they pretended you were doing it for some greater good.'

'I know,' she said softly.

'Get yourself sorted out, Louise. You shouldn't let anyone use you like that. Least of all someone whose only aim was to sell you out.'

She wiped her eyes again. 'I will.'

'Then give me a call.'

Tina looked up in surprise. 'What?'

Donovan mimed putting a phone to his ear. 'Phone me. Robbie'd like to see you.'

Tina smiled gratefully.

'So that's it?' said Jordan. 'We're just going to let them go?'

Macfadyen sighed. 'Ricky, if you don't shut up, I'll shoot you myself.'

'I'm just saying . . .'

'Don't say,' said Macfadyen. 'It's Den's call. Good on you, Den. Where are you going?'

'Home,' said Donovan. 'I've got some soccer kit needs washing. And beds to make. Shopping to do.' He grinned. 'A woman's work is never done, hey, lads?'

 # Three months later

The rooster kicked out and the metal spur attached to its claw ripped through its adversary. Blood splattered across the sawdust and the crowd cheered. Fistfuls of pesos were waved in the air, but Hathaway doubted anyone would bet on the underdog. There were few comebacks in cockfighting.

Hathaway wasn't a great fan of the Philippines, but it was the perfect place to hide, for a while at least. It was a country where pretty much anything could be had for a price, where security and privacy could be acquired, and where there were enough Westerners with shady pasts for another to blend in with few questions asked.

Hathaway had bought an isolated villa on the outskirts of Manila, made friends with the local police chief, and hired a dozen of the chief's men as his personal bodyguards. He never went anywhere without at least four of them, and as he stood at the edge of the cockfighting pit all four were within fifty feet, keeping a watchful eye.

Hathaway stiffened as he noticed that one of the few Westerners around the arena was looking in his direction. He was a man in his thirties wearing a beige safari suit. There was something familiar about the man. The man raised an eyebrow and nodded at him. Hathaway smiled instinctively, and nodded at the man. Was it a greeting from someone who recognised Hathaway, or just a nod of recognition between two outsiders?

Then Hathaway realised why the man seemed familiar and he smiled slowly. He was the spitting image of the French crooner, Sacha Distel. Hathaway relaxed. The guy was probably getting mistakenly recognised all the time. Hathaway gave him a small wave, then turned to watch the next cocks being prepared for battle. The man in charge of Hathaway's security had seen the unspoken exchange and looked at Hathaway for guidance. Hathaway nodded at him and mouthed, 'It's OK.'

In the pit, a pot-bellied man with a battered straw hat was attaching shiny metal spurs to a bird with jet-black feathers. Hathaway looked over at the black bird's opponent. It was a totally white bird with a scarlet crop. Hathaway smiled. He liked white birds. He waved a handful of pesos at one of the bookmakers and placed a bet on the black bird. Hathaway was feeling lucky.

STEPHEN LEATHER

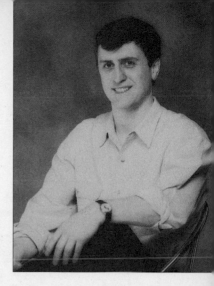

In most of his fast-paced thrillers, Manchester born Stephen Leather has written about criminals and how they operate, but in *Tango One* he says wanted to take a slightly different tack. 'Criminals, even big-time drug dealers, often have very ordinary personal lives, with wives and children in the background. I wanted to explore what would happen if a drugs baron, masterminding multi-million-pound deals, suddenly started having problems on the home front.' It's an unusual premise for a thriller, but in Den Donovan the author has created a very believable character who is forced to change as he juggles his criminal activities with trying to raise his young son.

Another aspect of the crime world that intrigues Stephen Leather is the relationship between undercover police officers and the criminal underworld they are trained to infiltrate. 'It always seems to me that the criminals—the ones at the top of their profession—drive the best cars, eat at the best restaurants and generally have very affluent lifestyles. An undercover officer has to have amazing self-control and moral strength not to be seduced by the lifestyle.'

Stephen Leather started his working life as a journalist, writing for newspapers such as the *Daily Mail*, *The Times* and the *South China Morning Post* in Hong Kong. But fiction was always his first love, and he became a full-time writer in 1992 with the publication of his fourth book, *The Chinaman*. Over the years, he has also carved out a reputation for himself as a TV scriptwriter. 'I wrote the scripts when two of my books, *The Bombmaker* and *The Stretch* were filmed recently by Sky, and I've written several episodes of a BBC series, *Murder in Mind*.' He also wrote three episodes of *The Knock*, a TV drama series about people working in the Customs and Excise service. This was very useful when it came to writing *Tango One*. 'I met quite a few Customs officers, and for a thriller writer it's useful to have friends who can fill you in on the mysteries of international drug trafficking!'

Paul Garrison
BURIED AT SEA

It's one thing to be on board a
fifty-foot sailboat when the seas are
calm and you're safe in the hands of an
experienced sailor.

It's quite another to find your
helmsman's been injured, leaving you
alone at the wheel and desperately trying
to outrun his deadliest enemies across
the world's roughest oceans.

I

STRONGMAN'S LAND

Nothing Jim saw, nothing around him, was familiar. Not the moving grey of the sea, not the shifting sky, not the ropes that were called lines nor the lines named sheets nor the pulleys dubbed blocks.

He had not seen another vessel in two weeks. On the chart that Shannon had found on the Internet when they decided he should take this crazy job, shipping lanes crisscrossed the North and South Atlantic like highways. But the ocean itself was as empty as space and almost as barren. The only living creatures were flying fish and a barrel-thick shark that sometimes swam in their shadow. His only companion: his employer, Will Spark.

It had to be the strangest gig ever. Personal trainer for a rich old guy on a sailboat in the middle of the ocean. This evening Jim was leading a spinning class, pedalling sprints and hill climbs beneath a heavy, cloud-jumbled sky.

Will, who was some kind of venture capitalist, had squeezed a pair of Schwinn Spinner Elite exercise bikes into his luxurious fifty-footer so they could work out just like they did back home in the health club. All by themselves, closing in on the equator, somewhere between Africa and Brazil.

Will Spark was dripping; his white hair was pasted to his scalp and matted to his chest; perspiration soaked his faded Yale running shorts. He was sucking air through his mouth, and it suddenly struck

Jim that he was utterly dependent on Will Spark to sail the boat to land. What if Will had a heart attack?

The personal trainer's nightmare: you let an aggressive type A geezer push too deep into oxygen debt and suddenly you're cracking ribs with your best CPR and praying the ambulance comes ahead of the negligence lawyers. That was on land. What would happen out here if the old guy fell over dead?

Jim knew a little about how to steer the boat, next to nothing about the sails, and even less about navigation.

'How you doing, Will?'

'Better than you, sonny.'

There was truth in that. Jim had been so seasick it had been two weeks before he could properly hydrate. His legs still felt like some vampire bat had drained his veins. Hard as he pedalled, the highest his heart-rate monitor would read was 175.

The boat topped a big wave just as Jim stood tall on the pedals. Glimpsing the view to the horizon, he was astonished to see a dark smudge, sharper than a cloud, smaller than a rain squall. A ship?

He probably should alert Will. The old man was kind of obsessed on the subject of ships. But this ship, if it was a ship, looked far away. And they were only twenty minutes into the class. Unlike most of Jim's private clients, Will was more interested in keeping fit than paying for a friend to talk at. The ship, if it was a ship, could wait.

Will was starting to tire.

'Listen to your body, Will,' Jim's voice boomed through the boat's loudhailer. 'And if you can, add a little more resistance.'

Jim concentrated on pedalling a smooth circle, knees in, shoulders back, head down. His body was a mess. With weeks to go before he could get off in Rio de Janeiro, he was asking himself, What in hell am I doing here?

He had hoped this voyage would be like a big-adventure bachelor party. But sailing across the ocean had imploded into 'go away and experience the world' when Shannon turned his proposal down point-blank. So he was stuck out here searching his soul to be sure he really wanted to marry Shannon—which he thought he had made clear by proposing to the woman.

Will glanced over and saw that Jim was struggling. Gasping, Will teased, 'You can take the mall rat out of the suburb but you can't take the suburb out of the mall rat.'

The old man was forever on his case for having been raised in the suburbs, because Jim made the mistake of asking where, among all the ingeniously stowed gear that made the sailboat self-sufficient, the dishwasher was hidden. The request had branded him the personal representative of every suburban cliché Will knew. No TV, either. Will had laughed. No Gap. No McDonald's. No surfing the Web.

They did have email, but it was a slow joke. You could send high-priced flashmails by satellite phone or you could transmit half a page in two minutes for free, if atmospheric conditions suited the battery-straining temperamental single sideband radio.

'What's up?' called Will when he saw Jim craning his head.

'I thought I saw a ship.'

Will Spark jumped off the Schwinn. 'Where?'

Jim pointed. Will focused his binoculars expertly. 'Sons of bitches.'

'What's wrong?'

'Take the helm. Head into the wind.'

Will ran forward to the mast, where he began yanking ropes from the rat's nest of halyards. Jim climbed down into the cockpit and took the big wooden steering wheel. Turning it automatically over-rode the autohelm. The boat heeled sharply.

'Other way,' yelled Will.

'Sorry.' Jim turned the other way. Both sails, flapping wildly, swung over the boat, the stiff fabric thundering. Will released a couple of ropes and down they came, burying the decks like snow crashing off a roof.

'What's going on?' Ordinarily, Will furled sails as precisely as a sky diver packing parachutes.

Will ran back. 'The bikes are made of steel,' he yelled. 'We have to get them below.'

The spinners each weighed ninety pounds with their massive fly-wheels and solid frames. Will released the jam cleats he had rigged to the car tracks and together they muscled them into the cockpit.

'OK, we're outta here.' Will put the engine in gear and accelerated. The propeller shoved the boat into a clumsy turn until at last her bow pointed into the wind and the smudge on the horizon fell directly astern. He engaged the autohelm and scanned the sea behind with his binoculars. 'You got good eyes, kid. I wouldn't have seen 'em in time.'

'Who?'

Will's jaw tightened. 'Son of a bitch, they're coming after us.' He looked around frantically. His gaze locked on the heart-rate monitor strapped to Jim's wrist.

'Where'd you get that? It's not your regular one.'

'My clients gave it to me. Like a *bon voyage* gift. They got together and gave it to me.'

'Which ones?'

'None you knew. I got a lot of new clients after you left.'

Will had worked out regularly for months in Jim's spinning classes at the health club, then suddenly disappeared. A year later, out of the blue, came the telephone call from Barbados. Will had offered Jim a two-month stint as his personal trainer and novice deck hand on a sail to Rio de Janeiro. Two hundred bucks a day for the experience of a lifetime.

'Let me see it.'

Jim unstrapped the wristwatch receiver. Will inspected it closely, shook it, held it to the sky. 'And the sensor.'

Jim unbuckled the chest strap that pressed the electrode to his chest. Will snatched it from his hand and examined it as he had the receiver. Then he plunged down the companionway steps into the cabin. Jim peered down through the hatch and saw Will hunched over the navigation table. He wrote something in the log. Then he jumped up and opened one of the big freezers in the galley.

'How about lamb for dinner?' he called in a tight voice.

'What?'

Will yanked a frozen leg of lamb from its Ziploc freezer bag and tossed it into the sink. Then he zipped both parts of Jim's heart-rate monitor into the plastic bag and hurried up the steps into the cockpit. The bag was ballooned with trapped air.

'What are you—Hey!'

Will leaned over the back of the boat, and Jim heard a splash. When he lunged to the stern rail, he saw his heart monitor bobbing away in the propeller wake. 'That's mine!'

'They're tracking us with it.'

'*Tracking* us?'

'They bugged your heart monitor. They put a homing device in it.'

Jim stared at the older man. 'Who are you talking about?'

'The sons of bitches on that ship.'

'What ship?'

'Look.' Will handed Jim the binoculars. 'See that dark area? That's a rain squall. They're behind it. Lucky break for us.'

'I don't see anything.' Jim lowered the glasses and looked hard at Will. He was used to working with people to help them overcome doubt and fear to fix their bodies. He could deal with the man's fear.

'Will, turn around. Go back and get my monitor.'

'What are you, nuts?'

'No. It's mine. It cost three hundred bucks.'

'I'll give you the three hundred bucks, OK?'

Jim was fully aware that he was arguing the wrong issue. This was not about the monitor, it was about Will's mysterious 'they'. If he could convince Will to turn the boat around, he might make him realise that he had temporarily lost his grip.

'They will kill us, Jim. There is no way we are going back.'

'Who will kill us?' Jim asked. 'Who are "they"?'

Will looked at him. 'You think I'm making this up? You think I'm crazy?'

Jim felt the first stab of fear.

How do we know he's a competent sailor? Shannon had asked Jim when Will first telephoned. Will's answer, which they had both found completely reassuring, was that he had bought his latest boat (his third) in Hong Kong and then sailed it halfway around the world to Barbados. Based on that feat, Jim had put his life in the older man's hands. And judging by the effortless way Will handled the boat, he couldn't have asked for a safer captain. Until now.

'No,' he said carefully. 'I don't think you're crazy. But I am very confused. What's going on?'

'Long story, kid. For the moment, let's just say we're goddamned lucky you spotted them in time.'

'Do "they" know we're sailing to Rio de Janeiro?'

Will paused to reflect. 'Probably,' he said. 'Though maybe not— considering they planted that homing device on you—but I'm not taking the chance.'

'What do you mean?' Jim asked.

'No way we're going to Brazil.'

'Where are we going?'

'Africa.'

'What are you talking about? My flight home leaves from Brazil.'

'I'll buy you a ticket from Lagos.'

'*Nigeria?* How long are we talking?'

'Month or so. Depending on the wind.'

'Or so? Five weeks?'

'Could be six or seven depending on conditions. We've got to get through the doldrums and sail the rest of the way across the Atlantic.' Will scanned the darkening water behind them. 'It's your watch. I'll go below and work out an exact course.'

'No, Will. We had a deal.'

'Don't blame me. It's *you* who brought them after us with that goddamned monitor.'

Jim waited in the cockpit, trying to figure out a way to talk sense to Will. There was no way he was going to Africa. He went below, down the four-step companionway into the luxurious main salon. Will was in the galley, an elegant workspace of brushed stainless steel and maple, knives like razors and spices Jim had never heard of. Will was peeling foil off the frozen leg of lamb.

Jim stood by the chart table opposite the galley. He noticed that Will had pencilled in their global positioning system fix. The chart showed that the water was shallower here, a mile deep instead of three. There was a kind of shelf midocean on which sat Saint Paul Rocks.

'I probably never really saw a ship. It could have been these rocks.'

Will shook his head. 'Doubt that.' He crossed the galley and reached past Jim to lift a fat green volume from the bookshelf. 'Nathaniel Bowditch, *American Practical Navigator*. Bowditch is the bible. And the bible says here that the distance you can see in miles is about one and one-seventh the square root of your height in feet. Figure your eye is eleven feet above the water. If so, the distance you can see to the horizon is about three point eight miles. Now, *Sailing Directions* say that the tallest of those rocks is sixty-five feet out of the sea. So, the square root of sixty-five times one and one-seventh equals . . .' He picked up the calculator, punched in a slew of numbers and showed Jim the screen. 'That increases the distance you could see them to about thirteen miles. But according to the GPS we are *fifty* miles from Saint Paul Rocks. So, sorry, you didn't see rocks, you saw a ship hunting us.'

'Maybe I saw a ship. But I didn't see a ship *hunting* us.' Jim looked around the main cabin. The polished teak, the leather-bound books, the banks of expensive electronics were all vivid reminders that Will Spark was a wealthy man who was accustomed to getting his own way. While Jim Leighton was a lopsided cross between employee and guest without a lot of say.

'Look, Will. A deal is a deal. You can't just change everything. I have a right to be dropped off where you promised.'

'I told you. That is no longer possible.'

'Will, don't make me force you to turn the boat around.'

'Force?' Will moved quickly towards him. 'You may be younger and stronger, sonny. But suburban college boys don't learn street fighting in health clubs.'

Jim had wondered about the scar tissue on Will's fists and the boxer's white ridges over his brow, and the time-bleached US Marine Corps *Semper fi* tattoo on his biceps, none of which fitted the image of a Yale man. Well, screw him. Jim *was* younger. Lots younger. And much stronger.

Will seemed to read his mind. He tapped Jim's chest hard. 'You have muscles like a pocket Schwarzenegger. But you have lousy bones. You're built too light in your knees and your wrists and your ankles. It must have taken twice the work to bulk up like that. What kind of problem drove you to put on all that muscle?'

'It comes in handy. At times like this.'

'Go ahead. Take your best shot.'

'Come on, Will. Turn the boat around.'

'Or what?' Will shot back. 'Even if you could take me, how will you sleep? You going to watch me twenty-four hours a day? You could always tie me to my bunk,' Will mocked. 'Except, how are you going to sail home alone?'

'All I'm saying is I want to go to Rio like you promised.'

'And I'm saying I apologise for dragging you into this mess. But the fact is, I've got no choice but to run. So you've got no choice but to run with me. Remember, if they catch me, they've caught you too. Lotsa luck explaining that you're just along for the ride.'

' "They" are in your head, Will. There is no "they". I'll prove it to you. Let's look on the radar.'

'We can't chance using the radar. What if they have ECM?'

'Excuse me, what's ECM?'

'Electronic countermeasures. They'd have our bearing and range in a microsecond.'

Jim slipped into the leather bench beside the nav table. The electric panel had a triple array of switches. He groped for the right one. Will reached past him and flicked a toggle marked MASTER SWITCH. The cabin went dark.

'You're out of your element, Jim.'

'If the ship is hunting us why doesn't it see *us* on *its* radar?'

'It can't. We're invisible.' Will laughed and turned the lights back on. 'Relax, kid. I'm not crazy. What I mean is we are invisible to radar. Mostly. Because we present a very small signature. There's not much on the boat to return a strong echo. Her hull's fibreglass, her spars are carbon fibre, the wheel's wood. Soon as we lowered the bikes into the cockpit, about the only steel above the water line was her winches.

'The only way those bastards can see us is to eyeball us—that's why I struck the sails. Our hull lies too low on the water to be seen from any distance, but the sails stand out like a bull's-eye . . . Any more questions?'

Jim shook his head. He didn't believe Will, but even if Will had lost his mind, he had an endless store of answers to fit every doubt Jim raised. Another thing was clear: Will Spark wasn't so scared any more. He wore the expression of a man at peace with a big decision. Back in charge. Unlike his clueless deck hand.

'Would you feel better,' Will asked gently, 'if you emailed Shannon? Tell her we got shoved east by heavy weather.'

'She'll know it's a lie. She's following the weather on the Internet. Why don't I just tell her you freaked out when you saw a ship.'

'Tell her what you want, just don't mention Nigeria in case they're breaking into our email.'

Jim looked at him in disbelief.

'Never heard of a computer program called Carnivore?' Will asked.

'Yes, the FBI uses Carnivore to scan email. Not some . . . wait a minute. Please don't tell me "they" are the FBI.'

'I'll tell you this, sonny: when these folks go head to head with the FBI, the FBI blinks.'

Jim gave up. What could he say about demons with a longer reach than the FBI?

Will's ThinkPad was connected to a satellite transceiver antenna attached to the stern rail. To send flashmail Jim had to log on as Will.

Guess what? I'm going to be away a little longer than we thought. Will's changing course, but I'll get home as soon as I can. I'm really sorry. I miss you.

Wait a minute, Jim thought. What am I doing? She doesn't care if I'm gone another month.

The boat rolled and he felt the seasickness coming back. A cloying mix of diesel exhaust and fibreglass gel coat clogged his mouth and nose. He punched DELETE and wrote:

I'm going to be away longer than I thought. Will's changing course. Looks like my big adventure's getting bigger.

Then he fled for the fresh air in the cockpit.

WHEN IT WAS fully dark they raised the sails, which steadied the boat considerably, and at their next watch change, midnight, Will noted their miles run with satisfaction. 'We're doing pretty good.' He took the wheel. 'Better catch some sleep, Jim. See you at oh-three hundred.'

They were standing watches: three hours on, three hours off. It was good manners, Will had explained, to arrive on deck, ready to go, five minutes before your time. Jim set his wrist alarm for ten to three.

Then, suddenly, Will was shaking him awake. He'd slept through his alarm.

'Sorry,' mumbled Jim. He struggled into his running shoes and followed Will up the companionway. The clouds had peeled back, revealing thousands of stars.

Will suggested that he shut off the autohelm and practise his steering. He showed him a star to steer by. 'It's good for fifteen minutes, then find yourself another. As soon as you get tired, put her back on the autohelm; we don't want to lose any time.' He started to go below. 'Oh, by the way, Shannon wrote back.'

'What did she say?'

'Quote: "Adventures should not run on schedule. Have a ball."'

It sounded to Jim like she didn't care, and he felt anew the sting of rejection. 'Shannon wanted me to do this trip,' he blurted.

'Why do I get the impression that Shannon does the thinking for both of you?'

'No, I liked the idea. I just probably wouldn't have come if she hadn't pushed me.'

If he allowed himself to get really paranoid, he would think she had seized on the voyage as an opportunity to start easing him out of her life even before he asked her to marry him . . . No . . . She had seemed genuinely surprised. By the time he had proposed, he had already accepted Will's invitation. Funny thought: had he proposed marriage out of fear of going away for a long time?

'She bought me the awesome Helly Hansen foul-weather gear.'

Will put on his 'me hearties' voice: 'Aye, ya looked ready for Cape Horn, matey,' and Jim couldn't help but laugh.

'Her parents chipped in—hoping I'd just keep sailing round the world.'

'Could it be the lass herself who paid you off? Not her parents.'

'She did not pay me to go away,' Jim shot back. 'She's giving me time to reflect on whether I really want to marry her.'

'Why wouldn't you?'

'None of your damned business.'

'Sorry. I'm a nosy old coot.' Will started down the companionway. 'It just seems there's a mystery about you two I don't understand.'

The first two hours of Jim's three-to-six watch were the longest of the night. It was a time to think the unthinkable: was this whole voyage truly his chance to opt out?

He had promised to think about what it would really mean to be married to Shannon. 'Really think, Jim,' were her parting words. 'I don't want to be your job. And I don't want a man who thinks he doesn't deserve more than a wounded bird.'

He had printed her last email. He read it by the glow of the compass, though he knew it by heart.

I wonder if a boy who struggled to make his unhappy mom happy will go way too far trying to make every girl he meets happy. So I ask you again: you've worked very hard to make a beautiful body. Why shouldn't you demand the same from your wife?

I can't walk. Remember? I am crippled.

Love, Shannon

She loved insisting on the word 'crippled'. 'Handicapped' didn't do justice to how thoroughly you could shatter bones by skiing into solid steel at fifty miles an hour. After six operations and a year of therapy she could stand, briefly, with crutches. 'Golfers,' she said, 'have handicaps; cripples have multiple compound fractures.'

'Crippled' was a much better way to describe the young woman whose family had hired him to work up an exercise routine to get the rest of her body back into shape. Holed up in her bedroom, hooked on painkillers and weeping with despair, she had rejected every physiotherapist they engaged.

Jim knew that he couldn't take much credit for slipping under her radar. The fact was that they had just plain liked each other from the very first day. And to Jim, at least, that friendship seemed to have grown into a firm basis for a marriage.

At last, a pale line began to form where the eastern sky met the sea. The stars faded quickly. Will came up, coffee mug in hand, eyes on the sails, at five minutes before six. He was humming a tune, which Jim took as a sign that the old man felt back on top.

Jim went below to read Shannon's email again.

SOARING ON TWIN HULLS like a gigantic manta ray, the huge catamaran, *Barcelona*, hurtled along at eighty miles an hour trailing wings of mist and spray.

The *Barcelona*'s glassed-in bridge offered a bird's eye view of the sea and there was ample room for the Australian captain, his first officer and the helmsman, as well as the American who had chartered her and his bodyguards. Three big blokes, two white, one black. Ex-US Navy SEALs, the captain guessed, judging by their swimmers' shoulders and barrel chests.

'Mr Nickels,' Captain Moser said, 'we're running out of time.'

Andy Nickels was not as tall as his bodyguards, but as lean in the gut and big in the shoulders. The captain rated him Special Forces, what with the buzz cut. His men looked the sort you might have a pint with, but there was a cold emptiness in Nickels's eye that warned he was one vicious piece of work.

It had been a long night and Moser was fed up. 'I said we're running out of time, Mr Nickels.'

The near silence on the bridge was broken only by the distant whine of the engines and the maddening on-again off-again *ping* of the homing signal. Finally, Nickels looked up. 'Shut your mouth.'

'You've no call to talk that way, chum. You know as well as I do that your ruddy bug has gone down. You paid for two days. You've had three and a half—that's it.'

Nickels spoke to one of his shadows, a man mountain called Greg, who strode swiftly from the bridge. Then he said, 'Stop the ship!'

Moser hesitated. Nickels's other shadows stepped forward like Rottweilers.

'Stop engines,' Moser ordered. The helmsman gathered the throttle clutches and hauled back. The big cat slowed rapidly as her hulls settled into the water.

Nickels stood up and tucked the homing monitor under his arm. 'What do you say we catch some air, Captain? And bring the mate.'

Captain Moser and the mate, Hoskins, followed Nickels through the main cabin, then downstairs and through an insulated door out to an abbreviated stern deck fifteen feet above the water.

Greg was waiting with a bucket of hamburger meat.

'Dump it all!' snarled Nickels.

Greg upended the bucket. The meat splashed red in the water and a moment later a long, dark shape cruised beneath the waves. Rolling sideways, it revealed a flash of white underbelly. When it straightened up, its fin cut the surface. A second shot through the bloodied water like a sinuous torpedo, then a third, accelerating with effortless strokes of its scythe-shaped tail.

'Throw the mate,' Nickels ordered.

Two men grabbed Hoskins and dragged him to the rail.

Moser could not believe they would actually throw the man to the sharks. Hoskins's terror gave him the strength to fight back. He broke loose and tried to run. They surrounded him in a flash and buckled him over with body punches. He went down, gasping for air.

'Stop them,' the captain yelled. 'I'll do what you want.'

Nickels's face hardened as they lifted the whimpering mate above the railing. The sharks broke the surface, wheeling in tight circles.

Suddenly, the homing receiver pinged rapidly. Nickels shoved past the struggling men and stared at the sea. 'What do you see?'

They scanned the water, searching for a sail. Nothing. But the receiver was pinging away, persistent as a car alarm. It sounded as if Will Spark's sailboat was less than a hundred feet away.

'There!' Nickels pointed. The sun flashed on a shiny ball, which the wind was bouncing across the waves. 'Captain!' he yelled. 'Launch a boat. You'—he pointed at his bodyguards—'go with him. Keep your eyes on that. Don't lose it.'

The men dropped the mate on the deck, grabbed the captain and marched him below. A pilot hatch opened and a rubber boat skidded down a ramp into the water. The sharks arrowed to it.

'Go!' Nickels yelled. 'Go now!'

One bodyguard shoved Moser into the boat. Greg took out a pistol and sprayed the water with automatic fire. But the sharks kept circling until the motor roared. The boat sped from the catamaran, Moser looking back to steer by Nickels's hand signals. The wind had blown the ball hundreds of yards before they lifted it from the sea.

'What is it?' Nickels snapped into his two-way.

Greg radioed back, 'I don't know, Andy. It's something in a bag.'

When he saw the contents for himself, Nickels slammed the heart-rate monitor to the deck and ground it beneath his boot.

'We wasted the whole damn night!' he shouted. 'We gave them all night to run. How far can he have gone, Captain?'

Moser concealed his glee at the American's misfortune. 'Assume the yacht's making six to seven knots.'

Nickels turned to Greg. 'Is that right?'

'No. He's an old guy and the kid is a novice. Besides, the wind was light all night. They made five knots if they were lucky.'

'All right, make it six knots,' said the captain. 'He must have spotted us before dark. After dark he wouldn't have seen us with no lights and we never picked up his radar. So at six knots he'd make seventy-two nautical miles in the past twelve hours. East, west, north or south?'

Greg shook his head. 'The wind veered east in the night. I doubt he beat to the east.'

'Could have used his engine,' Moser countered. 'At any rate, he's somewhere in a circle one hundred and forty-four miles in diameter. That's four hundred and fifty miles around. And that's an area of sixteen thousand square miles. One big patch of ocean.'

'East!' said Nickels. 'He would drop his sails to make a smaller target and motor east. Find him!'

'Now, hold on, Mr Nickels.'

Nickels turned beet red. 'Greg, take everybody up to the bridge.'

The heavy door sighed shut behind them.

Andy Nickels stalked to the rail. The sharks had gone, but not far. When he heaved the empty bucket into the water, grey shapes instantly razored towards the splash.

To the captain he said, 'For the rest of your miserable life, whatever I ask, you will always answer yes.' He seized the cringing mate by his belt and shirt collar. He lifted the man clear off the deck and began to spin in a circle, gathering momentum like an athlete throwing the hammer.

'You can't do that,' cried the captain.

'The hell I can't. We're in international waters.'

He whirled once, twice, three times and threw the screaming mate.

Captain Moser had already closed his eyes. When Hoskins's head crashed into his chest, he staggered and fell. Hoskins landed beside him, curled into a ball and wept.

'Captain?' said Nickels, looming over them.

'Yes.'

'What do you say you order full speed east?'

The captain radioed the helmsman with a trembling hand.

As the catamaran soared east at eighty miles an hour, Andy Nickels took his satphone and punched ENCRYPT for a secure line to Lloyd McVay. He hoped Val would answer. Val McVay was no less a ball-buster than her father, but it was the senior McVay that Nickels dreaded to disappoint.

Lloyd McVay picked up with a cold, 'What is it, Andy?' and Nickels knew he was in for a roasting.

'I'm very sorry, Mr McVay; he pulled another fast one on us.'

With his head down, Nickels watched his hightop Adidas trainers pace an ever-tightening circle. He had no one but himself to blame. Val McVay had arranged the tracking signal. His job had been to follow it. 'No, sir, I don't underestimate him . . . Don't you worry, sir, I'll get him.'

Suddenly, Lloyd McVay's tone softened. 'Now, Andy . . .'

Nickels braced for the bayonet in the ribs. How often had he himself delivered McVay's kiss-off: the foundation no longer needs your services.

'You may recall that I went to some length to emphasise the importance of the Sentinel project to the McVay Foundation.'

'Yes, sir.'

'Sentinel will change medicine as the world knows it—an advance greater than X-rays and antibiotics. With the health and happiness of all humanity in the balance, I was counting on an A-plus performance from you.'

'Yes, sir.' The breakthrough would not only earn the McVays more money on the Internet than Bill Gates, but would also win them a Nobel Prize. With that much at stake, the rules of engagement were no rules: do anything to get Sentinel back.

'I would define an A-plus as securing Will Spark immediately.'

'Yes, sir.'

'Then get cracking.'

JIM WOKE SUDDENLY. It was stiflingly hot in the cabin, but it wasn't the heat that had jarred him into a murky awareness. Something had changed. He dragged himself to the companionway and up the steps. The water looked glassy, but with a heavy swell under its surface, rising and falling. Without a breath of wind in the sails to stop the swell from rolling the boat, the mast was whipping across the sky, .They had stopped dead. Becalmed.

Jim saw Will at a halyard winch, cranking up the big, light air sail he called a blooper. The thin Dacron drooped from its halyard, like pantihose hung from a shower rod.

'What happened?'

'We ran into the bloody doldrums.'

Will gazed despairingly at the useless sail. Then he walked heavily back to the cockpit, plodding like an old man.

'Jim,' he muttered, as he slumped into a seat, 'do you ever ask yourself what you're doing with your life?'

'Sure. When I'm trying to decide what to do next—how long do these doldrums last?'

'Hours. Days. Weeks.'

'Weeks?' Jim stared at the glassy water. Unbelievable. And they had to get through this before they even got started to Africa. 'Look, Will, if "they" are following we should use the motor, right?'

'We'd run out of fuel.'

162

'We should at least do something to get away from them . . .'

'Don't you ever look back? No, you're too young. Just you wait, it comes to all of us. You'll look back and say, "Why didn't I make something of myself?"'

Jim couldn't help but laugh. 'What are you talking about, Will? You're rich. You've got a beautiful boat. Most people would kill to have your life.'

'They're welcome to it . . .' He trailed off, morosely.

Jim saw a little breeze riffle the water behind the boat. The sails filled tentatively and the boat began to move. Then a stronger gust fanned his face. On the road again, thought Jim. We're outta here.

A loud *bang* shattered the silence.

Jim tried to look everywhere at once. Then he saw the jib collapsing onto the foredeck.

'What happened?'

'We popped the headstay,' Will said calmly. 'Which means there's not much holding the mast. You want to jump below and bring me the red tool kit?'

Jim scrambled down the companionway, pawed frantically through the locker and ran back up with the red box.

Will had put the boat into a broad turn so the breeze was now behind them. 'We're going to jury-rig a temporary stay with a halyard. You take the wheel. Just keep the wind behind us.'

The old man loped forward and threaded a halyard through the bullnose hole in the centre of the bow, clipping it onto a sturdy mooring cleat. Jim couldn't help but admire his ease. The old man might be nuts, but when handling tools or cooking a meal or driving the sailboat through heavy seas he was always the best.

Will cranked a winch until the halyard ran taut from the top of the mast to the front of the boat. They furled the mainsail and the yacht started rolling again. 'The halyard will act as a stay to hold the mast up until we replace the headstay—you want to learn how to crimp wire cable?' He opened the red box, which contained his rigging tools. 'Flip a coin to see who goes up the mast.'

Jim lost.

ANDY NICKELS TURNED a slow, grim circle. The catamaran had covered eighty miles in an hour, a distance that would have taken Will Spark all night. He must have come this way, Nickels thought. I am so close.

But the equatorial ocean was flat and empty everywhere Nickels looked. Had he guessed wrong? Should he have gone west? Or north? Or south?

'How much fuel would he carry?'

The captain answered. The fight was out of him. 'Hundred, hundred and fifty gallons.'

'More like seventy-five,' Greg interrupted. Nickels had recruited him from the navy. So he ought to know about boats.

'Range?'

Greg said, 'Modern fifty-foot sailboat, he's got a seventy-five-horse diesel. Burns a gallon an hour at eight knots. Four hundred and fifty to six hundred miles.'

'So he can't keep on motoring?'

'Two or three days he'll be running on empty.'

'Captain, what do you make of the weather?'

'If he's come this way he's lost his wind.'

Nickels picked up a two-way radio and spoke to the lookouts he'd posted atop the *Barcelona*'s wheelhouse. 'Report.'

'Nothing.'

They were looking for a needle in a haystack. Nickels was wasting time out here.

'Captain. Where's the nearest land with an airport?'

'Cape Verde Islands.'

'Do it!'

Moser punched the Portuguese islands' coordinates into the GPS. *Barcelona* could cover the thousand miles in fifteen hours.

Nickels went down to the passenger cabin. Gradually, he formed a plan. The way to catch Will Spark was to station patrols at his likely stops: ambush him east, west, north and south. Deny him access to his lairs. Wear him down with disappointed hopes until the thief lost the strength to run.

Nickels took his satphone to a quiet corner and commenced a long day and night of encrypted conversations with arms dealers, soldiers, smugglers and cops in ports on both coasts of the North and South Atlantic. Ten years with the US Army Rangers fighting narcoterrorists had left him well connected. Problem was, it would be easier if Will Spark had gone west. But the thief was out here, somewhere, headed east.

IT TOOK HOURS to get the crimp right. When Jim was done, Will lowered him from the masthead, then went up himself to check it.

He came down, elated. 'I just saw cat's-paws a mile off and we've got some wind. Let's get the sails up. Nice job on the crimp.'

But moments after they got under way, the wind died again. Will's spirit plummeted deeper than before. Suddenly, he stood up and stared west.

'What do you see?'

'I'm not sure.' Will passed his binoculars to Jim. 'Your eyes are better. White on white—moving—almost dead astern.'

Jim swept the glasses over the horizon. The haze had lifted, but not by much. 'I don't see anything. Why don't you try your radar?'

'I told you. Our radar will give away our position.'

Jim shook his head, silently. If you wanted an answer, ask a paranoid. 'Why don't we start the motor?'

'Not yet. We need our fuel for the freezers and emergencies.'

'Maybe this is an emergency.'

'Jim, I'm sorry I got you into this mess.'

If I could only cheer him up, Jim thought, then maybe I could make him see sense. 'I could use some exercise. What do you say we hump the bikes up and do a hill climb?'

'No, thanks . . . You want exercise. Use the rowing machine.'

'What rowing machine?'

Will showed Jim how to inflate the yacht's rubber dinghy and launch it over the side. It bounced on the water like a toy. 'Be my guest.'

Stepping off the yacht into a tiny rubber boat in the middle of the ocean seemed foolhardy to Jim. What if the wind suddenly sprang up and blew him away? 'Any advice?'

'It's just like a rowing machine.'

'I've never seen a rowing machine jump around like that. I think I'd like a rope.'

A smile lit Will's face. 'I'll give you a three-hundred-foot line—you don't have to use the whole thing. Besides, we're not going anywhere.'

'WILL, LET'S TALK about "they".'

'What about 'em?'

It was five days since they had finally motored out of the doldrums. Lulled by the constant northeast trade winds, the thick heat and the regular watches, Jim had submitted to the reality that Will had added weeks to their voyage. But he still hoped that if he could convince his employer that 'they' were a fantasy, he would change course and let him off early. The books said that the Cape Verde Islands had an international airport and they were a lot closer than Nigeria.

'Who are "they", Will? Who's chasing you? And why?'

Will shrugged. 'Sometimes in business you disappoint the wrong people. Hey, it's hot as hell. Feel like going swimming?'

Jim looked over the side. The water sliding past was several miles deep, an unappetising grey colour, with God-knows-what swimming under its impenetrable surface. 'I'll pass. These people you disappointed? What kind of people are we talking about?'

'Angry people.' Will flashed his most engaging smile.

'Angry people usually sue when they're disappointed.'

'The people on board that ship don't mess around with lawsuits.'

'You're being hunted by criminals?'

'If they were common criminals, I could call the cops. I'm going swimming. You want to come?'

'If they're not criminals, and you can't call the cops, who are they?'

Will opened a hatch and pulled out a length of line and a safety harness, which he buckled round his chest. Then he climbed out of the cockpit and ran the line through a block at the end of the boom. He tied one end to his harness and ran the other through a deck block and wrapped it round an idle winch.

'Let out the main.'

Jim traced the mainsheet from the boom through the traveller and loosened the proper winch. The mainsail swung away.

'Cleat it off,' Will ordered when the boom was hanging six feet over the water. He handed Jim the end of his line and stepped over the safety lines and jumped. Then, dangling in his harness, hanging from the end of the boom, he yelled, 'Lower me into the water.'

Jim eased on Will's line until Will was dragged along the side of the boat, being alternately submerged and raised as the boat rolled.

'Fantastic!' he whooped. 'Oh man, this is beautiful.'

Watching him frolic, Jim began to feel the oppressive heat more than ever. Will looked as happy as a baby in a back-yard pool.

'You gotta try this. It's fantastic.'

But the water was grey, the body of it invisible. It looked like it was eating Will, who disappeared every time the boat dunked him.

'OK, haul me in.'

Jim cranked the winch, which raised Will out of the water. Will scrambled over the safety lines, laughing. 'Oh man, you gotta try it.'

Jim was afraid. What if there were sharks?

'You know what you are?' Will teased. 'You're the "Climate Control Kid". The CC Kid. If you're not in the air-conditioned mall with a roof over your head, you're scared.'

'Screw you. I'm not afraid. I'll swim if it makes you happy.'

'It'll make *you* happy.' Will laughed. 'You'll feel like you're flying.'

Flying turned out to be the perfect word. The boat rolled and the boom swept Jim high. It rolled the other way and it dropped him in the warm water. It was incredibly exhilarating.

'This is fantastic.' He should have done this days ago. As he rose from the water, he saw Will peering past him. Watching something. Something in the water.

Will leaned out. 'Jesus, is that a dolphin?'

The rolling boat plunged Jim into the water again. He craned his neck and saw a thick grey body draw near. 'It's a shark! Pull me in.'

'That's not a shark—hell, maybe it is.'

Trapped in the sling, bouncing in and out of the water, Jim panicked. 'Will, save me!'

'Easy. I got you.' But to Jim's horror, Will seemed to be moving very slowly, reaching for the winch handle as if he had all the time in the world. The thing in the water came closer and Jim screamed.

'I got you. Don't blow a gasket!' Will shouted from the winch.

'Get me up!'

Will cranked harder and Jim found himself clinging to the safety lines, imagining a shark sliding up the side of the boat and taking his foot in jagged rows of razor teeth. He fell into the cockpit, where he huddled, trying to contain his panic.

'Give you a tip,' said Will. 'If you want to swim with the sharks, you better swim with strong strokes; don't splash around like you're weak. Bump them back when they bump you. Show 'em you're still alive—though I got to tell you, that looked to me like a friendly dolphin. You got spooked by Flipper.'

Jim slowly caught his breath. Will was chuckling like it was the funniest joke he'd ever heard.

'The CC Kid,' he said. 'I'm shipmates with the CC Kid.'

Jim stood up. He wanted to take Will by the throat and squeeze the laughter out of him. He stared fixedly behind the boat. 'Here comes that ship again.'

Will went dead white. He spun round, pawed his binoculars from their rack and swept a completely empty horizon. Slowly the colour returned to his face.

'Bumped me back,' he said at last. 'Very funny. Didn't know you had it in you . . .' Then he fell silent.

As the old man slid down into his private world, the truth struck Jim like lightning. Will Spark truly believed he was being hunted.

JIM STARED at the screen. He was more baffled than ever by Will's behaviour.

Dear Shannon,

Funny thing happened the other day: I mistook a dolphin for a shark, which ordinarily wouldn't have mattered. But being in the water, swimming from the boom, it mattered a lot to me. Fortunately, Will was not fooled. So he took a long time to pull me out. A *Illlooooonggg* time. Huge laugh. But maybe you had to be here.

WILL'S SLOOP, *HUSTLE*, was both a rich man's toy and a potent machine, Jim came to realise. Shannon's father's health clubs were making money hand over fist, but nothing of all the stuff he owned—ski house, fast cars, diamonds for Shannon's mother—seemed as extravagant as Will's yacht.

'Do you mind me asking what *Hustle* cost?' Jim asked one evening.

'I bought her cheap,' Will answered casually. 'Hong Kong's the best place in the world to get a bargain on a boat.'

'Why are boats cheap in Hong Kong?'

'That's how far couples sailing around the world to save their marriage get before they admit it was a lousy idea.'

'Sailing or the marriage?'

Will grinned. 'Both. Don't get me started on marriage. I know you asked Shannon to marry you.' Will's grin broadened. 'Fact is, Hong Kong was the only place I could *afford* to buy. My last divorce really wiped me out. Ruinous—but worth every penny.'

Jim looked away, irritated by the bluster.

'Am I offending you?' Will asked.

'Like you said, I was hoping to get married. I'm looking at the upside.'

'Actually, I'm curious. Why'd she say no? Good-looking guy, sleepy eyes girls go for, and all them muscles . . . Did you tell me your parents were divorced?'

'No!'

Will gave him a quizzical look. 'Something tells me they should have been. Long time ago.'

'Why do you say that?'

'You're a nice kid. But you dislike older people. I'm guessing they put you through the wringer.'

Jim climbed out of the cockpit and headed forward.

It wasn't that he hated older people. He didn't hate anybody. But he did carry baggage—Shannon's word—filled with his mother's frustrated longings and his father's inability to do anything about them. In a way, Will had guessed right. He had always equated age with disappointment. And after three relationships with gloomy, troubled women he had begun to question whether he deliberately sought out disappointment. Then he met Shannon. She was sunny enough for both of them, baggage and all. His and hers.

'You can't fix my legs,' she had said when her father brought Jim into her bedroom.

Somehow he had known how to answer. 'I don't do legs. I'm here for the flabby arms.'

She had stared, stung. 'You'd be flabby, too, if you were stuck in bed for a year.'

'This is what I would do if I were stuck in bed for a year.'

Then he had startled the heck out of her, himself and her father, by lying down on the bed and curling ten reps of a five-pound dumbbell.

Face to face on the sheets, six inches apart, Jim had thought, God, what a pretty girl, and a smile had begun to light her blue eyes.

Their eyes still locked, Jim had rolled on his side, balanced on his hand and started one-arm pushups. The smile travelled over her face and she said, still holding Jim's gaze. 'Daddy, go away.'

Where, Jim still wondered, had he got the nerve? How had he sensed that she was ready to emerge from her despair. In any case, it had worked. He could never make her walk normally. No one could. But he could help her get strong. Though that success had led them both to a new form of despair. *I don't want to be your job.*

Suddenly the loudhailer clacked on. 'All hands to the galley. Them that helps bake apple pie gets a slice. Them that don't, starve.' Will did his cooking at night, when the boat was the coolest.

Jim joined Will below.

'There you are,' Will greeted him. 'You start the crust. Sift two cups of flour into the big mixing bowl. Put the bowl in the sink. Your only friend in a rolling galley is the sink.'

Jim put the bowl on the counter instead and immediately regretted it. Will helped mop up the spilt flour. His crust, Will promised, contained only half a stick of butter for the whole pie. He showed Jim how to cut the butter into the flour with two knives.

'Now I'm going to let you into a secret. Never trust anyone who covers an apple pie with a top crust. A top crust *steams* the apples— ruins them. Now I know what you're going to say, your mom makes a little chimney in the middle of the crust.'

'My mother bought pies at the Grand Union.'

'And I suppose your old man never taught you to change a tyre.'

'He called Triple A.'

'Your parents robbed you of a hands-on life. It's never too late to change. You did a good job crimping that headstay. All right, half the dough we'll roll out for our bottom crust. The other half, we'll put aside for our crumb topping.'

A wine bottle served as Will's rolling pin. He flattened the dough between sheets of waxed paper. 'You'll find the apples in the freezer.'

Jim pawed through the Ziploc bags of chickens, dry-aged steaks, pork chops and legs of lamb. Halfway down on the right he found a plastic bag of sliced apples, brown sugar, cloves, cinnamon and nutmeg—one of a dozen Will had prepared before he set sail.

The weather fax machine in the nav station beeped. Jim picked up the paper flowing from the printer. Superimposed across the weather map were three lines of block print.

'NO MAN IS AN ISLAND,
NOT EVEN A CLOD ON A YACHT.
COMMUNICATE, BEFORE WE CATCH A THIEF.'

'What the heck is this?' He recognised the fractured John Donne. But how had it got into a public broadcast of the weather report?

Will scanned it. 'Son of a bitch,' he whispered under his breath.

'Who's it from?' asked Jim.

'A poet who didn't know it.' Will crumpled the sheet.

Jim stared at him. Was Will's explanation about why he couldn't call the cops all bullshit? Was Will the criminal? Were the mysterious 'they' the law?

'How did it get into the weather fax?'

'I told you, they are powerful. Either they hacked their way in or they bribed some underpaid technician to look the other way. Pie filling, please.'

'What do they mean by "communicate"? Could it be an offer to negotiate?'

'If we were to slip this pie in the oven for an hour, we could build an appetite with a spinning class.'

'Communicate or else?'

'Empty threat,' said Will. 'As long as we keep our eyes peeled. *Ships* are a threat. They've got their hooks into the big shipping companies where they know the owners. Spinners on deck, Herr Instructor. *Mach schnell!*'

LLOYD MCVAY, a tall, stooped man in a plaid suit and florid bow tie, telephoned ports up and down the coasts that rimmed the Atlantic Ocean. His reach extended from Brazil to Antigua, from Miami to Senegal, on the great bulge of West Africa. Shipping agents, oil men and diplomats took his calls, eager to please.

Val McVay, his daughter and chief grant officer of the McVay Foundation for Humane Science, worked across from him, emailing yacht clubs and marinas on those same coasts. She was a pale woman, dressed in black; her face was as white as paper, her close-cropped hair ash-blonde, her eyes dark. She could see that her father was feeling pressed.

The disaster was writ large on the jumbo high-resolution flat-panel display that showed an electronic chart of the Atlantic Ocean. The red line that marked Will Spark's voyage from Barbados ran out abruptly in midocean. The nine million square miles of sea water depicted on the chart were empty. The enormous circle of blue that marked how far Spark could have sailed in the past week already encompassed an area larger than Europe.

Lloyd McVay said, 'I should speak with someone in the oil business, in the event Spark heads for his old stomping ground in West Africa.'

'Richard Hood at Shell? We gave his brother a lab grant.'

'Dick's an accountant. Bob Hunt oversees security.'

Val's grandfather had founded McVay Radio, building transceivers for the air force in the Second World War, and microwave generators for the then-new radar. After a long stint with the CIA, her father had taken over, developing transmitters and laser generators for the Defense Department, NASA and private industry. He had made a second fortune by jumping into PCs for ordinary people. McVay Computers sold cheap computer chips by the billions.

After graduating first in her class at Stanford, Val had joined him in the race to design high-speed browsers for the Internet. But their technically brilliant effort was steamrollered by Microsoft at the cost of much money and most of the McVay prestige. Silicon Valley now knew the tall, patrician Lloyd McVay as an older businessman who managed the benevolent-sounding, non-profit, tax-exempt McVay Foundation with his reclusive, thirty-something daughter.

In fact, under the cloak of their foundation, the McVays had set their sights on a third fortune that would dwarf the first two. Dispensing grants to an array of engineering projects, Val and her father had devoted the past six years to launching the next great breakthrough. They had finally found it in Sentinel—one of hundreds of developments the Foundation had financed. But first they had to find Will Spark, who had stolen it.

Val checked her list. Yacht clubs, merchant ships, work boats, fishing fleets and the possibility of enlisting the US Navy all covered.

For her, the worst part of this catastrophe was that she had come aboard late. When it first hit—when Will Spark first screwed them—they had decided that she would take care of day-to-day affairs, freeing her father to devote his full time to managing the crisis. But when Spark suddenly disappeared, Val had had to step in. She had discovered that her flair for conceiving and managing long-term projects was suited to fighting deceit with deceit. Coupled with her technical expertise, she had the powerful feeling that she could play the dark games even better than her father. Proof of this was her idea to trace Spark by bugging Jim Leighton's heart-rate monitor. An opportunity that Andy Nickels, her father's latest protégé, had squandered.

She watched an assistant slide an open folder onto Lloyd McVay's desk. Another handed him a wireless telephone.

'Bob Hunt! It's been too long since we've heard from you . . . How's that tennis game going?' His finger traced columns of print. 'Estelle is well, I trust?'

Val, who vastly preferred the bluntness of email to the chitchat required on the telephone, turned to her keypad to send blind copies to every yacht captain in her address file.

Have you seen the fifty-foot, one-off sloop *Hustle*? Centre cockpit, high aspect rig, Hong Kong registry, new teak decks, distinctive wooden spoked wheel, white hull.

Across the desk, Lloyd McVay was describing *Hustle* to the chairman of a Taiwanese container fleet.

Will Spark had contrived to lose himself on a big ocean. But for the owners of a foundation that underwrote research and development with grants and incubator money, disbursed first-class travel expenses to conferences and lobbied congressmen with studied generosity, the big ocean was surrounded by a very small world.

'SECOND-DAY PIE tastes better than first-day pie,' said Will Spark, savouring a forkful. 'So real wealth would be the means to employ servants to eat your first-day pie.'

'Who's chasing you, Will?'

'Question is, how wealthy are *you* going to get as a personal trainer? You ever ask yourself where it's taking you?'

Jim looked out at the water. His career future was not a happy subject. He was twenty-nine. Thirty loomed and cast a shadow over his limitations. 'I used to hope I'd get into the top ten of triathlon. My swimming was tops. I'm good on the bike. But I'm too slow a runner. I don't even compete any more.'

'So what are you going to do? Live off your wife?'

'No!'

'Hey, I'm just kidding. But how are you going to live?'

'I don't know, maybe I'll go back to school.'

Will's face scrunched up in an expression that scorned professional students. 'What did you study in college?'

'Lit and history.'

'No reason why you couldn't turn that into an MBA.'

'I don't want to be a businessman. I don't think I'm competitive enough.'

Will looked at him. 'What does Shannon want?'

'She *says* she wants a simple life. She doesn't want the whole two-jobs, half-the-day commuting lifestyle. And no time for the kids.'

'She sounds like a sensible girl.'

'Yeah, except that she doesn't have a clue about what it's like not to have money. Her father gives her anything she wants.'

'If I may be so blunt,' said Will, 'did you ever ask yourself what you were doing with this girl?'

More often than Will could imagine, Jim reflected, for reasons he would never know. 'We liked each other. In fact, we knew the second we met we were exactly what we wanted.'

'Several of my marriages started on that basis,' Will said acidly.

'Yeah, well, it used to amaze me how I loved her more every day.'

Will nodded. 'I underwrote some interesting research on a neuropeptide called oxytocin, which influences pair-bonding. It seems that rubbing your sexual parts stimulates the brain to release oxytocin—scientists call it the "cuddle hormone".'

Jim laughed. 'I still feel that way, even after she said no, and I gotta tell you, your long cut to Africa is killing me.'

Will said, 'Offshore, being a monk works best. Just shut it all down. What did you say her father does?'

'He's got a chain of health clubs in Connecticut. Just took over his sixth. That's how we met. He bought one of the clubs I was working in. The one you came to in Bridgeport.'

'And I bet that if Shannon married you, he would want you to manage one. You could live off your father-in-law.'

'I wouldn't be *living* off him. I'd be doing a job. I've got a lot of ideas. I'm thinking that the clubs could field bike-racing teams.'

'Those fat-assed old ladies aren't paying to race bikes, Jim.'

'You always came at the off-hours. There's plenty of young suits looking for a challenge.'

'If I wanted to run a gym, I'd do it in a big city. Give me a lean and hungry clientele.'

'I wouldn't live in a big city.'

'You really are a mall rat, aren't you?' Will chuckled. 'Ever think of breaking out of the suburbs?'

'I got mugged in New York City.'

Will looked hard at him. 'What happened?'

'I was down there for the AIDS bike-a-thon. Guy flashed a knife, "Gimme your dough." I threw my bike at him.'

'That where you got that?' Will pointed at a thin, white scar down the front of Jim's thigh.

'Naw, that was a crash. I slugged him and he ran.'

Will looked out over the sea. 'Do you ever think of going for the big time? Everyone else has got rich these days—why shouldn't you?'

'How? Are you backing a company I should know about?'

'My boy, we are sailing to the African coast. Who knows what opportunities may come our way in the next few weeks.'

'Is that why you're going there?'

Will looked back at the wake. 'You know why I'm going there.'

'No, Will, I don't. And I'd be grateful if you'd tell me.'

Will sprang to his feet, took the helm and overrode the autohelm. 'I told you already. There are people who want my guts for garters, but they're not going to get them.'

JIM LOOKED OVER his shoulder, up the open hatch, where Will was standing watch in the cockpit. He would send this one in a quick flash-and-delete.

Dear Shannon,
    The real reason we changed course is that Will got spooked when he saw a ship and convinced himself that the people on it wanted to kill him. I know that sounds crazy. I think he is. A little.

Jim checked his watch. The boat was an hour behind Greenwich Mean Time, four hours ahead of Connecticut. Shannon would be in her office. He switched on the satphone and flashmailed as Will. When he checked ten minutes later, there was a message from Shannon.

Jim, I'm so sorry I got you involved with a crazy man. Promise you'll learn immediately how to sail that boat by yourself. Immediately!

Jim clicked REPLY.

Hey, don't worry. I'm having a ball. I've already started to learn to sail.

After he mailed it, he noticed the flashmail status window. Email had come in for Will.

No need to ask for whom the bell tolls, Will Spark, it tolls for the thief.

Jim printed it.

It was early afternoon. The sun was blazing high overhead. Will, stripped to his shorts, was sweating in the shade of the canvas awning.

'What's up?'

'Another letter from John Donne. And it has your name on it.'

Will read it with a thin smile. 'Frustrated English professor.'

'This guy knows you. He used your name. Come on, Will. Who's the poet?'

'Beneath the veneer, he's a thug.'

'He calls you a thief, for Christ's sake. Did you rob him?'

'No!'

'Then why is he chasing you?'

Will sighed elaborately. 'OK, I'll fill you in as best I can . . . You know about moletronics?'

'Little computers?'

'Molecular electronics. Chips as small as molecules. Moletronics will completely reinvent computer design.'

'How small?'

'As small as a single cell. You could pop a data chip into a hypodermic needle, inject it into your brain. *Voilà!* Now you speak French.'

'How fast?'

'A billion times faster than anything on the shelf.'

'How do you know all this stuff?'

'I am what you could call a *proactive* investment banker. For the last big deal I was running, I rounded up a bunch of hotshot engineers who were out beyond the leading edge. I found them. I backed them. And I organised a breakthrough that paid off. Big time.'

'Congratulations.'

'I named it Sentinel. I've got Sentinel chips—right now—that outperform anything on the market by a thousand times. A hundred thousand times. Nothing stays new long, but a one-year lead in moletronics is like a century of the Industrial Revolution.'

'Why are you sailing to Africa when you should be cheerleading your engineers?'

'Because I'll put every billion-dollar chip factory in the world out of business overnight—you better believe there are people who don't want that to happen.'

'I'll bet.'

'That's who's chasing me.'

'Sounds a bit Oliver Stone, Will.'

'What do you mean?'

'A little heavy on the conspiracy theory, maybe? You're saying that legitimate corporations would try to murder a competitor?'

'Do you remember what happened in Barbados? Was I at the airport to meet you, like I promised?'

'No. You sent some taxi driver who couldn't speak English. Next thing I knew I thought I was going to drown on a fishing boat.'

'Don't you realise, now, why I had to leave before you?'

'Weather.'

'No. I got word they'd come to the island.'

Back to 'they', Jim thought in despair, as Will continued.

'I arranged for a taxi to meet your plane and hired a fishing boat to bring you out to *Hustle*. Wind was blowing up a gale and night fell dark as a bear's belly, so the Port Authority didn't notice me sail without clearance. I thought I was home free. Till you brought them down on us with that phoney heart-rate monitor.'

'Bullshit, Will.'

'Oh, yeah? You want to explain this letter?' Will waved the printout in Jim's face.

'I still find it hard to believe that legitimate corporations would—'

'Billions,' Will cut him off angrily. '*Billions and billions* of dollars. There isn't a human being alive that somebody wouldn't kill for billions. Besides, the suits don't pull the trigger. They hire a professional.'

'But even if you're right, Will. If you were killed, what's to stop your engineers from implementing Sentinel without you?'

'I'm the only one who has the whole picture. If I'm killed, it's over. The big boys'll catch up in time and cash in. If I can hide out till they do, maybe killing me wouldn't be worth the trouble.'

'Wait a minute. You knowingly put me in the line of fire?'

'That is not true. When I asked you to join me I thought I had pulled off a disappearing act. I just wanted a strong crewman and the company to Rio. I really thought I was home free.'

'But not when you ran from Barbados.'

'What do you mean?'

'You thought they were onto you and you let me come anyway.'

Will suddenly looked old. 'You're right. I should have left you.'

'Why didn't you?'

'I just wasn't up to the long haul alone. I figured if I got you aboard you'd be safe. No one would know we were heading to Rio. How was I to know you'd let them put the bug on you? So, let's say I apologise.' He reread the email. 'The guy is such a phoney,' he snorted. '"For whom the bell tolls . . .". So just because he can quote poetry means he's not a thug?' He shook his head in disgust.

'I'll get you out of this as soon as we hit Nigeria. Pal of mine's an oil man on the Bonny River. I'll get him to chopper you out to Lagos. Put you on a London flight, first class, then straight to New York.' He stuck out his hand.

Jim took it. 'Sounds great.' But just in case it wasn't, he vowed that he would continue to learn to sail the boat.

'Are you sure?' Will pressed. 'Something's on your mind.'

'What are you going to do after you drop me?'

'Shove off. That's the beauty of owning a boat . . . Here today, gone tomorrow.'

Which made this boat owner, Jim thought, not the sort of person to stake his life on—and his boat no place for a passenger, much less a novice deck hand.

Where are you, Will Spark?

Val McVay had met him only once. She had liked his ideas and liked him. She still couldn't believe she had slept with the man. That he was as old as her father hadn't mattered one whit during a long and memorable weekend. But conventional wisdom would deem it a stupid thing to do in the midst of negotiations.

The key to tracing Will Spark was still Jim Leighton.

She telephoned a private detective in Brooklyn. As always, he answered the phone like a starter pistol. 'Vinnie Thomas!'

'Do you know who this is?' she asked.

'Yeah, I know your voice.' She had originally hired the Brooklyn detective years ago to investigate a man she was considering for an occasional no-strings afternoon in the privacy of her Manhattan town house. Thomas had done a thoroughly professional job of confirming that the bored husband her prospect claimed to be was not a pervert or a fortune hunter. Since then, he'd been occasionally useful in her ongoing battle to stay a jump ahead of her father and Andy Nickels.

'We have another job for the woman you put into that spinning class,' Val McVay said.

'You are referring to the health club in Bridgeport, if I remember?'

'Mr Thomas, how many spinning classes do you infiltrate?'

'You'd be surprised.'

'It says here . . .' Jim climbed the companionway, book in hand, and inspected the sails—'if you tighten that'—he pointed at the boom vang, which had slipped loose—'then we'll go faster.'

Will returned an amused smile. 'Be my guest. Try it.'

Jim crawled onto the cabin roof and pressed the vang sheet back into the jaws of its jam cleat. He hauled on the line, the cleat gripped it and the vang pulled the boom down. The result of the effort was to slightly flatten the mainsail.

Will peered at the knot meter on the steering pedestal. 'Almost a tenth of a knot!' he laughed. 'Really tramping.'

'I'm not finished.'

Jim studied the mainsail. The taut triangular expanse pointed at the sky as trim as a spear. But a small flutter marred the trailing edge of the headsail. Aware that Will was watching his every move, Jim took a chrome handle from its socket beside the companionway, inserted it in the top of the winch controlling the jib and threw his weight into a half-turn. The jib sheet creaked with the strain. The fluttering stopped. The boat leaned a fraction and felt suddenly livelier.

'Half a knot!' Will called. 'Good on you.'

Jim grinned with satisfaction. He might not be a natural sailor, but he was beginning to get at least an inkling of how the boat worked.

That night, Jim wrote to Shannon. He was getting the hang of the SSB radio, which allowed him to send her a private letter and not worry about Will's paranoia—'Don't tell anybody we're sailing to Nigeria.' The fact was, even if Will's 'they' could intercept email, they'd have a heck of a time intercepting his and Shannon's because Shannon had secreted deep-cover private email addresses into the busy RileySpa website, to hide them from her mega-nosy mother.

I'm beginning to realise that this whole sailing thing is about form. On the bike, when my knees start wobbling I lose speed. On the boat, when a sail wobbles—'luffs' is the correct word—wind energy is wasted and she slows down. So maybe I'm becoming a sailor in spite of myself. Best news is, Will thinks we'll hit the Nigerian coast in THREE WEEKS!—Omigod, time for my watch. I'm going to practise steering.

He fired it off and ran on deck with five minutes to spare.

That night, Will gave him a big vote of confidence. For the first time, the old man slept in his luxurious cabin in the back of the boat, instead of in a hammock slung right beside the companionway.

Jim passed the first two hours steering manually. By day, surrounded by the featureless horizon, the compass needle was a tedious guide. By night, Will had taught him to steer by whatever distinctive stars or constellations lay ahead, and only occasionally check the compass needle as the heavens wheeled. Easier, but not easy. Finally he re-engaged the autohelm.

The night had started uncommonly bright, but gradually the stars began to disappear, until half were dark. Blind now, he tried to listen for clues. At first it all sounded the same, but when he strained he began to distinguish fluttering sailcloth from the hiss of waves, the smack of the hull cutting the water and the rush of wind.

Suddenly the boat heeled hard over. He couldn't figure out what had happened. Then he realised that the trade wind, which for days had cut across the bow at the same angle, had abruptly changed direction. *Hustle* lost speed. The sails went slack. The boat began rocking uncomfortably, pitching fore and aft, which caused the sails to slat and bang. Suddenly, the still air was stirred by a cold breeze.

Will ran up on deck. 'You should have woken me! It's going to hit us like a freight train.'

Now Jim saw what he had missed. A quarter of a mile off to the right, a heavy, bone-white line was bearing down on them like a huge grin in a dark face.

'Furl the jib! I'll reef the main!' Will leapt out of the cockpit and hastily lowered the mainsail halfway down the mast.

Jim, aware that he had screwed up by not paying attention to his surroundings, tried to furl in the jib. The line he was tugging turned a spool on the front of the boat that was supposed to crank the sail round its forestay like a vertical window shade. But it was jamming.

'Jesus, what were you thinking? When you see a squall coming, you have to act.'

'I didn't see it.'

A gust of wind struck the boat, icy cold and so strong that it ballooned the jib that Jim was struggling to furl.

'Will, I can't move it.'

Though Jim put all his strength against the winch handle, it wouldn't budge. The next gust shoved the boat so violently that it overrode the autohelm and turned downwind. Suddenly the sea was frothy white. The boom swung across the boat, slamming from left to right with a crash that shook the deck, and *Hustle* gybed about. Racing out of control, smashing sea to sea, she stampeded from the wind. A wave broke into the cockpit and poured down the companionway into the cabin.

'The washboards,' Will yelled over the roar of the water. 'Under the bench.'

Kneeling on the floor of the cockpit, Jim found the wooden boards and worked them clumsily into the vertical slots that flanked the companionway opening. When he was done and had the hatch closed tight, he realised that Will had somehow battled the boat around, back on course.

The wind was whining in the rigging and blowing cold spray. Neither man had had time to don a windcheater. The wind shifted again and knocked the boat half over. Jim was astonished to see the deck at so steep an angle it was nearly vertical. He smashed painfully into the lifelines that fenced the deck.

At the helm, Will played the wheel until the boat began to level off. 'We have to get that sail in. Here, you—'

An explosion cut off his words, a concussive *boom*. Where the jib had billowed full and white a second earlier, all that was left was a black hole fringed by flapping shreds of cloth. Released from the overwhelming pressure on the sail, the boat snapped straight up and forged ahead, the reefed mainsail driving her hard. The seas were suddenly flattened by a roaring cascade of hail that blinded them.

Pellets of ice raked the deck. They grew larger, the size of marbles, then golf balls. Jim saw a baseball-size chunk explode on the gunnel. Then he was knocked off his feet, stunned by a huge hailstone that had smashed into his face. He clapped his hand over his nose and it came away blood red. He tried to stand up just as a tremendous gust hit the boat full on her side. He reached for the lifelines but fell smoothly between them into the sea.

The water was warmer than the frigid wind, but it closed over his head with an awful silence. The hull shouldered past him and Jim panicked. The sailboat was plunging away from him into the storm and he would drown alone. His heart hammered in his chest.

Suddenly he was back in the water with the sharks the day Will had dared him to swim. The sharks that had turned out to be dolphins.

He tried to kick towards the surface. Immediately, his foot struck something hard. And he realised that, in his panic, what had seemed like hours in the water had been a fraction of a second. He was still beside the boat; its smooth side was slipping past his shoulder. He lunged for it, and felt Will's hand close on his.

Then hail was stinging his face and he was coughing and spitting, but he was sucking sweet air. He felt the boat roll violently and his hand began to slide from Will's, his strength overwhelmed by floods of fear-spurred adrenaline.

'I can't pull you aboard,' the old man rasped. 'I cracked a rib.'

Squinting up, Jim saw Will sprawled half over the side of the boat, his face contorted with pain as he stretched under the lifelines to hold Jim's hand.

Galvanised by Will's suffering, Jim called upon the discipline with which he had built his body. He had trained for years to override pain and expend his last reserves.

The boat rolled downwards. A lifeline stanchion was for a brief instant almost in reach. He flutter-kicked and seized it. 'Let go!'

'You sure?' Will gasped.

Jim grabbed the lower safety wire with his other hand. The boat was rolling, jerking him up, driving him down. He stopped fighting it and let his legs and torso rise with the flow. When he was skimming the surface, he tucked his legs into a tight ball and hooked a foot on the gunwale. The boat rolled up, nearly shaking him off. When it rolled down again, he used the force to tumble over the safety wires onto the hail-slicked deck.

Jim sank to the cockpit sole and rested his head on the bench, trembling from head to toe. He heard Will barking orders.

'Wake up, Jim. We're not out of this by a long shot.'

All Jim could think about was how close he had come to dying.

'Put on your harness.' Will shook Jim's shoulder.

Jim crawled to the bench hatch and pulled out a webbing harness. He slowly buckled it on.

'Clip onto the pedestal.'

The snap shackle clicked onto a steel ring tethering him to the boat by a six-foot length of braided nylon line.

'Help me into mine,' Will ordered, and Jim quickly buckled him into his harness. 'Now take the wheel and point her where I tell you.'

Jim discovered that with the jib in tatters it was a lot harder to keep the boat on course. Crazy wind gusts banged the sail and rattled hailstones in his face.

'We've got too much sail up,' Will yelled. 'I'm going to take another reef in the main.'

Jim watched in awe as Will, clutching his side, edged forward on the icy deck. His every motion was a model of economy as he tackled the sail. With clear arm gestures he showed Jim where to steer whenever the wind shifted. The crackling sail inched lower. When Will finally reeled back to the cockpit, his face was haggard with pain. He took the wheel with his good arm.

'Run below, get me two morphine tablets from the medicine kit.'

Desperate to atone for this catastrophe, Jim unclipped his safety harness and leapt towards the hatch. It was much quieter below deck. There were three drawers of medicine and first-aid gear in a cabinet by the nav station. As he started to open the morphine bottle, he had his first clear thought since the storm had struck, and he dried his hands before cupping two of the pills in his palm.

The coffee Thermos was nearly full. Jim brought it to Will along with the pills and a windcheater, receiving a gratifying, 'Bless you, my son.'

Some time before dawn the wind began to slacken. In the spreading light the sea remained vividly alive and frightening. The word *jagged* took hold in Jim's tired mind—the word he would use to describe the storm to Shannon. Jagged waves slashing at the sky, jagged cloud rocketing overhead, jagged tatters of sailcloth where the jib had blown out. His face hurt and his head throbbed. He was blind tired. And he blamed himself for the ruined headsail. But though he had nearly drowned, he was alive, and his spirit soared when Will put an end to his guilt with a cheerful, 'Think you could raise the number-three jib without falling overboard?'

It took an hour on the pitching foredeck to clear the ruined headsail and raise the spare. The boat responded by settling down to a more comfortable ride.

Will welcomed him back to the cockpit. 'May I presume that a fitness instructor is qualified to tape cracked ribs?'

'Absolutely.'

'Breakfast, first.'

'If I can get it.'

'Not based on what I've seen of your cooking so far. But if you can steer, and keep your eyes open in case that squall has any cousins, I'll pop another morphine and rustle up something to eat.'

IT SEEMED TO JIM like months since they had escaped the doldrums, though it was only three weeks. Even his memory of the squall had faded into an entry in the log—a waypoint in the 2,000 miles they had sailed east since Will had changed course. Their course had veered gradually north of the equator to pick up a boost from the Guinea Current. It swept them under the bulge of West Africa parallel to the coast.

> Dear Shannon,
>   Almost home. Just two more weeks or so, with luck. The area we're entering off the oil coast of Nigeria is called the Bight of Biafra. (A bight, in case you don't know, which I didn't, is an indentation in the shore that forms a big open bay.) Will says that the coast is rimmed by mangrove swamps, and is virtually impenetrable except where the rivers of the Niger Delta, the Bonny among the biggest (where we're heading, I think), empty into the sea. But, says Will, sandbars block the mouth of each river and they're pounded by heavy surf. Channels cut through some of the bars, marked with buoys. But when the channels shift, it sometimes takes a while for the Nigerians to realign the buoys.
>   Anyway, before we even reach the sandbars, we'll have to sail through a maze of offshore well heads and drilling platforms. Will says, quote, 'Many are lighted, some aren't. Some are marked on the charts, others are not.' If that weren't enough, he tells me that new wells are under construction. I couldn't resist telling him that it sounds more dangerous than the people chasing him.

Jim decided to spare her the information that, before they even got to the oil rigs, they would have to sail among scores of supertankers converging upon and steaming away from the Nigerian coast. Ships so big, Will noted cheerfully, that they could trample a sailboat like *Hustle* into the sea and never know they had done it.

SHANNON RILEY CHECKED her email from her chair at the front desk and laughed out loud.
'What's so funny?' her father called from his office.
'Jim, trying to keep me from worrying.'
Her father responded with his 'Oh, Jim' grunt.
'He's started to write wonderful letters.'
'That's nice,' said her father.
Up yours, thought Shannon. She clicked REPLY, then started to type like wildfire.

Jim!!! Look out for supertankers. They can't see you and they can't stop and if you think about it they're all over the place around oil wells. I'd never forgive myself if you got hurt because I pushed you there. Come home safe. Kisses

She deleted 'kisses'—it wasn't fair—and replaced it with

I've been loving your letters. I feel like I'm running around on the boat with you.

And flashed it off.

High heels clicked across the marble lobby and Shannon looked up from her computer. An unbelievably beautiful woman, dressed like a *Vogue* model, was heading towards the membership office with a worried smile.

Shannon smiled back. 'Can I help you?'

The woman had a European accent, very stylish-sounding. 'My membership—I am trying to make new?'

'You want to renew. Sure, which club?'

'No, not new. It is . . . How you say?. . . I am back . . . I was away.'

'Right. You want to start your membership up again. Do you have your card?'

'I have it some place.' She opened a Prada handbag. 'Here.'

Shannon swiped the card through the reader and brought up the woman's picture on her screen and the information that she had signed up several months ago, then frozen her membership. Reason: travel. Dina Usamov. She reached up to shake hands. 'I'm Shannon.'

'So now what am I to do?'

'It's done. We'll resume billing your credit card monthly.'

'That is it? Thank you. I am very happy to be back. Tell me, is my favourite spinning instructor back too? The boy named Jim?'

'No, not yet. Soon, I hope.'

'He went sailing, you know.'

'I know. We're friends.'

'Oh, he is the best boy.' Dina gave her a little smile. 'Do you know how he is doing? Does he telephone?'

'He emails me. Sometimes I feel like he's next door.'

'Please to email him my regards and I hope he comes home, soon.'

'Two weeks, I hope.'

'Where is he now?'

'Almost to Africa.'

'Where in Africa?'

'Shannon.' Her father came barrelling out of his office. 'Is my best girl going to have lunch with me today? Oh, sorry. Did I interrupt?'

Shannon was rolling her eyes at Dina when her telephone rang. Simultaneously a gang of stay-at-home moms came through the front door, several beelining for her with problems on their faces. The second line rang. The lull was over.

'Hello, thanks for calling RileySpa. Please hold—Dina,' she called across the lobby. 'Email him! He'd love to hear from a client. Here, I'll write it down for you: jleighton@rileyspa.com.'

Dina called her boss from the car and told him everything. Vinnie was pleased. 'Now that's the kind of detail that get you more jobs.'

'Happy that would be making me.' Dressing up, practising accents and playing assistant detective beat bartending between casting calls.

'Talk normal, for Christ's sake.'

'I'm staying in character.'

As Dina pulled out of the RileySpa parking lot, she saw the bright red BMW 740i with SHANNON vanity plates. An $80,000 car for a ditz of a receptionist dating a spinning instructor? No wonder she was so goddamned cheerful.

As she passed the 740, Dina saw the wheelchair emblem on the licence plate. Jesus H! she said to herself. The poor kid can't walk. She's disabled. She called Vinnie again.

'LET'S TAKE MY CAR,' said Shannon. She had mastered the motorcycle-like twist-grip controls on her 740, and when she was driving it was almost like the accident had never happened.

As they pulled out of the lot, her father said, 'I hope you don't mind, we're going to Emil's.'

'Why? We always go to The Fish House.'

'Uh . . . Fred didn't feel like fish.'

'Fred?'

'Fred Bernstein. You know—'

'I *know* Fred. Why is he having lunch with us?'

'Give the two of you a chance to get to know each other better. Hon, you're driving awful fast.'

'Did Mom set this up?'

Her father squirmed. Caught between her and her mother, he was like a toad trying to escape two angry cats. 'Remember, Fred sold the company.'

'You and Mom say "sold the company" like he saved the world or something. He sold his company for a bunch of money; now what's he going to do with himself?'

'It made Fred a very wealthy man. And how many men would . . .?' His voice trailed off.

'How many men would go out with a cripple?'

It was hard to separate her life from an injury that affected her every waking hour. But she was also still what she had been before the accident: the daughter of a competitive couple obsessed with getting rich. Her childhood had been a daily battle to escape from their single-minded pursuit of success. She knew plenty of kids like her. If they didn't become success-crazed like their parents they found ways to escape: doing drugs, or hanging with a gang, or, as Shannon had done, skateboarding. One extreme led to another, surfing, snowboarding, skiing. All had taken her further from her parents' obsessions. Until her luck ran out and left her their prisoner.

'The man is loaded,' her father said. 'He's young. Rich. He doesn't just want to date you. He wants to marry you. Hon, you're driving extremely fast.'

'You know why Fred wants to marry me? Because he thinks a crippled woman would be easier to control. I mean, think about it, Daddy, *I can't run away*. Pretty good deal for a guy who's built like a pear with dandruff.'

'He *sold* the company—dammit. I won't be around to take care of you for ever.'

'But Jim will. He doesn't want to control me. He likes me as I am.'

'He's a goddamned fitness instructor, for Christ's sake.'

'He's *my* fitness instructor.'

'If he loves you so much why'd he run off sailing?'

'I *made* him go sailing. I want him to have a chance to test himself. To grow up so he realises he can do better than a cripple.'

Ahead, an official-use-only cut crossed over the central reservation. Shannon squeezed the brakes hard and took the crossover in a haze of burning rubber.

'*Jesus Christ!* Hey, where are you going?'

'Back to the club. I'm not hungry.'

'Hon? Why are you crying?'

'I'm crying because Jim loves me and I don't want to wreck his life . . . If I were really a good person, I would write Jim never to come home because I'm marrying your goddamned Fred.'

'I was just trying to help.'

'I'll bet it never occurred to you that I have to wonder what's wrong with Jim that he needs a crippled girl?'

That silenced her father until he heard the siren.

'Brilliant. There's a cop chasing us.'

'I know.' She pulled over and extended her licence as the cop stormed up. He looked angry and wary.

'Step out of the car, miss.'

'Would you hand me my crutches, please? They're on the back seat. I'm crippled. I can't walk very far.'

The trooper registered the tears streaking her make-up. 'Are you all right, miss?'

'I'm OK.'

'Who are you?' he asked her father.

'I'm her father. I'm attempting to explain to my daughter that her mother and I love her very much and only want what's best for her.'

The trooper shook his head. 'Yeah, well you could start by telling her she's going to get killed driving like that . . . Miss, I'm going to issue you a verbal warning. These crossovers are reserved for police use.'

'I'm sorry,' said Shannon. She wiped her eyes and smiled.

The cop started to walk away. Then he turned and spoke in a low voice only Shannon could hear. 'Between me and you, miss? That was one cool turn.'

STILL A FULL week's sailing from the Niger Delta, they began to see the long thick silhouettes of oil tankers on every watch. They often had one steaming into view while another was still prowling the horizon—until the dry harmattan wind swirled dust off the African continent and blanketed the sea with haze.

With visibility unreliable, Will ran the radar day and night and set the collision alarm to sound whenever a ship came within three miles. At the same time, he moved back into his hammock for his off-watch cat naps. 'Not that I doubt you, CC Kid. But two sets of eyes are better than one.'

'How long am I going to remain the CC Kid?'

Will laughed. 'Till you tell me why you're afraid of the outdoors.'

'Hey, I'm pulling my own weight—starting to.'

'Given the choice, you'll stay indoors.'

Jim picked up the binoculars and scanned the haze, breaking the circle of the horizon into small increments as Will had taught him. At that moment, a battered tanker flying the Panamanian flag was drawing close. And a freighter heaped with oil derricks was crossing their wake.

'What flag is that freighter?' Will asked.

'I can't see his flag.'

'What colour is his funnel?'

The ship's smokestack was a stubby appendage to a murky-hued deckhouse. Seen through the haze it could be any light colour. 'I can't tell. White, maybe, with a couple of thin blue stripes.'

'Any red on the white?'

'It could be rust. It could be red.'

'*Russian*. Douse the sails!'

'What for?'

'I told you, they have their hooks in shipping. Douse 'em!'

II

AFRICA

A hundred miles from the Bonny River they turned north. The wind wheeled with them—a southwest monsoon that displaced the harmattan and built an enormous swell. That night, as they surfed the waves speeding towards the coast, the sky glowed red.

'Gas flares,' Will explained. 'Burning off waste gas from the oil-well heads. We're almost there. What do you say we celebrate our last night at sea?'

'Why don't we celebrate with one last spinning class?' said Jim.

Will turned his face to the wind. 'Maybe you're right.'

Jim winched the bikes up. Will patched the collision alarm into the loudhailer just in case a ship bore down on them. But the old man was in a playful mood and he rigged a strobe rescue light to flicker their shadows on the sails.

'Disco spin!'

By the flickering strobe light, Jim could see a jerkily slow-motion Will pretend to turn up his resistance. As for himself, Jim gave his all, anticipating several days of enforced inactivity, trapped in airless aeroplanes and departure lounges.

He was feeling some regret that the voyage was ending. The boat routines had become a comfortable habit and he had been learning so much that he hadn't had time to get bored. He looked over at Will. He would miss the old guy a little. Wouldn't miss his crazy demons, real or imagined. But what a trip!

He pedalled like he was flying. Eating the hill. Shannon was right.

The once-in-a-lifetime voyage had changed his life. He felt the tug of an endorphin high seeping into his brain. The music sounded unbearably beautiful. The strobe on the sails showed the boat for the splendid creature she was. God, she'd been good to them. The long voyage and all its hassles had been a crucible of friendship. Like team racing.

He could hear a loud thudding—his heart—a powerful *whomp, whomp, whomp*. The thudding grew louder, thundering, and suddenly something was very wrong. A blinding light from above seared his eyes. The thundering shook the bike and the decks, and a hard gust smacked the sails.

A ship, Jim thought. We're being run down by a ship.

An amplified voice thundered like the voice of God. 'What are you all doin' down there?' and Jim realised that a helicopter was hovering close overhead, beaming a light down on the sailboat.

'Douse that goddamned light!' Will yelled through the loudhailer.

The helicopter drew back fifty feet. In a thick American Gulf Coast drawl the pilot demanded, 'What the hell is wrong with you, blinking your 'mergency strobe when there ain't no 'mergency?'

Will shouted to Jim, 'Oil company rig tender. Way off base out here.'

The helicopter's searchlight locked onto Jim and Will dripping in their workout shorts. 'You all need rescuin' or not?'

'Hey, pal,' Will shot back. 'Be a good ol' boy and patch me through to Mr Kenyon.'

'Who?'

'Steve Kenyon. Your boss.'

'Kenyon's not with the company no mo'. Hasn't been here fo' two, three years.'

The helicopter veered away and thundered towards the invisible coast, leaving them in utter darkness.

'Bloody hell,' muttered Will.

As his eyes recovered from the glare of the searchlight, Jim looked over at Will. The old man was staring north at the red glow.

'Will, when where you out here last?'

''Ninety-six.'

'That's a long time ago.'

Will motioned to Jim to take the helm. 'Keep out of eyeball range of the platforms. I want to check the charts.'

WHEN WORD CAME IN on the satphone that Will Spark had been spotted sixty miles off the Bonny River in the Niger Delta, Andy Nickels was airborne in the wrong direction. He immediately instructed the McVay Foundation pilots to plot fuel and relief-crew stops for the long haul to Nigeria.

Then he woke an American operations superintendent in Port Harcourt whose responsibilities entailed security for offshore oil rigs, submarine pipelines and storage tankers. He told him that Greenpeace fanatics were headed for the Bonny River in a sailboat, intending to hook up with local dissidents to shut down oil production.

'When you find them we'll take custody.'

'You're welcome to 'em.'

JIM STAYED in *Hustle*'s cockpit, watching for ships and work boats and steering around oil platforms and the bright patches lit by burning gas glares. He was excited. Each of the rolling waves was shoving him closer to an airport and home.

Will brought him tea. 'We ought to see the fairway pretty soon— look for a couple of sea buoys. A four-second red blinker and a four-second green . . . What the hell is that?'

Jim looked to see where Will was focusing his night glasses. 'I see white . . .' It looked like a feather blowing along the orange horizon. 'I think it's moving.'

'It's a small boat throwing spray . . . Lost him . . . You know what worries me? Who told that cracker we were coming?'

'What cracker?'

'The helicopter pilot.'

'What are you talking about? He saw our flasher beacon. He thought we needed help.'

'Forty miles from the nearest oil rig?'

'I see a green flasher.' Jim counted, 'One . . . two . . . three . . . four-second green flasher! It's the sea buoy.'

'Find me the red. It should appear a hair to the left of the green.'

'I got it.'

'Good—what the hell is *that*?'

Jim saw another tiny splash of white whipping across their path. 'Is that the same boat?'

'No, too far away. Jesus, there's another.' Will leapt through the hatch to hunch over the radar screen. A second later he came up the companionway, shouting, 'Douse the sails! They're all over the place!'

'Who?'

'A whole slew of patrol boats. Douse the sails.'

Will cranked in the main. Jim furled the jib. Will started the engine and engaged the propeller.

'That goddamned cracker was looking for us. Somebody paid him to keep an eye peeled. And now they know we're coming.'

Jim couldn't believe this was starting all over again. 'Will, even if there is somebody chasing you, there's no way he's going to know you're on the Bonny River—*What is that?*'

Something tall and dark loomed nearby. Will grabbed the binoculars. Then he tossed them to Jim, spun the helm, and steered towards it. 'Good eyes, Jim. Get the mooring lines.'

When Jim returned with the lines, they were close enough to see what looked like the girders of a half-built office tower. 'What is it, an oil well?'

'Abandoned rig.'

'Where are you going?'

'Right inside. Any luck, the patrols won't distinguish us from the rig.'

They looked back. The lights of the patrol boats were still speeding in the orange dark.

As the sailboat motored closer and closer to the looming structure, Jim held his breath. The heavy swell was surging between the thick round legs, twenty storeys high, braced by cross girders.

'The mast is going to hit!'

'Optical illusion,' Will said coolly. 'Listen up. Take a line up to the bow. See that leg with the ladder? I'll get you in close, you loop onto a mooring cleat.'

Hustle's engine echoed against the steel as Will nosed the boat carefully between the stiltlike legs. Jim ran forward, knelt on the foredeck, leaned out of the pulpit and took a turn round a cleat heavy enough to hold a tugboat. The current swung the stern round and the boat drifted back on her mooring line, hidden under the tower.

'Keep your eyes open,' said Will, and went below.

Ten minutes later he called Jim down to the chart table.

'OK. What we're going to do is head for the Calabar River.'

'What's there?'

'Friends they won't know about.'

The chart showed the narrow Calabar River many miles to the east in the mangrove swamps—so far east that it formed the border between Nigeria and Cameroon.

'How do I get to the airport?'

'My pals will get you to Lagos.'

'Why don't we land at the Bonny River, like we were going to? Just long enough to drop me on the quay.' Port Harcourt was thirty miles up the river. From there he could catch a train to Lagos.

'They've probably got a dossier on me as long as your arm, so they'll know I was connected on the Bonny River. First place they'll look.'

Jim moulded his reasoning to fit Will's fears. 'If it's me you're worried about, don't. "They" won't bother me if I'm not with you.'

'Unless they torture you to death to find out where I am.'

Jim reminded himself that Will had a gruesome way of drawing him into his fantasy. 'How would I know where you went?'

'I can't take the chance they won't be waiting at the dock. The boat would be in clear view from the time we cross the bar.'

'Let's go now,' Jim suggested.

'Are you serious? God almighty couldn't cross that bar in the dark. No, we'll head for the Calabar River.'

'Well, if "they" have a dossier on you, "they" will look on the Calabar, too. Right?'

'Wrong. They won't connect me to the Calabar.'

While they were arguing, the wind swung round and the harmattan was back, blowing hard out of the northeast and throwing a gritty haze across the watery oil fields.

Will was delighted. 'It could last a week. We'll beat east along the ten-metre line. They can't see us from shore and they can't see us from offshore. The current is with us. With any luck, we'll make the Calabar before tomorrow night.'

Will led Jim up on deck. The 'patrols'—if they were patrols—had vanished in the haze. Will started the engine. 'Cast off, Jim. We're outta here.'

As HIS McVAY Foundation Hawker Horizon flew high above the dark Atlantic, Andy Nickels dialled Greg, who had arrived in Lagos.

Greg reported that the Joint Security patrol boats had found no sailboat anywhere near the Bonny estuary. He and his men were canvassing Will Spark's known haunts.

Nickels cut him off. 'Listen up, pal. We're getting indications Spark operated under another name out there.'

THE VOYAGE to the Calabar River took much longer than Will had predicted. 'Oil wells have grown oil wells since I was here last. The joint is jumpin'.'

Petroleum structures were strewn along the coast. Jim saw drilling rigs and huge production platforms and immense storage tankers.

And scattered everywhere was the dangerous debris of failed enterprises. Just before dawn, they cast their searchlight on a wreck. Masts rose out of the sea at crazy angles. The swells were smashing against the remains of a helicopter landing pad.

Dark was closing in again before they reached the Calabar. They dropped anchor outside the bar in ten metres of water. Will fixed their position precisely with the GPS.

A hideous night followed, with *Hustle* rolling violently. Huge waves shoved her to the right as they approached, then heaved her left as they passed under. Fetching in from the Atlantic, they came like clockwork, a big roller every forty seconds. Jim felt on the verge of throwing up all night.

At daybreak they saw white breakers foaming on a reef that marked the west side of the river. Will started the engine and piloted through the haze, repeatedly stopping to check the positions of the buoys marking the channels.

Gradually, like noticing a friend emerging from a crowd, Jim realised that he was looking at land. A low, flat coast lay grey-green in the haze. 'Land! I see land!'

'Welcome to Africa.'

The main channel was marked by a ghostly parade of ships—bulk carriers, container vessels and rusty old cargo freighters heading up-river to Calabar.

Will aimed for a secondary channel, and the numbers on the sonar began jumping erratically as the water shallowed, deepened, shallowed again. A sudden squall swept heavy rain across the estuary. It fell so hard they couldn't see the bow. Thunder cracked nearby. Lightning blazed. The squall passed, racing out to sea.

The wind slackened as the river narrowed. 'Run below and get the insect repellent from the medicine locker.'

Jim returned just in time. Mosquitoes swarmed the cockpit, whining in their ears. 'Slather it on,' said Will.

Suddenly Will spun the wheel and *Hustle* leaned clumsily into a sharp turn. Will pointed, and Jim saw floating just beneath the surface a submerged tree trunk as thick as a telephone pole.

'Missed!'

Heading upriver, checking the GPS and the depth finder, Will said, 'We're looking for a creek.'

Jim shielded his eyes from the hazy glare and scanned the low, green, featureless shore, where the trees grew right into the water.

'Is the creek buoyed?'

'There'll be a stake or two, if we're lucky . . . There!'

Will spun the wheel and *Hustle* nosed into semidarkness. Giant trees walled the sides. There was no wind. The air was thick, hot and hard to breathe. Will steered cautiously down the middle and throttled back to dead slow. The boat moved in near silence. After weeks on the open sea, Jim felt the close-dwelling walls of trees loom oppressively.

'A little creepy, isn't it?' said Will.

Ahead, the trees thinned at last. Jim caught glimpses of dull sky and finally the creek emptied into a broad lagoon. A village of stilt houses simmered in the afternoon heat, lifeless, except for the smoke that drifted over tin roofs. They dropped anchor a quarter of a mile across the water. The place looked deserted.

'Where is everybody?'

'The men are fishing. The women are indoors. Nobody but a damn fool goes out in the sun.'

Canoes and skiffs littered a mud beach beside the wooden pier. Some children gathered and Jim inspected them in the binoculars. Stick children, skin and bones, the smallest naked, the older ones in scraps of cloth, all barefoot. Suddenly they scattered. An outboard-powered canoe nosed out of a narrow tributary and headed for the pier.

A shapely young woman in a tight white dress ran down to the water, shielding her eyes with one hand and waving towards *Hustle* with the other.

'Well, I'll be damned,' said Will. 'Give me the glasses.'

'You know her?'

'Looks like I'm forgiven.'

'For what?'

'Leaving . . .'

Will passed Jim the binoculars. Jim adjusted the spread to his eyes as the woman hitched her skirt over her thighs and climbed down into the canoe. 'She's eating a lot better than those skinny kids. Who is she?'

'Old friend.'

She stood in the canoe, steadying herself on the shoulder of one of the men. The straps of her silver backpack tugged at her breasts. 'Jesus, Will, she doesn't look old enough to be that old a friend.'

Will shook his head. 'Strange.'

'What's strange?' Everything about the broad lagoon looked strange to Jim's eye—the deserted wooden shacks, the listing pier, the dark mass of the mangroves, the green, oil-streaked water.

'Strange that she's still hanging around here. I thought she lit out for Lagos. She sure didn't buy that dress here.'

'Will, I'm going to run ashore. Check out the flights.'

'Flights? From what airport?'

'It's late. I don't want to get stuck in the dark. Sooner I get going, the better.'

'OK, if you think you can handle it. Got any cash?'

Jim pulled out the wallet he'd stuffed into the pocket of his jeans.

'Don't flash your roll. Take fives—only fives. No twenties. And whatever you do, don't drink the water. They've got fleas swimming in it that will give you river blindness.' Will handed him a can of insect repellent. 'Better spray on some more. Mosquitoes carry malaria—you got your malaria shot?'

Even Shannon had laughed at all the shots Jim had had before he left. But he was glad of it now; this poison green swamp looked like a giant stew pot for every infection known to medical science.

Will helped him inflate the rubber dinghy and snubbed it close with the painter while Jim fitted the oars. When he started to shove off, Will held the rope. 'A word of advice about our Nigerian hosts. A Nigerian would rather shout than whisper. But what sounds like a bar brawl at home, here is just two pals saying hello.'

'Like guys yelling in the locker room.'

'Exactly.'

'Billy!' the girl called from the canoe. 'Billy C.'

'Who's Billy C?'

'Nickname.' Will glanced at the approaching canoe. 'Main thing is, never show fear—hang on a minute. You might as well say hello to Margaret.'

Margaret scrambled aboard, giggling and greeting Will with lipstick kisses on his cheeks. 'Billy. Billy. Billy.'

Jim hardly registered that the silent men in her boat immediately pushed off and motored away. Margaret was practically falling out of the dress. Her skin was very black and framed a friendly smile that gleamed like ice.

Will introduced Jim as 'my shipmate'.

'Hello, muscle man,' Margaret said in an English accent.

She leaned down towards Jim in the dinghy and extended a plump hand. The electric jolt of her skin and her generous décolletage were acute reminders that it had been six long weeks since he had even seen a woman.

'Nice to meet you, Margaret. I have to go. See you later, Will.'

She squeezed his hand with a wistful 'Later'.

Jim pushed off from *Hustle*'s high side, dipped the oars in the water and rowed clumsily towards the distant pier.

It was a hot pull over the still lagoon—long enough for a variety of erotic what-if scenarios to gallop through his mind. Margaret would fit any man's idea of adventure to a T.

As he looped the dinghy's bowline round a weathered piling, the rickety structure of the pier began to shake. He looked up to see four tall, gaunt teenagers. Machetes dangled from their waists. Their feet were bare, their plaid shirts were patched, and the cuffs of their trousers in tatters. The handles of their machetes were wrapped in frayed electrical tape, but the blades gleamed as silvery as the sharpest knife in Will Spark's orderly tool chest.

Jim looked up into the nearest face. 'Hey, how you doing?'

'Five dollar.'

'What?'

'You hear. Five dollar.'

Jim spoke slowly and loudly. 'I don't follow what you're saying.'

The answers came back fast and loud. Through the accents he heard a phrase they were repeating over and over.

'*Landing* fee?'

'Pay,' yelled one, sticking out his free hand, and his friends started chanting, 'Pay. Pay. Pay.'

Jim shot a glance across the lagoon to *Hustle*. Will was following the young woman down the companionway.

'Pay. Pay. Pay.'

I'm getting mugged, Jim thought, his temper rising. He jumped without warning, using his arms to pull himself up and bound onto the pier in a single motion. The two in front backed up a step, nervously fingering their weapons. They were emaciated, their skeletal chests barely as broad as his arms, and he saw fear in their eyes.

Then he stumbled. The pier felt like it was rolling under his feet. After six weeks on the moving boat, his slow-to-adjust inner ear was betraying his sense of balance on land.

They moved closer. One who had yet to speak demanded, 'You pay a five-dollar landing fee. It is the custom.'

Four against one. They had machetes. *Don't get killed for five dollars.* He kept his roll in his pocket as he peeled off one of the bills.

Out shot another hand. 'Five dollar.'

'I paid you. Get out of my way.'

They pointed their machetes at the rubber dinghy.

One kid explained, 'You pay five dollar. We protect your boat.'

Jim produced another five. Then he walked through them, towards the village. The entire place seemed to be nothing more than twenty shacks on stilts. Maybe the main village was further inland. There was a dirt road of sorts, which indicated that some vehicles had been through here at some point. The land was still rolling under him and he was still wobbly when the road forked. He followed it right. It narrowed and petered out at the edge of another swampy creek.

He walked slowly back. The left fork looked no more promising. Then he thought he heard music. A far-off pulse in the thick, hot atmosphere. So he took the left fork and walked for fifteen minutes. The land began to rise and the mangroves gave way to ordinary-looking trees. He heard people calling out and laughing.

Now he smelt food cooking in the still air. Climbing a steep rise, he found himself on a ridge. Below was a shallow ravine where scores of people were digging with picks and shovels. The cooking smells came from an open fire, where three women were roasting sweet potatoes on sticks. There was no village in sight, just a raw gouge in the earth, which looked like it had been dug that morning.

They had exposed a buried pipe. People were streaming down the slopes carrying buckets, jerry cans and plastic pails.

Jim was still trying to figure out what they were doing when suddenly a cheer went up. People started pushing and shoving, waving their buckets and pails. A sharp smell rose from the crowded pit— the nostril-pricking stink of gasoline.

A man carrying a brimming bucket in each hand climbed the slope nearby. Jim backed away quickly and bumped into someone. An old man had come up behind him.

'Excuse me, sir.'

'Sorry,' said Jim. 'My fault. You speak English?'

'Yes, of course.' He had an accent like Will's friend Margaret's.

His hair was white. He wore a rope for a belt and a Shell Oil cap.

'What are they doing?'

'Scooping,' said the old man. 'The white man's pipe runs under the land. They've made a little puncture to scoop some petrol.'

'That's a *gasoline* pipeline? They'll get killed if it blows up.'

'People have to survive. They mix it with oil to run a generator, or sell it to someone who owns an outboard motor.'

That explained where everyone had gone. The adventure seemed to have emptied every village for miles around.

'Is there a way I could get to an airport?'

'There is no airport.'

'A boat, maybe?'

'You might find someone with a motor canoe. Go to the lagoon.'

'I just came from there. No one's there.'

'When this is done, they'll come back. I wonder, sir, if you would have a dollar?'

Jim was reaching into his pocket when suddenly the eager shouts turned to cries of alarm. Flame leapt from a puddle of gasoline onto a man's shirt and he ran, screaming, while the fiery puddle spilled towards the pipe.

The burning man slipped and men pounced on him, beating the flames out with bare hands. Others kicked dirt on the fire. There was a moment of utter silence, then nervous laughter rippled through the crowd.

'We live,' the old man said, 'by the mercy of God.'

Jim turned away. Anyone who would risk being burned to death to steal gasoline was stuck in the Niger Delta worse than he was. The old man was still glued to his side. Jim pressed one of his five-dollar bills into his hand.

'God bless you, sir. God bless you and yours.'

Jim hurried back towards the pier, sweating in the heat.

One of the machete gang had climbed into *Hustle*'s dinghy.

The kid with the best English said, 'What do you want?'

'I need a ride upriver to Calabar.'

'How much you pay?'

Will had told him that daily income in the delta averaged thirty cents. Jim guessed a ferry price of twenty dollars.

The kid hooted with laughter. 'What's twenty dollars to a big man like you? Your family rich?'

'No.'

'They live in a big house?'

'I live in a little apartment.'

'They drive big cars. SUV cars.'

'I drive a goddamned Honda,' said Jim.

All three started shouting at once. 'You take our oil. You pay us with pollution. You kill our fish.'

'Wait a minute. I'm not the oil company. I'm just trying to go home.'

'Does your family miss you?'

Suddenly, they were extra alert, all four intent on his answer. Was he paranoid'? Or did they sound like kidnappers assessing his ransom value? He realised with a sinking heart that driving a cheap car didn't make him any less a jackpot to kids in bare feet.

A horn blast whipped their heads around. There, down the shoreline, something large was emerging from a creek overhung by mangrove trees. Salvation in the form of an ungainly workboat like the offshore rig tenders he and Will had dodged as they motored through the oil fields.

The workboat *Nellie H*, according to her smoke-stained stern, backed into the pier, which leaned and trembled from the strain. On her bow stood a soldier in uniform cradling a rifle.

A handful of black men trooped off the boat and wandered towards the huts. A heavily bulked-up white guy called after them. 'OK, boys, we'll be back for you in three days.'

'Hey, what's happening?' said Jim to the white guy.

'What the hell are you doing here?'

'Came in on that sailboat,' said Jim, extending his hand. 'Jim Leighton.'

'Frank Perry.' He looked Jim over. 'You a weightlifter, Jim?'

'A little,' said Jim. 'Not like you.'

'Man, I'm a mess. When I get home, it's going to take me six months to shape up for a pageant.'

Jim nodded in sympathy. Competing in a body builders' pageant required the classic Mr Olympia dimensions, which meant that Frank would have to burn forty pounds of fat into ten of muscle.

'Cast off!' boomed the loudhailer.

'Gotta go. You take care, dude.'

'Where are you heading?'

'Port Harcourt.'

'Could I catch a ride? I'm trying to get home.'

'Up to the old man,' the roustabout said dubiously. 'I gotta warn you, he is one pissed-off skipper. I'll take you up to him.'

Jim jumped into the boat and hurried forward with Frank Perry. 'Why's he pissed off?'

'We blew two cylinder heads 'cause the chief got drunk and the tide's going out and there's a hell of a squall coming in—buckets of rain, sixty-knot wind.'

The 'old man' was about Jim's age. He was slumped at the steering wheel, staring at the southern sky. Bloodshot eyes suggested that the 'chief' had not been drinking alone.

'No rides. Company policy.'

'I'll pay. I'm really stuck, Captain.'

'You can't pay me enough to get fired.'

'Hey, Cap,' said Perry. 'Give the man a break. How'd you like to be stuck in this shithole?'

'Perry, get out of my face . . . You come in on that fancy sailboat?'

'Yes, sir. We sailed from Barbados. I was supposed to crew to Rio, but the owner changed his mind.'

'Rio in Brazil? I'll say he changed his mind. What do you mean "crew"? You work for him?'

Jim decided that the workboat captain would not regard a personal trainer as a fellow working stiff. 'It's a job.'

'What's he paying you?'

Jim lied. 'Fifty bucks a day and a ticket home. From Brazil.'

'Jeee-zus . . . OK. OK. Give Perry a hand casting off.'

'Thank you, Captain. Thanks a lot. Can I get my stuff?'

'We're outta here in ten minutes. No way I'm crossing that bar at low tide.'

'I'll be right back.' Jim jumped into the rubber dinghy and rowed as fast as he could across the lagoon. His head swimming from the heat, he pulled himself onto *Hustle*, tied on the dinghy and leapt down the companionway.

Margaret lay on the cabin floor.

Jim was stunned again by her raw beauty. Her dress was hitched up her thighs. For a crazy instant he wondered if she had changed her clothes. Changed from the tight white dress into a combination white skirt and red blouse. But he was dreaming. Wishing. he red was her blood. So much blood that she had to be dead.

'Will?'

The only audible sound was the distant rumble of the *Nellie H*'s engines. Her captain was revving them, chafing to get under way.

The woman's mouth was wide open as if to scream. *What had the old man done?*

'Will?'

'In here, kid,' came the answer from Will's stateroom in the back of the boat.

Will was lying on his bunk, pointing a short-barrelled gun at the door. A sawn-off shotgun, Jim realised. Who would murder a beautiful young woman with a shotgun?

'Can you give me a hand, Jim?' Will was nearly sobbing. 'Pull the knife out.'

Jim looked again and this time saw a long knife sticking out of

Will's chest. He bent over the old man. Will was white from shock or blood loss. His pupils were dilated and he was gasping for air.

'I can't believe I fell for the oldest trick in the book.'

'I'll get a doctor.'

'There's no time. Pull the knife out.'

'I can't just pull it out. What if I cut an artery?' The blade had pierced Will where his breast met his shoulder.

Will bit his lips. 'I'll take the chance, for Christ's sake. Pull it out. It's killing me. I can't breathe.'

Left side. An inch from his heart? 'I can't. There's an oil-rig tender in the lagoon. Americans. They can radio in a helicopter. Fly you to a hospital.'

'*No!* They'll find me in hospital. They'll kill me.'

The *Nellie H* blew her horn. Jim whirled from Will's bunk and scrambled up the companionway. He thrust his head out of the hatch just as the rig tender began to depart. Perry waved frantically from the wheelhouse.

'*Jim!*' Will called. They said you saw your past flash by when you died; what Jim Leighton saw was his life ploughing across the lagoon, trailing a heavy wake.

'Run for it, Jim,' Will yelled. 'I'm a goner.'

Jim clung to the cockpit sill, watching the ponderous curl of the *Nellie H*'s wake roll towards the sailboat.

Then he saw its deadly threat.

He plunged down the companionway ladder, picturing the effect on the knife when the track of the passing vessel seized *Hustle* and threw her violently from side to side.

The old man was still conscious, eyes murky. Jim knelt beside the bunk and cradled him in his arms, hoping to cushion him from the rocking. No good. As the boat leaned into the cavity of the wake, Will's body shifted hard. Jim reached for the knife and closed his hand tightly round the handle. He braced every muscle in his body, counted to three, and yanked up.

Steel ground on bone. Will screamed.

The blade slid free. Jim flew backwards and crashed into the bulkhead before the rolling water tipped *Hustle* in the opposite direction and he fell face down on Will's bunk.

Fearfully, he watched the blood flow from Will's chest. The skin around the one-inch wound puckered, oozing red like a lipstick kiss. Jim noticed with faint hope that the blood was not spewing, this was not the rhythmic pumping from a sliced artery.

As gently as he could, he lifted Will to inspect his back. His skin was unblemished. The blade hadn't gone through. But God only knew what was going on inside the man.

'Jim,' Will groaned. 'Douse me with alcohol.'

'What?'

'Goddamned Africa. Every germ in the world. There's a bottle in the big medicine kit.'

He screamed when Jim dribbled the alcohol onto his chest, and Jim stopped automatically. But Will moaned, 'Sweet Jesus, get it over with. They probably cleaned fish with that goddamned thing. *Do it!*'

As Jim poured the alcohol into the wound, Will's whole body convulsed and he pummelled Jim with his fists.

Jim laid Will down again and the old man lay still, his breath whistling through his teeth. 'You have to pack the wound,' he said. 'Go to the medical locker. Get Iodoform gauze.'

Jim pawed frantically through the locker. 'I got it!'

'Stuff it in—Oh, Christ! . . . Good. Well done. OK, we have to get out of here. Before her people come back.'

'We have to find a doctor.'

Will closed his eyes. 'A doctor won't do us any good in a Nigerian jail,' he whispered. 'Do you want to defend yourself against murder charges in a lawless state?'

'Me? What about you?'

'I'll have worse problems. They'll kidnap me out of a hospital in twenty-four hours. Listen to me. It was self-defence. They sent her to kidnap me. Now help me up on deck. We've got to get out of here.'

He moved as if to swing his legs off his bunk, but fell back, sucking air. 'I can't move, Jim. It's up to you.'

THERE WAS NO TIME to waste booming the dinghy aboard. Jim tied it to a cleat, then hurried forward to figure out how to raise the anchor. Closer inspection revealed an up–down toggle that reversed the windlass. The chain began clanking aboard, dragging a stinking coat of mud and slime across the deck.

When the anchor itself finally emerged, it took Jim two tries to lock it into place. By then the boat was drifting towards the pier and he realised too late that he should have started the engine first.

When he tried the starter, it wouldn't fire. Again he pushed the starter button. Nothing—he had forgotten to flip the fuel switch. He cranked the starter again, and the diesel rumbled to life.

He steered for the narrow opening through which they had entered the lagoon. Under power, in these close quarters, the boat seemed extraordinarily long. She was slow to respond to the steering wheel and the creek mouth was coming up fast. Then the trees were hanging close and darkening the sky. *Hustle's* exhaust echoed in the tunnel-like space.

He was distracted by motion down the companionway. The dead woman seemed to be moving—her bloodied chest carpeted with flies. How long would they have to carry her body? He couldn't throw her overboard so close to the village. He'd have to wait until they were far out at sea.

Suddenly, directly ahead, loomed the ominous cylinder of a huge, waterlogged tree trunk. Jim spun the wheel, but it was too late. A loud *thunk* slammed through the decks and *Hustle* staggered.

What had he done? Had he damaged the hull? Terrified of sinking, he ran down the companionway, edged past the dead woman, and raced forward to the forepeak. He grabbed a flashlight and probed the cramped space, praying that the beam wouldn't reflect the gleam of water. Nothing. He cocked his ear, listening. Nothing. No gushing water; no dents or cracks. He couldn't believe that the hull would survive such a hit unscathed. He pulled up the floorboards and shone the light in the bilge. There was water, but no more than he had last seen under the floorboards.

Lucky, lucky, lucky.

Then he heard an engine approaching—like the high-pitched whine of the outboard-powered canoe he'd last seen heading out of the creek. Jim ran back through the main salon, climbed the companionway and looked out. The sound was close, coming from ahead. To the left he saw an indent in the bank. He swung cautiously into the opening, which led a hundred feet into the mangroves and then stopped at a wall of trees. An instant later, he felt the keel plough into the mud and then the sailboat was standing stock-still in the near darkness cast by the forest canopy.

Jim shut the engine down. How stupid could he be? In his panic he had trapped himself in a dead-end canal. As the outboard-powered canoe pulled abreast, a glance in the inlet would reveal *Hustle's* mast rearing straighter than the trees. He looked up. Could he pull the vines over the boat?

What had he told Will when Will had razzed him about bulking up? Muscle came in handy. Do it! He scrambled up the backstay, climbing the wire cable hand over hand. Fifteen feet above the deck, he let go with his right hand and lunged for a thick, leafy vine.

The vine and several attached to it swung closer to the mast. Giddy with fear and flying on adrenaline, he almost laughed at the sight he must make, suspended between the backstay and the vine like a crucified monkey.

The canoe pulled abreast of the inlet. Jim could see three men: one standing in the bow, one driving and one seated between them. The driver glanced down the inlet. The canoe flashed past and was gone.

When the noise of the motor had faded to a quiet buzz, Jim let go of the vine and slid down the backstay, burning his hands.

He started *Hustle*'s engine and engaged reverse. The propeller churned, then, with a heart-stopping series of hesitations, she began to move. Bumping bottom with her keel and dragging her spreaders through the branches, she backed out of the inlet. As soon as she reached the main channel, Jim shoved the throttle forward and drove her as fast as she would go towards the Calabar River.

Quite suddenly, the equatorial night was closing in. It was dark among the trees, but the slot of sky he could see above the creek began to glow from the distant offshore oil-well flares. Finally he saw the creek open into the Calabar River. He steered for the string of lighted buoys that marked the channel through the flat expanse of the estuary to the Atlantic. An expanse, he knew from their morning passage, that was shallow and treacherous.

The fairway buoys appeared sporadically, but ships' lights moving downstream gave him a clue to the deepest water. He could follow a ship out to the main channel, but what if the river pilots saw the sailboat? If they knew of a police manhunt, they'd radio his position.

He was getting ahead of himself. No one had seen the dead girl yet. Even if her friends realised she was missing, nothing he had seen ashore suggested it was the sort of place you dialled 911.

I'm overthinking this, he told himself. Just sail away. No one would know until he was a hundred miles at sea. Unless, of course, Will's mysterious 'they' really *had* sent the girl. Jim was so scared he couldn't think straight.

He ran below for *Sailing Directions* and brought the book up to the cockpit. The channel that Will had used was described as a minor channel, and local knowledge was strongly recommended. No way Jim could pilot it at night. But a secondary channel, too shallow for large vessels, crossed the wide flats where the river met the sea. Jim switched on the depth finder and steered a new course that would bring him across the main channel to the less populated route.

He crossed behind two ships, a tall container ship and a low-slung tanker. Suddenly, lightning flashed and Jim saw a third, smaller vessel between them, moving fast. A gun was mounted on the bow. A patrol boat? They hadn't seen him yet, because the sailboat was so low to the water. Surely they were tracking with radar, but Will had claimed that *Hustle* was 'invisible'. She'd better be.

He spotted a buoy marking the secondary channel and turned south, towards the sea. He held that course for more than an hour. Once he glimpsed the patrol boat's silhouette, tearing north at high speed. Then things quietened down and the sailboat was alone except for the distant ships plodding seawards. Ahead, he saw a lighted oil well, to the left of his channel. To the right he saw an angry white line on the water, and muted thunder confirmed that he was seeing surf—huge Atlantic waves breaking on Outer Reef. Now all he had to do was get past Outer Reef, skirt the oil fields and break for the open sea.

He locked the wheel and went below to check on Will. The old man was sleeping. His lips looked parched, so Jim dribbled a little water on them and then more as Will licked hungrily.

'What's happening?'

'Passing Outer Reef.'

'Well done, kid! . . . Which side?'

'We're east of it, in the second channel.'

'Steer clear of the oil rigs on the left. Have you seen any patrols?'

'One.'

'Call me if they get close.'

'You bet,' said Jim. That's all they needed: Will haemorrhaging all over the cockpit.

He took a fresh water bottle up to the helm. A couple of miles to his left the oil field sparkled with hundreds of lights. To his right, heavy seas pummelled Outer Reef. He steered a little closer to give the oil field a wider berth, and passed the reef. When next he looked, several miles of water lay between him and the foaming breakers.

His heart jumped. A helicopter was racing out from the now invisible shore. Helplessly, he watched it home in on *Hustle* as if they were attached by a wire. Then it stopped, midair, and hovered over Outer Reef, watching the channels.

Jim stopped the engine. The boat began to roll on the swell. He went back down to the after cabin.

The old man had fallen back to sleep, but the boat's clumsy roll woke him. Groggy and confused, he asked, 'What's up?'

'Helicopter. What do I do? We're three miles past Outer Reef.'

'Right . . . Listen to me. You have to fox their radar.'

'Radar? You said radar can't see us.'

'Airborne radar can. Looking down, they can pick up the steel in the engine. Now . . . Remember the wreck I showed you on the way in?'

'The masts.'

'Right. Drive the boat among the masts. Make your approach from downwind, real slow. Tie onto something solid and let her drift back a few yards. Keep watching your depth finder.'

Jim ran back to the cockpit. The wind had turned southerly and he smelt the wreck before he saw the masts—a coarse, lively odour of seaweed and barnacles exposed by the tide receding down the rusty flanks of the sunken ship. The masts jutted from the water in a dark and menacing cluster. When he slowed the engine, he heard the sea sluicing furiously in and out of the steel pillars.

How in hell was he going to get close enough to attach a rope without smashing into the wreck? The boat was lurching around on the swell, almost uncontrollable.

A heavy vibration shook the air. The helicopter was moving again in a broad circle over the water.

Somehow Jim had to point the boat and throw a line at the same time. Then it struck him that Will himself would never tie the boat to the mast. Will would have run in close circles. But he didn't trust Jim, a novice helmsman, to manoeuvre close enough to blend the radar signature of *Hustle*'s engine with the steel wreck without smacking into it.

Jim decided he liked those odds much better. He looked up at the helicopter thumping around the horizon. It was a good hiding trick Will had devised. A local helicopter pilot would be familiar with the wreck and recognise its radar position. He just had to keep the sailboat in its sphere until the helicopter gave up and went home.

But the swell was rising and falling sharply, which made controlling the boat extremely difficult.

Hustle was caught suddenly off-balance. The helm went dead in his hands and she made a nightmarish lurch. Jim felt something crunch underneath—the keel was scraping the wreck. He held his breath. If *Hustle*'s keel hung up—or worse, her rudder—the next swell would throw the boat into the masts and pin her in them until the swell pounded her to pieces. But she rose on the next sea and the propeller bit, driving her to temporary safety.

Jim battled the swell for an hour, repeating manoeuvres to hold the boat within the target range of the masts—all the while praying that the helicopter would give up.

Suddenly, it dropped to the water. A pinprick of light below it revealed the familiar shape of the patrol boat. Not only were they not stopping, the crews were coordinating to expand the search.

Jim circled closer to the masts. He saw the lights of the helicopter and the patrol boat diverge, the helicopter swinging towards the main channel, the patrol boat heading south on a course that would take it within eyeball range of the wreck.

A red flash lit the sky behind the boat.

They're shooting, thought Jim. They've seen us.

A second flash seared the clouds. A third turned the sky vermilion red. An immense din rumbled across the water, three massive explosions spaced like the flashes. A pillar of fire rose over the land.

The helicopter and the patrol boat wheeled towards the shore. Jim immediately steered away from the masts, regained the channel and headed south at full speed.

'What happened?' Will yelled. Somehow he had managed to unlock one of the ports that opened into the cockpit.

'Hang on, Will.' Jim was lining up a course between the lights of two distant oil fields. Then he set the autohelm and went below.

'What happened?'

'Something blew up.'

'Oil rig?'

'No. I think it's back behind the village. They were stealing gas from a pipeline. It could have been them.'

'Happens all the time, poor bastards. Where are the patrols?'

'It looks like they went to help.'

'God bless 'em,' said Will. 'Jim, I'm afraid I have to ask you to dump our friend.'

'What do you mean?'

'You know what I mean. I can't move. You have to throw Margaret's body overboard.'

Which meant picking it up. 'I won't do it,' said Jim.

'You won't and I can't,' Will replied slowly. 'But may I suggest it will be easier before she rots?'

Jim looked forward to the main salon. What remained white of her dress glowed like an angry glance.

'You've done yourself proud tonight, Jim. But you have to finish the job. There is no way we can sail all the way to South America with a rotting corpse.'

'We're sailing to *North* America,' Jim said firmly, and went to finish the job.

Will called after him. 'Wrap her in one of the big garbage bags.'

'I already thought of that.'

'But don't seal it. You don't want her to float.'

He hadn't thought of that.

WILL HAD WARNED him repeatedly about not wasting fuel. So when the wind swung, Jim raised the main and unfurled the jib and set a course south. Once the sails were pulling reasonably well, he shut down the engine, and in the deep silence that ensued, felt the boat come alive again. He sat in the cockpit all night, afraid to go below with the big ships converging on the oil fields.

At dawn he was stunned to see, looming on his left, two mountains, shockingly steep compared to the flat, swampy Niger coast. Jim located a drawing in *Sailing Directions* that identified the peaks as capping Isla de Bioko, which belonged to equatorial Guinea. Quickly, he turned the boat away from the island. When it was a safe twenty miles behind, he altered course, aiming for the point 900 miles ahead where Africa jutted into the Atlantic.

Will woke and called his name.

'How are you?' Jim asked. The old man looked awful.

'Hurting like hell. She did something to my lung . . . You have to douse my shoulder again. Infection will kill me.'

'Let me see if the bleeding has stopped.'

Jim stared at the wound, astonished. Some time in the night, Will had got up, walked to the first-aid kit in the main salon and repacked the wound. The pain must have been torture.

'I'm impressed. It's not bleeding.'

Will said, 'Listen, Jim. You have to hydrate me. There's a ton of saline and glucose bags in the medicine locker. You know how to hook up an IV?'

'I've had plenty of needles stuck in my arm. I'll figure it out.'

Jim hung the plastic bag from the clamp that held Will's ceiling compass. Then he wrapped a short length of elastic shock cord round Will's arm like a tourniquet. A fat vein popped up inside Will's elbow. He swabbed the skin with alcohol and attacked the vein with a sterile needle.

The boat's constant motion was a problem. A sudden lurch took him by surprise and he accidentally pushed in too deeply.

'Margaret was gentler than you are, for Christ's sake.'

Jim got it finally, taped the catheter to Will's forearm, and hurried to attach the clear tubing. The solution began to flow and Will sagged back on the sheets.

'Now,' Jim said, 'you're going to help me work out a course straight across the Atlantic Ocean to Florida.'

'They will kill us in Florida,' Will said flatly. 'And they won't bungle it like the Nigerians. They'll send professionals.'

Jim sat on the edge of the bed. 'Is it possible,' he asked gently, 'that Margaret stabbed you for her own personal reasons?'

Will's laugh came out half snort, half painful gasp. 'Crime of passion? Are you kidding?'

'You said you left her.'

'I didn't do anything terrible to the poor girl. We had a few laughs and then I left. She told me yesterday that afterwards she hooked up with the captain of an anchor handler. Jim, this is life. People do what they have to. They offered her enough money to do it.'

'If "they" are real.'

'As real as death,' muttered Will. His eyes were glazing over. 'I need morphine.'

Jim gave him two tablets. 'Sleep tight.'

It had taken a week to sail 900 miles into the Gulf of Guinea. So if the wind held, maybe another week to sail out. A week to get some rest for the long, long haul back across the Atlantic Ocean. Wearily, he went to email Shannon.

III

UNSHORED, HARBOURLESS IMMENSITIES

'Admiral Rugoff! So pleasing to hear your voice again. Your daughter is better? Excellent. Yes, yes . . .young people have to find themselves. Now, Admiral . . .'

Lloyd McVay described Will Spark's sloop, Will himself, and Jim Leighton, then gave the admiral Andy Nickels's guesstimate of its position in the Gulf of Guinea.

Rugoff—formerly admiral of the Soviet Navy's merchant fleet and now president of WorldSpan, Russia's largest privately held shipping conglomerate—said, 'It is a very big ocean, my friend. But perhaps my ships will get lucky. What do you want done with the yacht?'

'I want the yacht intact and Will Spark alive.'

'The young man?'

'Of no consequence.'

'How valuable are they?' the Russian asked.

McVay was confident that the admiral's greed would be tempered by good sense. 'Between you and me, Admiral, you can name your price.'

He punched END, and looked at Val. 'Your ears pricked up.'

'What or who was "of no consequence"?'

'Spark's crew.'

'Dad, he's just a kid along for the ride.'

'Who knows what ideas Spark has put in his head.'

'All the more reason to keep him in the circle.'

Lloyd McVay shot an angry look at his daughter.

Val McVay returned a self-contained stare, defying him to challenge her. 'If you had read his files as I have, you would conclude that Will Spark always teams up with some malleable young person whom he can control. It doesn't take a genius to imagine that if Will Spark happened to fall overboard, Jim Leighton might know plenty about Sentinel—such as where Will put it.'

McVay snapped his fingers for a phone. 'Get me Admiral Rugoff again . . . Admiral, I'm sure it doesn't matter, but the nervous Nellies on my staff want the young man, too.'

Val was shaking her head at her computer.

'Now what?' McVay asked when he was done with the Russian.

'Jim and Shannon are not emailing each other.'

'Jim and Shannon?'

'We've been monitoring RileySpa.com since I got Jim's address. Nothing.'

'RileySpa is owned by Shannon's parents. Young lovers might well maintain separate email accounts for privacy. May I presume that you are also searching for those accounts?'

'I am, but it takes time. There are two thousand five hundred and forty-eight separate addresses registered to the RileySpa website. They offer their employees free email and every damned one of them uses seven screen names.'

SHANNON'S REACTION when she got Jim's email was to dial 911. She had to tell someone who could help that Jim was in trouble. But who could help him hundreds of miles from shore in international waters?

She showed her father Jim's email. 'Daddy, is there some way you could get the navy to help him?'

'Never happen. Even if an American citizen could call up the US navy, what would I tell them? The reason this guy I know needs rescuing is that he's sailing with a man who shot a Nigerian woman? Sorry, hon.' He turned back to the email. 'Hey, this reads like he's home free.'

'If he can sail the boat all by himself.'

'I can't believe they shot somebody. Must have been—'

'Jim didn't shoot anybody.'

'Honey, you've really got to wonder what Jim's mixed up in.'

Shannon was worried sick.

WILL SPARK'S 1987 edition of *Ocean Passages of the World* looked like it had endured most of them. The navy-blue cover was rubbed smooth, with threads showing dirty white through the cloth. The pages were thumbed and coffee-stained. On the title page, Will had printed the names of his three yachts, *Cordelia*, *Runner* and *Hustle*.

Chapter One began matter-of-factly: '*Ocean Passages of the World* is written for use in planning deep-sea voyages.' It made the challenge sound doable. To exit the Gulf of Guinea, Jim had to reverse their inbound route. At Cape Palmas on the southwest tip of the bulge of Africa, he would hang a shallow right and sail northwest to the Cape Verde Islands. From there, it was 2,980 miles to New York.

Except it was winter and *Ocean Passages* said that in winter the New York route was beset by gale winds, heavy seas and bitter cold. He found a southern route to Florida that looked warm and peaceful by contrast—a sun-drenched novice's voyage he would find all the easier because the trade wind and the North Equatorial Current were both going his way.

Ocean Passages gave him the courses to sail to each waypoint and he learned to punch them into both the mast-mounted GPS and Will's handhelds. Which meant he could set the autohelm and check his accuracy with the electronics.

So it was with a sense of optimism that he next emailed Shannon.

Things have settled a little. Will's still out of it. But I'm fine. And I'm coming home! I know I can do it. I can navigate by the book. By the charts. And by the electronics. I can handle the boat as long as I keep it simple. No fancy sail changes. I'll just stick to the roll-out jib and the easily reefed main. The one thing I've got pretty good at is steering . . .

Often, he took over from the autohelm to practise—particularly at night by the stars. On this western track, paralleling the distant shores of Nigeria, Togo, Ghana and Liberia, he watched Orion rise directly behind him after sunset.

The fact is, if worst comes to worst and Will doesn't make it, I can probably do it all alone.

He deleted 'probably'.

WHEN SHANNON RILEY began to investigate Will Spark, she first pulled his membership file from the RileySpa computer, which stored the addresses of inactive members. His membership photograph showed an older, white-haired man in glasses looking away from the camera. He had given his address as the Larchmont Yacht Club, which right away made her wonder why he had joined a Bridgeport health club, thirty miles away in a lower-rent area.

Most members paid their monthly dues by credit card. Will Spark had paid cash. He had left the space for his business address blank, so too the notify-in-case-of-emergency line.

None of this really meant anything.

Shannon telephoned the Larchmont Yacht Club and asked for Will Spark's business address. The yacht club did not give out such information, she was told frostily.

'Is he still a member?' Shannon asked. The yacht club did not give out membership information, period. The person hung up on her.

JIM WAS CATNAPPING in the cockpit, waking regularly to check for tankers, when around noon his attention was drawn to a column of rain a quarter of a mile from the boat. He thought it was another shower, but it was spinning as it descended from a black cloud.

A second whirling column of water rose up from the sea. The two columns joined, tripled in height and thickness and began to dart on the sea's glassy surface like a hungry tongue.

As Jim started the engine, the waterspout came straight at the sailboat. Jim tried to steer away from it as it tore through the sea leaving wild white water in its wake and racing off towards the horizon. It had almost disappeared when it split vertically into two spouts that ran back at him like a pair of giant legs and flanked the boat. Water cascaded onto the decks as Jim shoved the throttle, but the engine was already running wide open.

The legs merged a hundred yards ahead of the boat and formed a single column again. Suddenly it collapsed, half its water tumbling back into the ocean, half vanishing in cloud.

> Dear Shannon,
> I just saw a waterspout. Awesome. I had always assumed waterspouts were mythic phenomena like mermaids.
> I'm getting very lonely. Maybe because I don't get sleep running the boat. I feel like some homeless guy who keeps getting woken up by the cops. Move along, pal! Trim the jib, reef the main, look out for that supertanker.

He sent the message and found an email from Shannon waiting for him, titled, 'Who is Will?!?'

> I've been looking into Will's background and I'm afraid that I sent you sailing with somebody pretty mysterious, like he's a criminal or a spy or something. Maybe this wouldn't mean much, if he hadn't killed that girl. I wonder who he really is?

Jim quickly wrote back. Will might be a little crazy but they had been through a lot together. He had to set Shannon straight.

> He killed the girl in self-defence. So don't worry. I think of him as my friend. I know I don't know much about him. Though since he got stabbed I'm more inclined to believe his story about being chased. I've grown to like him very much. And don't forget he saved my life when I went overboard. As far as my safety is concerned, I'm in charge now. Even if Will is 'bent' or a thief or whatever, he's flat on his back. He can't do anything to me. And frankly, he wouldn't even if he could. We've become shipmates. So relax. I can handle this and I can handle Will.

He radioed that and checked a few minutes later for Shannon's reply.

> Just think about what I've said. Your 'shipmate' is possibly a very dangerous man. You've seen him kill somebody. And I can't find his name anywhere.

Jim went to Will's cabin and watched him sleep. The old man's sunken cheeks quivered as he breathed. Jim hoped that Shannon was wrong. But how could he be surprised? *My pal in Lagos. My pals in Calabar. Helicopter to the airport . . .*

Access codes blocked the files in Will's laptop. And his teak desk, which was built into the forward bulkhead of the main cabin, was always locked. But there was a brass key on the lanyard that secured his bosun's knife to his shorts.

Jim took the shorts, knife and all, to the main cabin and worked the key into the lock. Inside, the desk was much deeper than it appeared from the front and riddled with cubbyholes, slots and shelves. They contained a row of green clothbound books, magazine and newspaper clippings, a red cloth sack of krugerrand gold coins and an antique pocket watch.

The 'books', Jim discovered, were hard-bound accordion files in which Will had stowed letters and invoices. Jim riffled through the paperwork for the endless expenses required to keep *Hustle* afloat: jib-furler replacement in Hawaii, freezer repairs in Panama City, shackles, blocks, line, oil filters, batteries.

Jim noticed that a well-thumbed cover had peeled apart, the cloth separating from the cardboard. The file was empty but, when Jim picked it up, a folded blue paper hidden between the cloth and cardboard fell out.

It was a letter, hand-written in green ink. The opening lines told him that it was personal and he didn't want to read it. The greeting read, 'My dearest Billy'—which was what Margaret had called him. It was signed, 'Yours always, Cordelia.'

Big deal. So he'd had a girlfriend named Cordelia—which anyone could have guessed as he had named an entire boat after her—and Cordelia called him Billy. Plenty of guys named William were called Billy.

He pondered a moment. If he were going to put Shannon at ease, he had to read the damn letter, personal or not.

He had guessed right. It was a long, sad goodbye. Cordelia forgave Billy, she said, for running out on her. But she could not forgive his business—'a dirty business', she called it—and so she was saying goodbye. 'I do not set myself up as an angel, but I cannot knowingly entwine my life with a thief, which is what you are, my dear, even though I know that I will miss you far, far more than the thief will ever miss "his Cordi".'

Jim turned on Will's laptop and, when prompted for a password, typed 'Cordelia'.

Invalid.

The password prompt was blinking. He typed 'Cordi'.

Yes! He got up and stepped back to Will's cabin. Out like a light. Excited, he sat back down at Will's computer and opened his email files, which went back six years. They were mostly reports heavy on the computer lingo from Kin Yiu Lam, Choy Yee and Pather Singh, who sounded like his moletronics engineers.

Lam, Yee and Singh all referred to the microprocessor they were developing as 'the project'. Their letters were laced with requests for more research funds, which he kept on paying. Then, after four years, a new series of letters started.

Using the name Sentinel for the first time, Will applied for a research grant from the McVay Foundation for Humane Science to fund the moletronics programme at the Computing College of West Virginia. Money started coming in. But despite claims that Sentinel would revolutionise medicine, for over a year it seemed small time.

Suddenly it happened. The Foundation's chief grant officer, a woman named Val McVay, pressed Will for specifics about the sources of his software. Will dodged repeated requests. A month later, Val McVay's father, the head of the Foundation, stepped in.

The numbers were mind-boggling. Will seemed on the verge of reaping hundreds of millions of dollars. But, like his daughter, McVay pressed for more details about Will's laboratories and engineers. Their exchanges grew terse, the mood cool. Finally, McVay used the word 'withholding'. With that, the letters stopped abruptly. A year and three months ago. The same month that Will had disappeared from Jim's spinning class.

He checked on Will again. Still sleeping. Jim made his rounds on deck, had some soup and returned to Will's desk.

The antique watch was beautiful. The lid opened on a face mysterious with dials. It even showed the phases of the moon. Turning it over in his hands, Jim noticed a second lid on the back side. He popped it open. An inscription was etched on polished gold: *For Billy Cole, who 'can cure' what ails.*

Jim closed up Will's desk and put Will's key back. Before shutting down his computer, he sent an email.

Dear Shannon,
  Try 'Billy Cole'.
  I love you,
  Jim

HE AWOKE with a vague sense of disquiet. Something was wrong. He catapulted out of the hammock and up the companionway. The boat was off course. The rising sun was throwing daggers of heat from the left instead of from behind. He went to the wheel to figure out why the autohelm had gone wrong.

'Morning, sleepyhead.'

Jim whirled round. There on the cabin roof was Will Spark, looking as though his flesh had been liposuctioned from his frame.

Will's voice was reedy from disuse. 'They used to hang people who slept on watch.'

'Are you OK? You've been out for five days. I got a little water into you but I couldn't get you to eat.'

'The IV helped, thanks. Made a mess of my arm, though. Feels like you were using it for fencing practice.'

'How's the wound?'

Will's face clouded. 'Something's going on I don't like. Damned infection or something.'

'Does it hurt?'

'More than it should. That's why I think it's infected . . . Listen, now that you're finally awake, give me a hand shifting the jib car.' He pointed at a pulley that adjusted the jib. 'Your jib's too flat.'

'When I bring her back on course she'll be fine.' Jim turned to the helm.

'Leave it,' said Will. 'She's on course.'

'She is not. She's veered south thirty degrees.'

'She's on course.'

'For where?'

'Buenos Aires. Argentina.'

Dumbfounded, Jim asked, 'Why?'

'Because it's my boat.'

Jim stared a moment in disbelief. 'No,' he said finally. 'Right now, for all practical purposes, this is *our* boat.'

'I can see that playing captain has given you some delusions.'

'You got in trouble, which put me in trouble, too. This boat is our ticket out of Africa—away from that girl you shot—and this boat is going to Florida, where I'm getting off on safe American territory.'

Will looked surprised by Jim's sudden determination. And he looked, Jim noted with no little pride, like he believed him. Instead of arguing, Will retorted in a grave voice, 'If you make me sail to Florida, I'm a dead man.'

'I don't care. We're sailing to Florida.'

'You have a short memory. Who pulled you out of the drink? I saved your life, Jim.'

'I've got a much longer memory for the trouble you've got me into.'

'Please, Jim. I've got friends in Buenos Aires.'

'You had friends in Nigeria. Loved them.'

'You don't understand. You just don't—'

'That's right. I don't understand. I have no facts. Spill it, Will. What the hell are you mixed up in?'

Will started to cough. He pointed feebly at Jim's water bottle and Jim thrust it towards him.

He watched Will fumble the bottle to his mouth. 'Let me help you below. You've got to lie down. I'll bring you some soup.'

'Just hang on a minute . . . Look, I admit that I've been less than truthful with you, Jim.'

'Things like your name being Will Spark instead of Billy Cole?'

Will blinked. 'Where'd you learn that?'

Jim had said more than he intended to. 'I broke into your desk. I found your watch. "For Billy Cole"?'

Will shrugged. 'I was just trying to keep it simple.'

'So what's your name?'

'Will Spark. Do you recall Sentinel? My microprocessor?'

'Faster than a speeding bullet, years ahead of the competition. The one that's going to put all the chip factories out of business so they're going to kill you.'

'It will put them out of business, but that's not who's going to kill me. It's my former business partners. They want to kill me.'

Jim sighed. 'Will, please go below and rest.'

'Shut up and listen,' Will shot back fiercely. 'There is a powerful foundation that believes I possess the prototype of a superminiature, ultrafast microprocessor.'

'The McVay Foundation for Humane Science. I know. I read your file.'

'They're the "they". What do you know about molecular diagnosis?'

'Only what I read in the *New York Times* and *The Economist*.'

'Such speed on such a tiny scale offers a total revolution in medicine. A watchman of the body—which is why I named it Sentinel. Goddamned Sony already had Watchman . . .' He stared at Jim. 'Sentinel offers medicine's Holy Grail. Diagnostic sensors small enough to sail the human bloodstream.'

'I rented the video. *Fantastic Voyage*.'

'This is *real*! With Sentinel, a doctor can inject you with a molecular microprocessor that will cruise through your entire body checking it out for the earliest signs of anything wrong. Anything. The *first* cancer cell. The initial bulge of a stroke. The microscopic narrowing of an artery. It runs through you twice a year and cross-checks any problems against every data bank in the world via the Internet.

'It never occurred to me until it was too late that what the McVays wanted with my breakthrough was to destroy the entire medical establishment—doctors, hospitals, insurance companies.'

'Why?'

'So they could build a new system and put themselves in it.'

'But wasn't that your goal?'

'No. I wasn't thinking on such a cosmic scale. I just saw Sentinel as a major breakthrough that could make me very rich. Nor did it occur to me that they would have to kill me to silence me.'

'That doesn't make sense.'

Will stared at him.

'Would it be safe to say,' Jim asked, 'that you switched from trying to rip them off in a small way to ripping them off in a big way?'

Will laughed.

'What's so funny?'

'I'm very impressed. You've been listening.' For a long moment he regarded Jim with genuine pleasure. 'You're right. Of course I did. I'm going to bring Sentinel to market myself.'

'You cheated your partners.'

'Before they could cheat me—I would have been lucky to see one per cent out of it.'

'So you stole it.'

'Call it what you will. I'm walking dead, Jim. The McVays wrote the book on ruthless.'

'They're not killers. They're scientists.'

'Where'd you get that idea?'

'You had the Foundation's annual report in your files.'

Will rolled his eyes at Jim's naiveté. 'Lloyd McVay is ex-CIA. His old man got rich bribing congressmen, senators and generals, not to mention tinpot dictators all around the world. They made their fortunes selling weapons.'

'I read they were high-tech.'

'High-tech *weapons*. They know the military-industrial complex inside out. And when they shifted into consumer technology they bribed their computers into half the schools in the nation.'

'But now all they have is a nonprofit foundation.'

Will turned red in the face. 'It's a goddamned tax-dodge front for stealing new technology from gullible fools like me. Lloyd McVay is a poetry-quoting, Ivy League *thug*.'

'You really don't like him.'

'He represents the worst of the unearned-privileged class.'

'What about his daughter?'

'Val?' Will ran his hand through his hair. 'Val's a somewhat differ-ent case. I sort of liked her, actually. She used to be a sailor—big time. Raced in the Southern Ocean. Strange woman, pale as a vampire, smart as hell. I could never figure out how she could stand being under the thumb of that manipulative old bastard.'

'Did you make it with her?'

'That's not a gentleman's question, Jim.'

'Forgive me. I was hoping in my ill-mannered way that we might have a friend in that "powerful foundation" that's trying to kill us.'

Will answered him seriously. 'I suspect that Val is as vicious as her father. Lloyd is vicious for the fun of it. She would be vicious just to get the job done.'

'A thugette?' Jim asked with a smile.

'No joke, Jim. Those two took a very public shellacking in the Internet market. The McVays will do *anything* to claw their way back on top, and thanks to me they are homing in on the richest prize in the world. Three *trillion* dollars a year. That's how much Americans and Europeans alone spend on healthcare.

'Lloyd and Val McVay will kill for the power of Sentinel. They've hired the worst gangster scum you could imagine to do their dirty work. His name is Andy Nickels. A mindless destroyer. I made the deadly mistake of thinking that was all he was. He almost nailed me with your tracking device.'

Suddenly Jim believed Will's weird tale. What tipped it, he thought, was that offhand remark about not being able to call Sentinel 'Watchman'. Will seemed genuinely annoyed with Sony for taking the name for their mini-TVs.

And then, before he could stop himself, Jim asked a question that he knew he shouldn't. Not if he truly wanted to get home to Shannon safe and sound to work for her father managing a health club. 'So where's the prototype?'

Will smiled. Only his lips moved. 'In a safe place.'

Jim said, 'You don't trust me.'

'I don't trust anybody.' A speculative gleam revived Will's eyes. 'What do you want, Jim? A piece of it?'

'Well, what if I did?'

'Your shot at the big time?' Will asked mockingly.

'Why not? Like you said, everyone else has got rich. So why shouldn't I?'

'Cashing in could get pretty dicey.'

'How far is Buenos Aires?'

Will studied him carefully for a moment. Then he said, 'Why don't we look it up?'

Jim got *Ocean Passages*. From where they were, off Cape Palmas on the southeastern tip of Liberia, it looked the better part of 4,000 miles. The GPS confirmed it: 3,848 miles. Will predicted that *Hustle* would average 150 miles a day. A thousand miles a week. A month if they were lucky. 'Figure more like six weeks,' said Will. 'Seven to be on the safe side.'

'Do you think that you can last seven weeks?' Jim asked.

'I don't know,' Will answered simply. 'I certainly hope so.'

'So where is the prototype?'

'In my head. Literally.'

Jim got what Will was saying straight away, but he couldn't quite believe it. Then he laughed out loud.

Will returned a weak smile. 'Better make sure I don't fall over-board.'

Jim laughed again. 'I'm going to tie you to the mast . . . Wait a minute, Will. How do you get it out?'

'A lab procedure. I have a place I can go to in Argentina.'

Jim studied him closely, peering at his bony skull and trying to visualise the microscopic instruments flowing through the narrow capillaries that fed the brain.

SHANNON RILEY found Billy Cole through the Connecticut State Interlibrary Nexis newspaper connection. But when the headline first leapt off the screen, Shannon got confused. It read: CANCURE.COM MEDICAL STOCK FRAUD WILL SPARK AGGRESSIVE PROSECUTION.

But she was searching for Billy Cole.

Then it hit her. Could this headline have given him a joke idea for a new name? Very funny. But when she read the article it was clear that he had needed a laugh. Billy Cole's CanCure.com rip-off had taken Seattle investors for millions.

Shannon found a Seattle magazine with a photo of Billy Cole in handcuffs, being escorted off his boat by the FBI. She wondered if she had made a mistake. The mastermind of the CanCure fraud looked frail and much older than the Will Spark Jim had described. If anything, he looked like the old man on Will Spark's health club membership card. She compared the two photographs carefully. It was a neat trick. He wore spectacles and looked down from the camera. In the magazine he had lowered his arms to shrink his shoulders. The overall impression was of a bent old man.

The article quoted the prosecutor lamenting the mild sentence— millions of dollars had been stolen, little of the money returned to the bilked investors. But his case had been weak. The jury had returned minor convictions on a technicality, and William Cole was released soon after with time off for good behaviour. Upon his release he had boarded his sailboat, *Runner*, bound, he claimed, 'For a sunny beach where I hope to live out my days trading seashells.'

HUSTLE CROSSED the equator on a dark night. There was some custom of the sea where sailors who had 'crossed the line' initiated those who hadn't. But Will was fast asleep, zonked out on penicillin and morphine, so Jim sat alone in the cockpit.

The South Atlantic spread to the ends of the earth. The boat was doing six knots, which made the vast sea meaningless. Three thousand four hundred miles to go.

He found *Moby-Dick* on Will's bookshelf and thumbed through it, looking for what Melville said about crossing the equator. He couldn't find it but he did stumble over the phrase 'unshored, harbourless immensities', which aptly described what lay ahead.

We are not lost, he thought. We are only hiding.

WILL WALKED SHAKILY into the galley. Something about him looked better. His cheeks were pink and smooth.

'You shaved,' Jim said.

'Of course. How many times do I have to remind you that cleanliness, careful stowage, kitchen skills and a decent bottle of wine are the requisites for civilisation.'

'I see you're feeling much better.'

'Not quite up to the bottle of wine.'

'Hungry?'

'I would kill for French toast and black coffee. And then I think it's high time we gave *Hustle* a spring-clean.'

With Will directing, Jim mixed dried eggs and long-life ultrapasteurised milk. Then he cut thick chunks of bread. He glanced at Will, and the instant the old man started to speak Jim chorused with him, 'Now, here's the secret of French toast.'

'OK, wise guy. You know the secret?'

'Tell me the secret.'

'Patience. Most people don't wait for the bread to be fully soaked.'

Will tried to help clean the galley, but he quickly tired. Jim said, 'Why don't you check your email?'

When he glanced over Will's shoulder, he saw that the screen was a crazy quilt of numbers and symbols.

'What's with the squiggles? Secret formula for Sentinel?'

'It's encrypted. I told you the McVays can intercept email.'

Will leaned forward and typed in a command. The laptop now displayed an ordinary email letter. Jim saw the greeting, 'My very good friend.'

'Who's that?'

'One of my engineers. Wants to know why he isn't rich yet.'

JIM READ SHANNON's email over and over. He didn't want Will to be a crook. And he sure as hell didn't want Sentinel to be a fraud. He wanted a piece of something that was real.

Will Spark/Billy Cole landed in jail because he suckered people into investing money in so-called high-tech, medical research that was nothing more than a scam. I'm sorry, darling, but your shipmate is a con man.

He started to type back, 'You have no absolute proof that Will and this Billy Cole are the same . . .' He stopped. Of course she had proof. *Runner* was Will's last boat, previous to *Hustle*. He flipped open *Ocean Passages*. The names of three boats were written on the title page. *Cordelia. Runner. Hustle.* Jim looked into Will's cabin. The old man appeared to be asleep. But he opened his eyes.

Jim said, 'Will. We have to talk. Shannon checked you out on the Internet. She found Billy Cole and CanCure.com.'

'Clever Shannon.'

'Did you go to jail?'

'Most people my age have a past.'

'Do you deny being a crook?'

'I denied it at the trial. The jury didn't believe me.'

'Are you saying you were innocent? Why'd you run if you were innocent?' Be innocent, Jim thought. Tell me you're not a crook . . . Tell me that Sentinel is real.

'Run? In a sailboat?' Will sighed elaborately.

'That's what the papers said. The FBI caught you in San Francisco.'

'They were waiting at the quay when I sailed *Runner* into Frisco.'

'Were you surprised they were waiting for you?'

'I'll tell you something, Jim. The Feds had their laugh. I had mine.'

'What do you mean?'

'There was money involved. A considerable amount of cash.'

'So you *were* guilty.'

Will ignored that. 'I deep-sixed the money.'

'What does that mean?'

Will sighed. 'Doesn't anybody read any more? It means to throw overboard.'

'You threw the money overboard?'

'In shallow water. I weighted the waterproof container so it would sink and marked the spot with the GPS. When I got out of prison, I dived for it. Then I bought a new boat. If you have a boat, people assume you're rich. Keep that in mind, Jim. Here, I'll tell you a trick that never fails. Say you make landfall where you don't know a soul. You drop anchor off the richest house you see. Row ashore and ask permission to anchor for the night. You don't need permission— they don't own the water—but it's polite. Nine times out of ten, they'll ask you in for drinks, dinner follows naturally. And what kind of host would let a charming sailor row home in the dark?'

'Who's going to have the last laugh this time?'

'Me,' Will shot back. 'Just like last time. And you, if you continue to play your cards right.'

Jim flinched. 'Why'd you have to be a crook?'

Will looked at him. 'What is your problem, Jim? You're taking my past mistakes personally.'

'Wasn't sailing enough, goddammit?'

'Why are you so upset?'

'I'm not upset. I am merely asking.'

'You're clenching your fists.'

'I look at the way you and the boat are one and how you can fix anything and read the water and I think: if I could be so good at something, I'd be completely satisfied.'

'You're making me into a role model!'

Jim blundered out of the cabin, ran up the companionway and stood in the cockpit, turning in circles. Then he hurried back to the stern and leaned over the bubbling wake. He felt trapped on the boat: trapped with Will, trapped with himself and his disappointment. He walked forward again, and on impulse began to haul himself up the jackstay, climbing to the top spreader fifty feet above the deck. He stood on it, breathing hard, his arms burning with lactic acid. Standing on the spreader he looked out at the sea. A gust heeled the boat. His perch leaned out over the water and he could see past the foresail.

'Jesus!'

A huge ship lay dead ahead—waiting for them.

It was a dirty red, and as square as a factory. Containers stacked high from bow to stern made it look even bigger than it was. And closer, Jim realised. Another three miles and he'd have run smack into it. A blue and white ensign flew from its telemetry mast. Russian merchantman colours.

Jim descended the wire as fast as he could, burning his hands, and hit the deck running. No point in dousing the sails; even if the Russians had posted a blind lookout they'd have seen him by now. His fastest move was to flee south on a broad reach. He steered off the wind, let out both the main and jib sheets, and started the diesel. The engine gave him another knot.

The ship had a lifeboat hanging from the stern. He focused hard with the binoculars and saw the propeller. Motor driven. If they lowered that boat, he was dead.

'Hey,' Will called. 'What's with the engine?'

'There's a ship. Russian.' He heard the fear in his voice and thought, I'm as paranoid as he is now.

Will climbed the companionway. He reached for the binoculars. 'A goddamned Russian. Why isn't he moving? Did he spot us?'

'I don't see how he could miss us. I wonder why he isn't chasing.'

'I just hope he doesn't send that lifeboat after us.'

Slowly, the three miles increased to four. At five, the monsoon haze softened the boxy silhouette. At six, they were alone on the sea.

'Back on course?' asked Jim.

'Let's give him a few more miles.'

'Good idea. God that was close.'

Will asked, 'How long did the Russian see you before you saw him. Long enough to see we're heading for the Río de la Plata?'

'I don't know. Maybe we'd better not go to Buenos Aires.'

'I'm running out of places, son. Jesus, what a lousy break.'

JIM STUDIED what he had written.

> Dear Shannon,
> Will Spark and Billy Cole are definitely the same guy. But I don't believe that Will's dangerous. Maybe I wouldn't buy stock from him, but I'm not afraid to turn my back on him either. We are still on course for Buenos Aires.

Shannon wasn't fooled.

Dear Jim,

But you *are* buying 'stock' from him. You're 'investing' your safety by helping Will sail to Argentina, for which you're hoping to be paid a piece of his so-called microprocessor. What makes you think that Sentinel isn't as phoney as CanCure.com?

That, of course, was the big question. Jim had to know the truth. So he waited until Will's defences were low to pop the question.

Right after they saw the Russian, Will's fever bounced to 103. Jim rigged another saline drip and sat on the edge of his bunk as the old man lay with his eyes closed.

'So, Will. Can I ask you something?'

'Shoot,' he whispered.

'Is the microprocessor any better than CanCure.com?'

'What do you mean?'

'Is Sentinel real? Or is it just another scam?'

Will was quiet. After a while Jim feared that he had slipped into a deep sleep. As he started to leave him the old man spoke.

'Jim, I spent my whole life trying to hit a home run. Other men my age have built something solid but I was always striking out. But now it's my turn. Sentinel is my home run.'

He smiled at Jim and the expression on his face was so hopeful that Jim didn't have the heart to ask again if it was just another scam. But Will knew what was on his mind.

'Is Sentinel real?' Will said. 'Why don't you ask the McVays? They think Sentinel's real enough to kill for.'

LLOYD MCVAY REFILLED Admiral Rugoff's glass and asked, 'To what do we owe the pleasure of your presence in our remote corner of New Jersey, Admiral?'

'Coincidence,' said his Russian visitor. 'I happened to be doing business in Port Elizabeth when one of my captains reported that he had sighted a yacht that fits your profile in the South Atlantic.'

'Why didn't he seize it?'

'His ship had broken down. He was making repairs.'

'Couldn't he have sent a boat after it? They carry lifeboats, don't they?'

The old admiral looked at him curiously and McVay realised that his nerves were showing. He glanced at Val. She was waiting, as still as an ice sculpture.

'They do carry a lifeboat. If the ship is sinking and the crew is sufficiently sober and the davits haven't frozen with rust from inattention to maintenance, they might be able to launch in half an hour. At which point, if they are very lucky, the motor will start. Pursuit was not an option.'

'Did they happen to notice which way the sailboat was headed?'

'When it sighted my ship it bore away to the south. But before they changed course they were headed south by southwest. Their exact compass course was two hundred and twenty degrees, magnetic.'

'What does that mean?'

'That would put them on course for the River Plate. You'll find him in Buenos Aires or Montevideo.'

TWO NIGHTS AFTER he dodged the Russian ship, Jim lost the wind. The southwest monsoon had grown weaker by the hour and quite suddenly it was gone. *Hustle* wallowed on a confused sea for half the night, sails banging in the dark. Then, just as suddenly, the southeast trade wind filled the sails.

He woke to a changed ocean—a crisp blue sea different from any other he had seen. Well into the South Atlantic, a hundred miles east of Ascension Island, the sky was sharper and brighter. The vistas lengthened. The horizons seemed more distant yet more distinct—dark blue sky and darker sea in sharp divide.

The southeast trade wind bore a hint of far-off cold. Jim rummaged around for the sweatshirt he had packed in Connecticut. When he checked on Will, the old man was huddled under a sheet. Jim draped his bony back with a blanket. Will muttered gratitude.

'Who's Cordi?' asked Jim.

'What?'

'You said, "Thanks, Cordi".'

Will opened his eyes. They were red from fever and flickering with confusion. 'Where are we?'

'Eight degrees south, thirteen east,' said Jim. He watched anxiously as Will tried to fix latitude and longitude on the chart he carried in his head. The fever and the massive doses of antibiotics he was ingesting were scrambling his mind. His condition had been vacillating between good days and bad days. Today was beginning to look like a bad one. But Will surprised him.

'Make sure you don't run into Ascension Island. The Brits lease out an air base there. They might take offence.'

'Maybe we should go there, Will. If they have a base they will have a hospital.'

Will shook his head. 'I had a bit of a mix-up in London several years ago. An equities situation. Purely a misunderstanding—but I thought it best to leave British territory.'

'By "equities situation" you mean a stock swindle?'

'Absolutely not. But Johnny Law has a long memory. And John Bull a long reach.'

Annoyed, Jim backed out of the cabin. 'I'll make us some breakfast. Will you eat?'

'I'd better. I feel like hell.'

'And while I'm doing that, maybe you could write me a list of countries where you're not being chased by the cops or the robbers. It shouldn't take too long.'

Will nodded. 'There's truth in that, son.'

The southeast trades grew stronger. Steadying up, they gave *Hustle* her first 200-mile run, averaging more than eight knots for the next twenty-four hours. Jim spent nearly all that time on deck, basking in the sheer beauty of the blue, blue ocean and the black and starry night. Around the time of the false dawn, he fell into a deep sleep on the cockpit bench. He was ripped awake by a loud *bang*.

He saw, silhouetted against the pale sky, a halyard swinging from the masthead, angling down through the main hatch. He heard the busy click-click-click of a winch and then, to his disbelief, one of the Schwinn spinners came smashing up the companionway, gouging wood and fibreglass.

Jim saw Will at the mast, madly cranking the winch halyard.

'What the hell . . .?'

'Spinning class!'

Gently, but firmly, Jim removed Will's hands from the winch. 'OK, Will, let's just go back—'

'You're not putting me below.' Will's body stiffened and he grabbed Jim's arm in a clawlike hand. 'Jim, what's wrong with me? I'm losing my mind.'

'You'll be better in the morning.'

'Jim, promise me something.'

'What?'

'If I die, promise me you'll deliver my body to Buenos Aires.'

'You're not going to die. Come on back to the cockpit before we fall overboard.'

'Promise!'

'OK, I promise.'

'The doctor. You have to take me to the doctor.'

'What doctor?'

'The one who's going to remove this chip from my head.'

Suddenly, Will wasn't sounding so crazy any more. 'What's the doctor's name?'

'Angela Heinman Ruiz. Her address is in my book. Promise.'

'I promise.'

'She's part English, part German. Married an Argentinian—lovely woman. Used to be a real looker—prefers Rio—has a practice there, too. Plastic surgeon. Her husband was a shrink. They had a hell of a business going.'

JIM FOUND HIMSELF in touch with Dr Ruiz sooner than he had expected. It started with an email message to Will—encrypted like the messages from his engineers.

> Dear One,
>   It sounds like you're in an awful fix and of course I'll help. The knife surely penetrated the pleural cavity, causing the pneumothorax that collapsed the lung. As you are no longer experiencing shortness of breath, apparently your collapsed lung has self-corrected, but your wound is almost certainly infected. Draining the abscess now, rather than later, is paramount. I'm particularly concerned that the abscess might break and travel down the path of the knife into your lung.
>   Love, Angela
>
> YOUNG MAN, READ THIS VERY CAREFULLY
>   Your goal is to incise and drain an abscess. Once you have enlarged the opening of the wound, you will use your gloved finger to break the little pockets of pus into a unicameral single-cavity pocket which you will push out through the larger hole you are making . . .

'I presume I'm the young man,' said Jim.

'Are you up to it?'

'I've taken a whole mess of first-aid courses but I've never cut anybody open.'

'No problem,' said Will. 'I'm open already.'

'What do we do about the pain?'

'I swallow morphine. You shoot the area around it with local anaesthetic. Marcain.'

'You have *Marcain?*'

'Of course I have Marcain. This is a blue-water boat. I can't call an ambulance.'

'Maybe I'd better strap you down so you can't start thrashing around in the middle of it.'

'Not necessary. We'll localise me until I'm numb as a piece of wood. I won't feel a thing.' He winked, but he looked as scared as Jim did. Angela had advised them to do it outside, not in the cabin.

The light is better outdoors. And as the procedure will turn messy, much simpler to hose down the cockpit afterwards, wouldn't you think?

'Thoughtful of her,' Will grunted. 'Any suggestions about how to control the bleeding?'

Jim was rereading anxiously. 'She says that I'm supposed to pack it with Iodoform gauze and I should press on anything that bleeds and hold it for a while. Do we have a retractor? I might need it to hold the incision open while I poke around inside.'

'Yes.'

'Can't we get her on the radio so she could guide me?'

'There's no privacy on the radio. They'll know we're here.'

'Who's going to find us in the middle of nowhere?'

'How about that Russian you almost ran into? There are ships everywhere. Or some goddamned do-gooder will lend a hand and we'll end up "rescued" on the six o'clock news. No radio.'

'It's your life.'

A SHARK WAS PACING the boat like a malevolent shadow.

Will saw it when they came up on deck. 'Oh, that is a lousy omen.'

For a moment, Jim couldn't take his eyes off the animal. But with a pan full of surgical tools in one hand and Will's shrunken arm in the other, a shark was the least of his worries.

'It's just a shark.'

'It's a blood omen. Listen, Jim, if I die—'

'You're not going to die,' said Jim. What else could he say?

'Listen!' Will turned towards him and for a moment he was the old Will, strong and healthy. 'If I die . . . take my body to Buenos Aires. Bring it to Angela.'

Jim heard his voice slide into personal trainer mode, taking charge of the client. 'Will, you're not going to die. But if you did, we're at least three weeks from Argentina and you'd be a very smelly corpse.'

'Put my body in the freezer.'

'The freezer isn't big enough.'

'Then put my head in the freezer.'

'Will, are you asking me to cut off your head?'

'Put it in the freezer and take it to Angela. Use the serrated Global bread knife. Did you know that the Japanese make the Global the same way they made Samurai swords?'

'No way, Will.'

'If you want what's floating around my head you will do it.'

Jim knew that there was no way on God's earth he would cut Will's head off if he died. Sticking him with the Marcain syringe was hard enough. Will bit his lip and braced himself as Jim pierced the tender skin, squeezing the local painkiller from the hypodermic.

It was the first close look at the wound that Will had allowed him, and it dispelled Jim's last doubts about the intentions of Margaret in the white dress. When the blade slid between Will's second and third ribs, only dumb luck prevented it from ripping through his heart.

Jim picked up the scalpel.

'I'm really starting to float out on the morphine,' Will whispered. 'I don't feel a thing.'

'How about this?' It was now or never.

'Jesus!' Will gasped.

Jim jumped back. Blood was oozing from a half-inch slit that lengthened the knife wound.

'Do it!' said Will. 'It didn't hurt. It just surprised me.'

Jim cut into the flesh. Blood welled. He mopped with the cotton sponges, which instantly became soaked. He cut again, lengthening the incision and working deeper. Soon he started to feel detached, far from the rolling boat and the clean wind but close to the blade and the job he was trying to do.

Something dark and greyish appeared inside the wound. He couldn't see it clearly through the welling blood and he wondered whether he had exposed an artery. Would his next stroke send Will's lifeblood geysering in his face? But there was no pulse to it.

Jim probed it tentatively and pushed his finger in. Grey pus oozed. An overwhelming stench filled his nostrils, and Jim sensed that this was the infection that had been dogging Will. 'Irrigate the incision' Angela had written. If there was any pure water left in a polluted world, the boat was sailing on it. Jim dipped the bucket they used to swab the decks, scooped it back by its rope and sluiced the contents into the gaping wound.

Will shouted. 'That's cold!'

Jim sluiced the gash again and again. The salt slowed the bleeding. He took a long hard look at his handiwork. Something gleamed. He leaned closer and saw to his astonishment a small piece of metal winking from the depths of the wound. He found a pair of forceps in the medical locker, wiped them with Betadine and probed for the metal. He felt it scrape on the forceps, gripped it and withdrew it. The tip of Margaret's fish knife must have broken off. It was half an inch long and heavy enough to *clink* when he dropped it in the pan.

He irrigated the wound again and when at last he saw no more pus, he packed the incision with the iodine-treated pads and pressed them until the bleeding stopped.

'How do you feel, Will?'

'Stoned.'

Jim carried Will as carefully as he could to his cabin, laid him on his bunk and covered him with a sheet. Then he climbed back on deck, cleared up the mess and sank exhausted into the cockpit seat.

JIM FELT PROUD at first. Will's soaring energy and strength to complain how clumsily Jim had 'butchered' him seemed proof that the operation was a success. Will had not regained all his strength, however. He couldn't crank a winch, much less wrestle the sheets as they changed from tack to tack. Instead he steered, and for a while he started eating again, resurrecting joints to roast and long-frozen stews from the freezer. The hot meals were welcome as they neared the thirtieth parallel and the wind grew cooler and stronger.

After a week, Jim asked if Will was ready for him to stitch the wound. But Will put him off. It was around that time that Will got on Jim's case about maintenance.

'You've got to keep on top of it, Jim. Daily rounds, checking lines, blocks, sheets, chafing. I'll show you how to tear down the starboard sheet winch, get the crud out of it and grease the bearings.'

Jim held tools. Will enumerated the steps. After lunch, he said, 'I want you to run up the mast and grease the halyard sheaves.' From the masthead, Jim communicated by the clip-on VHF he wore, with Will talking him through the inspection and lubrication of the blocks. When Jim described them as 'pulleys',Will corrected him. '*Blocks*. As in blockhead.'

Next they made the rounds of all the winches. Jim finished reassembling the halyard winch as dark was falling. Cold spray hissed across the foredeck and the cabin roof. He was looking forward to drying off below and eating something warm.

'OK, let's service the autohelm.'

'It's getting dark,' Jim protested.

Will disengaged the automatic steering, locked the rudder so the boat would hold her approximate course, and began pulling parts from the autohelm, which he passed back to Jim.

'You'll find half the day is dark, but there are certain jobs that won't wait—like things to do with the steering—so it's kind of helpful to know your way around in the dark.'

'Will, wait.You're riding me hard. Either something is bothering you, or you're trying to tell me something. Why don't you just say it?'

'I'm not trying to tell you something. I'm trying to *teach* you to take care of the boat. I should have started months ago.'

'But you didn't. And now all of a sudden you're putting me through a crash course.'

'You're in need of one. You're in the middle of a serious ocean. You're not quite a novice any more, but you're no pro.'

'Will, are you all right?'

'I'm not sure,' Will answered. 'I think I ought to talk to my doctor.'

Will meant actual voice talk, not email, which indicated to Jim how seriously concerned he was, because he had said repeatedly that the McVays might track him by phone or radio signals.

Will couldn't get a connection with the satellite phone. 'I'm getting a recording—no longer in service. Bloody awful time for a screw-up,' he muttered to a worried Jim, who stood behind him at the nav station, wondering whether a new infection had invaded Will's wound.

'ONE WAY OR ANOTHER, Shannon Riley will lead us to Jim Leighton, and Jim Leighton will lead us to Will Spark,' Andy Nickels said.

'What do you mean, "one way or another"?' asked Val McVay.

'As you know, we're watching the girl in Connecticut twenty-four seven. They will talk on the telephone when the boat lands. I've got people on the phones for when he tells her where he is.' He glanced at Lloyd McVay and added, 'Or Ms McVay might still get lucky with that email address she turned up.'

Val ignored the jibe, saying only, 'What if Shannon goes to him?'

'Yes,' said her father. 'They might meet where Will Spark lands the boat.'

'In which case,' said Andy, 'we will follow Shannon to Jim.'

'What if neither of those things happen?'

'We can always take her hostage.'

'Kidnap her?'

'Do you have a problem with that?' He glanced at Lloyd McVay.

'I have a huge problem with that,' Val shot back. 'A million things can go wrong.'

'No way it'll come back to us.'

Val said, 'Get real, Andy. Just follow her. It can't be too hard to follow a girl in a wheelchair.'

'WHAT DOES THE DOCTOR say?' Will called from his bunk. He was in great pain and profoundly weak.

'Her email account seems to be shut. And when I finally got the high-seas operator to put me through, her answering machine said she was away for a week.'

Jim couldn't meet Will's eye. They had tried every antibiotic in the well-stocked medicine locker, but the infection just wouldn't go away. It was too late to try to sail back to Ascension Island. The Argentine capital was closer, but still a week off. They could try to contact a ship, but a freighter's sickbay wasn't likely to contain any more exotic antibiotics than *Hustle* already carried.

They were out of options and Will knew it. His face hardened. 'I'm dying.'

'I'll get you to Buenos Aires as fast as I can.'

Will cast a miserable look out of the port. 'But we're still in the variables.'

'The wind's swinging west.'

'Great. Then we'll butt heads with the westerlies.'

'I'll do what I can.'

To Jim's surprise, a warm smile softened Will's expression. 'I know you will.'

'I just wish I was a better sailor.'

'Listen, Jim. This whole mess is not your fault. Don't start blaming yourself if I don't make it.'

'You'll make it,' Jim retorted.

BUT THE NEXT MORNING the wind failed them. *Hustle* banged along in choppy seas, losing much of the time Jim had gained by driving her hard all night. Now, when speed was everything, the variables had turned contrary.

Jim did his rounds, then scrambled some freeze-dried eggs and brought them to Will. The old man's face was pink with fever. Jim was shocked.

Will took a tentative forkful. 'Very nice. I'll make a civilised man of you yet. Could I borrow your spare heart monitor?'

'What for?'

He looked at Jim. His eyes glistened. 'I want to see how I'm doing.'

Jim got the monitor from his bag and helped Will strap the sensor round his chest. His ribs pressed his flanks like a fish skeleton. Jim looked at the read-out. The man's heart was racing as if he were climbing a hill.

'Get your breakfast,' Will said. 'I want to talk to you.'

Deeply concerned, Jim made a second batch of eggs and returned to the cabin. Will waited until he was done.

'I haven't been totally honest with you.'

'I've heard this before.'

Will returned a beaten, weary look. 'Humour me, please.'

He sounded frightened. Jim turned his full attention to the old man.

'Do you remember that I asked you to take my body to Buenos Aires if I die?'

'You're not going to die.'

'Take it to Angela. There's a list of addresses in the drawer under the chart table. Angela's lab and a safe house in Buenos Aires and some friends who can help.'

'What if your friends can't or won't help me?'

'If something happens to Angela, bail out and head for the Falklands.'

'The Falkland Islands?' The Falklands were about a thousand miles from Buenos Aires.

'A woman there will help you. Her farm is marked on my chart.'

'And what if *this* friend can't help?'

'Run south, kid. Don't stop till you hit Antarctica.'

'So what happens when they find me there? I go to the South Pole?'

'No one will find you there.'

'Will, I'm so tired I can't see straight, much less deal with your fantasy. I'm going to sleep.'

'I've written my will.'

'What are you talking about?'

'It's in the nav station drawer. When I die you get everything.'

'You're making me your heir?' Tired as he was, Jim stood up straight, his mind swarming.

Will said, 'I see I have your attention at last.'

'How can I be your heir?'

'I have no kids of my own and I'm not leaving it to my ex-wives. There's no real money to speak of. But you can have all my possessions and all my royalty rights—which includes Sentinel.'

Good luck cashing that in, Jim thought. And then, as if from a distance, he heard Will say, 'And *Hustle*.'

'You're giving me the boat?'

'I am *willing* you my yacht.'

Light was pouring in the ports, glowing on the varnished wood. There were times when Jim hated being stuck on *Hustle*, but she was a fine and beautiful object.

No. It was too crazy. Besides, he couldn't afford to run her. He'd seen the bills in Will's desk: thousands a year just to keep her in trim.

As he had so often in their conversations, Will read Jim's mind. 'You could charter her out. People go nuts for the workmanship. They want excellent food, first-class accommodation, a pleasant captain and his beautiful first-mate-slash-wife.'

'Sounds great, Will, but I can't. Shannon couldn't do it.'

'Why the hell not?'

'She's crippled. She can't walk more than a few steps on crutches.'

'You never said anything . . .' He trailed off, his expression hurt. 'Why didn't you tell me?'

'I didn't want to talk about it, Will.'

'You poor kids, you—'

'We're OK,' Jim cut in. 'It's not like she's paralysed or anything. We have a sex life—'

'I'm really sorry, Jim . . . What happened?'

'She got creamed in a ski accident. Multiple compound fractures, both legs. So I don't see her doing yacht charters.'

'Why don't you let Shannon decide what she can and can't do. Decide together when *Hustle* is yours. If . . .'

'If what?'

'If you put my head in the freezer and deliver it to Angela.'

'I told you, I can't do that.'

'This is a dying man's last wish.'

'You're not—'

'I am, Jim. The infection is burning me up. I'm sailing on fire like a dead Viking.' He lunged at Jim, grabbed his arm with astonishing power. 'Jim, the McVays are the last people on the planet who should have the power of my processor. You must not let them get it.'

'Will, I'll do everything I can to keep it for myself.'

'Promise you'll take my head to Angela.'

'I promise.'

As a scientist, Val McVay held a belief that there was no such thing as an indecipherable code. But even Val had to admit that if there was an utterly secure secret communication, it would use code similar to the one Will Spark used in his email correspondence.

Having failed to crack emails intercepted to and from his Sentinel engineers, Val knew she hadn't a hope of reading the contents of the long messages he had exchanged with Dr Angela Heinman Ruiz of Rio de Janeiro. A clue to his destination? Perhaps.

Cross-checking revealed that Dr Ruiz was a plastic surgeon, but she had practised microsurgery years ago. Although she was busy most of the time in Rio, she had a second practice in Buenos Aires. The problem was, Dr Ruiz was currently in neither of her offices.

JIM WENT UP ON DECK and trimmed the main and the jib. All he could do was try to make the boat go faster.

To hell with the McVays. They were Will's problem. His goal was clear: sail *Hustle* close enough to Buenos Aires to radio a medevac helicopter. Nurse Will along. Then helicopter him to hospital.

He ducked below. Will was sprawled on the couch in the main cabin. He thrust his arm towards Jim and pointed at his heart-rate monitor. 'I'll bet you've never seen numbers like these.'

Jim looked. His own heart jumped. Will's pulse had fallen to forty beats a minute.

Jim said, 'I'll radio Angela.'

He switched on the single sideband. If he couldn't get Angela, he would broadcast a distress call on 2182. Some doctor somewhere would tell him what to do.

Will laughed.

'What?' Jim turned from the radio. There was a finality in Will's tone, like a solid door swinging shut.

'Jim, don't forget our deal.'

As he spoke, an errant swell smacked *Hustle* on her port side, staggering the sloop and throwing Will off the couch. Jim jumped to catch him but, before he could swing his legs out from under the desk, the old man tumbled to the deck.

Jim knelt and turned him over. Will was struggling to pull something from his pocket. 'This is for you.'

'Hang on to it,' Jim said.

'See this key?'

'Yes.' The key he had stolen to open Will's private desk. 'It opens the desk in the bulkhead. Keep anything you want.'

'Let me help you into bed.'

'I'm outta here. It's all yours, Jim. Just make sure you get my head to Buenos Aires.' He closed his eyes. 'Watch this.' He raised his arm.

The heart-rate monitor was recording a deadly thirty beats a minute. And as Jim watched in helpless fascination, the numbers spooled down to zero.

FOR THE FIRST TIME in his life, Jim understood the phrase 'a bag of bones', as he carried Will into his cabin and laid him on the bed.

> Dear Shannon,
>   Will died at nine twenty this morning. We sailed from Barbados to Nigeria together and then back across the South Atlantic. Thousands of miles. I know he was a con man and a liar. And it looks like he was a thief, too. But he was fun to sail with and he was so full of hope. He made me want to be an optimist, like you.
>   I love you. I wish you were here with me.
>   Jim

He entered Will's death in the log. He wrote the time he died, *Hustle*'s position, and his opinion that he died from an infection resulting from a knife wound suffered in Nigeria.

He stood in the main cabin for a while, not knowing what to do next. Air. He needed air. He hurried up the companionway. The wind was chilly, like the first cool day of autumn.

It *is* autumn, he thought. And there's a dead man below whose head I'm supposed to cut off and put in the freezer. Thank God they were out of the tropics. The cool weather bought him a day or two to make up his mind.

He went below, sat down at the nav station and opened the drawer. There was a business envelope with his name written on it in Will's handwriting, a single sheet folded inside. Jim took it up to the cockpit. It began in the same clear hand.

> *I, William Spark, AKA Billy Cole, AKA Pendleton Rice, AKA Randell Smythe, AKA Micky Creegan . . .*

What a time Shannon would have with all those names.

> *. . . being sound of mind and frail of body, write my last will and testament. If Jim Leighton, my good friend and loyal shipmate, delivers my body—or, failing that, my head—to Dr Angela Heinman Ruiz in Buenos Aires, Argentina, I bequeath to him all my worldly possessions, including my yacht, Hustle, and royalty rights to all my patents.'*

Maybe if he covered Will's body with a blanket and wrapped his head in a towel . . . *Am I losing my mind?* Jim thought.

If Jim Leighton fails to hold up his end of this bargain, everything goes to Ms Cordelia MacDonald, Borlum Farm, East Island, Falkland Islands.

No surprise there. Perform, or you get nothing.

Will had signed it *William Spark*, and dated it, *Aboard the yacht Hustle, 32 degrees south, 40 west.*

Finally, Will had scribbled a note on the bottom of the page:

JIM: JUST HANG ON TO MY HEAD. Keep it in the freezer. Even if you screw up, and everything goes to Cordi, you can keep the boat. Cordi hates sailing.

Will had scribbled some more in a scrawl so chaotic it was almost impossible to read:

You're in a win–win situation, kid. Just do the right thing.

Jim said, 'Do the right thing? Oh give me a break.' Will was manipulating him to the end. Even after the end. The right thing was to bury Will at sea and sail home an honest man. But Will had backed him into a trap. I want it all—and I want to take care of Shannon, if she'll let me. All I have to do is butcher my former shipmate.

LIKE THE OPERATION, this post-mortem decapitation would be less messy on deck. What if someone sees? But Jim was on his own and no one would ever know. Except for Dr Angela Heinman Ruiz when he handed her Will's head.

He carried Will up to the cockpit and wrapped a towel round his head. Maybe there wouldn't be much blood, but who knew? Jim was feeling sick to his stomach.

He laid the body across the afterdeck where he had 'operated' on Will's wound. Operation successful, patient dead. He picked up the serrated Global knife, looked around the empty ocean, and glanced at the compass, which showed them heading due north.

'*North?*'

He leaned closer. The needle spun until it pointed due east. He stepped back and it spun west. He was holding the knife. The steel was affecting the compass, throwing it off. He looked at the finely scalloped edge. A beautiful tool, Will had called it. A thousand years of Japanese war technology tamed for the kitchen.

Jim threw the knife high in the air and watched it gleaming in the sun. Maybe someone else could do this, he thought. But not me.

The knife sliced without a splash into the sea. The compass swung southwest and stayed there, steady as a rock.

It seemed foolish to waste an anchor, but he couldn't just drop Will's body over the side and let it drift. So he pulled out one of the spinning bikes and muscled it up the companionway. Then he tied Will's arms and legs to it. He squatted down, gathered Will and the heavy bike in his arms, and lifted them over the stern rail.

With a concussive splash, Will and the spinning bike cannonballed a hole in the water. Jim leaned out, trying to distinguish the spot, but it was lost in the wake.

Feeling numb, Jim wrote in the log: *Will Spark, buried at sea.*

He noted the time, the date and *Hustle*'s position on the GPS, and signed his name.

Had Sentinel just gone overboard? Was it really *in* Will's head? Or only in his imagination?

If Will's enemies wanted what was in his head they could keep on chasing him. Jim was going home. If the McVays asked, he would tell them that Will had faked his death and that the old man had gone ashore in Uruguay. At home, if they hassled him, he would dial 911.

Ocean Passages of the World said that the best way home was to head north to a waypoint off Cabo Calcanar on the bulge of South America, then to steer 3,460 miles northwest to New York.

Jim didn't even know if he had enough food and water left to sail straight home. Maybe he should just pull into Rio de Janeiro? Why not? He had an open plane ticket.

No, he wanted to keep the boat. And if in the long term he couldn't keep it, he was at least determined to sail it home. Besides, Rio, Bermuda and the Caribbean all presented the same obstacle: how to prove to Immigration or Customs that he owned the boat?

Jim started to get really paranoid: What's to say I didn't kill him? How do I prove I didn't throw him overboard to keep the boat? An autopsy would confirm how he died. But no body, no autopsy.

He had no appetite, nor was he tired. He had only a desire to make the boat go faster, so he kept driving her through the evening and into the night.

Moonlight suddenly broke through the swift-moving cumulus clouds, which were splashed dark and light as they galloped across the moon, covering and uncovering it. Will used to call it a *Treasure Island* sky. And then, when he least expected it, Jim began to cry.

IV

VILLA MISERIA

Jim slept in the cockpit, waking hourly to shorten sail. At dawn it was blowing thirty knots. The seas were streaked with foam and salt crusted his hair. A vote of confidence from the weather: go home.

He cooked some breakfast and then found two emails waiting. One was titled: Returned mail. It was the letter he had written to Shannon right after Will died. The other was headed: SEE YOU SOON! A quick glance stopped him cold.

> Dear Jim,
>
> People have been asking questions about you—on the phone—and they're insinuating that you're involved in some kind of criminal activity. I'm sure that your friend Will is behind it. Daddy is really pissed and he's actually *ordered* me to stop writing you until you come home and explain yourself. He says he'll fire me if I disobey him.
>
> So I wrote myself a $10,000 cheque on the company credit card and bought a ticket to Buenos Aires.

'*No!*'

> I'll be waiting for you at the Plaza Hotel on the Plaza San Martín. They said anyone can tell you how to get there—it's right in the middle of the city. I'm leaving tomorrow morning. You must be pretty close to Buenos Aires by now, so with any luck I will see you in just a few days. Until then, olé—or whatever they say in Argentina.
>
> PS: I closed both my email accounts.

Who the hell was asking questions?

Was it someone investigating one of Will's scams? Or the McVays? If they were asking questions at the club, then they already knew about Shannon and him. What would happen when she left Westport? Would they follow her?

The broad reach on which Jim had been sailing home was a close-hauled battle when he turned the boat round. Worse, he had to tack, approaching the Río de la Plata obliquely, with his bow never pointing directly at Buenos Aires.

A GUY IN A BASEBALL JACKET was following her in a beat-up Toyota. Shannon wouldn't have paid him much mind if she hadn't seen him the night before and if she weren't a little jumpy about getting to the airport without her parents finding out.

A private detective, she guessed, working for one of Will Spark's victims. Maybe an undercover cop looking for Will. Whatever, there was no way she would let him follow her to Kennedy Airport.

She headed towards the club. It was early, but traffic was getting heavy on I-95. She speeded up and swung into the passing lane. The Toyota followed, pulling up close to keep her in sight. Shannon shifted to the middle lane, passed a Lincoln Navigator and tucked in front, leaving no room for the Toyota. The guy actually pulled alongside her and pretended not to glance over. When he did, she gave him a little wave. He was bracing to shove between her and the Navigator. She squeezed the brake lever with her left hand. The Navigator's tyres screamed and would have hit her if she hadn't swung onto the shoulder and across forty feet of grass. She hit the southbound passing lane right in front of a Lexus and swivelled her twist-grip accelerator as hard as she could. Horns shrilled. People screamed at their windscreens. Like anyone could hear them at seventy miles an hour.

'"WE'RE WATCHING HER twenty-four seven",' Val McVay mimicked Andy Nickels.

'She pulled a cute one.'

'She's *handicapped*. Our best link to Will Spark cannot *walk* and you let her disappear.'

'This is a temporary setback,' Andy replied coolly. 'I've got people fanning out all over Buenos Aires—Will Spark's destination.'

'Assumed destination,' Val reminded him. 'The fact is, Dr Angela Heinman Ruiz was last seen in Rio de Janeiro.'

'We're watching her apartment in Buenos Aires. And'—Nickels played his trump card—'I put the ex-resident on the payroll.'

Lloyd McVay banged a big hand on his bony knee. 'Well done, Andy!'

'The "ex-resident"?' demanded Val. 'What does that mean?'

Nickels explained that the former CIA station chief in Buenos Aires had been hired to enlist the city's famously corruptible *Policía Federal* to watch the airports and tourist hotels for an American girl in a wheelchair. 'Plus, we've put a bounty on them.'

'Alive!' warned Lloyd.

'Of course, sir. The second they make contact with the girl, we've got them.'

Val stood up. 'I'm going down there.'

Andy turned to her father. 'Mr McVay, BA is one tough town. I'm dealing with scum. The bosses should stay home.'

Lloyd McVay shook his head emphatically. 'You're forgetting your Shakespeare, Andy. We'll be pulling many strings in Buenos Aires, calling in a lot of favours.

> '"The presence of a king engenders love
> Among his subjects and his loyal friends."

'Go! Both of you. Retrieve Sentinel!'

JIM WAS STILL 120 miles from Buenos Aires. It was the closest he had been to Shannon in three months and he practically wanted to climb the mast for an early look at her. He was touched that she would come all this way. Touched—and hopeful. Had she changed her mind about marrying him? Or was it just her sense of duty? And what would she make of him? Would she notice a 'new Jim'?

Sailing Directions warned bluntly of sudden lethal changes in the weather, particularly the ferocious squalls—*pamperos*—that thundered off Argentina's pampas. Conditions were ripe, with a warm wind blowing from the north and the barometer indicating a gradual drop in pressure.

While the estuary of the Río de la Plata was as broad as an inland sea, much of it was shallow. With traffic funnelled into the dredged channels, Jim soon found himself in busy waters.

Thank God for Will's electronics. The GPS, the knot meter, depth finder and radar showed him where he was on the chart, how fast *Hustle* was moving, whether there was enough water under her keel, and warned when he was about to run into something. He was good to go, as long as none of those instruments stopped working.

'THEY FORGOT TO LOCK the gates of heaven. An angel has escaped.'

'Are you talking to me?'

This was what the guidebooks called *un piropo*, the Argentine male's poetic pick-up line. He had come over from a nearby table with another young guy. It would have been hard not to smile.

She let him do all the work. 'You're American?' he exclaimed. 'I have travelled throughout America and have never saw a woman so beautiful in your entire country.'

'Thank you. But I'm waiting for my boyfriend.'

'Not yet engaged?'

'Not yet.'

'Then I still have a chance.'

Shannon laughed. 'Not a chance in the world.'

'My name is Carlos. May I show you Buenos Aires?'

'No, thanks.' She indicated her forearm crutches leaning against her chair in the lobby of the Plaza Hotel. A turnoff if ever there was one. 'I really can't get around too easily.'

The *porteño* never blinked. 'My cousin Ramón has a car. We will drive you everywhere.'

He was so cute. He had curly black hair, dark eyes and that smile. Shannon flashed him one back. 'Could we drive to the harbour?'

JIM GOT WORRIED when he started seeing islands where the chart showed no islands. He climbed the mast and in the rising light of morning saw that the 'islands' were clumps of trees dotting a land as flat as the ocean. The trees shaded ranch houses and vast, prosperous-looking barns.

It occurred to him that Will's enemies were expecting him to arrive in Buenos Aires by boat. Why not dump the boat now and catch a bus or a train? He'd slip in the back door while they were watching the waterfront.

The bay of San Clemente looked like a good possibility. He sailed southeast on a course that paralleled the shoreline. When it curved to form the bay, he looked for other sailboats to moor among. He wanted a private landing where he wouldn't have to get into passports and Customs. Here and there, single boats were moored at the foot of large lawns that flowed from mansions down to the water's edge. He steered for the biggest estate, which had a huge two-masted schooner tied to its mooring. Such an estate looked ready-made for Will's rowing-ashore scam.

He dropped anchor a hundred yards off, furled the sails and inflated the dinghy. Then he quickly shaved and combed his tangled hair. He put on a clean polo shirt and jeans, then lowered the dinghy, climbed in and rowed to the quay.

So far, this beat landing in Nigeria. There were no teens with machetes, although the sad-faced middle-aged man hurrying down the lawn did have a gun on his hip. '*Buenos días,*' he called.

'Good morning, sir. I don't speak Spanish. I'm Jim Leighton.'

'Captain Rodolpho Faveros, navy of Argentina, retired.'

Of all the dumb luck: a naval officer who'd probably call Immigration. 'Would it be all right if I anchored off your home?'

'Where are you from, Mr Leighton?'

'I've just come in from Nigeria. I have to meet my girlfriend in Buenos Aires.'

'And before Nigeria?'

'I live in Connecticut.'

Captain Faveros brightened. 'I know it well.' He caught the dinghy's painter and extended a hand to Jim. 'Steady!'

The quay felt like it was rolling. Faveros grabbed his arm. 'The walk to the house will restore your land legs.'

'Would it be all right if I left the boat?'

'It'll be safe here. We have our "pirates", but they won't fool with the navy.' Steadying Jim, Faveros steered him up the lawn. Jim found the colours of the gardens painfully intense after so many weeks of sea blues and greys.

'Have you had lunch? Perhaps my wife . . .' Faveros's voice trailed off and the sad expression darkened his face again. Jim saw a woman watching from the windows of the house. She drifted away like a ghost.

'I ate, thanks,' said Jim. 'I've got to get to Buenos Aires as soon as possible. Is there a bus? Or a train?'

Faveros said, 'I'll drive you to the train. It is close.'

It turned out to be forty miles, but Faveros wouldn't hear of Jim hiring a taxi. In the car he started talking, and the words were soon gushing, as if he had been rehearsing them for days in his head. 'If only things were better at home, but we've had a tragedy. Our son has left. He's searching to find his so-called "real" parents. He's adopted. But I am his father "really". As is my wife his "real" mother. His biological mother is almost certainly dead. This is not uncommon.'

'What is not uncommon?' asked Jim.

'You know, of course, of Argentina's *desaperacidos*? It means the disappeared?'

Dazzled by the speed of the car, Jim was trying to follow Faveros. 'I'm afraid I don't know much about it.'

'Twenty-five years ago, Argentina had many terrible problems and the military government tried to reorganise the nation. Many left-wing radicals were killed. Prisoners were thrown from planes into the sea. *Desaparecidos* . . .' Faveros gesticulated with his left hand. 'It was a desperate time. Sometimes the *desaparecidos* left children behind. Orphans. Those children were adopted.'

Faveros gave a desolate shrug. 'So now we spend our days waiting for my son to come to his senses. My wife has gone back into therapy and so have I.' He tried to smile. 'Psychoanalysis is the Argentine vice . . . We would give our son anything. But all he wants is his so-called "real" mother. And she is surely dead.'

Tears trickled from his eyes, then, to Jim's horror, his entire face seemed to crumple. He wept violently, heaving tears, gulping for air. He slammed on the brakes and stopped in the middle of the road.

'I'm sorry,' said Jim, trying to comfort him. 'I know what you're going through.'

'You can't possibly. No one could who's not been here.'

'I've been here,' said Jim, surprised by himself and wishing instantly he could take the words back. 'On your child's side.'

'What are you saying? Oh! You mean you were adopted?'

'No, I wasn't adopted.'

'You were either adopted or not, young man. Which was it?'

Suddenly Jim was on the verge of blurting out a secret he had never told anyone except Shannon.

'My mother "confessed" to me, once.' He swallowed hard.

Faveros was watching him closely.

'My mother's life hadn't worked out as she had hoped. She was always searching . . . Meditation. Gurus. Erhard seminar training—EST. She told me that my real father—my biological father—was a trainer she'd met at an EST retreat. A rugged, outdoors type. The direct opposite of the man I thought was my father.'

'How old were you when she told you?'

'Fourteen.'

'*Qué macana!* She obliterated your adolescence.'

Jim shook his head. 'No, I didn't know what to do with it.'

'If you hadn't just sailed in single-handed from Africa, I would think you would detest anything that evoked your mother's out-doorsman lover. Ah! Perhaps you are trying to emulate him. Transference.'

'I had this secret. I knew this thing my mother had done to my father, but I couldn't tell him.'

Faveros looked Jim directly in the eye. 'It was not for you to betray your mother's confidence.'

'She did worse than betray him. She tricked him into raising a kid who wasn't his.'

'Your father had eyes. He should have confronted her! Ha! Hear me talking.' He laughed bitterly. 'The "father" expert.'

'I'm not talking about simple cheating on her husband. I'm talking about my *father*.'

'Which one? The father who raised you? Or the father who doesn't know you exist?'

Jim stared, silenced. Neither one, he thought. The tearful feeling passed and he felt as light as air. I got lucky, he thought. Will Spark made me his heir. For a moment, I got myself a *real* father.

Faveros smiled at him. 'I warned you about Argentina, young man. You have made an excellent landfall if you wish to be analysed.'

AS VAL MCVAY PACED the floating pontoons on her third visit to the Argentine Yacht Club, her eye was drawn repeatedly to a giant black catamaran. Two knife-thin hulls straddled the water in a wide stance that promised it could carry an awesome spread of sail. The 100-foot-long hulls and rigging were as black as night, except for the red letters that spelt out her name: *JoyStick*. It intrigued her for some reason she couldn't explain. Surely she wasn't getting a yen to sail again?

'Val!' An old friend smiled down at her from a high-tech ketch.

'Watson!' She hugged the charter captain, a handsome, sea-worn Brazilian. 'What are you doing here?'

'Leaving for the Med, soon as that bloody front passes. Do you have a boat?'

'I'm just looking around.'

Val was stunned by the sudden desire to simply sail away. Forget about goals—forget about Sentinel. Just meld into the sea. 'Have you seen a sloop called *Hustle*? Fifty foot. Centre cockpit. Tall rig.'

Watson shook his head. 'I got your email. Never saw the boat.'

'What's the *JoyStick*?' Val asked.

Watson explained that the catamaran had been gearing up for an around-the-world race when her owner went bankrupt.

'Is she as fast as she looks?'

'A cruise missile, downwind. I hear she's a serious machine. Were you thinking of "persuading" someone to buy her for you?'

'No, Watson. I'm thinking of buying her for myself.'

A taxi stopped on the sea wall. Andy Nickels got out, scoping the marina like a hungry wolverine. 'Gotta go,' said Val, kissing her friend's cheek. 'Happy voyage, Watson.'

TO JIM'S EARS, attuned to the wind and water, Buenos Aires was a thunderstorm of noise. And even though the cars were old, and the buildings in disrepair, and the trees browning in the dry southern autumn, to his eyes the colours seemed as bright as fire. He climbed out of a taxi a few blocks down a wide boulevard down from Shannon's hotel so he could check it out and avoid blundering into Will's enemies.

He was pretending to browse at a newsstand when he suddenly realised that every newspaper had a picture of the same middle-aged woman on the front page. He didn't have to read Spanish to understand the name in the picture caption: Dr Angela Heinman Ruiz.

He bought an English-language paper called the *Herald* and read in disbelief that Dr Ruiz had fallen from her high-rise terrace while attempting to escape kidnappers.

It had to be the McVays, trying to get to Will.

He walked as fast as he could to the Plaza Hotel.

Shannon's laugh filled the lobby as he entered. He whirled towards the unmistakable sound with an overwhelming sense of relief. She was at the bar, surrounded by guys, waving her empty Coke glass for a refill. Jim's heart jumped.

Shannon sensed his rush. She stared blankly, then broke into a big smile. 'Omigod! Jim!'

She threw her arms around him. Jim lifted her off the stool, felt the familiar strong grip of her arms and the perfect fit of her lips.

The men burst into applause and started pounding Jim on the back. He leaned close to whisper in Shannon's ear. 'We've got to get out of here. It's not safe.'

'Did Will—?'

'Will is dead.'

That stopped her. 'Oh, Jim. You poor thing.'

'So is a friend of his he was supposed to meet here—Oh shit. Those suits over there are watching us.'

Shannon said, 'They're hotel security. They're in the lobby all the time.'

Is this what it was like for Will when I wouldn't believe him? Jim wondered.

Shannon saw how troubled he was. 'Let's go to our room. Bye, guys. We're going to go—'

'You must dine with us.'

'Later, Carlos. Talk to you later.'

He scooped her up and she grabbed her crutches. 'Tenth floor.'

'Who are those guys?'

'Carlos and Ramón? They drove me to the harbour every day to look for you. Are you jealous?'

'I would be, if I wasn't scared. Didn't it strike you as just a little too convenient?'

'Listen to me. When I checked into the hotel I went to the workout room. I made friends with a trainer and I asked her about these boys I saw every afternoon in the lobby. She told me they were cousins who often stopped for coffee. OK?'

'All right. I guess they were safe. But Will got me into bigger trouble than we thought. We're getting on a plane home.'

'Help me pack, then.' She pulled a travel bag from under the bed. 'You've changed, Jim. You're more direct.'

'Can you stand it?'

'I think so.'

'God, Shannon, I'm so happy to see you.'

There was a knock at the bedroom door. 'Room service. *Amigos* send champagne.'

Through the peephole in the door, Jim saw a waiter with an ice bucket. 'It's champagne, all right. I wouldn't mind a glass.'

As he opened the door, Shannon said, 'Wait! It's a hundred and fifty a bottle. No way they—'

The waiter was already coming through the door, launching a kick at Jim's groin.

Shannon's warning saved his balls. He was stepping backward as the kick brushed past him, and he was able to catch the guy's heel and keep lifting. The waiter landed hard on his back in a shower of ice cubes and water.

The hotel security men Jim had seen in the lobby sprang from either side of the door. The first lost his footing on the bottle and fell. The second attacked Jim with a blizzard of kicks and punches.

The man was big and devilishly fast. He landed a shoe to Jim's stomach and two punches to his head. Jim fell back to cover Shannon. He felt wonderfully clear. The blows were bouncing off muscle. The months of learning to survive at sea had tempered his strength and boosted his reaction time.

When the guy stepped closer, Jim wrapped him in his arms and squeezed with all his might. The man screamed. Jim felt something snap and the body went limp.

Shannon screamed, '*Jim!*'

The other security man jumped off the floor like a jack-in-the-box. Jim threw the man he had bearhugged and the two went down in a heap, just as the waiter rose on one knee, yanking a gun from his cummerbund. Jim dived at him, trying to grab his hand. The waiter jerked the gun in a wide arc past Shannon into Jim's face.

Jim seized his wrist with both hands and bent it back, trying to make him drop the gun. The waiter's arm just kept bending and bending, and suddenly the gun fired with a dull thud.

'*Jim!*'

'I'm OK.' He rose slowly, staring at the fallen waiter. 'It hit him not me.'

The man Jim had bearhugged lay like a bent paperclip.

'Where's the other one?'

'He ran. Look out—'

The bent paperclip was straightening, pulling something black from his jacket. Jim flattened him with the bottle. The man's hand convulsed. A black wallet flipped open as it fell. Shannon snatched up the telephone. 'I'll call the police.'

A gold and black badge shone in the light that spilled from the corridor. Jim kicked the ice bucket out of the way and closed the door.

'No, don't call. They *are* the police.'

'WILL WARNED ME.' Jim was breathing hard, taking the steps two at a time down a utility stairwell. Shannon, as light as a feather on the tenth floor, was getting heavy. 'He told me the people who want Sentinel are connected all over the world.'

'Why didn't they just arrest us? Why try to trick us?'

'It wasn't official until one of them got shot.'

One flight below the lobby floor, a corridor opened onto a loading bay. In the street, sirens sounded in the distance.

'There's a taxi.' Jim got Shannon inside. 'US consulate. Palermo. *Por favor*.'

The driver drove like a madman through the evening traffic, crossing the Retiro barrio and skirting a dark shantytown. Suddenly they were there, the driver slowing in a traffic jam caused by a dozen police cars blocking the front of the US consulate.

'Oh shit.'

'Now what?' asked Shannon.

'I don't know.' If the cops were looking for them at the consulate they'd be watching the airports, too.

'Where's the boat?' Shannon asked.

'About a hundred miles downriver.'

The boat was low on diesel but they could sail out of the Río de la Plata and into the open Atlantic in half a day. Low on diesel, low on water, low on food, but gone.

They changed cabs and told the driver to take them back towards Retiro. Police cars were screaming all over the place. Every traffic cop seemed to stare at the taxi. The driver kept watching them in the mirror.

'Stop the car,' Jim said.

The guy mumbled, '*No entiendo*,' and kept going, eyes darting, clearly looking for a cop. Jim closed his hand on the driver's shoulder, found the radial nerve and sent a twinge travelling down the man's arm into his fingers. The driver pulled over and Shannon paid. They got out on a wide boulevard beside a park and waited until a raging chorus of horns forced the taxi to move.

'He's going straight to the cops.'

Jim reached for Shannon to pick her up again. She stopped him. 'We're too conspicuous. Let me use the crutches.'

Balancing herself on one crutch, she struggled into her backpack. 'I'll get myself to that café.' She pointed. 'Go the other way and find another cab.' She moved off.

It beat standing there waiting for the cops.

When he looked back, Jim saw Shannon had stopped to buy something from a street vendor—a hat to cover her blonde hair. The city was so dense with cars and pedestrians, within a hundred yards he was out of sight of anyone who had seen them get out of the cab.

He was looking for another cab when he noticed bicycles gliding past on a newly paved bicycle path. The third rider he called to spoke English. The nearby Velodrome had a rental kiosk, she told him. And there Jim got lucky.

Shannon was sitting at an outside table, watching the road for taxis, so Jim saw her before she saw him. She had covered nearly 200 yards on the crutches, a brutal haul. But her face lit up when she saw him pedalling towards her.

'You genius! A bicycle built for two.'

He helped her onto the front seat, got her feet on the pedals, and strapped her crutches alongside her backpack.

The flat path was easy going for a couple of miles, then it petered out and they were on a narrow, rutted dirt road that entered a neighbourhood of low brick houses. The road zigzagged and the houses, which stood cheek by jowl, began to squeeze it hard.

Here, the people staring at them looked totally different from anyone they'd seen so far—smaller, darker, and dressed in rags. Jim steered round a pile of garbage and wove a path through people pushing rusted shopping trolleys.

'Jim, I think we should get out of here,' said Shannon.

The street grew narrower still and the houses had turned to shacks made of corrugated metal and scrap lumber. The bike was too long to turn round. Jim stepped off and walked it, looking for a turnoff.

A little kid in ripped jeans and a dirty T-shirt shook a torn paper cup in Jim's face. In an instant they were surrounded by ragged children, reaching for their packs and grabbing at their pockets.

The children were so silent that Jim and Shannon could hear the distant whine of a train. Jim saw a flash of steel and felt something sting his thigh. When he looked down he saw that they'd slashed right through his pocket. A walnut-sized fist emerged from the cloth, stuffed with money.

They were pulling the bike, dragging it with Shannon still on the seat. He pulled her off and the bike vanished. Jim backed against a wall, gripping Shannon in the crook of his left arm, and fending off the silent, swarming kids with his right. A ten-year-old grabbed one of Shannon's crutches. Without them she was helpless and Jim felt her erupt into a torrent of frightened muscle. She thrust the other crutch like a cue stick and the kid let go.

Jim started to remove his backpack. 'Give them your stuff.'

But before hands could close on his pack, the children scattered. Six teenagers, as silent as the children, stood staring at Jim and Shannon. Five held knives. The sixth had a pistol. He gestured with it for them to follow him.

Jim had no choice but to swing Shannon into his arms and walk with them through the maze of narrow streets. They stopped in front of a brick house and the door opened instantly. The leader gestured again with the gun. The door closed behind them. They went through a series of rooms and narrow doorways, descending finally into a dank cellar—a low-ceilinged room crowded with children. In the glare of several oil lamps, they saw a broad, squat man sitting at a trestle table.

Jim felt Shannon shudder. The man's face was grotesquely scarred. He had no eyebrows and, Jim realised with a twisting stomach, no ears. One arm was a withered claw. The other, gracefully muscled, seemed to be the last remnant of a once strong and handsome man.

His milky left eye was blind. The other flicked from Shannon to Jim and back to Shannon's crutches. Then he smacked the table, and announced with childlike glee: 'Word of an Englishman! You found them. Welcome, Shannon. Welcome, Jim.' He snapped his fingers. 'Tell Eduardo we have them.'

Two boys hurried out. The children—a dozen or more—crowded closer.

'Who,' asked Shannon, 'is Eduardo?'

'Eduardo, pretty woman, is my negotiator. He will help set the price for the famous Jim and Shannon everyone is looking for.'

'You're going to turn us over to the police?' Jim asked.

'No, my muscled friend. The *policía* do not pay us. Put your pretty woman down. We'll bring her a chair. It is hard to stand on crutches, is it not?' He pointed at his useless legs.

They brought a cracked plastic chair and Jim lowered Shannon onto it. He was racking his brains, wondering if they could buy their way out of this with the gold krugerrands in his pack, when Shannon broke the silence.

'Your English is excellent. Where did you learn it?'

'I was born Brazilian. When Portuguese is your native language, you are wise to learn new tongues.' He looked down at his shrivelled body. 'My nurse spoke English—a nun. Here in BA, of course, there is much English, so mine has been exercised. I am called Stallone, by the way,' said the mutilated man. 'My "surf tag". May I ask what happened to your legs?'

Jim felt Shannon stiffen. She had told him only once the horror story of her accident and made him swear they would never speak of it again.

'An accident,' she answered. 'And yours?'

'An accident.'

Shannon and Stallone stared at each other for what seemed to Jim a very long time. Then Shannon said, 'Skiing.'

'Surfing,' said Stallone.

Shannon looked at him, clearly surprised.

Stallone laughed. 'Train surfing. *Surfistas* ride on the train's roof, dance in the wind. It feels wonderful, but there are problems. Falling off is one problem. The train runs over you. Or you land on your head at a hundred miles per hour. The other problem is electrocution. The electric cable that powers the locomotive is just above the roof. Four thousand volts. You start to fall, you grab the cable. You can't help it.'

He flashed white, even teeth, which, like his beautiful arm and hand, had survived intact. 'The electricity burned the fat right out of my legs and this arm.'

Shannon said, 'My father is a very wealthy man. He will pay you for us.'

Stallone shook his head. 'Sadly, your father is not nearly so wealthy as the people Eduardo is dealing with. Nor is he here. These people have been asking for you all over BA. They tell the police, the mafia, the gangs of the *villas miserias*: whoever finds the pretty blonde girl who can't walk, whoever finds her muscle man—name your price. Jim and Shannon are a very popular couple.'

'Double your money,' Jim said. 'It's me they want. Not her. Sell Shannon to her father. Sell me to the—'

'No,' said Shannon.

Stallone said, 'Be quiet, pretty woman. Your muscle man has a good idea.'

His eye glistened as Shannon said to Jim, 'Please don't leave me.'

Stallone jabbed a finger at Shannon's crutches. 'How did skiing do that to you?'

Jim started to speak in her defence, but Shannon's hand bit into his, and he listened as she challenged their captor.

'I did something as stupid as you did.'

Stallone's twisted body seemed to swell up. He gripped the table with both hands. 'What did you do?' he hissed.

'I went onto the ski mountain at night. When it was closed.'

Stallone nodded, though it was doubtful he had ever seen skis. 'You didn't pay?'

'Not a peso. It was free.'

'And you *felt* free?'

'All alone racing down the mountain. The snow glowed blue.'

'Fast?'

'Very fast. Fast as a train.'

Stallone flashed another smile. 'You crash.'

'I soar like a bird and I float to the ground. My knees bend to take the shock; they cushion the landing and I make a magnificent turn through a blue-glowing curve . . .'

'Then?'

'There, in front of me, is a snow cat. A tractor they drive up and down the mountain to groom the snow trails. It had broken down. It was a dark, silent mound of steel. I couldn't stop. No one could have.'

Stallone stared at Shannon. He whispered, 'I know. I knew I was reaching for the cable. I couldn't stop myself. I was afraid to fall.'

Abruptly, he swivelled to look round the cramped, dim room. Children and teenagers gazed back impassively. Stallone shrugged. 'What do these people want from you?' he asked Jim.

'Something I don't have.'

'They'll expect a better answer than that.'

'I don't have it.'

'They will "ask" until you give it to them. Or die. Her, too.'

He cocked his ear to a sound Jim couldn't hear. Those who had gone out earlier had returned with those who would do the asking. Two Americans, by the look of them. Soldiers or cops, the leader with arms and chest that said he could benchpress 400. Andy Nickels? His back-up was taller, with a swimmer's chest and shoulders. Buzz cuts, smooth-shaven, hard-planed faces.

'Where's Will Spark?' asked Andy.

Jim squeezed Shannon's hand lightly, trying to beam a thought into her brain: *Don't tell them Will is dead. If they think we have Sentinel they will torture us to death to get it.*

They had one hope—that the McVays would chase Will, believing him to still be alive.

'Last I saw he was headed east. Ten miles off Montevideo.'

'Where were you?'

'On the ferry to Buenos Aires. Will dropped me at Montevideo.'

'No one saw him there.'

'It's a big port. He dropped me right at the main quay.'

'Where is he headed?'

'I told you. East.'

'For where?'

'I don't know. What the hell is this about?'

'Why didn't he tell you where he was headed?'

'He claimed somebody was chasing him and that it would be better if I didn't know. I'm beginning to believe him.'

Was this the one who had bungled kidnapping Dr Ruiz? Jim wondered. Or had they hired locals? Or bought cops to do it?

'You're lying. If Will Spark had sailed east our people would have stopped him.'

'It's a big river. A hundred miles wide. You'd need a lot of people on a lot of boats to spot one little sailboat.'

'We have both.' He turned to Stallone. 'All right. We'll take them.'

Stallone said, 'Show me the money.'

Andy's henchman, Greg, tossed an orange and blue FedEx package onto Stallone's table.

'Open it.'

Every child in the room eyed the switchblade that Greg used to slash open the envelope. He dumped the contents on the table.

Stallone nodded at the banded stacks of twenty-dollar bills. He looked up at Nickels. 'I accept this money as ransom for you and your friend. A guide will lead you safely out of my barrio.'

'*What?*'

Greg and Andy Nickels exploded into motion. Each whipped a pistol from an ankle holster.

Children scurried. A box-cutter laid a deep, red track across the back of Greg's hand; his gun fell to the dirt floor. Two razors brushed his throat.

'Tell them to stop,' said Nickels. Blood was pouring from his hand, too, but he still held his pistol level at Stallone. 'Now!'

Stallone said, 'Check out the ceiling.'

Jim looked up and flinched. Children in the rafters were aiming short-barrelled shotguns. Greg said, 'They've got sawn-offs.'

'Do you know who you're cheating?' Andy asked Stallone.

Stallone pounded his chest. 'Here ,I am king. You are nobody.'

Nickels put down his pistol. Small hands fished his cellphone, his wallet and another gun from his pockets.

Raging, he turned on Stallone. 'If you cheat us we will hunt you to the end of the earth.'

Stallone shrugged. '*This* is the end of the earth. No one who enters leaves unless I say so—no cop, no gang, no yankee foreigner.'

Nickels turned to Jim. 'Give me Will Spark. Name your price.'

'I told you, Will is sailing east. All we want is to go home.'

'We will help you go home. We'll protect you from the cops.'

Jim looked at Shannon. 'Do you believe that?'

Shannon said, 'No.'

Stallone laughed. Then he said to Nickels, 'My little friends will show you out—the long way.'

STALLONE BRUSHED aside their stunned thanks. 'Surfers and skiers hang together. Besides, I keep the money.'

'You saved our lives.'

'Temporarily. You are safe only as long as you stay in my *villa miseria.* How will you get home to America?'

'We have a boat. It's just north of San Clemente.'

'San Clemente is far from my kingdom. Have you any money?'

'I have some gold krugerrands in my pack.'

'Gold is good. There is a person in La Boca who drives a van to Mar del Plata. San Clemente is on the way there. For gold he might take you.'

'What kind of shipment?' Shannon asked.

Jim said, 'We don't want to know.'

'Correct,' said Stallone.

AT DAWN, thousands of garbage trucks began their daily shuttle between the city's residential neighbourhoods and the shantytowns where they dumped their loads. One that trundled full into Stallone's barrio left still carrying a cardboard refrigerator box. As the truck passed through the Retiro barrio, the refrigerator box was buried under office trash and restaurant waste. Filled to the brim, the truck groaned on into the old working-class barrio of La Boca, where it disappeared into the loading bay of a hospital.

The Fiat van that pulled out of the hospital minutes later sped south on Route 2. Twice it was stopped by police, who took their regular bribe and waved the driver on. He told Jim and Shannon that he was a university student and only dealt drugs to his friends.

The third stop was at the hands of the provincial police, who were not at all friendly. Huddled under a blanket in the back, Jim and Shannon listened fearfully as the police circled the van. At last, they accepted the driver's bribe and waved him on.

An hour later, Jim directed him to Captain Faveros's front gate. Jim waited for the van to go before he rang the bell. After a few minutes, Captain Faveros came down the driveway in an open Jeep.

'I see you were successful, my young friend. *Buenas tardes, señorita.*'

Jim made the introductions and Faveros hesitated when he saw Shannon's crutches. 'Welcome, Señorita Riley. Come in, come in.'

Jim felt an immense relief as the Jeep rounded the first curve in the driveway and they were no longer visible from the road. 'Could you drive us right to our boat? We have to sail immediately.'

'I recommend you wait. There's a cold front approaching. You might encounter the *pampero.* Stay the night. Sail in the morning.'

Jim saw little choice but to be up-front. 'Captain Faveros, I have to tell you, the police are after us. We did nothing wrong, but the sooner we're out of here, the better for us. And for you.'

'Not to worry. I'll telephone my friend the district commander.'

'It's the federals from Buenos Aires. If we leave immediately, no one will know we were here.'

Captain Faveros stopped the Jeep as the quay came into view. Jim's heart jumped. There was a patch of empty water where he had anchored *Hustle.*

'Where's my boat?'

Faveros ignored his question. 'You must realise, it would be my duty to report your presence.'

'I swear to you we did nothing wrong.'

'That would not be for me to judge. What you tell me explains what I've been hearing on the marine radio channels. They are looking for your boat.'

'Who?'

'Private interests, shall we say. Certain fishing boats—smugglers—even a Customs cutter that I happen to know is crewed by thieves. It appears there's a sizable bounty.'

Jim heard him through a roaring in his ears. Would the McVays never give up?

'May I ask—without prejudice—did you steal your yacht?'

'No!'

'I took the liberty of taking it off the mooring.' Faveros put the Jeep in gear and drove to the quay. 'She's there, behind mine.'

Jim saw her, squeezed between the quay and Faveros's huge schooner. Only *Hustle*'s mast would be visible from the water. You would have to come within a hundred feet to distinguish the sloop from the bigger yacht.

'You'll be safe till dark,' Captain Faveros said.

'Why are you helping us?'

Captain Faveros looked down at his shoes. 'I know that I cannot undo my mistakes but perhaps if I can help you, and you are truly innocent, God will return me to my son's heart.'

Jim felt Shannon's gaze and he was struck by how totally responsible he would be for her safety once they set sail. 'What do you think?' he asked her.

'I can't believe you sailed all the way across the ocean on that.'

Huddled in the lee of Faveros's enormous yacht, Will's sloop looked small and insignificant.

'She's a solid boat,' he said firmly.

Faveros chimed in, 'I would imagine she is very forgiving.'

'Very forgiving,' said Jim, wondering what the naval veteran had picked up to guess that he was an amateur. 'Shannon, let's get aboard.'

'If there is anything I can do?' Faveros asked politely.

'Let me buy some diesel.'

'Yes, of—Excuse me.' He touched the beeper on his belt and punched a reply number into his cellphone. '*Sí . . . sí . . . Gracias.*' He holstered the phone and turned to Jim. 'The police have arrested a drug smuggler who claims to have dropped you off at my gate. They're coming now.'

Jim scooped Shannon off the quay and swung her into the cockpit. 'Help me cast off,' he said to Faveros.

Faveros sprang into action. He untied his yacht's stern line and carried it across Jim's afterdeck and onto his.

Jim started the engine and ran forward to untie the bowline. Standing on the afterdeck of his schooner, Captain Faveros leaned his weight on a boat hook and poled off from Jim's hull. Jim engaged his propeller and backed out.

'I'll keep them at the gate,' Faveros called. 'Bon voyage. Look out for the *pampero*.'

JIM LOOKED over his shoulder as the diesel engine roared. They were a mile from Faveros's mooring already. Which boats in the fishing fleet were angling for the bounty? Did the cops have a boat? He picked up the binoculars and focused on a yellow vessel putting to sea.

'Hey, Captain,' Shannon called. 'What's a *pampero*?'

'Local storm that comes screaming off the pampas. Humongous gusts and sheets of rain.'

'Would it hide us?'

'If it doesn't kill us.'

'While hiding us from the people who want to kill us.'

They both laughed. She looked as frightened as he was, but she said happily, 'Neat boat, Captain. Would you show me around?'

'I'll show you how to steer.'

It was humbling to see how fast she got it. In minutes she was laying down a respectable wake. Jim jumped below and brought up the storm jib. To their left, west, was a chequerboard sky of bright white clouds on a field of black.

The yellow boat was catching up, probably making a third again their speed. Already Jim could distinguish its round bluff bow and boxy cabin.

'You'd think,' said Shannon, 'that with the sky looking that way he would turn around and head home.'

'If he was just going fishing.'

Jim went below, put on his oilskin jacket, and brought one up for Shannon. The sky was now more black than white and *Hustle* was rolling in the brisker seas outside San Clemente Bay. Jim looked back. The yellow boat's bluff was throwing out clouds of spray.

A mile or so ahead, on a line with the Punta Rasa lighthouse, he could see whitecaps. A curtain of black descended to the estuary and seemed to be curling ahead of them, too.

'The boat's catching up,' said Shannon.

Jim realised with a start that less than 200 yards separated them. There was no one on the yellow boat's deck, but he could see several forms through the wheelhouse glass. Yard by yard it drew nearer.

Suddenly the wind stopped.

Hustle staggered and her sails hung slack. She lost two knots with only her engine to drive her through the thickening seas.

Two men dressed in sea boots and oilskins stepped out of the yellow boat's wheelhouse. They were twirling ropes, one moving towards the bow, the other towards the stern.

'Look out! They're throwing grappling hooks.'

Jim spun the wheel. Always slow to respond when driven by her propeller, *Hustle* veered clumsily. The hooks lofted through the air. The forward one splashed into the sea. The other crashed on the deck, bounced wildly, banged against the backstay, clanged on the aftmost safety-line stanchion, and, miraculously failing to hook it, fell into the water.

As Jim changed course, the yellow boat circled closer and the men hauled in their hooks.

The stern man threw again. Jim slammed the wheel over and the hook splashed harmlessly behind him. Then, as the second hook came flying across the water, he realised they had set him up. It was too late to do anything but shove the wheel into Shannon's hands and run forward, pulling Will's bosun's knife from his pocket.

The hook caught the bow pulpit. The rope jumped as taut as a steel bar and *Hustle* lurched into a clumsy, wallowing turn, dragged behind the fishing boat. Jim frantically sawed at the rope with the knife. A full sea nearly knocked him overboard as the rope parted with a loud bang. He ran back to the cockpit.

Shannon was fighting the wheel, trying to turn away from the high yellow bow at their stern. It was so close that Jim could see the expressions on the faces of the fishermen twirling the grappling hooks: triumph fired their eyes. Instead of a huge tuna or swordfish, they were going to hook a sailboat. Suddenly their expressions changed to abject terror. Jim looked over his shoulder. The black sky was yards from his boat—pounding down like a cataract.

'Hold on!' he yelled to Shannon.

A tremendous gust of wind slammed into the sails and knocked

Hustle onto her side. A slab-fronted sea struck before she could straighten up. It smashed against her hull like a bulldozer. The impact reverberated through the decks and, as sea water burst over his head, Jim thought, If she were made of wood she'd be splinters.

A second gust held her down. Heeled steeply, she shed the water from her decks, leapt up, and ran before the wind. Jim caught a single glimpse of the yellow boat's black bottom, and then it was gone and he was battling for their lives.

It was so dark he had to turn on the binnacle light to read the compass. They were headed due east, pushed by a westerly wind, straight at Cape San Antonio.

'Shannon! Grab this!' He handed her the mainsheet. 'Haul it in when I tell you.' He put the wheel hard over and held it, as *Hustle* cut across a sea that looked like a brick wall. She swung north. 'Now!' As the mainsail swept across the cabin, Shannon hauled in the slackening sheet.

A lightning bolt struck the land a quarter of a mile away and illuminated the sandbar, which was exploding with surf beside the boat. A gust veering north banged the sails, and *Hustle* slid closer to the bar. Another gust, from dead ahead, seemed to stop her in her tracks. Jim could hear the surf thundering and could feel it through the hull. When the lightning flashed again, he could see, close enough to touch, the line of breaking seas grabbing at the boat like a long white tentacle.

The wind wheeled—a powerful blast from the northeast. The sails crashed around and *Hustle* stampeded off on a starboard tack, racing away from the shallows. Jim couldn't believe how close he had just come to losing her. She'd been ten feet from impaling the bar with her keel—ten feet from falling on her side, seas battering her mast under water, smashing her down.

Beside him Shannon was hanging on like a bronco rider. He put his mouth to her ear. 'Are you OK?'

She turned to him, her eyes huge, and yelled, 'This is so cool!'

THE RAIN SLACKENED and Jim checked their GPS fix against the chart. 'We're miles clear of the point.'

'Nice going, Captain. I'm impressed.'

Jim's spirits soared. It looked like they had made it. The wind was swinging south and the temperature was dropping, which indicated the end of the *pampero*.

'She's a good boat. Will gave her to me.'

'You're kidding.'

'In his will. She's ours. If we want her.'

'Wow. Well, we have plenty of time to think about it. Right now I'm starving.'

'I can't leave the cockpit. Too many ships.'

'I'll make something. Don't worry, I'll find my way around.'

He showed her how to open the hatch and remove the washboards. Shannon lowered herself into the cabin. The last he saw she was locating light switches with a penlight she had found in Will's oilskins.

Half an hour later Shannon pulled herself up through the hatch. She was wearing another jacket and Will's sea boots. Having attained the cockpit, she reached down and produced two insulated mugs of soup.

'I tried the radios,' she said. 'The short-range. I heard a lot of *"Hustle"*. They're still looking for us.'

'Lots of luck. It's a big ocean.'

'But you said we're nearly out of fuel. And low on water. And I didn't see much food. Where can we get enough to sail home on?'

Jim was bone-weary. 'Let's just get through the night—put some miles between us and them—and we'll tackle a plan in the morning. Why don't you catch some sleep?'

'I'm staying with you.'

'One of us has to watch for ships.'

'We'll take turns. You first.'

IT WAS A PITCH-BLACK NIGHT without a star in the sky. When the wind ceased to gust and finally settled into a cold breeze from the west-southwest, Jim unfurled a bit of jib. An hour later, with weather conditions easing, he shook the second reef out of the main. *Hustle* responded with a gratifying eight knots. It felt wonderful to be in control of the boat again.

Twice, while Shannon slept, Jim slipped below and listened to the radio traffic. It was sprinkled repeatedly with the name of their boat. Returning to the cockpit, he covered Shannon with a heat-retaining, waterproof foil space blanket from one of the survival kits. Then, while monitoring the dark and the compass, he held Shannon in his arms and tried to put himself in Andy Nickcls's mind.

What if it was true that the McVay Foundation possessed the enormous state-within-the-state power that Will had claimed? If McVay wanted Sentinel enough to kill for it, wouldn't he use his power and money to divert ships to hunt Will down?

Nickels knew his speed. All he had to do was draw a circle from the Río de la Plata determined by time and speed and hunt within it. When the circle got too big, he would cover their likely landfalls.

Which left him and Shannon with the problem of where in hell to replenish supplies. The entire Argentine coast was out, and most parts of the Caribbean. No wonder Will had fled to Hong Kong.

At sunrise, Shannon was curled beside him, her head on his lap. Her face looked free of care, sure he would protect her. Her trust made him happy. She opened her eyes and smiled at him. Birds were wheeling and darting at the water. Foaming crests were tinged red by the dawn. 'It's so beautiful.'

'"Red sky at morning, sailors take warning."'

'It's still beautiful.'

V

THE ICE FIELD

'We're going south,' he said. 'The Falkland Islands.'

'How far?'

'Eight hundred miles.'

'Could we talk about this?'

'Well, sure, I mean . . . but what's to talk about?'

Shannon took his hand, opened it up and traced the lines in his palm. 'We've both been operating alone for the last three months. I think we have to sort of reboot—if we're going to be together.'

Jim laughed. 'If there wasn't an "if" in the middle of Buenos Aires, why would there be an "if" out here?'

'Don't take it for granted. That's one of the things that worry me about not being able to walk. You think I can't run away.'

'Are you happy to see me again?'

'I'm thrilled. I told you. My heart flipped when I saw you.'

'So, why would you want to run away?'

'The point is that you think I can't. That allows you to behave as if I won't. Like announcing, "We're going south." That affects our relationship.'

'Shannon, could we decide on our course before we discuss the relationship?'

'It's been on my mind, is all. I've been thinking a lot about us. I don't want you to think that I'm the best you can do.'

He was about to say that she was the best he *wanted* to do. But her face was closing down and he could hear his own voice getting louder. 'I might have felt that way sometimes in the past. I don't now.'

'Will you think about it?'

It occurred to him in the nick of time that this was not an argument to win. 'Yes,' he said. 'I will think about it.'

Shannon brightened immediately. 'So what's the scoop on the Falkland Islands?'

'Number one, being British territory they're the nearest place the Argentine cops can't touch us. Two, the McVay Foundation might not have much clout there, either. Three, they're probably expecting us to go north. Four, the Falklands are just a week or two away and we need food, water and fuel. Five, they might even let us get on a plane to London.'

'And leave the boat?'

'We'll have to talk about the boat . . . Six, Will had an old girlfriend there. If we need to we could go to her. Maybe she can help us.'

'But if the McVays knew about Will's doctor, wouldn't they know about his Falkland partner in crime, too?'

'She wasn't that kind of partner. She dumped Will because he was a crook.'

Shannon said, 'OK. Six good reasons. Any reasons not to?'

'Yes. One big reason. Very heavy seas.'

'Too heavy for the boat?'

'The boat can handle it. The question is, can we?'

'You were great yesterday.'

'Thanks. How do you feel about it?'

Shannon stretched her arms and took a long look around. The sun was burnishing *Hustle*'s wet decks red and gold. 'I am so happy to still be alive. And I am *so* happy to be with you again. Right now, if you said, "Let's sail to the North Pole," I'd say, "Why not?"'

'OK, we're going to hang a ninety-degree right. We've got the wind behind us, so we're going to let that mainsheet out, and the jib sheet.'

'Well, don't we sound nautical.'

He eased the jib sheet and helped Shannon with the main, then turned the wheel until the compass needle pointed 190 degrees—just west of due south.

'*Sailing Directions* recommends hugging the coast to avoid the current, but I'd rather fight the current than any ships they've got covering that angle—I'll show you on the chart. We'll figure out an exact course on the GPS.'

'I'm starving again.'

'I'll bring you a morsel. Then I'll charge the batteries and there'll be some hot water if you want a shower.'

'I would kill for clean hair.'

JIM WAS STUDYING a sobering weather fax at the nav station when Shannon emerged from her shower. She wore a towel like a turban on her head and a thick terry robe she had found in Will's locker.

Shannon reached for the heavy-weather teak handholds that lined the cabin ceiling. Strong arms rippling, she moved towards him by swinging herself from handhold to handhold. She made it look effortless, but traversing the twenty feet from the head to the nav station left her gasping for breath. 'Whew! Beats crutches. What's that? Oh, the weather fax . . . Those are depressions, aren't they?'

'Moving right across our path.'

'How much time before they hit us?'

'Tonight, tomorrow morning.'

'Then we've got time.'

'For what?'

'I'll meet you in bed.'

Jim went up on deck to check the sea. The wind was getting colder. He took a third reef in the main and looked once more for ships. All alone. Still, he switched on the radar and set the collision alarm before he joined Shannon in the aft cabin.

She was sitting up in bed, still in her robe. 'It's been so long I feel like it's our first date.'

'You wouldn't sleep with me on our first date.'

'Come here, Jim, let me hold you . . . I loved your emails. When you told me stuff you were thinking and feeling I really felt close to you. Do you know what I mean?'

'Shark attack.'

'That was obviously hard to write. You didn't say much. It was all between the lines. But I was really glad that you tried. You were talking to me, at last.'

'I worried I was moaning too much. It's hard to open up to somebody who's said, "No, thanks." I didn't want to be a pest. And I didn't want to sound more miserable than I was.'

'You told me what you were feeling. Like when Will was sick . . . It was like meeting somebody new.' She laughed. 'It makes me feel kind of funny being in bed with you. Like there are two of you, the Jim I used to be with and my new email Jim. Why are you laughing?'

'I'm not laughing. But, if you've ever had a threesome fantasy, now's your chance.'

IN THE HASTILY ASSEMBLED satellite receiver room, cooling fans hummed, keyboards chattered and light danced on the flat-panel displays.

Val McVay was tired after the fourteen-hour flight home from Buenos Aires—most of it spent on the satphone with the engineers setting up this war room.

She clicked her remote and zoomed in on the southwestern quadrant of the South Atlantic Ocean. 'You see those ships?' she said to her father. Each ship icon she activated with her laser pointer: a Taiwanese bulk carrier, two British, and a Russian.

'We "see" them by high-resolution infrared because they are steamships. Their smokestacks expel sufficient heat to penetrate the cloud.'

'But there is no smokestack on a sailboat.'

'It's getting cold. I would expect them to have a heater, venting through the top of the boat.'

Lloyd McVay peered intently at the monitor. 'We see the heat of their fire?'

'Yes. Burning diesel or bottled gas.'

On screen appeared a modified cruising hull, rigged in cutter mode.

Lloyd McVay said quietly, 'It matches. That's Will Spark.'

Val clicked again and data appeared in the lower-left corner. *Hustle? POS: 42° 21 S, 61° 17 W. SPEED: 5.4 knots. COURSE: 190.*

'South?' said her father. 'He's headed south?'

'Straight at the Falkland Islands. Could be that he intends to provision in Stanley.'

Her father studied the chart. 'Who do you think is on the boat?'

'Will Spark. And I presume Jim and Shannon joined up with him.'

'But you don't know for sure.'

'Andy was told that a sailboat outran a fishing boat that had gone out for the bounty.'

'So Andy told me on the satphone. Did they actually *see* the old man?'

'I believe that the fishing boat sank in the *pampero*.'

'Andy told me that, too. Though he didn't explain how Spark's sailboat survived.'

'It was more up to the job . . . Wait, we're about to receive the next live images.'

Val began clicking. Nothing changed on the monitors. The computer continued mindlessly panning the model, giving the false illusion that old information was new. Val tapped some more. 'Clouds. Dammit. We lost half the day's data stream except for the radar and it's not enough on its own.'

'*Twelve hours* since anything new?'

Val gestured at the bleak stats on the weather monitor. Thickening overcast stretched from the fortieth parallel south to the Falklands.

Her father said, 'Twelve hours. They could have sunk to the bottom of the sea, for goodness' sake.' Val suddenly got to her feet. 'Where are you going?'

'Tierra del Fuego.'

'What for?' Her father was clearly caught off balance, a rare and deeply satisfying sight.

'The Argentine Air Force has granted permission to land the Hawker at their Río Grande base. Andy and his men are picking me up in a boat I bought in Buenos Aires.'

'Don't be ridiculous.'

Val McVay fixed her father with a cold eye and then, in a move more mocking than tender, straightened his bow tie. 'What is ridiculous about tracking Will Spark by satellite and recapturing Sentinel with a faster boat?'

'Look, Val, you'd best stay here until we positively ID Spark's yacht.'

'It's all set up, Dad. The team here will handle the tech side. All you have to do is relay their position.'

'Dammit, it will take Andy a week to sail there.'

'I bought a rocket ship. They tied up an hour ago.'

JIM HAD FINALLY caught up with his sleep, napping in Will's hammock by the companionway. The weather fax showed no big depressions for a while. They had crossed the forty-third parallel. And Shannon was taking to the boat like she was born on it.

With Jim's help she had rigged a line from a clamp on the backstay that she used to swing herself from the back of the cockpit to the companionway. There she fastened the line for when she came up and lowered herself down into the cabin.

'No stars tonight, Captain?'

'Rain. *Mucho* rain.' He could see it marching ponderously out of the west. It would reach them around dark and probably pour all night. Fine with him. Steady rain beat by a long shot the squalls that had knocked them around the first two days out of the Río de la Plata.

'I'll get a clean sail later and see if we can catch some rainwater.'

'Oh, Jim,' said Shannon. 'It's so *gorgeous* up here. I don't want this to end.'

'Don't you think we should get home safe, as soon as we can?'

'Yeah, but I don't want to.'

'Well, we need food and diesel.'

'We've got two months of emergency rice and a ton of beans.'

'We could freeze if we run out of diesel.'

'We've got about five gallons left. If we just use the engine to charge the batteries, the heater doesn't burn much. And if we sail somewhere warm, we won't even need that.'

Jim said, 'Why don't we see what we find in the Falklands? If we find plenty of food and fuel in Stanley, we can talk about sailing home. Or maybe we can just fly home and come back in the future.'

'What would we do with the boat? Just leave it?'

'Maybe we could anchor her at Will's friend's place.'

'And spend a fortune on ten-thousand-mile plane tickets back and forth. Money that could go into maintaining *Hustle* instead of abandoning her.'

'You are talking about her like she's your cat.'

Shannon turned away. 'She has a soul. Maybe you don't feel it, but I do.'

Jim went below to Will's desk and opened his old logs. It was ten years since Will had sailed in. Would the approach to Cordi's home on West Falkland Island be the same?

Will had meticulously recorded the course into a bay he had dubbed 'Cordi's Bay'. He had noted landmarks—a tall rock, an abandoned jetty—into the inner anchorage, 'Cordi's Cove', where he lined up a white house with the peak of a rocky hill.

What if they got caught? According to *Sailing Directions* a military commissioner maintained security in the British Crown Colony. On the other hand, the two main islands and hundreds of smaller ones had an 800-mile coastline and a landmass the size of Connecticut. An excellent place to get lost. Who would notice a single sailboat?

He took some tea up to Shannon in the cockpit.

'I've been thinking,' he said. 'We could have problems in Stanley. Your passport was stamped in Argentina and Barbados is my last stamp. In. I never got one going out. So if we try to clear Customs we could have hassles, which could lead to "Where-is-Will-Spark?" hassles.'

'They'll figure it out. I mean, you didn't kill him. He died.'

'Yeah, they'd figure it out eventually. Problem is, when they do they might seize the boat.'

'Why?'

'I told you. Will said he was wanted for fraud in the UK. The Falklands are part of the UK.'

'So what are you thinking?'

'What if, instead of going to Stanley, we just "popped in" on this Cordi friend of Will's? Show her his will—she gets everything but the boat. Maybe she could sell us food and diesel and we could just head north. She's way down on the southwest coast of West Falkland Island. Stanley's a hundred miles away.'

Night was nearly fifteen hours long this far south. Jim thought that they could mask most of their approach in darkness, timing their arrival so as to navigate the dangerous coastal waters in the light of dawn.

'Maybe we could just slip in "under the radar",' he said. 'We'd have a short day there and slip out just before dark.'

'Slip out on the boat?'

'Well, yeah, that's what I'm saying.'

'Stay on the boat?'

'Isn't that what you wanted?'

'I would love that so much.'

DAWN FOUND THEM skirting the west coast of West Falkland Island. The reassuring eighty-metre readings on the depth finder did not prepare them for the sight of the heavy seas pummelling steep cliffs.

Jim headed up into the west wind. Close-hauled, shoved by the swells and gripped by currents he hadn't noticed in the dark, *Hustle* seemed caught by the opposing forces. She clawed off and fell back, clawed off again and fell back again. Jim continued hand steering, coaxing the boat. Shannon was trying to match the coast to the chart.

'I think we're supposed to be on the other side of that point.'

The point was marked by a stony bluff barely visible a mile ahead.

Jim marked its bearing on the compass and watched tensely for an indication of movement either way. The first clue that the boat was making way was the sight of a string of hills behind the cliffs. The boat was moving off.

Jim sailed off for nearly an hour before he felt safe to try to swing round the point. He was planning the steps he had to take to gybe between the headlands that sheltered Cordi's Bay, when he heard a deep ripping noise approaching from the west.

With a sudden shrieking crash, an enormous dark-coloured fighter jet screamed overhead, skimmed the cliffs and thundered east. They waited for it to swoop round for a second look. Jim couldn't meet Shannon's eye. If the military plane spotted them they would have no choice but to radio who they were and try to clear Customs.

A minute stretched to two and slowly to three before Jim said, 'Maybe he didn't see us.'

The entrance between the cliffs was a third of a mile wide. They lined up and swung nearly north, the sails banging around in a hard gybe. Jim felt the seas start to shove her off course. Then *Hustle* accelerated. He engaged the propeller for more push and drove the final quarter of a mile into a bay surrounded by low, rocky coast.

He powered into the wind, steering for the abandoned jetty Will had noted.

'There's the tall rock.'

'And there's her house.'

A whitewashed stone cottage with a slate roof slid into view. Smoke was curling from the chimney. There were long glass structures on either side, greenhouses that flanked the old house like gossamer wings.

When the peak of the rocky hill appeared to be behind the stone house, Jim motored into Cordi's Cove, and steered for a sturdy pier that projected from the rocky beach.

'Someone's coming,' said Shannon. She waved.

A white-haired woman was running from the house, pulling on a windcheater, calling 'Billy!'

The woman caught the line Jim tossed and took a wrap around a piling while he backed *Hustle* against the quay and jumped onto it with the stern line.

'Where is Billy Cole?'

'Are you Ms MacDonald? Cordi MacDonald?' Jim asked.

'Yes.'

'I'm sorry. Billy was—injured . . . He died three weeks ago.'

'Oh, my Lord.' She looked like she was going to faint.

Jim grabbed her arm. Shannon dragged herself closer and took Cordi's weathered hand in hers.

'Would you like something?' she asked Cordi. 'Tea?'

Cordi blinked. 'Where are my manners? Come inside.'

'Are you sure you're all right?'

'I'm fine. It's just a bit of a shock, that's all.'

'I DON'T WANT IT.'

'It could be worth a lot some day.'

'I don't want anything that Billy left because anything he left he likely stole.'

. Jim said, 'I had the impression this Sentinel was actually legitimate. The patents and royalties could be worth something—though who knows where it is.'

'That's Billy in a nutshell.' Cordi folded the will and handed it back. 'It's very good of you to bring this to me. But I don't want it.'

While making tea in her comfortable kitchen, Cordi kept glancing out of the window. 'I would get the boat off the mooring sooner rather than later. We've got a blow coming in.'

'I'm curious,' said Jim. 'How did you know this was Will's boat?'

'He sent me a snap when he bought her. Told me about the refit.'

'You stayed close?' asked Shannon.

Cordi turned to her with a smile. 'I loved him with all my heart, loved his enthusiasms, loved his charm. But for all his talents, Billy would prefer a dishonest penny to an honest pound. That was bad enough, but when he got older, he grew greedy.' She stared out of the window. 'One of the things I've enjoyed about getting "of an age" was finally knowing when to say no . . . Excuse me.'

A radio was crackling. She opened a cabinet and donned a headset. 'Cordi here . . . Who's that? . . . Thank you, Willard . . . Out.'

She turned to Shannon. 'Did you report in to Stanley?'

'No. We sailed right in.'

'It seems that British Security has put out an alert about your boat. An RAF pilot tried to raise you and got no reply.'

'We left the radio off.'

'Well, you're going to have to do something about it. The fisheries inspectors will be on the lookout. And the RAF. And anyone with a radio. Which is everyone.'

Jim and Shannon looked at each other. Jim said, 'Could you ask someone in Stanley if there are any Taiwanese or Russian ships in the harbour?'

'Whatever for?'

'Will—Billy—had some dealings and they are—'

'Say no more. I can imagine any number of Billy scenarios provoking hordes of Chinese and Russians.'

Cordi radioed her friend Dora. She switched on the speakers so Jim and Shannon could listen in. Dora reported that a Russian container ship had steamed away three hours ago.

'They just don't give up,' said Jim.

Cordi's friend said, 'A ginormous racing yacht put in this morning. A ruddy great black thing—a catamaran.'

'Odd time of year to race,' said Cordi.

Dora agreed. 'Americans racing in the winter! With a woman, no less!'

Jim asked, 'Did she say Americans? What's the boat called?'

'Does the boat have a name, Dora?'

'*JoyStick*,' came the reply. Cordi ended the call.

Jim shrugged. What name was he expecting? McVay Foundation Chase Boat?

'Let's just go,' Shannon said. 'Cordi, could we possibly buy some food from you?'

Cordi laughed. 'No farmer ever turned down cash. I've got potatoes, leeks, onions, turnips and Brussels sprouts—all of which should keep well on the boat. And I've got lashings of tinned meat and fish, biscuits, pasta.'

'Is there any place we could buy diesel fuel?'

'Not from me. I'm waiting on the tanker—I'm down to fumes. But I've got a friend. You can raft up with him and pump it into your tanks.'

They loaded the boat quickly, Jim wheelbarrowing bags and boxes of food from Cordi's store to the quay, Shannon stowing it below.

Cordi's friend, Peter, met them in sheltered water just inside the mouth of the bay. The young fisherman had a hand-cranked pump. Jim took turns with him, transferring seventy gallons from the big fishing boat into *Hustle*'s tanks.

Peter, like Cordi, agreed to payment in half-ounce gold krugerrands. 'We've got a blow coming,' he told Jim quietly. 'Get far offshore. Immediately.'

'I want to head north.'

'Not on your life. You'll end up on the rocks.' The young

Falklander spoke firmly, as if to a child wandering in traffic. 'If it were me, I would sail south for deep water then run east before the wind. Only don't go too far south or you'll find yourself on the Burdwood Bank.'

The Burdwood Bank was marked clearly on the chart, a 200-mile-long, sixty-mile-wide patch less than 100 metres deep. It didn't take an old salt to picture the effect of storm-driven Cape Horn seas rolling over its shallow waters. But Peter cautioned anyway, 'It will not be pretty.'

JIM HAD NEVER SEEN anything like the seas piled up by the low-pressure systems sweeping in from Cape Horn. With darkness falling, they had just crossed the 200-metre line into deep water and he made the mistake of switching on the work lights. *Hustle* was at that instant perched on the crest of a wave, and the powerful lights gave Jim a frightening view of swiftly moving mountains of white water. They looked taller than the boat and twice as fast.

As it raced ahead, the sailboat descended into a deep trough. Suddenly they were at the bottom of the pit, and in the shuddering beams of light Jim glimpsed the next wave. A white slab of water was erupting behind the boat, taller than a truck. But *Hustle* climbed it. She attained the crest then started sliding down the back as the wave raced on.

Jim saw that there was order out here. The seas were advancing as implacably as an army, but they marched in harmony. He could deal with that. So, too, could the autohelm. He set it to take the waves at a slight angle to the stern. The big rollers overtook the boat, gave her a boost, and raced on. The boat was on course. Rest when you can, Will had told him, so he went below.

They ran with the storm the full length of the Falklands' south coast, covering 100 miles by dawn and forty more by noon. The wind had backed north in the night and driven them much closer to the Burdwood Bank shallows than Jim had intended. The depth finder still read a reassuring 1,000 metres of deep water under the keel, however.

The afternoon light was strong. A thin wintry sun lit miles and miles of desolation. Somewhere in their wake lay the Falkland Islands. Far to the south was Antarctica. Ahead, the ocean stretched across the planet, empty all the way to South Africa. But, as *Hustle* lingered high on the crest of a great comber and Jim looked back, he was amazed to see another boat.

JOYSTICK'S STEERING stations were set aft on each hull. Val McVay was steering from the port station, constantly moving her head to keep one eye on the following seas, the other on the mast.

She and Greg and Pete and Joe were sharing the helm, an hour on and three off to keep their concentration. It was focus or die.

JoyStick felt remarkably steady—an ocean straddler with the light stance of a water spider. But she was not stable, as several hairy near broaches in the night had demonstrated. She had pitched forward twice since they'd gone screaming out of Tierra del Fuego, simultaneously burying her knife-thin bows under tons of sea water while flinging her rudders uselessly in the air.

So far Val had been able to manoeuvre out of the nose dives, but it was only a matter of time before the cat stuffed a bow while one of the guys was at the helm. And with the exception of Greg, the former SEALs had little experience on cats.

Val gave her crew high marks for keeping busy. When they weren't sailing the boat, they were fixing something, and when they weren't fixing something, they were cleaning their weapons. In between watches and chores, they slept like wolves digesting their last kill.

This was especially important as they were short-handed. Ideally she'd race *JoyStick* with a crew of eight or ten. They were five. But Will Spark was short-handed, too. Nor was this race destined to last long. The satellites were homing in on him. And her boat could sail three times as fast as his.

Andy Nickels had risen in her estimation. He was no sailor, but he had quickly learned to puke downwind. He displayed no interest in the boat other than as a means to catching Will Spark. Whereas Greg was in his element. At daybreak, he had climbed the mast, and was scoping the sea from the top spreader, 150 feet above the deck. Now, he spoke in Val's radio headset. 'Can you bear right five degrees, ma'am? I think I see something.'

JIM WOULD NEVER have seen the boat behind them at such a distance if it weren't black—the one colour that stood out in the swirls of grey cloud and white water. 'A ruddy great black thing' Cordi's friend had called the racing yacht in Stanley.

The next crest lifted *Hustle* until the sea again spread before him. The tall, spiky silhouette looked closer. He counted the rollers that separated them—it looked like eleven. From the next sea, he saw it again, ten crests back. Time to speed *Hustle* up. He was struggling to raise the main when Shannon came scrambling through the hatch.

'More sail?'

'Look. Ten crests back. You'll see in a sec.'

'Wow, is that the racer Cordi's friend saw?'

'I don't know. Can you count how many crests back he is?'

'Looks like . . . seven, eight . . . nine.'

'He's gaining on us.'

'What's that yellow thing up on top?'

Jim passed Shannon the binoculars just as a roller lifted them up.

'Jim, there's a guy on top with some kind of telescope. It's too big a coincidence. He's got to be looking for us.'

'THEY'RE RAISING another sail,' Greg reported from the masthead.

JoyStick sprang to the top of a crest and there they were, half a mile in front. Val watched with some alarm as the main sail rose jerkily up the mast, from a triple-reef position to a double.

She said to Andy Nickels, 'Better get somebody into a wet suit.'

'What for?'

'They're carrying too much sail. If they broach we've got to pull Will Spark out of the water.'

'The water's freezing. He'll be dead in three minutes.'

'Then prepare *now* to get him out in *two*. He's probably got Sentinel on his person. But if he's left the prototype on the boat, we've got to find out where before it sinks.'

Val concentrated on keeping the catamaran under control. It had not occurred to her until this moment that she might frighten Will into accidentally sinking himself.

JIM WAS SHOCKED by the black boat's speed. It had halved the distance between them and was suddenly little more than a quarter of a mile behind. Startling, too, was its size. Its spire of sail and mast scraped the sky like a black steeple.

Shannon was studying it with the binoculars. 'Two hulls. No wonder she's fast . . . There's a guy standing on the first spreader and three in the back . . . I think the guy on the spreader has a gun—Jim, get down! It's them. He's aiming it.'

Pushing off from the cockpit coaming with her arms, she threw herself at Jim. They sprawled to the narrow deck between the benches. A high-power bullet whipped past the mast with a *crack*.

The wind banged into *Hustle*'s mainsail and an errant cross sea smacked her bow. The combined force overrode the autohelm, and the boat turned into the wind, baring her hull to the following sea.

Jim lunged for the helm. 'We'll broach! I gotta steer.'

A second murderous *crack* drove them back to the deck. The sea reared and a wind gust crashed into the mainsail. Knowing what was coming and helpless to stop it, Jim grabbed Shannon and held her tightly as the boat fell on its side.

The icy water broke over them, flooding the cockpit. The rolling sea filled the mainsail and held the boat flat like a pinned wrestler. Shannon screamed. Jim yelled, 'She'll come up. She has to.'

'LOST 'EM,' GREG RADIOED.

'What do you mean, "lost"?'

'They fell behind a wave. They're gone.'

'They can't be gone,' Andy Nickels yelled into his mike. 'They're only two hundred yards ahead. Look for them.'

JoyStick rocketed to the top of a high crest. At the helm, Val could see for miles. From *JoyStick*'s bows to the dark horizon, the jagged, blistered sea was empty.

WE'RE GOING TO DIE right here and now, thought Jim. The sea must have smashed a hatch and *Hustle* was filling with water. Why else would she lie on her side like this? Thousands of pounds of lead in her keel should have whipped *Hustle* upright.

Instead, she lay flat, her mast, storm jib and mainsail submerged. Then, with a loud, wet, whooshing sound, the sails tried to spill their load of water.

'Here we go. Hold on, Shannon.'

Jim grabbed the helm as *Hustle* sprang upright. The black boat had passed them, running with the wind at an incredible speed, leaving them in its wake.

'They couldn't see us when we got knocked down.'

'They'll see us now.'

And indeed, before the catamaran had raced half a mile, the crew must have spotted them, because she suddenly changed course, peeling away to the north.

'Where are they going?'

'It's a catamaran,' said Shannon. 'They can't sail as close to the wind as we can.'

'At that speed they don't have to.'

'What are we going to do?' asked Shannon.

Jim looked around frantically. The knockdown had been a blessing in disguise. But it was the only gift they'd get, and they'd better not waste it. The only direction he could go that the catamaran couldn't was south. But the Burdwood Bank lay south.

He watched the black boat skimming the edge of a roller.

Shannon had it in the binoculars. 'They're turning.'

'How many crew?' he asked.

'I see five.'

'They must have their hands full.'

When it was a mile behind and closing fast, Shannon said, 'He's not aiming the gun yet.'

'Get down.' He dragged her off the bench onto the floor of the cockpit. Scalp prickling, Jim poked his head up to judge the distance. 'OK, get ready. We're going to do a one-eighty to starboard.' He reached up to the controls and shoved the throttle to full power.

The black boat was only 200 yards behind, its bows rising like a pair of knives. Jim waited until the last second, then hauled himself up on the helm, turning it as he climbed to his feet.

Hustle swung sharply to starboard, right in the path of the black catamaran. He saw immediately that he had cut it too close.

He thought he heard the man on the mast yell as the twin hulls bracketed the slow-moving sailboat. He felt the propeller bite tentatively. The sloop swung through the wind. The sails shifted from port to starboard and she accelerated across the path of the catamaran, which sheered to port. Jim braced for a hull-splintering crash. But a wave shoved them roughly aside as the huge cat roared past.

'Jim! Look out!'

A diver in a wet suit strode in long bouncing leaps across the net between the two hulls. Using the springy material like a trampoline, he launched himself over the side and into *Hustle*'s cockpit.

A hightop Adidas trainer came flying at Jim's face. He blocked it with both hands and the diver soared over him and fell against the sail. His face mask was ripped off in the fall and Jim saw that it was Andy Nickels, whom they'd last seen in Stallone's *villa miseria*. Nickels jumped to his feet and drew a bayonet. 'Where's the old man?'

'Left!' yelled Jim. Shannon turned the helm hard left and *Hustle* heeled sharply to port. The wind smacked into the sail and the boom whipped across and swept Andy Nickels into the sea.

THE BLACK BOAT was two miles behind, circling to pick up the fallen man. Shannon was watching with binoculars. 'They're hoisting him up with a halyard. I hope that bastard freezes to death. Oh God, here they come again.'

'OK,' Jim said. 'We're going south, as close to the wind as we can.'

'That'll put us on the Burdwood Bank.'

'It's too rough for them to make speed. All we have to do is get away from them in the dark. By daylight tomorrow we'll be a hundred miles from here. They'll never find us.'

JIM HAD EXPECTED to be bounced around. He'd even expected to be seasick. But he had not expected that he and Shannon would be thrown around the cabin like ping-pong balls. Bruised, cold and exhausted, they both struggled to hold the boat close to the wind while driving her across the bank. It was a long, brutal night and an equally grim day.

As night gathered in the east again, the crashing and banging had still not ceased.

'At least,' said Shannon, 'we got rid of them. I was so afraid they'd stay right behind us.'

Some time after midnight the fierce chop began to level out and the pounding slowly eased. By dawn, *Hustle* was ploughing a somewhat smoother course, climbing and descending long, deep Southern Ocean swells.

Between snow squalls, Jim went up on deck to make his rounds. He discovered that the spinnaker pole had gone overboard some time in the night. The massive spar had been plucked from its cradle like a strand of linguine. They had no spare but, on the upside, he had no intention of flying a spinnaker in the Southern Ocean. He smelt coffee brewing and he was heading with a grateful smile to the companionway when he saw silhouetted in the east a tall, black spike.

Without pausing to think, Jim leapt to the mast, let fly the halyards and dropped the mainsail on the cabin and the storm on the foredeck.

Shannon opened the hatch. 'What is going on?'

'They're back.'

Jim started the engine and put the boat back on course, tight into the wind. How in hell had they found them? Or was it just bad luck?

The cold wind turned suddenly colder. The source, they saw, was a new line of snow squalls roaming out of the west, bunched like a herd of woolly black mastodons.

He looked at Shannon. She shook her head in resigned disbelief. 'Do it,' she said.

He altered course to intercept the darkest squall, and before *Hustle* had closed within a mile, snow was swirling around her. Jim looked back and watched the black spire dissolve into a soft white horizon.

By nightfall they had lost count of how many squalls they had fought. They strapped themselves into the pilot berth, grateful to have escaped the black boat and too tired to care about the weather.

JIM WOKE UP, thirsty, hungry and tired. Something had jarred him out of sleep. Then he heard a sharp *thump* against the hull. He pulled on his foul-weather gear and went up on deck.

It was pitch-black and he shone a spotlight around the boat. Chunks of ice were floating in the water. Ahead of the boat the beam reflected off a piece as big as a car. He took the helm and steered round it. For a while he saw nothing, but he was afraid to return to sleep in case they ran into another piece. Thus he was still at the wheel when dawn broke. He took a long, careful look for more ice, then ducked below.

'You poor thing,' said Shannon. 'I'll watch for a while.'

He collapsed into the pilot berth and closed his eyes. Hours or seconds later, he knew not which, Shannon called urgently and he sat up with his heart pounding.

'What? What?'

'They're coming up behind us.'

WILL'S SLOOP could sail closer to the wind than the catamaran. But though they could manoeuvre in directions *JoyStick* couldn't go, the cat had a terrifying genius for finding them again.

'How can they always know where we are?' asked Shannon. 'Radar?'

'According to Will, they'd have to have an immensely powerful radar, and there's no way they would generate enough electricity on a sailboat. It's something else, like satellites. Will said the McVays were big in military electronics.'

'So what do we do?'

'I don't know. Try to outsail them?'

They pored over the chart. The easier routes were downwind to Australia.

'We can't go downwind, they'll catch up in a flash.'

'The wind is west. The only thing west is Cape Horn.'

It was 300 miles to Cape Horn. They made fifty miles in two days. It seemed that every other wave smashed the sloop back two yards. When the immensely strong Kevlar jib broke, they finally admitted they could not even reach Cape Horn, much less round it.

They bore off to the northeast. But no sooner had *Hustle* settled onto the easier course than they saw the black steeple spike the horizon. They retreated in the only direction left to them. South into the violent seas of the Drake Passage.

HUSTLE WAS PLODDING warily somewhere off the Antarctic Peninsula—an ever-shifting world of drifting packs, towering icebergs and pressure ridges thrust up like Gothic castles.

They had no business being here. *Hustle*'s fibreglass hull was no match for the floating ice. But now, two grim weeks and 1,000 miles south of Cordi's snug farmhouse in the Falkland Islands, *Hustle* was running out of ocean.

Jim began to laugh. 'Will said to keep running even after Antarctica.'

'Where?' Shannon asked.

'I don't know. The South Pole. Jesus, what a mess.'

'It doesn't sound like him to say that.'

And suddenly Jim realised why Will wanted him to flee.

'Oh my God. We're running for him.'

'What do you mean?'

'Will is using us. He set us up to draw the McVays away from Sentinel. It isn't on the boat.'

'Of course it isn't. It's in Will's head at the bottom of the ocean.'

'It's at the bottom of the ocean, all right. But not in Will's head. Will *said* it was in his head and I believed him. Oh my God. I've finally figured him out.'

'You're tired, Jim. You're not making sense.'

'Yes, I am! Will conned me into continuing the wild-goose chase . . . I finally understand him. He told me that for the first time in his life he had hit a home run. For the first time Will Spark wanted the prize more than he wanted to play the game.'

'What are you saying?'

'Will was so desperate for his home run that he kept the microprocessor for himself. He hoped to escape the McVays and still cash in. But when I spotted their ship at the equator he panicked. So he "deep-sixed" it along with my heart-rate monitor.'

'Are you saying Will threw Sentinel overboard in the middle of the ocean?'

'Yes! I didn't register at the time, but Will threw two things overboard. My monitor in a plastic bag and a second item—a waterproof container holding the microprocessor. That's what splashed.'

'What splash?'

'I heard a splash. The plastic bag wouldn't splash. He threw the microprocessor overboard at the same time . . . I'll show you. Take the helm.'

Jim dived below and checked Will's entry in *Hustle*'s log for the day they spotted the ship hunting for them near Saint Paul Rocks. Sure enough, Will had noted the sighting of the ship. He had determined their exact position by GPS.

Jim returned to the cockpit in a daze. 'He meant to go back. I just looked at the chart. All you have to do is punch in the coordinates and follow the GPS back to that spot. Just like when the FBI caught him. He deep-sixed his money and dived for it when he got out of jail.'

'But the ocean must be miles deep.'

'Actually, its less than a mile deep where he dropped it. I'll bet you anything that right until the second he died he thought he would somehow manage to sail back there.'

'And then what? Scuba-dive a mile deep? No way, Jim.'

'So he must have had another plan—some way to make Sentinel float to the surface.'

'How would he activate it?'

Jim looked to the north as if his eye could magically see the hot pearly sky of the equatorial ocean. Instead he saw the black catamaran looming out of the wind-driven snow.

THE HUGE CAT was racing east to west on a broad reach. Zigzagging. Jim studied it with the binoculars, puzzled.

'Ice dead ahead!' Shannon cried.

Jim dodged the submerged floe. That's why the catamaran was zigzagging. They were dodging ice, too.

He put the helm hard over.

'Where are we going?'

'Either they'll crash into a hunk of ice and sink. Or we'll lose ourselves in the snow.'

'They won't sink,' she said. 'Catamaran hulls are full of watertight compartments.'

Crack! A high-powered slug smacked past the mast.

'Get down!'

Crack! The second shot passed the backstay.

Down he went, flat on his face. The cat had come about and was clawing closer to the wind to intercept them, while the gunman on its mast was pinning them down so they couldn't sail *Hustle*. Flat on the cockpit sole, Jim was out of tricks.

Shannon said, 'Promise me you won't do anything stupid when they come aboard.'

Jim said, 'Can you get below? Will's shotgun is in the aft cabin in one of the bunk drawers. Pass it up to me.'

Shannon shook her head, but slid the hatch open and slithered down the companionway. Jim took another look. The cat was nearer, starkly visible through the snow.

'Jim!' Shannon opened the port in the side of the cockpit and passed Will's sawn-off shotgun through it. Jim took the stubby stock. Her gloved hand reached through with three cartridges. 'Do you know how to use this?'

'I shot clay pigeons in Boy Scouts.'

He took a quick look through the binoculars. The cat had closed to within 200 yards. Andy Nickels was braced on the first spreader with a rifle. Another man was on the bow spotting ice. They made tempting targets in their yellow foul-weather suits. But he didn't have a prayer of winning a gunfight with heavily armed professionals.

In another second, they were so close that the rifleman on the spreader could look down over *Hustle*'s sail and shoot him where he lay on the floor of the cockpit. It was now or never. Jim rose on one knee and took aim at the halyard winches clustered at the base of *JoyStick*'s mast. The shotgun's report was a deafening boom. The recoil staggered him. Quickly he jammed another shell into the breech and fired again. But the boats were moving apart and already the catamaran was out of shotgun range.

As the boats separated, Andy Nickels saw Jim grab the wheel. He raised his weapon and took careful aim. He began to squeeze the trigger, intending to take out the shotgun by shattering Jim's shoulder with a high-powered slug.

Focusing intently on a difficult shot between two boats in wild motion, he ignored the high-pitched shriek of a broken halyard wire flying up its channel inside *JoyStick*'s mast. Only when a shadow passed over his face did he look up. Like the wing of a giant albatross, fifteen storeys of black mainsail tumbled down the mast and enveloped him in thundering, wind-struck folds.

VAL SAW CHAOS ERUPT. Everything went wrong at once. The mainsail fell, billowing like a parachute, blocking her view of the water ahead. A sixty-knot gust filled the jib at the same instant and with no mainsail to balance the foresail, the wind slewed the cat into a ninety-degree skid.

She was sailing blind at twenty-five knots when the port bow struck ice. The deck slammed under her feet and Val felt herself go flying. Suddenly she saw grey water coming at her face.

Next thing she knew, she was under water so cold that the exposed skin on her face felt like it was burning. Her buoyant dry suit floated her to the surface just as *JoyStick* flew away.

She watched in utter disbelief as the huge catamaran careened out of control, racing for the horizon. Suddenly it reared up on its starboard hull, dipped its mast in the water and turned upside-down.

The snow descended like a dark blanket and she was alone, floating up to her chin in freezing sea water, fully aware that her HPX Ocean Dry Suit would keep her alive for two hours. Viewed logically, this was not an acceptable option.

Sentinel was lost. No. *She* had lost Sentinel. How could she have been so stupid as to go sailing? *She*, who knew that the quintessence of computer science was to dominate events from the distance. She had succumbed to a romantic hands-on impulse. It was unacceptable. She tore open the front of her suit and stretched the latex neck seal. The wave that poured in was cold enough to stop her heart. Within moments of embracing the intense cold, she wanted to sleep. She closed her eyes in a dreamy delirium. Here's a quote for you, Dad: 'To sleep, perchance to dream.'

There was a shrieking in her ears, so loud it hurt. She wanted to die in peace. Something was shaking her by the dry suit. It actually lifted her out of the water. Her peace was disturbed by the purposeful click, click, click of a yacht winch. Suddenly there was a hard deck under her and Shannon Riley was shrieking in her ear, 'Wake up!'

A man shouted, 'Let's get her below. If that pack ice gets around us, we're dead.'

Val's last conscious thought was that she hoped the pack ice crushed them. Later, she became aware that she was out of the wind and snow. She heard Jim Leighton struggling up on deck. Shannon was screaming at her to wake up.

Val said, 'Tell him to fly a storm sail and a Yankee jib.'

JIM WENT BELOW to fetch the Yankee jib. Shannon removed the dry suit from the woman they had winched out of the sea and strapped her into the leeward pilot berth. She lay dead to the world, eyes shut, barely breathing. Her skin was paper-white. Pale as a vampire—in Will's words. Val McVay.

Jim dragged the sail through the cabin.

'Where is Will Spark?' she whispered.

'He died last month in the South Atlantic.'

'That's not possible. Why didn't you—'

'Tell your killers in Buenos Aires? We hoped they would chase Will and leave us alone.'

'Where is Sentinel?

She had huge dark eyes, but they weren't focusing. Jim looked deep into them and said, 'Sentinel is where it always was: in Will Spark's head.'

THREE DAYS LATER, halfway across the Drake Passage, the wind dropped and the sea flattened out. Shannon handed up leek and potato soup in two mugs and joined Jim in the cockpit.

'Jim, I've been thinking,' she said.

'About what?'

'If Will knew that Sentinel was sitting on the bottom of the ocean, why did he insist you put his head in the freezer? And if you had put his head in the freezer what's the one thing you would hang on to?'

'The freezer! But why?'

'He must have hidden a device to signal the microprocessor to surface. In the freezer.'

'See if you can get Val to come up on deck. I'll look for it.'

JIM LEFT the extremely low frequency underwater radio transmitter hidden where he found it, beside the freezer's compressor. It was bigger than a brick and weighed as much, consisting mostly of a powerful battery, which Will had hard-wired through the freezer to keep it charged.

Jim entered into the GPS the exact location where Will had thrown the heart-rate monitor and microprocessor overboard. Then he worked out a course to set *Hustle* towards that point—3,540 miles to the north.

They told Val they were sailing to Florida. She was proving a placid shipmate. She made no attempts to communicate with the outside world and stood her watches faithfully. Off watch she worked hard, cleaning and maintaining the battered sloop.

She appeared to have shut down emotionally and slept long hours in the forward cabin. Her only complaint was the cold, which lasted well north of Buenos Aires; her only request was that they keep the stove burning for warmth.

'DO YOU THINK she's beautiful?' Shannon asked one night when they were alone in the cockpit.

'I'm a blue-eyes man myself.'

'It is not necessary to say things like that to make me feel secure.'

'I'm saying that because I love you.'

'Why?'

He took her hands in his. 'Shannon, if I could tell you why I love you, it probably wouldn't be love. It would be like a job description.'

'You could try.'

'All I know is I get excited when you come up on watch. I like the world with you in it. Everything is fun. Hey, relax. I'm not going to bug you to marry me. The only woman I'll ever marry is going to be a volunteer.'

'What if we find Sentinel?'

'I think we should split fifty-fifty. You do what you want. I'll do want I want. Maybe some day we can do it together.'

Shannon sat quietly digesting that. Then she gave him a teasing punch on the arm. 'Hey, Muscles, what's the first thing you'll buy when you're rich?'

'A refit for poor *Hustle*. What will you buy first?'

'I don't know. Maybe a new spinnaker pole.'

VI

THE HOME RUN

With the three of them sharing watches, *Hustle* made a fast passage to the equator, covering the distance in less than a month. Jim and Shannon had pushed the boat very hard on their last several watches, their excitement growing as they neared the exact spot where Will had deep-sixed Sentinel.

It was nearing noon. Jim rigged the stainless-steel dive ladder off the stern and was about to lower it into the water when Val came up the companionway. She took the binoculars from their rack and focused on the western horizon.

'What do you see?' Jim asked.

Val handed him the binoculars. Jim exchanged a puzzled look with Shannon and raised the glasses. His hands started trembling.

'What is it, Jim?' asked Shannon.

'A very fast ship, coming this way.'

Shannon's face fell. 'Val? Did you betray us?'

'Only by omission. I omitted to tell you that I designed a system to track this boat with satellite data. At first I didn't give a damn whether my father continued using it or not. Then it became obvious that Will did not take Sentinel to his watery grave.'

'How?'

'Most coincidences can be explained by the data. You two were beelining for Saint Paul Rocks like your lives depended on it—very near where Will got away from me last winter.'

'Val, we saved your *life*.'

'Did you expect me to say, "Oh, by the way, my father is tracking your course. Be on the lookout if you are attempting to retrieve what was stolen from us"?'

'But we connected. I thought we were friends.'

'Shannon!' Val said sharply. 'I don't *connect*. I excel.'

Shannon looked as stunned as Jim felt. They'd led the McVays straight to their goal. There was no way their sailboat could outrun the high-speed ship, which was soaring up on skirts of spray.

It swooped in a tight bank and the thunder of its engines ceased. The ship came to a stop and drifted down on *Hustle*. Armed men appeared on the stern deck in diving gear.

'Who's the tall guy in the bow tie?' asked Jim.

'That is my father, Lloyd McVay.'

Jim focused the glasses on the 'poetry-quoting thug' who had hunted him across three oceans. Lloyd McVay looked almost quaint in his bow tie and lightweight suit.

Jim shifted the glasses and got another shock. 'Your Rottweiler, Nickels, got rescued, too. Something happened to his face.' He handed Val the binoculars.

Val's jaw tightened. 'It looks like Andy lost his nose to frostbite.'

'He's lucky to be alive—just like you.'

Luckier than you think, Val thought. With a month to worm his way into my father's good graces. She was going to have serious problems.

Her father called down. 'Is that you, Val? My goodness, I feared when you lost your boat you lost your life.'

'I hope you didn't grieve too deeply.'

'I took comfort in my hymnal and never lost hope: "And while the lamp holds out to burn, the vilest sinner may return."' In other words, he would never forgive her for striking out on her own.

'It appears you also took comfort from my tracking system.'

His answer confirmed her fears. 'Andy is due much of the credit. He discovered that, in an earlier incarnation, Will stashed ill-gotten gains on the sea bottom. Course projections for this boat led Andy and me to draw the obvious conclusion. Young man,' he called to Jim, 'You have stopped Will Spark's boat precisely where he escaped from me last February.'

'So?'

'So if you don't have Sentinel, you had better have a way to retrieve it.'

'It was in Will's head when I buried him at sea.'

McVay gestured. Seamen secured *Hustle* fore and aft. Andy Nickels descended to the foredeck and steadied the ladder for the older McVay.

Lloyd McVay brushed his daughter's cheek with his thin lips. 'High marks for survival, at least.'

To Jim he said, 'Andy brought what used to be quaintly called a truth serum.' He looked at Shannon. 'It will be administered to the young lady.'

The men on the ferry started flinging meat into the water.

McVay said, 'Will Spark must have left behind some sort of flotation signal instrument. If you hand it to me in less than sixty seconds, Andy will not throw young Shannon overboard.'

Before Jim saw the first shark, he knew he was beaten. 'It's behind the freezer, next to the compressor.'

The ELF transmitter had a telescoping antenna with a cuplike protuberance at the end. They lowered it into the water and turned the instrument on. It beeped at ten-second intervals.

'How long, Val?' asked McVay.

Val was already calculating in her mind the time for the signal to reach the microprocessor in the mile-deep water. 'Ten minutes, I would guess.'

At the end of ten minutes, all that was visible in the bloodied water was a pair of blue sharks.

'There!' shouted Andy.

Fluorescent orange dye spread on the surface, twenty feet from the sailboat. In its midst was an orange balloon.

'Dive!' yelled Andy.

The divers hesitated. The sharks were circling. In that moment of confusion, Jim saw a chance to turn the tables. It was a chance to keep the prototype out of McVay's hands. But more important, it was his only chance to save Shannon. He had no doubt that the instant Lloyd McVay had Sentinel, the big ferry would smash *Hustle* and her witnesses under the sea.

Jim lowered himself smoothly into the water before anyone noticed. Careful not to splash, he swam a swift breast stroke towards the floating canister.

A dorsal fin cut the surface. Fear sucked the breath from his lungs. A ten-foot blue shark smacked into him, rasping his skin with its rough hide. Fighting panic, Jim slammed his elbow as hard as he could into its flank. He sensed another rush and kicked it full in the nose. Both animals veered away. Jim resumed his smooth swim into the orange stain.

He plucked from the water a shiny canister, the size of a beer can. 'Good lad,' called Lloyd McVay. 'Now just bring it here.'

Treading water, Jim ripped away the float bladder and held the canister over his head. It was heavy, made of stainless steel.

'Guns overboard!' Jim yelled. 'Or I dump it.'

Lloyd and Val McVay couldn't take their eyes off the canister.

'A million dollars!' shouted Lloyd McVay.

'*Ten* million dollars,' shouted Val. 'Get out of the water.'

'Jim!' Shannon pleaded. 'Get back on the boat.'

'Guns overboard.'

'Do it!' yelled Lloyd McVay. 'Weapons over the side. Now.'

Assault rifles and pistols rained into the sea. Trying to keep track of the sharks, Jim scissor-kicked towards *Hustle*.

'Help him,' snapped Val, and Nickels reached out to pull Jim aboard.

'Back off,' shouted Jim. 'Shannon, the dive ladder.'

Shannon dragged herself out of the cockpit and across the stern deck, and shoved the ladder into the water. Jim climbed partway up, inches ahead of another blue shark.

'Here's the deal. Everyone off the boat into our boat. As soon as we can figure out how to drive yours, I'll throw you the canister.'

Red with anger, Lloyd McVay ordered his crew to abandon ship.

Jim watched all six men clamber down to *Hustle*'s foredeck. The huge ferry loomed to his left, rubbing *Hustle*'s port side as the two vessels moved in the swell. He climbed another rung on the ladder and looked around, gauging his next move.

The six men were ahead of the mast, fifty feet from where he was holding the canister over the water. Shannon crouched beside him on the stern deck. Val was twenty feet straight ahead on the cabin roof. Andy Nickels and Lloyd McVay were standing near her, eyes flickering between the canister and the shark-roiled water at their feet.

'OK, Shannon.' He touched her arm. 'Can you pull yourself up that ladder?'

Shannon grasped the rope they'd hung from the backstay and swung across the cockpit towards the nearest ladder dangling from the ferry. As she did so, a swell tilted the boat, causing her to swing wide. Nickels was on her in a flash, encircling her waist.

'The party's over. If it sinks, she sinks. Give it to Mr McVay.'

Jim felt himself die inside. But Will, the great optimist, had laughed on his deathbed.

'Catch!'

He lobbed the canister in the direction of Nickels and McVay, along the side of the boat.

'Catch that, Andy!' Lloyd McVay shouted.

Nickels released Shannon and lunged, bobbling the canister on the stumps of frostbitten fingers. As it bounced free, he tumbled towards the water, caught himself on the lifelines and hung half over the side. The taller McVay reached further, shoes planted on the gunwale, one hand grasping the lifeline.

The canister containing Will Spark's microprocessor danced on the tips of his fingers. As it bounced away, he let go of the lifeline and with a cry of triumph, closed his hand.

Teetering on one foot, he hooked a finger of his other hand around the safety lines. Directly under him, Andy Nickels screamed in terror as a shark smacked the hull beside him. Swinging his legs desperately out of the water, Nickels kicked the lifeline from McVay's grasp.

McVay looked down in sudden amazement, as if noticing the churning water for the first time. He froze, suddenly rigid with fear. Sentinel slipped away from him and splashed into the sea.

'Val!' he shouted, grasping for her hand, eyes riveted on the sharks.

Val McVay did not hesitate. She had a split second to weigh her future. The Sentinel concept was still viable. But developing it would demand single-minded effort and unquestioned control of the McVay Foundation for Humane Science.

'You're forgetting your Shakespeare, Dad.'

'Help me!'

'It's serpent's tooth time.'

THE FERRY HAD VANISHED over the horizon with Val and Andy and their crew. But only when the sharks had finally gone did Jim and Shannon speak, and then only in stunned whispers.

'Why didn't they kill us?' Shannon asked.

'Val's not a killer.'

'From where I was watching, she could have saved her father.'

Jim shrugged. 'He might have pulled her under . . . Will used to say to me, "People do what they have to do. It's the real world, Jim." Then he'd laugh at me like I was totally naive.'

Shannon was looking at him strangely. 'Didn't that bother you?'

'Why should it? I *was* naive. I had a lot to learn. He had a lot to teach.'

'You really admired him.'

'Shannon, we've been through this. I liked him, warts and all.'

'I think you should sit down.'

He sat beside her on the cockpit bench. 'I'm sitting.'

'There was never time to talk about this. And then when we finally did have time Val was around. Maybe I used her as an excuse. But I didn't know what to do with it.'

'With what?'

'I don't know what it means, but I have to tell you. When I first telephoned the Larchmont Yacht Club, hoping to learn about Will, they hung up on me. Then, after you found out about Billy Cole, I drove over there. They were very nice to me. I said I was looking for my grandfather, Will Spark. "It's simply ages since we've seen Mr Spark," they said. Anyhow, I kept smiling around until in comes an old friend of Will's—"Hello, Bunky. Meet Will Spark's granddaughter." Bunky and I start talking. When we're alone, he goes, "Will never had a granddaughter."'

'You were caught.'

'Egg all over my face. Except I got this brainstorm. I said, "Billy Cole had a granddaughter." Bunky just laughed. "Billy didn't either. And don't tell me it was Mick Creegan."'

'Mick Creegan! I think that was Will's real name.'

'It was. Bunky knew Will way back when. They had always stayed in touch.'

'What did he tell you about him?'

Shannon reached for Jim's hand. 'Jobs he'd had. He'd been a teacher. He taught Outward Bound. And sailing.' She stroked his hand. 'Back in the 1970s, he was an EST trainer.'

'What?'

'He led EST retreats. In California. In the mountains.'

A hundred thoughts scattered. A thousand fell into place.

Shannon said, 'My head was spinning. Could your mother have—?'

'I don't know. Jesus. I don't know *what* my mother . . . Did the old guy know about me?'

'No.'

'Is that why Will gave me the boat?'

'He gave you the boat because you were ready for the boat,' Shannon said firmly. 'A gift from a teacher to his prize student.'

'But if he was more, if he was—' Jim couldn't speak the word. 'Why wouldn't Will tell me?'

'I thought a lot about that. Maybe he was ashamed of himself.'

'He could have told me.'

'Jim, I think he tracked you down. He joined the Bridgeport club to take your classes . . . He checked you out . . .' Shannon touched Jim's cheek. 'And liked what he saw . . .'

Jim pressed her fingers to a smile that opened up his face. Sentinel was lost on the bottom of the ocean. They were low on food and water, far from any shore. They were broke. The boat needed work. The hurricane season had begun. And all was right with the world.

'He took me sailing.'

PAUL GARRISON

For reasons of privacy, Paul Garrison likes to keep details of his personal life vague. He talks, therefore, in tantalisingly cryptic terms about his background. 'I was born in Manhattan but left soon after on a boat. I guess my fate was sealed,' he says, referring to his lifelong passion for the sea and sailing. Like a number of his fictional characters, Garrison has faced many a stormy sea, though he says he would never claim to be a sailor of the calibre of Will Spark, the millionaire helmsman in *Buried At Sea*. He finds sailing both exhilarating and terrifying. 'Getting beat up at sea always makes me ask, what am I doing here? Why did I volunteer to do this?'

'I've worked around boats and ships most of my life. I've also built houses and driven trucks and worked in the woods,' he says of his life hitherto. 'Business used to keep me in the Far East, but now I am able to devote most of my time to writing. You could say I'm a late bloomer. I worked at a variety of careers before I discovered that writing fiction stirred my creative juices more than anything else. I come from a line of storytellers, so fiction has always seemed a likely thing for me to do.'

The inspiration for *Buried at Sea* came during a transatlantic sailing trip. 'I was on a forty-nine-foot sloop that rolled like a bathtub. It gradually dawned on me that the guy who owned the boat was something of a lunatic. And I started thinking of the fictional possibilities: what if it was just him and me on the boat in the middle of the ocean? In those circumstances I wouldn't be able to sleep that well off watch, and I wouldn't have great faith in making it to the other side. I discovered the character of my hero, Jim Leighton, in a New York health club when I was researching my second novel. He was a very hard-working and dedicated young instructor, who took his job of helping people very seriously. It made me wonder what would happen to someone like him if he were trapped alone on a boat with the lunatic.'

Garrison, who is married and 'happily child free', currently has 'a base in the northeastern United States—inland, but close enough to the coast to hitch a ride on a boat.' Asked if he has any unfulfilled ambitions, he laughs and says that one day he would like to write a huge novel about William Shakespeare that would then be turned into a smash Broadway musical. 'But for now, I'm hard at work on the next novel!'

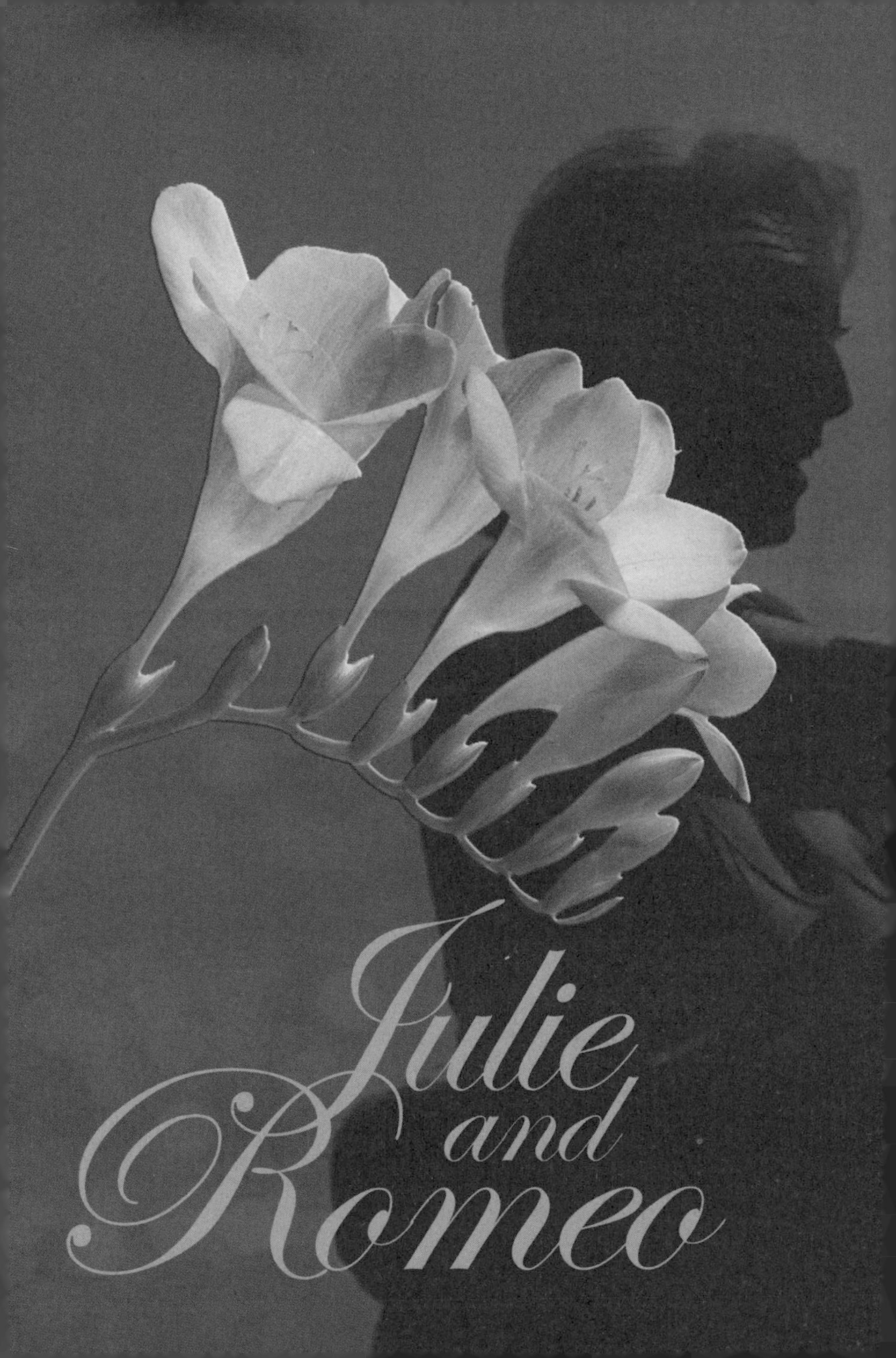
Julie
and
Romeo

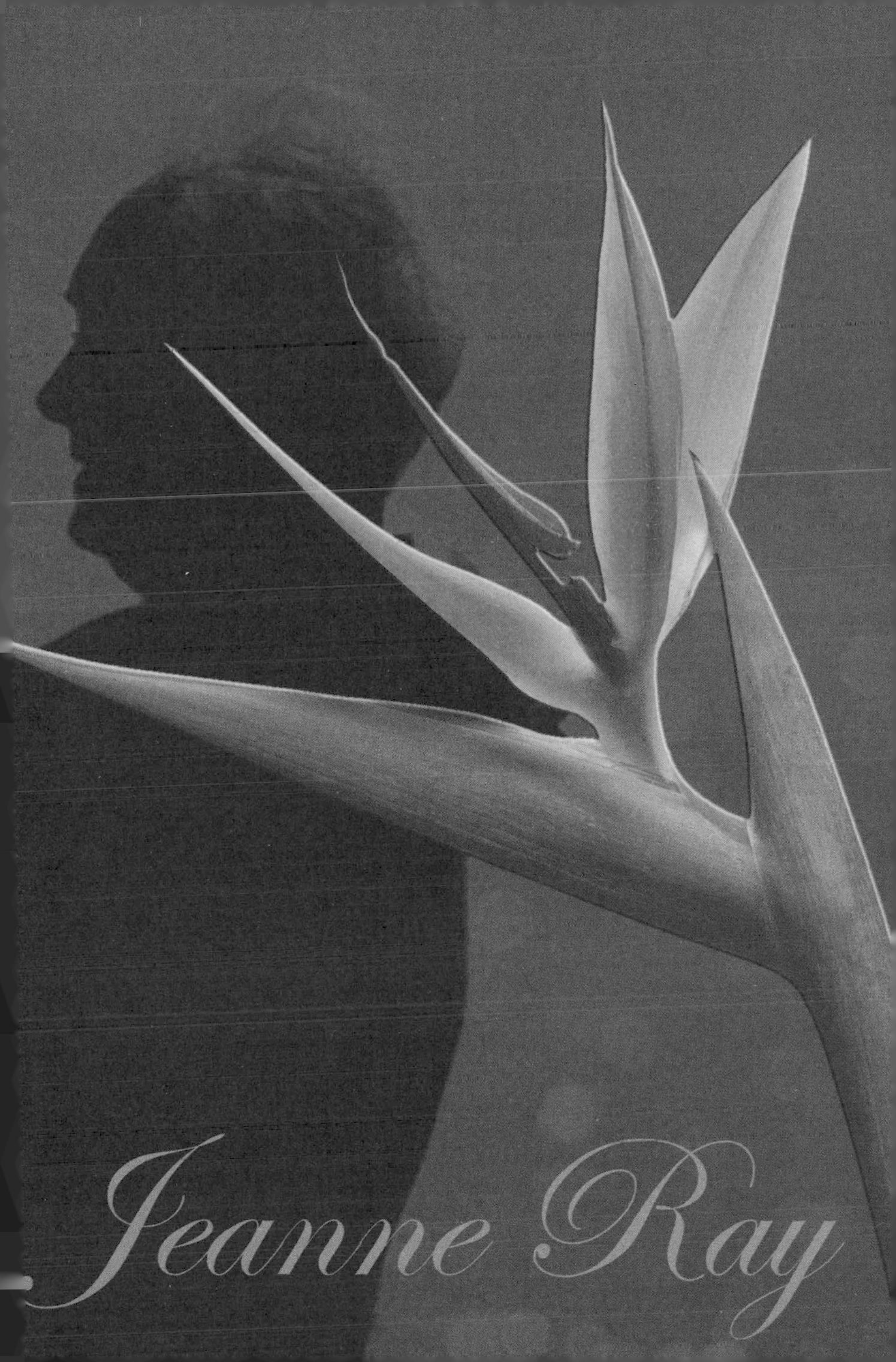
Jeanne Ray

Julie Roseman could never have imagined she would speak a kind word to Romeo Cacciamani. For as long as she can remember their two families have had nothing good to say to one another.

But there he was. This Italian guy, probably around sixty, like her. Good-looking. Nice smile. Nice teeth. Asking would she like a cup of coffee . . .

Chapter One

The first time I heard the name Cacciamani, I was five years old. My father said it, and then he spat. The spitting I had seen before. I watched my father spit out his toothpaste into the sink. I had seen him spit once while mowing the lawn, when he claimed to have taken in a mouthful of gnats. But this particular spitting, the spitting done in association with the word Cacciamani, was done directly onto the cement floor of the back room of Roseman's, our family's florist shop. That floor, like everything else in my father's world, was kept meticulously clean—nary a leaf hit that floor—and so, even as a child, I recognised the utter seriousness of his gesture.

'Pigs,' my father said, referring not to himself for what he had done to his floor, but to the name that had led him to do it.

I wish I could remember the rest of this story, how the Cacciamanis had come up in the first place, but I was five. Fifty-five years later, only the highlights of such memories remain.

People love to say that hate is a learned thing. Children mimic their parents; every contemptible piece of narrow-mindedness is handed down from generation to generation like so much fine family silver. I doubt it is as easy as this, as I know my own two daughters have picked up a few things in this world I will not take responsibility for, but then I think of my father and the small, shimmery pool of his spit on the floor. I hated Cacciamani with all the passionate single-mindedness of a child, without even knowing what or who it was. I decided it was a fish. My father, who loved just about everything, was not a fan of fish, and so I assumed the conversation must have gone something like this:

MY MOTHER: Howard, I got some nice fresh Cacciamani for dinner tonight.
MY FATHER: Cacciamani! [Spit] Pigs!

For the next several years I imagined rubbery, pale-fleshed bottom feeders, the dreaded Cacciamani, snuffling around blindly in Boston harbour. When exactly I made the transition from fish to family, from family to rival florists, I don't know. My path did not cross with the Cacciamanis'. We did not go to the same school. Their name was rarely spoken, and when it was, there was a great fanfare of unexplained wrath that I gladly participated in. We were a liberal family, aware of the recent persecution of our people and therefore unlikely to persecute others. As far as I knew, the only prejudice we had was against the Cacciamanis. And back then there were only three Cacciamanis for me to hate: a father, a mother and a son. I remember seeing the mother at Haymarket several times on Saturdays. She was beautiful—tall and thin, with black hair and red lips. Still, I thought it was an evil sort of beauty. Then their son grew up, married, and had six children, many of whom married and had children of their own. The Cacciamani clan grew by leaps and bounds, and as far as I was concerned, the whole lot of them were worthless—a fact that was reinforced when Tony Cacciamani tried to marry my daughter Sandy when they were in high school.

So that was how I came to hate Cacciamanis. Now let me tell you how I stopped. It was five years ago when I came to hate my husband, Mort Roth. Mort ran off with Lila, a thirty-eight-year-old bouquet-grasping bridesmaid he met at a wedding while delivering flowers. Apparently he met her at several weddings. She was practically a professional bridesmaid—many friends, few dates. There went Mort and Lila. After that I knew what it was to really hate someone for your own reasons, which is much more poignant than hating on someone else's behalf. I didn't know I had ceased to carry an axe for the Cacciamanis. I simply hadn't thought of them for years. And then one day, while attending a seminar at the downtown Boston Sheraton called 'Making Your Small Business Thrive', I practically walked into a man with the name tag ROMEO CACCIAMANI. I steeled myself for the great wave of fury, but nothing, not even a twinge. What came instead was this thought: Poor Romeo Cacciamani; his shop must be going bust, too, if he's at this thing.

He tilted his head. 'Julie Roseman,' he said, reading my tag.

And there he was, a nice-looking Italian guy sitting right at sixty. He was wearing pressed khaki trousers and a white polo shirt. No gold chains. I was so surprised by my utter lack of hostility that I wanted to laugh. I wanted to shake his hand, and I would have, except I had a Styrofoam cup of hot coffee in one hand and several folders in the other. 'Romeo Cacciamani,' I said with wonder.

'It was something else, wasn't it? Roth?'

I nodded. 'Roth,' I said. 'And Roth no more.'

He raised his eyebrows in a not-unfriendly way, as if he should be shocked and wasn't. Something occurred to me then: Did Cacciamanis still hate Rosemans? I knew that Mort and Romeo had got into it over the years, but now Mort was gone and my parents were dead and my younger brother, Jake, scarcely a Roseman at all, was making furniture in Montana. That left me and my daughters, Sandy and Nora. 'Are your parents . . .'

'My father's been gone eleven years now. My mother lives with me. Almost ninety. When is the last time I saw you?'

No sooner had he said it than he remembered the answer to his own question. I could see the edges of his ears turn red. 'Fifteen years,' I said, and left it at that. That was the last time we had seen each other, but that was not the last time I had seen him. Over the years I had seen Romeo often—as we drove past each other in our cars, as I turned my grocery trolley into his aisle and then caught the mistake in time. For all I knew, he had been studiously avoiding me as well. We both lived in Somerville, a big enough place to avoid someone for years. We owned the only two florist shops in town, so it stood to reason that if one of us was providing the flowers for a wedding or funeral, the other one wouldn't be there.

'How's Sandy?' he said.

'She's good.' I wasn't going to be asking about his Tony.

'Things turned out for her OK?'

I shrugged. 'You have kids. You know how it is. Her marriage didn't work out. She's back home with me now. Two children.' I felt awkward. I wanted to say everything was fantastic for her, say it not for myself, but for Sandy, who in her weaker moments still felt the loss of Tony Cacciamani.

Romeo scratched the top of his head, where all of his hair appeared to be intact. 'That was a sad thing,' he said. 'A very sad thing. What my son was doing with a Roseman—'

'A Roth,' I corrected. 'Sandy was a Roth.'

He smiled. 'You're all Rosemans as far as I'm concerned. And your husband was the biggest Roseman of them all.'

'My husband only looked like a Roseman. In the end he proved to be otherwise. He met somebody else.' I don't know what possessed me to include this last bit of information, but once it was said, there was no taking it back.

Romeo nodded sadly. Maybe he thought he'd known what kind of guy Mort was all along, or maybe he felt sorry for me, but either way I knew it was time for our reunion to come to an end. 'I need to get going,' I said, struggling to get a look at my watch. 'I want to get a seat for the advertising lecture.'

He let me go graciously, said something about it being nice to see me again. Had he always had such a nice face?

'Romeo?' I said. I don't think I had ever called him by his first name. It was always 'Mr Cacciamani', even though we were the same age. Besides, I thought Romeo was a ridiculous name for an adult. 'I read in the paper about your wife. I was sorry about that.' It was so long ago—three years, four? I should have sent a card at least.

He nodded a little. 'Thank you.'

'I didn't know her. I mean, I think I only met her twice, but I had a lot of respect for her. She seemed like a lovely woman.'

'Camille was a lovely woman,' he said sadly; then he turned away.

AFTER THE LECTURER announced that it was essential for every small-business owner to set aside 10 per cent of gross revenues for advertising, I stopped listening. A great idea, unless you plan to make payroll or have dinner every now and then. Instead my mind drifted back to what Romeo had said about Mort being the biggest Roseman of all. It hit the nail on the head, and I wondered how a Cacciamani could have so much insight into my life.

The whole time I was growing up, I worked in my parents' shop. Even as a little girl, I was in the back room filling up the water picks or wrapping corsages with florist tape. When I got older, my father moved me out front to work the cash register, and when I was in college, I came in early to do the arrangements for the day. I loved the shop when I was young: the cool, dark world of the walk-in on a hot summer day, the bright yellow of an African daisy in February, the constant, dizzying perfume of the gardenias. But then I met Mort, and he started hanging around the store, so helpful, so polite. From our second date my mother was saying, 'When is he going to marry you?' Like he'd been stringing me along for years and I was about to let my best chance get away. I was all of twenty-one, just minutes away from being yesterday's fresh pick. Six months later Mort asked my father if he could marry me, which might have been construed as charming and old-fashioned, but nobody asked me anything. Me they told. 'Julie, Julie!' my mother said when I walked into the store, and my father's eyes were beaming from all the tears, and Mort was just standing there, a grinning idiot, like I was going to be so proud of him. They'd sold me off, or at least that's what it felt like. My brother had bailed out on the business, and in Mort they had found a responsible son to assume the Roseman mantle. I was nothing but the conduit for the transaction. But this is my memory speaking. I'm sure I was happy at the time. I have a vague idea that I loved Mort then.

I made my own bouquet for the wedding: white tuberoses, white hydrangeas, white peonies. It was the most beautiful work I'd ever done. Then at the end of the reception I walked to the front of the banquet hall. All my single girlfriends were there—Gloria, my maid of honour, all the bridesmaids. I turned my back, and with all my might I threw my beautiful bouquet up over my head. The flowers sailed right out of my hands. It was nearly thirty-five years before I got them back again.

Mort didn't want me in the shop. This was rule number one when we got back from our honeymoon. My parents agreed. They could only afford one employee, and since Mort would be taking over sooner or later, what mattered was that he learn the business. I could work as a secretary, with the understanding that I would quit as soon as I got pregnant. Nobody put a gun to my head. That was just the way things went. Mort became the Roseman, and I became his wife.

My parents retired, safe in the knowledge that Mort was there, and they died before he got round to proving them wrong. For this I am grateful. At least he didn't cause my parents any pain. But for all their love and unquestioning trust, they did one very strange thing: they left me the shop. Just me. Mort cursed and raged for weeks. 'What a slap!' he said. 'A betrayal!'

I didn't understand what he was talking about. 'It's ours,' I said. 'My name, your name, what difference does it make?'

Mort said it made a big difference, and he was after me to sign over the title. While I've done a lot of dumb things in my life, I'm pleased to report that this wasn't one of them. He groused. I stalled. He left. It turns out Lila had her eye on my parents' shop. Mort and Lila's Flowers. The very thought of it makes me weak.

A lot can change in thirty-five years. While I was driving school runs and taking Nora and Sandy to tap and ballet classes, the world of flowers was moving forward. I went into the shop from time to time, but I was surprised one day when I noticed that the cash register was a computer and no one had told me about it. Shipping, billing, trucking, taxes—the depth of my ignorance was bottomless. I had never noticed that we now sold fancy ribbon and vases. There was even a wire rack of greeting cards beside the door. Mort didn't leave a manual when he and Lila packed off for Seattle. Nor did he leave much money. He just left.

What a beautiful story this would be if the wronged wife pulled it out of the fire and took the business straight into the top 500 companies listed in *Fortune* magazine. It didn't work out that way. I stayed in bed for a while, and when I got up, I found a lot of rotted flowers and unpaid bills. I couldn't sell the store. It had been my parents' entire life, and as little as I knew about flowers, I knew less about just about everything else. Five years later I was spending money I didn't have on a seminar that was telling me to put 10 per cent into advertising.

My hips were getting stiff in the folding chair, and my coffee was cold. Fortunately, I had taken a spot at the back of the auditorium, and I slipped out into the hallway. It was empty except for an orange bench on which sat one Romeo Cacciamani.

The first time I saw Romeo in the Sheraton, I was amazed to find I no longer hated him. The second time I saw him, I was considerably more amazed to find my heart jumped up as if there had been a tiny trampoline installed in my chest.

He glanced up at me and then looked down at his hands. 'Oh,' he said, his voice disappointed. 'You've got coffee. I was going to ask you if you wanted a cup of coffee.'

I looked at the white cup in my hand. There wasn't a trash can, so I dug it into the sand of an ashtray. 'I'd like a cup of coffee,' I said.

ROMEO CACCIAMANI held open the door of the Boston Sheraton for me, and I stepped outside into a beautiful late spring day. There were a million things that should have been going through my head: Why has he asked me for coffee? Does he want to talk about what happened with the kids? Is he going to tell me he hates me in the fine tradition of his family? But in truth, the only thing I was thinking was, Wouldn't Mort just die? Please, God, let Mort be in Boston on business. Let him be across the street watching us. Let Mort think that we are wildly in love and that I am planning on signing over every last petal I have to this man. Nothing would kill Mort faster.'

At a Starbucks down the street we found a table among the full-time students and unemployed writers who believed that coffee shops were libraries. Romeo paid for my light grande latte and got himself a cup of black coffee.

'Two bucks for a cup of coffee,' he said, sinking into his chair. 'Why didn't I think of that one?'

'Beanie Babies,' I said. 'I should have come up with those.'

'We sell them at the store,' he said. 'I hate them. People call all day long, "Do you have Spots? Do you have Gobbler?" We had to put in an extra line so the flower calls can come through.'

Not only had I not thought of making Beanie Babies in time, I hadn't even thought of selling them. 'So business must be good.'

He glanced down at our mutual stack of small-business folders. 'You know how it is.' The thought seemed to depress us both, and for a while we just sipped our coffee in silence.

'I've thought over the years maybe I should write to you,' Romeo said. 'And then I saw you today, and I thought—'

But he stopped, and I was too curious to wait politely. 'What would you write to me about?'

'Oh, the family stuff.' He stopped and shook his head. 'Sandy. I look back on all that, and I think I just didn't . . . I didn't handle that whole thing so well. All the yelling and Camille crying. I still think they were too young to get married. It may have been OK to bust up the wedding, but I don't think we should have busted *them* up. That was about us, not about them.'

It had been a terrible night, freezing cold and pouring rain. Tony Cacciamani had actually brought a ladder to our house. Sandy was going to climb down the ladder and they were going to get married, but it fell and there was Sandy, hanging off the sill of her first-floor bedroom window, screaming. We said it was all a Cacciamani plot, that Tony was really trying to kill Sandy.

'That was a long time ago,' I said. And it was, but it made me sad to even think about it.

He nodded. 'A long time. I have one daughter. Plummy. I don't know if you know that. She's twenty now, at Boston College. Such a smart kid. I wonder where she came from. She's not like anybody else in the family. But when all that happened with Sandy and Tony, Plummy was just a little girl. I didn't know anything about girls then.'

I was remembering Sandy, sixteen years old, up on her bed crying and crying and Tony Cacciamani calling the house all the time and

Mort hanging up on him. Mort told Sandy that Tony had never called her. I never thought about it any more. It was a dark chapter in my parenting history. 'I understand,' I said. 'We don't have to talk about this.' Anyone who knows me knows that 'We don't have to talk about this' is a very simplistic code for 'Stop talking about this'. Romeo did not know the code.

'What I mean to say is,' Romeo went on, 'now Plummy is a young lady, grown up. I think I have a better understanding now of how it must have looked from your side. When you have boys, you think that all the world's problems come from girls. Then you have a girl, and man, you start to take another look at all the boys out there. The world starts looking like a dangerous place.'

That made me laugh. I tried to snap myself out of the past.

'Kids are going to make mistakes,' I said. 'Big mistakes. All we can do is teach them what's best and then stand by to bail them out.'

'Well, that's what you did. You protected your daughter,' Romeo said. 'That's what I would have said in that letter I didn't write to you.'

'We didn't do such a great job ourselves. We weren't exactly models of civility. Mort said some awful things about Tony, about you. God, the screaming that went on.' I tried to remember what I thought about Romeo Cacciamani when he and his wife had sat on our couch. Was he nice? Was he bright? Did I think he was a good-looking guy? Was it possible that he had simply become such a good-looking guy in the last fifteen years?

'Mort hated us. That was for sure. Mort Roseman's daughter sneaking off with a Cacciamani.' He shook his head. 'That's powerful stuff.'

'Roth,' I reminded him. 'Mort Roth.'

Romeo shrugged.

'I hated you, too,' I said, and then was horrified by my own sudden inclination towards candidness.

But as far as Romeo was concerned, I hadn't confessed anything more serious than a dislike for decaf. 'Cacciamanis and Rosemans,' he said. 'Very bad blood.'

I saw this as my opportunity to get the answer to a question that had been bothering me for years, one that I could never ask my family because it was too obvious and I was too stupid. 'Why do we hate each other?'

'I'm not sure.' Romeo took a long drink of his coffee. 'I could say it was because of what happened to Tony and Sandy, but I certainly hated all of you a long time before that. My parents hated your parents. Whew!' He shook his head. 'Now that was hate. My mother crept into your parents' yard one night and poured salt on the roots of all your mother's roses.'

'She killed the roses? Are you kidding me? My mother always said it was a Cacciamani curse.' They had simply withered up, and after that she couldn't make a single thing grow there.

'It was Cacciamani table salt. Maybe the same thing. One time— I must have been in about the eighth grade—I had gone to a birthday party, and you were there. I didn't talk to you or anything. I knew better than that. But that night I told my father that I thought you were sort of cute, and he washed my mouth out with soap. Ever had your mouth washed out with soap?'

I shook my head. I tried to assume the least coquettish tone possible. 'So you thought I was cute?'

'I was at that age. I was trying to hack my father off, even though I didn't know it would hack him off that much.' He looked out of the window. 'But yeah, I thought you were cute then. Actually, I think you're cute now.'

Let me establish something here: things had not been so hot between me and Mort in the years before he left. Since Mort, nothing. I was not proud of this, but I had no idea what to do about it. I had no time to do anything about it, not between working round the clock and taking care of the house and helping Sandy out with her kids. I had some attributes left, and yes, there were times that people flirted with me. But a real compliment from a seemingly nice man, well, that hadn't happened for a very long time. It was like a faint song—sweet and far away.

'I don't remember you at a party,' I said. 'I wish I did.'

He smiled. 'I was very cool. I came and stood round the edges for a minute. Then I left. That was my style.'

As much as I wanted to see where this might go, I couldn't get my mind off the salt. 'So why did your mother kill our roses?'

'That part I could not tell you. I always thought you knew. The way they said the word Roseman around our house, you'd have thought there'd been a murder somewhere along the line.'

'I don't think my parents killed any Cacciamanis.'

'What about your grandparents?'

'Jews in Lithuania. They didn't get to Italy much. I hear the train service was bad. But your mother is still alive. Can't you ask her?'

'Salting the roses is what I *know* she did. The things I don't know, I wouldn't want to know. My mother is a tough lady. She would be capable of some pretty serious stuff. If she hasn't told me by now why she hated the Rosemans, she's never going to tell me.'

'What about your kids?'

Romeo drummed his fingers on the top of the table. He had nice hands, thin and strong like maybe he played the piano. He still wore his wedding ring. 'I'm afraid that one is my fault.'

'Ah, don't worry about it. Mort and I didn't exactly talk you up to our girls over dinner.'

'They hate us?'

Nora hated. Nora with her Lexus and her cellphone, her tax-attorney husband, and blisteringly hot real-estate career—Nora hated the Cacciamanis with a passion that would rival anyone's in the family. She was a daddy's girl. She would walk out of her best friend's wedding if the Cacciamanis had done the flowers. Sandy hated them, too, but for her own reasons—because she really did love Tony. She named her little boy Tony, which I thought was a very questionable move, but I never said a word. 'They hate you.'

'My boys get a grudge, and that's it—real Cacciamanis all of them. Plummy I'm not so sure about. She does her studies. She dances. She works in the shop. I don't think she's got time to hate anybody. So you don't seem to hate me, and I don't seem to hate you. What do you think happened to us?'

I explained how things changed for me after Mort. I told him that, if someone had asked me how I felt about the Cacciamanis this morning, I would have said something awful out of the sheer reflexive habit of it all, but that when I saw him, just another failing small-business owner like myself, it all seemed to be gone.

He was a good listener. 'I understand,' he said. 'When Camille died, well, I changed my mind about a lot of things. I would have been happy to go on hating the Rosemans like always, but when I lost Camille, I lost all my energy for trivial things. I inherited her good sense when she died.'

'That's quite a gift.'

'Quite a gift,' Romeo repeated slowly. 'So really, it's not so different. We both lost the person we loved, and the hate just went with it.'

'It's not the same. I didn't love Mort. Not like you loved Camille.'

'Nobody loves the same way, but you loved Mort. You must have. Otherwise you wouldn't have stayed with the idiot for so many years.'

I laughed, and Romeo laughed, then he put his hand over my wrist and patted it. It was nice, a friendly little touch.

When we stepped outside, the sun was still bright and the air was crisp and as sweet as hyacinth. Romeo Cacciamani bounced on his toes a couple of times. 'The lecture on self-employed retirement accounts starts at three,' he said.

'So, what good is that going to do me? I don't have any money for a retirement account. Besides, I'm never going to be able to retire.'

'Me neither,' Romeo said. 'Too many kids.'

'How many kids?'

'Six. The five boys and Plummy.'

I whistled.

'So, no more lectures. I guess it's back to Somerville.' He looked down the street as if he were expecting a car to pull up and take him home. 'You drive?'

'Are you crazy? Parking was a fortune. I took the bus.'

He nodded, and again he scanned the street, looking as far away from me as possible. 'Ever walk to Somerville?'

'From downtown?'

He nodded. 'I noticed your shoes. You wear sensible shoes. You could walk in those.'

I had given up on sexy shoes when the girls were born. I was extremely, irrationally flattered to think that he had looked at my feet. 'I'm a florist,' I said. 'I stand up all day.'

'But you told your family you were going to be at the seminar till at least five, right? You have plenty of time still.'

'I don't think I've ever walked that far in my life.'

'It isn't that bad. You walk that far every day just round the store. I do. Let's say we give it a try, and if it doesn't work, we split a cab back.'

There was no sign of rain, and I had had the good sense to leave my folders on the table in Starbucks. There had been a freak snowstorm in April, but every last bit of slush and grey ice had melted away. The sidewalks looked clear and dry, appropriate for travel. I nodded. Where had I come to in my life that walking from Boston to Somerville could seem like an act of wanton recklessness? 'Sure,' I said. 'Hell, yes.'

And so we started back, out of the shadow of the Prudential Center and off towards Massachusetts Avenue. We made the very, very long trip over the Massachusetts Avenue bridge, where the sky reflected pink light onto the Charles River and the last of the day's sailing boats skated across the water. Who knew that walking to Somerville could be such a beautiful thing to do?

It was a longer trip than we expected. Romeo suggested we stop in La Groceria and have a plate of spaghetti for dinner. They had a very nice bottle of not-so-expensive Chianti. What was funny was we didn't talk much about our families. We talked about movies and a television show we both liked. We talked about growing up in Boston and the trips we had taken. After dinner we walked for a long time without saying anything at all. It was pretty, the houses at dusk, all the warm orange light coming from the windows. It didn't bother me, not talking to Romeo. I never felt that we had run out of things to say; we were two people who knew each other well. Two people who had nothing but time.

As SOON AS I SAW the silvery Lexus in the driveway, I knew I was in serious trouble. I was late. I had forgotten that it was Sandy's night for school and I was supposed to be watching the kids. She must have waited and waited and finally called her sister as a last possible resort for child care. I sat down on the low brick wall round my little front yard, wanting to put off for a moment what I knew was coming. I loved Nora, but she did not tolerate forgetfulness nor suffer inconvenience gladly. I wanted just a minute to think about my happy evening. Romeo, thankfully, had veered off towards his own home five blocks ago. I would not have wanted him to see me hiding from my daughter in my yard.

I touched my fingers to my lips to make sure I wasn't showing any breadcrumbs, and then I went inside. Nora had every light in the house blazing. My grandchildren, Tony and Sarah, eight and four respectively, were both up. They were both crying.

'My God!' Nora said, coming towards me like a train. 'I was just telling the children I was going to have to call the police. Mother, where have you been? I was absolutely sure you were d-e-a-d.'

'You were dead!' Sarah wailed, and shimmied up into my arms. Tony banded himself round my waist.

My back is not the back it once was. I tried to steady myself beneath the weight. 'I'm not dead. Shush. Look at me.' Such a wealth of tears! 'Do I look dead?'

Sarah shook her head, but the crying had taken on a life of its own and could not be stopped. I rubbed small circles on her back. 'Tony,' I said, looking down on his head. 'Are you all right?'

Tony, never much of a talker, nodded into my waist, moving around an extra ten pounds I should lose. The whole thing broke my heart. There was so much passion in their fear. I looked at Nora, who spread her hands open as if to say, Look at all the suffering you've caused.

'I just forgot,' I said. 'I forgot it was Sandy's school night.'

'So where were you?' Nora said.

I felt very bad, yes, very guilty, but I could see the irony of my situation. In high school Nora put us through hell, staying out until four in the morning, saying she was running down the street for a Coke and coming back six hours later on the back of some boy's motorcycle. This well-dressed real estate broker with the lizard shoes and the diamond earrings, who now folded her arms across her chest, had been grounded by me, her mother, more times than I could count. 'I went to the seminar. I ran into a friend. We had dinner and walked home.'

'Walked home? From the Sheraton?'

Enough was enough. I put Sarah down and peeled Tony off me. They tottered towards the sofa, drunk with their grief. 'Nora, I'm sorry you had to come over here, and I thank you for your help with the children.' I tried to put the mother-note of authority back into my voice, not that it had ever meant a thing to her, anyway.

'Alex and I were on our way out the door to dinner when Sandy called. She said you were only going to be a few minutes late. She didn't tell me she hadn't even heard from you.'

'I'm sorry.'

'We had reservations at Biba.'

I didn't know what that was, but I apologised again.

The children had returned to their normal breathing patterns and fell into an exhausted stupor on the sofa. Nora put on her coat, which was cut like a trench coat but was made from a pale yellow silk that looked simply lovely on her. I never could get over the way Nora had turned out, so successful, so striking, so, frankly, rich. Never write off a kid who gives you bunches of trouble—I suppose that's the moral of the story. 'You look so nice,' I said.

'Well, we were going out.' Nora shrugged and picked up her handbag. Then she smiled at me. 'It's OK. I forget things, too.'

Slightly patronising, but I'd take it.

'Who did you run into, anyway?'

I laughed at the thought of it, the whole happy absurdity. 'You'd never guess. Never in a million years.'

Nora returned my happy look. It was a little game. 'Who?'

'Romeo Cacciamani. Can you believe that?'

I should have lied. Just because I had run into the enemy of all Rosemans and found nothing in my heart but peace did not mean that such peace would be shared by all members of my tribe.

Nora dropped her purse. 'You *what*? You did *what*?'

Tony and Sarah, even in their diminished states, heard the shift in tone and raised their sleepy heads.

'Nora,' I said quietly. 'Go home. We can talk about this some other time.'

'Tell me!' Nora said. Nora actually roared. She was capable of that.

I kept my voice very soft, but there was no undoing this. 'I ran into Romeo Cacciamani at the conference. We got talking, we had dinner.'

'Cacciamani? You ate dinner with a Cacciamani?'

It was amazing. She sounded exactly like her grandfather when she said the word. I half expected her to spit.

'I asked myself, What was this huge feud all about, anyway?'

'You don't *know*? Why don't you ask Sandy? Sandy *knows*.'

Now the children had heard their mother's name, and all the crying started up again. 'I mean before that. Nora, let it drop. He's a perfectly decent person.'

'I'm not hearing this,' Nora said. Then a thought of utter horror occurred to her. 'Did you *walk home* with him?'

'No,' I said. 'Of course not.'

'He let you walk all the way from downtown alone?'

'Stop this. Stop. Go home. I'm going to put the children to bed.'

'Mother, swear that you will never see that man again.'

'He lives in Somerville. I'll see him at the grocery store.'

'You know what I mean.'

'Good night, Nora.'

'Swear it. I am absolutely not leaving until you swear it.'

For a second, a picture of that reality crossed my mind. 'Sure,' I said. 'I swear it. Now go.'

Nora blew out like a storm. Not a word to me or the children. So I swore; what did it mean? I hadn't seen Romeo in fifteen years, and it would probably be fifteen years before I saw him again. So what?

I put the children to bed, the last vestiges of any happiness from my evening stomped out like a bug beneath my heel. I was sixty and back to buttoning up flannel pyjamas. But they were sweet children, and even though I wished that Sandy's marriage had worked out and that they all lived happily in another house, most days I didn't mind having them there.

'You're not going anywhere, are you?' Tony said, his voice all trembly. He was such a little boy for eight.

'Down the hall and straight to bed is the only place I'm going.' I leaned over and kissed him hard on the forehead until he giggled.

I kept my word to Tony and went straight to sleep. But I did have a dream that bears mention. Romeo Cacciamani was throwing pebbles at my window. I got up in the dark and opened the window to stick my head outside. In the dream my window opened easily, and there was no screen to contend with. I was wearing a very pretty white nightgown.

'What do you want, Romeo Cacciamani?' I said.

He was standing in the middle of the street in his khaki trousers and windbreaker, looking up at my window. He looked so handsome in the moonlight. How had I always missed that? I wanted to put my hand on his cheek.

'I had to see you,' he said. 'I couldn't sleep. I knew I was never going to go to sleep again if I didn't get to see you.' He smiled at me and waved. 'Good night, Julie.'

'Good night, Romeo.'

And then I woke up. Here's the worrisome part: I was standing at the window. I've never been a sleepwalker, and I wondered if I could have fallen out. Then I remembered that the windows were all painted shut. I looked out onto the dark street. There was no one there, and I was a nut.

IN THE MORNING Sandy came into my room and closed the door behind her. It was 6.00am, and the children weren't awake yet. She was wearing sweatpants and a Celtics T-shirt. She had her glasses on, and the curls of her hair had yet to be brushed down. 'You went out on a date with Romeo Cacciamani?'

'Absolutely not,' I said. I had been lying in bed staring at the ceiling, thinking about ordering carnations. 'We ran into each other at this conference and had dinner. End of story.'

Her lip began to quiver. 'Why would you do that to me?'

I sat up, alarmed. 'No, honey, not to you. This had nothing to do with you.'

'Why else would you have dinner with him?'

'Sandy, I don't know. It was such a small thing. We ran into each other. We started talking. We got hungry. We ate. That was it. I promise you.'

'You hate the Cacciamanis.' She was wiping beneath her glasses with the back of her hand. She was so sensitive, poor Sandy.

'I did hate them. You're right. But when I saw Romeo yesterday, I just didn't hate him any more.'

'He's Romeo now?' She came over and slumped down on the end of my bed. She was too thin. Ever since her divorce, I could see her shoulder blades sticking out behind her like wings. 'If he was around, if I had to hear his name, I really don't think I could stand it.'

'He isn't around. He isn't here.'

'So you won't see him any more?'

'I'm not seeing Mr Cacciamani. I just ran into him.'

Her face brightened a little. She wiped again beneath her glasses. 'So you aren't going to see him again?'

These girls, they did not give me an inch. What difference did it make? It was an easy thing to promise. I wouldn't see him. 'I won't.'

Sandy crawled up to me on the bed. She was thirty-two years old, but sometimes she reminded me of Sarah, who was very mature for four. She put her arms round my neck and lay down beside me. 'I really love you, Mom.'

I told her the truth without explaining how extremely complicated that truth felt to me at the moment. I told her I loved her, too.

Chapter Two

When my girls were growing up, I believed them to be the beating heart of the world, the very centre of the universe. Unfortunately, they knew I believed this, and so they came to believe it themselves. As far as they were concerned, I was their mother, pure and simple, even after they were grown-up. They could not imagine I wouldn't do what they wanted me to do, as that was the nature of our relationship. And maybe they were right. We were talking about Cacciamanis, after all. I could hate Romeo again—I was sure of it, even though I had been thinking of him all morning in distinctly unhateful ways. Sixty years of hate versus one plate of spaghetti and a long walk? No contest.

SANDY HAD DROPPED out of college in the beginning of her junior year. She was bored with the work and happily in love with a fellow whose name was also Sandy. They married and became Sandy and Sandy Anderson, believing the novelty of a shared name would be enough to sustain their relationship. They were wrong. Now Sandy the husband lived in Maui, where he taught surfing, got stoned, and forgot to pay his child support, and Sandy the wife went to school three nights a week in hopes of becoming a nurse. During the day she helped me out at the flower shop, and I paid her a salary I could not afford in hopes of giving her a sense of independence. She was a good worker. She was charming to the customers and had a nice way with flowers. Her arrangements were pretty and cheerful. She was also very good about deliveries. She never dawdled, and she had a brilliant sense of direction, which she certainly did not inherit from me.

The day after my dinner with Romeo, Sandy and I went in early to get the morning's deliveries ready and then packed them into my car. We had always had a white Ford van with the name ROSEMAN'S painted on the side along with a big bouquet of roses. I loved that van. It made me feel successful. But when times started getting tight, the van was the first thing to go.

Sandy looked over the delivery sheet. 'Well, at least everything is nice and close today. I shouldn't be gone long at all.'

As she left, I told her to be careful. I always worried about her knocking on the doors of strangers.

I took my time sweeping up and wiping down the glass door. I moved a bucket of Star Gazer lilies out to the sidewalk. It was a cool day, and we needed to sell them soon if they were going to have any petals left on them.

The phone rang: some guy wanting to send an apology bouquet. 'I've been bad,' he told me.

'I understand.' He said he wanted to spend seventy-five dollars, not including tax and delivery, so I figured he had been really bad. 'What do you want to say on the card?'

The line was quiet for a while. 'Don't know. What would you want to hear?'

'I don't know,' I said. 'You haven't done anything to me.'

'But what do other guys say? I'm no good at this.'

'The basics are usually safe: "I love you." "I'm sorry."'

'I like that. Write that down.'

'And her name?'

'Catherine.'

'Catherine with a C or a K?'

Again there was quiet. 'No idea.'

I sighed and wrote it out with a K. 'If it's wrong, I'll tell her it was my fault.'

'That's brilliant,' the man said. 'I only wish I could blame the rest of it on you, too.' He gave me his credit-card number, and I wrote it down.

I pinned Katherine's order to the corkboard and then went into the cooler and started changing the water and clipping back the stems so that everybody would get a better chance at life. For all the years I'd been in the store, I'd never got tired of the flowers. I'd got tired of the accounting and the credit-card companies and the bad cheques, but the flowers themselves still amazed me. I was in the business of happiness. There were funerals, of course, hospital stays, but even then the role of the flowers was to cheer. Mostly it was about love. Flowers provide a means of expression for people who don't know what to say. Hand the person you love a bundle of flaming poppies, their twisted stems heading in every direction, their petals waving out like wind-blown flags. They look so promising, so much like life. They'll get the message.

We weren't open yet, but I had unlocked the door to put the lilies outside. I was in the back, working my knife across a bunch of rose stems, when I heard the doorbell chime. I wiped my wet hands on my jeans and went out to the front.

There between a display of potted chrysanthemums and a bucket of expensive freesias stood Romeo Cacciamani.

'You've got a real nice store,' he said. 'I've never actually been in here before. My parents used to tell me the Rosemans sold voodoo stuff—dried bats, eye of newt. Do you have any eye of newt?'

What I thought: Why am I wearing this disgusting shirt of Mort's?

What I thought next: How long ago did Sandy leave?

What I said: 'No newts.'

He nodded. 'You've never been in Romeo's, have you?'

Romeo's was the name of his store, named for him by his parents, a tribute to their one and only child. It was a romantic name, of course, a flower-giving sort of name. It also drove my parents insane because they came before us in the phone book.

'I've never darkened your door.' I was so glad to see him you would have thought he was dropping off my lottery cheque. How could I be that glad?

He knelt down beside some sweet peas I had just got in and began to fluff them out a little. I was thankful he was focusing on the sweet peas, which were hard to come by, reasonably priced, and dazzling in their freshness. 'I think you'd brighten the place up.' He did not look in my direction, and it would have been reasonable to assume he was talking about the flowers.

'So maybe some day I'll see your store.' What was he doing here, exactly? Out at the Mount Auburn cemetery my father was doing loops in his grave. Cacciamani hands on our stalks. Besides, if Sandy was to walk in the door, there would be a meltdown to rival anything in Chernobyl.

'Julie Roseman,' he said to the flowers. The way he said my name caused my heart to stop for a beat. 'I had a very nice time last night.'

'I did, too,' I said. 'Until I got home.'

Then he looked up at me. 'You didn't tell them, did you?'

'I don't know what I was thinking. It was a huge mistake.'

Romeo shook his head. 'I told everybody I went to a movie by myself. I do that sometimes.'

'I wish I'd thought of that. How many do you have at home?'

'Well, there's me, and there's my mom. Plummy's living at home because I am barely making tuition at Boston College. Then Alan, he's my youngest son—he's thirty-two. He got laid off last year. He had a really good computer job and then nothing, so now he's home with his wife, Theresa, and their three kids. They've got a dog, too. Junior. Do you count the dog?'

'I do.'

'OK. So there's nine of us.'

'You were smart not to tell them. But, my God, dinner. You'd think we'd committed a crime.' I looked at my watch. 'Listen. I don't mean to rush you, but Sandy is going to be back here any minute, and I'm just not up for a repeat performance. I know that's terrible. Everyone should be over this dreaded curse by now, but they aren't, so . . .' I shrugged.

'So why did I come?'

'We might need to jump ahead to that point, yes.' I could feel the sweat coming up under my arms, the sweat of fear—Sandy looking for a parking space; Sandy locking the car.

'I haven't done this in such a long time. I was nineteen when Camille and I got married. A guy gets out of practice.'

And then, of course, I saw it. Maybe in another setting, another time, I would have strung it out and enjoyed it, but now I was only in a hurry. 'Would you like to have dinner with me?'

He smiled a smile so grateful, so relieved, that I wished I had asked him the minute he'd walked in the door. He nodded his head.

'Good. When?'

'Tomorrow.'

Curse fate and baby-sitting. 'Can't,' I said. 'Sandy has school tomorrow, and I've got the kids. Sandy, Sandy. You really need to get out of here.'

'Tonight.'

'Tonight. Would you mind going out the back?'

'Fine,' he said. He started to stand up and then reached for my hand. He had been squatting with those flowers a long time. I pulled him to his feet. For a second I held his warm hand. I felt a small current zip up my arm and into my chest.

'I'll pick you up.'

'No, no,' he said with a certain panic in his voice. 'Can't do that. What if we meet at the library?'

'My grandson likes to go to the library. He'd tell.'

He closed his eyes. 'Why can't I think?'

'The CVS drugstore in Porter Square,' I said. 'Seven o'clock.'

And then I saw her, Sandy, through the window. 'Out,' I said, pointing to the back. 'Go, go, go!' For a sixty-year-old man whose legs were stiff, he managed to fly when he needed to. And I, for the first time in thirty-nine years, had a date.

ALL DAY LONG I worked to keep my fingers free of the scissors' blades. I knew that I was bound to chop one off. I mixed up orders and forgot to hand out a single packet of cut-flower food.

'What is it?' Sandy kept asking me. 'Are you mad at me about this morning? Are you worried about Tony and Sarah?'

'I'm just tired,' I said. 'I didn't sleep well.'

Finally she relented. It was time to pick up Sarah from preschool. We weren't busy, so I told her to take the rest of the day off. I tried to sound magnanimous. Once she was gone, I called my best friend, Gloria. Gloria had suffered mightily through her first marriage and had been rewarded in her second one. We had been friends since the seventh grade. She was my maid of honour and the person who drove me to my divorce hearing. Gloria and I go way back.

'Cacciamani!' she said. She was laughing so hard that she finally had to put the phone down and get herself a glass of water.

'I'm insane,' I told her.

'You were insane for hating the guy all those years. You aren't insane for going out with him. I think he's nice. He's good-looking.'

'You know him?'

'I don't *know* him, but I've bought flowers from him.'

'What were you doing buying flowers at Romeo's? I thought you bought your flowers at Roseman's.'

'I always buy them at Roseman's now, and I usually did before, but, honey, I've got to tell you, Mort drove me crazy. The man could not stop talking. If I was in a hurry, it was just so much easier to go to Romeo's.'

'You have a point there. So you don't think I'm awful? The girls are going to hate me.'

'The girls will never know, if you have an ounce of discretion in you. You're an adult, after all. Besides, I never could figure out what in the hell this family feud was all about, anyway. Why did you all hate them so much?'

'That's the weird part. I don't know. And Romeo doesn't know why they hated us. Just a tradition, I guess.'

'So the tradition is over. Where are you going?'

'We're meeting at the CVS drugstore in Porter Square.'

'That pretty much leaves all of your options open. Do you know what he likes to do?'

'He likes to walk.'

'So flat shoes. Put perfume behind your knees. Men love that.'

'I don't think he'll be coming in contact with the backs of my knees.'

'You're better off if you're prepared, emotionally speaking. You have to think through all of the scenarios.'

But I couldn't think through any of them. Suddenly I was paralysed with a kind of fear I hadn't known since Mort told me about Lila. 'Listen, Gloria. Will you come over tonight and pick me up? Show everybody that we're going out to dinner and then drive away with me. The girls will get suspicious if I go out again tonight.'

'You want me to drive you to the drugstore?'

'If you could,' I said, ashamed of how pathetic I sounded.

'Sure, Julie,' she said. 'I'll be your alibi any day.'

I closed the shop a half-hour early and went home to sit in the bath. The house was empty, and the quiet gave me a false sense of peace. Maybe we would have a nice dinner and nobody would find out.

SANDY, TONY AND SARAH returned from McDonald's at six o'clock. At six fifteen Nora walked in. I would have bet money on it. Sandy was in the kitchen, encouraging the children to sit in chairs while eating some ice cream.

'I was just showing a house down the street,' Nora said, perfectly cool. 'I thought I'd drop in and say hello.' Nora had on an emerald-green suit with a Hermès scarf tied loosely round her neck.

'You look awfully nice,' I said.

'You look nice yourself,' Nora said. 'Going out?'

'I am, actually. Gloria and I are going to dinner.'

'In the middle of the week?'

'We eat during the week.'

'Just wondering,' Nora said. 'Maybe I'll stick around for a minute. I haven't seen Gloria in ages. She's happy with Buzz, isn't she?'

'Things turned out very well for them.'

Nora paced around a little, smoothing down her skirt, readjusting a lampshade. She didn't want to be there. She wanted to get home to Alex, but she still had to check up on me. I couldn't be too mad at her, considering that her worst suspicions of my character were exactly correct. 'How are things going at the shop?' she asked.

'Not good. You know that.'

'I don't see why you just don't give it up. Take the capital out and get yourself a condominium.'

'I want to make this work.'

'It's not *going* to work, Mother. The business falls off every year. Everything Daddy worked for is going to be for nothing.'

'It was never your father's work. It was my father's work.' I had made a solemn vow to myself never to talk Mort down to the girls, but where business was concerned, I failed. Mort had made the place thrive, but he never cared about flowers. And in the end he didn't care about me, either. I was in no mood to hear about how I was ruining his hard work.

'Call it whatever you want,' Nora said. 'What I'm worried about is you. It's the Cacciamanis. You know that's the reason the business is failing. They poison our name in the community every chance they get. The big weddings, the fund-raising dinners—that business is all going to Cacciamanis.'

'We do plenty of weddings. In fact, I've even been thinking about starting a wedding-planner business on the side. I'm always helping girls find a caterer and pick out their bridesmaids' dresses.'

'I think they're anti-Semitic.' Nora never listened to me.

'That's crazy. You can't call someone anti-Semitic just because they don't like you. Are we anti-Catholic?'

'Of course not. You just don't understand.'

'Oh, please,' I said. Then the doorbell rang, and I was awash with gratitude. I went into the kitchen and kissed Tony and Sarah good night. Sandy looked at me wistfully for a minute, and so I leaned over and kissed her, too.

Nora had let Gloria in, and they were standing in the living room laughing, the best of friends. 'Time to go,' I said.

'Maybe I could come,' Nora said. 'Alex has a meeting tonight, and I don't have any plans. It could be fun, just the girls.'

Gloria took a deep breath and put her hand on Nora's shoulder. 'Honey,' she said, 'forgive me, but I need your mom all to myself tonight.'

'Is everything OK?'

Gloria shrugged and managed to look both hopeless and brave. 'I've just got some things I need to talk to her about. She's such an angel to me, you know.'

'Hi, Gloria,' Sandy called from the kitchen.

'Hi, sweetheart. Kiss the kids for me. We're running.' Then Gloria put one arm round my shoulder and manhandled me out of the door before any further discussion could evolve. I got into her Plymouth, and she all but floored it getting off my street. 'I thought you were just being a wimp wanting me to pick you up tonight, but that felt like a regular jailbreak.'

GLORIA PULLED UP in a red zone in front of the CVS. It was ten minutes to seven. 'Do you need me to pick you up?'

I shook my head. 'I'll get home fine.'

'Or maybe you won't.' She gave me a kiss. 'Think positive.'

I wondered what I could have been thinking of, asking a man to meet me in a store with fluorescent overhead lighting. Slowly, casually, I began to make my way up and down the aisles, trying not to look so incredibly suspicious that I would be arrested for shoplifting before he even got there. In the make-up aisle bottles of tan foundation claimed to make your skin young and dewy. There was a lipstick called French Kiss. Skin creams offered the miracles of youth, the overnight face-lift, and an age-recovery combination. The magazine aisle was not kinder. 'How to Make Him Beg for More', 'Great Sex at 20, 30 and 40'. I stopped and picked that one up. What happened to great sex at fifty? And what about sixty? Were we finished? Unentitled? Too thrilled to be taking our grandchildren to swimming classes to even think about sex?

By the time I had wandered over towards the pharmacy, I was ready to call it a night. Lubrication creams next to adult undergarments. A wall of condoms in every conceivable colour and texture, all promising protection against sexually transmitted diseases. I had forgotten about those. The magazine was right. I was over, out of business. I was standing there staring at the boxes, reading the hideously depressing slogans—'For Feeling Like Love'—thinking that sex was for the young, when I felt a tap on my shoulder.

'Shopping?' Romeo said.

I wasn't wearing my glasses, and so my nose was approximately three inches away from a box of condoms. 'I think this may be the single worst instant of my life,' I said.

'Good,' he said. 'Then things can only go up from here.' Romeo smiled at me. He took my hand and led me out of the contraceptive aisle, which was considerate because if left to my own devices, I would have tried to claw my way out through the floor.

'Do you eat sushi?' he asked.

'Raw fish?'

'Plummy got me into it. It's what college kids eat. If you don't want to do that, we can go somewhere else.'

'No,' I said. 'Given the circumstances, I would say raw fish is exactly what we should be eating. It's reckless food, don't you think?'

'I do.'

As we left CVS and walked towards the car, Romeo kept holding my hand. It's a wonderful thing to have somebody hold your hand. The last time Mort held my hand was as we were walking back down the aisle after our wedding. After that I held hands with my daughters when they were little, crossing the street. I was glad to have Tony and Sarah to hold hands with again. I was gladder still to be holding hands with Romeo, especially since I knew he had picked mine up not because he was afraid I might dart out into traffic, but because he liked the way my hand felt inside his own.

A piece of dating advice for the out-of-practice: if you're nervous about a date, especially if it is a date with your sworn enemy, try shaking off that nervousness by doing something that you would feel even more nervous about, say, skydiving, armed robbery, or eating sushi. The restaurant, in Harvard Square, was pretty, very quiet, with papered walls and soft lighting. There was an ikebana arrangement at the entrance that Romeo and I both admired. I let him order, because not even the most enlightened feminist knows how to order sushi if she's never eaten it before. The waitress brought us a bottle of sake. 'Never pour your own,' Romeo said, filling my glass. 'It's bad luck. Plummy told me that.' Then he handed me the bottle, and I filled his glass. 'To the most beautiful florist in Somerville,' he said.

'Don't sell yourself short.' I touched my glass to his glass.

'No, really,' he said. 'It's you. It is absolutely you.'

I felt drunk after two sips, and it had very little to do with the sake. Then a black lacquered tray arrived, covered in slabs of raw fish perched on top of tiny bricks of white rice. Suddenly the thought of having to eat my dinner seemed so much more frightening than having a date that I didn't feel nervous around Romeo at all. To celebrate, I popped a piece of salmon into my mouth. It wasn't bad. The eel I spat discreetly into my napkin, as I did the abalone, which was a little bit like biting into a human ear.

'I used to do that, too,' Romeo said. 'You get used to it.' He stretched his arms across the table, and for a second he touched my hands. 'I still can't believe I'm having dinner with you.' Then he took his hands back again. 'I have to tell you, you didn't bump into me by accident at that seminar.'

'What?' I left one hand on the table just in case he wanted it.

'I was walking through, and I saw this woman, this beautiful woman. I only saw her for a second, but—I don't know—I felt like I knew her.'

I wasn't loving this story.

'So I circled back round so I could see the name tag, only you didn't see me.'

'Me?'

'Then I came back a third time. I practically walked right into you. We talked for a minute, and then you were gone.' He snapped his fingers. 'I completely lost my nerve. I thought, Well, that's it. I had every intention of leaving, but I found myself waiting for you out in the hall. Do you ever just have a feeling about something—you know you've got to do it no matter what?'

'Not until recently,' I said. I picked up the bottle of sake and refilled Romeo's glass.

'I'd like it if we could get to know each other better,' he said. 'As people, you know, not just as Rosemans and Cacciamanis.'

'I think that's a fine plan,' I said. 'So, tell me about your children.' Children were always a big part of the story.

Romeo smiled and leaned back in his chair. He liked his children, I could tell. 'Oh, let's see. Camille and I started early. Joe, the oldest, he's forty. He owns a trucking company, and he's doing OK for himself. He's married and has three kids. Then there's Raymond. He's still single. He works with me in the shop. Nicky is in the air force, stationed over in Germany. He married a German girl about five years ago, and now they have two kids. Then there's Tony.' He sighed. 'He's thirty-three now. He works for the World Health Organisation. He's in Ecuador giving out vaccinations.'

'Did he ever get married?'

Romeo shook his head. 'Nope. I have to tell you, I think I really screwed things up for Tony. He was in love with Sandy, and not just kid stuff. I don't think he ever got over all that.'

I thought of poor Sandy at home with her kids and their Happy Meals from McDonald's, her nursing books, and her homework. She never got over it herself.

'Anyway, Alan I told you about. He and Theresa are at home with their three. And then there's my Plummy. It was such a wonderful thing for Camille to have a girl. She's a real treat.'

'And a real surprise, it sounds like.'

'Five boys, we thought we were through with that. We thought we had the whole rhythm thing down, and then Plummy. We named her Patience, because Camille said that's what it took to get a girl. The boys called her Plummy. They'd say, "Isn't she just plummy?" I think they picked it up from the Beatles. The boys were crazy about her.'

I liked the idea of all those children—all their friends, their boyfriends and girlfriends, and later their children. 'It sounds nice.'

'Camille made it nice. She was a wonderful mother. I think back on all the things she had to do. I didn't understand it until she was sick, until I had to start doing them myself. She took care of us.'

We ate green tea ice cream for dessert and drank tea out of little cups. We talked about the flower business. We laid out every trade secret we had, both of us, and I learned more over dinner than I ever had from a seminar. I told him how I wanted to do a little wedding planning on the side. That was the thing I was really good at: big parties, organisation. Romeo said he admired that; he was crummy at organisation. Romeo had taken on too many members of his family, and, while he said his product was good, he had a tendency towards disorder. He once missed an entire wedding. He had it marked down for the next week. I, on the other hand, still didn't feel like I had a handle on what I was doing, and every month the revenues slipped. We were both going broke.

It wasn't exactly a light-hearted conversation we'd stumbled into, but still, I felt like singing when we left the restaurant. Romeo said he would drive me home or at least to the end of my street. When we got there, he pulled over and turned off the engine. 'No one ever told me Rosemans were such good company,' Romeo said.

'When we're not selling the dried beaks of nightingales.'

'When Camille died, I thought, That's it. I'd known her since eighth grade. We were each other's family. I thought, There's never going to be enough time to get to know somebody like that again.'

'Sure,' I said. From a distance I could see my house. All the lights were off. My own family safe asleep.

'But the thing is, I do know you. I've been hearing stories about the Rosemans since I was born. They weren't the right stories maybe. . . .' He stopped and drummed his thumbs against the steering wheel.

'I know what you mean,' I said. 'In the end a Roseman and a Cacciamani are all the same thing.'

'All the same thing,' he said. He had a way of repeating what I said, and I liked it; he was really listening. And then Romeo Cacciamani did something truly miraculous. He leaned over, and he kissed me. It was just on my lower lip at first, and then my upper lip. Little kisses, and after each one he'd pull away from me like it was over, but then he would come back for more. He put his hands on my face; then he kissed my eyelids, then my forehead, and then the parting in my hair. I put my hands on the back of his neck and kissed his mouth, his neck. This was the part that no one had told me while they discussed the evils of the Cacciamanis. No one said they were such good kissers. I was dreaming, sinking, swimming in a warm dark river of kissing. I could smell the soap on his skin and the fabric softener in his shirt. Oh, Romeo, this makes it all worthwhile, all those nights of working late and coming home alone, crying over the books and the roses that came in with brown spots, the worrying about Sandy and Nora and the children, the anger at Mort, the missing my parents. All of it was washed back by the sea of tender kissing, maybe not for ever but for now.

I knew nothing about time, but after a while we decided it was late enough. 'Can I walk you down?' he said.

'Better not.' I leaned forward and kissed him again.

'We'll manage this, right? We'll find a way to do this.'

'I have every intention of it,' I said. I put my hand on his hand and then let myself out of the car. I had walked all the way from Boston to Somerville. Tonight I felt like I could walk past my house and keep heading west. I could walk to Cleveland, to Nebraska, over the Rockies until I got to Oregon, and even then I wouldn't stop if I didn't want to. I could go into the ocean; I could swim. I was that sure of myself tonight. I could go on for ever.

I WENT UP THE STAIRS to my room in the dark. My lips were puffy, and I kept touching them with my fingers, my tongue. They still had the goods. After such a period of neglect, what a thrill to find they still had all their spring intact. I turned on the lamp beside my bed, sat down on the edge, and bounced a couple of times. If I had been twenty, I would have gone to bed with him. I would not have known how to get out of the car after kissing like that. But now I was more sensible. I was supposed to believe in getting to know a person. I was supposed to be grateful for what I got.

So why did I want to go running down the street to see if I could catch up with his car? Here alone in a room with a bed, I wanted to put my head through the wall, I was so eaten up by desire. I had not had sex in, let's be honest, more than five years. Five years plus the last four or five months when Mort was here and we didn't have any sex and I didn't much care because I didn't know he was going. And before that, how long had it been? My fifties had more or less been a sexual wasteland, good years that I could have been burning down the house night after night had there been someone who wanted me, someone I wanted. So maybe tonight I had a chance, and I decided what . . . to wait? Why? Because I wanted to get to know him better? Who did I know better than a Cacciamani? Because I didn't want him to think I was that kind of woman? I was that kind of woman! Just give me the chance. I fell face down on the bed and bit into my pillow to keep from screaming.

There was the strangest noise outside. It sounded like hail, almost like little stones hitting the side of the house. Then I realised it *was* little stones hitting the side of the house. I looked out of the window, but I couldn't see anything, so I went back and turned out the light. There on the sidewalk outside my house stood Romeo Cacciamani.

I put my shoulder onto the window frame and tugged with both hands. Damn Mort, who said he could paint the windows himself! He probably knew that some day Romeo would come here at night and I'd never be able to get the damn thing open. He'd painted me in! Helpless, trapped, I looked down at Romeo and saw he was motioning, saying something without making any noise.

Come down, he was saying.

I flew down the stairs, three at a time. I was out of that door and back into the night and into his arms before I even knew I'd left the bedroom, back into the universe of kissing. It had been what? Ten minutes? Fifteen? But I had felt the loss of him more than I can ever remember feeling anything.

'I can't believe you came back,' I said. I kissed him again.

'I didn't know where to go,' he said. Stop, kiss. 'I just kept driving around.'

'Come inside.' Kiss.

322

'I can't come in. You know that.'

The front door was wide open, and the house was dark. He was right. Not inside. 'Your house?'

'No, no, no.'

'A hotel. I have credit cards.'

He stood back for a second. We were dizzy. 'Really?' he said. 'You'd go to a hotel?'

'Isn't that why you came back?'

'I just had to see you again. I didn't want to get my hopes up.' He kissed me, hard this time, the kind of kiss that makes it abundantly clear what the other person has on his mind. It was joy. 'I know,' he said. 'My shop. There's a place in my shop.'

I went and closed the front door quietly; then we took off in his car. We kissed at every stop sign. Why did car manufacturers think bucket seats were a good idea? I think it was all part of a conspiracy. When we were repressed, they gave us bench seats, but once we figured out how to use them, they stuck a gear lever right in the middle of everything. I put my hand inside his shirt and touched the hair on his chest. Five years and four months makes a woman forget herself, and I had forgotten everything.

I had driven past Romeo's shop before, but it goes without saying that I had never been in it. Inside, it was dark, and in the dim shadows that the streetlight threw in from the window, I could see it was mostly bare. All the flowers would be in the cooler. I couldn't tell if it was nice or not, but I imagined it was beautiful. He locked the door behind us. 'I have a little place in the back,' he said. 'I sleep here sometimes when I have a really big job to get out. I like to work at night.' He took my hand and squeezed it, but we were both suddenly shy, unsure of where to turn next.

'Show me around,' I whispered. I didn't want to make a sound.

'With the lights off?' he whispered back.

'Why not? You know where everything is.' I wanted it to be this way. I wanted to slow things down, just for a few minutes, just so I could revel in what it felt like to want someone so badly and know I was going to get him.

He held on to me. 'The plants are over here—mums, azaleas, some little potted perennials, African violets.'

'Do you sell a lot of azaleas?'

'They fly out.'

'I always figured people bought those at nurseries.'

He kissed me until my knees felt loose and I had to lean against him. Had I known that such kissing existed in the world, I would never have married Mort.

'And these, these are my pride. Wait, let me get the flashlight.' He disappeared into the darkness and came back with a circle of light. He shone it across a table of orchids. 'Look at them,' he said. 'Aren't they something else?'

And they were, like flowers from a lusher, more ingenious planet: big ones, white and heavy as saucers of cream, little amethyst ones, tiny yellow spiders the size of thumbnails. 'I never had the nerve to try orchids,' I whispered.

'They aren't so hard. You just have to understand what they need. I think they are the most beautiful flowers.'

'Show me the cooler,' I said.

'Really?'

I took his hand, kissed his fingers. Romeo Cacciamani, whose name I was never allowed to say at the dinner table, I kiss your hands.

He pulled open the big steel door and we stepped inside. There was a dim automatic light. It was exactly like mine. There was just enough room for the two of us to stand. The flowers were up on shelves: bundles of roses in plastic wrap, gerbera daisies and lilies, pink and yellow stock, larkspur, Japanese iris, buckets of ferns. They pressed in against us. I loved the smells blending, becoming one another. Then, up on the top shelf, I saw a beautiful arrangement.

'Who did that?'

Romeo looked up. 'I did it. Who do you think does the flowers around here?'

'You made that?' I said, my voice so soft it was hardly my voice at all. 'You did that yourself?'

'Sure.'

'Oh my God,' I said. 'You really are a better florist than I am. That's brilliant. I mean it. That's one of the best-looking arrangements I've ever seen.' It seemed reckless and at the same time had perfect balance. I never would have thought to use the tiny lilies of the valley and the foxgloves in with those giant white peonies. And then there were white English roses, as big as the peonies. White tulips came up from everywhere, and all of it balanced, balanced like it was a painting, a perfectly composed still life, a carving in white-pink marble. It was like something that had simply occurred in nature and soon would grow and spread and take over the room. I had been looking at flowers for as long as I could remember, and I had never seen anything so perfect. 'I think you may be a genius.'

'What a nice thing to say.' And when he kissed me this time, we both knew we were ready. If there had been more time or more light, I might have thought about my weight, my underwear, but maybe not. In that moment I was so happy with Romeo, I felt happy with myself. Where else should two florists come together than in a walk-in cooler stuffed to the rafters with flowers? We took off our clothes and stood together naked and holding each other as much for warmth as for love.

'Julie, it's freezing. There's a bed in the back.'

To all the magazines that only document sex up to forty, I say this: have you ever walked naked with your lover through a florist's shop at midnight? No? Then don't tell me about sex.

The way was dark, and he held my hand, stopping to kiss me and touch me. The very hands that had arranged those flowers arranged me now. We were Adam and Eve, and this was a dark, flowered Eden. 'In here,' he said.

'Who's that?'

'Romeo?' I whispered. 'Is that you?'

'Raymond?' said Romeo.

'Dad? Dad, is that you?'

Maybe a better woman would have stuck by her man, but I was fly-ing naked through the store. The lights came on just as I leapt for the cooler door. I pulled it tight behind me and cursed the safety precau-tions that did not allow me to lock it from inside. Our clothes were all over the place, strung over dahlias, crushing down the gypsophila. I untangled mine and inserted myself as quickly as any human being has ever put on clothing. As for my passion, my heart's desire, forget about it. All I wanted now was to get away.

There was a knock on the door. Romeo was calling my name, wanting to know if I was all right.

'Sure,' I said. 'Absolutely.'

I was pretty much put together when he came in wearing a ratty plaid bathrobe. 'That's my son Raymond. He was working late. He fell asleep.' Romeo dressed quickly. 'We have to go out there now.'

'I'd rather not,' I said. 'I'm fine in here.'

'I have to take you home.'

'I don't see how,' I said, but I knew he was right. He took my hand, and together we came out of the cooler.

Raymond was standing there in his boxer shorts and T-shirt, his arms folded across his chest. He was bigger than his father, softer in the face and with less hair, but still a nice-enough-looking guy. He had a big grin on, like this was a very funny moment, until he saw who I was.

'Raymond,' Romeo said. 'This is Julie Roseman.'

'I know. And she can get the hell out of this store.'

'Raymond!' Romeo said. It was his parental voice. Even though the son was in his thirties, the tone had some effect on him.

'How could you bring . . . bring'—he was struggling to find a properly awful word. He did not succeed, thank God—'*her* here?'

'Mrs Roseman and I are friends,' Romeo said.

'How you could bring her into Mama's shop. What is Grandma going to say, you bringing a Roseman here to—'

'Raymond, stop it.'

'I won't stop it,' Raymond said, his own voice raised. 'Not a Roseman. Not a Roseman in this store. Not a Roseman with my father.'

I must confess this outburst had very little effect on me, except to increase my wonderment at what, exactly, had gone so wrong between us. Raymond was not so different from my own girls.

'I'll take you home, Julie.'

'She can walk,' Raymond said.

At that point Romeo went at him, I think to strike him, but Raymond held up his palms. 'Forget it,' he said, and turned to walk out of the room. But before he left, he did the most remarkable thing. He said my name, and then he spat.

Chapter Three

'We are cooked,' I said on the drive home. We had both been quiet for a while, both of us stunned as if by a sharp blow.

'Raymond,' Romeo said, shaking his head. 'If it had been Joe, all hell would have broken loose. If it had been Nicky or Alan, even Tony, I might have believed it. But Raymond is so easy-going. Of all my boys, I would have guessed that he would be the one who wouldn't care.'

'Do you think he's going to tell?' I asked glumly.

Romeo sighed. 'I guess I better get back there and try and talk him out of it. Raymond I can deal with, but if they all get into this, it's going to be impossible.' He pulled up in front of my house. Too much had happened for us to try to play it safe.

'Not to sound too much like a teenager, but do you think I'm going to see you again?' I asked.

'You're going to see me. I'm crazy about you, Julie Roseman.'

I kissed him again. I knew I was crazy for him, too. I said good night, and for the second time that night I went upstairs to my room.

I would have thought I'd spend the night staring at the wall and wringing my hands, but I don't think I'd ever been that tired in my life. I barely struggled out of my clothes and fell into bed.

WHEN SANDY WOKE ME, it was bright outside—not just light, but daytime. 'I took the kids to school already. Are you feeling all right? Did you and Gloria tie one on last night?'

I really had to think about what she was talking about. I could hardly open my eyes. Dear Sandy had brought me both a cup of coffee and an alibi. 'Gloria is such a bad influence on me,' I said.

'White wine?' Sandy asked.

'Manhattans,' I whispered. 'Then pinot noir with dinner.'

'Grape and grain. You shouldn't ever do that. Red wine always does me in.' Sandy patted my knee beneath the covers. 'Well, I'll go on in and get things started at the shop. You come when you can.' She smiled at me, her heart full of sympathy for my hangover. She closed the door quietly behind her.

I leaned over and called Gloria.

'Naked?' she said. 'You met his son naked?' She was laughing to the point of blind hysteria. I thought about hanging up on her, but she was my only ally.

'Shut up,' I said. 'I have no sense of humour this morning.'

'OK,' she said, sputtering. 'I'm with you.'

'I wasn't naked when I met him. I made it back to the cooler and put my clothes on.'

'So you had sex before you met the son or after?'

'Neither. We never got there. Believe me, after I met the son, sex was no longer on the agenda. I don't know if it's ever going to be on the agenda after last night.'

'Raymond's going to tell, you know. I'm afraid you're going to have some major repercussions from this.'

'Poor Romeo,' I said.

'I'm not talking about Romeo. I'm talking about you. Those people hate the Rosemans, Julie. You watch your back.'

Gloria read detective stories. She liked to use phrases like 'Watch your back'. I told her I would.

I SHOULD HAVE SPENT the day in bed with cucumber slices on my eyes, but I pulled my hair into a ponytail and headed to the shop. Work was the only way to take my mind off my problems. I couldn't imagine how I would see Romeo again, but when the despair felt like it was going to strangle me, I would remember those kisses—in the car, in front of the house, by the orchids, in the cooler. Those kisses were my salvation.

As I parked the car, I saw Sandy through the shop window talking to a customer. Even from a distance I could tell Sandy was cowering. I headed in and heard a loud voice. I stepped up my pace. I thought at first that we were being robbed. I was ready to jump him. A fistfight would have been right up my alley this morning.

'Hey,' I bellowed, slamming the door behind me. 'What's going on here?'

Sandy slumped against the counter, tears streaming down her face. 'How could you?' she said to me.

'How could I what?'

Then the man turned round. Who knew which Cacciamani he was? Probably the military son, flown in from Germany just to kill me. This one was bigger than Raymond. This one was huge, the seams of his T-shirt hardly holding the fabric together over so many muscles. Still, though, he had Romeo in his face, and I felt at once fear and a weird sort of fondness for him.

'So you're Mrs Roseman?'

There was no sense splitting hairs on my title. I told him I was.

'I was just telling your daughter here what a tramp her mother was. I guess it runs in the family. She didn't catch my brother Tony, and you're not going to get your hands on my father or our business.'

Sandy sank down into a little wicker chair behind the counter and gave herself over to her grief.

'Look, Mr Cacciamani,' I said. 'I would like nothing better than to set things straight between our families, but this isn't the way we're going to do it. Now, I need to ask you to leave my store.'

'No, you look. I don't want any of you coming near my family. I can make you very sorry, Mrs Roseman. A few insults, the cold shoulder, a little bit of screaming now and then, that was fine for my grandparents, my parents. But you're dealing with a different generation of Cacciamani now, capisce?'

I opened the door. 'Out.'

He leaned back against the counter and folded his arms, which barely made it across his massive chest. 'Not till I know that you understand what I'm saying. I know you Rosemans aren't so quick.'

Maybe I should have been afraid of him, but I just kept thinking, No way is Romeo's son going to slug me. This was all some ridiculous war, and it was up to me to not buckle under to it. 'Which son are you?'

He held up one finger to illustrate his rank. 'Joe.'

'Joe, you take your threats against me and my family and get out of my store, or so help me God, I'm calling the police.'

'It's OK,' he said. 'Maybe you do know what I'm talking about.' There were five pots of tiny daffodils on the counter, and he leaned over and pinched off all their heads and held them in his hand. While he was stripping my plants, he said to Sandy, 'Tony was never going to marry you. He told me you weren't any good.'

She didn't even seem to register it. She kept her head down.

'Think about it, Mrs Roseman,' Joe said as he walked through my store dropping a careful trail of daffodil heads.

I locked the door behind him. 'What a gorilla!' I admit it, the flame of hatred for all things Cacciamani shot up in my chest. I did my best to turn it down. Joe didn't understand, just as, until very recently, I had not understood. He probably wasn't such a bad guy.

I walked back behind the counter and started rubbing Sandy's back. Poor Sandy, it was a much bigger blow for her than it ever could be for me. 'Sandy, are you all right, honey?'

'Don't touch me.'

I held my hand still. 'Did something happen before I got here?'

She kept her head down. Her mass of tiny dark curls covered her face and shoulders. 'He said you were chasing Mr Cacciamani through his shop last night when his brother Raymond came in and made you stop. He said you were naked.'

'Oh boy.'

Sandy flipped her head up. '"Oh, we were drinking Manhattans last night,"' she said in a high-pitched voice. '"Gloria and I drank a whole bottle of pinot noir." Did you actually make it all up in advance, Mother?'

'No.'

'All I asked you was to not go out with Mr Cacciamani. I thought you would understand.' She started to cry again. 'Everything about Tony, that part of my life—that was really painful for me, and so I asked you please do not go out with him. It wasn't like I was asking so much. After all, you always hated his guts. You couldn't respect me that much? You had to just look me right in the face and lie to me? Poor, stupid Sandy, just tell her what she wants to hear.'

I looked at the little daffodil plants, their healthy green stalks pointing energetically to nowhere. I could see it both ways, her way and mine. Mothers don't like to hurt their children, not even when all they're doing is trying to have a life of their own. 'Sandy, I am just so sorry I hurt you, and you're right: I never should have lied to you. But if you could see it from my perspective . . .'

'I don't want to.'

'Well, give it a try, anyway. When you were in high school, you loved Tony, and your dad and your grandparents and I all took it very personally. We thought you said you loved him just to make us angry. But I know now that wasn't true. You didn't care that he was a Cacciamani. He was just Tony, the boy you loved. We were wrong to tell you not to see Tony any more. You've got to understand that where you were fifteen years ago is where I am right now. I'd like nothing better than to wake up tomorrow and find out Romeo had a different last name. But it's not going to work that way. I really like Romeo. You should understand that better than anybody. I don't understand about all this hate, but I'm ready for it to be over.'

Sandy took a deep breath. 'That's pretty much what I said to you when I was in high school. And you know what you said to me, Mother? You said, "Get over it."' Sandy straightened up her shoulders and looked me dead in the eye.

'Get over it,' she said.

SANDY TOOK the rest of the day off, which was to say she picked up her bag and walked out of the store, tears streaming, hair springing along behind her. How had I come to this in such a short time? Things were bad, and I could only guess that they'd get worse. I wondered if Romeo knew by now that Joe had come to see me. I couldn't call him for fear of who might pick up the phone, and no doubt he was feeling the same way about calling me. The simple thing to do would be to knuckle under and give him up. But I didn't want to. He was right; we had been enemies for so long that we had bonded together. All the passion of hate had become the passion of love. The ions that had bound us together from the start had simply reconfigured.

All day long I went through my responsibilities in the dullest way. I handled the flowers as if they were spatulas. Every arrangement I put together I tore apart again, remembering the perfect bouquet in Romeo's cooler. I left the little headless daffodils in their place, even though all my customers remarked on them. 'These didn't do very well,' they said sadly.

'No,' I said, as if I hadn't noticed. 'I guess not.'

I kept waiting for the other Cacciamani boys to come and harass me. I thought it would be like a fairy tale. Each one who came would be bigger than the last, their threats scarier, until finally some fire-breathing Cacciamani boy, nine foot tall and covered in hair, would break down the door to my shop. 'Release my father!' he would shout, and his breath would singe off my eyebrows.

But even under such duress I'd say to the fire-breather, 'Sorry. No can do.'

And when I had stood up to the very worst of them, the spell would be broken. They would all be restored to regular guys, decent sons who would dance the lambada at our wedding. It would be explained to me then: we were all victims of some ancient curse having to do with a slight made to some witch 2,000 years ago for which we could not possibly be responsible. The phone rang, and suddenly my heart was filled with hope.

'I'm waiting for you at your house,' Nora said. Then she hung up.

So the path to broken curses was going to be a little more treacherous than I had imagined. I flipped over the CLOSED sign and went to meet my fate.

I LOVED NORA; I know I have mentioned this before. But the sight of that Lexus in my driveway struck greater fear into my heart than the sight of Joe Cacciamani decapitating miniature daffodils ever could.

'Alex and I have talked it over, and I've told Sandy that she and the kids can come and live with us,' Nora said. This before, Hello, Mother. This before, Heard you had a rough day.

'Nora, ease up on me, will you?'

'No, Mother, I will not ease up on you. When you look me in the eye and you swear something, I expect I can take you at your word. What can we count on now, huh? Can you tell me that? What else are you lying about?'

'OK, you win. You were adopted.' This conversation was taking place in the hall. My bag was in one hand, my keys were in the other. 'Where are the kids?'

'Sandy thought it would be better if they didn't see you just now.'

'Why, because I'm such an evil influence? A sixty-year-old woman goes on a date, and the children have to be evacuated from the house?'

'This *date*, as you call it, isn't the issue, though you have a hell of a definition of a date, from what I hear. The issue is—'

'Hang on to that thought for one second, sweetheart, your mother needs a glass of wine.' I dropped my keys into my bag, dropped my bag onto the floor, and then headed for the kitchen. Nora followed close behind in her smart grey trouser suit. I wanted to tell her I couldn't argue with her while I was wearing dirt-covered jeans. It put me at a terrible disadvantage.

'The issue is trust,' she continued. 'The issue is *family*. The Rosemans do not keep company with the Cacciamanis. That was your guiding principle when we were growing up.'

I took the wine out of the refrigerator and held it up to her. She shook her head, and so I poured for one. 'I made a mistake,' I said. 'I'm sorry. No one knows what we did to them or what they did to us. What happened with your sister in high school could have happened to anybody. It's time to put that one behind us.'

'I can't believe I'm hearing this.'

'Believe it.'

'So you're telling me you're going to see him again?'

I took a sip. For a minute there I really wanted to open up to her, tell her about the jam I was in. Why did we always tense our backs before we spoke to each other? 'I don't know. I'd like to. I keep thinking this all might blow over and I could go out with Romeo. He's so nice, Nora. That's the thing you won't believe. He's the nicest man I've ever met.' I had tried talking to her one way; now I was banking on compassion. Never bank on compassion where Nora is concerned.

'So that's your answer,' she said. 'I'm taking the kids.'

'For what *reason*?'

'If you don't see it by now, I can't explain it to you.'

'Well, are they coming back tonight?' For all the times I'd wished that Sandy would pull her life together and get a place of her own, suddenly the thought of them leaving seemed so awful to me. And maybe I was proving myself to be a lousy mother, but I was one hell of a good grandmother.

'Sure,' Nora said, looking at her watch. 'They'll be back in a few minutes.'

'And then they're going to your house?'

'Not tonight,' Nora said. 'I have to show a new listing, and Alex has a meeting. In fact, I need to get going.'

'So you're moving Sandy and the kids out because I'm an unfit influence, but at a time that is more convenient to you?'

Nora started to say something, but she thought it over for a couple of seconds, raised her eyebrows and nodded. 'More or less.'

'I won't hold my breath.'

'Think about what I said, Mother.' Nora was back in her yellow silk coat and sailing out the door.

I had about ten minutes to finish off my wine and stare vacantly at the wall in the kitchen, in which time I came up with the idea of painting everything pale yellow. Then Sandy and the kids came home. Whatever my girls had been plotting, at least they had the decency not to tell the children about it. Tony and Sarah came flying at me like I had just come home from a tour in the Peace Corps.

'We didn't see you last night, and then we didn't see you this morning,' Tony said breathlessly. 'We haven't seen you in ages.'

'Ages,' I said, kissing his head madly and then his sister's head as well. I looked over at Sandy, who was hanging back by the door. She had a guilty look for having foisted Nora onto me. I think she realised the punishment did not fit the crime.

'I drew you a picture,' Sarah said. 'Because you were gone for such a long time.' She extracted a drawing from her pink Cinderella backpack. It was a stick figure with her hair flicked up, and she was holding a giant bunch of flowers.

'It's divine,' I said.

'It's you,' Tony said.

After Sandy went to school, I shifted into total indulgence mode. I made popcorn balls with syrup and played Go Fish with real enthusiasm. We watched the video of *Lady and the Tramp*, a movie that moved me almost to tears in my present circumstances. I identified with both Lady and Tramp. Since it was Friday, I extended bedtime by an hour. In short, we partied. Maybe I was trying to secure my place in their hearts, but I really think that had already been done. I wasn't going to risk my family, and I wasn't going to be bossed. The trick was finding the line between those two things.

IT WAS STILL DARK when I felt a hand shaking my shoulder. I used to get up on my own.

'Grandma?'

I rolled over. 'Tony, baby, what is it?'

'Somebody's stealing your roses.'

The clock said five forty-five. 'Are you having a bad dream?'

He shook his head. 'It isn't a dream. It's a lady. There's a really old lady outside, and she's stealing the roses.'

Tony's bedroom was at the front of the house, his window above the roses. I was up and in my bathrobe in a heartbeat.

'Don't go down there,' he cried. 'She'll do something awful.'

'Not a chance, baby. I know who it is. It's a friend of mine. She's going to borrow the roses. I'll just go down and say hello to her.'

'It's too early.'

'You're absolutely right. I thought she was coming later. You sleep in my bed, and I'll come up in a minute, and we'll sleep in together.'

Again I was running down the stairs, running through the door and into the garden. The grass was cold and wet. The old bat had attached my hose to the tap and was watering the roses. It was too early for blooms, but they had their leaves already and some nice little buds. I could see it all there: a spade and two empty, giant-sized boxes of kosher salt. She had to use kosher.

'Hey,' I said. 'Turn my hose off!'

She looked good for almost ninety, still tall and thin, with a bunch of steel-wool hair. She looked at me with utter contempt. 'What are you doing up so early?' she said. 'Rosemans are a lazy bunch. Everybody knows that.'

I ripped the hose out of her hand and threw it back into the boxwoods, still running. I didn't care how old she was, I was going to take her out. 'Get away from my flowers. Get away from my family.'

'No, *you* get away from *my* family, you tart.' She poked her bony finger into a soft spot beneath my collarbone in a way that hurt quite a bit. She knew just where to aim. There was a blue Dodge idling in front of my house, and when the old bat poked me, out flew yet another Cacciamani boy, this one not quite as big as the other two, which ruined my theory of expanding sons.

'Hey, you,' he said. 'Get your hands off my grandmother!'

Old woman Cacciamani smiled and folded her arms, her Rottweiler boy bounding up on me.

'Do you have eyes?' I said. 'Do you see who is poking who here?'

'Whom,' the old woman said. 'Who is poking whom.' She turned to Wolf Boy. 'It's appalling. They can't even speak.'

'Please,' I said. 'Both of you stay exactly where you are. This time I am calling the police.'

'Everybody in town knows you're a crummy florist,' the old woman said. 'You probably think salt is fertiliser.'

'Shouldn't you be dead already?' I asked.

'Hey,' Cacciamani Boy said, lunging again.

She raised up the skeleton of her hand, which was draped in a layer of parchment paper so thin it let through the first rays of morning light. 'Alan,' she said. 'Wait for me in the car.'

'I'm not leaving you alone with her. It isn't safe.'

'Alan. The car.'

What a short leash these men lived on. In miserable obedience he slunk back to the Dodge. He didn't get in, but leaned up against it.

'I've had it with you Rosemans,' she hissed. 'I'm an old woman, and I've lived to protect my family from the likes of you, your parents, and your whorish little girls. I will not leave this earth until I know that my people are safe from yours.'

'For the remark about my daughters alone I should break your sorry neck.'

'Come near my Romeo again, and you'll know all about broken necks.'

I tried to control myself. This could be my big chance after all, my shot at the truth. 'Since you have ruined my sleep, frightened my grandson, and killed my roses, will you at least do me the courtesy of explaining to me what the hell your problem is?'

'You are unfit to be in the same room with my son.'

'Fascinating. I mean before that.'

'Your daughter tried to trap my Tony into a life of misery.'

'Well, Tony surely contributed to that one.'

'If he was going to marry her, it's because she lied to him. She probably told him she was pregnant. She probably tricked him.'

'Please,' I said, breathing deeply. 'Before I am forced as a mother to cut your heart out, I want you to think back before the business with Sandy and Tony. What went on between you and my parents? I know this didn't start in the previous generation, because your crowd and my crowd did not run together in the old country.' My hands were shaking. Every fibre of my being wanted to throw her to the ground and jump up and down on her. I have never felt such seething hatred in my life.

'Why should I tell you?'

'Because this is madness! It's insanity.'

She looked at me for a while. 'I owe you nothing.' She went to poke again, but I saw it coming this time, and I stepped aside, at which point she fell face forward onto my lawn.

I backed towards my door, my hands raised as a clear sign that I had not touched her and would not touch her. Cacciamani Alan came running back and scooped the old pile of sticks up in his arms. I went inside and closed the door, utterly indifferent as to whether she was dead or alive.

I OPENED SANDY'S DOOR. She was asleep in a cloud of curls. 'Get up right now,' I said without much tenderness. 'I need your help.'

She sat up quickly. She was a mother. She slept in her track suit and was used to waking up in a hurry. 'What is it?'

'The roses,' I said. 'We've got to move fast.'

Nora would have rolled over and gone back to sleep, but Sandy knew by the tone of my voice that I wasn't kidding around. This was a higher priority than whatever argument we were having. I went to the linen closet and got a stack of sheets and towels. I went to the kitchen and got a box of garden refuse bags. I went to the garage and got two shovels. There wasn't much time.

'What is it?' Sandy said, scurrying behind me.

'That old Cacciamani bitch salted my roses!' When I threw open the front door, I half expected the paramedics to be there resuscitating what was left of her, but all the Cacciamanis were gone, swept away in the blue Dodge. The only trace that they had been there at all were the two empty boxes of salt. She had taken the spade, so I guessed she wasn't terminal.

'She salted the roses?' Sandy stopped to stare at me in horror.

'Yeah.' I stuck my shovel in and heard a crunch. Sandy grabbed the other one, and we were digging.

'That's what General Sherman did after he burned down the South,' Sandy said. 'That's like the lowest thing one human being can do to another. He wanted to ruin all the farmland so the people who came back after the fire wouldn't be able to feed themselves.'

'I think she was operating under a similar impulse.' I spread a sheet over the lawn. 'Put all the earth here. We might have a chance, but it's going to be tough. She took the time to water it in.'

'She *watered* the salt?' Now Sandy was really throwing her back into the digging. She wasn't hurt any more. She wasn't scared. She was angry. She was my girl. 'Only a total sociopath would stop to water the salt.'

'That's not all,' I told her. 'It turns out she salted my mother's roses, too. Years ago. We didn't know it, of course. We just knew they died and nothing could ever be planted in that spot again.' One good thing was the old woman wasn't strong enough to dig very deeply. There were still pockets of coarse kosher salt in the ground. You had to kind of admire her for doing it herself, for making Alan stay in the car while she marched up my path like Sherman to repeat the crime.

'How did your mother find out who did it?'

'She never did. Romeo told me.' I pulled up the plants and

gently loosened the soil from their roots, then wrapped each of them in a towel. My Queen Elizabeth, my London Best, my Pink Lady.

'You think about this, Mother. You think about the kind of family who would do this.'

I thought about it while I dug even deeper to get out any salt that might have trickled down. 'I'm thinking about it, Sandy. I'm thinking about very little else.'

We went to the garage and began lugging out fifty-pound bags of soil and fertiliser. We loaded up the ground with the best compost money could buy. Then I rinsed off the roses' roots in the street, and together Sandy and I planted them all back again. By the time it was over, we were mud-caked, exhausted and proud. Sandy came to me and hugged me for a long time.

'She didn't win,' I said.

'The grocery store is full of salt,' Sandy said.

'Then I'll dig them up as many times as I have to.'

'What are you going to do, Mother?' Sandy said.

'I don't know yet.' We sat down together on the front porch.

'I've been thinking about what you said. I want to try and see it your way.'

'I appreciate that.'

Sandy looked down the street in both directions. 'Did Mr Caccia-mani say anything about Tony?' she asked tentatively.

Maybe this would hurt her; maybe it wouldn't. All I was sure of was that I shouldn't lie to Sandy about anything. 'He never got married. He's in Ecuador giving out vaccines.' I reached over and took her filthy hand in mine. 'Romeo said he was so sorry about what he had done to break you up. He said that Tony had really loved you, that he never got over you.'

Sandy kept her head down for a minute, and I didn't know if she was going to start crying again. 'I know this is terrible of me,' she said finally. 'But I think that's the nicest thing that anyone has ever said.'

SATURDAYS WERE ALWAYS a juggling act. The store tended to be packed for the first half of the day and utterly dead after two o'clock. Usually we just brought Tony and Sarah with us. Tony liked to work in the back. The more tasks you gave him, the happier he was. While he was perfectly willing to sweep the floors and unpack boxes of ribbon, nothing gave him a sense of purpose like filling up water picks, which he accomplished to absolute perfection. What he wanted to do was strip the thorns off roses, but I was twelve before my father let me have a knife. Sarah, on the other hand, was an up-front girl. I believe that 'May I help you?' was her first complete sentence. People were very charmed. That kid could have sold water to fish. When there were no customers around, she would check all the plants for dead leaves. She pinched them off gently, carefully, and stuck them into her pockets.

The four of us worked briskly. Sandy and I were both invigorated by our morning's triumph over the salt and our own tenuous reconnection. But even in the midst of all the good feelings I could not help noticing the man who was parked in an older black Ford across the street. He would sit there in his car reading; then from time to time he'd get out and stretch up on his toes. Then he'd feed a couple of quarters into the meter and get back in his car for more reading. Then he drove away; then he came back. He was a heavy man in a black raincoat, with a full head of close-cropped silver hair. He looked Italian.

Sandy didn't see him. I know that because if she had, she would have called the police. I knew there was no point in doing that now. As much as I knew that man was there for me, I couldn't call and complain about someone who was parking.

At two o'clock, as usual, customers stopped coming in. Sandy rounded up the kids to go home. I would stay until five, cleaning up and working on the books. People like to know you're open until five on Saturday, even if they never come by.

'OK,' Sandy said. 'We're off.' She kissed my cheek in celebration of our good day together. I held on to her for a second. I didn't know what was coming, but I knew it might be bad.

'Go,' I said, trying not to choke up. 'Have a fantastic day.'

I stood at the door and waved goodbye to them. Tony and Sarah loved to wave and be waved to. After they had gone, I just stood there at the door. He watched Sandy and the kids drive away, and then he tossed his magazine onto the seat beside him, got out of the car and came across the street. I was sick with dread but wanted to appear brave. I held the door open for him.

'My,' he said, 'that's service.'

He was dressed as a priest. I was sure he caused less suspicion that way. 'What do you want?' I said straight out.

He looked at me a little puzzled. 'Want? Oh yes, some flowers. I was thinking about getting something different for the altar. We're in a bit of a rut.'

I sighed. All the work of my day fell on me all of a sudden. I felt old. 'Just get to it,' I said. 'I'm really tired of you people. If you're going to shoot me, shoot me, whatever.' There was not one chance in the world that he was a priest who had spent the entire day in his car trying to figure out what floral arrangement he wanted for his church.

Now the man looked very puzzled. 'Shoot you?'

'Whatever your plan is—threaten me, scare me to death. Whatever it is you have to do, I just want to get it done, OK?'

'Do you know me?' the man in black asked.

'Sure. You're the guy who's been parked across the street off and on since nine o'clock this morning, waiting for my daughter and my grandchildren to leave so that you could have a private word with me. Am I right so far?'

'Oh, I am bad at this,' he said, looking genuinely crestfallen. 'It never occurred to me that you might notice.'

'And this has to do with the Cacciamanis, correct?'

'How do you know all this? This is very impressive. Romeo was right: you really are something. Except for the shooting part. You're wrong about that. I have no intention of shooting you.'

'Romeo?'

'I'm Father Alphonse,' he said, sticking out his meaty hand. 'You can call me Al.'

'Father Al?'

'Just Al is fine. You're Jewish, right?'

I nodded. 'Romeo sent you?'

'It isn't really part of my job description, but he's stuck. He's being watched by his family. You're being watched by your family. The idea is that no one suspects a priest, which is funny because you did. You really do break all the rules.'

'I've been told that.'

'Romeo and I go way back. From first grade at St Catherine's. He was lining up for the priesthood himself, you know. Did he tell you that? Then he met Camille on a bus. He made the right choice. She was a great woman, Camille.' He gave me a nervous look. 'Meaning no disrespect to you.'

'None taken.'

'When God took Camille, Romeo never thought there was going to be anyone else for him. He thought his life was over. And he kept on thinking that until he met you.'

'Me?'

'Romeo is crazy about you,' the priest said.

Crazy about me? 'Nobody else in his family is.'

'Have they been giving you a bad time?'

'I wouldn't know where to start.'

Al shook his head and clucked his tongue. 'Romeo was afraid of that. He's very worried about you. There's a lot of bad blood between your families, a great deal of pain.'

I looked at him. 'Say, you wouldn't happen to know what's behind all this, would you? You're a priest. People tell you things.'

'People do tell me things, but I'm not allowed to repeat them.'

'Not even in emergencies?'

'Sorry.' He took an envelope out of his coat pocket and handed it to me. 'I can give you this, though.'

The envelope said 'Julie' on it. I wish I could say my heart leapt at the sight of Romeo's handwriting, but I had never seen his handwriting before.

'Go ahead,' Al said, 'read it. I'm supposed to wait for a reply.' He turned his back and stared at the asters. He leaned over to sniff them. I opened the note.

Dear Julie,

I told you when I met you again that I had been wanting to write you a letter. Well, here it is. Sorry doesn't begin to express how terrible I feel about everything that has happened. If you are in half the trouble that I'm in, then you know what I'm talking about. As much as I know the answer is to walk away from each other and forget about it, I just can't do that. Please meet me tomorrow morning in the CVS at nine o'clock. Tell Al I'll go to Mass tonight. Give me one day so that we can, at the very least, make things right between us, even if we can't make things right between our families.

Love,

Romeo

'Oh,' I said, holding on to the paper.

'Good news, I hope,' Al said.

'I don't know,' I said. 'I don't know what constitutes good news any more.'

'Well, you don't have to give me an answer now.' He took out his wallet and gave me a card. There was his name, his number, and the address of St Catherine's Church. 'You can call me. I have an answering machine.' He tapped the card. 'That's my private number.'

I turned the card round and round in my fingers, trying to figure it all out. 'Listen,' I said. 'I know you've already been here all day, but could you stick around for ten minutes?'

'Sure,' he said. 'I've got ten minutes.'

I put the letter and the card in the pocket of my smock. 'Come in the back with me. I'll make you an arrangement. You said you wanted something new for the altar?'

'Oh, I was just making small talk. Romeo gives us our flowers.'

'Well, this week the flowers at St Catherine's are brought to you by Roseman's. That will be a first, Jewish flowers.'

'Flowers are flowers,' he said. 'I'd never turn them down.'

I got Al a stool, and he sat with me while I worked. The new flowers would come in on Monday morning, and so I used up everything I had. It took me a lot longer than ten minutes, but I gave him my masterpiece. The flowers were graceful, towering. It was not as good as Romeo's, but it was a deeply ambitious arrangement. It was all Al could do to work it into his car. He held my hand. He could not thank me enough.

'No,' I said. 'Thank you.'

'Anything else?' Al asked me at the kerb.

'Yes,' I said. 'Tell him yes.'

I CLOSED UP EARLY. Why not? There were no more flowers. I called Gloria. 'I need to shop,' I said. 'And I need advice.'

'My two favourite things in the world. Buzz drove up the Cape this morning to fish. According to my calculations, he is absolutely stuck in traffic on Route 6 about now. I'll pick you up.'

Over the years I had wondered many times why my marriage to Mort couldn't have been more like my friendship with Gloria. Not that I needed Mort to go shopping with me, but I wished I could have called him when I needed advice and thought he might be willing to drop everything. Mort would tell me to hold on, whatever it was could wait while he puttered through the tasks at hand. And even when I had his attention, it would wander. 'Julie, look at that,' he would say as I was pouring out my heart. 'Do you see that water stain on the ceiling? How long has that been there?' Over the years I just stopped asking. If I had a little success that merited celebration, Gloria was the one I called. If it was a problem, a failure, a questionable lump that required someone sitting with me in the doctor's office for three hours, it was Gloria who was there. She had seen me through Nora's biker phase and Sandy's would-be childhood marriage. I had seen her through her daughter Kate's anorexia and her son Jeff's arrest after a one-night spree of stealing car radios. What Mort didn't understand was that I wanted someone to hash things out with, somebody who paid attention and remembered. That was Gloria. That was not my husband.

I told her about old woman Cacciamani on our way to Saks. I told her about Al the priest as we pulled into the parking lot. When we had parked the car, I showed her the letter.

'You were holding out on me,' she said, digging through her bag for her glasses. I handed her mine. 'This should have been first.' She read it carefully. 'This is good. And you said yes?'

'I said yes.'

'I never would have thought otherwise.'

We got out of the car and walked towards the store. I had no business spending money on anything, but after the last couple of days I'll admit I felt like I deserved a treat.

We swung through the doors, and immediately I felt comforted by the smell of perfume and face powder and new shoes. Gloria stopped at the Chanel counter, politely brushed off the salesgirl, and ran three different stripes of lipstick across the top of her hand. 'Now, the first thing you want my advice on is your clothes. That's the easy part. The second thing you want my advice on is Sandy and Nora.'

I picked up a tube called Splendor and drew a line across the inside of my wrist. 'Precisely.'

'I want to tell you to lie. Every instinct I have thinks that you should lie. But you won't, because you really can't. On the other hand, telling them is just going to be hell.'

'Think Saigon in 1972.'

'Right,' she said. 'That's your problem in a nutshell.'

'And the answer?'

Gloria smiled at me sadly. 'There isn't an answer, angel, because there isn't a question. You know you're going to tell them, you know it's going to be awful, and that's really all there is to it.' Her eyes teared up a little bit.

I felt comforted by the depth of her sympathy. With Mort I was always trying to convince, to state and prove my case. Gloria only wanted to help me come to my own logical conclusions. 'So I guess that's solved,' I said heavily.

'Well, at least that leaves us the fun part. Don't forget you're going to spend the day with Romeo tomorrow.'

'Given how this day started, it seems hard to believe.'

Gloria discouraged me from buying the cotton sweater that came down almost to my knees. She encouraged me to buy a matching lace underwear set in a colour called champagne. Then she steered me towards a phone in the women's lounge. 'You need to call Nora now and tell her to come over.'

'I can call her once I get home.'

Gloria looked at me hard and handed me a quarter and a dime. 'Tell her you're on your way and you want to meet her there.'

I took the change and called my oldest daughter, who, to my complete surprise and disappointment, answered the phone. I requested the meeting.

'This is Cacciamani business, isn't it?'

'It is.'

Nora sighed. 'Sandy's already told me about salting the roses.'

'Well, there's more.'

'So much more you can't tell me over the phone?'

'It would be a lot easier if I could talk to you both together.'

Nora sighed again. 'All right. I'll be there in half an hour.'

I hung up the phone and looked at my watch. 'She said half an hour. We're going to have to really move it to be there on time.'

'You have to stop being so afraid of her,' Gloria said.

'Why?' I said. 'She's scary.'

Gloria drove me back to the flower shop so I could pick up my car. 'You're going to have a wonderful time tomorrow,' she said. 'We'll look back on all of this and have one hell of a laugh. It will be years from now, but it will happen.'

'I'm going to have to take your word on it.'

She tapped the horn twice and waved as she drove away. I wished that she could have come home with me; but she didn't offer, because she knew it wasn't right and I knew it wasn't right and neither of us had to say it.

SANDY AND NORA were sitting in the kitchen.

'So here's the thing.' I sat down opposite them. 'A priest came to see me at the shop today, a Father Al, and he brought me a letter from Romeo.'

'After I left?' Sandy asked.

'Actually, yes. You had just gone.'

'You're getting letters from Catholic priests now?' Nora said incredulously.

'He didn't write the letter. He only delivered it. And you might want to pace yourself, because there's more to come.' I couldn't help but think about the night I had called both of the girls home to tell them Mort had left with Lila. Sandy was married then, and both girls brought their husbands. It was so humiliating to have to announce to them all that my marriage had failed and that their father preferred a much younger, much more attractive woman to me. Both girls cried. They had counted on us always being together. I thought that night was the hardest thing I was ever going to have to do. It turns out I was mistaken.

'He wants to see you,' Sandy said.

Bless her for that. 'Tomorrow morning.'

Nora looked at her watch. 'Well, seeing as how it's seven o'clock now, I don't think you're calling us over so we can discuss this.'

'I wasn't planning on asking permission, if that's what you mean.'

'The answer is no,' Nora said, standing up. 'We've been threatened and harassed. Property has been damaged.' Nora took anything concerning property very seriously. 'These aren't just people we don't like any more. These are dangerous people. You just can't keep thinking that you're the only person in this world whose needs matter. You have to think about your family.'

'I'll admit things have got out of hand, but I want to see Romeo again. I just don't want to lie to you.'

Sandy was thinking about it, holding the past in one hand and the present in the other, making her silent assessments. I asked her where she stood on all of this.

'I think these are really, really crazy people,' she said quietly. 'And I think you're making a mistake.'

I could live with that.

'Don't call me,' Nora said. 'I have to detach myself from this.' She picked up her bag and said good night.

'Does that mean "Don't call me and let me know how it goes", or does that mean "Don't ever call me again"?'

'I'll let you know,' Nora said, and then she was gone.

I had a real lump in my throat. It wasn't that I needed her approval or that I was worried she'd never come back. But we had been having the same old fight for so many years that it just made me sad beyond measure. She had been my baby. We had shared a body for a while. It seemed like ever since then I'd been missing her.

'So you aren't going to walk?' I said, turning round to Sandy.

'I'm not moving out. But I think this is a serious mistake. That's what you told me, and maybe for my age, for that time in my life, you were right.'

I was fairly stunned by her admission. I reached out and stroked her hair. 'I'm just so much older.' I felt so much older.

'I know,' she said without any unkindness. 'That's why you should know better.'

Chapter Four

I was up at six—up meaning out of bed. I had been awake since three. I conditioned my hair and blew it dry. I used some of Sandy's face scrub. I put on my champagne underwear. It was pretty. It would have been much prettier on the girl who sold it to me, but it would have been too big for her, and anyway, she wasn't here. I changed clothes three times. I thought that I had outgrown the ability to look into a full closet and think that there was nothing there. Finally I chose a pair of heavy linen trousers and a dark blue boat-neck sweater, an outfit that I thought made me look smart but unconcerned. I was growing less concerned by the minute. All of the things I should have been worried about were falling away: Nora's wrath; all the Cacciamani boys' threats; the old matriarch, who may or may not have died on my lawn yesterday. The hardest thing to put aside was Sandy, but I did that, too. I was happy. I was a woman getting dressed for a date with a man I knew I was crazy about. I put on the little amber drop earrings that I always got the most compliments on. I put on lipstick. I slipped on my most sensible walking shoes.

Sandy was in the kitchen with a cup of coffee, reading the paper. 'You look so nice,' she said. She looked mostly tired herself, like she might have been sitting there all night.

'I really appreciate that.'

'Don't. I'd rather you didn't look nice. I thought about nailing your bedroom door shut, but then I figured the hammer might wake you.'

'I always was a light sleeper.' I poured myself a cup of coffee.

'I just decided there comes a point in every woman's life when she has to accept the fact that her mother is all grown up and she should be allowed to make her own mistakes.'

'Are we there already?' I sat down beside her. 'It seems like only yesterday I was holding your head back and trying to pour liquid penicillin down your throat because you were half dying of something but you didn't like the taste of the medicine.'

She smiled a little. 'I don't remember that. I remember the scene, but in my version I'm pouring it down little Tony. Maybe that's why this whole thing is harder for Nora. She hasn't had kids of her own yet. She isn't used to being bent to somebody else's will. Kids make you good at not getting your own way any more. I don't like what you're doing, but at least I understand that there's nothing I can do about it.'

'Thanks, honey.'

'Do you want me to drive you over there?'

I shook my head. 'It's not far. I'm going to walk. It's nice outside.' I stared at the clock. 'It isn't time to go yet.'

'Here,' Sandy said, shoving half the Sunday paper towards me. 'I'm going to make waffles for the kids.'

I spread open the paper. I went through all of it while the kids watched cartoons. Then I put on an apron and washed the dishes. After which I alphabetised all the spices in the spice rack.

I looked at the clock again. 'I could go now.'

'If you want to be absurdly early.'

'Where you going?' Sarah said.

'Grandma's got a play date,' Sandy said. She looked at me with some fondness. 'Get out of here.'

I kissed them each goodbye. It was too early, but I couldn't control myself, and I started walking. I was thinking only about Romeo now, how much I used to hate him and how much I didn't hate him any more. I was thinking about his hair, which was rough as a brush, half black and half grey. By the time I got to the end of Cedar and turned onto Elm, I was repeating his letter again and again in my mind. *Love, Romeo.* I was walking faster. It was eight thirty when I got there, and I had a light sweat on my forehead. I went into the store and went straight to the condom section, where lo and behold, a full half-hour early, Romeo was waiting.

We stood there for a minute, grinning stupidly at our own good fortune.

'You met Al,' he said.

'A great guy.'

'He liked you. He said you thought he was going to shoot you.'

'I'd had a bad couple of days.'

'You are so beautiful.'

'I was just thinking the same thing about you.'

He reached out and took my hand. I stepped towards him, and then he kissed me. Very few people were in CVS at eight thirty on a

Sunday morning. There in the condom aisle I wrapped my arms round his neck and he crossed his fine hands behind my back. That kiss was worth everything. Even if every rose had died, that kiss would have made it right. It was tender and passionate. We must have made a sight, two sixty-year-old people looking like they might just drop down and do it there in the birth-control aisle.

'OK,' he said. 'OK.' He kissed my chin. 'We've got a big day ahead of us.' He took my hand again, and we went outside and got into his car. He held the door open for me.

'So, where are we going?'

'Surprise,' he said. 'Are you hungry?'

The thought of food was impossible at the moment. I shook my head.

'Me neither.' Romeo was a good driver. 'So, you met my mother?'

I looked out of the window and watched Somerville shooting past me. 'I didn't kill her, did I?'

'She's fine. Just a little scratched.'

'She poked me once. Then the second time I dodged it. I swear to God, I never touched her.'

'She poked you?'

'She did. See?' I pulled down the neck of my sweater to show him the round purple bruise and also the strap of the champagne bra for good measure.

He looked while driving. 'The Cacciamani stigmata!' he said. 'I've had that exact same bruise for probably fifty per cent of my life. She has it perfected. It hurts like hell. None of us are ever smart enough to duck. We just stand there and take it.'

'You've got a tough mother, if you don't mind my saying.'

'I have a tough mother,' he said with gravity. 'She was a good mother in a lot of ways. She worked so hard for the business. She took good care of me and my dad. I think about what it must have been like for her, a pretty girl coming over from Italy all by herself, not speaking a word of English. But I'll tell you, she rules. When I married Camille, we bought the duplex underneath my parents' place—how's that for genius? I don't know how Camille stood it. My mother just took over everything she touched. It was like my kids had two mothers, one who was sweet to them and one who kicked their butts.'

'She poked your kids?'

'She poked the kids. She poked my father. She even poked the mailman once for being late.' He laughed a little. 'Now she's poking you.' He shook his head. 'I really am sorry about that.'

'If my daughter Nora had seen you, she would have done more than poke. How much trouble are your kids giving you?'

'I have to tell you, it's been a real surprise to me. I dropped the whole Cacciamani–Roseman thing so many years ago. I never would have imagined they'd keep the torches burning.'

'So it's bad?'

'Very bad. Except for Plummy. She doesn't get it. She just shrugs the whole thing off and goes to school.'

'Did you ever ask your mother, you know, what it's all about?' Not that I would blame him for a minute if he hadn't.

'She poked me and told me to mind my own business.'

I stuck my elbow out of the open window. I loved having somebody else drive. 'I don't care,' I said, leaning my head back. 'Tomorrow, yes. Today, I am through with the whole thing.'

Romeo reached over the gear lever and squeezed my hand.

As we took the expressway north to New Hampshire, we commented on the price of blossoming cherry boughs. We talked of the years we were broke and the years we were flush. We talked about how to raise a first-rate orchid. After crossing the New Hampshire state line, we drove on to Canobie Lake Park. I hadn't been to the park since the girls were at school.

Everything was different if you didn't bring the children. I was always nervous in amusement parks—the revolting food, the creepy-looking ride attendants, the kids shooting off in every direction. But in the daylight, my two girls grown and my grandchildren safely at home, Canobie Lake Park seemed remarkably wholesome, if tattered.

'Does your family know you're here?' I asked Romeo.

Romeo shook his head. 'I just sneaked out. Sixty years old and I'm sneaking again. I haven't had any reason to sneak in a long time.'

'I wonder what would have happened if we had met when we were young?' I said, staring out at the beautiful day in front of me. 'I mean, what if you had come up to me at that party in eighth grade? What would have happened if we had fallen in love in high school?'

'The same thing that happened to Tony and Sandy, only worse. Our parents would have killed us. Your father would have killed me, and my mother would have killed you.'

'So, it was better that we didn't meet then.'

'My family doesn't like you now, but at least they won't kill you.'

I thought about mentioning Joe, who certainly seemed capable of killing me if he had a mind to, but why spoil the day?

'Do you ride the rides?' I asked him.

Romeo stood behind me and put his arms round my waist. He bent over to put his chin on my shoulder. 'I used to when I was a kid,' he said softly into my ear. His voice made me shiver. 'One of us would steal our parents' car, and we'd drive up here at night, jump over the fence. We'd buy one ticket for the roller coaster, and then we'd just refuse to get off. After the first couple of rides they'd quit trying to fight us, and they'd just leave us on all night.'

'Bad kids,' I said, feeling strangely breathless as his hand slid under the back of my sweater. 'My father would have been right to keep me away from you.'

'You want to try it?'

I'd never been on a roller coaster. I had always been the one to stay on the ground and hold the popcorn bags. They scared the living daylights out of me, but not as much as sushi. 'Sure,' I said. 'Anything once.'

THAT WAS HOW things started. It was the roller coaster and then the Scrambler, the Zipper. We took it all on. When we wanted to scream, we screamed. We held each other's hands and raised them over our heads. We went back to the roller coaster. The world spun in dazzling colours—yellow tents, black-haired children, dull grass, gold streamers. We stumbled to the Paratrooper. We did loop-the-loops and hung upside-down suspended from our harnesses. We did not care. Gravity had no effect on us. I no longer knew when I was right side up or upside-down. And it felt right. Now my body matched my life. I was reckless, disorientated, drunk with confusion and desire. As soon as the young man with the tattoo and the whisky breath locked us in our cage, we were at each other like two mammals for as long as the price of admission allowed.

By noon I could no longer put together full sentences. 'I think I need . . .' I no longer knew what it was I needed.

'Rest. I need to rest,' Romeo said. He took my hand, and we stumbled to the far side of the park. 'Do you play Fascination?'

'What is it?'

'All you need to know is that you sit down and nothing moves.'

The idea sounded so wonderful that tears came to my eyes.

The Fascination Parlour was some combination of Skee-Ball, tic-tac-toe and bingo. We cashed in notes for a handful of quarters and took two red vinyl stools at the end of long steel cages.

'This is where you win me cheesy stuffed animals that I keep in my bedroom,' I said. 'Nora always had a hundred of those things.'

'I'm not going to win you anything,' he said, feeding two quarters into the slot. 'I've always been rotten at Fascination, and right now my head is so screwed up I don't think I could tie my shoes.'

He tossed a rubber ball up the rubber ramp and into the cage. Sure enough, it hit one wall and then the other and then came bouncing back to him.

'That's something,' I said. 'Do you bowl?'

'About like this, except the ball never rolls back to me.' He threw another, which reached the same conclusion by following a completely different path.

With every loss I found myself more profoundly attracted to him. He seemed so happy to lose. Mort would have stormed off four quarters ago, making it clear to everyone within earshot that the whole thing was rigged and nobody could win no matter how good they were.

Romeo gave me the quarters. 'Go to work,' he said.

I picked up the rubber ball and sank it in the middle square.

'Hey,' he said. 'You're a ringer.'

'I have good hand–eye coordination.' I sank the next one in the upper left-hand hole. Maybe I had beginner's luck. Ball three.

'Number seven!' the caller said. 'Number seven wins the prize.'

I had to check my seat to see if I was seven. When did I get to be so lucky? I told Romeo he had to pick the prize. He chose a stuffed cat with a small stuffed fish in its mouth. The fish had a huge smile on its face, as if it was thrilled to be devoured alive. 'My granddaughter will like this,' he said. 'She has a thing for cats.'

'Does she have a cat?'

Romeo shook his head. 'One of my mother's rules—no cats.' Should I worry about a man who lived with his mother? What difference did it make? I was never going to get anywhere near the old woman. Whatever relationship we had in the future would surely consist of long car drives and sneaking around. All around us people ate toffee-apples and held hands. They screamed for their children and laughed outrageously at nothing. Romeo had one arm round my shoulder and one arm round the stuffed cat he called Tiger. This was a wonderful day, but it was as little like anything in my real life as I could possibly imagine. We went to a stand and bought clam fritters and Cokes.

'Hey,' I said. 'Not to spoil the mood or anything, but do you have any thoughts on, you know, this? Us? I keep going over it, and the only really logical thing to do is quit before we get started, but then, I think we've already started.'

He kissed the top of my head. 'Part of me says my family comes first,' he said. 'That's the primary law with the Cacciamanis, and I believe in it. I don't want to hurt my mother, and I especially don't want to hurt my children. The other part of me says to hell with that. We're not hurting them. You're not a bad person. You're not going to tear my family apart.'

'I don't think Nora is speaking to me. Sandy is speaking to me, but she's profoundly disappointed in my actions. I don't know how long I'm going to be able to hold up under that kind of pressure. I mean, you and I aren't going to run off and ditch our kids, never see our grandkids again.'

'Maybe, over time, they'd get used to us together.'

But neither one of us said anything to that. Every interaction I had with Cacciamanis, other than Romeo, only made things worse.

'Look,' I said, pointing to a tent up ahead. 'That's what we need, spiritual guidance.' That's what the tent said: PSYCHIC READINGS AND SPIRITUAL GUIDANCE. PALMS, TAROT, CRYSTAL BALL.

'Oh, Al loves to give sermons on those things.'

'I suppose he's against them.'

'Al thinks you should take your spiritual guidance from God.'

'Well, Al doesn't have children. We need extra help.' All I wanted was a second opinion.

'I don't know,' Romeo said, eyeing the tent like it was a centre for some cult religion that snatched up teenage runaways and forced them into saffron robes.

'Hey, I rode the Zipper,' I said. 'I've made my leap of faith for the day. You need to make yours.'

We walked over, and after a moment's indecision about how to proceed, I rapped on the wooden sign. A woman in her sixties, who looked like every woman in my neighbourhood, stuck her head out from the flap. She had short salt-and-pepper hair, a light blue pullover, a little pink lipstick. She smiled at us and waved us in. It was cramped and dark inside. There were candles and a little electric fan. The fortuneteller was wearing jeans and clogs. I was disappointed. I was hoping for something a little more exotic.

'You wanted Mata Hari,' she said brightly. 'I'm Ellen. I used to be Madame Zikestra, but the wig and the robes drove me insane.'

'No, you're fine,' I said. 'I mean, I'm sure you're fine.' Did she read minds or did everybody ask her the same question?

'I only do one at a time,' she said pleasantly.

I shook my head. 'This is a joint deal,' I told her. 'What we need to find out, we need to find out together.'

'OK,' Ellen said. 'But for the two of you it's twenty bucks.'

I reached into my bag and put a twenty down on the table.

'There's only one chair,' she said.

So Romeo and I split the chair, each hanging one leg off the side. 'All right. Let me see those hands.'

We put our hands palms up on the table. Romeo had on his wedding ring, and Ellen tapped it. 'You're not married,' she said.

'Not to her,' Romeo said.

'Not to anybody,' Ellen said in a matter-of-fact tone. 'Not to anybody alive, and we can't be married to the dead. That's the first thing I have to tell you.'

Romeo looked more interested then.

She traced her nail lightly across my palms and then went to Romeo's, then back to mine. 'Most days I sit in this tent and all these little girls come in. "How many babies will I have?" "Does he really love me?" "Am I going to get a car for my birthday?" On and on and on. The things I see I could never tell them, anyway. They're only children, after all. They should have their happiness. For example, if you had come in here at fourteen,' she said to Romeo, 'you wouldn't have wanted to hear that you were going to fall in love with a very kind woman and that you'd have seven children together and one of those children would die when she was a little baby. I couldn't tell you that later on your wife was going to get breast cancer and die. To know all of that before would be unbearable.' She shook her head in sympathy for it all. 'If you had heard it and believed me, you would have thought it would be impossible to survive. But people survive terrible things. Now all those facts are history. Now I can tell you the truth. But if I had told you then, it would have been cruel.'

Romeo closed his hands together like a book.

'Oh, come on. Don't do that,' she said, and patted his hands. 'Don't make me feel bad for talking. It's already happened. I didn't do it. It's good to see people who've had some life, people who want to know true things.'

But I wasn't sure I did want to know. I wanted Madame Zikestra. I wanted twenty dollars' worth of reassurance that everything was going to be fine. 'I think we should go,' I said.

She ignored me. 'Open your hands again,' she said to Romeo.

He did what she told him.

'There are so many funny things here, the two of you. I get the strongest sense of memory, like I've seen these two sets of hands before. Years ago two children came into my tent. I was still doing the whole magic fortuneteller thing then. They said they had to come in together. I set their hands up just this way, and I saw an amazing thing: the two of them had the same lines. Not the details, but in the big things they were twined together. I felt very sorry for them because I could see that they really were in love but that this love would separate them and whip them all across the world before they came together again. But I didn't tell them anything. I said what they wanted to hear—their parents would forgive them, there would be joy in their families, blah, blah, blah. It was true, but it was so far away. They never could have stood the pain if I had explained it to them.'

Ellen had the careful, cheerful tone of someone who was giving you very complex directions to the expressway.

'And now I see the same two hands. You were right to say you had to come together. You were right to wait until now. If I had seen the two of you at fourteen, it would have been the same story, and I would have told you the same lie. But all the storms are clearing now, and the world is bringing you together again, as it should be. Just don't ever regret the past. It was all for a reason. You loved your wife,' she said to Romeo, and then she turned to me. 'And you, so you had to wait longer for love, but you had your girls, and so the waiting became another kind of love.'

I nodded. I felt physically ill. Maybe the rides were catching up with me. Mostly it was the awful notion of Sandy and Tony sitting in this tent fifteen years ago.

'So what do we do?' I said. 'About the storm?'

'It's been a hell of a storm, but every storm in the world runs its course sooner or later. Two hands like these don't happen very often. Love each other madly. Do you understand what I'm saying?'

I suppose it was clear enough. At any rate, I would have agreed to anything if it meant getting out of there. Romeo picked up the stuffed cat. We said goodbye and stumbled out of the tent.

'I'm sorry,' I said to Romeo. 'I'm so sorry about that.'

'Come on.' He took my hand. 'We're leaving.'

I followed him to the car. I wanted to ask him about the baby he and Camille had lost. I wanted to ask him if he thought it was possible she was talking about our children, but I felt too awful about dragging him in there in the first place. I felt like I wanted to go to a dark place and sleep.

Five miles outside of Canobie Lake, we came to a little green and white motel called the Sylvan Park. Romeo pulled into the parking lot and told me to wait. I stared at the bushes, the cracked asphalt, and tried not to think about anything. He came back with a key. 'Twenty-three,' he said. He drove to the end of the row and parked the car. We went into the room and fell down on the bed without turning on the lights. I didn't think it was strange we had wound up here. I think it was the only place for us to go. He held me close to him. 'I found you,' he whispered into my hair. 'I found you.' Romeo and I passed out together, tangled up, face to face, fully dressed.

Sleeping with someone is the ultimate intimacy, I think. Through sleeping we establish trust. When we woke up, we were already kissing. I let my shoes fall to the floor. I slipped out of my sweater and crumpled linen trousers. Romeo took off his shirt and jeans. He touched the champagne underwear lightly with his fingers; he ran the palms of his hands over the cups of the bra, as if he had never seen anything so remarkable in his life. He was the one I was waiting for.

Sex stays with you, even in the years you never call it into service. When you call it up again, it's there, full of memory and response. Romeo's hands, Romeo's mouth, the lines of his naked legs, the warmth of his chest against my face—every corner of him brought me back to life. The sweet forgetfulness of where you leave off and the other person begins. We were the roller coaster now, the Scrambler, the Zipper. Love rolled us together and tossed us into the air. We were bigger than gravity. We stretched into it, closed our eyes, held on to each other, held tight. We slowed down and memorised each other's fingers. I held his ear lobe between my lips. He traced my eyes with his tongue. We made love so deeply that I felt the very shape of my body changing. I whispered. He sang. Somewhere in it all, Romeo told me he loved me. I returned the compliment.

IN SOMERVILLE, the houses were all dark, but my porch light was still on. We kissed good night.

'We never did come up with a plan,' I said.

'We're the plan. The rest of it will just have to fall into place.'

I got out of the car and waved. My bones felt soft. I felt like I could slip underneath the door and float up to my bedroom. Instead I got out my keys and let myself inside. I flicked on the hall light.

There was someone sleeping on my sofa. The light seemed to wake him up, and Mort rolled over, stretched and smiled.

'Hey there, Julie,' he said.

Chapter Five

Mort liked that couch. It wasn't like I'd never seen him there before. One way or another he and that couch had logged in a lot of hours together over the years. It had been reupholstered, but it was still essentially the same piece of furniture, which is to say that Mort did not look out of place there even though I hadn't seen him in five years.

'Ah, Mort,' I said. What was there to say? Should I scream, yell? Certainly that would come, but at that moment my heart was too full of goodwill. Besides, I was more than a little relieved that it wasn't one of those hulking Cacciamani boys come to murder me for corrupting his father.

'You look good, Jules,' Mort said. 'A little rumpled, but good.'

'And you've come to tell me this?' Why didn't this whole thing seem stranger to me? Even with the five-year lapse, I was still so used to talking to Mort.

Mort sat up and stretched as if trying to realign his entire body. He was the most unabashed stretcher I'd ever seen. Even after a nap on a plane he would throw his arms over his head and roar. Then he would roll his shoulders, scratch his stomach, give his scalp several vigorous rubs with his fingertips.

Suddenly I had a terrible thought: What if something had happened with Lila? What if he was here because he wanted me back? 'Mort, why are you here? You haven't come to tell me something horrible?'

He shook his head. 'Nothing horrible, or at least nothing horrible in which you are not an active participant.' He was starting to look righteous. He was waking up.

'Romeo?'

'Nora called me. She was sobbing on the phone. I have to fly all the way across country to try and straighten things out. Do you ever stop to think about what you're doing to the girls?'

As of today I was starting to think of myself as lucky, maybe for the first time in my life. All those years I had conversations with Mort in my head and thought of what I should have said. Now here was a chance to vent my spleen. 'What *I'm* doing to the girls?'

'What you're doing,' Mort said, not giving an inch.

'I'm a single, sixty-year-old woman getting on with her life. That's what I'm doing. I'm not married and neither is Romeo. We're not busting up any families, betraying any confidences. You want to talk about the girls? Let's talk about the girls, Mort. Let's talk about what the divorce did to them.'

'You can't throw this off on my shoulders. This isn't about me.'

'You're damn right it isn't about you. So get your sorry ass off my couch and get out of my house.'

Mort got up off the couch. He looked good himself, I was sad to say. He was thinner. He was wearing nicer clothes. 'We'll talk about this tomorrow when you're a little more rational. When you haven't been out half the night on a date.' He managed to get a very nasty spin on the word 'date'.

I looked at my watch. 'It isn't even midnight. And we have talked about this. We're not talking about this any more.'

Mort pointed at me, the veins bulging out on his temples where he had once had hair. 'I'm not going to watch you throw my business and my family down the tubes over a stinking Cacciamani.'

I opened the door. 'Out.' We had been here before, this hallway, these words—only it was his sex life we were screaming about then.

'Grandma?' Tony called down from the top of the stairs.

'It's OK, baby. I'm home. I'm sorry we woke you up.'

'Is Grandpa still here?'

'You've seen the kids?' I said to Mort.

'What do you think, I sneaked in and got on the couch?'

'He's right here,' I called up to Tony. 'We were just talking.'

Tony came padding down the stairs in his pyjamas. 'Hey, Grandpa.'

'Hey, Killer,' Mort said. Why would you call a child that?

'Are you going to spend the night?' Tony came over and looped himself in my arms.

'I'm going to spend the night at Aunt Nora's. I'll be back tomorrow when you get out of school.'

'And Lila?' he said suspiciously.

'Lila's here?' I said.

'She's at Nora's.'

'She played poker with me,' Tony said. 'She's not very good.'

'Here?' I said. 'She came here?'

'I wanted to see Sandy and the kids,' Mort said. 'What was I supposed to do, leave her in the car?'

'Yes, you were. Why are you bringing Lila out here, anyway?'

'She wanted to visit friends, and Nora sent us two plane tickets.'

I put the heels of my hands over my eyes. 'No more,' I said, as quietly as possible so as not to frighten Tony. 'Good night.'

Mort leaned over and kissed Tony on the top of his head. 'You're getting so big.'

'You told me that already,' Tony said.

Mort finally said good night, and left.

'You and Grandpa don't get along,' Tony said.

'Not particularly, but it's nothing that you should be worried about.'

'I can't believe he likes Lila better than you,' Tony said.

And on that bright note we went upstairs.

The night I had planned went something like this: I go up to my room, maybe light a candle. I take off my clothes and put on my nightgown, fluff up my pillows and slide into bed. I don't go to sleep for a long time. I take my time to replay every second of happiness over in my mind. That's what I was going to do.

Instead I tuck Tony back into bed and then go into my room and try very hard not to slam the door. Just who in the hell did Mort think he was, showing up and telling me how I'm supposed to conduct my life? I tore off my clothes, including my champagne underwear, and threw them into a ball at the foot of the bed. My hands were shaking as I swallowed two sleeping tablets without water, got into a T-shirt and sat down on the bed. Lila in my house? Playing poker with my grandchildren? And what about Nora? It was one thing to deal with her harping disapproval, but for her to call in the National Guard to prevent me from having my one shot at happiness—that was more than I could easily forgive. And why did it have to happen *tonight*? Why did they all have to come in and chop down the best day I've had since I don't know when? I shut my eyes and tried to think of Romeo, but all I could see was Mort's bald head, his face contorted in righteous indignation. I used to feel so terrible when he looked at me that way, and while I still felt terrible, it was a different kind of terrible entirely.

My problems were too big for sleeping pills, and by five o'clock the next morning I was downstairs relining the kitchen cabinets. I'd had the new shelf paper for about a year, and I knew it was the only thing standing between me and a nervous breakdown. In the store I had thought it was incredibly cheerful—yellow with a pattern of tiny daisies—but now the daisies looked like little scurrying bugs.

'This is bad,' Sandy said when she came downstairs at six. 'I haven't seen you paper the shelves since you and Dad were splitting up.'

'Well then, it's time. Does this look like bugs to you?'

Sandy peered at a shelf. 'Sort of. So is this because you had a bad time with Mr Cacciamani yesterday or because you know that Dad is in town?'

'Dad and Lila,' I corrected. 'And Nora bought the plane tickets.'

'Not to be a turncoat or anything, but I didn't know about this until they were on the plane coming out here.'

'I appreciate that.' I started to cut another piece of paper.

'So are you going to see Dad?'

'I saw him last night.'

'He came back?'

'He was on the couch when I got home.'

Sandy got herself a cup of coffee. 'He shouldn't have done that. He said good night. He left. I didn't want you to get ambushed. Did it go very badly?'

'Would you want to come home from a date in the middle of the night and find Sandy Anderson asleep on your couch?'

'I'd be so grateful to have a date, I doubt I would have cared.' Sandy smiled at me. 'I do get your point, though. How was your date, anyway?'

At the very thought of it I slumped down and threw aside the paper roll. 'The date was great. Not that I can remember it very well now.'

'Where did he take you?'

I eyed my younger daughter. 'Honey, I don't mean to sound paranoid, but this is just between you and me, right?'

A cloud passed over Sandy's face, and a hurt look set in. 'I was trying to show some interest. If you don't want to tell me, don't. I'm not Nora.'

'Of course you're not Nora. I'm sorry. It's just that with—'

'I don't like this whole Cacciamani business. I think they're a bunch of thugs, but I'm trying to respect your choices. I should just stay out of it.' Sandy walked out of the kitchen, and when I called her name, she did not come back.

Canobie Lake Park, I wanted to say. We went to Canobie Lake Park.

I cleaned up the paper scraps and put the plates back where they belonged. Then I got dressed and went to work. It was barely light outside, and I had already blown it at home. I liked to go in early on Mondays anyway so I could get all the new flowers unloaded and in their buckets before the customers came in.

I went in the back door, and as soon as I was inside the shop, I felt better. I ran my hand over the wooden workbenches my father had built, and looked at my scissors and clippers hung neatly up on the pegboard on the wall. It was more my home than my house was. It was the place that always calmed me down. The years I was married, I hardly ever came here, so I didn't associate the place so much with Mort. When I took it over again, it was like coming back to my family. I became a Roseman again. I understood, I guess, why my father thought I couldn't take care of the business, but I wished he could have seen me trying. I wished he could have known that I loved the store like it was family.

When I went to the front to wash the windows, I saw a box lying flat on the sidewalk, pressed against the door. It was a florist's box—of which I had a thousand—with a huge yellow bow. I wondered if it was some sort of weird return. I unlocked the door and brought the box inside. The sticker on the front said ROMEO'S. Written beneath it in handwriting I now recognised, it said *Keep Flat. This Side Up.*

Flowers? No one had ever sent me flowers. 'Like bringing coals to Newcastle,' my father liked to say. My heart was beating like crazy. Romeo, Romeo. It felt too heavy to be flowers. I took the box to the bench, slipped off the ribbon, and pulled off the lid.

Vegetables.

Vegetables like flowers.

The tiniest leaves of spinach I had ever seen lined the whole of the bottom of the box like a cloud of florist's tissue. At the top there were two purple cabbages trimmed in white. Around them in a halo of red were twelve small tomatoes, then stalks of tender green asparagus sprouting leaves of six miniature Japanese aubergines. At the bottom there was a row of courgettes, then red new potatoes, then baby carrots, their fernlike tops still intact. The note was on a white florist's card that had HAPPY BIRTHDAY printed at the top with a line drawn through it.

> *Carissima Julie,*
> *Did you know you were a very hard person to buy a present for at 6.00am on a Monday?*
> *I love you,*
> *Romeo*

There was an arrow, and I turned the card to the back. *When is your birthday, anyway?*

I will admit it: I held the card to my heart. I dipped my face down to smell the asparagus. Could he have been at the front door as I was coming in the back? Had I missed him? Beautiful, beautiful vegetables. All was redeemed.

'Vegetables?' Gloria said over the phone.

'I know it sounds funny, but you should see them. It's art, I swear.'

'OK,' she said, and I heard her take a sip of coffee. Gloria was nothing without coffee. 'So was the underwear a hit?'

'Don't you want to hear about the day first?'

'I want to hear about the underwear first.'

So I told her. I wanted to tell. Then I told her about the park. I told her about Mort.

'Mort? Excuse me?'

'I'm not kidding. He was there when I got home. Nora sent for him and Lila so that he could talk some sense into me.'

'I take it all back—you should be scared of Nora.'

'Right now I'm just angry. Look, Gloria. Would you do me another favour?'

'To aid the course of true love or thwart your ex-husband, anything.'

'I'm going to owe you big after this. Go to Romeo's and tell him I got the vegetables. Tell him I'm crazy about the vegetables.'

'What do you want me to say, exactly?'

'It doesn't matter,' I said, knowing that Gloria and I were of the same mind on these matters. 'Just go and talk about love.'

SANDY WAS STILL SULLEN when she came to work at ten, but being that it was Monday, there was a lot to do and she had to get over it quickly. Actually, there wasn't as much to do as there should have been. Both of our flower shipments came up short, and since I had given everything left from the weekend to Father Al, there were no stragglers to back us up. There were no deliveries, so we stayed in the shop together, going over the plans for a big wedding.

Gloria swept in. 'I saw him,' she said. 'I was just there.'

'Saw who?' Sandy asked.

Gloria shot me a look, but I said, 'Romeo. I asked Gloria to go over and thank him for a present.'

'He sent you a present?' Sandy said suspiciously.

'Come on,' I said. I took them both into the cooler and pulled the lid off the vegetable box. I dazzled them with my dinner.

'Wow,' Sandy said, extending one tentative finger to an aubergine. 'Are they real?'

'They are.'

'They're stunning,' Gloria said. 'You were absolutely right. Now can we get out of the freezer? I know you are used to it, but I'm not.'

We came out with the vegetable box.

'And you had to send Gloria over to thank him?' Sandy said. 'You can't even go and see him?'

'Not exactly,' I said. 'You know how his family feels about me, and he knows how you and Nora feel about him. We're trying not to step on too many toes here.' I wanted a few points for sensitivity.

Sandy picked up an asparagus stalk, twirled it gently in her fingers. 'A guy who'd do something like this . . .'

'Is a wonderful guy,' Gloria said. 'Julie, you were right not to go over there. The place is crawling with Cacciamanis.'

'What did he say?' Sandy asked, replacing the asparagus stalk carefully.

'Well, the first trick was getting him alone. I told the thug at the cash register that I wanted to discuss the flower arrangements for my husband's funeral and that I would rather speak to the owner in private. Did you know he has an office? Why don't you have an office?'

'You told him Buzz was dead?'

'I only told the first guy Buzz was dead. I told Romeo the truth when we were alone.'

'So what did he *say*?' Sandy repeated.

Gloria looked at her. 'He said he was crazy in love with your mother, OK?'

'That's enough for me,' I said.

'He said he's thinking maybe you could go to dinner in Newton tomorrow night. He says he doesn't know anyone in Newton. I told him we know everyone in Newton.'

'Tomorrow's my night with the kids,' I said. 'Maybe Wednesday.'

'I can get a baby sitter,' Sandy said.

'Are you saying you're going to help me go on a date?' Gloria and I were both staring at her.

'I'm saying those are very nice vegetables,' Sandy said wistfully. 'You don't see something like that every day. That's all. I'm going to go watch the front. You two talk.' Sandy left us alone.

'That's a girl you can trust,' Gloria said. 'She's warming to this.'

'It comes and goes. Tell me, what else did Romeo say?'

'Everything right. He said he couldn't stop thinking about you. He had a wonderful time at Canobie Lake, though to hear him tell it, you drove up there, played a couple of rounds of Fascination, and came home.'

'Did you tell him about Mort?'

Gloria shook her head. 'I figured what's the point in making the poor guy crazy.'

I heard the front doorbell and then Sandy's voice. 'Hi, Dad.'

There was a pause, some footsteps, and then Mort. 'Would you look at this place? It's a dump. She's turned it into a dump.'

'Speak of the devil,' Gloria said. 'Do you want me to stay?'

'I think you've done enough for one day.'

'Mom?' Sandy called. 'Could you come out here, please?'

Gloria went first, smiling. 'Mort!' she said. 'Imagine us both showing up at Roseman's.'

Mort kissed her on the cheek. 'You look good, Gloria.' He said it in the same surprised and humbled tone he had used to tell me that I looked good. I wanted to kick him. 'How's Buzz?'

'Just great. In fact, I'm off to see him right this minute. The next time you're coming to town, let me know first.' Gloria gave Sandy a kiss and waved goodbye.

'So I guess she's in on this whole thing,' Mort said, watching her walk away. 'Your great conspirator. She must be loving this.'

'Nobody is loving this,' I said. With Gloria gone, I felt less confident.

Mort started pacing the shop from corner to corner. 'I see you're killing the shop. Is that part of the romance? He talks you into tanking the business so he can be the only game in town?'

'Mort.'

'Where are all the flowers? Can you tell me that? This is a flower shop. You're supposed to have flowers.'

'There was some kind of trouble with the shipment, all right? It's just today. You want to tell me in all the years you worked here you never had a problem with delivery?'

'I had my problems, but I was always on the phone yelling at somebody. Who have you called this morning?'

I hadn't called anyone. The vegetables came and then Sandy and then Gloria. I didn't even think about it. 'I'll run my store my way.'

'Your store. That just galls me.'

Sandy cleared her throat. 'Mom, Dad, if you don't mind, I'm going to go now.' Somehow she had made it all the way over to the door without our noticing.

'Ah, honey,' Mort said. 'Your mom and I are just talking.'

'Talk all you want,' Sandy said. 'I just don't want to hear it.'

She went through the door like a bullet. I watched her curls bounce away. Sandy's hair went a long way towards giving her levity. No matter how hard she tried to storm away, she always bounced.

I went over and moved two pots of hydrangeas out of the late-morning sun. 'Sandy's right,' I said. 'We shouldn't be talking like this.' I stopped and looked at Mort, my husband for more than half my lifetime. 'Mort, just go, OK? We're only going to get into a horrible fight. You and Lila can have a nice vacation in Boston. See the kids, don't see me, tell Nora whatever you want to tell her. That isn't such a bad deal, is it?'

'So you'll stay away from the Cacciamani. Is that what you're telling me?'

I sank down into a little wicker chair. 'How in the world could that be what I'm telling you?'

'Because that's what this is all about. Your father said that Rosemans and Cacciamanis had to keep away from each other. It was my job to make sure they did. That whole business with Sandy nearly broke your parents' hearts.'

'I told you not to tell them.'

'You don't understand, Jules. This Cacciamani bastard isn't just some guy I don't get along with. I've seen him operate for years—first with his old man and then with his pack of boys behind him. These aren't your average bad people. They're probably Mafia.'

'Give me a break, Mort. What did the Cacciamanis ever do to you? Do you even have any idea what this whole feud is about?'

'What it's about?' Mort said. 'What it's about? Julie, what rock have you been living under? It's about business. It's about them smearing our name all over town, saying we used old flowers for weddings. Saying we went to the cemetery and picked up our bouquets after funerals. They kept me out of Rotary. And it didn't start with Romeo. It goes back to his old man and that evil bag he was married to, may they rot in hell.'

'Not so fast. She isn't dead yet.'

'Is that possible?' Mort shrugged. 'Then they're waiting for her. They're sharpening up the pitchforks. Those people undermined us in every way possible. They'd call our big accounts and say we had cancelled, that they were going to be doing the flowers. And God forbid a Monday morning ever rolled by when I wasn't here to meet the shipment. Every rose in the bunch would have its head twisted off.'

OK. That one I believed. I had seen a Cacciamani behead a plant before. 'So if this is true, some of it, any of it, how many of those same things did my dad do right back to them? And what did you do? Do you expect me to believe the Cacciamanis threw all the punches and the Rosemans stood there and took it?'

Mort looked like he couldn't possibly be hearing me right. 'Of course I went after them. So did your folks. When we got hit, we hit back. That's called life, Julie.'

'Life, fine, but then after a couple of generations, who throws the first punch? Are you reacting, or are you going out there to nail them?'

'What in the hell difference does it make? These are Cacciamanis we're talking about. All that matters is that we get them before they get us.'

'But don't you see, Mort? It's a game. They played dirty. We played dirty. Everybody hates everybody. But if we decide to stop it, if both sides choose not to fight any more, the game is over. It's that simple.'

'That simple if you were playing with fair-minded people, which you're not. What I'm saying is that love blinds us.' For a second he looked like he was as tired out by this whole thing as I was. 'We don't always see the whole picture. That's why the people who are responsible for us have to step in and save us sometimes.'

'But I don't need saving. When you ran off with Lila, I didn't believe she wanted what was best for you. But it was your life, and you were entitled to your own mistakes.'

'I'm not going to let this drop, Julie.'

'You're going to have to. Sooner or later you have to go home.'

Mort sighed and looked around the shop. Without a moment's hesitation he picked up the best pot of purple cyclamen from a bunch of pots on a low platform and put it next to the cash register. 'Got to get them up to eye level. You know that Lila and I have a shop now. Lila picked up on the business fast. She has a real good head for flowers.'

'I'm glad to hear it.'

Mort put his hands on his hips and surveyed the store, the lord of all he saw. 'This is a great place. Do you know that? The space, the light. You couldn't find a place like this in Seattle. It could use some updating, but the feel of it . . . I always had a real connection here. From the first time you brought me in, I really believed that one day this was all going to be mine. I loved this shop.'

'I know you did.'

'Let me see the books, Julie. I know you're running the whole thing into the ground.'

'It's my store now. Forget about it.'

'I know it's your store, but I still have feelings for the place. Just give me a couple of hours. If the place was on fire, would you turn away my bucket of water?'

'Don't be stupid.'

'No, *you* don't be stupid. I might be able to help you put out the fire. Why don't you try loving Roseman's more than you hate me.'

It was only my vanity that stopped me. But the truth was that he was great with the books, and I was turning them into soup. He was right: we were going down. I did need help. 'OK,' I said finally, waving him back towards the desk. 'You know where everything is. Nothing has changed.'

'Oh, Julie,' he said sadly. 'Everything's changed.'

THE ONE GOOD THING about having Mort look over the books was that it took his mind off Romeo. 'Aargh!' he would yell while I was waiting on customers.

The customers would look towards the back of the store. Some appeared frightened; others were simply confused. 'He's trying to move the desk,' I said calmly. 'It's very heavy.'

At one point Mort tore open the curtain that separated the front of the shop from the back. 'What are you trying to do? Kill us?'

'Kill me,' I said. 'Not us. It's mine to lose.'

'Well, congratulations on your new-found liberty, because you've lost it.'

'How was I supposed to know what to do? For thirty-four years you never let me in the store, and then you run off to Seattle with Lila. There wasn't time to take a course in accounting. I had to get to work.'

'That's why you pay people, Julie. They're called accountants.'

'With what, Mort? You got the money, remember? That was the deal. The house is mortgaged to the gutters. I got a loan on the shop.'

'You took a loan against Roseman's!'

I hadn't meant to tell him, but in the next thirty minutes or so he would have found out, anyway. I felt my eyes welling up with tears. I was overcome with shame and guilt. I had mortgaged my parents' store, borrowed against the very thing they had worked their whole lives to pay off. 'I didn't know what else to do.'

'You should have called me.' Mort was seething.

'I wasn't going to call you. You know that.'

Mort closed the curtain again and went back to work. I did a little watering. What would happen if I lost Roseman's? Who would I be without the flower shop? Nora didn't care a thing about flowers, but I wanted it to be there for Sandy if she wanted it. One day she could give it to Tony and Sarah. To think, out of sheer incompetence I could have frittered away the only legacy my family had—it absolutely killed me. I went into the back. 'Just forget about it,' I said to Mort. 'You can't fix it. Go home to Lila. She must wonder where you are.'

Mort didn't look up. He was punching on a calculator just as fast as his fingers would go. He had a pencil behind each ear. 'Leave me alone. Get out there and sell some flowers.'

I closed the curtain. I felt very weepy now. The way I saw it, I had lost or would eventually lose my marriage, my business, my daughters, and Romeo. Somewhere my parents were looking down on me and shaking their heads in despair.

Mort asked me to go out and get him a sandwich at one o'clock and said he'd watch the store. I bought myself a yoghurt but then didn't even have the appetite for that. I stuck it into the cooler behind some daisies and resumed my worrying.

From two to five was usually when I worked on the books, but Mort was still back there, swearing under his breath. Today the bell rang at two thirty and in walked a very nervous-looking Romeo Cacciamani. He was wearing grey trousers and a nice white shirt with rolled-up sleeves. He looked almost unbearably handsome.

'My God,' I said, my voice automatically dropping to a whisper. 'What are you doing here?'

'Your friend Gloria said this was when Sandy went to pick up her kids from school. Is this all right? Is Sandy here?'

I glanced behind me and moved quickly to the front of the store. I kissed him. I couldn't help it. I was so glad and so sorry to see him. 'She isn't here, but you have to go. Really.'

'I'm sorry. I know I shouldn't have come. I've been driving round the block for half an hour telling myself not to come. But I had to see you.'

'I loved the vegetables.'

'Did you? I just didn't know what to send. I wanted to buy you something big, like, say, California, but there wasn't time.' He put his arms round me. 'What about dinner tomorrow?'

'Sure,' I said. 'I can work something out, but you have to go now.' I wanted him to stay and stay. I wanted to tell him everything that was happening.

'Is everything all right? You seem so upset.'

'It's a stressful time,' I said, and then, as if to prove my point, Mort came out from behind the curtain with three spiral ledgers. He dropped them.

'Cacciamani!' he yelled. 'Get your lousy mitts off my wife.'

Wife? I thought. Where was Lila?

'What's he doing here?' Romeo asked, his tone more curious than alarmed. He kept his mitts firmly on me.

'None of your damn business what I'm doing here. Now get out before I set you on the kerb in pieces.'

Romeo seemed to smile a little in spite of himself. 'I haven't heard that one in a long time.'

'I swear, Cacciamani, get out of here now. You do not want to get into it with me.'

'Of course I don't want to get into it with you. What in the hell is your problem, Mort?'

'My problem? My *problem*? You're my *problem*, buddy. You always have been. Except when I was here, you knew enough to stay away. Now I'm gone, and you're sniffing around my wife, ruining my business.' Mort shook the few papers he was still holding in his hands. Somehow it seemed the two problems had become conflated in his mind. Now it was Romeo's fault that Roseman's was sinking, Romeo's fault that I wasn't sitting at home. The budget deficit—that was probably Romeo's fault as well.

Romeo scratched his head. 'Your business? Your wife?'

'Well, they sure as hell aren't yours.'

'Listen, Mort. Enough with the tough-guy talk. We never got along. So what? This isn't a turf war.'

'It is a turf war, if that's your terminology. I want you off my turf.'

Romeo took a small step away from me, towards Mort. 'You don't live here any more, unless I've got the story wrong.'

'Let me tell you, Cacciamani, you've got everything wrong.' Mort came out from behind the counter.

'Look,' I said. 'This is a ridiculous mistake. Mort is visiting, and Romeo is leaving. Let's just drop it.'

'I'm not leaving,' Romeo said. Mort was taller than Romeo, but Romeo was built like somebody who could throw an ox through a wall, or at least he could have twenty years ago.

Mort nodded, the veins coming up. 'Well, good. That's really fine, because you're the one I've been wanting to talk to, anyway. You just saved me a trip.'

'Mort,' I said in a tone used to soothe nervous Doberman pinschers. 'Settle down.'

'Stay out of this, Julie. You,' he said, pointing at Romeo, 'need to stay away from my family. You stay away from Julie. You stay away from my girls. You stay away from my store.'

'You can't tell him to stay away from me, Mort, or the store.' It wasn't that I was completely against him at that moment. He had spent the day trying to rescue my books. He was tired and hugely frustrated, and I liked to think that had this meeting taken place at another time, it might have gone better.

Mort turned to me. 'Are you on his side?'

'Please. Let's just all walk away from this.'

'After everything he did to me?'

Romeo asked, suddenly enraged, 'Did to you? If he wants a fight, I'll give him a fight. I had put the past in the past.' He turned to Mort. 'But if you want to bring it up, I'm sure I can remember.'

'A fight?' Mort said, his eyes bright as dimes. 'You want to fight?'

Who said these things? Fighting was only in the movies.

'If that's what you're looking for, come on.'

No sooner were the words out of Romeo's mouth than Mort had the cyclamen in his hand and was hurling it straight at Romeo's head. Mort had been state-ranked in baseball when he was in college. They called him the Arm. The pot hit Romeo on the left temple and exploded into a fan of earth, petals, stems and terracotta shards. Romeo went down.

For all his fits of rage, I had never seen Mort strike another person. He didn't even spank the girls when they were little. I knelt beside Romeo. His head was bleeding spectacularly, and I was trying to brush the soil out of his eyes. I loved him. It was one of those moments in life when you're sure.

'Mort, you stupid sonofabitch, you could have killed him!'

At the very mention of being killed, Romeo rose up from the ground and flew at my ex-husband like a creature with wings. He got his hands round Mort's throat and started beating his head into the counter. Mort somehow landed a hook on the exact spot where Romeo's head was already split open. Romeo, reflexively, brought up his knee.

It never occurred to me that intelligent grown men still fought, and yet there I was, watching it as if the whole thing were taking place under water. I thought that fighting had rules. I was wrong. They were slugging, pulling. I think I saw Mort bite. They knocked over the card rack and smashed the African violets. 'Stop it!' I screamed. 'Stop it!'

With that simple command they fell apart, panting, bloody and dislodged. They lay on my floor amid the soil and the blossoms. In less than a minute they had both been ruined, the store had been ruined, I had been ruined. I went to Romeo, whose whole head was covered in blood. Both his forehead and his lip were bleeding now, and his left hand was turned at an unnatural angle. There was a bright red pool forming under his head.

But it was Mort who really concerned me. I think most of the blood on him was Romeo's, but there was a horrible swelling on the side of his head. I couldn't get him to respond to me. He lingered in a mumbling, half-conscious state and then slipped out of it. I put my head down on his chest and listened to his heart.

Romeo dragged himself into a sitting position, wincing at every inch. 'Dear Mother of God,' he said. 'Tell me I didn't kill him.'

'You didn't kill him,' I said. 'But I'm calling an ambulance.'

Time happened in a dream. It seemed like the second the phone was in the cradle, the ambulance guys were rushing through the door. Because I had told them, when asked over the phone, that the cause of injury was a fight, they sent the police as well. Blue and red lights flashed brightly through the window, and Ginger, the woman who runs the dress shop next door, came over to see if I'd been murdered.

'Do you know these men?' the young officer asked me as two para medics started working on Mort and the third applied pressure to Romeo's head.

'Ex-husband,' I said, pointing. 'New boyfriend.'

He nodded and closed his book.

'We've got a concussion here,' one paramedic said of Mort.

'This one is losing a lot of blood,' Romeo's paramedic said.

Romeo allowed himself to be hoisted onto a stretcher. They already had Mort's limp body tied onto a gurney, and side by side, like bunkmates at camp, they were slid into the ambulance. I got in between them for the short ride, just to make sure nobody woke up and tried to get things going again.

Inside the emergency department, they took Mort and Romeo off quickly. I called Sandy. 'Listen carefully,' I said. I told her to call Gloria to come and watch the kids. Then she should call Nora and come to the hospital. 'Your father has been in a fight.'

'The two of you were fighting?' Sandy said. 'Fistfighting?'

'It was Romeo,' I said. It didn't matter if she knew or Nora knew or any of them knew. It was over. No one could come back from something like this.

'How bad is it?' Sandy said, her voice tentative.

'Not bad like death. Not even bad like permanent injury. But bad,' I said.

'How's Romeo?'

'Um, I'd guess about the same. I have to call his family.'

I sat with the phone in my hand for several minutes before I pulled myself together and called the store.

'Romeo's,' a voice said.

I asked to speak to Raymond. Despite our unpleasant first meeting, I remembered Romeo saying he was the most rational of his sons.

'You bet,' the voice said, so cheerful, so helpful. It sounded like the place was packed. There was a pause, and I tried to keep from sobbing. A different yet very similar voice came on the line. 'Raymond Cacciamani.'

I cleared my throat. 'Raymond, don't hang up the phone. There's been an accident, and your father's in the hospital. This is Julie Roseman.' I thought it was best to put that fact at the end.

'Somerville Hospital?' he said, like he was taking a delivery order.

'Yes.'

Raymond hung up the phone. Personally, I would have asked a couple of questions. For all he knew, Romeo was dead. I was planning on begging him to come alone. I was going to tell him it was only a cut and everything was fine. Too late for that. I didn't think there was any point in trying again.

I went to the nurses' station and made enquiries.

'Are you a relative?' the nurse asked without looking up.

'Ex-wife to one and friend to the other—girlfriend.'

'So not exactly family in either case. Nobody's ready to have company right now, anyway. Why don't you just wait another minute?'

So I slumped down into a yellow plastic chair and waited, waited for Nora and Sandy and the Cacciamanis. Waited to pay the price for a little happiness.

A BROKEN EX-HUSBAND, a battered new lover, two hysterical daughters, and a whole host of raging Cacciamanis—that was what I braced myself for. What I forgot, amazingly enough, was the one thing that would truly, deeply disturb me: Lila the wife. When she clicked through the electric doors in her high heels, Nora close behind, I felt the last bits of whatever inner glue I had holding me together give way. Lila Roth, both bridesmaid and bride. We had met before, or if not met, passed each other in the driveway while she was helping Mort move out and I was leaving so as not to watch.

Lila was a blonde. Maybe real, maybe not. She had a certain kind of thinness that smacked of self-obsession. She was wearing eye shadow; her nails were shell pink; she wore stockings with open-toed shoes; her teeth were bleached a toilet-bowl white. Need I go on? Not a single detail escaped me.

'Where is he? What have you done with him?'

What have I done with him? Like maybe I had put him in a storage closet? 'Mort's going to be fine.' I had no data with which to support this. 'He's being seen by the doctors now.'

'The doctors!' she said. 'He's with doctors!'

'This is a hospital.'

'Mother, what happened?' Nora said, looking a little less confident than usual, as if perhaps even she understood her own culpability in the day's events.

'Your father showed up at the shop, and then Romeo showed up. I wasn't expecting either one of them. They got into a fistfight.'

'So your boyfriend did this. You admit it!' Lila said.

'I admit it,' I said.

'Nora, you're my witness.' She turned to me. 'I will sue you, so help me God.'

But Nora was falling down on her witnessing duties. She was dialling her cellphone and pacing off across the lobby for privacy. 'I don't know what you're going to sue me for exactly,' I said. 'I wasn't involved in the fight.'

Lila was stumped only for a second. 'It happened in your store. That means you're liable.'

'Well, seeing as Mort threw the first flowerpot, I would say you were liable, if I was the kind of person who sued other people, which I'm not.'

'You bitch,' Lila said. 'I told Mort this was lunacy, flying across the country to try and straighten out your love life. But he had to help you. He had to be the good guy. This is how you thank him.'

'This is how I thank him,' I repeated. 'Aren't you a little curious about how he's doing? Don't you want to talk to his doctors?'

Lila flashed her blinding incisors at me and then stomped off.

'I can't believe you let this happen,' Nora said. 'Alex is on his way over. If she talks about suing again, maybe he can shut her up.'

I hit Nora once when she was fifteen. She came home drunk at four in the morning after I had spent the night on the phone with the police and local area morgues. She came in the front door and proceeded up to her bedroom without stopping to say hello. When I called out her name in a mixture of relief, joy and fury, she told me to drop dead. I slapped her open handed across the face, exactly the way every child psychologist will tell you you must never do. I replayed that scene over in my mind for years, trying to think how I could have handled it differently, properly, but to this day smacking her seemed like the only logical response to her actions. There in the hospital waiting room I put my hand on her shoulder. 'If you want to see your father and his wife, you invite them out to see you. Buy them plane tickets, I don't care. But don't you ever, ever conspire against me with anyone again and expect me to forgive you because I am your mother. I am sick and tired of forgiving you, Nora.'

Nora now wore the same look of utter incredulity that she had worn at fifteen, the imprint of my hand fresh on her cheek. 'I was trying to *help* you,' she said. 'I called Daddy so he could talk sense into you. Clearly, Mr Cacciamani is a dangerous man. Do you still think he's so wonderful after what he did to my father?'

'Nora,' I said, trying very hard to keep my voice steady. 'I think you should go and comfort your stepmother, because if I have to talk to you about this for one more minute, I'm going to say something we'll both feel bad about later.'

Again with the open mouth, the disbelieving hurt. I was sure I was doing the wrong thing. I could not help it. Not every relationship works out. It hadn't worked out with Mort; it wasn't going to work out with Romeo. Was it possible I could ever come to such a point with a daughter to say, 'Enough's enough' and 'See you around'?

God forgive me for what I know to be a small-minded slur against Romeo's family, but when they came in the door, I couldn't help but think of *West Side Story*: the Jets walking down the streets of Hell's Kitchen snapping their fingers. There were so many of them, and they all looked so much alike. The wives all looked like sisters, and though I had met four of his sons before (counting Tony, who was still in Ecuador), I couldn't remember which was which. My only lucky break was that the old woman didn't appear to be in attendance. They came towards me in a mass, and just as I thought they were going to stomp me to death, the whole pack veered to the left to the nurses' station. There was a flurry of enquiries, some raised voices, and then they disappeared through the swing doors marked NO ADMITTANCE: HOSPITAL PERSONNEL ONLY. That was it.

Two minutes later Father Al came in looking flustered and concerned. 'Al,' I said, and waved him down.

I could see the confusion on his face. He was trying to place me as a parishioner, and then he remembered. 'Julie, oh. Julie. Are you all right?' He patted my hand. It was such a relief to have someone pat my hand.

'I'm fine.'

'What about Romeo? Raymond called me. He said there was an accident, and he said something about you.'

I could imagine what the something was, but Al was a priest and wouldn't say. 'He's going to be fine, I think. He got into a fight with my ex-husband.'

'Mort? Mort's in town?'

'You know Mort?'

'I don't know him myself, no, but I've heard plenty about him.'

'Well, they ran into each other.'

'And Romeo's children'—he looked around nervously—'have they come in yet?'

'They're already in the back with him. I don't even know if they saw me.'

'This is going to be bad,' he said. 'Romeo will be fine. He was such a scrapper when we were in school. I thought he had outgrown it.'

'He probably had. He was provoked.'

'We'll keep that between us.' Al looked towards the doors. 'I really should go in there.'

'Will you let me know how he is? Tell him I'm out here? I know they'll never let me in to see him, but I don't want him to think I just walked away.'

'He knows that.'

I suddenly felt a great sob come up before there was time to properly suppress it. 'I'm absolutely prepared to give him up. I don't mean to sound so melodramatic, but I can't keep causing him all this trouble with his family. I love Romeo. I only want what's best for him. You know that, don't you?'

Al took me in his arms and let me cry on his black shirt for a minute. Gloria would have done the same thing. I pulled myself upright and ran my hands beneath my eyes. 'Go on,' I said. 'I'm fine.'

Al nodded and smiled at me; then he went through the doors without even stopping to ask the nurse's permission.

What if Romeo thought I had gone? What if he didn't even know I was out in the waiting room? All I wanted was to hold his hand, to tell him everything was going to be fine. I wanted the chance to tell him all sorts of comforting lies about how everything would turn out fine. But once Mort threw that pot of flowers, I lost all of my rights, or I realised I'd never had any to begin with.

Sandy came in next. It was starting to feel like a terrible episode of *This Is Your Life*. If I stood there long enough, my third-grade teacher would come in. 'I always thought that Julie Roseman was trouble,' she'd say.

'Dad?' Sandy asked me.

'I don't know. Nora and Lila are back there with him now. I'm afraid I'm *persona non grata* on both sides. No one has come out to tell me anything.'

Sandy, never a take-charge sort of girl, went up to the nurse and asked for the status of Mort Roth and Romeo Cacciamani.

'Are you a relative?' the nurse asked. She'd seen a lot of relatives.

Sandy told her yes. 'Roth is my father and Cacciamani is my uncle.'

'They're related?'

'By marriage,' Sandy said. 'Not blood. They hate each other.'

'Obviously,' the nurse said. She thumbed through some papers and then nodded her head. 'Hang on a second.' She picked up the phone.

'You go in and see your dad,' I said. 'I can wait here.'

'Then I'll wait with you for a minute. Dad's got Lila and Nora. That's a pretty full house.'

I wanted to kiss her. I kissed her. 'How are the kids?'

'Their life is a party. They couldn't believe Gloria was coming over. She's going to take them shopping.'

'OK,' the nurse said, putting down the phone. She looked at me. 'You're the ex-wife slash girlfriend, correct?'

'Correct.'

'What the hell, it's nothing serious. Many bruises for both parties. Roth looks like a concussion and two broken ribs. They'll keep him overnight for observation, but he should be out of here with a splitting headache by morning. Cacciamani had eighteen stitches, a broken left wrist, and, coincidentally, two broken ribs. They'll let him go in about an hour.'

Sandy and I took our places in the chairs. 'What a day,' I said. 'What a horrible, horrible day.'

'Do you want to tell me what happened?'

'Not particularly.'

'I was just starting to like him a little, the idea of him at least.'

'Romeo?'

Sandy nodded.

'That's really nice. I'm giving him up now. Nobody needs all of this. My love is going to kill him, and I couldn't stand that.' I felt like I was going to start crying again. 'Go and see if your father's awake.' Mort had ruined my life once again, but I still couldn't help feeling vaguely responsible for his pulverised state. If it wasn't for me, he wouldn't be bleeding now. Of course, if it wasn't for Mort, I wouldn't have been dating to begin with.

Sandy pushed out of her chair. 'I'll be back in a minute.'

'Take your time,' I said. 'I'm not going anywhere.' I was so tired I thought about stretching out over the chairs and slipping off into a coma. I hoped they would notice me in a day or two and give me a room, hook me up to a nice glucose drip. I couldn't imagine going back to work, and I couldn't imagine going home. The hospital seemed like a fine place to set up camp.

There was a pretty, waiflike girl with long black hair and a dark purple scarf looped round her neck wandering through the waiting room. She would stop in front of people and ask them a question. They shook their heads, and she moved on to the next group. She looked like the gypsy princess in every film that had a gypsy princess—huge sad eyes and exceptional posture. She started to walk towards me. 'Mrs Roseman?' she asked.

I looked up at her and blinked in agreement.

'I'm Patience Cacciamani.'

'Plummy?'

She nodded. She had tiny gold rings on her fingers, and one of her ears was pierced three times. On her this looked like a good idea.

'My dad wanted me to tell you he's OK. He made everybody else go out in the corridor so he could talk to me alone. He wants to know if you're OK.'

The fact that she was talking to me was so confusing that I could barely understand her words. 'I'm OK.'

She sat down in Sandy's chair. 'You don't look so great, if you don't mind me saying.'

'I don't mind at all.'

'I had wanted to meet you, but it never occurred to me it would be like this.'

'You wanted to meet me?'

'Sure,' she said. 'Dad's crazy about you.'

'But what about your brothers?'

She waved her hand. 'They're idiots. Not idiots, really. They're good guys one at a time, but when you put them together, they're like—I don't know—a bunch of moose or something.'

This made me smile.

'They won't actually hurt you—I hope you know that—but they do seem to despise you. I don't mean to be rude, but I think we should be able to speak frankly.'

Where this child came up with this much poise was beyond me. It made me want to go out and have a couple more holes put in my ear. 'I agree. Absolutely. Tell me about your father.'

She stared off into the middle of the waiting room trying to conjure him in her mind. 'Stitches here,' she said, and drew a line with her finger across her own temple. I could see the flowerpot landing there now. 'And here.' She touched her lip. 'He broke his wrist, but only one little bone, and there are two cracked ribs.' She pressed a hand into her ribs. 'It must have been one hell of a fight.'

'It was.'

'How's the other guy, your ex?'

'I hear he has a concussion. They're keeping him overnight.'

'That's good. I don't mean good that he's hurt, but this way the boys will be able to say Dad won. Dad doesn't have to spend the night.'

'That is good.'

'My family has some wicked problem with your family. I think everybody needs to let go of their anger.'

'That makes two of us.'

'Well, you and Dad like each other. That's a positive start, don't you think?'

'I did think,' I said. 'But right now it's all a little confusing.'

She nodded and gave me a sad smile like the statues of Mary that were everywhere in this town. She looked towards the double doors and sighed. 'I guess I should be getting back. They're going to be releasing him soon. We're supposed to take cars and pick him up round the back. It was very nice meeting you.'

'You, too. You'll tell your dad I hope he's OK?' Romeo, Romeo. All I wanted was to hold him in my arms.

'I'll tell him,' she said. Plummy leaned towards me and brushed my cheek with the back of her hand. 'You get some rest.'

She wasn't two steps away from me when her extended family started pouring into the waiting room.

'Plummy!' the big one yelled. 'You get away from her.'

'Shut up, Joe,' Plummy said without the slightest inflection.

They came towards me in a clump.

'I thought I made things clear to you,' Joe said, pointing a finger in my direction. His face was red and he was breathing hard.

'Joe,' Plummy said. 'Do you want me to get Dad out here and have him see you talk to Mrs Roseman this way?'

'Shut up,' he said to his sister.

She walked up to him. She was taller than I had realised. She got her face very nearly in his face. 'No, you shut up, Joseph.' She kept her voice low. 'People are staring at you. They're going to throw you out of the hospital. Leave Mrs Roseman alone, OK? That's what Dad told me to say. Leave her alone, or I'm telling.'

I wanted to be this girl. I had never in my life possessed one ounce of her confidence.

Joe gave me one more point. 'You're ruined.' He and his pack retreated.

Plummy looked at me and shrugged. 'Forget him,' she mouthed. Then she added in a bright voice, 'Bye, Mrs Roseman.' She followed them out of the door.

Chapter Six

It was a very tentative time in my family. The things that had been said in the hospital were put aside. The next afternoon, when Mort was released and went back to Nora's, there was an unspoken agreement that we would all play nice for his sake. Everyone moved slowly and with exaggerated politeness. I waited almost a week before visiting so as not to ruffle any feathers. 'Would you like a cup of coffee, Julie?' Lila asked me.

'Oh, no, but thank you.' I stood on the front steps of Nora's house balancing a casserole dish on my upturned palms. Macaroni and cheese. Mort's all-time favourite. I was sure it would be swirling down the garbage disposal before I got my car started again.

'Don't you want to come in, say hello to Mort?' It sounded like she was singing the invitation. *'Don't you want to come in-n-n-n-n, say hel-l-l-l-oooo?'*

Actually, I did want to see Mort. I'm not exactly sure why. Maybe it was because since the fight I'd felt like everything had changed, and I wondered if he felt it, too. 'Let him get his rest,' I said, the thing I knew Lila wanted to hear. 'If he wants to call me later, I'll be glad to come back over. How is he doing?'

'Oh, the doctor says he's super. The swelling in his face has gone down a lot. Really, it's just his ribs that hurt. We should be going home soon.'

'Mother?' Nora called out. 'Is that you? Won't you come in?'

'I'm just dropping off a casserole. I need to get to work. Tell Mort

I hope he feels better.' Notice I said 'Mort' and not 'your father', so as not to make Lila feel excluded. I went down the steps, turned and waved. Nora and Lila stood at the door waving back. What a pretty pack of Stepford Wives we made.

I hadn't talked to Romeo all week. I sent him a get-well card—who knows if he got it? He sent me a note saying that he would call as soon as the dust settled. But this was a Sahara sort of dust. It never settled, not even for a minute. Every day after that there was another note from him, saying that he loved me, saying that he missed me. I sat on my bed and read them and cried and cried. I was ruining his life, ripping up his family, and getting him punched, and that wasn't the thing to do when you loved someone as much as I loved Romeo. The right thing to do was to walk away. I understood how much I loved him then, when I knew I was going to walk away.

I didn't talk about Romeo, though I thought of nothing else. It would have conflicted with the Geneva Accord of Good Manners. At home Sandy was so nice to me you would have thought I had a terminal illness. She worked harder at the store, harder around the house. In the evenings she took Tony and Sarah over to see Mort, and all her reports were glowing. 'He looks fantastic,' she said. 'You'd hardly know that anything had happened to him.'

I imagined the same was true of Romeo. I imagined that everyone was getting back to normal, except for me.

Gloria was helping out all over the place—at home, at work. She had bought a couple of new outfits that she thought would look good in a florist shop: drawstring trousers made out of natural hemp and loose linen jackets covered in a cabbage rose print. She looked more like a florist than I ever did. She had gone in with her spare set of keys the night of the fight and cleaned everything up. She swept all the evidence into plastic garbage bags.

'You can't keep working for me like this,' I said. 'It's too much.'

'I like it,' she said. 'I haven't had a job since Buzz and I got married.' Buzz owned an insurance company.

'But nothing's wrong with me.'

She put down a bucket of gypsophila. 'Julie, you've got to call him. You've got to straighten this out.'

'Nothing to straighten,' I said. 'Nothing at all.'

'He loves you.'

'I'm destroying his life. I won't do it any more.'

And so I continued to make my way through the fog. I spent so much time thinking about things I shouldn't have been thinking about that I failed to notice what was going on around me. It was Gloria who called the obvious to my attention a few days later.

'Julie, there aren't any flowers.'

'Huh?'

'There aren't any flowers coming in.'

'What?'

She put her hands on my shoulders and turned me round so that I had to look at her square in the face. 'There are *no* flowers.'

I sniffed the air. With a couple of good sniffs I could take a pretty accurate inventory. Gloria was right. We were down to a handful of carnations, some fern, and one bucket of homegrown gladioli.

'I kept thinking you'd notice. I kept thinking they'd show up.'

I thought about Mort. *Get on the phone, yell at somebody.* I ran past Gloria and took my place at the desk. I called the first number, but there was no one to yell at. The receptionist put me on hold and left me there for fifteen minutes. When I called again, she sent me back to hold. When I called back a third time, she hung up on me. My second distributor at least did me the courtesy of telling me my account had been cancelled before he hung up on me. I called people I used for special occasions and was told they no longer delivered to my neighbourhood. I called people I had never used before and was told they were no longer taking on new accounts. Everywhere I went, I hit a wall.

'How bad is it?' Gloria said.

'Very bad.'

'Very bad like a screwup or very bad like a Cacciamani?'

'The latter.'

'You have to call him,' Gloria said. 'I'll call him. He wouldn't let this happen to you. He doesn't know about it.'

'I'm sure you're right,' I said. 'But Romeo didn't do it, and he's not going to be able to undo it, either. Joe runs a trucking company. He's got roots in the business that spread all the way to Idaho.' I tossed my pencil down onto the table. 'I'm wrecked,' I said. 'Simple as that.'

'No,' Gloria said. She had tears in her eyes. She was taking this hard, as I would once I was able to grasp what had happened. 'You have to fight.'

'I can't keep on fighting. I've lost. This just polishes off what I started.'

Gloria sat down on the floor and put her head between her knees. 'I think I'm going to be sick.'

'That makes two of us.'

I put a sign in the window: ON VACATION.

I was going to tell Sandy what had happened when I got home, but she was on her way out of the door to Nora's with the kids as I was coming in. 'Dad and Lila are going home in the morning,' she said. 'I'm going to go over and say goodbye. Do you want to come? I know he'd like to see you.'

Tomorrow was Sunday. I didn't have to tell her about the shop right now. 'I don't think so, honey. It seems like it would be better if I sat this one out. You say goodbye to him for me, OK?' I kissed the kids. 'Sandy, ask Nora to come by on her way home from the airport tomorrow. I'd like to talk to her.'

'Another family conference?' Sandy asked suspiciously.

'Not exactly. I just think I'm a little out of touch.'

After they left, I made myself a bag of microwave popcorn for dinner, washing it down with a bottle of wine. When that was over, I went to bed.

It was after ten o'clock when the phone rang, and for one brief instant I was hopeful. But it was Mort.

'Jules? Can you hear me?'

'Sure,' I said. 'Why are you whispering?'

'Sandy and the kids left a little while ago, and everybody is going to bed. I'm down in the kitchen. I told Lila I wanted a glass of milk.'

'You hate milk.'

'She doesn't know that. Listen, Julie, I was sorry I didn't get to see you to say goodbye. We never seem to do a good job at ending things.'

'Yeah, well, I wanted to say I was sorry about your head. I think it was largely your own fault, but I know that if it wasn't for me, it wouldn't have happened.'

'I threw the pot at the guy.'

I was stunned. What he said sounded almost like an admission of something, and that wasn't Mort's style.

'I've had a lot of time to think, even with my sore brain.'

'So what do you think?'

'It's been nice, being back. I've liked seeing the girls, and Tony and Sarah. I just thought if things were more OK between us, then it would be easier for me to come back and see them. We don't have to be in some huge fight all the time, do we?'

I told him we did not.

'You're a real trouper, Jules. And the Cacciamani stuff—'

'Don't even go there.'

'Really, I have to say it. I think the guy's a jerk, but I understand that it's your business. We're all entitled to throw away our own lives, right?'

Sandy must have been working on him in his reduced state. 'Don't worry about it, Mort. Romeo and I are through. Nobody bounces back from a fight like that.'

'I bounced back,' Mort said.

'Well, you're tougher than the rest of us.'

'About the store,' he said, and I felt my heart freeze inside my chest. 'I got a lot of work done before the fight, but you need to see an accountant. I'll pay for it. I know you don't want me to, but that store matters to me a lot. I don't want to see it go under just because you don't know what you're doing.'

My eyes filled up with tears. Mort would hear the truth later from one of the girls. Let him have a good night's sleep. Let him get on that plane tomorrow for Seattle. 'OK,' I said. I had forgotten to pull the blinds down on the windows, and now I could see the moon setting off the tender spring leaves on the trees. It was a beautiful thing.

'I don't mean to say you haven't done a good job. You've kept the place afloat. And the flowers look great. It's just the books.'

'I understand.'

'I should go,' he said. 'They're going to find me down here. They've kept real tabs on me. You'd think I was an old man.'

Then the tears were running down my cheeks. 'Good night, Mort,' I said.

'Good night, Jules.'

WHEN I OPENED my eyes and looked at the clock, it was ten thirty and the room was flooded in light. I had not slept until ten thirty since I was in junior high school. I leaned over and checked my watch on the bedside table, thinking the clock must be wrong, but it wasn't. I got up, brushed my teeth, and got dressed. It was Sunday morning, and the kids were downstairs watching cartoons.

'We kept the volume down,' Tony said. 'You're sleeping.'

I waved to them and wandered into the kitchen. Nora was there at the table with Sandy, and they were drinking coffee and talking.

'God, did I oversleep. I'm sorry.' I got myself a cup of coffee and joined them. 'You should have come up and got me.'

Nora shook her head. She looked positively happy. Maybe she was just glad to have got rid of her houseguests. 'I just walked in from the airport. Besides, you needed to get some rest.'

'Did Lila and your dad get off OK?'

'Not a hitch. Dad even made a fuss about carrying his own suitcase,' she said.

'Good,' I said. 'That's good.'

'So now life gets back to normal,' Nora said. She reached over and gave me an uncharacteristic squeeze on the wrist.

I looked at both my girls—smart, good-looking girls, girls whom I loved even as they drove me insane. I wanted to remember them in the last peaceful moment I was going to see for a while. 'Not exactly.'

Both of them set their coffee cups down. They clicked against the table at the exact same instant. 'I knew it,' Sandy said.

'It's Roseman's,' I told them slowly because I didn't want to repeat myself. 'There were a lot of problems to begin with.'

'What happened?' Sandy said. The two words were like heavy stones thrown off the side of a building.

'All our flowers have been cut off. I've called every supplier I could think of. No one will deliver to us any more.'

'How is that possible?' Nora asked.

'Cacciamani,' Sandy said. 'They've ruined us. That's it, isn't it? They've frozen us out.'

'I don't know that,' I said.

'You know what's happened.' Sandy stood up from the table and walked over and closed the kitchen door so that Tony and Sarah wouldn't hear us. 'You can figure this out.'

'I can figure it out.'

I wouldn't have expected this. Sandy was ready to toss the kitchen table through the window, but Nora was just sitting there staring into her coffee cup.

'We'll get round it,' Sandy said. 'I don't care if I have to drive to New Hampshire every morning and bring the flowers back myself. They are not going to close us down.'

'I don't know,' I said.

'I know!' Sandy said, and hit the table with her fist. 'Damn it, Mother, snap out of it. You're going to have to fight them.'

'We don't have to fight them,' Nora said. 'We already won.'

Sandy stopped and looked at her sister.

'How did we win?' I said.

Nora didn't look smug. I'll give her that much. She just laid out the facts like she would on any other deal she had closed. She was a powerful businesswoman, my older daughter. I forgot that sometimes. 'I bought the Cacciamanis' building. I did some research. It turns out they never owned the place. They had rented it all these years. They had a great deal. A classic old Somerville deal where the owner seemed to forget they were there and never raised the rent.'

'You bought the building?' Sandy said, sitting down.

'I sent them the eviction notice yesterday. They have two weeks to get out. The way I see it, they probably don't have anything saved. There are too many kids for that. They'll never be able to find another place for what they were paying. They'll stumble. They'll fall. They'll never get up.'

'Whew,' Sandy said. 'I hope you never get that mad at me.'

'It's business,' Nora said.

What surprised me was that I didn't feel angry at Nora. I had to be fair. If I could see the reasoning behind Joe Cacciamani's attempt to destroy me, then I had to be able to see the logic of Nora bringing down Romeo. This was where we had come to. This was who we were.

'Come on,' I said. 'Get the kids and get in the car.'

'Where are we going?' Sandy said.

'The Cacciamanis'.'

'I'm not going,' Nora said calmly.

'We're all going,' I said. 'All of us together. This is the last absolute dictate I will issue as your mother, but you are going.'

Nora sat there for a minute. I thought there was going to be a fight. Instead she walked to the sink and rinsed out her cup. 'All right.'

'Why do we have to go?' Tony said when I told the kids.

'Because there are no adults to stay home with you,' Sandy said.

'Who are these people again?'

'Friends of Grandma's,' she said. 'Sort of.'

SOMERVILLE, LIKE ROME, was a city built on seven hills. I lived in Spring Hill. Romeo lived in Winter Hill. I had been to his house once before, years ago during the whole Sandy and Tony affair. There had been two meetings: one at our house, one at theirs. He lived on Marshall Street. I remembered it clearly.

'What are you going to say?' Nora asked. She was driving, and I was giving directions. Sandy and Tony and Sarah were in the back.

'I just want to tell them it's over: all the fighting, the undermining. The Roseman family is now officially out of the game.'

'What about the building?' Nora said. 'I've closed on it.'

'Then you'll rent to them. You'll give it to them. I don't know. You'll figure it out. All I know is that I want us to be a certain kind of people. I want us to be decent people.' I felt a sense of lightness in my chest. In Somerville the irises and peonies were blooming with mad abandon. Everything felt so easy all of a sudden. We may not get our heart's desire, but we could all be decent people.

Sandy was quiet in the back seat. Tony was reading all the street signs to Sarah. Sandy must have been to this house before. She must have sneaked in a back door in the dark.

On Marshall Street I told Nora to slow down. I was looking at all the houses. 'It's up there on the left,' Sandy said. 'The one with the balloons on the mailbox.'

'Balloons!' Sarah said. Sarah was mad for balloons.

'Maybe they were expecting us,' Nora said.

There was definitely something up at the Cacciamanis'. We had to drive all the way round the block before Nora found a parking space. 'Couldn't we do this later?' she said. 'When they aren't having a party?'

'We'll never come back. You're right, maybe the timing isn't great. But I really think it's now or never.' Even if we were interrupting something, we were doing so in the name of peace. They'd be happy to hear they hadn't lost their store. That fact alone would counteract our presence at their party.

'Never is not a bad option,' Nora said.

'Do we have a present?' Tony asked.

'Sort of,' Nora said, and opened her door. 'It's called real estate.'

Sandy and Nora and I made slow time up the block. Tony and Sarah kept racing ahead and then coming back for us.

'Come on, come on,' they yelled, most likely figuring that where there were balloons there was usually cake. I figured we had almost no shot at the cake.

The house was a double-decker with four units, meant to manage a large Catholic family. On one door there was a wreath of flowers, pink and white roses all the way round. It was so simple, so utterly charming, I knew it had to be Romeo's. My heart rose and sank a hundred times just going up the path.

'I don't know about this,' Sandy said quietly.

'Are we going in or what?' Tony said. He ran ahead and pushed the doorbell three times and then ran back and stood behind us. The way we froze to the sidewalk, you would have thought he had pulled the pin out of a grenade.

'Mother,' Nora said. 'If you're trying to teach me a lesson about taking responsibility for my actions, I have now learned it. Turn around with me and start running like hell.'

I was about to agree when a tanned young man I didn't recognise swung open the door. He was wearing a pink paper hat that had *90!*

sticking out of the top. He had a beard and was wearing shorts and a World Health Organisation T-shirt. He looked at us for one second and then made what can only be described as a high-pitched sound of almost unbearable happiness. He ran to Sandy and picked her up by the waist. He swung her round and kissed her neck. He said her name over and over again.

'Do we know him?' Tony said.

'He was a friend of your mom's a long time ago,' Nora told him.

Tony Cacciamani put my daughter down. 'My God,' he said. 'How did you know I was back? I only got here two hours ago.'

'I didn't know,' Sandy said. 'Are you OK?'

'I'm fine. I'm so good now. You look so beautiful. You're all grown up.' He looked at the rest of us. 'Hey, Mrs Roth. Hey, Nora.'

'Hi, Tony,' I said. I had no idea that Tony knew Nora. For the first time, it occurred to me that my older daughter must have helped my younger daughter to plan her trysts.

'And who are you?' he said to Tony and Sarah. 'Nora, are they yours?'

'Mine,' Sandy said. There was, of course, some embarrassment in the introduction of her son, Tony, to Tony Cacciamani.

'Hello,' Tony said, shaking their hands, his voice more serious now.

'Sandy's been divorced for three years,' Nora said. 'Let's just skip right ahead to that.'

For once I was grateful for Nora's directness. Tony brightened and invited us inside. 'You came for my grandmother's birthday party? Man, things really have changed since I've been gone.'

'It's Mrs Cacciamani's birthday?' I said.

Tony nodded his pink hat and put his arm casually round Sandy's shoulder, as if it had never left that spot. 'Ninety today.'

The living room was packed with Italians in party clothes, laughing and drinking, every one of them wearing a pink paper hat with 90! sticking out of the top. There were tables full of sandwiches and vegetable trays, a punch bowl the size of a large fish tank, a pink and white cake that took up one whole card table. In the corner there was an accordion player grinding through 'That's Amore!' It was one hell of a party. No one seemed to notice we were there. I ploughed into the room looking for Romeo, and everyone smiled and tried to scoot over to give me enough room to get through.

'Have you seen Romeo?' I asked a little boy at the punch table.

'I think he's in the kitchen,' he said, and pointed. 'That way.'

I thanked him and pressed on to the kitchen door.

Plummy and her father were struggling with a bag of ice that had frozen together. He didn't look happy. There were lines of stitches in his forehead and near his lip and a plaster cast on his wrist.

It was the moment I was most afraid of—that he would not be glad to see me. I wondered if it was the last time I would ever see him. 'Romeo,' I said.

But when Romeo looked up and saw me, his mouth fell open and for a second he seemed to be caught just between laughing and sobbing. He smiled at me like his son had smiled at Sandy. He said my name over and over. He came to me and hugged and kissed me. 'My God! You're here!'

'I've got to straighten things out, with you, with your family.' I wanted to be serious and brave. I wanted to melt into him for ever.

'I'm going to take this out to the living room,' Plummy said, scooping up the ice bag. She smiled at me on her way out. 'Hi, Mrs Roseman.'

'I love that girl,' I said to Romeo.

He kissed me gently, because of his lip. The kitchen door swung shut, swung open. Two young men I didn't know walked in. By the expressions on their faces you would have thought they had caught us dissecting the family dog.

'Julie,' Romeo said with some hesitation. 'These are my sons Alan and Nicky. Nicky came all the way from Germany for the party.'

'Julie Roseman?' Nicky said. Alan went back through the door.

In half a minute they were all there. I could hear Nora's voice rise above the others in the living room. Then we were all back in the living room, and everyone's voice seemed to go up. The accordion player stopped in the middle of his song.

'Rosemans!' I heard the old woman yell. 'There are Rosemans in my house!' We were easy to spot. We were the ones without hats.

'I'm sorry. I'm sorry,' I said. I turned to Romeo. 'Listen. This is so important, or I would never have come. I know about the lease.'

Romeo frowned. 'Let's do this later,' he whispered.

'What about the lease?' Raymond said.

'Nora bought your building.'

'*Your* Nora bought it?' Romeo said.

At the mention of her name, Nora squared her shoulders and came across the room. 'I'm Nora Bernstein,' she said. 'I bought the building.'

'*You* evicted us?' Romeo said.

'She evicted us?' Raymond said.

'I was going to tell you after the party,' Romeo told his son. 'I didn't know who bought it.'

'Get them out of my house!' the old woman screamed. She was wearing a blue trouser-suit and had a pink paper hat that was bigger than everyone else's. It said *I'M 90!* on the top. She was pretty far away from me, which gave me some peace of mind.

'Come on,' Raymond said, and put a hand on Nora's arm. 'Let's go.' Nora stared at him until he took it away.

'I bought it because I was trying to protect my mother. You cut off all her flowers. She's ruined because of you.' This was less than true, since Nora had bought the building before she had heard about the flowers, but she should be allowed to keep her dignity.

'I cut off her flowers?' Romeo said. 'What are you talking about?'

'We don't need to get into that,' I said to Nora.

'Yes, we do. You said this is honesty time.' She turned to the crowd and clapped her hands three times. 'Listen, people. There's going to be a game: true confessions. I bought Romeo's flower shop and evicted him. He contacted every flower distributor in the area to cut off my mother's supply and ruin her business.'

The crowd collectively inhaled at this information.

'Wait a minute,' Romeo said. 'I never did that.'

Joe lumbered forward from the crowd. His *90!* hat seemed barely bigger than a folded Kleenex on his head. 'I did,' he said. 'She'll never get her hand on another flower as long as I live.'

'You ruined her?' Romeo stepped towards his son. 'You black-balled her?'

'You were right, Mom,' Nora said. 'This is so much better.'

I took Romeo's arm. 'It went both ways. That's the whole point. We have to stop this right now.'

'Come in the kitchen,' Romeo said to me, then he raised his voice in the crowd. 'Cacciamanis, Rosemans, in the kitchen. No cousins, no kids. Mother, in the kitchen.'

'I'm not going in there with them,' she said.

Nora went over and whispered something in her ear. The old woman looked furious but followed us in.

'How did you do that?' I whispered to Nora.

'I told her she wasn't allowed in the kitchen.'

Tony and Sandy were already in there. I don't know how they managed that. They were sitting at the table holding hands and looked surprised to see us.

'That's the girl!' the old woman said. 'Get her off of Tony.'

Romeo held his hand up to his mother. 'Hang on a minute. So, Joe, you went behind my back to ruin Roseman's?'

'She had it coming.'

'Out,' he said.

'What?'

'Out of my house.' Romeo stood, feet apart, his arms crossed. It was a stance that meant business.

The point was to figure out how to make peace between Caccia- manis and Rosemans. The last thing I wanted to do was separate Romeo from his first-born. 'No,' I said. 'You can't do that. We're going to fix this.'

'Don't you tell my father "No",' Joe said, pointing a finger at me.

'We just need to stop it,' I said, my voice sounding a little frantic. 'We need to make an agreement once and for all. If you and I can't see each other any more, I can accept that, but I don't want to live like crazy people.'

'We can't see each other?' Romeo said. He looked at me as if such a horrible outcome had never occurred to him before. I thought at that moment I would cry for loving him so much.

Plummy, who was wearing a little lavender sundress with a black cardigan, clapped her hands together. She was clearly ready to make order out of chaos. 'OK,' she said. 'Once and for all we're going to get to the bottom of this, and then we're going back to the party. Now, somebody here knows this story.' She bit her lip and looked around the room. 'Grammy,' she said finally. 'What's the story?'

'The Rosemans are pigs,' she said.

'OK, that's a start. Now, why are the Rosemans pigs?'

That was the question. Why were Rosemans pigs? Why were the Cacciamanis slimy fish?

'Come on,' Plummy said.

'It's my birthday,' the old woman said. She reached up and touched her hat as if to drive her point home.

'Happy birthday,' Plummy said. 'Everybody wants to eat the cake and watch you open your presents, but that isn't going to happen un- til you confess.'

'I want to go now.' She was trying to pass herself off as feeble, but it didn't wash.

'I'm really sorry,' Plummy said. 'But you can't go until you tell us what happened. We've all waited long enough.' The clear fact was that Plummy Cacciamani ruled. She was a kind and modest dicta- tor, but she was a dictator nonetheless.

'I don't know anything,' she said. 'Don't you believe these lying Rosemans.'

'You don't know anything?' Plummy asked.

The old woman looked away from her. 'Nothing about them. Who'd want to know about Rosemans?'

'What about the letters?' Plummy said.

'What letters?'

Plummy looked like the very picture of innocence. She reached up and twisted one of the gold hoops in her ear. 'The letters under your mattress in the pink silk handkerchief. The ones that all start, "My darling . . ."'

The eldest Cacciamani turned with flames in her eyes. She raised a finger to poke, but Plummy gently pushed it down. Everyone shifted to make sure they had a very clear view of the action. 'Why are you reading my letters?'

'I clean your room, Grammy. I flip your mattress every month. I never thought it mattered before, but now I think it does.'

'They're none of your business.'

'I know that,' Plummy said calmly. 'That's why I never mentioned them before. But now we have this problem.'

The old woman took a deep breath and leaned against the refrigerator. She looked trapped. 'I'll tell you later,' she said.

Plummy went and put her arm round her grandmother. She kissed the old woman's cheek. 'You tell me later, and I'll just have to get everybody together again so I can tell them what you said. Tell me now,' she whispered kindly.

We were all waiting—five sons, three wives, my two girls, Plummy, me and Romeo. Mattresses? Letters? We leaned towards her, mesmerised. Plummy let her grammy twist in the wind.

'Come onto the porch,' the old woman said weakly.

Plummy nodded her head and patted the old woman's hand. She led her grandmother past the rest of us and out onto the back porch. We waited.

'How's your head?' I asked Romeo. 'Does it hurt any more?'

'Nah. Just the ribs a little when I breathe. How about Mort?'

I told him that Mort had healed up and gone home this morning. Romeo smiled. 'That guy has a hell of an arm.'

We waited and waited. In the other room people had started laughing again. The accordion had started up again. They had forgotten about us. They were there for a party. Finally Raymond went and looked out of the back window.

'Can you see anything?' Romeo asked.

'Grammy's in the chair, and Plummy's kind of leaning over her. It looks pretty intense. I can't see what they're saying.'

'I don't know why we have to shake her down on her birthday,' Alan said. His pretty Italian wife stood next to him, nodding.

'Because we're not going to do this again next week,' Nora said. 'It isn't that much fun.'

'Wait!' Raymond pulled back from the window. 'She's coming in.'

Plummy came back alone.

'Where's Grammy?' Raymond said.

'She's sitting down outside for a minute. She wanted some air.'

'So what's the story?' Nora said.

'The story is this.' Plummy leaned against the counter. She spoke to Nora. 'My grandmother and your grandfather had a love affair.'

'My grandfather?' Nora pointed at her chest.

'The hell they did,' Joe said.

Plummy held up her hand but didn't look at him. 'Please,' she said. 'This was a very long time ago. The Rosemans had their shop in Somerville, and Grammy and Grampy had a shop in the North End. Grammy met Mr Roseman buying vases, and they fell in love. I guess it was all pretty hot. Grammy wanted to be closer to Mr Roseman, so she talked Grampy into moving their shop to Somerville. She told him it was a better place to raise children. Daddy was three years old then, and they called the place Romeo's. The way I understand it, Mr Roseman strung Grammy along big-time. He kept promising Grammy that he was going to run away with her, but every time she was ready to go, he would come up with some lame excuse and they never did it. After a while Grammy got really angry, and I guess she started doing things to the Rosemans. She said it started out small at first—she'd badmouth their flowers to other people. She threw a stone through their window once. Then she hid a dead fish in their storeroom, a flounder. That was when Mr Roseman got mad at her, and he paid a kid to dump a box of fleas in their store. It was back and forth, one thing and then another. Grammy told Grampy that the Rosemans were trying to ruin them to get their customers, that the Rosemans were trying to force them out of the neighbourhood, and that they had to fight back. Who knows what Mr Roseman told Mrs Roseman? No one actually got ruined until now.'

'And they fell for it?' Nora asked her. 'My grandmother and old man Cacciamani? They just picked up the feud and ran with it without any more information than that?'

'Well, all of us did, too. Our families hated each other and we didn't even have the fleas to deal with.'

'You expect me to believe that?' Raymond said.

'Go ask her. She's told it once now. I bet she'll tell it again. Or go and read the letters under the mattress. They're pretty steamy.'

'But she hated Mr Roseman,' Nicky said. 'She hated him more than any of them.'

'That's the way it works sometimes,' Plummy said thoughtfully. 'Big love makes for big hate.'

'I still hate him,' old Mrs Cacciamani said. She was standing at the door, suddenly looking older than ninety. Her trouser-suit was wrinkled, her party hat tipped to one side. 'And I'll hate every last one of them until I die.'

My father? I thought. My father and the Wicked Witch of the West? The woman he hated above all other life forms? I could still hear his voice clearly in my head. I could hear every terrible name he called her. Of all the possible explanations, I had to admit this one seemed the most implausible to me.

'Mama, are you sure about this?' Romeo asked.

'Of course I'm sure. What do you think, I don't know who I was in love with?' Then, with surprising vigour, she slammed through the kitchen door and back into her party. It swung open, shut, open, shut, behind her.

The rest of us stood there listening to the accordion music coming through the wall.

'Just to recap,' Nora said. 'What this means is that the birthday girl was in love with my grandfather, my mother is in love with your father, and my sister is in love with Tony here.'

Sandy looked mortified.

'That's what it's looking like,' Plummy said.

Nora continued. 'So the basis of this tedious, never-ending fight is that three generations of Cacciamanis and Rosemans have been in love with each other.'

The room took a moment to digest this information. Then Nora started to laugh, and pretty soon Sandy was laughing, too. Then Plummy joined in. At that point none of the rest of us got the joke.

'Mr Cacciamani,' Nora said. 'Keep your store. Think of me as your benevolent landlord. You,' she said, pointing to Joe. 'Turn the delivery service back on for my mother's flowers tomorrow. Now I want to get out of here. I'm taking my car.' She looked at me and Sandy. 'Something tells me you two will find rides home.'

Epilogue

The story ends with a wedding, right? These stories practically have to. This wedding was on July 1. Some people said it was awfully quick, but once they heard the whole story, they had to agree it was, in fact, a long time coming. The roses were fantastic. We're talking garden roses. When we were done, it looked like we had got our hands on every rose in Massachusetts. Romeo and I did the whole thing together. That was how we got the idea of combining our stores in the first place. We worked together like a dream. I made the bride's bouquet. Every colour I could find went into that bouquet. It was even better than the one I had made when I married Mort. The wedding was in my garden. We had a justice of the peace so that no one would get their toes stepped on religionwise, but Father Al was there, and I saw him moving his lips. Nora was the maid of honour. She insisted on the title. She said she couldn't bear to be anybody's matron of honour. Joe was the best man. Little Tony and Sarah did the rings and the flowers. It was a small wedding, except that no Cacciamani wedding could ever really be considered small.

Tony and Sandy went to the Cape for their honeymoon. They're saving to buy a house. For the time being, they are living with me.

Everyone was asking at the wedding when Romeo and I were going to get married. But for us it isn't such an issue. We'd never get all his family and all my family into one house, anyway. We're together, trust me on that. The rest of it will fall into place over time. We keep a little apartment that none of the kids know about. It isn't a whole lot bigger than the bed we dragged into it. We've got two cups there, a corkscrew, a couple of old quilts for when it's really cold, some towels. It doesn't take much to make a place feel like home. To anyone who ever thought that love and passion were for the young, I say, think again. I am speaking from personal experience here.

Romeo says we live together at work. Most couples work apart but live in one house. We're just doing it the other way round. Things have got busy, now that we're doing the wedding and party-planning service. It turns out we need all the various family members we've got on the payroll. We're always at the same store—one day his, one day mine. The next thing we knew, they were both ours. It's Romeo and Julie's now. Two locations to better serve you.

JEANNE RAY

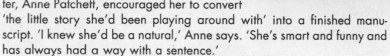

The successful publication of *Julie and Romeo*, Jeanne Ray's first novel, came as something of a shock to her. She was looking forward to retirement, after a busy forty-year career as a nurse, when her novelist daughter, Anne Patchett, encouraged her to convert 'the little story she'd been playing around with' into a finished manuscript. 'I knew she'd be a natural,' Anne says. 'She's smart and funny and has always had a way with a sentence.'

Without more ado, she took her mother's script to her own agent, who 'rushed it off to half of New York'. And Anne's confidence in her mother's abilities proved to be well founded. Within weeks, book rights were sold and then the film rights were snapped up by Barbra Streisand, with Al Pacino tipped as her co-star. Following publication, the book began to climb the best-seller charts, and suddenly Jeanne Ray was a celebrity, with an exciting new career ahead of her.

So what inspired this glamorous grandmother to write an 'extremely funny book about sixty-year-olds finding true love'—as one reviewer described it? Jeanne Ray says she was browsing through a magazine display shortly after her sixtieth birthday when she noticed that none of the cover lines referred to her age group. 'I felt angry that somehow society had forgotten I was still an intelligent, attractive, sexual human being, and I wanted to get it off my chest. I thought people in their sixties needed a love story . . . We can be in love—we're not just dried-up old beans.'

One piece of good advice that the author is eager to pass on to older readers is 'don't waste time'. 'I never thought that at this age I'd be an author. Now is the time to pursue artistic things, to travel or take up a hobby you've always dreamed about. And if love comes along, grab it! I hope to show people life isn't over at sixty. Seize the day—it's never too late.'

DEAD SLEEP

GREG ILES

When Jordan Glass chances upon a portrait by an unknown artist in a Hong Kong gallery, she is stunned. The face in the painting is that of her twin sister who vanished without trace from New Orleans thirteen months earlier.

More shockingly still, when she contacts the FBI they link her evidence with the disappearance of eleven other women over the past eighteen months.

Jordan teams up with special agent John Kaiser to unearth the identity of the mystery artist, and in so doing places herself directly in the killer's sights . . .

1

I stopped shooting people six months ago, just after I won the Pulitzer Prize. People were always my gift, but they were wearing me down long before I won the prize. Still, I kept shooting them, in some blind quest that I didn't even know I was on. It's hard to admit that, but the Pulitzer was a different milestone for me than it is for most photographers. You see, my father won it twice. The first time in 1966, for a series in McComb, Mississippi. The second in 1972, for a shot on the Cambodian border. He never knew he'd got that one. The prize-winning film was pulled from his camera by American marines on the wrong side of the Mekong River. The camera was all they found. Twenty frames of Tri-X made the sequence of events clear. Shooting his motor-drive Nikon F2 at five frames per second, my dad recorded the brutal execution of a female prisoner by a Khmer Rouge soldier, then captured the face of her executioner as the pistol was turned towards the brave but foolish man pointing the camera at him. I was twelve years old and 10,000 miles away, but that bullet struck me in the heart.

Jonathan Glass was a legend long before that day, but fame is no comfort to a lonely child who didn't see her father nearly enough. Following in his footsteps has been one way for me to get to know him. I won my Pulitzer with his battle-scarred Nikon. He'd probably joke about the sentimentality of my using his old camera, but I know what he'd say about my winning the prize: 'Not bad, for a girl.'

And then he'd hug me. God, I miss that bearlike hug that sheltered me from the world. I haven't felt those arms in twenty-eight years, but they're as familiar as the hypnotic fragrance of the sweet olive tree he planted outside my window when I turned eight.

For most photographers, winning the Pulitzer is the point at which your telephone starts ringing with the job offers of your dreams. For me it was a stopping point. Of course, new assignments poured in. But I declined them. I was thirty-nine years old, unmarried (though not without offers), and I'd passed the mental state known as 'burned out' five years before. The reason was simple. My job, reduced to its essentials, has been to chronicle death's grisly passage through the world. And like other professionals who see the face of death as a manifestation of evil—cops, soldiers, doctors, priests— war photographers age more rapidly than normal people. The extra years don't always show, but you feel them in the deep places, in the marrow and the heart.

And yet it wasn't this that made me stop. You can walk through a battlefield and come upon an infant lying atop its dead mother and not feel a fraction of what you will when you lose someone you love. When my father turned his camera on that murderous Khmer Rouge soldier, he must have known his life was forfeit. He shot the picture anyway, and it went a long way towards changing the mind of America about that war. All my life I lived by that example, by my father's unwritten code. So no one was more shocked than I that, when death crashed into my family again, the encounter shattered me.

I limped through seven months of work, had one spasm of creativity that won me the Pulitzer, then collapsed in an airport. The doctors called it post-traumatic stress disorder and told me that I had to stop working for a while. I agreed. The problem was, I didn't know how.

Thankfully, a solution presented itself. Several New York editors had been after me for years to do a book of my war photographs. In exchange for letting an editor at Viking do an anthology of my war work, I accepted a double advance: one for that book, and one for the book of my dreams. The book of my dreams has no people in it. No faces, anyway. Its working title is 'Weather'.

'Weather' was what took me to Hong Kong this week. I was there a few months ago to shoot the monsoon as it rolled over one of the most tightly packed cities in the world. This time Hong Kong was only a two-day way station to China proper. But on the second day, my entire book project imploded.

A friend had convinced me that I had to visit the Hong Kong Museum of Art, to see some Chinese watercolours. He said the ancient Chinese painters had achieved an almost perfect purity in their images of nature, so I figured the paintings were worth a look, if only for some perspective. After twenty minutes inside the museum, perspective was the last thing on my mind.

The guard at the entrance was the first signpost, but I misread him completely. As I walked through the door, his lips parted slightly, and the whites of his eyes grew in an expression not unlike lust. I still cause that reaction in men on occasion, but I should have paid more attention. Because to Chinese men I am *kwailo*, a foreign devil, and my hair is not blonde, the colour they so prize.

Next was the tiny Chinese matron who rented me a Walkman, headphones, and the English-language version of the museum's audio tour. She looked up, smiling, to hand me the equipment; then her teeth disappeared and her face lost two shades of colour. I felt like someone had just walked over my grave. I shook it off, put on the Walkman, and headed for the exhibition rooms.

My friend was right. The watercolours floored me. As I moved among them, the internal darkness that is my constant companion began to ease. But the respite was brief. While studying one particular painting—a man poling along a river in a boat—I found myself being stared at by another blue-uniformed museum guard, whose eyes conveyed something between fascination and fear.

Thoroughly unsettled, I hurried through the next few exhibition rooms with hardly a glance at the paintings. I turned down a short corridor, hoping to find a short cut back to the entrance. What I found instead was an exhibition room filled with people.

Hesitating before the arched entrance, I wondered what had brought them there. The rest of the museum was virtually deserted. Were the paintings in this room that much better than the rest? The visitors stood silent and apart from one another, studying the paintings with eerie intensity. Posted above the arch was a plaque with both Chinese pictographs and English letters. It read:

NUDE WOMEN IN REPOSE
Artist Unknown

When I looked back into the room, I realised it wasn't filled with 'people'—it was filled with men. Every man in the room was Chinese, and every one wore a business suit. I fast-forwarded the Walkman until I came to a description of the room before me.

'*"Nude Women in Repose",*' announced the voice in my headset. '*Seven canvases by the unknown artist responsible for the group of paintings known as "The Sleeping Women" series. The Sleeping Women are a mystery in the world of modern art. Nineteen paintings are known to exist, all oil on canvas, the first coming onto the market in 1999. Though all the paintings were originally believed to depict sleeping women in the nude, this theory is now in question. The early paintings are so abstract that the question cannot be settled with certainty, but it is the later canvases, almost photographic in their accuracy, that have created a sensation among collectors, who believe the paintings depict women not in sleep but in death. The last painting in the series, titled "Sleeping Woman Number Nineteen", sold to Japanese businessman Hodai Takagi for one point two million pounds sterling. As for the artist, his identity remains unknown. His work is available exclusively through Christopher Wingate, LLC, of New York City, USA.'*

I took a deep breath and went in.

My arrival caused a ripple among the men, as though they were ashamed of their presence in this room. I met their fugitive glances with a level gaze and walked up to the first painting.

It was quintessentially Western, a portrait of a nude woman in a bathtub. A roundeye woman like me, but ten years younger. Maybe thirty. Her pose—one arm hanging languidly over the edge of the tub—communicated an undeniable peace, though I couldn't tell whether it was the peace of sleep or of death.

Sensing the men behind me edging closer, I moved to the next painting. In it, the female subject lay on a bed of straw spread on planks, as though on a threshing floor. Her eyes were open and had the dull sheen I had seen in too many makeshift morgues and hastily dug graves. There was no question about this one; she was supposed to look dead, though of course that didn't mean she *was* dead.

Again I heard men behind me. Shuffling feet, irregular respiration. Were they trying to gauge my reaction to this Occidental woman in the most vulnerable state a woman can be in? Someone paid $2 million for a painting like this. A man paid that, of course. A woman would have bought this painting only to destroy it.

Two men stood before the next painting, but they weren't looking at the canvas. They gaped like clubbed mackerel as I approached, then they backed quickly out of my way to clear the space before the painting. As I turned towards it, a premonitory wave of heat flashed across my neck and shoulders, and I felt the dry itch of the past rubbing against the present.

This woman was naked as well. She sat in a window seat, her head and one shoulder leaned against the casement, her long hair falling on her shoulders like a dark veil. Her eyes were half open, but they looked more like the glass eyes of a doll than those of a living woman. Though she had been sitting face-on to me from the moment I looked at the canvas, I suddenly had the terrifying sensation that she had turned to me and spoken aloud. My heart ballooned in my chest. This was not a painting but a mirror. The face looking back at me from the wall was my own. The body, too, mine: my feet, hips, breasts, my shoulders and neck. But the eyes were what held me, the dead eyes—held me and then dropped me through the floor into a nightmare I had travelled 10,000 miles to escape.

THIRTEEN MONTHS AGO, my twin sister Jane stepped out of her house on St Charles Avenue in New Orleans to run her daily three-mile round of the Garden District. Her two young children waited inside with the maid, first contentedly, then anxiously as their mother's absence stretched beyond any they remembered. After ninety minutes, the maid called Jane's husband Marc at his downtown law firm.

Knowing you could walk one block out of the Garden District and be in a free-fire zone, Marc Lacour immediately left work and drove the streets of their neighbourhood in search of his wife. Then he left the Garden District and questioned every porch-sitter, shade-tree mechanic, crack dealer and homeless person he could find on the adjoining streets. No one had heard or seen anything of Jane. A prominent attorney, Marc immediately called the police and used his influence to mount a massive search. The police found nothing.

I was in Sarajevo when Jane disappeared, shooting a series on the aftermath of the war. It took me seventy-two hours to get to New Orleans. By that time, the FBI had entered the picture and subsumed my sister's disappearance into a much larger case, designated NOKIDS in FBI-speak, for New Orleans Kidnappings. It turned out that Jane was fifth in a rapidly growing group of missing women, all from the New Orleans area. Not one corpse had been found. Not one relative had received a ransom note, and in the eyes of every cop I spoke to, I saw the grim unspoken truth: every one of those women was presumed dead. With no crime-scene evidence, witnesses or corpses to work with, even the Bureau's vaunted Investigative Support Unit was stumped by the cold trail.

I should clarify something. Not once since my father vanished in Cambodia have I sensed that he was truly dead, gone from this world. Not even with the last frame of film he shot showing an executioner's pistol pointed at his face. Miracles happen, especially in war. For this reason I've spent thousands of dollars over the past twenty years trying to find him, piggybacking my money with that of the relatives of Vietnam-era Missing-In-Action personnel.

With Jane it's different. By the time my agency tracked me down in Sarajevo, something had already changed irrevocably within me. As I crossed a street once infested with snipers, a nimbus of dread welled up in my chest—not the familiar dread of a bullet with my name on it, but something much deeper. Whatever energy animates my soul simply stopped flowing as I ran, and I felt as though a bullet *had* punched through me, taking with it something no doctor could ever put back or put right.

Quantum physics describes 'twinned particles', photons of energy that behave identically, even though separated by miles, when confronted with a choice of paths. It is now thought that some unseen connection binds them, defying known physical laws. Jane and I were joined in this way. And from the moment that dark current of dread pulsed through my heart, I felt that *my* twin was dead. Twelve hours later, I got the call.

Thirteen months after that—two hours ago—I walked into the museum in Hong Kong and saw her painted image, naked in death. I'm not sure what happened immediately after. The next thing I remember is sitting in this first-class seat on a Cathay Pacific 747 bound for New York. My eyes are dry and grainy, stinging. I am cried out. My mind gropes backwards towards the museum, but there is something in the way. A shadow.

Gradually, in the wake of my third Scotch, things begin to return. Flashing images at first, then jerky sequences. I'm standing before the painting of a naked woman whose face is mine to the last detail, and my feet are rooted to the floor with the permanence of nightmares. The men crowding me from behind believe I'm the woman who modelled for the painting on the wall. They chatter incessantly, puzzled that I am alive, angry that their fantasy of 'Sleeping Women' seems to be a hoax. But I know things they don't. I see my sister stepping out onto St Charles Avenue. Three miles is her goal, but somewhere in the junglelike Garden District, she puts a foot wrong and falls into the hole my father fell into in 1972.

Now she stares back at me with vacant eyes, from a canvas as deep as a window into hell. Having accepted her death in my bones, having mourned and buried her in my mind, this unexpected resurrection triggers a storm of emotions. But somewhere in the chemical chaos of my brain, my rational mind continues to work. Whoever painted this picture has knowledge of my sister *beyond* the moment she vanished from the Garden District. He knows what no one else could: the story of Jane's last hours, or minutes, or seconds. He alone in the world can give me what has eluded me for the past year. Peace.

As I stare into my sister's painted eyes, a wild hope is born in my chest. Jane *looks* dead in the picture. But there must be some chance, despite my premonition in Sarajevo, that she was merely unconscious while this work was done. Drugged maybe.

A particularly loud burst of Chinese snaps the spell of the picture, waking me to the tears growing cold on my cheeks. I have a wild urge to reach up and snatch the canvas from the wall, to cover my sister's nakedness from these prying eyes. But if I pull down a painting worth millions of dollars, I will find myself in the custody of the Chinese police. I run instead. I run like hell, and I don't stop until I reach a darkened room filled with ancient documents under glass. My hands are shaking in the dark, and when I hug myself, I realise the rest of me is shaking too. In the blackness I see the painting back in the exhibition room. It is not Jane's corpse, but it may be the closest thing anyone will ever find to it. It's a starting point. With this realisation comes another: there are other paintings like Jane's. According to the audio tour, nineteen. As far as I know, only eleven women have disappeared from New Orleans. Who are the other eight?

Stop! snaps a voice in my head. My father's voice. *Forget your questions! What should you do NOW?*

The audio tour said the paintings are sold through a US dealer named Christopher something in New York. Windham? Winwood? Win*gate*. To be sure, I pull the Walkman off my belt and jam it into my crowded bumbag. One thing is obvious: if Christopher Wingate is based in New York, that's where the answers are. I try to second-guess what the boy geniuses of the FBI's Investigative Support Unit would want from this place. The paintings, obviously. I can't take those with me. But the next-best thing is not impossible. In my bumbag is the small, inexpensive point-and-shoot camera I always carry in case a world-class tragedy explodes right in front of me.

I retrace my steps to the exhibition room. With my sudden reappearance, the milling Chinese draw together in excited knots. I shoot two pictures of the woman in the bathtub. The flash of the little Canon sets off a blast of irate Chinese. Moving quickly, I shoot two more paintings before a museum guard gets a hand on my arm. I turn to him and nod as though I understand, then break away towards the painting of Jane. I get off one shot before he blows his whistle for help and locks onto my arm again.

Sometimes you can bullshit your way out of situations like this. This is not one of those times. If I'm still here when Someone In Authority arrives, I'll never get out of the museum with my film. I double the guard over with a well-placed knee and run for the second time.

The police whistle sounds again. I skid to a stop beside a fire door and crash through to the outside, leaving a wake of alarms behind me. For the first time I'm glad of the teeming crowds of Hong Kong; even a roundeye woman can disappear in less than a minute. Three hundred yards from the museum, I hail a taxi and order him to my hotel. Inside my room, I throw my clothes into my suitcase, pack my cameras into their aluminium flight cases, and take a different cab to the new airport. I intend to be out of Chinese airspace before some enterprising cop figures out that, while they may not have my name, they have a perfect likeness of my face on their museum wall. They could have fliers at the airport and the hotels in less than an hour. I'm not sure why they would—I've committed no crime, other than stealing a Walkman—but I've been arrested for less before.

Hong Kong International Airport is a babel of Asian languages and rushing travellers. At the Cathay Pacific counter, I let the ticket agent gut me for full fare on a first-class ticket to New York, leaving in thirty-five minutes. The money would buy a decent used car in the States, but, after what happened in the museum, I can't sit shoulder to shoulder with some computer salesman for twenty hours.

Which puts me where I am now: three Scotches down and my short-term memory back in gear. The alcohol is serving several functions, one of them being to damp the embers of grief stirring in my soul. But nineteen hours is a long time to hide from yourself. I have a supply of Xanax tranquillisers in my bumbag, for the nights when the open wound of my sister's unknown fate throbs too acutely for sleep. It's throbbing now, and it's not even full dark yet. I pop three pills with a swallow of Scotch and take the Airfone out of my armrest.

There's really only one useful thing I can do from the plane. After a few swipes of my Visa and some haggling with directory assistance, I'm speaking to the operator at the FBI Academy in Quantico, Virginia, who transfers me to the offices of the Investigative Support Unit. Daniel Baxter, the chief of the unit, must be fifty, but he's a lean and hungry fifty, with a combat soldier's eyes. His record of success is legendary in a war where victories are few and the defeats almost unbearable. To wit, my sister and her ten sisters in purgatory. Baxter's unit scored a big zero on that one. But the grim fact is, when a certain kind of shit hits the fan, there's no one else to call.

'Baxter,' says a sharp baritone voice.

'This is Jordan Glass,' I tell him. 'Do you remember me?'

'You're hard to forget, Ms Glass.'

I give Baxter as lucid a summary as I can manage, then wait for his response. I expect some expression of astonishment but I should have known better.

'Did you recognise any other New Orleans victims?' he asks.

'No. But I never studied the photos of those beyond number six.'

'You're sure it was your sister's face in that painting?'

'Are you kidding? It's *my* face, Baxter. My *body*.'

'OK . . . I believe you.'

'Have you ever heard of these paintings?'

'No. I'll talk to our fine arts people. And we'll start taking this Christopher Wingate's life apart. When will you be in New York?'

'Nineteen hours. Around five pm New York time.'

'I'm going to book you a flight to Washington from JFK. American Airlines. It'll be an e-ticket, just show your passport. I'll have an agent pick you up at the airport. Now get some sleep. I need you sharp and thinking.'

'It's nice to be needed.' I terminate the connection and replace the Airfone in the armrest.

You didn't need me thirteen months ago, I say silently. But that was then. Now things have changed. Now they'll want me around until they get a handle on the significance of the paintings. Then they'll cut me off. Exclusion is the worst fate for a journalist, and a living hell for a victim's family. As the chemical fog descends over my eyes, a last cogent spark flashes in my brain, and I take out the phone again. Ron Epstein works Page Six at the *New York Post*; he's a human who's who of the city. Like Daniel Baxter, he's addicted to his work, which means he's probably there now, despite the early hour in New York. The *Post* operator puts me through to him.

'Ron? It's Jordan Glass.'

'Jordan! Where are you? I thought you were off in the hinterlands, taking pictures of clouds or something.'

'I was. Ron, have you ever heard of Christopher Wingate?'

'The art dealer? *Naturellement.* Very chic, very cool. Everyone wants Wingate to handle their stuff, but he's very picky.'

'I want to talk to him. Can you get me his phone number?'

'If I can't, no one can. But it may take a while. Are you somewhere I can call you?'

'No. Can I call you tomorrow? I'm going to sleep for a while.'

'I'll have it for you then.'

'Thanks, Ron. I owe you dinner at Lutèce.'

2

Two hours before the Cathay Pacific jet landed in New York, I called Ron Epstein and got Christopher Wingate's number. It took an hour of steady calling to get the art dealer on the phone, but he was intrigued enough by my modest celebrity to see me at his gallery without explanation. I couldn't tell much about him from his voice, which had an affected accent I couldn't place. He did mention my book-in-progress, so my guess is that he thinks I'm looking for a dealer to sell my photographs to the fine art market.

Meeting Wingate alone is a risk, but my work has always involved calculations of risk. I have to assume he's heard about the scene at the museum by now. He won't have my name, but he will know that the woman who caused the disturbance looked exactly like one of The Sleeping Women. Does he know that one of The Sleeping Women looks like the photographer Jordan Glass? He knows my reputation, but it's unlikely that he's seen a photo of me. The real danger depends on how involved Wingate is with the painter of The Sleeping Women. Does he know that the subjects in the paintings are probably dead? If so, then he's willing to turn a blind eye to murder in order to earn a fortune in commissions. How dangerous does that make him? One thing is certain: If I go straight to Washington now, the FBI will never let me close to him. Every piece of information I get will be second hand, just like it was after Jane disappeared.

After I clear customs at JFK, I roll my bags to the American Airlines gate, collect my e-ticket to Washington, and check my bags on that flight. Then I walk out of the airport and hire a cab. Before going to Lower Manhattan, I have the cabby take me to a pawnshop on 98th Street. There I buy a can of Chemical Mace.

When the cab pulls up to Wingate's 15th Street gallery in the failing light of dusk, I find a simple brownstone house like a thousand others in the city, with a bar on one side and a video rental store on the other. After paying the cabby to wait, I get out. There's a buzzer by the front door. I slip on sunglasses as I approach, in case there's a videocam. There is. I push the buzzer and wait.

'Who are you?' asks the voice I recognise from my earlier call.

'Jordan Glass.'

The buzzer burps, the lock disengages, and I pull the door open. The ground floor of the gallery is half illuminated by fluorescent light from the first floor, spilling down an iron staircase. With my sunglasses, it's hard to see, but the paintings look modern for the most part. 'Do you like that Lucian Freud?' asks the voice I heard on the speaker outside.

There's a man standing on the landing. He is wiry and balding, but he compensates for the baldness with a shadow of trimmed black stubble. In his black jeans, T-shirt and leather jacket, he looks like the midlevel mafia thugs I saw in Moscow a few years back: underfed but fiercely predatory. 'Not really,' I confess, with a quick look at the painting hanging nearest me. 'Should I?'

'*Should* doesn't come into it. Though it would have a better chance of impressing you if you took off those sunglasses.'

'I wouldn't like it any better. I'm not here to see this.'

'What are you here to see?'

'You, if you're Christopher Wingate.'

He beckons me forward, then turns and starts back up the stairs. I follow. We continue up to the second floor. This is clearly where he lives. It has a Danish feel, all Scandinavian wood. Standing in the middle of the room is a large, unsealed wooden crate with packing material spilling out of its open end. There's a claw hammer lying atop the crate, a scattering of nails around it. Wingate brushes a proprietary hand against the crate as he passes the crate.

'What's in the box?'

'A painting.'

I gesture at the crate. 'You work up here? This looks like your apartment.'

'It's a special painting. It may be the last time I see it. I want to enjoy it while I can. Would you like an espresso? Cappuccino?'

'Cappuccino.'

He walks to a machine on a counter behind him and starts to fill a cup. While his back is to me, I move to the open crate. Peeking between the box and the heavy gold frame, I can just see the upper torso and head of a nude woman, her eyes open and fixed in a strangely peaceful stare. Wingate is still dispensing the cup as I back away. 'I'm a huge fan of your work,' he says to the wall. 'You have a pitiless eye.'

'Is that a compliment?'

'Of course. You don't shy away from horror. But there's compassion there, too. That's why people connect with your work. I think there would be quite a demand, if you were inclined to market it as fine art. Not much photography qualifies, but yours does.'

'You're not living up to your advance billing. I heard you were a son of a bitch.'

He turns with a grin and offers me a steaming cup. The pure blackness of his eyes is startling. 'I am, to most people. But with artists I like, I'm a shameless flatterer.'

'What painting is so wonderful that you have to keep it this close to you?' I ask abruptly, pointing at the packing crate with my free hand.

Momentarily off balance, he answers without thinking. 'It's a painting by an anonymous artist. His work fascinates me.'

'You like looking at pictures of dead women?'

Wingate freezes, his eyes locked onto mine. 'No one knows if they're dead or not.'

'I want to meet the artist.'

'Impossible.'

'May I see the painting?'

He purses his lips. 'I don't see why not, since you already have.' He walks round to the open side of the crate, braces his feet against the bottom and reaches in for the frame. 'Could you give me a hand?'

I hesitate, thinking about the claw hammer, but he doesn't look like he wants to bludgeon me to death, so I set my cappuccino on the floor and take hold of the other side of the crate, while he slides out a padded metal frame that holds the gilt frame inside it.

'There,' he says. 'You can see it now.'

The woman looks like 10,000 others in New Orleans: a mixture of French blood with some fraction of African, resulting in a degree of natural beauty rarely seen elsewhere in America. But this woman is not in her natural state. Her skin should be *café au lait*; here it's the colour of bone china. And her eyes are fully open without a hint of life in them.

'*Sleeping Woman Number Twenty*,' says Wingate. 'Do you like it?'

Only now do I see the rest of the painting. The artist has posed his subject against a wall, knees drawn up to her chest as though she's sitting. But she's not sitting. She's merely leaning there, her head lolling on her marbled shoulder, while around her swirls a storm of colour. Only the woman herself is presented with startling realism.

'I don't *like* it. But I feel . . . whoever painted it is very talented.'

'Enormously.' Genuine excitement lights Wingate's black eyes. 'He's capturing something that no one else today is even close to.'

'What do you call this style?'

Wingate sighs thoughtfully. 'Hard to say. He began with almost pure Impressionism, which is *dead*. But the vision was there. Between the fifth and twelfth paintings, he began to evolve something much more fascinating. Are you familiar with the Nabis?'

'The what?'

'Nabis. It means "prophets". Bonnard, Denis, Vuillard?'

'What I know about art wouldn't fill a postcard.'

'Don't blame yourself. That's the American educational system. They simply don't teach it.'

'Are you American?'

A bemused smile. 'I usually lie when someone asks that question. I don't want to insult your intelligence, so we'll skip the biography.'

'Hiding a dark secret?'

'A little mystery keeps me interesting. Collectors like to buy from interesting dealers. People think I have mob connections, criminal clients all over. In New York, that kind of reputation doesn't hurt.'

'Do you have prints of other Sleeping Women I can see?'

'There are no prints. No photos. No copies of any kind. I guarantee that to the purchaser.'

'Why?'

'Rarity is the rarest commodity.'

'How long have you had this one?'

Wingate looks at me from the corner of his eye. 'Not long.'

'How long will you have it?'

'It ships tomorrow.'

He takes hold of the metal frame and motions for me to brace the crate while he pushes the painting back inside.

'For a series of about eight paintings,' Wingate continues, 'he could have been one of the Nabis. But he changed again. The women became more and more real, their bodies less alive, their surroundings more so. Now he paints like one of the old masters. His technique is unbelievable.'

'Do you really not know if they're alive or dead?' I ask.

'Give me a break. They're models. If some horny Japanese industrialist wants to think they're dead and pays millions for them, I'm not complaining.'

If Wingate doesn't know the women are real, he's about to find out. As he straightens up I turn squarely to him and take off my sunglasses. 'What do you think now?'

His facial muscles hardly move, but he's freaked all right. 'I think maybe you're running some kind of scam on me.'

'Why?'

'Because I sold a picture of you. You're one of The Sleeping Women.'

He must not have heard about what happened in Hong Kong.

'No,' I say softly. 'That was my sister. We're twins. Identical twins.'

He shakes his head in amazement. 'I think you know more than I do about this. Is your sister OK?'

I can't tell if he's sincere or not. 'I don't know. She disappeared thirteen months ago. When did you sell the painting of her?'

'Maybe a year ago. To a Japanese businessman called Takagi.'

'Look, I want you to understand something. I don't give a damn about the police or the law. All I care about is my sister. I think she's dead. I think all the women in these paintings are dead. And so do you. But I can't move on with my life until I *know*. I've got to find out what happened to my sister. I owe her that.'

Wingate looks at the crate. 'Hey, I can sympathise. But I can't help you, OK? I really don't know anything.'

'How is that possible? You're the exclusive dealer for this artist.'

'Sure. But I've never met the guy.'

'But you know he's a man?'

'I'm not positive. I've never even seen him. Everything goes through the mail. Money in train station lockers, like spy novels—what do they call that? A blind drop?'

'How do you pay him? You can't leave millions in train station lockers. Do you wire the money to a bank account somewhere?'

A languid expression comes over Wingate's features. 'Look, I sympathise with you. But I don't see that is your business. If what you say is true, the police will be asking me all this soon enough. Maybe you'd better talk to them. And I'd better talk to my lawyer.'

A buzz of alarm begins in the back of my brain. Christopher Wingate does not look like a man who would welcome the attention of police. Yet he's stalling me by claiming he wants to wait until they become involved. It's time to get out of here.

'Who knows about all this, anyway?' he asks suddenly.

I'm wishing my hand was in my pocket, wrapped around the Mace can, but he's watching me closely and the hammer is within his reach. 'A few people. The FBI.'

Wingate bites his bottom lip like a man weighing options. Then a half-smile appears. 'Is that supposed to scare me?' He picks up the claw hammer, and I jump back. He laughs at my skittishness, then grabs a handful of nails, puts a few in his mouth, and begins hammering the side panel back onto the crate. 'Every cloud has a silver lining, right?' The nails between his lips make him answer out of one side of his mouth. 'The FBI starts investigating these paintings in a murder case, they become worldwide news. I'm going to make a *lot* more money on this painting than I thought. Maybe double the bid.'

'Why are you selling these paintings in Asia rather than America? Were you trying to delay the connection to the missing women?'

He laughs again. 'It just happened that way. A Frenchman from the Cayman Islands bought the first five, but he'd spent most of his life in Vietnam. Then a Japanese collector stepped in. A Malaysian. Also a Chinese. There's something in these images that appeals to the Eastern sensibility.'

'Where is this one going?'

'An auction house in Tokyo.'

'Why go to that trouble? Why not auction them here?'

Pure smugness now. 'It's like Brian Epstein with the Beatles. You're number one in England, but at some point you have to take them to America. Maybe the time has come.'

Wingate's arrogance finally triggers something deep within me, a well of outrage that explodes despite my best efforts or interests.

'I was lying about the FBI,' I say in a cold voice. 'I haven't told them about the paintings yet. I wanted to talk to you first. But since you're being such a prick, I *am* going to tell them. Do you know what will happen then? This canvas you're drooling over will become evidence in a serial murder case, and it'll be confiscated. And you won't make jack*shit* off it. Not for a very long time.'

Wingate straightens up with the hammer and turns to face me. 'What do you want to know?' he asks.

'I want a name. I want to know who paints these pictures.'

He hefts the hammer and drops its head into the palm of his other hand with a slap. 'If you haven't told the FBI yet, you're not in a very good position to make that kind of demand,' he says.

I back towards the iron staircase, finding the spray nozzle with my finger as I go.

'Where are you going, Jordan?' He takes three quick steps towards me, the hammer held waist high. As he does, a new scenario hits me with chilling force. What if the painter isn't the killer at all? What if

Wingate kills the women and merely commissions the paintings from some starving artist? His dark eyes flash as he moves forward, and the violence in them unnerves me.

In one movement I whip out the Mace can and blast his face from six feet, the powerful stream filling his eyes, nose and mouth with enough chemical irritant to set his mucous membranes on fire. He screams like a child, drops the hammer and starts clawing his eyes. As I whirl towards the stairs, a giant invisible hand swats me back into the room and a fusillade of distant cannon hammers my eardrums.

When I open my eyes, I see grey smoke. I scrabble to my knees and crawl towards the staircase, but the smoke only gets thicker. The lower floors of the gallery are on fire.

'Is there a fire escape?' I shout, but Wingate doesn't hear me. He's still running round the room, wailing, '*My eyes! I'm blind!*'

'Shut up!' I shout. 'You're not blind. I maced you! Where's the fire escape? If we don't get out we're going to die.'

'Bedroom. Back . . . back wall.'

He doesn't move until I yank his arm hard. Then he starts crawling beside me. I go through the bedroom door first. The smoke here is not as bad. As I crawl towards the window, Wingate grabs my ankle. 'Wait!' he rasps. 'The painting! I can't leave it!'

The pressure of his hand on my ankle is gone. When I turn back, I see no sign of him through the smoke.

'Forget the goddamn painting!' I shout into the grey wall.

'Help me!' he calls back. 'I can't move the crate alone!'

'Leave it!'

No reply. After a few seconds I hear something whacking the crate, then a creaking sound like tearing wood. I don't much care if Wingate wants to commit suicide, but it suddenly strikes me that women's lives may depend on that painting. I take a deep breath and crawl towards the sound of coughing.

My head soon bumps something soft. It's Wingate, gagging in the smoke. The flames have reached the top of the stairs, and in their orange glow I see the painting, half out of the crate. Unzipping my bumbag, I take out my Canon, pop off three shots, then zip it back up. I grab Wingate's legs and try to drag him to the bedroom, but the exertion makes me dizzy. I'm near to fainting, and fainting here would mean death. Dropping his feet, I rush to the window, flip the catch and shove it upwards.

The outside air fills my lungs with rich oxygen and clears my head. Below me is the iron framework of a fire escape. It's the classic New

York model; one floor down, a latched ladder awaits only my weight to send it to the street below. But when I crawl down to the platform and pull the latch, the ladder stays where it is. The fire escape isn't functioning. It's fifteen feet to the cracked cement of the alley below, so I crawl over the railing and lower myself until I'm hanging by my hands from the edge of the platform. I'm five foot eight, which shortens the drop to about ten feet.

What the hell. A broken ankle is nothing compared with Wingate's fate. I open my hands and drop through the dark. My heels strike the cement and fly out from under me, leaving my right buttock and wrist to absorb the main force of the impact. I yell in pain, but the exhilaration of escape is a powerful anaesthetic. I get to my feet and look up. The window I just crawled through is spouting fire.

I look down the alley, and what I see there sends a cold ripple along my flesh. There's a man standing at the far end, watching me. I see him only in silhouette, because all the light is behind him. As I stare, he moves towards me. My hand goes to my pocket, but the Mace is not there. I lost it upstairs. I whirl and run towards the other end of the alley, towards the banshee wail of sirens.

CAREERING OUT of the mouth of the alley, I come face to face with a spectacle I covered dozens of times early in my career. The classic fire scene: engines with red lights flashing and hoses spraying; squad cars arriving; cops yelling; a crowd of spectators. The police are trying to herd them behind a taped perimeter. I walk past the biggest cop and point my camera at the fire.

'Hey!' he yells. 'Get back behind this tape!'

'The *Post*,' I tell him, holding up my camera.

'Let me see your card.'

'I don't have it. I was having a drink in the bar with some friends. Give me a break, man, I'm the first one here. I can scoop everybody.'

As the cop deliberates, I turn back to the mouth of the alley, but no one comes running out of it. The corner wall blurs for a moment, though, the vertical line of brick seeming to wrinkle in the dark. Was that him? Is he trying to figure a way to get to me even now?

Finally, the cop jerks his head towards the building. I'm past him in a flash, moving along the perimeter of the crowd, shooting as I go. No one seems to notice that I'm shooting the crowd and not the fire. If the guy in the alley didn't set this fire, the person who did is probably in this crowd. Arsonists love to watch their fires burn, they almost have to do it. I may already have his face on film.

As I turn back from the burning building, a furtive movement registers in my peripheral vision. Wide eyes dropping below the back edge of the crowd, off to my right. People are standing five deep at the tape now, and I can't see the eyes any more. But as I watch, a sock cap begins to move along the back of the crowd, coming in my direction. Throwing up my camera arm, I pop off a shot over the heads of the crowd. The head disappears, then reappears still closer. I squeeze the shutter release again, but it won't depress. I'm out of film.

The sock cap moves forward now, pushing slowly towards me through the crowd. What if he's carrying a gun? Glancing round, I rush to the fire captain, who's standing by the one of the engines.

'Captain! Jane Adams, from the *Post*. I was shooting the crowd, and I passed a guy who smelt of gasoline. When I said something about it, he started following me. He was wearing a sock cap.'

The fireman's eyes go wide. 'Where?'

I turn and point to the spot I left moments ago. There, for an instant, I see a bearded face and blazing eyes beneath the sock cap.

The fire captain races towards the tape.

'What was that?' asks a cop who suddenly appears at my side.

'I smelt gas on a guy over there. He went to check it out.'

'No shit? Good work. This is one fucked-up crime scene.'

'What do you mean?'

'They just found a guy dead in a car across the street.'

'What? How did he die?'

'Somebody cut his throat. Like a slaughterhouse in that car.'

The fire captain is already pushing back to us, shaking his head. 'Guy could be two feet away, we wouldn't know except by the smell.'

The guy *could* be two feet away. And there isn't any gasoline smell. It's time to go. But how? My cab is long gone, and walking isn't on. As I ponder my options, a yellow taxi pulls to the end of the block and disgorges a kid with cameras hanging from his neck. The official press. I start running. '*Taxi!*' I yell. '*Don't let him go!*'

For some reason—maybe because he's seen my camera—the photographer holds the cab.

'Thanks!' I tell him, jumping into the back seat. I thump the plastic partition. 'JFK! Move it!' With a screech of rubber, the cab is rolling towards the Queens-Midtown Tunnel.

MY FLIGHT LANDS at Reagan National in Washington at 10.15pm, and when I step off the plane, there's a man in a suit waiting for me at the gate. He's holding a white cardboard sign that says 'J. GLASS'.

'I'm Jordan Glass.'

'Special Agent Sims,' he says with a frown. 'You're late. Follow me.'

He sets off down the concourse at a rapid clip and walks right past the down escalator marked 'Baggage and Ground Transportation'.

'I have some bags down there,' I call after him. 'My cameras. They were on the earlier flight, so they're probably in storage.'

'We have your cases, Ms Glass.'

Agent Sims leads me through a door marked 'Airport Personnel Only', and a blast of cold air hits my face. Sims helps me onto a baggage truck and signals its driver, who takes off across the airfield.

In less than ten minutes we're descending over Quantico in a Bell 260 chopper. There's an agent waiting on the FBI helipad, to take my baggage, but I follow Sims into the maze of the Academy building.

'Wait here,' says Sims, having escorted me into an empty room, sterile and white, like some convention-hotel meeting space.

The door shuts, then locks from the outside. Two minutes later the doorknob clicks. Then the door opens and two men walk in. The first is Daniel Baxter, dark-haired and compact, about five foot ten and corded with muscle. His eyes are brown and compassionate but steady as gunsights. The man behind him is taller—over six foot—and at least ten years older, with silver hair, an expensive suit, and a bluff Yalie look. Baxter speaks as he takes his seat.

'Ms Glass, this is Dr Arthur Lenz. He's a forensic psychiatrist who consults for the Bureau.' Lenz nods in my direction as Baxter gestures for me to sit down. 'I suppose you have an explanation for missing the plane I booked for you?' Baxter continues.

'Well—'

'Before you go any further, let me advise you that Christopher Wingate has been under Bureau surveillance since you called me.'

I wasn't sure whether I was going to admit being at the fire. Now there's no way to deny it. 'You had people outside his gallery? Then why didn't they bust in there and try to save us?'

'We had one agent at the scene, Ms Glass, doing surveillance from his car. The fire started on the ground floor, and it was explosive in nature. An incendiary device made of gasoline and liquid soap.'

'Homemade napalm.' I know it well.

'Yes. The sprinkler system was disabled prior to the device being detonated, the fire alarm as well. We've since determined that the fire-escape ladders were also wired in the up position. All inoperative.'

'You think you're telling me something? I had to jump to save myself. Your guy couldn't do anything to help?'

'Our guy did do something. He died there.'

A wave of heat tells me my face is red.

Baxter's eyes are merciless. 'Special Agent Fred Coates, twenty-eight years old, married with three kids. When the bomb went off, he called the fire department, shot some pictures of the first people on the scene. Then he called the New York field office on his cellphone. He was talking to his Special Agent in Charge when somebody reached through the window and slit his throat. The killer stole his camera. He missed one flash memory card that had fallen between the console and Agent Coates's seat. That's where we got the shot of you. We lost his pictures of the crowd.'

'Jesus. I'm sorry.'

Baxter spears me with an accusing look. 'What the hell did you think you could achieve there? I told you to come straight here.'

'Don't put this on me! Whoever killed him would have set that fire whether I was there or not. And I *do* have pictures of the crowd.'

Both men lean forward, mouths open. 'Where?' asks Dr Lenz.

'We'll talk about that in a minute. I want to clarify something right up front. This isn't going to be a one-way conversation.'

'Do you realise how important every minute is?' Baxter asks. 'By withholding that film—'

'My sister's been missing for over a year, OK? I think she can wait another twenty minutes.'

'You don't have all the facts.'

'And that's exactly what I want.'

Baxter shows his exasperation. 'Ms Glass, that fire bomb was planted to kill Wingate and destroy his records. You're lucky you didn't go up with the rest.'

'It was Wingate who almost killed me. He died trying to save the stupid painting.'

'What painting?' asks Lenz.

'*Sleeping Woman Number Twenty.*'

'I wonder why,' Lenz says softly. 'Surely it would have been insured.'

'The insurance wouldn't have been enough. When I told Wingate I was going to the FBI, that the women in the pictures were almost certainly the victims from New Orleans, he was ecstatic. He said the new canvas would probably sell for double the standing bid on it.'

Baxter reaches into a file, removes a photograph, and pushes it across the table at me. It's a head shot of a young, dark-haired woman.

'That's her. *Damn* it. The woman in the painting. Who is she?'

'Last known victim,' Baxter replies.

'How long ago was she taken?'

'Four and a half weeks.'

'What was the interval between her and the one before her?'

'Six weeks.'

'And before that?'

'Fifty-four days. Seven and a half weeks.'

This decreasing time span bears out the reading I did after Jane was taken. One theory says that as serial offenders get a taste for their work, their confidence grows and they try to fulfil their fantasies more and more frequently. 'So you figure he's due for another soon?'

The two men share a look I cannot interpret. Then the psychiatrist gives a slight nod, and Baxter turns to me.

'Ms Glass, approximately one hour ago, a young Caucasian woman disappeared from the parking lot of a New Orleans grocery store called Dorignac's. She left her house a few minutes before the store closed—eight fifty pm Central Time—to get some sausage. By nine fifteen, her husband started to worry, so he got the kids out of bed and drove down to see if his wife had a dead battery.'

'He found her empty car with the door open?'

Baxter gives a sombre nod.

This happened to two victims before Jane. I'm about to speak, when shock steals my breath. 'Wait a minute. The man who took the Dorignac's woman couldn't have killed Wingate.'

Baxter nods slowly. 'Nine-one-one in New York got the call about the Wingate fire at seven fifty-one pm. Eastern Time. The Dorignac's victim disappeared between eight fifty-five and nine fifteen Central Time. That's a maximum difference of two hours twenty-four minutes.'

'So there's no way the same person could have done both.'

'There's one way,' says Baxter. 'The incendiary device had a timer on it. If it was set long enough in advance, the same person could have got back to New Orleans in time to take the woman from Dorignac's.'

'But it wasn't,' I think aloud. '*He* wasn't.'

'How do you know?'

'Because I saw him.'

I describe the drama of the man from the alley, shooting the blind photo over the crowd, and sending the fireman and cop after him.

'Where's your film?' asks Baxter, his eyes burning with excitement.

'Not here, if that's what you're thinking. So are you saying there's more than one person behind the disappearances?'

'The evidence points to two UNSUBs, not one,' says Lenz. 'The killer's in New Orleans, the painter in New York.'

UNSUB is FBI-speak for Unknown Subject.

'But Wingate was killed in New York.'

'Different motive. That was self-preservation.'

'I had the same thought up there. So the New Orleans guy kidnaps the women. How does the New York guy do the paintings? He works from photographs? Or he flies to New Orleans to paint corpses?'

'If that scenario is the answer,' says Baxter, 'I pray to God he flies. We can take back data from airline computers and work out a list of potential suspects. We're due for a break in this case.'

I nod hopefully, but inside I know better. 'If Wingate was killed to silence him, how do you think it happened? The logic of it?'

Baxter leans back and steeples his fingers. 'I think Wingate told the UNSUB in New York about the Hong Kong incident. Wingate's phone records show a call from the curator of the Hong Kong exhibition to his gallery within an hour of your making the disturbance.'

A hot flush brings sweat to my face. 'Wingate knew about Hong Kong? So what if he was setting me up for the killer and got caught in his own trap?'

'Quite possible,' says Baxter. 'If Wingate somehow knew it was you in Hong Kong, then he knew your sister was in one of the paintings. Maybe he knew everything about the crimes. He calls the UNSUB and tells him you're coming to the gallery, but he doesn't want any violence there. He also wants to know who you've talked to. The UNSUB sees his chance to take you both out.'

'I'm not sure he knew that much. He *said* he'd never seen the artist's face. It was all done with blind drops or something.' I quickly summarise Wingate's explanation of how he received the paintings, and the subsequent drops of cash in train station lockers.

'I suppose it could have happened that way,' Baxter concedes. 'But what I need right now is the film you shot tonight.'

'Once I give you that, you're going to cut me out.'

Baxter starts to speak, but the psychiatrist cuts him off with a wave of his hand. Lenz obviously pulls a lot of weight in the ISU.

'Ms Glass, I have a proposal that might interest you.'

'I'm listening.'

'Fate has handed us a unique opportunity. Your appearance in Hong Kong caused a disturbance because you looked exactly like a woman in one of the paintings. Imagine, therefore, the reaction you might cause in the killer if you came face to face with him.'

'Go on.'

'Forensic art analysis has come a very long way in the past twenty years. I believe the paintings will lead us in short order to a suspect, or perhaps a group of them. And once we have those suspects, Ms Glass, *you* are the weapon I would most like to use against them.'

So, they do need me. They cooked all this up before I got here.

'How would you feel about that?' asks the psychiatrist. 'Posing as a special agent at interviews while Daniel and I observe suspects?'

'She'd kill to do it,' says Baxter. 'I know that much about her.'

Lenz fires a harsh look at him. 'Ms Glass?'

'I'll do it on one condition. That I'm in the loop from now till the day you get the guy. I want access to everything.'

I expect Baxter to argue, but he just looks at the table and says, 'Done. Where's your film?'

'I dropped it in a mailbox at JFK near the American Airlines gates. It's addressed to my house in San Francisco.'

'We'll get it. We can develop it at the lab right here.'

'I figured you guys had mastered mail theft.'

Baxter stifles an obscene reply and takes out a cellphone.

'One other thing,' I add. 'I shot three photos of *Sleeping Woman Number Twenty* before I escaped the building.'

With a look of grudging admiration, Baxter dials a number and tells someone to find out who the postmaster general is and get him out of bed. When he hangs up, I say, 'I want digital copies of those pictures emailed to the New Orleans field office. I'll pick up prints in the morning.'

'You're going to New Orleans?' asks Lenz.

'That's right.'

'It's too late to get a flight tonight.'

'Then I expect you guys to get me a plane. I only came here at your request. I need to tell my sister's husband what's happened. Before he hears about it some other way.'

Baxter sighs. 'Look, Arthur is going to New Orleans in the morning, to speak to some art dealers there. Why don't you fly down with him then?'

'I'd be happy to fly down tonight,' Lenz says, 'if Ms Glass feels such urgency. Can the plane be made ready?'

Baxter considers this. 'I suppose. But, Ms Glass, please urge your brother-in-law to be discreet. If you're going to be effective in our investigation, no one can know you're in town.'

'Agreed. But I want a full update on the plane. That's the deal.'

Baxter sighs and looks at Lenz as if the psychiatrist has named his own poison. 'Arthur can handle that.'

3

The FBI Learjet hurtles into the Virginia sky at 3.00am, after a long wait for mechanical checks, refuelling, and a fresh flight crew. I should have waited for morning, but I couldn't. I learned unflappable patience during thousands of hours behind my camera, but Jane's disappearance robbed me of that. Now, if I'm standing still, I have too much time to think. Motion is my salvation.

The interior of the jet is configured for work, with two seats facing each other over a collapsable desktop. Dr Lenz seems accustomed to the cramped quarters of the cabin, despite his heavy frame. I imagine he once shuttled between murder scenes the way I shuttled between wars.

'Ms Glass,' he says, 'we have a little over two hours together. I'd like to spend that time as profitably as we can.'

'I agree.'

'Interviewing you—particularly since you're an identical twin—is almost like being able to interview your sister before the fact. I'd like to ask you some questions, some of them very personal.'

'I'll answer what I think is relevant.'

He blinks once, slowly, like an owl. 'I hope you'll try to answer them all. By withholding information, you may prevent my learning something which could advance our efforts to find the killer.'

'You've been using the word "killer" since I arrived. You believe all the women are dead?'

His eyes don't waver. 'I do. Does that bother you?'

'No. I feel the same way. I do have one question, though. Are you aware of the phone call I received eight months ago?'

'The one in the middle of the night? That you thought might be from your sister?'

'Yes. The Bureau traced it to a train station in Thailand.'

Lenz grants me a smile of condolence. 'It's my opinion that the guess you made the following morning was correct. That it was someone you'd met during your efforts to locate your father.'

'I just thought maybe . . . me finding the paintings in Asia—'

'We'll certainly look into it. But I'd like to move on now. I understand you weren't that close to Jane as an adult, so I'd like you to tell me how you grew up. What shaped her personality. And yours.'

It's times like now I wish I smoked. 'OK. You know my father was a war photographer. Well, that meant he was almost never home.'

'How did the family react to that?'

'I handled it better than my sister or mother did. I understood why he went, even as a child. Why on earth would you hang around the Mississippi backwoods if you could be roaming the world?'

'Why did your mother marry a man who would never be home?'

'She didn't know that when she married him. He was just a big, handsome Scots-English guy who looked like he could handle anything that came along. And he could, pretty much. Except married life in Mississippi. A nine-to-five job. That was hell for him.

'He tried to do right by her, to keep her with him as his career took off. He even moved her to New York. She lasted until she got pregnant. During her eighth month, he went on assignment to Kenya. She went back to Oxford, Mississippi. If she hadn't been pregnant when she left, Dad probably never would have come back home. But he did. Not that often, but when he did, it was paradise for me.'

'What about Jane?'

'Not so much for her. We were twins, but emotionally we were different from early on. Some of it was just bad luck.'

'How so?'

'Jane was mauled by a dog when she was four. It really tore up her arm. It made her fearful for the rest of her life.'

'Did Jane resent your father's absences?'

'Yes. I think she got to hate him before he disappeared, because of how sad Mom was, and because money was so tight.'

Lenz holds up his forefinger. 'You used the word disappeared. Isn't it generally accepted that your father died in Vietnam?'

'Yes. Cambodia, actually. But I've never accepted that. I never felt that he was dead, and over the years there've been occasional sightings of him in Asia by former colleagues.'

'What sort of scenario do you envision? That he chose not to return to America? That he abandoned you?'

'Probably so.' I pull back my hair, digging my fingernails into my scalp as I go. 'I always suspected that he had a woman there. In Vietnam. Maybe another whole family. Lots of servicemen did. Why should photographers be any different?'

Lenz's blue-grey eyes flicker with cold light. 'Could you forgive him that?'

The central question of my life. 'I've spent a lot of time photographing distant wars, just as he did. I know how lonely it can be.'

'You said you never *felt* your father was dead. What about Jane? Do you feel she's dead?'

'I felt it twelve hours before I got the call.'

'So you shared the sort of intuitive bond that many twins speak of?'

I nodded. 'It's a very real thing, in my opinion.'

'I don't dispute it. You're being very forthcoming with me, Jordan, and I appreciate that. I think we could save a lot of time if you describe what you consider the seminal events in your lives as siblings. Your high-school days, for example.'

'Look, I don't see how questions about my high-school life are going to help you understand Jane. Let's move on to something that might actually help you find Jane's killer. That's the goal here, right?'

Lenz only watches me. 'You're a photographer. You use filters to produce certain visual effects, yes? Human beings use similar filters. Emotional filters. They're put in place by our parents, our siblings, our friends and enemies. Before we bring you into contact with any suspects in this case, I must understand you. I need to be able to correct for your particular filter.'

I look out of the porthole window to my left. Lenz wants my secrets. But some things are between me and my conscience, no one else. Still, I feel some obligation to cooperate. Lenz is trusting me not to screw up his investigation. I suppose I have to trust him a little.

'The years after my father disappeared were difficult. Jane's strategy was assimilation. Conformity. She studied hard, became cheerleader, and kept the same boyfriend for three years. I give her a lot of credit. Being popular isn't easy without money.'

'Money seems to be a recurring theme with Jane.'

'Not only with her. Before Dad was gone, I didn't realise how poor we were. But by thirteen, you start to notice. Material things are part of high-school snobbery. Clothes and shoes, what kind of car you have, your house. Mom had started drinking and wrecked our car, and after that we didn't have one. It was embarrassing. One day, prowling through the attic, I discovered some old camera equipment. Mom told me that when she got pregnant, she persuaded Dad to open a portrait studio, to try to make their lives more stable. It never came to anything, of course. But he kept the equipment. A large-format camera, floodlights, a background sheet, darkroom equipment, the works. I taught myself to use the stuff. A year later, I was running a portrait studio out of our house. Our lives improved. I was paying the light bill and buying the groceries, and because of that, I could pretty much do what I wanted.'

Lenz nods encouragement. 'And what did you want?'

'My own life. Oxford's a college town, and I rode all over it on my ten-speed bicycle, watching people, shooting pictures.'

'It sounds like an idyllic childhood,' Lenz says. 'Was it?'

'Not exactly. While other girls my age were riding out to Sardis Reservoir to fumble around in back seats with guys from the football team, I was doing something a little different.'

A deep stillness settles over Lenz's body. Like a priest, he has heard so many confessions that nothing could surprise him.

'The first week of my senior year, our history teacher died. He was about seventy. To fill his shoes, the school board hired a young alumnus named David Gresham. Gresham had been drafted in 1970, and served one tour in Vietnam. He came back to Oxford wounded, but his wounds weren't visible, so the school board didn't notice them. But I did. I watched Mr Gresham very closely, because he'd been to the place where my father vanished. One day after school, I stayed to ask him what he knew about Cambodia. When he asked why I was interested, I told him about my father. I hadn't meant to, but when I looked into his eyes, my pain and grief poured out like a river through a broken dam. A month later, we became lovers.'

'How old was he?' asks Lenz.

'Twenty-six. I was seventeen and a half. A virgin. We both knew it was dangerous, but there was never any question of him seducing an innocent child. I knew exactly what I was doing. He taught me a lot about the world. I discovered a lot about myself. And I gave peace to a boy who had been broken in some fundamental way that could never be corrected, only made less painful.'

'It's amazing that you found each other,' Lenz says without a trace of judgment in his eyes. 'This did not end well, of course.'

'We managed to keep our relationship secret for most of the year. But in April, one of David's neighbours saw us kissing at the creek behind his house, and took it upon himself to report it to the school board. The board gave David the option of resigning and leaving town before they opened an investigation that would destroy both our futures. To protect him, I denied everything, but it didn't help. Two nights later, he went down to the creek and managed to drown himself. The coroner called it an accident, but David had enough Scotch in him to sedate a bull.'

'I'm sorry.'

My eyes seek out the porthole again, a round well of night. 'He probably thought his death would end the scandal, but it only got worse. Jane had a breakdown brought on by social embarrassment. My mother just drank more. When I went back to school my Star Student award was revoked. Then my appointment book went blank. No one wanted me shooting their family portraits. When I refused to abase myself in contrition, various mothers told the school board that they didn't want their daughters exposed to a "teenage Jezebel". They really called me that. At that point, I did what David should have done. I had three thousand dollars in the bank. I took two thousand, packed my clothes and cameras, rode the bus to New Orleans, and scratched up a job developing prints for the staff photographers at the *Times-Picayune*. A year later, I was a staff photographer myself.'

'Did you continue to support your family financially?'

'Yes. Then in college Jane met a guy from a wealthy family in New Orleans. Married him in his senior year of law school. She found the handsomest, most reliable provider she could, married him, had two kids, and lived happily ever after.'

For some reason this inaccurate summary brings a wave of tears to my eyes. 'I need a drink. Do you think they have any of those little airplane bottles stowed on this plane?'

'No. Jordan, I want you to—'

'Get off it! OK? You wanted our story, you've got it. We're poster girls for nurture in the nature-versus-nurture debate. We're physically identical but emotionally we're opposites. Jane acted like she despised me, but she was so jealous of me it made her sick. Was she weak? Yes. But weaker people can't help being weak. Now Jane is alive or she's dead. Either way, I have to know. But your games aren't taking us any closer to an answer. I don't think anything connects these victims, except the fact that they're women.'

'Jordan, don't you want to—'

'What I *want* is what Baxter promised me. A complete breakdown of the FBI's investigation so far. And I want it now.'

Lenz splays his age-spotted hands on the desktop and leans back. 'Did that outburst make you feel better?'

'Start talking, damn it!'

'There's not much to tell. We're now gathering at the National Gallery in Washington every known painting that belongs to The Sleeping Women series.'

'How many do you have so far?'

'None. Four will arrive by plane tomorrow, more the next day. Some collectors have refused to ship their paintings but agreed to allow Bureau forensic teams to travel to their collections. First we'll try to match the paintings to the known victims in New Orleans. We'll also be searching the canvases for fingerprints, hairs, skin flakes, other biological artefacts. Experts will make studies of the painter's style and try to draw comparisons with known artists. And that's only the beginning of what the paintings will go through.'

'Who's in charge of the case for the Bureau?'

'Daniel Baxter will run the Washington track; he'll be in charge of all profiling, with me consulting. The New Orleans Special Agent in Charge will run that end of the case.'

'Who's the SAC? Same one as last year?'

'No. Patrick Bowles. He's a competent man.' Lenz looks as though he's about to continue, but he stops himself.

'What is it?'

'Another man in New Orleans may be playing the primary role in the investigation at this point.'

'Who?'

Lenz sighs. 'His name is John Kaiser. He's a journeyman agent now, but two years ago he was a member of the Investigative Support Unit.'

'In Quantico? With Baxter?'

'Yes.'

'Why is he in New Orleans?'

'He transferred out of the Unit. He's the only man in the area with any real experience in cases like this—full time, on the ground.'

'Has he made any headway?'

'No one had, until you found those paintings. But I've no doubt that John Kaiser knows more about the victims and attacks than any man alive. Except the killer, of course.'

'Was this Kaiser good when he was at Quantico?'

Lenz looks over at the porthole. 'He had a very high success rate.'

'But you don't like him.'

'We disagree about fundamental issues of methodology.'

'That's psychobabble to me, Doctor. I've learned one thing in my business, like it or not.'

'What's that?'

'You don't argue with results.'

A high beeping sounds in the cabin. Lenz reaches into his jacket, removes a cellphone and presses a button. 'Yes?' As he listens, he seems to shrink in his seat. 'When?' he says. 'Yes . . . . Right.'

'What's happened?' I ask as he drops the phone in his lap.

'Twenty minutes ago, two teenagers found the body of the woman taken from Dorignac's grocery store. She was lying on the bank of a drainage canal, nude. Her husband just identified the body.'

This news nauseates me, but not because of its ugliness. 'It wasn't him,' I say quietly. 'If they found a body, it's unrelated.'

'Not necessarily. It could still be him.' Lenz nods with a strange intensity. 'Think about it. It's been four and a half weeks since the last victim. The New Orleans UNSUB was on the prowl tonight—maybe all afternoon. He may have known what happened in Hong Kong, but he didn't know that his partner was about to silence Wingate, along with you. He snatches the woman from Dorignac's and takes her back to his house. When he arrives, he finds an urgent message on his machine from his partner. Or maybe he gets a call, telling him Wingate is no longer a problem, and also that Jordan Glass got away. The investigation is about to get very hot. So, instead of painting this woman, he kills her and dumps her. Some time in the last seven hours.' Lenz slaps his knee with excitement. 'No, we can't discount this victim just because we found her body.'

I want to believe him, but for some reason I don't. 'But we know he's smart enough to dump the body without it being found.'

'That's the point!' Lenz snaps. 'He's *letting* us find her, in order to confuse the trail.'

'But isn't that risky, if he's actually had her in his possession? I mean, with all the forensics at your disposal?'

The psychiatrist smiles for the first time in a long while. 'Yes, it is.'

THIS MORNING I SLEPT IN. Except for my right flank, which feels like a mule kicked it, my muscles have that deliciously liquid feeling that only sex or too much sleep can give. It's been a while since I had the former, so I owe my thanks to a quiet hotel room. I ate breakfast in the lobby, then called Budget and rented a Mustang convertible. After travelling in the East for months, riding in underpowered taxis, cyclos and rickshaws, an American muscle car feels exactly right. It's late October in New Orleans, but I have the convertible top down. The leaves are green and still on the trees, and the morning sun tells me the temperature could hit eighty by lunchtime.

I'm late for my meeting with the FBI because nobody bothered to tell me they moved the field office from downtown. The brand-new building is a massive four-storey brick structure designed to look like a college campus building, but the closer I get, the more it looks like a fortress. The armed gate guard checks my driver's licence, radios upstairs, then raises the barrier and waves me into the parking lot.

As I lock the Mustang and walk towards the entrance, I sense that I'm being watched on screens inside. A metal detector at the door leads me into a small vestibule not unlike a doctor's office, where a female receptionist assures me someone will be down for me in a minute. Thirty seconds later, a door opens and a tall man with deep-set eyes and a day's growth of beard steps through.

'Jordan Glass?'

'Yes. Sorry I'm late. I went to the old federal building downtown.'

'That's our fault, then. I'm John Kaiser.'

This guy does not look like the FBI agents I've known. He's six foot two, lanky, and looks as comfortable in his white shirt and sports jacket as a cowboy in a tuxedo. His dark brown hair is past the unwritten regulation length, and his aura is about as unofficial as anything I can imagine. He looks like a law student who's been study-ing for three days without sleep. A forty-five-year-old law student.

'You don't look like an FBI agent.'

A lopsided grin. 'My SAC is fond of telling me that.'

'Are we going upstairs?'

He lowers his voice. 'To tell you the truth, I'd rather talk to you alone first. Do you like Chinese food? I haven't eaten since last night, so I ordered some. I ordered for two.'

'I like Chinese. But why don't you want to eat it in your office?'

Kaiser has hazel eyes, and they focus on mine with subdued urgency. 'Because I'd rather talk without any interference.'

'From whom?'

'You met him last night.'

'So the dislike is mutual?'

'Afraid so.'

'You can't keep Dr Lenz out of your office?'

'I'm not sure. But I can definitely keep him off a picnic table on Lakeshore Drive, especially if he doesn't know I'm going there.'

'I'll go if we take my car.'

'You read my mind, Ms Glass.'

Kaiser collects his takeout bags and follows me through the main doors. 'We got your film from the fire scene,' he says.

'What did it show?'

'New York is busting its collective ass trying to trace every face in the crowd shots. It's a big job. The good news is, the video store had a list of members, and the bartender says a lot of his patrons that evening were regulars.'

'I thought maybe I got a shot of the guy who set the fire. It would have been a downward shot, at the back of a crowd.'

Kaiser gives me a strange look. 'You won't believe this, but you got the top of some heads, and a Caucasian hand flipping you the finger.'

'You're kidding me.'

'My sense of humour doesn't extend to cases like this one. You think the UNSUB saw what you were doing in time to duck down and flip you off?'

'He saw what I was doing, all right. He was moving along the back of the crowd, following me. I think he was trying to get close enough to kill me. That's why I got the firefighters after him.'

'That was smart.'

'I thought I got that camera up quick enough. Damn.'

'It's in the past,' he says. 'You can't change it, so forget it.'

'You make it sound easy.' I stop beside the Mustang. 'This is it.'

Kaiser flashes a broad smile of pleasure as he folds his long frame into the passenger seat beside me. In seconds we're roaring down Lakeshore Drive, headed for the green expanses beside Lake Pontchartrain. He leans his head back and looks up at the sky.

'Damn, this feels good.'

'What?'

'Riding in a convertible with a pretty girl. It's been a long time.'

Despite the strangeness of the situation, I feel a little flush of pleasure. Minutes later, I nose the Mustang into a cement semicircle by a wooden bench on the lake side of the road. Kaiser carries the food to the bench, straddles one end, and lays out the cardboard containers and drinks in front of him. 'I got Peking Chicken and Spicy Beef,' he says. 'Also some shrimp fried rice, egg rolls, and two iced teas, unsweetened. Take whatever you want.'

'Peking Chicken.' I straddle the other end of the bench and reach for one of the cups.

'Do you want to start?' he asks. 'Or do you want me to?'

'I will. First of all, have you formed some picture of whoever's behind all this?'

'I've tried, but there's not much to go on. No corpses. No witnesses. No evidence. The victims might as well have been kidnapped by aliens. And that frightens me more than anything.'

'Why?'

'Because it's hard to hide a body well. Especially in an urban environment. Corpses stink. Dogs and cats root them out. Homeless people discover them. And nosy neighbours see everything.'

'There's a lot of swamp around New Orleans,' I point out.

Kaiser shakes his head. 'We've been dragging the swamps for months with no results. And those swamps aren't empty. There are hunters, fishermen, oil people. Think about it. If the UNSUB dumps a woman off a causeway, she's going to float within sight of some-body. Eleven bodies in a row? Forget it. No, if they're dead, he's burying them. And the safest place to do that is beneath a house. A house he's living in. Toss in a little lime every now and then, they wouldn't even stink.'

'Excuse me . . . you just said *if* they're dead. Dr Lenz is positive they're dead.'

'The doctor and I disagree about a lot of things.'

'But what makes you think they might be alive? Where could they possibly be?'

'It's a big world, Ms Glass. There's something else, though. The autopsy on the Dorignac's victim is mostly complete. We took some skin from beneath her fingernails. It could be very important. We also found a strange burn on her neck. The kind of contact burn consistent with an electrical stun device, like a taser.'

My pulse quickens. 'What does that tell you?'

'That the UNSUB may not have wanted to kill his victims.'

'Oh God. Please let that be it.'

'I don't want to create false hope, but it's a good sign in my book.' Kaiser gives me a measuring look. 'A couple of other things make this UNSUB very interesting to me. One, he's the only serial offender I know of to earn enormous profit from his crimes. Two, he's not after publicity. Not the usual kind, anyway. He's not send-ing severed fingers to relatives or the TV stations. So for him, the women are simply part of the process of creating the paintings. That's what this is all about. The paintings.'

'But aren't the paintings a kind of publicity in themselves?'

'Yes, but a very specialised kind. Publicity and profit are linked here. If the artist were painting solely to fulfil his private needs, he wouldn't sell them. Think of the risk he's taking by putting them on the market. That's the only way we've learned anything about him.'

'How are profit and publicity linked?'

'He wants the art world to see what he's doing. Maybe critics, maybe other painters, I don't know. The money might not be impor-tant in and of itself. It wouldn't surprise me if he hasn't spent a dime of it.' Kaiser looks at his watch. 'I'd like to ask you about something personal, if you don't mind.'

'What?'

'The phone call you got from Thailand. Would you mind telling me about it?'

'Not if you think it might help you.'

'It might.'

'It was five months after Jane disappeared. A bad time for me. I was having to sedate myself to sleep. Anyway, the phone rang in the middle of the night. It must have rung a long time to wake me up, and when I finally got to it, the connection was terrible.'

'What was the first thing you heard?'

'A woman crying. The woman sobbed, "Jordan." Then there was static. Then: "I need your help. I can't—" Then there was more static, like a bad cellphone connection. Then she said, "Daddy's alive, but he can't help me." Then: "Please," like she was begging, at her wits' end. At that point I felt that it was Jane, and I was about to ask where she was when a man in the background said something in French that I didn't understand. Then in English the man said, "No, *chérie*, it's just a dream." And then the phone went dead.'

My appetite is gone. A clammy sweat has broken out under my silk blouse, sending a cold rivulet down my ribs.

'What happened next?'

'I thought the whole thing might have been a delusion. But I reported it to Baxter, who traced its origin to a station in Bangkok.'

'When you found that out, what did your gut tell you?'

'I hoped it was my sister. But the more I thought about it, the less I believed it. I know a lot of Missing in Action families, from searching for my father for so long. What if it was a female relative of an MIA in the middle of a search?'

'But MIA relatives go over to try to help the missing soldier. Not the other way round.'

'Yes,' I acknowledge. 'So, what do you think?'

He idly pokes his beef. 'I think it might have been your sister.'

I take a deep breath and try to steady my nerves. 'This is why you didn't want Lenz here, isn't it?'

Kaiser looks at the ground. 'If your sister *is* alive, it throws Lenz's present theory into question. Lenz talks a lot about how everything is possible, how there are no rules, but deep down he's wearing blinkers. He probably asked you about all sorts of family stuff. Right?'

'Yes.'

'That's the way he works. I'm not criticising him for it. He did some ground-breaking work early in his career.'

'That's pretty much what he said about you.'

'Really? Well, I won't kid you, I don't think he should be involved in this investigation. I don't trust his instincts. He was involved in a case a while back that turned into a real clusterfuck. And Baxter places too much weight on what he says, because of their history.'

'What do you think about his plan to use me to rattle any suspects you dig up?'

'It's not as simple or safe as it sounds. The results could be inconclusive, and it could put you right in the killer's sights.'

Since Kaiser took the conversation into personal territory, I feel justified in doing the same. 'What about you? Why did you leave Quantico?'

'I burned out. It happens to everyone in that job, sooner or later. I just snapped more spectacularly than most.'

'What happened?'

'After four years at Quantico, I was pretty much Baxter's right hand. I was handling far too heavy a load. Child murders, serial rapes, bombers, kidnappings, the whole sick spectrum. It got to where I was actually living at the Academy. When my personal life fell apart, I hardly noticed. Then one day the inevitable happened.'

'What was that?' I ask. 'The inevitable?'

'Baxter and I were out at the Montana State Prison, interviewing a death-row inmate. He'd raped and murdered seven little boys, and this guy was really enjoying telling us what he'd done. I just couldn't detach myself. I couldn't stop thinking about this one little boy, screaming for his mother while this guy shoved power tools up his rectum.' Kaiser swallows hard, like his mouth is dry. 'And I lost control, nearly killed him.'

'Jesus. How did you keep your job?'

Kaiser slowly shakes his head, as if gauging how much to tell me. 'Baxter covered for me. He told the warden the con jumped me and I defended myself.' Kaiser looks away. 'I guess you're going to go all liberal on me now, tell me I violated his civil rights?'

'Well, you did. You know that. But I understand why. It sounds to me like you had a delayed reaction to something else.'

He looks back at me as though surprised. 'That's what it was, all right. I'd lost a little girl a week before. Working a rape and murder case in Minnesota. I was advising Minneapolis Homicide, and we were really close to getting the UNSUB. But he strangled one more little girl before we did. If I'd been one day faster . . . well, you know.'

'It's in the past. Isn't that what you told me? So forget it.'

'Glib bullshit.'

His honesty brings a smile to my face.

'A while ago you said "clusterfuck". That's a Vietnam term, isn't it? Were you there?'

He nods distractedly. 'Yeah.'

'You look too young for it.'

'I was in the army. I was there at the end of the ground fighting. Seventy-one and -two.'

Which makes him forty-six or forty-seven, if he went over when he was eighteen. 'Were you drafted?'

'I wish I could tell you I was. But I volunteered. What did I know? I was a kid from Idaho. Went to Ranger School, the whole nine yards.'

'How did you feel about journalists over there? Photographers?'

'They had a job to do, like I did.'

'A different job.'

'True. I met a couple who were OK. But some of them just stayed in the hotels and sent Vietnamese out to get their combat shots. I didn't care much for them.'

'That still happens. But there are plenty of good photographers, too. The ones who know the danger, they're scared shitless, but they do it anyway. They crawl right into the middle of it, where the mortar rounds are dropping and the machine guns are churning up the mud.'

'That's the kind of courage I respected over there,' Kaiser says quietly. 'I knew some soldiers like that.'

'That's the kind of courage my father had,' I tell him. 'He wasn't that gifted a photographer. His composition wasn't great. But when you're that close, composition doesn't matter. Just the shot.'

His face is lined with silent grief; I wonder if he knows it. 'Something tells me you were a soldier like that,' I say quietly.

He doesn't respond to that, but continues, 'I've seen your name under some pretty rough pictures. Why do you do it?'

'Because I have to. It isn't a conscious choice.'

'Are you trying to change the world?'

I laugh. 'In the beginning I was. I'm not that naive now.'

'You've probably changed it more than most people ever will. You change people's minds, make them see things in a new way. That's the hardest thing to do in this world, if you ask me.'

'Will you marry me?'

He laughs and hits me on the shoulder. 'Are you that starved for affirmation?'

'This past year has really sucked.'

'The past two have sucked for me. Welcome to the club.'

Kaiser's cellphone rings. He looks at the display and presses Send. 'Kaiser.' His face grows tight as he listens. 'OK.' He hangs up. 'What happened?'

'I don't know, but Baxter wants me back at the field office and he said to bring you with me. They're setting up a video link to Quantico. Something's popped somewhere.'

4

The FBI field office is run from the third floor, which was designed so that you see nothing but hallways and doors unless you walk through one of the doors. We stop in front of one marked 'Patrick Bowles, Special Agent in Charge', and Kaiser gives me a look of encouragement. 'Don't be shy. Just say what you think.'

'I usually do.'

He nods and ushers me into a large L-shaped room with a broad window overlooking Lake Pontchartrain. There's a desk in the dogleg of the L, and sitting behind it is a florid man with quick green eyes and silver hair. On the way over, Kaiser told me that SAC Bowles is the senior FBI official in the state of Louisiana, in charge of 150 field agents and 100 support personnel. When he gets up to greet me, I see that he's wearing a three-piece suit that never hung on any department store rack, silver links in his French cuffs, and a silk tie.

'Ms Glass?' he says, offering his hand, then motioning me towards a leather chair in a group.

Glancing to my left, I see Arthur Lenz on a sofa in a private seating area in the deep leg of the L. The good doctor doesn't look happy, but he stands and walks over to us. Kaiser sits in a chair opposite mine, and SAC Bowles retakes his place behind his desk and glances at his watch. 'Daniel Baxter wants to discuss something. We'll have a satellite video link in about thirty seconds.'

Bowles pushes a button on his desk, and a three-foot section of wall slides back, revealing an LCD screen. 'There's a camera above the screen,' he says. 'Baxter can see us all in a wide-angle shot.'

Suddenly, Daniel Baxter's face fills the screen, and his voice emanates from hidden speakers. 'Hello, Patrick. Hello, Ms Glass. John. Arthur.'

The ISU chief looks directly at me as he speaks. 'Ms Glass, from the moment you called me from your return flight from Hong Kong, we've been using the combined weight of the Department of Justice and the Department of State to gather The Sleeping Women paintings for forensic analysis. We now have six paintings in our possession, including some of the first. We've already begun our analysis, and the bad news is, we've found no fingerprints preserved in the paint.'

'Damn,' curses Bowles.

'We *have* found traces of talc in the paint, which suggests that the artist wore surgical gloves while doing his work. We've made arrangements for eight paintings to be shipped to us in Washington. The owners of six more have given us permission to send forensic teams to their homes or galleries to make the necessary studies.'

'That leaves five,' says Kaiser. 'Nineteen total, right?'

Baxter nods. 'The remaining five are owned by a man named Marcel de Becque. De Becque's father was a French colonial businessman who put his money into tea plantations in Vietnam.'

'And he lives in the Cayman Islands,' I finish.

'How did you know that?' Baxter asks sharply.

'Wingate mentioned him.'

'De Becque won't send us his paintings?' asks Kaiser.

'He's not only refused to ship his paintings to us, but also refused to allow our forensic teams to go to his estate to study them.'

'Frog son of a bitch,' growls Bowles. 'What's he doing in the Caymans? Probably running from something.'

'He is,' Baxter confirms. 'Word is, de Becque was heavily involved in the unofficial war economy throughout the Vietnam conflict.'

'Black marketeer,' Kaiser says with obvious distaste.

'Four years ago,' says Baxter, 'Marcel de Becque was implicated in a stock-fraud scheme on the Paris Bourse. He had to flee the country, but he netted close to fifty million from the deal. He's immune to pressure from us because he's committed no crime on US soil.'

Kaiser unexpectedly voices my thought for me. 'What does all this have to do with Jordan Glass?'

Baxter turns to me again. 'Monsieur de Becque has made an unusual proposition. He told me he would allow his Sleeping Women, as he refers to them, to be photographed—not forensically examined, mind you—but only if the photographer was Jordan Glass.'

'Why in the world would he ask for me?'

'I was hoping you could shed some light on that,' says Baxter.

'Maybe de Becque is the killer,' suggests Bowles. 'He killed Jane

Lacour, and now he's discovered she has a twin sister. He wants to do her as well. Make a set.'

'De Becque is seventy years old,' says Baxter. 'He falls well outside all profiles for serial murder.'

'This may not be serial murder,' says Kaiser. 'And de Becque could easily be behind the selections. We need to find out if he's come to New Orleans in the past eighteen months, and if so, how often.'

'De Becque owns his own jet,' says Baxter. 'A Cessna Citation. We're trying to trace its movements now. He says he'll send it to pick up Ms Glass and her equipment. The catch is, she has to go alone.'

Kaiser looks incredulous. 'You're not actually considering this?'

'John, we have to look at those paintings—'

'I'll do it,' I tell them.

'If you do,' says Baxter, 'it won't be under de Becque's conditions.'

'Under no conditions,' says Kaiser. 'We have no control down there.'

'Let me get this straight,' I say to Kaiser. 'You think a seventy-year-old man is going around New Orleans kidnapping women in their twenties and thirties? Without leaving a trace? My sister ran three miles a day and worked out with weights. She could kick the crap out of most seventy-year-old men, pardon my French.'

'If de Becque is behind it,' says Kaiser, 'I see him commissioning the paintings. Paying one or more men to take the women for him, and one artist to paint them.'

'An elegant scenario,' says Lenz. 'But if de Becque commissions the paintings, why wouldn't he have them all?'

'He could be selling them,' says Baxter.

'A guy worth fifty million?' asks Bowles.

As they bat ideas back and forth, something occurs to me. 'Wingate told me de Becque bought the first five Sleeping Women,' I tell Baxter. 'So how did you test some of the first paintings for talc?'

'They didn't sell in the order they were painted,' he replies. 'We tested some of the first ones *painted*. Some of the more abstract ones. His Nabi period. It was the realistic ones that sold first and started the phenomenon.'

'Did de Becque know I'm already involved with you?' I ask.

'He seemed to,' says Baxter.

'How the hell would he know that?' Kaiser asks. He turns to Bowles. 'How tight have you kept this?'

The SAC's lips tighten. 'If there's a leak, it's not our people.'

Kaiser doesn't look convinced. Neither does Lenz.

'So, what are we going to do?' asks Bowles.

'I'm going to Grand Cayman,' I tell them. 'One way or another.'

Lenz nods approval, but Kaiser says, 'We have no idea what's going on in this case, no idea about motive. De Becque could have people in New Orleans right now. They could snatch or kill her any time. She needs protection.'

'Agreed,' says Baxter. 'Patrick, could you put one of your agents with Ms Glass until we contact her?'

Bowles nods assent.

'Ms Glass,' Baxter says in a conclusive tone, 'I appreciate your willingness to go through with this. And if Agent Kaiser knew you like I do, he'd know there's no point in arguing with you.'

Bowles looks at Kaiser. 'Take Ms Glass outside and find her some protection, John. Somebody you'll be satisfied with.'

Kaiser gets up and walks out without a glance in my direction. I stand and say, 'Gentlemen,' with the panache I've developed over twenty years working in a profession dominated by men.

Kaiser is waiting for me in the corridor, his jaw tight. 'Your work has dulled your ability to assess risk,' he says. 'You think because you've tromped through a few battlefields, a visit to the Cayman Islands is nothing. But there's a difference. In a war zone, a journalist's enemy is bad luck. You might take a stray bullet, but nobody's trying very hard to kill you. De Becque may have nothing else on his mind *but* killing you. You have no business taking that kind of risk.'

'Do you have a sister or a brother, Agent Kaiser?'

'Yes. A brother.'

'So why are we arguing?'

He sighs and looks at the floor. I start past him, but he takes hold of my shoulder. 'What about the protection?'

'Find me somebody who's not a robot, and I'm fine with it.' I touch him lightly on the elbow. 'I'm not stupid, OK?'

'What do you plan on doing his afternoon?'

'Buying presents for my niece and nephew. I'm supposed to stay with them tonight. My brother-in-law's house.'

'That's where your sister disappeared. The Garden District.'

'Which proves no neighbourhood's safe, right? I don't guess *you're* available to guard me this afternoon?'

He chuckles. 'No. I've got someone good in mind, though.'

I'M SITTING on St Charles Avenue in my rented Mustang, a little way up from my brother-in-law's house in case my niece and nephew are watching through the windows. My bodyguard is standing thirty yards away, beneath a spreading oak. Agent Wendy Travis, the female operative Kaiser has chosen to protect me, looks as if she could be an accountant, but for the pistol visible through the opening in her jacket. She's attractive in a well-scrubbed American way, twice as fit as me and a member of the SWAT team. I feel safer than I have in years.

She kindly followed me around town this afternoon while I searched for presents for my niece and nephew. Henry is eight, and Lyn is six. I've only seen them once since I left New Orleans eleven months ago. I promised myself I would visit more often, but that was a hard promise to keep. The reason is simple: I look like their missing mother so they end up confused and crying when I visit.

Wendy knows I'm nervous about the visit. An hour ago I persuaded her to take me to a funky little bar on Magazine. She didn't drink, but I had two gin and tonics. To keep my mind off what was coming, I asked her about the New Orleans field office and Agent John Kaiser in particular. Kaiser, it seems, is the resident hunk of the office. All the assistants and secretaries flirt shamelessly with him, but he has never asked one for a date, patted a rump, or even squeezed a shoulder, which impresses Agent Wendy no end. His record with the Investigative Support Unit was stellar until he snapped under the pressure. When I told Wendy I knew that already, she couldn't hide her suspicion. How, she wondered, had I learned something in one day that it had taken her weeks to discover?

'His wife left him,' she said. 'Did he tell you that?'

'No.'

A satisfied smile. 'She couldn't take the hours he put in. That's pretty common. But he didn't even stop working then, to try and sort it out. He just let her go.'

'Kids?' I asked.

She shook her head.

'He told me he served in Vietnam. Do you know anything about that?'

'He doesn't talk about it. But Bowles told my SWAT commander that he'd seen John's service record, and that he has a bagful of medals. My commander approached him, to try to get him to join the SWAT team, but he wasn't interested.'

'It doesn't surprise me. Men who've seen a lot of combat don't have many illusions about solving problems with weapons.'

Wendy bit her lip and wondered if that was an insult. 'You've seen it?' she asked. 'Combat, I mean? You've taken pictures of it and all?'

'Yes.'

'You ever get shot?'

'Yes.'

I instantly went up two notches in her estimation. 'Did it hurt?'

'I don't recommend it. I took a piece of shrapnel in the rear end once, too. That hurt a lot worse than the bullet did. Talk about *hot*.'

Wendy laughed, I laughed with her, and by the time we finished talking, I knew she was more than half in love with John Kaiser.

I climb out of the Mustang with my gift-wrapped packages and suitcase and walk up the block to my brother-in-law's house. I mount the porch and swing the brass knocker against the oak door. Marc himself opens the door.

You'd think people would be blessed with money or looks, not both, but Marc Lacour shatters that assumption. He has sandy blond hair, blue eyes, a chiselled face, and a muscular frame that looks ten years younger than its forty-one years. He smiles when he sees me, then pulls me to him for a hug, which I return.

'Jordan,' he says as I draw back. 'I'm glad you're here.'

He takes my case and leads me through the huge central hall, into the formal living room. As I perch on a wing chair and he closes the door, I hear the patter of small shoes on the hardwood floor of the hall. Then a small face appears from behind the living-room door-post. Lyn's face. A physical echo of my own. With her large dark eyes, she looks like a fawn peeking from behind a tree. As her mouth falls open, Henry's blond hair and blue eyes appear above her. Henry blinks, then disappears. I smile as broadly as I can and hold out my arms. Lyn looks at her father—then steps into the open and runs to me.

It takes a supreme effort to keep from crying as her little arms wrap round my neck like a drowning child's.

Marc ushers Henry towards me with his hands on the boy's shoulders. 'This big guy here is Henry, Aunt Jordan.'

'I know that. Hello, Henry. I brought you a present. Would you like to see?' I say, proffering one of the wrapped packages.

'*Yeah!*' He attacks the package, and in seconds exposes a box that says 'Panasonic'. 'It's a DVD player, Dad! For the car!'

Lyn is standing quietly at my knee, watching me. She doesn't even ask if I got her anything.

'And this is for you,' I tell her, handing her the smaller box.

She carefully removes the bow and sets it aside, and by this simple act breaks my heart again. She learned that frugal habit from Jane, as Jane learned it from our mother. At last the box becomes visible.

'Is it a camera?' she says, removing the two-piece body from its plastic housing.

'Yes.'

'Is it a kid's camera, or a grown-up camera?'

'It's a grown-up camera. A digital camera. You have to be careful while you learn to use it. But don't be *too* careful. It's only a tool. What's important is your eyes, and what you see in your head. The camera just helps you show other people what you see. Do you understand?'

She nods slowly, her eyes bright. 'Will you teach me how to use it?'

'I sure will. The pictures from this camera go into a computer before they go onto paper. I'll bet you have a computer.'

'My dad has one.'

'We'll just borrow his until he gets you your own. Right, Dad?'

Marc shakes his head, but he's smiling. 'Right. OK, who's ready for supper? Annabelle!'

The clicking of heels comes up the hallway, followed by an elderly black woman's voice. 'What you hollerin' about, Mr Lacour?'

'How's supper coming?'

'Almost ready.' Annabelle appears in the doorway. She has a warm smile on her face until her eyes settle on me. It fades instantly.

'Annabelle, this is Jordan,' says Marc.

'Lord, I see that,' she says softly. 'Child, you the spittin' image of . . .' She glances at the kids and trails off. 'God bless you,' she says, taking my hand and squeezing it. Then she goes to Henry and Lyn, bends nearly double, gives each a hug, and walks back to the door.

'You can go on when supper's done,' Marc says. 'Have a good night.'

'I'll be gone as soon as I get the biscuits out the oven,' she says.

By the time we reach the dining room, the table is laden with food. A pork loin with what smells like honey-and-brown-sugar glaze, cheese grits, biscuits, and a token salad.

Lyn and Henry take the chairs on either side of mine, and we all dig in. It's surprising how quickly we fall into a natural rhythm of conversation, and the only awkward moments come in the silences. The children look at me as though they've lost all sense of time, and I know they are reliving hours spent at this table with their mother. Once, even Marc's eyes seem to glaze over, as he slips into the same dimension the kids visit so much more easily.

After we retire to the living room, I give Lyn a lesson on the digital Nikon. She is deft with her hands, and after she shoots a few test shots, I load them into Marc's notebook computer. The results are good, and Lyn practically bursts with pleasure. Marc tries to get the kids to bed, but they refuse, crawling into my lap for me to argue their case. I oblige, and before long Henry is zonked out. Marc sits in a chair across the room, half watching a stock market report on CNBC, so he doesn't notice Lyn staring up at me, her chin quivering.

'What is it, honey?' I whisper.

She closes her eyes tight, squeezing out tears as she turns her face into my breast and sobs. 'I miss my mama.'

This time there's no stopping my tears. I have never known a protective instinct as powerful as the one that suffuses me now. I would kill to protect these children. But who can I kill to protect them from the loss of their mother? All I can do is caress Lyn's forehead and reassure her about the future. 'I know you do, baby. I do, too. But I'm here for you now. Think about happy times.'

'Are you going to stay with us tonight?'

'I sure am.'

Marc looks over at us, his eyes suddenly alert. 'What's the matter?'

'Nothing a little hugging won't fix,' I tell him, rocking Lyn as best I can with Henry weighing me down. But what I'm hearing in my mind is the voice on the telephone eight months ago. *God, let that have been Jane*, I pray silently. *These children need more than I can ever give them.*

A half-hour later, Marc and I carry the kids to their beds. When we get back to the living room, he opens a second bottle of wine and refills our glasses. 'Sit down, Jordan. There's something you should know. I've told the kids that Jane is dead.'

The voice that emerges from my mouth sounds like a stunned four-year-old. '*But . . . you don't know she's dead.*'

Marc sits on the ottoman and shakes his head. 'How long are you going to wait before you accept it? Your father's been dead almost thirty years and you're still looking for him. The kids can't wait that long. I had to tell them.' He drains his glass and his eyes mist over. 'I'm just trying to make things as easy on them as I can.'

I give him a conciliatory nod. 'I understand why you did this. But it's not right, Marc. What will you feel if it turns out you're wrong?'

He snorts. 'You don't really think those women are alive, do you?'

'I honestly don't know. But I won't give up until I see her body. I wish you wouldn't either. In your heart, at least.'

'My heart?' He gestures towards his chest with the goblet. 'For the last thirteen months, my life has been shit. If it weren't for those kids, I might not even be here.'

'Marc—'

He covers his eyes and begins sobbing. Alcohol and depression definitely don't mix. I feel a little awkward, but I get up, walk over to him and lay my hand on his shoulder.

'I know it's hard. I've had a tough time myself.'

He shakes his head, as though to deny the tears, then wipes his face on his shirtsleeve. 'Goddamn it! I'm sorry I got like this.'

I sit on the ottoman and put my hands on his shoulders. 'Hey. You've been through one of the worst things anyone can go through. You're allowed.'

His eyes seek out mine. 'I just can't seem to get it together. But I'm glad you came. I can't believe how the kids responded to you.'

'I can't believe how I responded to them. I almost feel they're mine.'

'I know. Just . . . thanks for coming.' He leans forward and embraces me. The hug does me good, too, I must admit. But suddenly a current of shock shoots through me. There's something moist against my neck. *He's kissing my neck.*

I go stiff in spite of my desire not to overreact. '*Marc?*'

He takes his lips away, but before I can gather my thoughts, he's kissing my mouth. I jerk back and put my hands on his arms to restrain him.

His eyes plead silently with me. 'You don't know what it's been like without her. I can't even *look* at another woman. All I see is Jane. But watching you tonight, at the table, with the kids . . . you almost *are* her.'

'I'm not Jane.'

'I know. But if I let my mind drift, it's like you are. You even *feel* like her.' He pulls his arms free and squeezes my hands. 'Your hands are the same, your eyes, your breasts, everything.' His blue eyes fix mine with a monk's intensity. 'Do you know what it would mean to me to have one night with you? It would be like Jane had come back.'

'*Stop!*' I hiss, afraid the children will wake. 'Do you hear yourself? I'm not Jane, and I can't pretend to be! Not to ease your grief. Not for the kids, and especially not in your bed. In *her* bed. My God.' Without knowing how I got there, I find myself standing three feet away from him with my arms crossed over my breasts. 'I think it would be best if I stay at a hotel tonight.'

He blinks. 'Don't do that. I didn't mean to upset you.'

I find my suitcase in the hall, and feel thankful I didn't unpack yet.

'What do I tell the kids?' he asks.

'Tell them I got called away to a photo shoot. I'll be back to see them soon.'

He looks penitent now, but before he sinks into drunken apologies, I leave. As I hit the sidewalk, a car door opens a few yards away and a dark figure floats in front of me.

'Jordan?' says a female voice. 'What's the matter?'

'I'm fine, Wendy. I'm just staying elsewhere.'

'What happened?'

'Men problems,' I murmur.

'Gotcha. Where are we going?'

'A hotel, I guess.'

She takes my suitcase and starts towards the Mustang, then pauses. 'Um, look . . . I don't know how you feel about hotels, but I've got an extra bedroom at my apartment. I've got to stick with you no matter where you go, so, you know. It's up to you.'

There have been nights I would have killed for a hotel room. But tonight I don't want a sterile, empty place. I want real things around me, a humanly messy kitchen and CDs and a crocheted comforter on the couch. 'That sounds great. Let's go.'

I'm about to start the Mustang when my cellphone rings. 'Hello?'

'Ms Glass? Daniel Baxter.'

'What's up?'

'I've been negotiating with Monsieur de Becque of the Cayman Islands. He says you can go on our plane, and you can bring one assistant to help with lighting, et cetera. Agent Kaiser has volunteered.'

I smile to myself. 'Great. When do we leave?'

'Tomorrow afternoon. I'll call you in the morning to give you the travel details.'

'I'll talk to you then.'

5

Most flights to the Cayman Islands depart from Houston or Miami, but with the FBI Lear, things are simpler. It's Kaiser, me, and two pilots up front for the two-hour run from New Orleans to Grand Cayman, largest of the three islands that make up the British colony.

We've been in the air for just over an hour, and Kaiser is uncharacteristically quiet. Or perhaps I'm radiating enough hostility to discourage conversation. I can still feel my brother-in-law's lips against my neck, and the emotional fallout is hard to shake on top of everything else.

'Are you sleeping?'

I blink from my trance and look across the narrow aisle at John Kaiser, who is studying me with a worried gaze. He's wearing navy slacks, a polo shirt, and a tan suede jacket that fits perfectly. I dressed for this trip in tailored black silk trousers and a matching jacket, with a low-cut linen blouse. A kinky old Frenchman might just respond to some tasteful décolletage. 'No. Just thinking,' I reply.

'What about?'

'We don't know each other well enough for you to ask that.'

He gives me a tight smile. 'You're right. Sorry.'

I straighten up in my seat. 'You probably have some grand plan for this meeting, right? A strategy?'

'Nope. Dr Lenz would have one. But I go on instinct a lot of the time. We're going to play it by ear.'

Eventually, below us, the white beaches of Grand Cayman come into view. Our pilot swings round North Bay to show us de Becque's estate: a gated compound that stands on a jutting point of land near the marina. Then we land at the airport near Georgetown. A white Range Rover awaits us on the runway. Customs having been taken care of in advance by the Justice Department, a Caucasian driver and his Caymanian associate load my camera and lighting equipment into the back of the Rover, and we drive northwards.

A high wall surrounds de Becque's estate, but when our driver opens an iron gate with a coded remote, I see a British colonial mansion that, like some embassies, gives the impression of a fortress. The driver pulls the Range Rover into a crescent drive and stops before wide marble steps. His assistant gets out, opens our doors, then motions us upwards.

The massive door opens before we ring the bell, and I find myself facing one of the most beautiful women I have ever seen. With fine black hair, light brown skin and almond eyes, she possesses that rare combination of Asian and European features that makes it impossible for me to guess her age.

'*Bonjour*, Mademoiselle Glass. I am Li. Please come in.'

I step inside, followed by Kaiser, who with the driver brings in the aluminium flight cases. They set the cases down in the foyer.

Li smiles at us, and says, 'If you will follow me, *s'il vous plaît?* Your equipment will be taken to the proper room.'

Our journey through de Becque's mansion is an education in

understated elegance. There's a Zen-like simplicity to the spaces and to the furniture that adorns them. All lighting is indirect, and the few visible beams fall upon paintings spaced at tasteful intervals.

Our destination is a large, high-ceilinged room with a massive wall of glass facing the harbour. In the distance, a dozen boats ply the waters of North Bay, and as I watch them I realise a man is standing at the lower right edge of the glass, watching me.

'*Bonjour*,' the deeply tanned man with a full head of close-cropped silver hair says. 'I am Marcel de Becque.' He walks forward and, before I know what he's doing, takes my right hand, bends, and kisses it with courtly grace. 'You are far more beautiful in person, *ma chérie*. I thank you for coming.'

Despite the strangeness of the situation, I feel my face flush. 'This is my assistant, John Kaiser.'

De Becque smiles in a way that lets us know he will play along with this fiction. Then he waves his hand towards the wall to my right, which holds a large display of black and white photographs. Most of them appear to date from various phases of the Vietnam War, and each is clearly the work of a master photographer.

'Do you like them?' de Becque asks.

'They're remarkable. Where did you get them?'

'I knew many journalists during the war,' he says. 'Photographers as well. They were kind enough to give me prints from time to time.'

Not all the photos are of military subjects. Several are studies of temples and statuary; still others groups of khaki-clad men with the stateless look of war correspondents. On closer inspection, I recognise several photographers: Sean Flynn, Dixie Reese, Larry Burrows. As I move to the next photo, my blood goes cold in my veins. Standing alone by a stone Buddha is my father. Jonathan Glass.

'Where did you get this?' I whisper.

'Terry Reynolds shot that in seventy-two,' says de Becque. 'I knew your father well, Jordan.'

I try to maintain my composure as I speak. 'Monsieur—'

He stops me with an upraised hand. 'I'm sure you have a thousand questions. Why don't you photograph my paintings first? Then you may return here and satisfy your curiosity.'

PHOTOGRAPHING The Sleeping Women is a simple exercise, technically speaking. Kaiser does his best to follow my orders in setting up the lighting, but it's clear to Li—whom de Becque sent along to make sure we don't get too close to the canvases—that my 'assistant' has never handled a softbox or barn door in his life.

I shoot the paintings with a thoroughness bordering on compulsion, but I try not to look too hard at them. There's no denying their remarkable power. Unlike the painting I saw in Wingate's gallery, the women in these canvases are saturated in colour rather than surrounded by it: vivid blues and oranges highlighted with whites and yellows. Two are lying in bathtubs, posed much like the woman in the first painting I saw in Hong Kong, but their faces are less defined than hers. If I didn't know these women might be dead, I would believe them asleep, for their skin fairly hums with light.

I fire off two more shots of the last painting and remove the exposed film. 'I'm done,' I say. 'Let's go see de Becque.'

THE OLD FRENCHMAN is waiting in the glass-walled room. He gestures us towards a pair of sofas that face each other before the great window. Li pours wine for us, then vanishes without a sound.

'You wish your "assistant" to join us?' de Becque asks, one eyebrow arched.

I turn to Kaiser, who sighs and says, 'I'm Special Agent Kaiser, FBI.'

De Becque walks forward and gives Kaiser's hand a light shake. 'Isn't that a relief? Deception is a wearying art. Please, sit.'

Kaiser and I take one sofa, de Becque the one facing us.

'Why have I brought you here?' the Frenchman says to me. 'That is question number one?'

'That's a good place to start.'

'You're here because I wanted to see you in the flesh, as they say. It's that simple. I knew your father in Vietnam. When I learned you were involved in this case, I took steps to meet you.'

'How did you learn Ms Glass was involved?' asks Kaiser.

De Becque makes a very French gesture with his opened hands, which I translate as *Some things we must accept without explanation.* Kaiser doesn't like it, but there's not much he can do about it.

'How did you meet my father?'

'I collect art, and I consider photography an art. My tea plantation in Vietnam provided a good base for those journalists whom I invited to use it. My table was famed throughout the country, and I enjoy good conversation.'

'What do you know about my father's death?'

'I'm not at all sure he died when the world believes he did.'

There it is. Spoken by a man in a position to know.

'How could he have survived?'

445

'While the Khmer Rouge generally killed journalists out of hand, not all Cambodians did. I believe Jonathan was shot, yes. But he could well have been nursed back to health. And like you, I've heard reports over the years that he has been sighted.'

'If he survived,' says Kaiser, 'and he considered you a friend, why wouldn't he seek you out?'

'He may have. But I had sold my plantation by the time he went missing.'

'Do you think he could still be alive?' I ask.

A smile of condolence. 'It would be too much to hope for, I think.'

I sigh. 'We're here for another reason, of course. But may I telephone you later for specifics?'

'I'll make sure you have my numbers before you go.'

Kaiser leans forward, his wine glass between his knees. 'I'd like to ask you a few questions.'

'Of course. But I may be selective about my answers.'

'Do you know the identity of the artist of The Sleeping Women?'

'I do not.'

'How did his paintings first come to your attention?'

'I was acquainted with Christopher Wingate, the art dealer. I'm in the habit of buying new artists whose work catches my eye. When he introduced me to The Sleeping Women I told him I would buy all he could get me.'

'And he got you five?'

'Yes. I made the mistake of letting certain Asian acquaintances see my paintings. The price skyrocketed overnight. After the fifth, Wingate betrayed me and began selling to the Japanese.'

'Did you have any idea that the subjects might be dead?'

'Not at first. I assumed the poses were of sleep, as everyone else did. But after I saw the fourth, I began to get a feeling. Then I saw the genius of these paintings. They were paintings of death, but not in any way that had been done before.'

'How do you mean?'

'In the West, the attitude towards death is denial. In the East it's different. Death is part of life in the East. For many it's a sweet release. That is part of what I see in The Sleeping Women.'

'An interesting interpretation,' says Kaiser. 'You know that at least one of the subjects in the paintings is missing and probably dead?'

'Yes. This poor girl's sister.'

'How do you feel about that? How do you feel about the fact that young women may be dying to produce these paintings?'

De Becque gives Kaiser a look of distaste. 'Many human endeavours are begun with the knowledge that they will cost human lives. Bridges, tunnels, pharmaceutical trials, exploration and, of course, wars. None of these goals even approaches the importance of art.'

Kaiser sighs and puts down his wine. 'Why wouldn't you send your paintings to Washington for study?'

'I am a fugitive. I don't trust governments, particularly the American government. I had many dealings with it in Indochina, and I found American officials naive, hypocritical and stupid.'

'That's something, coming from a black marketeer.'

De Becque laughs. 'You hate me? For the black market? You might as well hate rainfall or cockroaches.'

I give Kaiser a sharp look and turn to de Becque. 'You've seen me in the flesh now,' I tell him. 'What do you think?'

His blue eyes twinkle like Maurice Chevalier's. 'I would love to see you au naturel, *chérie*. You're a work of art.'

'Would naked be enough? Or would naked and dead be better?'

'Don't be ridiculous. I am a libertine. I celebrate life.'

'Did you commission the painting of my sister?'

His humour vanishes. 'No.'

'Did you try to buy it?'

'I never had the chance. I never saw it.'

Kaiser says, 'When did you first learn of Ms Glass's existence?'

'When I saw her name beneath a photograph in the early eighties.' De Becque chuckles. 'I nearly jumped out of my skin. The credit read "J. Glass", same as her father's.' He nods thoughtfully, and looks at me. 'Do you think your sister might still be alive?'

'I didn't until I saw her painting in Hong Kong. Now I'm not sure.'

When de Becque makes no comment, I ask, 'Do *you* think the women are alive or dead?'

The Frenchman sighs. 'Dead, I would say. Although I would not assume all these women share the same fate.'

'Why not?' asks Kaiser.

'No plan is perfect. I wouldn't think it absurd to hope one or more out of nineteen is alive somewhere.'

'Is it nineteen women?' Kaiser asks. 'There are only eleven victims in New Orleans. If each painting is of a different woman, then there are eight victims we don't know about.'

'Perhaps those eight are simply models?' de Becque suggests. 'Paid off long ago and forgotten.'

'We'd like that to be true, of course. But the abstract nature of the early paintings has made it impossible for us to match the faces to victims. We haven't even matched them to the eleven known victims yet.'

'If any of these women are still alive,' I ask, 'where could they possibly be? Why wouldn't they have come forward by now?'

'The world is very wide, *chérie*. And full of people with strange appetites. I'm more concerned about you. Your involvement with the FBI may bring you to the painter's attention. I would not have anything happen to you.'

'She'll be protected,' says Kaiser.

'Good intentions aren't enough, monsieur. I haven't much confidence in your FBI, to be frank.'

'I appreciate your concern, monsieur,' I say, 'but I want to remain part of the effort to stop this man.'

'Then take a word of advice. Be very careful. I would not like to see you come up for auction some time soon.'

'If I do, buy me. I'd rather hang here than in Hong Kong.'

A white smile cracks the Frenchman's face. 'I would top any price, *chérie*. You have my word upon it.' At that moment I see genuine affection in his eyes, and I'm suddenly sure he knew my father far better than he claimed.

'I think it's time to go,' I tell Kaiser. Then, rising to my feet, I remember something. 'Your numbers!' I say. 'I never got them.'

'They're waiting in your plane.'

Of course they are.

THE RANGE ROVER hums towards the airport. Bright sunlight glints off the bonnet, chasing a blue iguana beneath a green roadside bush. As the reptile vanishes, The Sleeping Women I saw in de Becque's gallery flash through my mind, and a minor epiphany sends a chill along my skin.

'I just realised something. Those women are being painted in natural light.'

'How can you tell?' asks Kaiser.

'Twenty-five years of experience. Light is very important to colour. I'll bet artists are even pickier about it than photographers.'

'If he's painting the women outdoors, that would mean a really secluded place. There's lots of woods and swamp, but getting there with a prisoner or a body could be tough.'

'A courtyard,' I tell him. 'New Orleans is full of walled gardens and courtyards. I think that's what we're looking for.'

Kaiser squeezes my arm. 'You'd have done well at Quantico.'

As soon as we are safely on the Lear, he says, 'De Becque is in this thing up to his neck. I can feel it.'

'Maybe the women really *aren't* being killed,' I say. 'Maybe they're being held somewhere in Asia.'

'Moved there on de Becque's jet, you mean?'

'Maybe. Have you traced its movements over the past year?'

'We're having some trouble with that. But Baxter will stay on it. He's a bulldog with that kind of thing. I'll call him for an update.'

Kaiser walks forward, takes the seat by the bulkhead, and in moments is holding a special scrambled phone to his ear. The jet begins to roll, and soon we're hurtling north. After about ten minutes, Kaiser hangs up and comes back to the seat facing me. There's an excitement in his eyes that he can't conceal. 'We just hit the jackpot. The DC lab traced two brush hairs they took from the paintings. They come from a rare type of kolinsky sable, and the brushes are handmade in one small factory in Manchuria. There's only one American importer, based in New York. He buys two lots a year, and they're sold before he gets them. To repeat customers.'

'Any in New Orleans?'

Kaiser smiles. 'The biggest order outside New York went to New Orleans. The art department of Tulane University.'

'My God. Wasn't one of the victims kidnapped on the campus?'

'Two. Another from Audubon Park which is close by Tulane. Baxter's meeting the president of the university now. By the time we land, he'll have a list of everyone who's had access to those brushes.'

My stomach feels hollow. 'This might really be it.'

Kaiser nods. 'You know something? De Becque lied to us in there. He told us he never saw the painting of Jane. This is a guy who can get on his private jet and fly to Asia any time he wants. He's pissed at Wingate for selling the later Sleeping Women out from under him, to Asian collectors. But do you think he didn't fly to Hong Kong the minute they went on exhibition there?'

'It's hard to imagine him not doing that.'

'He's got a thing about those paintings. And a thing about *you*. I'll bet he's got a streak of kinkiness that's off the chart.'

'So, what are you saying?'

Kaiser looks out of the porthole window, his face blue in the thickly filtered sunlight. 'This is like digging up a huge statue buried in sand. You uncover a shoulder, then a knee. You think you know what's down there, but you don't. Not until it's all out of the ground.'

6

In the main conference room of the New Orleans field office, a strategy meeting is deciding what direction the NOKIDS case will take from here. I am not at that meeting. I've been banished to SAC Bowles's office. Once again, exclusion defines my status as an outsider. The meeting is being chaired by a deputy director of the FBI, and includes the US Attorney for New Orleans, the New Orleans chief of police, and various other big shots.

Bowles's door opens and Kaiser walks in. I catch sight of Agent Wendy looking in from the hall.

'You ready?' he asks.

'What's happened so far?'

'Lots of nothing. The bureaucrats had to weigh in. The Deputy Director and the US Attorney are gone now. The big news is, we have four suspects. And all of them were here in town the day Wingate died in New York. We'll hear the details in there. When we get done, I'd like to talk to you alone. We never got dinner. Maybe we can have a late meal, if you're up for it.'

'Sure. Wendy, too?'

He blows air from his cheeks. 'I'll handle that. Let's go.'

It's a quick walk to the conference room, which is stunning in size with a panoramic view of Lake Pontchartrain. The conference table is thirty feet long and surrounded by massive blue plush executive chairs with the FBI crest embroidered in the upholstery. At the near end of the table sit the usual suspects: Daniel Baxter, SAC Bowles, Dr Lenz, and Bill Granger, the head of the Violent Crimes Squad. I take a seat beside Kaiser.

'Ms Glass,' says Baxter, 'we've made phenomenal progress in the past eight hours. The sable brush hairs led us to the Tulane University art department. With the help of the president of the university, we've determined that the order was placed by one Roger Wheaton, the artist in residence at Newcomb College, which is part of Tulane.'

'The name sounds familiar.'

'Wheaton is one of the most highly regarded artists in America. He's fifty-eight years old, and he came to Tulane just two years ago.'

'About the time the disappearances started,' says Bill Granger.

'The main point is,' Baxter continues, 'that Wheaton didn't order the special sable brushes only for himself. He has three graduate students who have been studying under him since he arrived. Two are male, and followed him down from New York. The other is a Louisiana woman.'

'One of your suspects is a woman?'

'She has access to the brushes, and the taser used in the snatch of the Dorignac's victim makes a female perpetrator possible.'

'When are we talking to them?'

'Tomorrow. Before we go into details, though, you should understand our position. The Investigative Support Unit normally works in an advisory capacity for state or local police agencies. We provide expertise relating to serial offenders, but the police do the legwork. However, in cases like this, where we have knowledge that crimes will likely be committed in the future, we become involved in all aspects of the investigation. There are over two dozen detectives working this case, from the seven separate New Orleans police departments. We're presently leading the joint task force.

'All four suspects have been under surveillance from the time they were identified, but they won't be approached until after we go in tomorrow. While we interview Roger Wheaton at the university, NOPD will be searching his residence from top to bottom. We're already turning his life inside out, in so far as it exists on paper. His three students get the same treatment, though investigating art students is like investigating waiters; they almost don't exist on paper. Right now none of the four has a paper alibi for the Dorignac's snatch. All four were at an opening at the New Orleans Museum of Art until seven thirty pm. Beyond that we know nothing.' Baxter's dark eyes burn into mine. 'Tomorrow, Ms Glass, we are the point of a very bulky spear. We have to hit our target. If we miss, we lose the best chance we have to surprise our UNSUB into a confession.'

'I get it. Let's have the details.'

Baxter shuffles a stack of papers. 'I'm going to give you a quick sketch of each,' he says. 'This is for John's benefit, too.'

SAC Bowles gets up and kills the lights, and a large screen hanging from the ceiling at the end of the room comes alive with white light.

'I want you to see all four first,' Baxter says. 'See if any look familiar. These images are being relayed from our Emergency Operations Centre.' Baxter leans forward and addresses the speakerphone on the desk. 'Give us the composite, Tom.'

Four photos appear simultaneously on the screen. None looks familiar, or even like what I expected, but why should they be? When

I hear the word 'students', I think of people in their twenties. The oldest here—Roger Wheaton, I presume—is wearing bifocal glasses and reminds me of Max von Sydow, the actor. Severe and Scandinavian-looking, with shoulder-length grey hair. Beside his photo is a fortyish guy who looks like an ex-convict: hollow-eyed, unshaven, tough. Then I realise he's actually wearing prison garb.

'Is that guy a convict?'

'He's done two stretches in Sing Sing,' says Baxter. 'We'll get to that. These faces ring any bells?'

'Not so far.'

The other man in the composite is stunningly handsome, and my sixth sense tells me he's gay. The woman is also attractive, with long black hair, light skin and black eyes. But despite her skin tone, something about her features suggests African blood.

'The older man is Roger Wheaton,' says Baxter. 'The convict is Leon Isaac Gaines, aged forty-two. Raised in Queens, New York. The third man is Frank Smith. He's thirty-five, and also a New York native. The woman is Thalia Laveau, thirty-nine, a native of Terrebonne Parish here in Louisiana. All four suspects lived in New York for a time, so all could have ties to whoever killed Wingate.' He leans towards the speakerphone. 'Put up Wheaton alone.'

The composite vanishes, replaced by a shot of Roger Wheaton.

'Before we do his bio,' says Baxter, 'let's deal with why Wheaton came to New Orleans. Three years ago, this reclusive artist of international reputation was diagnosed with scleroderma, a potentially fatal disease.' Baxter turns to Dr Lenz. 'Arthur?'

Lenz inclines his head towards me as he speaks. 'Scleroderma is vascular in nature, and causes scarring and eventual failure of the internal organs. One symptom in Wheaton's case is called Raynaud's phenomenon. This is a spasm and constriction of the blood vessels of the extremities—usually the fingers, but sometimes the nose or the penis—which is caused by contact with cold temperature. These attacks completely cut off circulation to the digits, sometimes causing irreversible tissue damage. Sufferers frequently wear gloves.'

'Wheaton moved south to avoid this?' I ask.

'Apparently.'

Baxter takes over here, in the tone of a man reading from a cue card. 'Roger Wheaton. Born 1943, in rural Vermont. Youngest of three brothers. He had no formal training as a child, but showed phenomenal talent as an artist, and at seventeen left home for New York. We don't have a lot of information on this period of Wheaton's life, but in interviews he's said he supported himself doing odd jobs and painting portraits on the street. He was unsuccessful as an artist, and in 1966 he joined the Marine Corps. He did two tours in Vietnam, earning a Bronze Star and a Purple Heart. You should also note that he instituted a disciplinary action against members of his platoon for raping a twelve-year-old Vietnamese girl. He lost one brother there.'

Baxter shuffles some papers. 'After Vietnam, Wheaton returned to New York, enrolled in the art programme at NYU, and slowly made a name for himself painting portraits. He supported himself this way for years, while he worked on his private obsession, which is landscapes. For the past twenty years, he's painted the same subject over and over again. It's a forest clearing, and every painting in the series is called 'The Clearing'. He began in a very realistic style, but over the years he's gone more abstract. The paintings are still called The Clearing, but they're not recognisable as such. The early, more realistic ones showed a Vermont-style forest clearing, but also jungle foliage typical of Vietnam—and sometimes the two mixed—so there's no telling about the real origin of the image, or its significance.'

'A progression from realistic to abstract,' says Kaiser. 'The exact opposite of The Sleeping Women.'

'Wheaton's progression is much more marked,' says Lenz. 'His style is so defined now that it's spawned a genre or school in the worldwide art community. They call it "Dark Impressionism". Not because the paintings themselves are necessarily dark—though most of his recent work is—but because of their dark content. As for him painting The Sleeping Women, two connoisseurs have already told us that The Sleeping Women share no similarities whatever with the paintings of Roger Wheaton.'

'Could one man paint two radically different styles and an expert not be able to tell he did both?' asks Baxter.

'If he did it to prove a point, probably. But over the course of a body of work, certain idiosyncrasies reveal themselves.'

Baxter says to the speakerphone, 'Put up Gaines, Tom.'

The photo of Wheaton is replaced by a mugshot of the convict. This guy I would walk across a busy interstate to avoid. Crazed eyes, pasty skin, tangled black hair, a stubbled face, and a broken nose. The only paintbrush I can see him holding would be six inches wide.

'Leon Isaac Gaines,' says Baxter. 'His father and mother were both drunks. The father did a stretch in Sing Sing for carnal knowledge of a fourteen-year-old girl. Leon was arrested repeatedly as a juvenile. Burglary, assault, peeping, arson, you name it.'

Kaiser grunts, and I know why. Arson is one leg of the 'homicidal triangle' of indicators for serial killers as children. Bed-wetting, arson, and cruelty to animals: I remember them from my reading.

'Gaines is a two-time loser, once for aggravated battery, once for attempted rape,' Baxter is saying. 'He never picked up a paintbrush in his life until his first term in Sing Sing—1975. Gaines showed so much promise that the warden showed his stuff to some New York dealers. During his second hitch, he attracted the attention of the New York art community.'

'What does he paint?' asks Kaiser.

'He started with prison scenes. Now he paints nothing but his girl-friend. Whatever girlfriend he has at the time.'

'So Gaines is essentially painting a series, as well?' I ask. 'The same subject again and again? Just like Wheaton and the UNSUB?'

'The others are too, in their ways,' says Lenz. 'Wheaton used this as a criterion in his selection. He's on record as saying that only deep study of a particular subject can produce deeper levels of truth.'

Baxter continues. 'You should note that, as far as we can tell, Gaines regularly abuses every woman he's been with. NOPD has been called to his duplex several times by neighbours, but the girl-friend has yet to swear out a complaint. Gaines is usually drunk when they get there.'

'I think we've got the picture on Gaines,' says Kaiser.

'OK,' says Baxter. 'Let's have Frank Smith, Tom.'

Gaines's face is replaced by the angelic visage I saw earlier.

'Frank Smith,' says Baxter. 'Born into a wealthy family in Westchester County in 1965. He focused on art from an early age, and took an MFA degree from Columbia. Smith is openly gay, and he's painted homosexual themes from his college days.'

'Not nude sleeping men?' asks Kaiser.

'If only,' says Baxter. 'By all reports, Smith is enormously talented, and paints in the style of the old masters.'

'What about the girl?' says Kaiser. 'What's her story?'

'Waste of time,' Lenz says. 'There's no precedent for a woman committing this type of murder.'

'We don't know they *are* murders,' Kaiser says.

'Thalia Laveau,' says Baxter, trying to tamp down any flaring tempers. 'Born on Bayou Terrebonne in 1961. Father a trapper.'

'What did he trap?' asks Kaiser.

'Anything that didn't trap him first,' I answer.

'You know about these people?' Baxter asks.

'We did a story down there when I was on the *Times-Picayune*. It's another world. The whole place smells like drying shrimp.'

'Chime in with anything relevant,' Baxter says. 'Racially, Laveau is part French, part African-American and part Native American.'

'A redbone?' asks Bowles.

'No, that's different,' I tell him. 'Thalia Laveau is what's called a Sabine. Sabines are trappers and fishermen,' I add, thinking back. 'They live in shacks along bayous that lead to the Gulf of Mexico. They're Catholic, but have strange superstitions. There's some voodoo in there, I think. Inbreeding, too. They range from white-skinned, like this woman, to very dark. They're tough people, clannish.'

'As far as we know, Thalia Laveau had no formal training as an artist,' Baxter adds. 'She just started drawing one day and showed a knack for it. She quit school at seventeen and went to New York. There she supported herself in various ways, from waitressing to working in art galleries. She's also worked as an artist's model at Tulane University, and some of that is nude work. The most significant thing we've heard so far is that she's a lesbian.'

'Is that rumour or fact?' I ask.

'Unconfirmed.'

'What does Laveau paint?' asks Kaiser. 'Nude women?'

'No. She goes into the homes of strangers, lives there for a while, then starts painting their lives. Her work doesn't sell for much.'

'Do Leon Gaines's pictures sell?' I ask.

'Somebody paid five thousand for one. He could make a living at it, if he wasn't so deep in debt. He's borrowed to the hilt on student loans, rumoured to have a heroin habit, and owes bookies as well.'

'Laveau and Gaines live pretty close to the bone,' says Kaiser. 'Where are the millions earned from The Sleeping Women?'

'Good question.'

Dr Lenz says, 'Right now I like Wheaton or Frank Smith. They're already wealthy, so they would have the knowledge to hide the money. Gaines is too obvious. And Laveau . . . is a woman.'

'I'm not excluding anybody,' says Kaiser. 'After visiting Cayman, I'm convinced Marcel de Becque could be behind it all. He could easily be commissioning someone to paint the pictures and paying them peanuts compared to the overall take.'

'If de Becque is behind this,' Lenz counters, 'why draw attention to himself by demanding that we send Glass to see him in exchange for photos of his paintings?'

'He's a ballsy guy. He's not scared of us.' Kaiser looks at Baxter without waiting for a response. 'How are we going to handle the approach? Who's going in?'

Baxter walks to the wall and switches on the overhead lights.

'John,' he says, 'I know you've been out at the front on this thing for a long time, which counts for a lot in my—'

'Damn it,' Kaiser mutters.

Baxter implores Kaiser with his hands. 'Listen, John. Because of Wheaton's artistic stature, and because of his medical condition, I'm inclined to let Arthur take the lead on this one.'

Kaiser sits in silence. The medical angle makes argument pointless.

'Normally, I'd be going in as well,' Baxter concludes. 'But because I think you should be there, John, I'm sending you in in my place. If you feel some path is not being explored, you can go down it. OK?'

'Where will you be?' Kaiser asks in a taut voice.

'Surveillance van outside. Arthur's going to wear a wire. It's a major break with Bureau policy, but the Director has personally approved it.'

'And Glass?' Kaiser says without looking at me.

'She'll be in the van with me until Arthur cues her. The code phrase is, "I'm sorry, our photographer was supposed to be here ten minutes ago." That's the story for the suspects: we're not confiscating their paintings, just photographing them. Once we've finished, though, NOPD will be confiscating everything in sight. When Jordan comes in, she won't look directly at the suspect. This will make someone who's shocked by her appearance have to work harder to confirm what his eyes are telling him. The innocent people won't look at her twice—though I'm sure Gaines will ogle her a little. If you come out and say somebody's dirty we bring them in for interrogation.' Baxter looks around the table. 'OK. We'll have another strategy meeting tomorrow morning, here, seven am.'

I try to catch Kaiser's eye, but he gives me nothing. 'I need a bite to eat and some sleep,' I say, rising from my chair.

'Take Agent Travis with you,' Baxter says, meaning Wendy.

'I will.'

'The Camellia Grill is still open,' Kaiser says in an offhand voice. 'You know it?'

'I probably ate there a hundred times in my younger days.'

'Get some sleep, Jordan,' says Baxter. 'Tomorrow's a very big day.'

'I'll see you here at seven.'

Kaiser gives me a wave as I depart, but Dr Lenz simply watches, his wise eyes missing nothing.

THE CAMELLIA GRILL stands at the intersection of Carrollton and St Charles, with the river rolling past just beyond the embankment. Agent Wendy and I have been here long enough to get menus when John Kaiser walks through the door and comes over.

'Could I see you alone for a minute?' he asks Wendy.

She gets up without a word and follows him outside. When they come back in, Wendy goes to the far end of the bar while Kaiser takes her stool beside me.

'What did you say to her?' I ask.

'That I needed to talk to you without Lenz hearing.'

'I see. She's got a crush on you.'

'I never encouraged it.'

'You think that makes it any better for her?'

Kaiser picks up a menu. 'She's a good girl. She can handle it.' He glances up at me, and his eyes seem to hold more understanding than his words. The skin around his eyes is dark with fatigue.

'OK,' I say, looking at my own menu. 'What are we doing here?'

'This is our first date, isn't it?' He says it deadpan, and I laugh.

'Come on. What's going on?'

'Just what I told Wendy. I want to talk to you without Lenz around. I have a certain amount of anxiety that whoever's running this kidnapping thing is ahead of us. Maybe way ahead.'

'What are you going to do about it?'

'We'll get to that. Let's order.'

Kaiser signals a waiter, and we order omelettes and orange juice. Glancing to my left, I catch Wendy watching us over her shoulder.

'What will Baxter say about you talking to me alone?'

'I don't think Wendy will tell him. She'll give us the benefit of the doubt this time. But he certainly wouldn't like what I'm going to say.'

'Which is?'

Kaiser puts his elbows on the counter and rotates his stool so he faces me more directly. 'If I got you a handgun, would you carry it?'

'What would Baxter think about that?'

'He wouldn't like it. And the Office of Professional Responsibility would probably fire me.'

'So why are you suggesting it?'

'Because I think you're in danger. If the UNSUB wants you, he could shoot Wendy before either of you knew he was there. If you're armed, you might have a chance to react in time.'

'You mean kill him?'

'Could you do it?'

'If he shot Wendy in front of me? You're damn straight.'

Our omelettes and juice arrive, but neither of us lifts a fork. Finally, he says, 'May I ask you a personal question?'

'You can ask.'

'You've never been married?'

'That's right. Does that shock you?'

'It surprises me. Not many heterosexual women who look like you make it to forty without getting married at least once.'

'Is that a nice way of asking what's wrong with me?'

Kaiser laughs. 'It's a nice way of being nosy.'

'You'd think I'd be a prize catch, wouldn't you? But in reality it goes like this. I meet a guy. Good-looking, successful, independent. Doctor, journalist, investment banker, A-list actor. Whatever. He can't wait to go out with me. I'm a not-so-ugly woman in what a lot of people see as a glamour job. The first few dates, he shows me off to his friends. We like each other. We get intimate. Then, in a week or a month, I get a new assignment. Afghanistan. Brazil. Bosnia. Egypt. A month on the ground schlepping cameras. Maybe this particular guy is making international partner the next week and wants me at his celebration party. Maybe the Oscars are next week. But I take the assignment. And by the time I get back, he's decided maybe the relationship isn't working out after all. Most guys simply can't take the fact that I have a higher priority than them in my life.'

'I know I'm not the highest priority in your life,' says Kaiser. 'And I'm perfectly OK with that.'

I watch him as he pours hot sauce on his omelette, but I can't read anything in his eyes. 'What are we talking about?'

'I think you know.'

'Well, at least we're on the same page.'

He smiles, and this time his white teeth show and his eyes sparkle. 'I didn't really come here to say that, but I'm glad I did. I feel awkward because of your sister.'

'That has nothing to do with my sister. What happened to Jane only confirmed something I learned long ago. If you wait to do things you want to do, you may be dead before you get the chance.'

'I learned that too. In Vietnam. But it's easy to lose sight of it in the rush of everyday life.' He pauses, then says, 'Can you handle another personal question?'

'Might as well.'

'Lenz told me you weren't close to your sister. Yet you seem to have made it your mission to find her. How do you explain that?'

How do I explain that? 'I didn't tell Lenz everything. Jane and I had problems growing up, yes. Some of those problems lasted into adulthood. But as time passes, family starts to matter. And with our mother in the drunken shape she's in, Jane and I only had each other.'

'You're speaking in the past tense.'

'I don't know what I believe right now. All I know is that I have to find her. Dead, alive, whatever. She's my blood, and I love her. It's that simple. I have to find my sister.'

Kaiser reaches out and squeezes my wrist. 'You will, Jordan.'

'Thanks.'

'Have you ever wanted to settle down, have your own family?'

'I hear the clock ticking. I visited my nephew and niece last night, and my feelings for them overwhelmed me.'

He glances down the counter. 'Wendy said there might have been some trouble over there. At your brother-in-law's.'

'You know, I can take you guys in my life up to a point. But I won't give up all my privacy to be protected.' I take a long sip of my juice and try to keep my temper in check. 'Just what do you know about me, anyway? My medical records? Everything down to my bra size?'

'I don't know your bra size.' His face is absolutely serious.

'Do you want to?'

'I think I'm up to investigating the question.'

'Given adequate time, you mean.'

'Naturally.' He takes a sip of his juice. 'But sadly we don't have adequate time tonight.' He looks again at Wendy, who's making a point of not looking at us. 'The task force is meeting right now. I have to get back, and I don't know when I can get out of it.'

'Speaking of that, you told de Becque you're having trouble matching the abstract faces in the paintings to victims, right?'

Kaiser nods. 'Eleven victims, nineteen paintings. Two major problems. There could be victims we don't know about. Maybe they were hookers or runaways, and nobody reported them missing. Maybe we've actually found their bodies, but since they match the more abstract paintings, we can't tell. But I have gone over every homicide and missing person in New Orleans for the past three years, and we only have a handful of possibles, none very likely.'

'How many paintings have you matched to known victims?'

'Six definitive matches. Two probables. But the faces are so vague in some of the paintings that we're not getting anywhere with them.'

'Who do you have working on them?'

'The University of Arizona. They've done great work for us in the past with digital photo enhancement. But it's not happening this time.'

'I think that's because what you want in this case isn't really photo enhancement. The distortions you want to correct aren't the result of blur or a lack of resolution, they're distortions created in the mind of a human being, perhaps an insane one.'

'What do you suggest?'

'I recall a colleague telling me about a system that was being developed for the government. Its purpose was to try to bring visual coherence out of chaos. He called it Argus. You know, the mythical beast with a hundred eyes?'

'I'll ask Baxter to see what he can find out.'

'OK. There's my contribution. Is the Bureau buying this meal?'

'I think the Bureau can afford it.' Apropos of nothing, Kaiser reaches out and touches my hand, and a thrill races up my arm. 'Look,' he says, with another glance at Wendy, 'why don't we—'

I pull back my hand. 'Let's not push it, OK? It's there. We know it's there. Let's see what happens.'

He nods slowly. 'OK. It's your call.'

Outside, Kaiser bids us farewell and leaves for the field office. Wendy doesn't talk on the way back to her apartment. Much as I like her, I think tomorrow would be a good day to find a hotel.

7

I'm sitting in a cramped FBI surveillance van on the campus of Tulane University. The oaks are still in leaf and the lawns shine in the sun. Twenty yards away from the van stands the Woldenberg Art Centre, a stately old brick complex that houses the university's art departments and the Newcomb Art Gallery.

Thirty seconds ago, John Kaiser and Arthur Lenz went through the doors of the gallery to meet Roger Wheaton, the artist in residence at the university. The president of the university had set up the interview an hour ago, asking Wheaton to cooperate with us, even though he thought the idea that Wheaton could be involved in any crime was absurd.

The interior of the van is uncomfortably warm, even at 9.00am. 'Before there were female agents,' says Baxter, 'we stripped down to our shorts in these things.'

'Don't hesitate on my account. I'll strip myself if I have to stay in here much longer.'

Baxter laughs. At his request, I'm wearing a skirt suit and heels, so that I'll look more feminine to the suspects when I go in. A female field agent was dispatched to Dillard's department store this morning with a list of my sizes. Getting the store to open early was apparently no trick for SAC Bowles, but trying on the various selections caused me to miss most of this morning's strategy meeting.

'Wheaton had no problem with being questioned?' I ask.

'Not so long as we talked to him while he's working. Apparently he's obsessive about his schedule and currently working on a painting that takes up a whole room. Multiple canvases stretched over curved frames to form a circle, to create a feeling that you're walking into this clearing he's painting.'

'We're going in,' says Lenz into his concealed microphone.

A knocking sound reverberates from the small monitor speaker on the console before us. Then the sound of a door opening.

'What the hell?' says Kaiser.

'It's the painting,' says Lenz. 'Keep going. There, to your right.'

There's a pause. 'Are you Roger Wheaton?' asks Kaiser.

A deep voice says, 'Yes. Are you the gentlemen from the FBI?'

'I'm Special Agent Kaiser. This is Dr Arthur Lenz. Dr Lenz is a forensic psychiatrist.'

'How curious. Well, good day to you both. How can I help you?'

'We have some questions for you, Mr Wheaton. They shouldn't take too long.'

'Good. I like to get the paint on quickly.'

'This painting is . . . stupendous,' says Lenz, his voice filled with awe. 'It's your masterpiece.'

'I hope so,' Wheaton replies. 'It's my last.'

'The last "Clearing" you mean? But why stop now?'

When Wheaton answers, his voice is heavy with regret. 'My health isn't what it once was. You have some questions, the president said?'

'Mr Wheaton,' says Kaiser, 'as you are probably aware, over the past eighteen months, eleven women have disappeared from the New Orleans area without trace. We're here about those disappearances. You see, some of the victims have turned up, in a manner of speaking.'

'You've discovered some bodies?'

'Not exactly. We've discovered a series of paintings depicting these women.'

'*Paintings?* Paintings of the missing women?'

'Correct. In these paintings, the women are nude, and posed in positions of sleep. Possibly in death.'

I touch Baxter's arm. 'I thought Dr Lenz was going to take the lead on the questions.'

'Arthur wanted John to ask the questions that have to be asked. He'll jump in when he's ready. Arthur's a subtle guy.'

'Mr Wheaton,' says Kaiser, 'in examining these paintings forensically, we've recovered some hairs from them. The hairs come from a special type of paintbrush. A very fine grade kolinsky sable produced by one small factory in Manchuria. There's only one US importer, and he sells a very limited quantity. To select customers.'

'And Tulane University was one of those customers. Now I see. Of course. I placed that order. I use them for fine work in my oils.'

'Have you always used the rare kolinsky brushes?'

'No.' This time the pause seems interminable. 'Three years ago I was diagnosed with an autoimmune disease that affects my hands and fingers. I've had to alter the mechanics of my brush stroke. I experimented for a while, and finally discovered the kolinskys. They worked so well that I encouraged my students to try them.'

'I see. How many people have access to these brushes?'

'My graduate students, of course. But anyone could walk in here and take one if they really wanted to. We'd have to have twenty-four-hour guards to keep them out.'

'Mr Wheaton,' Kaiser says in an apologetic tone, 'I hesitate to ask this, but would you have any trouble providing alibis for a group of dates over the past eighteen months?'

'Are you saying I'm a suspect in these terrible crimes?'

'Anyone with access to these brushes is by definition a suspect. Do you know where you were three nights ago, after the opening at the museum? Say from eight forty-five to nine fifteen?'

'I was at home. And I foresee your next question. I was alone, as it happens. Should I contact an attorney?'

'That's your prerogative. I wouldn't want to influence you either way.'

'I see.' Wheaton is answering more slowly now.

'Would you mind telling us how you selected each of your graduate students?' asks Kaiser.

'I suppose not. Each applicant submitted paintings for review. I initially looked at photos sent through the mail. Then I flew down and examined a group of paintings by each of the finalists.'

'Could you give us a verbal sketch of each student?'

'I really don't know that much about them.'

'Frank Smith, say.'

There's a long silence. 'I'm very fond of Frank,' Wheaton says finally. 'He's a talented boy. He's never known financial hardship, but I think his childhood was difficult. He had one of those fathers, you know. Great expectations, of the conventional kind. I don't know what else to say.'

'Have you ever seen Frank Smith get violent?'

'*Violent?* He's passionate about his work. But violent? No. He rubs a lot of people up the wrong way, though. Frank knows everything there is to know about art history, and he doesn't suffer fools gladly. You can imagine how that affects a man like Leon Gaines.'

'Why don't you tell us?'

'Leon would probably have killed Frank by now if it wouldn't put him in the penitentiary for life. It would make him a three-time loser, you see. They'd never let him out again.'

'Tell us about Gaines.'

Wheaton sighs loudly. 'Leon is a tortured soul who'll never rid himself of his demons. Not even through his art.'

'Are you aware that Gaines beats his girlfriend?'

'I have no idea what Leon does in his spare time, but nothing would surprise me. And his paintings are full of that kind of thing.'

'Do you think he's capable of murder?'

'We're all capable of killing, Agent Kaiser. Surely you know that.'

'You served in Vietnam,' Kaiser says. 'Is that right?'

'You must know I did.'

'You had quite a distinguished record.'

'I did what was asked of me.'

'You did more than that. You won a Bronze Star. They didn't hand out medals for digging foxholes.'

'No. It was a straightforward enough action. My company was pinned down in a paddy field. Our sergeant had stepped on a mine that took off his leg above the knee. Two men went out after him. Both were shot dead by a sniper. The weather was too bad to call in napalm on the sniper, and our artillery couldn't seem to get him either. The sergeant screamed that if anyone else came out after him, he was going to pull the pin on one of his own grenades. But he was bleeding to death, so I went and got him.'

'Just like that?'

'That's the way it was sometimes. The sniper shot at me but missed.'

'That's the way it is, all right.'

'You were in Vietnam?' Wheaton asks Kaiser.

'Yes. What about the rape incident?'

More dead air as Wheaton adjusts to the shift of conversational gears; Kaiser has gone from comrade-in-arms to adversary in two seconds. 'What about it?' he asks eventually.

'It must have cost you some friends, to push it as far as you did.'

'I was raised to treat women with respect, Agent Kaiser. No matter what language they speak or what colour they are.'

I feel like cheering aloud.

'Was it an attempted rape, or a fait accompli?'

'I walked in on the crime in progress. We were checking a ville for weapons caches, and I heard screams from a hootch near the back.'

'And what did you do?'

'I told them to stop, but they just laughed, so I held up my weapon and threatened to shoot them.'

'What happened next?'

'They cursed me and threatened to kill me, but they stopped.'

'You reported the incident right then?'

'That's right. Is this relevant to your investigation?'

'I have no idea, sir. But we have to ask about everything. I appreciate your being frank with us, though. That says a lot in your favour.'

'Does it?'

The sound of fabric rubbing against the mike tells me Lenz is moving around the room. 'Mr Wheaton, as a forensic psychiatrist, I'm also a medical doctor. If you don't mind, I'd like to ask about your disease, and how it's affected your work.'

'That's something I'd prefer not to talk about.'

Lenz doesn't immediately reply, but I can imagine the laserlike stare that must be searching Roger Wheaton's face at this moment. 'I understand,' the psychiatrist says finally. 'But I'm afraid I must insist. Such diagnoses deeply affect human psychology, as I'm sure you know. I see you're wearing gloves. Has the move south relieved your Raynaud's phenomenon to any degree?'

'Somewhat. But I still have frequent episodes.'

'Are you being treated?'

'I fully understand my situation, Dr Lenz. I'm an artist. I have no family. My priority is my work and I shall do my work for as long as I can. When I die, my work will live after me. That's more satisfaction than most men will ever know.'

'Come on,' Baxter murmurs, anxiously tapping the console before him. 'Get her in there.'

But Lenz doesn't know when to quit. 'I'd like to move on to—'

'I apologise, Mr Wheaton,' Kaiser says sharply. 'Our photographer was supposed to be here ten minutes ago. If—'

'*Go!*' Baxter says, slapping my knee.

I throw open the van's rear door, and in seconds I'm clacking across the sidewalk, fighting to keep my balance in unfamiliar heels, my heart pounding against my sternum.

The smell of oil paint hits me as I go through the door, and grows stronger as I move towards the Newcomb Art Gallery where I find myself facing a curved white wall. Then I see wooden framing: the back of Wheaton's room-sized canvas circle. To my right is an opening in the curved wall. As I go through, I concentrate on Baxter's instructions to act detached and professional, but my first sight of the painting stops me in my tracks.

The circle of joined canvas panels is eight feet high and at least thirty-five feet across. The scale alone inspires awe. But it's the image itself that takes my breath away. I feel as though I've walked into J.R.R. Tolkien's Mirkwood, a shadowy world where roots wind around the feet and gnarled limbs bind the throat, where tangled vines conceal things we wish would remain out of sight. Through this dark world winds a narrow black stream, occasionally rippling white over rocks or fallen branches. The scene shocks me because I expected something abstract, as all Wheaton's later work has been. Only one curved panel is unfinished, and before it stands Wheaton himself, paintbrush and palette in his white-gloved hands.

The size of the artist is my second shock. The head shot I saw last night gave me the impression of a slight man, but Wheaton is only an inch shorter than Kaiser, who stands six foot two. He has wiry arms but large hands, and shoulders only slightly bowed by age. He has a full head of silver hair that sweeps back from his forehead, some of it reaching his shoulders. He gives the impression of a man who has reached a place of extraordinary peace.

'Is this your photographer?' he asks, and then he smiles at me.

Wheaton's smile fades as he turns to Lenz, who like Kaiser has not even heard the artist's question, so intent is he on picking up signals of recognition in Wheaton's face. I could save them the trouble. This guy has never seen me before in his life.

'Yes, sir,' I say loudly, trying to snap them out of it.

Wheaton turns back to me. 'What are you here to photograph?'

'Your work.'

'Well, fire away. As long as your pictures will be held by the FBI, that is. I don't want reporters seeing this until I've completed it.'

'Absolutely,' Kaiser says. 'They'll be held in strict confidence.'

Kaiser glances at me, and I see instantly that he too shares my judgment of Wheaton. The big Vermonter has no idea who I am. With the Mamiya camera I used at de Becque's, I take a few flash shots of various panels of the painting, but it's all a sham. Many of Wheaton's paintings will be confiscated as soon as this interview ends, and I feel guilty being part of this charade.

As I work, Wheaton drags a ladder to the unfinished panel, laboriously climbs it, then begins painting with small strokes about seven feet up. A few times in my career, I've sensed I was in the presence of true greatness. I have that feeling now. I have a powerful desire to shoot Wheaton, to document the artist at work. After a moment's hesitation, I take a few shots of him, and he doesn't seem to mind.

Lenz and Kaiser have moved across the room to confer quietly, and I sense that they're ready to move on. Sure enough, Kaiser catches my eye and nods at me to wrap it up. I finish out the roll then walk up to the ladder and offer Wheaton my hand as a gesture of thanks. Leaving his brush and palette atop the ladder, Wheaton climbs down and gives my hand a gentle shake.

'Thanks for making that easy for me,' I say.

The artist smiles shyly. 'It's very easy to tolerate the attentions of a pretty girl.' He looks up, his eyes narrowed behind the bifocals. 'Have you always worked for the FBI?'

'No. I was a photojournalist before.' This is not exactly a lie.

He studies me a bit longer, then smiles again. 'Please stop by and tell me about it some time. Photography interests me.'

'I'll try to do that.'

'Mr Wheaton,' says Kaiser, 'I want you to know how much we appreciate your help. The New Orleans police will probably want to talk to you as well. My advice is to cooperate as fully as you can. It will end the ordeal sooner than anything else.'

Dr Lenz says, 'We must also ask you to refrain from contacting your graduate students about this. I'm sure you understand.'

The artist looks as if he understands all too well.

'Oh, one more thing. Leon Gaines paints women exclusively. Sometimes nude, sometimes not. Frank Smith paints nude men. Have you ever known him to paint nude women?'

Wheaton shakes his head. We are nearly to the door when he calls: 'Thalia Laveau paints women. Is that important?'

'What do you mean?' asks Kaiser. 'Women working in their homes? Like that?'

'No. Her documentary paintings actually surprised me. Because the audition paintings she submitted were nude studies.'

'Of women?' Lenz almost whispers.

'Exclusively.'

'COME ON!' Baxter shouts from the open door of the surveillance van. 'Get in! The NOPD surveillance team has just reported that Leon Gaines is fighting with his girlfriend right now. They can hear him yelling out in the street.'

We scrunch into the cramped van and squat in the heat, our faces inches apart.

'What do we know about the girlfriend?' asks Lenz.

'Name's Linda Knapp,' Baxter replies. 'She's twenty-nine and a barmaid. He's been with her on and off for a little over a year. So. Do we talk to him now or do we wait?'

'Now,' says Kaiser. 'Go in hard, settle him down, then bring Jordan in.'

Baxter turns to me, and says, 'This isn't like talking to Roger Wheaton, Jordan. Gaines is a violent felon.'

'I signed your release this morning. Kaiser's armed, and there'll be cops outside. I'm ready.'

Baxter slaps the panel separating us from the van's driver. The motor roars, and we lurch backwards, then forwards. As we roll off the campus, Kaiser catches my eye and gives me a nod of gratitude.

LEON GAINES lives in a house on Freret Street, near the river. It's in a mostly black neighbourhood, where people mind their own business. Our driver stops a couple of driveways up from Gaines's place.

Baxter opens the door. Kaiser gets out and starts up the cracked sidewalk, Dr Lenz working hard to keep pace with him. After a few seconds, Lenz's nervous voice comes from the speakers. 'I can hear Gaines yelling from here,' he says.

Their shoes bang on wooden steps; then a hard knocking echoes through the van. 'Leon Gaines!' shouts Kaiser. 'Open up! FBI!'

The unmistakable sound of a door being jerked open comes from the speakers. Then a New York accent laced with alcohol booms, 'Who the hell are you? Pencil-dicks from the finance company? If you are, I got something for you.'

'I'm Special Agent John Kaiser, FBI. And I've got something for you, Leon. A search warrant. Step back from the door.'

'FBI?' A puzzled silence. 'Search warrant? For what?'

'We've got two choices here, Leon,' Kaiser says in a voice I hardly recognise. 'We can step inside and talk, or we can search this dump. Right now I just want to talk. But if I don't like what I hear, we'll have to search, and we might conceivably stumble across some drugs. Or a gun. Either beef would put you right into Sing Sing—'

There's a scuffling noise as they move inside. 'What do you want to talk about?'

'Eleven women have disappeared from New Orleans over the past year and a half. You know about that?'

'Yeah. So?'

'We found a series of paintings that show these missing women. In the paintings, the women are nude and posed like they're asleep or dead.'

'So?'

'The last sold for over a million bucks.'

'Do I look like I just made a million bucks to you?'

'Your paintings reveal a predilection for violence,' says Lenz.

'Who the hell are you?'

'This is Dr Lenz, Leon,' says Kaiser. 'You speak to him with respect, or you'll be funding the Vaseline concession at Sing Sing.'

Gaines says nothing.

'This artist doesn't sign his work. But we've found some rare sable brush hairs in the paint on some of them. Sound familiar?'

There's a pause as Gaines works it out. 'It's those expensive brushes Wheaton got us. Right?'

'Right. So where were you three nights ago, after the opening at the museum?'

'Right here.'

'Can anybody verify that?'

'*Linda!*' Gaines yells, clipping the mike Lenz is wearing.

There's a pause; then Kaiser says, 'Ms Knapp?'

'Who's asking?' says a scratchy female voice.

'I'm with the FBI. Could you tell us—'

'Tell these guys we were here after the NOMA thing,' Gaines cuts in. 'They don't believe me.'

'Shit,' mutters Baxter.

'That's right,' the woman says. 'We came straight home. We were here all night.'

'Can anyone else confirm that?' asks Kaiser.

'No,' says Gaines. 'We were having some quality time, you know?'

'Right,' Kaiser says wearily.

'That's all,' Gaines says, dismissing his girlfriend.

'Tell me about Roger Wheaton,' Lenz asks.

'The guy's dying, but he keeps working and he doesn't bitch. Sometimes his fingers turn blue, man. *Blue*. There's no blood going to them. It's agony. But he just sits down and waits until it stops, then goes right back to work.'

'You clearly respect him,' says Lenz. 'What about Frank Smith?'

Gaines makes a spitting sound.

'You don't like Smith? What about his paintings?'

Gaines laughs in derision. 'The nude fag series? He copies the old masters so the stuff looks less like porn, then pawns it off on ignorant queens from New York. It's a sweet scam, I'll give him that.'

'What about Thalia Laveau?' asks Lenz.

Another pause, as though Gaines is debating whether to answer. 'She's a tasty piece, if you like dark meat. But she just paints the poor and downtrodden. Who wants to buy that?'

'Do you know a man named Marcel de Becque?' asks Lenz.

'Never heard of him.'

'We're going to want to take some pictures,' Kaiser says in a detached voice. 'Our photographer was supposed to be here already, but I'm sure we can find something to talk about in the meantime.'

Baxter slaps my knee. '*Go*. And if it gets rough, hit the floor.'

He opens the door, and I'm on the concrete, moving up the line of houses. I feel a moment's trepidation as I reach for the handle to Gaines's door, but the knowledge that Kaiser has a gun settles me enough to knock and go through.

The first thing that hits me is the smell. The scents of paint and oil that made Wheaton's studio so pleasant are here smothered by the stink of mildew, stale beer, rotting food, tobacco and marijuana.

'Who's this?' asks Gaines.

There's a strange caesura as Kaiser and Lenz judge his reaction to me. I busy myself with my camera.

'She's our photographer,' says Kaiser. He points at a large easel standing in a corner, a cloth thrown over it. 'Is that painting yours?'

'Yeah,' Gaines replies, and from the sound of his voice I can tell he's still looking at me.

I give him my face, searching his eyes for signs of recognition. They're dark coals set in yellow sclera, and they look permanently wide, like a hyperthyroid patient's, the effect exaggerated by dark half-moons beneath them. Three days' growth of beard stubbles his face.

'Take the sheet off the painting so she can shoot it,' Kaiser orders.

Because I expected so little, Gaines's painting is startlingly power-ful. A lank-haired blonde woman with a hard face sits at a kitchen table in the harsh light of a bare bulb. She's surrounded by dirty cereal bowls and her shirt is open to the waist. Her hollow eyes look out from the canvas with the sullen resignation of an animal that has helped build its own cage. It's hard to imagine such truthful art coming from the creature standing across the room.

I set the flash on the Mamiya and start shooting, doing my best to ignore Gaines, whose eyes I feel like greasy fingers on my skin. Gaines moves closer to me. 'I can tell you like my picture. You ought to come back later and let me paint you.'

'*Shut up, you cheating bastard!*'

I whirl to find the blonde woman from the painting charging into the room. Wild eyes flash in her pale face and a livid red mark the size of a fist covers one cheek from eye to mouth.

'Get back in there!' Gaines yells, his right hand balled into a fist.

Kaiser interposes himself between Gaines and the girl, who's wear-ing only a thin nightgown. 'Has this man assaulted you, miss?'

'He fucked me over, is what he done!' The girl looks at me with a defiant rage. 'Don't let them crazy eyes get you, honey, he's a loser.'

'Like you'd know?' Gaines yells. 'This lady's got class.'

'Yeah? That means she don't lay down with trash like you.'

Gaines lunges at her, but Kaiser does something with his foot and suddenly Gaines is on the floor, clutching his knee with both hands.

'I think you'd better come with us,' Kaiser tells her.

'I got nowhere to go he can't find me.'

'We can arrange a shelter. A protected place.'

'You try it, slut,' Gaines groans.

'Maybe I will go with you,' the girl says to Kaiser.

When he nods, she runs into the back of the house, and after some scuffling sounds, returns with a bag and a holdall filled with clothes.

'You can forget what I said before,' she says. 'I don't know where he was three nights ago. He was supposed to come back after the NOMA opening, but he never did.'

Gaines stares up from the floor with murder in his eyes.

'Well, Leon,' says Kaiser, walking towards the door. 'I think you've got a problem. The NOPD will be in touch.'

Once on the sidewalk, Kaiser signals to someone I can't see. A man in plain clothes and a shoulder holster jogs up the street, con-fers with Kaiser, then leads Gaines's girlfriend away. The three of us gather by the opened rear door of the van.

Baxter looks expectantly at us. 'What do you think?'

'It's not Gaines,' says Lenz. 'Jordan didn't spook him a bit. He'd never seen her before.'

Baxter turns to me. 'What did you think about him?'

'I know he seems too obvious. But there was something in him that repelled me on a whole other level. Does that make sense?'

'Yes,' says Kaiser. 'I felt it too.'

Baxter says, 'NOPD's ready to go in now and tear the place apart. Is that what we want?'

'They're bound to find drugs or weapons,' says Kaiser. 'We could put him in Sing Sing and see if the kidnappings stop.'

'For all we know, the painter is a replaceable element in the equation,' says Lenz.

'But we'll learn more by trailing him than jailing him,' Kaiser says.

Baxter looks at Lenz, who nods.

Baxter presses a button on the console and speaks into his headset mike. 'Ed? Roust Gaines, but if you can keep from arresting him, we'd like you to leave him in place . . . . Thanks.' He knocks on the front panel, and the van heads for the more agreeable ambiance of the French Quarter.

8

'Roger Wheaton called Frank Smith and warned him we're coming,' Baxter says, pulling off his headset. 'Wiretap just picked it up.'

We're parked across the street from a beautiful Creole cottage on Esplanade, the eastern border of the French Quarter.

'The call actually makes Wheaton look less suspicious,' Kaiser says. 'He's not stupid. He knows he's a suspect, which probably means a wiretap, but he made the warning call anyway. That's what somebody does when they're innocent and pissed off.'

'Has he made calls to Thalia Laveau or Leon Gaines?' asks Lenz.

'Not yet,' Baxter replies. 'Only Smith.'

Kaiser and Lenz leave the van and slam the door.

Baxter presses his face to the van's tinted porthole window. 'Hey, look at this.'

I put my cheek to his, and my eyes to the darkened porthole.

Frank Smith stands waiting for Kaiser and Lenz on his porch. He's sleek and handsome, his tan set off by white tropical clothing, linen or silk. He has large vivid eyes and an ironic smile on his lips.

Through the speakers, Frank Smith's voice has the festive tone of a man greeting party guests. 'Hello! Are you the gentlemen from the FBI? When do the storm troopers arrive?'

'What a smart-ass,' mutters Kaiser. 'There are no storm troopers, Mr Smith. Because of certain evidence, you've become a suspect in some very serious crimes. We're here to ask you some questions.'

'Well, I don't have an alibi for the night the woman was taken from Dorignac's. I was here, alone, listening to music.' Smith holds out his hands as if for handcuffs. 'Let's get it over with.'

'We can talk here, in a civil manner,' says Kaiser, 'or the police can haul you downtown.'

Smith laughs. 'My God, it's Humphrey Bogart in platform shoes. Why don't we go into the salon? I'll have coffee brought in.'

Footsteps and a closing door echo in the van, then Smith says, 'Juan? Three coffees, please.'

'*Sí.*'

'Mr Smith,' Lenz begins, 'I'm Arthur Lenz, a forensic psychiatrist. This is Special Agent John Kaiser. We—'

'Let me save you both some time,' Smith interrupts. 'You're here because of the women who've been vanishing. You've discovered that the series of paintings known as The Sleeping Women depicts these women. Some bit of evidence has led you to Roger Wheaton's programme at Tulane, so you're questioning Wheaton and the rest of us.'

'You sound as if you were already aware of The Sleeping Women,' says Kaiser.

'I was. I heard about them from a friend in Asia.'

'How did you feel about the prospect that women might be dying to produce those paintings?' asks Lenz.

'I haven't seen the paintings, so that's difficult to answer.'

'Do you mean the quality of the paintings would determine your view of the morality of women dying to produce them?'

'To paraphrase Wilde, Doctor, there's no such thing as a moral or immoral painting. A painting is either well done or badly done. The circumstances involved in their creation are irrelevant.'

'That sounds familiar,' says Kaiser.

'How so?' asks Smith.

'Do you know a man named Marcel de Becque?'

'No. But I did know Christopher Wingate.'

'Why would you bring up Christopher Wingate?' asks Lenz.

'Let's not play games, Doctor. I heard about Wingate's death. I knew he was the dealer for The Sleeping Women. I thought nothing of it at the time. But now that the paintings are connected with possible murders, I see his death in a different light.'

'How did you know Wingate?' asks Kaiser.

'A mutual friend introduced us at a party in New York.'

'I'm going to ask you a sensitive question,' says Lenz. 'Please don't take offence. This is very important. Is Roger Wheaton gay?'

Smith barks a little laugh that's hard to read. 'Did you ask Roger?'

'No. I wasn't sure, and I didn't want to offend him.'

'I'm offended for him.'

'When people are dying, private matters often must become public. If you won't answer the question, I will have to ask Wheaton. Is that what you want me to do?'

After a pause, Smith says, 'I wouldn't say Roger is gay.'

'Have you ever seen him out with a woman?' Lenz asks.

'Roger doesn't "go out". He's either home or at the university. And yes, he has female guests.'

'Does he have particular male friends?'

'I flatter myself that I'm his friend.'

'Would you have any problem giving us your whereabouts on a particular set of dates?' asks Kaiser.

'I wouldn't think so. But I happen to know that the incidence of homosexual serial killers is zero. So I think you'd have some difficulty persuading a jury I'm a good candidate for harassment in this case.'

'We're not focusing on you as a suspect,' Lenz says. 'You're simply one of four people with access to particular brush hairs taken from Sleeping Women canvases.'

'Tell me about these hairs.'

Kaiser quickly summarises the link between the factory in Manchuria, the New York importer and Wheaton's special orders. Then he asks, 'What do you think of Roger Wheaton's work?'

'Roger isn't like the rest of us. He paints from within. I try to do it. But the external is an important part of the process for me. I plan, I use models, rigorous technique. I strive to capture beauty, to freeze and yet animate it. Roger doesn't use models or photographs. When he paints, the divine simply flows out through his brush.'

'Do you know anything about the clearing he supposedly paints? Is it a real place?'

'I assume it is, or was, but I really don't think it matters.'

'It may well matter in relation to these crimes,' says Lenz.

'Are you really looking at Roger as a suspect? That's ludicrous. He's the gentlest man I know. Also the most ethical.'

'This is a waste of time,' Kaiser says testily. 'Our photographer should be here any minute.'

Baxter takes hold of my elbow. 'Move. Go, go, go.'

I cross Esplanade to Frank Smith's cottage. My knock is answered by a beautiful Hispanic boy of about nineteen. Juan, I presume.

'I'm from the FBI. I'm here to take some pictures,' I tell him.

'*Si.* Follow me.'

A few steps and a left turn take us to the salon, where the others sit drinking coffee. Frank Smith looks up as I reach the door, and though I intended to keep my eyes on my camera, I find myself looking square into his face. The young painter has sea-green eyes, an aquamarine shade I've only seen in the eyes of women. They're set in a deeply tanned face, above a Roman nose and sensual mouth. Suddenly recalling my purpose for being here, I blink and turn to Kaiser. 'I'm sorry I'm late. What do you want me to shoot?'

'Anything by Mr Smith here.'

Frank Smith hasn't taken his eyes off me, and I'm eerily certain that he has seen me before. Me or my sister.

'I beg your pardon,' he says. 'Have we met?'

I clear my throat. 'I don't think so.'

'In San Francisco, perhaps? Have you been there?'

I live there when I'm not working . . . 'Yes, but not for—'

'My God, you're Jordan Glass.'

Kaiser, Lenz and I stare at one another like fools.

'I might not have recognised you,' Smith says, 'but with the camera, something just clicked. Don't tell me you've joined the FBI?'

'No.'

'Well, what in the world are you doing here?'

The truth has a voice of its own. 'My sister was one of the victims.'

Smith's mouth drops open. 'Oh, no.'

Kaiser is glaring at me like I shouldn't have given away the game, but once Smith recognised me, there was no point in continuing.

'We were identical twins,' I explain.

The artist's eyes narrow as he tries to understand; it doesn't take him long. 'You're a stalking-horse! They're using you to try to panic the killer into revealing himself.' He shakes his head in amazement. 'Well, I'm happy to meet you, despite the circumstances. I love your work. I have for years.'

'Thank you.'

'How did you recognise her?' asks Lenz.

Smith directs his answer to me. 'Someone pointed you out to me at a party in San Francisco.'

'I love the cottage,' I tell him, laying a hand on his arm to gauge his reaction. He clearly enjoys it. 'Do you have a garden?'

Smith beams. 'Of course. Follow me.' Without paying the slightest bit of attention to Kaiser or Lenz, he escorts me to a walled garden filled with citrus plants, roses, and a gnarled wisteria that's probably as old as the house. Rushing water from a three-tiered fountain fills the courtyard with sound, but what holds me rapt is the light—glorious sunlight falling softly through the foliage with the same clarity I remember so clearly from Marcel de Becque's Sleeping Women.

'It's lovely,' I say, wondering if my sister ever lay unconscious or dead on the paving bricks before me.

'You have a standing invitation. Please call any time.'

My second invitation today. 'I just might do that.'

Footsteps sound on the porch behind us. Kaiser says, 'Mr Smith, we'd like you to keep Ms Glass's presence in New Orleans to yourself.'

'Spoilsport,' Smith retorts, cutting his eyes at me. 'They're no fun at all, are they?' Taking my arm, he leads me back through the house to Esplanade Avenue. 'Remember,' he says. 'You're always welcome.'

I nod but do not speak, and without a word to Kaiser or Lenz, Smith turns and goes back into his cottage, leaving us on the street.

THALIA LAVEAU LIVES on the first floor of a three-storey Victorian house near Tulane University. Nine other women and two men live in the house, which is a nightmare for the NOPD surveillance team.

The door to Thalia's apartment stands at the head of some rickety wooden steps attached to the peeling clapboard exterior of the house. I cling to the handrail as I climb the steps, since I'm about as comfortable in heels as I would be in snowshoes. I knock loudly and wait, wondering if I was crazy to persuade Baxter to let me do this interview alone. The odds of Thalia Laveau being involved are low and I thought I'd be able to get her to open up far more to me alone than to Kaiser and Lenz. After a moment, I hear footsteps.

'Who is it?' calls a voice muffled by the wood.

'My name is Jordan Glass. I want to talk to you about your paintings.' Discreetly, I check that the microphone clipped to my bra is still securely in place.

There's a sound of bolts sliding back; then the door opens to the length of a chain lock. One dark eye peeks out and examines me.

'Who did you say you are?'

So much for my face rattling her into a confession. 'Ms Laveau, do you know about the women who've been disappearing from New Orleans over the past eighteen months?'

'What about them?'

'One of them was my sister. I'm trying to find out if she is alive or dead, and the FBI is helping me. Or letting me help them, rather.'

The dark eye blinks. 'I'm sorry. But what's that got to do with me?'

'I found some paintings of the victims. They're all nudes, posed like they're either dead or asleep. The FBI found special sable paintbrush hairs stuck in the paint, and they traced them to Roger Wheaton's programme at Tulane. No one really believes you're involved, but the fact that you have access to these special brushes forces the FBI to try to rule you out.'

I hear her sigh. 'I guess you want to come in?'

'I'd like to, if you'll talk to me.'

The eye disappears and the door closes. The chain rattles, and then the door opens again. I slip through before she can change her mind.

Facing Thalia Laveau at last, I realise how misleading her photograph was. In the pictures I saw yesterday, her black hair looked cornsilk fine, but today it's done in long thick strings that look like dreadlocks. Her skin is as light as mine, despite her African blood, but her eyes are a piercing black. She's wearing a colourful robe that looks Caribbean, and her expression is that of a woman comfortable in her own skin and amused by the pretensions of others.

'Come into the back,' she says. Her voice is without accent, which tells me she's worked hard to get rid of the sound of her childhood. I follow her through an empty door frame into a larger room, furnished with spartan taste. There's a sofa, which she motions me to, and a chair, which she takes. After she sits, a heavy striped cat that looks half wild creeps from behind her chair and settles in her lap. Thalia sits with remarkable ease, waiting for me to explain myself.

'I won't lie to you, Thalia,' I start. 'After I leave, the police are going to come here and question you about your whereabouts on the nights the women disappeared. Will you have any trouble giving alibis for those nights?'

'I don't know. I spend a lot of time alone.'

'What about three nights ago, after the NOMA event?'

Confusion clouds her eyes. 'The papers said the woman taken that night was unrelated to the others.'

'I know. The FBI has its own way of working.'

'Then—oh God. He's still taking them. And you think I—'

'I don't think anything, Thalia. I was just asking a question and hoping you had an answer that could keep the police off your back.'

'I came straight home and did some yoga.'

'Did anyone see you or call you? Anyone who could confirm that?' Lines of worry now. 'I don't think so. Like I said, I'm alone a lot.'

I nod, uncertain which way to go with her. 'Thalia, why did you want to study under Roger Wheaton?' I ask finally.

'Are you kidding? It was a one-in-a-million opportunity. I always loved his paintings. I couldn't believe it when he selected me.'

'I believe you submitted female nudes for your audition paintings?'

'Yes.' Her hand goes to her mouth. 'My nudes make me look like a suspect, don't they?'

'To some people. Why did you switch from nudes to painting people in their homes?'

'I don't know. Frustration, I guess. My nudes weren't selling, except to businessmen who wanted something for their offices. Something arty with tits, you know? I wasn't put on earth to fulfil that function.'

I nod in understanding. 'Thalia, do you know a man named Christopher Wingate?'

She shakes her head. 'Who is he?'

'A big art dealer in New York. He's the man who sold the paintings of the victims. The series is called The Sleeping Women.'

'Do they sell?'

'The last one sold for two million dollars.'

'*God.*' She closes her eyes and shakes her head. 'The buyer was a man, of course.'

'Yes. A Japanese.'

'Isn't that typical? A dead, naked woman sells for two million dollars. Do you think a landscape by the same artist would have sold for that?'

'I don't know.'

'Of course it wouldn't!' Thalia sits with her mouth shut tight, as though she refuses to lower herself to discuss what makes her so angry.

'Tell me about Leon Gaines. What do you think about him?'

'Leon's a pig. He's always sniffing around, telling me what he'd like to do to me. He offered me five hundred dollars to model nude for him. I wouldn't do it for ten thousand.'

'Does he know you're gay?'

Thalia's body stiffens, and her eyes go on alert. 'Why do you say that? Has the FBI been spying on me?'

'No. But the police have. Only for one day, though.'

She looks relieved.

'The FBI want to know whether you're gay or not. They do a lot of psychological profiling in these cases, and they feel that's important.'

She looks down at the coffee table between us, then raises her eyes to mine and smiles. 'I'm strange. I have a sex drive like anyone else, but I don't trust it. It betrays me. It makes me want to use sex to get noticed. So when I need someone, I go to women.'

'What about love and tenderness?'

'I have friends. Mostly women. Do you have a lot of friends?'

'Not really. I have colleagues, people who do what I do and understand the demands of my life. I'm a photojournalist and I spend so much time travelling that it's hard to make new friends. I have more ex-lovers than friends.'

She smiles with empathy. 'Friends are hard to find when you're forty. You really have to open yourself up to people, and that's hard to do. If you have one or two friends left from childhood, you're lucky.'

'Do you have friends left back home, in Terrebonne Parish?'

'One. She's still down on the bayou. We talk on the phone sometimes, but I don't go back to visit. Do you have any kids?'

'No. You?'

'I got pregnant once, when I was fifteen. By my cousin. I had an abortion. That was that.'

'Oh.' I feel my face growing hot. 'I'm sorry.'

'That's why I left the place. My father abused me from the time I was ten, my cousin later. It really messed me up. I ran away when I was old enough, but I've never really got over it. That's why I choose women. It's like a safe harbour for me.'

'I understand.'

She looks sceptical. 'Do you? Were you abused as a child?'

'Not like that. Not by family. But . . .' I'm suddenly hyperconscious of Baxter and Lenz and Kaiser in the surveillance van, monitoring every word. I feel like a traitor, both to Thalia and to myself.

'Take your time,' she says

'I was raped,' I say softly, not quite believing the words as they fall from my mouth. 'It was a long time ago.'

'Time doesn't mean anything when it's that.'

'You're right. I was in Honduras, during the war in El Salvador. I'd been photographing this refugee camp with a couple of print reporters, and we got separated. They left without me and I had to walk back to the town. This car came along and stopped for me. There were government soldiers in the car, four of them, one an officer, all polite and smiling. They said they'd take me into town. It was a long way. A mile down the road, they turned off and drove me into the jungle. So far that no one could hear me screaming. I know, because I lost my voice that night.'

'It's all right,' Thalia murmurs. 'I'm here with you.'

'I know. But it's not all right. It's never got all right. I'm more ashamed of that than anything I've ever done.'

'You didn't *do* anything, Jordan. What did you do? You accepted a ride from men who said they'd help you.'

Tears of anger and self-disgust sting my eyes. 'I'm not talking about the rape. I'm talking about after. It went on for hours, and at some point during the night I passed out. At dawn I woke up with my arms numb but my hands no longer bound. I followed the tyre tracks out to the road, then limped into town. I didn't tell a soul what they'd done. I thought if the people I worked for found out what had happened, they'd pull me out of there. I've been haunted ever since by the women who might have been raped after me because I didn't report those men.'

Thalia shakes her head. 'You've punished yourself enough. What matters is how you are now. That's the only thing you can change.'

'I know that.'

'You're afraid for your sister, aren't you? Afraid she'll have to go through something like that.'

'Or worse.'

'OK, but you're doing everything humanly possible to find her.'

'I have to know, Thalia.'

'You will, honey. You'll know.' She walks over and pulls me to my feet. 'Come in the kitchen. I'm going to make you some green tea.'

'I'm sorry I did this. You're the first person I ever told that to, and I don't know why I did. I don't even know you.'

Thalia Laveau places both her hands on my shoulders and looks deep into my eyes. 'You know what?'

'What?'

'You just found a friend at forty.'

AN HOUR LATER, back in the shower in my hotel room, I turn the water as hot as I can stand it, my eyes closed against the spray even as I see the four strange souls I encountered today: a dying man, a

violent man, a feminine man, and a wounded woman. Yesterday I
had some hope of resolution, fooled by the confidence of men in
their systems and their evidence. What are those men saying now,
after the failure of their grand plan? Baxter. Lenz. Kaiser. They
paraded me past their suspects and saw not one flicker of panic. Not
even a flinch at my face—

A telephone is ringing. I pull back the shower curtain and see a
phone mounted on the wall. I press my right palm into the white
towel on the rack, then pick up the receiver. 'Yes?'

'It's John Kaiser.' He sounds uncomfortable.

'Oh. What is it?'

'I'm sorry we heard your conversation with Thalia Laveau,' he
says. 'I'm sorry it happened to you.'

'I don't want to talk about it.'

'I'm downstairs right now. We're about to have a meeting. Before
the official task force meeting. Baxter, Lenz, Bowles and me. I know
you're upset, but I thought you might be more angry if you missed it.'

As badly as I want to crack open the minibar and flop onto my
bed wrapped in towels, I know he's right. I'll feel worse if I don't go.

'I'm in the shower. Give me five minutes.'

THIS TIME WE MEET where we did the first time: SAC Bowles's office.
Kaiser leads the way with a perfunctory knock, and though I hear
voices, the office appears empty. Walking further in, I see Baxter,
Lenz and SAC Bowles waiting in the private seating area in the deep
leg of the L.

Kaiser and I sit side by side on a sofa, facing Baxter and Lenz.

Kaiser looks at Baxter. 'What's the new development you mentioned on the phone?'

I look up in surprise. John hadn't mentioned this.

'Even though Wingate's murder and the Dorignac's snatch were
only two hours apart,' says Baxter, 'I've had a half-dozen agents
checking manifests between New York and New Orleans for flights
in surrounding hours. It finally paid off. One hour after Wingate
died, a lone man paid cash for a flight from JFK to Atlanta, then
cash again for a flight to Baton Rouge.'

'Who was he?' I ask.

Dr Lenz answers. 'A false name, of course. It could be that the
UNSUB who killed Wingate was already in New York when you
upset the applecart in Hong Kong. He silenced Wingate, then flew
straight—or almost straight—to New Orleans to warn his partner.

The plan may have been to paint the Dorignac's woman, but the New York UNSUB made the prudent decision. Do her and dump her.'

Baxter gives the psychiatrist a sharp look. 'That's possible. But no matter who the New York UNSUB is, someone already in New Orleans had to kidnap her. Probably the painter.'

'You have a description of the New York UNSUB?' asks Kaiser.

'Very general. Mid-thirties, muscular, hard face. Casual dress. And there's something else. Linda Knapp—Gaines's girlfriend—turned up back at Gaines's place thirty minutes ago. She told NOPD that whatever nights they needed alibis for, he was home with her.'

I recall how angry and desperate to get away from Gaines the woman had looked. Now she's back with him, protecting him from the police. This is a common mystery I've never understood.

'As far as the others are concerned, initial questioning by NOPD hasn't turned up any rock-solid alibis. It's not surprising, really. Almost all the kidnappings happened during the week, between ten pm and six am.'

As Baxter speaks, a strange epiphany occurs at the dark centre of my mind. 'I've thought of another possibility,' I say quietly.

The others turn to me.

'What is it?' Kaiser asks.

'What if one of the four suspects that we saw today is doing the murders, but doesn't *know* he's doing them?'

No one responds. Baxter and Kaiser look stunned by the suggestion, but Dr Lenz is sanguine.

'How did you come up with that?' asks the psychiatrist.

'The old Sherlock Holmes theory. After you exclude all impossibilities, whatever is left is the solution, however improbable it may seem.'

'You're talking about MPD,' says Lenz. 'Multiple-personality disorder. It's extremely rare. Much rarer than films or novels would have you believe.'

'When it does happen,' says Bowles, 'what causes it?'

'Severe sexual or physical abuse in childhood,' says Lenz. 'Exclusively.'

'What do we know about the childhoods of the three men?' I ask. 'We know Laveau had that kind of problem.'

'Not much,' says Baxter. 'Wheaton's childhood is pretty obscure. We do know his mother left the home when he was thirteen or fourteen, which could be a sign of abuse, but we don't have details.'

'We should ask Wheaton about that,' says Kaiser.

'What about Leon Gaines?' I ask. 'Didn't you say his father did time for carnal knowledge of a minor? A fourteen-year-old girl?'

Baxter nods. 'That's right. We'd better dig deeper on the father.'

'Frank Smith,' says Kaiser. 'What do we know about his childhood?'

'Wealthy family,' says Lenz. 'Not the kind where abuse would be reported. I'll try to contact the family doctor.'

As we ponder this angle in silence, the SAC's phone rings. Bowles goes to the phone. When he hangs up he returns to us, a tight smile on his lips. 'Frank Smith's Salvadorian butler just told NOPD detectives that Roger Wheaton has visited Frank several times at night. He's stayed over twice. And get this. On those nights, he's heard them screaming at each other. Heard it through the walls.'

Dr Lenz looks more excited than I've seen him to date. 'We've got to see both of them again,' he says.

'No doubt,' agrees Baxter. 'How should we approach them?'

'I think I should talk to Frank Smith,' I say firmly.

They all look at me. 'Alone?' asks Baxter.

'He invited me back, didn't he?'

'She got Laveau to trust her,' Kaiser reminds them.

Lenz nods. 'Smith really responded to her. We have to go with the best odds.'

Baxter sighs. 'OK. Jordan will talk to Smith.'

'Arthur and I can see Wheaton,' Kaiser says. 'We should have the phone company fault their lines. We don't want any more warnings passing between them.'

'Sounds like a plan,' Baxter concludes. He looks at his watch. 'We need to go.' Turning to me, he says, 'Jordan, we still need you to stay isolated from any friends from your former life here.'

'No problem. I'm beat. I'm going back to my hotel, ordering room service and racking out.'

Baxter slaps his thighs and stands, and the other men follow suit like football players rising from a huddle.

'Let's go talk to the boys in blue,' says Baxter.

Baxter leads the way to the door, headed for the Emergency Operations Centre, which I have yet to see. Bowles follows, and Lenz falls into line behind him. Only Kaiser hangs back, contriving to walk beside me. 'So, you're going to bed early?' he says softly.

'Yes.' I pause at the door and watch the others move down the corridor. 'But maybe not to sleep. Call me from the lobby.'

Looking up the corridor, he touches my hand and squeezes slightly, then without a word follows Dr Lenz. I give him a few seconds, then go round the corner to the elevators, where Wendy is waiting for me.

9

I've been asleep for a while when the phone rings beside my bed. I pick up the phone. 'Hello?'

'It's me. I'm downstairs.'

John Kaiser's face appears in my mind. 'What time is it?'

'Well after midnight. The police questioned each suspect for hours. We had to hear it all. Look, if you're too tired, that's all right.'

Part of me wants to tell him I'm too tired, but a little tingle between my neck and my knees stops me.

'No, come on up.'

'On the way.'

I hang up and stumble into the bathroom, the fuzzy heaviness of fatigue telling me the last few days have been more stressful than I thought. I brush my teeth, wash my face and pull on a white cotton T-shirt and jeans.

Kaiser knocks softly to keep from alerting Wendy next door. I check the peephole to make sure it's him, then quickly open the door. He steps inside, then smiles and sets two sweating Coke cans on the desk. He opens one and offers it to me.

'Thanks.' I take a long sip. 'I need some caffeine. You tired?'

'Pretty tired.'

'How do you feel about the case?'

He shrugs. 'Not great.'

'What's the deal with Lenz? He doesn't say much in front of you, does he?'

'Since leaving the Bureau, he's found out how quickly you can be forgotten. He'd like to show that what Quantico has now is the second string.'

'He wasn't surprised when I asked if one of the suspects could be killing people without knowing it.'

'He didn't seem to be.' Kaiser gives me a knowing look.

'Do you like that theory?'

'No. It's hard for me to picture someone that messed up pulling off eleven abductions and possibly painting like Rembrandt as well. But I'll research it anyway.' He takes a sip of his Coke. 'Are we going to talk business all night?'

'I hope not.'

I sit on the foot of the bed. Kaiser takes off his jacket and sits opposite me, his gun still on his belt.

'What should we talk about?' he asks.

'Why don't you tell me what's on your mind?'

A hint of a smile. 'You are.'

'Why do you think that is?'

He shakes his head. 'I wish I knew. You know how sometimes when you lose something, it's only when you're not looking for it any more that you find it?'

'Yes. But sometimes by then you don't need whatever it was.'

'This is something everybody needs.'

'I think you're right.' I feel warm inside, but a deeper hesitation keeps me from giving in completely to the moment. 'I told you about some of my problems with men. With dating. Now I want to know about you. What drove you and your wife apart?'

He sighs and sets down his drink can. 'It wasn't that I let my work take over my life—though I certainly did that. If I'd been a doctor or an engineer, she wouldn't have minded. It was that the things I saw every day simply couldn't be communicated to someone normal. "Conventional" is probably a better word. I'd come home after eighteen hours of looking at murdered children and she'd be upset that the new drapes for the living room didn't quite match the carpet. She didn't want to know the unvarnished truth. Who would, if they didn't have to? She shut all that out, and I got shut out with it.'

'Do you blame her for that?'

'No. It showed she had good survival instincts. It's healthier not to let those things into your head, because once they're in, you can't get them out. You know. You've probably seen more hell than I have.'

'I don't think you can quantify hell. But I know what you mean about communicating it. I've spent my whole career trying to do it, and I sometimes wonder if I've succeeded even once.'

Kaiser's eyes hold an empathy I haven't seen in a very long time. 'So here we sit,' he says. 'Damaged goods.'

What I feel for this man is not infatuation, or some neurochemical attraction that compels me to sleep with him. It's a simple intimacy that I've felt from the hour we first rode together in the rented Mustang. He has an easiness—and also a wariness—that draws me to him. John Kaiser has looked into the deep dark and is still basically all right. I know I would feel as safe with this man as it is possible to feel.

'So, you want kids,' he says, picking up last night's conversation from the Camellia Grill.

'Yep. Have to start pretty soon. How about you? You want kids?'

He looks back at me, his eyes twinkling. He's clearly enjoying himself. 'Only one a year for five or six years.'

My stomach flips over. 'I guess that lets me out of the race.'

'I'm kidding. Two would be nice, though.'

'I might be able to handle two. Maybe we should spend the night in this bed together. If we're still happy in the morning, you can pop the question.'

He barks a laugh. 'Jesus! Were you always like this?'

'No, but I'm getting too old to waste time. If you're just up here to get laid, I think you'll have better luck next door.'

His smile vanishes. 'I like this room just fine.'

He takes hold of my wrists and pulls me to my feet, which brings my face to the level of his chest. Then he slips his arms round my waist and looks down at me. He peers into my eyes and pulls my waist to his. Then he lowers his face and touches his lips to mine. My heart thumps against my sternum, as I knew it would, but it's nice to have my instinct confirmed.

I kiss him, opening my mouth to his. Then I pull back. 'Maybe I should start using your first name now.'

His eyes shine with delight. 'Whatever you want.'

'We'll make the first occasion momentous. Ready?'

'Ready.'

'Make love to me, John.'

He smiles, then lifts me into his arms the way they do in old cowboy movies. I expect to be lowered onto the bed, but instead he carries me into the bathroom. 'It's been a long day. You'd like me better after a shower.'

'Or maybe during one,' I reply, laughing.

He laughs and sets me on the counter, then turns the shower taps. Steam begins to fill the room as he takes off his shoes.

'I forgot this.'

There's a rip of Velcro, and then he's holding a small revolver in a nylon holster. 'This is for you,' he says. 'It's a Smith and Wesson .38-calibre featherweight. You know how to use it?'

'Yes.'

'Good. I'll put it out on the desk.'

When he returns to the bathroom, I wriggle out of my T-shirt and jeans and step towards the curtain. As he slips off his trousers, his eyes take me in from head to toe. 'You're beautiful, Jordan.'

The truth of his belief is plain in his face. 'I feel beautiful right now.'

He takes my hand, then pulls back the curtain and helps me into the tub. The shock of the hot water is wonderful, and having him under it with me even better. He soaps my back, and I soap his. Then we soap fronts, which is much more interesting.

He leans down and gently kisses my breast. His lips slide up my neck to my chin, then my mouth, and then a clamorous ringing shocks us motionless. The bathroom phone. I dry my hand, then pick up the phone. 'Hello?'

'Jordan, it's Daniel Baxter.'

I mouth 'Baxter' to John, who quickly turns off the water.

'What's going on?'

'Ah . . . is John up there with you?'

'Just a second, the TV's too loud.' I press my hand over the transmitter. 'He wants to talk to you. Shall I say you're not here?'

He shakes his head and takes the phone. 'What's up, boss?'

As he listens, his eyes flick back and forth with growing intensity. Something terrible has happened. 'We'll be right there,' he says. He then hangs up, his eyes cloudy with confusion. 'Thalia Laveau has disappeared,' he tells me. 'Daniel thinks she's been taken by the UNSUB.'

Nausea rolls through my stomach. '*Thalia?* But . . . but she was under surveillance.'

'She evaded it purposely.'

'*What?*'

'He wouldn't give me the details over an unsecure phone. We won't know anything more till we get there. Jesus, why her?'

Several answers come to me, as my heart balloons with terror for her, a woman who fled her home and family to escape sexual abuse, who is now at the mercy of a man without mercy.

THE EMERGENCY OPERATIONS Centre, which has been kept from me until now, is the pounding heart of the NOKIDS investigation. It's huge—more than 3,000 square feet—with long rows of tables marching towards the front of the room. Behind each row sit rows of men and women with banks of phones before them. John posts Wendy at the door of the EOC, then leads me in. Wendy was quiet during the ride over. I felt for her, but there's more to worry about now than hurt feelings.

At the front of the room, facing the tables, is an array of oversized computer monitors showing views of various buildings: live television surveillance of the residences of the four main suspects.

'So this is it,' I say softly. 'Where are Baxter and Lenz?'

'Right here,' says a voice behind me.

'Joined at the hip,' I say, turning to face them.

'How did she do it?' asks John.

'Her room-mate helped her,' says Baxter. 'Loaned her a coat and umbrella to fool the surveillance guys.'

'How did you figure it out?' I ask.

'Earlier today, Laveau called a woman friend from the campus and arranged to meet her at eleven tonight. When Laveau didn't show by midnight, the friend called the NOPD. NOPD called us.'

'The woman claimed Laveau was coming over for tea and sympathy,' says Lenz, 'but obviously it was more than that. She evaded our surveillance to protect her lover's identity. They had a long-standing relationship. The woman can alibi Thalia not only for the Dorignac's snatch, but also for at least five of the other abductions.'

I jump in. 'Maybe we're missing the obvious here. Maybe one of the male suspects has been lusting after Thalia. Our questioning rattled him. He knows it's a matter of time before he's nailed. Faced with that, he decides he has nothing to lose by indulging himself with Thalia.'

'All three were under round-the-clock surveillance,' says Lenz.

'Thalia didn't have any trouble eluding it.'

Baxter sighs and turns to John. 'Frank Smith was in a restaurant at the time Laveau left her house, and afterwards. Gaines was at his house on Freret. Wheaton was painting at the Woldenberg Centre.'

'What about Jordan's idea of natural light?' asks John. 'Have we got aerial shots of all the courtyards or enclosed gardens in the city?'

'That's just not practical,' says Baxter. 'This city stretches over two hundred square miles. The painting house could be anywhere in that area.'

'No. The painter wouldn't want to drive twenty miles every time he wanted to work on a painting. Wheaton and Gaines live within a mile of the university. Frank Smith lives at the edge of the French Quarter. Let's get aerial photos of every square block of those areas. Then we'll look for sheltered courtyards where the painter would have good natural light.'

'The leaves are still on the goddamn trees,' Baxter argues.

'Then get architectural plans!' John snaps. 'We should have agents at the courthouse doing title searches on every building in those two areas. We may find some connection to one of the suspects.'

'I guess that's all we've got,' Baxter concludes. 'Other than Wheaton's nocturnal visits to Frank Smith.'

'And we're on that in the morning,' John says.

'What time are we talking to Smith and Wheaton?' I ask.

'Be here by eight,' Baxter replies. 'Agent Travis will drive you over.'

'Eight, then,' I say, and walk to the door where Wendy awaits.

NEW ORLEANS STEAMS in the morning after rain. Dr Lenz has decided he wants me in on the second Wheaton interview. I'm not sure why, and I didn't have time to ask him. When I arrive at the field office, the building is besieged by camera crews. Thalia Laveau's disappearance has already started a new wave of panic.

This morning's interview with Wheaton will take place at the artist's temporary residence on Audubon Place, a private street of palatial homes adjoining the Tulane campus. John, Lenz and I approach the front door together. Before we reach it, Wheaton walks onto his porch in blue trousers, a sweatshirt, his wire-rimmed bifocals, and his trademark white cotton gloves.

'I saw you through the window,' he says as we mount the steps to the front gallery. 'I saw a news report. Has Thalia really disappeared?'

'I'm afraid so,' says John. 'May we come in?'

'Of course.'

Wheaton leads us through a hall into a magnificently appointed drawing room. John and I sit together on a sofa opposite the artist, and Lenz takes a chair to our right.

'Hello, again,' Wheaton says as I sit, his long face conveying silent grief. 'Are you taking more photographs today?'

'I wish I was. You're a wonderful subject.'

'We just came from working another case,' says Lenz. 'We didn't want to leave our photographer in the car.'

'Gentlemen,' says the artist, 'do you believe Thalia was taken by the same person who took the others?'

'Yes,' says John. 'We do.'

Wheaton sighs. 'What do you require of me?'

John looks at Lenz, who decides to lead with his chin. 'Mr Wheaton, we're told you've made several visits to Frank Smith's home.'

Wheaton's face tightens. 'Did Frank tell you that?'

Lenz does not respond directly. 'We're also told that you argued vehemently with him on these occasions. We'd very much like to know the reason for these visits, and for the arguments.'

Wheaton shakes his head and looks away, his desire to help apparently gone, or at least tempered by disgust. 'I can't help you with that. All I can do is assure you that those visits have nothing whatever to do with the crimes you're investigating. You'll have to trust me that far.'

'I'm afraid in these circumstances,' Lenz says, 'your word as a gentleman will not be enough. I can assure you that all answers you give will be held in the strictest confidence.'

This, of course, is a bald-faced lie. Wheaton doesn't respond, instead he looks at me and says, 'Why are *you* really here?'

'I am a photographer, Mr Wheaton, but I don't work for the FBI. My sister was a victim of whoever is taking these women. She disappeared last year.'

Wheaton's lips part in amazement. 'I'm so sorry. What is your name?'

'Jordan Glass.'

'Well, let me assure you, Ms Glass, that if I had information which could possibly help, I wouldn't hesitate to give it to you.'

'Mr Wheaton,' John says, 'I appreciate your desire for privacy. But it might be that you have information you aren't qualified to judge the importance of.'

Wheaton looks at the ceiling. 'You're saying I might possess information that proves Frank is behind these disappearances and not know it?'

'It's possible.'

'It's *not* possible. Frank couldn't have anything to do with these crimes.' Wheaton's face is red now, and he fixes John with his deep-set eyes. 'However, because Ms Glass has made me acutely aware of the stakes in this case, I will tell you something that's been bothering me. I hesitated before, because Leon Gaines makes such an easy target. But on the few occasions when I brought my graduate students together, both at the university and here at this house, I observed Leon making inappropriate remarks to Thalia, sexual remarks. And, once I saw him wait for her by her car. It was several weeks ago.'

'What happened?' asks John.

'She handled him with the firmness she always used. Thalia is a beautiful girl, and she seemed accustomed to dealing with that kind of attention.'

'She drove away alone on that occasion?'

'Yes. I think Leon kept at her because he knew she posed nude for a graduate painting class. He took this as sexual advertising.'

'You were right to tell us,' says John.

'I hope so. But now, gentlemen, I must ask you to leave. I need to work.'

'I hate to intrude further,' says Lenz. 'But we're unclear on some biographical points in your life.'

Wheaton bunches his brows in consternation.

'Published interviews say very little about your background beyond a certain point, but we know, for example, that you were reared in a rural part of Vermont, and that your father was a farmer. We also know that your mother left home when you were thirteen or fourteen.'

Wheaton looks ready to throw Lenz bodily from the house.

'I realise this is painful,' says the psychiatrist. 'But we need to know. Why did she leave without taking her children with her?'

Wheaton swallows and looks at the floor. 'I don't know. My father believed she met a man and ran away with him. I never did. It's certainly possible that she fell in love with another man—my father was unpleasant—but she would never have left me—us—behind.'

My throat feels tight; pressed mercilessly by Lenz, Roger Wheaton is articulating my own deepest fear and hope.

'I believe she put herself into a vulnerable situation,' he says, 'and something bad happened to her. And either my father didn't tell us about it, or no one knew who she really was. If she were hiding her identity to be with someone else—in New York, for example—I can see how it would happen.'

'Was your father "unpleasant" to the degree that he abused your mother?' asks Lenz.

'By today's standards? Undoubtedly. But this was the 1950s.'

'Did he abuse you and your brothers?'

Wheaton shrugs. 'Again, by today's standards, yes.'

'What about sexual abuse?'

The artist's deep sigh conveys utter contempt for the psychiatrist. 'Nothing of the kind.' Wheaton wipes his forehead with a gloved hand. 'Now, I really must insist that you go.'

Lenz fires a last shot as he gets to his feet.

'Mr Wheaton, would you simply tell us whether you're homosexual or not? It would prevent a lot of further prying into your life.'

Wheaton seems to sag under the weight of the question. 'The answer is academic, I'm afraid. My disease rendered me impotent over two years ago.' He glances at me, and the wounded pride in his face makes me look at the floor.

'Thank you for your time,' I say before Lenz can press him further. I back towards the hallway. 'I appreciate your honesty about Gaines. It really might help find Thalia and my sister.'

Wheaton steps forward and takes my hand between his two white gloves. 'I hope so. I care a great deal for Thalia. She's a wounded soul. Call me if you'd like to take more photographs. I'd like to paint you. We could do an exchange.'

'I would like you to paint me some time. I'd like to see how you see me.'

'It would be a pleasure, my dear.' Wheaton moves from the door so that John and Lenz can get into the hall. 'Goodbye, gentlemen.'

Dr Lenz tries to shake the artist's hand, but Wheaton takes a step backwards and gives him a tight smile. Then the three of us are outside again, walking towards the FBI sedan parked on the street.

'He just told us to go to hell,' says John.

Lenz nods. 'But he certainly pointed his finger at Gaines.'

'After saying nothing yesterday. I wonder why.'

'He told you why,' I say irritably. 'He doesn't like talking about anybody's personal business. Even an asshole like Gaines.'

John opens the front door of the car for me. 'I hope you have better luck with Frank Smith. You still want to go in alone?'

'Absolutely.'

'Let's get to the Quarter, then.'

THE MEDICAL TAPE holding the T-4 transmitter at the small of my back chafes as I climb the steps of the Creole cottage on Esplanade and knock on the door. Frank Smith opens the door with a broad smile. 'Is this visit social? Or government business?'

'I wish I could say the former, but it's not.'

Smith arches his eyebrows. 'Then I don't think I'm at home.'

His movie-star handsomeness is starting to irritate me. 'Have you watched any TV this morning?' I ask.

'No.' His green eyes narrow. 'Don't tell me he's taken another one.'

'He took Thalia. Last night.'

This is the first time I've seen Frank Smith lose his perfect control. 'May I please come in?'

He steps out of my way, and I walk inside. Instead of going into the salon, I walk straight through the house and into the courtyard. There's a small wrought-iron table under the gnarled wisteria, and I take a seat there. Smith sits across the table from me. 'How could Thalia be kidnapped when she was under surveillance?' he asks.

'What makes you think she was under surveillance?'

'Well, *I* am. Where are your FBI friends today?'

'I asked to come alone.'

He mulls over my answer. 'What is it you want to know?'

I quickly explain that the Bureau knows Roger Wheaton spent several evenings at this house, and also that he and Smith argued.

'I wondered why Juan didn't show up this morning,' Smith says. 'I suppose they threatened to deport him?'

'I don't know, Frank. I'm sorry. But this is life or death. Thalia could still be alive. We have to help her.'

'Yes, but what you're asking has nothing to do with this case.'

'That's what Wheaton said.'

Smith turns up his palms as if to say, *Next subject.*

'Look, if you guys are having a relationship, admitting it is the quickest way of getting the FBI out of your life. They honestly don't care what you or Wheaton do for sex. What worries them is other possibilities.'

'Like?'

'Like you're in a conspiracy to produce The Sleeping Women.'

'Ridiculous.'

'I think so too. But I don't run the FBI. Come on, Frank. What's the deal? Is Roger Wheaton gay?'

'Have you asked him?'

'He evaded the question.'

'Well he would, wouldn't he? He grew up in rural Vermont. He's fifty-eight years old. He's another generation altogether.'

'You're saying he's gay?'

'Of course he is. He's simply not comfortable with the kind of attention that comes with being gay and famous.'

'Are you and he lovers?'

Smith shakes his head with what looks like regret. 'No.'

'But if the visits were about friendship, what were the arguments about? The yelling?'

Smith shakes his head again. 'I can't answer that.'

Filled with frustration, but also understanding Smith's reluctance to violate Wheaton's privacy, I lean forward, reach into my blouse and pull the tiny mike from my bra.

'I'm switching off,' I say loudly. 'Don't come in.' Then I unthread the wire, rip the transmitter from the skin of my back, drop the medical tape on the table between us and switch it off.

'We're no longer live, Frank. It's you and me.'

He looks ready to throw me out of his house.

'Listen,' I say with the conviction of my own pain. 'My sister had two small children that she loved more than her life. She was yanked off the street by some predator, and she's probably rotting in the swamp somewhere right now. There are eleven other women just like her. If your arguments with Wheaton have nothing to do with this case, all the effort the FBI puts into investigating them is wasted. Do you want that wasted effort to cost Thalia her life?'

Smith closes his eyes, takes a long breath, then expels it slowly and opens his eyes again. 'It's simple. Roger wants me to kill him.'

A rush of heat passes over my face. 'What?'

'His disease is steadily worsening. It's in his lungs now. The end will be . . . unpleasant. He wants my help when the time comes.'

I feel like slinking away in shame. Suddenly everything is clear, Wheaton's reticence most of all. 'You get it now?' asks Smith.

'Part of it. But why the arguments? You refused to help him?'

'That's right. I thought Roger might be motivated by clinical depression. I think he has a lot of great paintings left in him.'

Finally I say, 'I'm sorry. How did he want you to help him? Did he have a method in mind?'

'Insulin. It's a peaceful way to go, he says. He's researched it. Sleep, coma, then death. The problem is that sometimes you don't die. You just get brain damage.'

'That's why he needed your help?'

'Yes. He wanted me to find some drug that would stop his heart after the coma.'

'Jesus. OK.' I stand and gather up the transmitter and microphone. 'I'll tell the FBI they're barking up the wrong tree.'

'Thank you.' Smith forces a smile. He gets to his feet and leads me back through the house to the front door. He yanks open the door and stands clear of it. 'Come again soon, now.'

I walk out into the pale sunlight and the door closes behind me. It's been a long time since I felt this low. Probing private lives has never been my thing. All photojournalism is essentially exploitative, but in photography you intrude from a distance. Just click, click, click.

I turn towards the Mississippi and start to walk, knowing that the FBI sedan bearing Baxter, Lenz and John will come alongside at any moment. They'll be pissed I pulled the wire, which is fine. I'm pissed I've played the role of pawn in their dead-end investigation.

The hum of a motor announces my escorts. The sedan pulls up to the kerb on my left and, when I don't stop, keeps pace as I walk.

Baxter rolls down the passenger window. 'Why did you kill the wire?' he asks.

'You know why,' I reply, looking straight ahead.

'What did he tell you?'

'He convinced me that Wheaton's visits there have nothing to do with the case.'

'Do you think you're the best judge of that?'

'As good as any of you.'

'OK. We're going back to the office now. Call if you want to talk. Wendy has a cellphone.'

The car stops and Wendy gets out, wearing her usual skirt and jacket combo, the jacket there to hide her pistol. She falls into step a couple of yards behind me, and the sedan pulls forward and then passes us. As it recedes, I see John looking back over the rear seat.

10

As I turn onto Royal Street, Agent Wendy still trailing a few yards behind, my mind swirls with images I have no desire to ponder, land my stomach rolls with the low-level nausea I've felt since Dr Lenz badgered Roger Wheaton into telling us his disease rendered him impotent years ago. At St Philip I break left, making for the river. With every step the Quarter grows more commercial. There are restaurants and pubs now, lawyers' offices, hotels. Yet still the odd doorway leads down a tunnel that opens onto a secluded courtyard, beckoning with the promise of midnight trysts and masked soirees. I shudder in sudden awareness that The Sleeping Women may have been painted in one of these courtyards.

Joan of Arc awaits me on her golden horse at the Place de France, a little concrete island in the traffic. Wendy moves alongside me here, for suddenly we are awash in a sea of humanity; surging waves of tourists and merchants hawking vegetables, coffee and souvenirs.

'Where are we going?' asks Wendy.

'The river. There's a walkway across the streetcar tracks.'

'I know. The Moonwalk.'

She stays at my shoulder as I climb to the brick walkway atop the embankment. The Mississippi is wide here, and the water high for this time of year. We walk towards Jackson Square.

We're not alone on the walkway. There are tourists with cameras, joggers wearing headphones, buskers. As we approach and pass each, I feel Wendy tense beside me, then slowly relax.

Then out of the blue she says, 'I don't want to offend you or anything, but I heard you told Laveau you got raped once. Is that true?'

I feel a flash of temper, knowing the story is probably making the rounds of the field office, but it's hard to be angry at Wendy, whose curiosity seems part of an eternal quest for self-improvement. 'It was a long time ago.'

'I've never had trouble like that. A baseball player got really pushy with me in college once, in the back seat of his car. I waited until he exposed himself, and then I made him regret it.'

'Good for you.'

'Yeah. But something like this, where they snatch you off the street, someone who's all prepared with a rape kit—'

'We don't know the victims are being raped,' I remind her.

'Well, right, except for the woman taken from Dorignac's.'

A wave of heat comes into my cheeks.

'I shouldn't assume anything about the others from that,' Wendy goes on. 'We don't know for sure the UNSUB took her.'

Her words stop me dead on the walkway. 'The woman taken from Dorignac's grocery was raped?'

Wendy looks confused. 'Well, they found semen inside her. She could have just had sex, of course, but I think the opinion of the pathologist was that she was raped.'

As I stand speechless in the wind, a drop of rain touches my face.

'I just put my foot in my mouth, didn't I?' says Wendy. 'They didn't tell you. I guess they didn't want you to suffer any more than you had to, with your sister and all.'

My rising anger is dwarfed by hurt at John's betrayal. How could he hold this back from me? But then come images of Jane suffering terror and rape—

I turn and continue along the embankment despite the rain. Two men are approaching, a young one with jeans and a beard, and behind him a man wearing khakis and a teal button-down shirt. Wendy tenses, watching the bearded man as he passes. While she watches him, the man in the teal shirt brings up his right arm, and polished nickel gleams in the rain.

I shout a warning to Wendy, and before the sound fades she's in front of me, her hand flying to the pistol holstered under her jacket.

A gunshot explodes over the embankment, and something hot and wet stings my face. Wendy seems to stutter in place, then falls backwards onto the bricks with a flat thump. My white blouse is spattered with a fine red mist. Wendy's blood. Screams erupt from the parking lot, and I sense more than see people diving to the ground.

The man in the teal shirt charges me, his gun pointed at my chest, and grabs my arm with his free hand. 'Move your ass!' he shouts.

My eyes are locked on Wendy, who lies on her back, eyes fixed on the sky, blood bubbling on her lips. As I stare, my captor pulls up his gun and shoots her again, this time in the side.

I try to yank my arm free, but he swings the gun in a quick savage arc against my forehead, and the world blanks out for a moment.

'Move or I'll kill you right here!'

A jumble of thoughts: his tremendous strength; his lack of hesitation in shooting Wendy; the realisation that he shot Wendy to get to me; that this is *him*—the kidnapper, the UNSUB, the bastard who took my sister. Now he has me.

As he drags me towards the streetcar tracks, I notice a man in the parking lot with his arms levelled in our direction. John Kaiser.

'Jordan!' he cries. 'Drop!'

As I start to fall, my captor jerks me in front of him like a shield, and fires three times in John's direction. John spins, trying to avoid the shots, but his spin continues to the ground and he does not get up.

'Dead cop,' says the voice in my ear. The barrel of his pistol touches my temple. 'Move.'

My mind flashes onto the gun John gave me, but it's lying useless in its holster in my rented Mustang, parked at the FBI office. The only weapon I have is the knowledge that the man holding me doesn't want to kill me here. He has a much more exotic fate in mind.

'We're going to my car,' he says, seizing my arm. 'If you fight, I'll shoot you in the spine. You'll go limp as a rag doll, and I'll have to carry you, but you'll still be nice and warm between the legs and you'll still make a pretty picture for the man.'

The icy conviction in his voice paralyses me, wiping out every emotion but terror as he pulls me back across the walkway.

Thirty yards away, John lies on his stomach, struggling to reach his knees. When we pass him, my attacker will fire a bullet into him, just as he did with Wendy. My limbs are heavy with the inevitability.

'*Jooordan!*'

The scream stops me cold. Twisting my neck, I see Wendy lying on her stomach, propped on her elbows, her pistol clenched in both hands. An arm whips round me to aim at her, but I bat it aside and throw myself down. Orange flame bursts from Wendy's gun.

An explosive grunt sounds beside me. My attacker staggers, then Wendy's gun spits again. He bellows in rage and pain, then charges her with blind fury. Wendy fires again but misses, and he starts shooting, round after round, until I know that she's gone.

He turns back to me, but he's wounded and can't move well. From twenty yards away, he raises his gun and points it at me. He means to kill me now.

The gun wavers, steadies, then flies skywards as thunder booms behind me and ricochets back from the far shore. I whirl to find John kneeling at the edge of the embankment, his .40-calibre automatic levelled with absolute stillness. 'Hit the bricks!' he yells.

I dive onto the walkway, and John empties his clip, blast after blast roaring across the river. When I look up, my attacker is gone.

As the last shot fades, I crawl across the bricks to Wendy, hoping it's not too late. The hair at the back of her head is a mass of blood, and my heart knots against the truth.

I get slowly to my feet and walk to the top of the wooden steps that lead down to the water. The man in the teal shirt is doubled over near the bottom step, gasping for breath and trying to hang on to a wooden chain post. As I watch, my heart empty of pity, his hand slips off the post and he tumbles headfirst into the river.

After a moment he bobs to the surface, floating in place, his mouth opening and closing like that of a landed fish. Then he turns away as the current pulls him along the bank. I realise then that if the river takes him, we may never know who he was, never find Thalia, or Jane, or any of the others—or even learn what happened to them.

Hopping over the chain, I try to keep pace with him by running along the treacherous embankment. Navigating the grey rocks without breaking an ankle is difficult, and the high water carries him rapidly along, not only downriver but into the main channel.

'Help!' he shouts, panic filling his dull eyes. 'I can't breathe!'

'Go to hell!' I yell, though I need to save him.

He's twenty-five feet into the channel now, turning in slow circles in the wake of a distant tug. Then, as his face comes round again, he shouts, 'Your sister's alive!'

A bolus of adrenalin flushes through my veins, and I have to fight every muscle to keep from leaping in after him. That's just what he wants, of course. He has to be lying. 'Where is she?' I cry.

'Save me!' he yells again. 'I can save her! Please!'

I struggle down to the river's edge, where a piece of driftwood lies wedged in the rock. It's a long branch, worn smooth by the water.

'Jordan!' shouts a voice from miles away. It's John, back at the steps. 'Bring him in with the branch!'

I pull at the limb with all my strength, but I can't free it from the rocks. Every second he slips further downstream, my sister's fate going with him. I can't save the bastard without jumping in myself, and that would be insanity.

Suddenly, without conscious thought, my hand flies to the zipper of my bumbag, and my hand jerks out the Canon point-and-shoot I used at the gallery fire in New York.

I point the lens at the drowning man and shoot three or four exposures, then his head slips below the surface and does not return.

Panting with exhaustion, I climb carefully up the embankment. John is sitting on top of the steps, fifty yards away, a cellphone in his hand. As I trot down to where he sits, he puts down the phone and tightens his belt, which he has tied round his thigh.

'You're hit in the leg?' I ask.

Clearly in great pain, he nods, then points down the steps. 'See if you can find his gun. He might have dropped it. Finger prints.'

I work my way down the steps, but there's no gun. Dropping to my knees, I feel my way along the first submerged step, but a soft splinter is my only reward. Moving sideways, I feel among the submerged rocks, and again find nothing. But as my hand comes out of the murky water, I freeze. Lying between two rocks in a pool of oily water is a cellphone. Retrieving it, I climb back up the steps.

'Son of a bitch,' John groans when he sees it. He takes the phone by its antenna. 'This phone's getting on a plane to Washington. Don't mention it to any beat cops. Wait for Homicide.'

He points towards the French Market, where two mounted policemen are spurring their horses across the streetcar tracks.

I sit beside John, and in the first seconds of stillness, I start to shake. I wring my hands, trying to make them stop. 'Wendy's dead,' I say softly.

He nods. 'She was a good kid.'

'She wasn't a kid. She was a hero. She deserves a medal.'

'Goes without saying.'

'So what the hell were you doing here?'

'I didn't feel good about you walking around the Quarter. I knew you were upset and I've always felt you were in more danger than anyone realised.'

I squeeze his hand. 'I'm glad you're paranoid.'

'What did the guy say to you down there?'

'He said Jane was alive.'

John looks at me, his eyes hard. 'Did you believe him?'

'I don't know.' I pause. 'He said something else, John.'

'What?'

'If he had to shoot me in the spine, it would still be nice and warm between my legs, and I'd still make a pretty picture for the man.'

John's face pales. 'He said that? "For the man"?'

The clatter of hoofs on brick is closer. John takes his wallet out of his trousers and opens it to show his FBI credentials. Two cops—one black, one white—stare down with drawn guns.

John holds up his credentials so that the cops can see them.

'Special Agent John Kaiser, FBI. This crime scene is to be secured for the joint task force. I've been shot, so you men get to it.'

THE WAKE of Wendy's death is a blur to me now, as I ride the elevator up to the third floor of the FBI fortress on Lake Pontchartrain. While John spent ninety minutes in the accident room at Charity Hospital downtown, I sat in a waiting room with enough armed special agents to make me feel like the First Lady. I was lucky that one of my new protectors was a female agent. She brought me a new blouse from her car and bagged up the bloodstained one.

John came through surgery fine, but his doctor didn't want to release him for twenty-four hours. John thanked the man, picked up the stick a physiotherapist had deposited in his room, and limped out of the hospital to a waiting FBI car.

Baxter, Lenz and SAC Bowles are waiting for us in Bowles's office.

'How is it, John?' Baxter asks as I help him sit down.

'Stiff, but fine.'

Baxter nods. Nobody's going to tell Kaiser to take sickness leave. Baxter turns to me. 'How are you doing, Jordan?'

'Holding it together.'

'I know that wasn't easy, seeing what happened to Wendy.'

I want to stay silent, but I feel I should say something. 'You should know this. She did everything right. Nobody could have done better.'

Baxter's jaw muscles clench as pain and pride fight for dominance in his eyes.

'We still don't have the guy's body?' John asks Baxter.

'No. Divers are searching, but we may never find it.'

'What about the cellphone?' John asks.

'No prints. It was wiped clean. This UNSUB was taking extreme precautions, but the Engineering Research Facility at Quantico is checking the memory chips now. We should get a report any time.'

'What about my pictures?' I ask.

'That's the one bright spot. They were blurry but usable. The University of Arizona produced a decent enhancement of the best one, and it's running on the local TV stations.'

'Well,' John half groans. 'We rattled the hell out of somebody. We just got a delayed reaction, and it was tougher than we expected.'

'Yep,' Baxter agrees.

'Where were the three musketeers while this went down?' John asks.

'Wheaton was painting at the Woldenberg Art Centre. Had been since you talked to him this morning. After Jordan left Smith's house, Smith lunched at Bayona, then went back home. Gaines and his girlfriend woke up at ten in the morning, started drinking, then arguing. They stopped long enough to have sex, then passed out.'

'Any of them make suspicious calls?' John asks.

'Nothing.' Baxter looks from John to Lenz. 'I want to hear thoughts. Anything. Gut feelings, whatever you've got.'

'What about Jordan's split-personality idea?' John asks. 'We didn't get anything out of Wheaton or Smith on childhood abuse, but that concept has stuck with me. Is it possible that an artist with a split personality could paint in two completely different styles?'

Lenz steeples his fingers and leans back. 'There are cases of MPD on record where one personality required heart medication to survive, and another did not. So—two completely different painters occupying the same body? It's technically possible. But given the scale of this case, the extraordinary lengths to which the dominant personality would have to go to conceal his acts from the others—'

'Wait,' says John. 'Not all the personalities know what the others are doing?'

'Correct. Generally one is dominant and knows everything, while the others remain partially in the dark.'

The phone on Bowles's desk rings. The SAC answers, then holds out the phone to Baxter. 'ERF at Quantico.'

The ISU chief gets up and takes the phone. 'Got it,' he says finally.

'What?' asks John as Baxter hangs up.

Baxter lays his hands flat on Bowles's desk. 'It was a stolen cellphone, reprogrammed. No way to trace the UNSUB from that. But ERF salvaged the chips. They got the speed-dial numbers programmed into the phone. One belonged to Marcel de Becque. I'll get the EOC to find out where he is right now.'

Before Baxter can make the call, Bowles's phone rings again. This time Baxter picks up. 'Baxter here.'

Baxter listens and even his poker face betrays excitement as he scrawls an address on a file folder. 'We owe you, Henry,' he says and hangs up. 'Chief Farrell of NOPD's got a widow lady out in Kenner who says she rents a room to the guy whose photo is showing on TV.' He activates the speakerphone and punches in a number.

'Forensics,' says a female voice.

'Two-twenty-one Wisteria Drive, Kenner. Take the whole unit. We'll meet you there.'

SITUATED IN A WARREN of streets just north of New Orleans's International Airport, 221 Wisteria Drive is a typical suburban house with a two-storey clapboard garage behind it.

As Baxter kills the engine, a woman with a cigarette in her mouth walks out of the carport door, waving a set of keys.

John reaches for the door handle. 'Here we go.'

'You got here quick, I'll say that,' Mrs Pitre says in a smoke-parched voice. 'I've been worried Mr Johnson would come back before you got here.' She sticks out her right hand. 'Carol Pitre, widowed four years since my husband got killed offshore.'

'Special Agent John Kaiser.' He shakes her hand. 'Mr Johnson won't be coming back, ma'am.'

'How do you know? What's he done, anyhow? The police said he was a federal fugitive, but that doesn't tell me anything.'

'That's all we can say at this point, ma'am.'

The forensic unit's Suburban pulls into the driveway with a roar and a squeal of brakes. A second one pulls in behind it.

'Mrs Pitre, did Mr Johnson show you any identification?' asks John.

'Hell, yes. I asked for it, didn't I? World's full of crazy people.'

'What did he show you?'

'Voter registration card. He had a New York driving licence, too.'

'Thank you. We would like to go up now, Mrs Pitre. Is it just one room over the garage?'

'Two rooms and a bathroom.'

'I see.' John turns to me and pulls me aside. 'I'm going up with Daniel and Lenz for a quick look. I'd like to take you up, but it wouldn't fly with the forensic unit.'

'I'm OK. Go on.'

While John, Lenz and Baxter climb the stairs inside the garage I sidle back to the FBI sedan. I settle in for a wait, but within minutes

John limps down the bottom four steps, followed by Lenz.

'Is it your leg?' I call, getting out and hurrying towards him.

'No.' There's an evidence bag in his hand. He waves to the forensic unit, and a platoon of technicians hurry towards the garage.

'What is it? What did you find?'

'The UNSUB knew we were coming. The place was wiped clean, like the cellphone. But waiting for us on the kitchen counter was a perfect row of photographs.'

A strange chill runs along my shoulders. 'The victims?'

'Yes. Eleven. Not the woman from Dorignac's or Thalia.'

'So he didn't take the Dorignac's victim.' I realise John is still holding the evidence bag. 'What's in that?' I ask, my chest tightening.

John sighs and touches my arm. 'Jane's photo. If you're up to it, I'd like you to see if you can tell me where it was taken.'

'Let's see it.'

He hesitates, then opens the Ziploc and slides out the photo. It's a black and white print, shot with a telephoto lens. The depth of field is so poor that I can't distinguish the background, but Jane is clear. Wearing a sleeveless sweater and jeans, she's looking towards the camera. As I study the image, searching for some telling detail, anything that might yield a clue to her fate, my heart clenches like a fist and my skin goes cold. 'Look at her arms, John.'

'What about them?'

'No scars.'

'What?'

A wave of vertigo throws me into a spin, though I know I'm standing still. 'Jane was attacked by a dog when she was little.'

The photo begins to quiver in my hand as realisations clamour for attention. Fighting tears, I press the picture to my chest.

'Careful,' John warns. 'There might be fingerprints.'

'Look!' Dr Lenz says over John's shoulder. 'There's something written on the back.'

John leans forward and studies the back of the print. 'It's an address. Twenty-five-ninety St Charles.'

'That's Jane Lacour's address,' says Lenz.

'There's a phone number, too. It's Manhattan 555-2999.'

'I know that number,' I whisper.

'Whose is it?' John asks.

'Just a second.' I try to think back. 'Oh my God . . . It's Wingate's gallery. Christopher Wingate. I dialled this number from the plane back from Hong Kong.'

'That's everybody tied in the same knot. Wingate, the UNSUB and de Becque,' John says.

'Wingate's number on a victim's photo,' muses Lenz. 'That could mean Wingate selected Jane Lacour.'

'How?' asks John. 'He hasn't been in New Orleans for years.'

'He didn't choose Jane,' I whisper. 'He chose me.'

THE PICTURE JOHN PULLED from the Ziploc bag floats in my mind like an emblem of guilt as I drive towards John Kaiser's house in the rented Mustang. John sits beside me in the passenger seat, the seat fully reclined so he can stretch out his wounded leg. I've placed the photo now. It ran in several major newspapers two years ago, when I won the North American Press Association Award. Wingate must have accessed some database that contained that picture, printed it, and sent it to the UNSUB in New Orleans.

'I know what you're thinking, Jordan,' says John. 'A little survivor guilt is normal, but this is crazy.'

I squeeze the wheel, trying to bleed off the exasperation I've felt since the forensic unit confirmed the handwriting on the photo was Wingate's, but it does no good. 'Somebody outside New Orleans chose me as victim number five, and it got Jane killed,' I cry.

He bites his lower lip and shakes his head. 'If I had to pick someone, I'd pick Marcel de Becque.'

'What if he *ordered* me, John? The way you'd commission any painting? He tells Wingate he wants me in the next painting, but since I'm travelling all the time, Wingate takes Jane instead.'

'There's one big hole in that theory. Every other victim lives in New Orleans. But for some unknown reason, de Becque chooses you—a world traveller based in San Francisco—as victim number five. To fill de Becque's order, Wingate decides to use your twin sister as a substitute. And that substitute just *happens* to live in the same city as all the other victims? That's a statistical impossibility.'

A low pounding has started at the base of my skull. I reach down to the floor and unzip my bumbag, looking for my pill bottle.

'What's that?' John asks as I bring it up.

'Xanax. I need to calm down. It's no big deal.'

'Xanax is a chemical cousin of Valium. We've got another fifteen minutes in the car.' His hazel eyes are filled with concern. 'You're not going to fall asleep at the wheel, are you?'

I laugh. 'Don't worry about that. Two of these would put you out, but they'll barely dent me.'

I park in the driveway of John's suburban ranch house, then help him out of the passenger side. Thirty seconds after he read Wingate's number off the back of my photograph he collapsed in Mrs Pitre's driveway, and Baxter had ordered me to take him home to rest.

Under the carport, he punches a security code into a wall box and opens the back door, which leads into a spotless white kitchen.

'You obviously never cook,' I remark.

'I cook sometimes. But I'm basically a neat guy.'

'I've never met a neat guy I'd want to spend the night with.'

He laughs, then winces.

'Your leg?'

'It's stiffening up fast. Let me just get on the couch there.' Beyond the kitchen counter is a dining area with a large arch leading to a decently furnished den.

He limps to the sofa with his weight on the stick, but I take his hand and pull him past the sofa towards the hall. 'I don't want to sleep,' he complains, pulling back against my hand.

'We're not going to sleep.'

'Oh.'

His resistance stops, and I lead him towards a half-open door at the end of the hall, where a cherry footboard shows through. Like the rest of the house, the bedroom is clean; the bed is neatly made. I pull back the covers and he eases himself onto the edge of the bed, then lies back on the pillow with a groan.

'Bad?'

'Not good. I'm OK, though.'

'Let's see if I can make it better.'

I slip off my shoes, then climb onto the bed and carefully sit astride him. 'Does that hurt?'

'No.'

'Liar.' Leaning forward, I brush his lips with mine and pull back, waiting for him to respond. He kisses me back, gently, yet insistently enough to remind me of the passion I felt in the shower last night. A warm wave of desire rolls through me, which suppresses the shadowy images bubbling up from my subconscious.

'I want to forget,' I whisper. 'Just for an hour.'

He nods and pulls my lips to his, kissing me deeply as his arms slip round my back. After a bit, he nibbles my neck, then my ear, and the warmth escalates into something urgent enough to make me squirm in discomfort.

I slide off him and begin unbuttoning my blouse. When the blouse slips off my shoulders, John's breath goes shallow. I slide off my jeans and pants, then climb back to the spot I was in before. I touch his lips with my finger.

'Five minutes ago I felt as low as I ever have. I thought we were going to come in here and have violent sex that would exorcise our demons just long enough to let us sleep. But that's not what this is.'

He nods. 'I know.'

'You make me happy, John.'

'I'm glad. You make me happy too.' He nods down towards his leg. 'I'm not exactly in top form.'

'One critical part is still in working order.'

He shakes his head and laughs. 'You're not shy, are you?'

'I'm forty, John. I'm not a Girl Scout any more.' I reach back and undo his belt and trousers.

He pulls my face down and kisses me again, gently despite his need. I playfully bite his bottom lip.

He lays his hands on my thighs and slowly presses up into me, taking my breath away. Then he begins to move.

It's been almost a year since I made love with a man, and I feel as though I'm recovering from a sort of physical amnesia. When he collapses onto the pillow, I fall beside him.

'Jesus,' he says breathlessly.

'I know.'

'You're amazing.'

'Take it easy. You're in shock.'

'I think you're right.'

I rub my hand slowly over his abdomen. 'Why don't you sleep for a while?' I say.

He shakes his head. 'I can't. Not with Thalia still out there. I can never sleep when things are breaking.'

'You want me to make coffee or something?'

'Coffee would be good. And would you mind bringing those Argus photos in here?' John had only agreed to go home if he could take the latest Argus-generated enhancements of the abstract Sleeping Women with him.

I retrieve the thick manila envelope from the coffee table and toss it onto the bed. 'Pace yourself. Coffee and biscuits, coming up.'

I walk back to the kitchen and orientate myself, but I've got no further than running water when John's voice echoes up the hallway.

'I know this woman,' he says, shaking a piece of paper at me as I run through the door.

'From where?' I ask, taking the picture from him. It's a facial shot of a young blonde woman, maybe eighteen. 'Is she one of the missing persons you've been studying?'

'No. I saw her *years* ago. In Quantico. Every year we have city and state cops coming through our National Academy programme. Most of them have a case that's dogged them for years, one they couldn't solve or get out of their minds. A police detective showed me this woman at Quantico.'

'A New Orleans detective?'

'That's the thing. He was from New York. This is a really old case.'

My head is buzzing with a strange excitement. 'How old?'

'Ten years? Listen, serial offenders don't just wake up one day and start killing people in middle age. Baxter's unit was checking all four suspects' past residences for similar unsolved crimes. Vermont, where Wheaton's from. Terrebonne Parish, where Laveau grew up. Those were easy. That left New York, for Smith and Gaines. In fact, all four suspects have ties to New York. But when you're talking about missing persons—which is what this case is, because of the lack of corpses—you're talking about thousands of victims, even if you only go back a few years. But I thought, What if there were unsolved homicides in New York that had only one or two similarities to this case? Women taken from grocery stores, jogging paths, et cetera, snatched off the street without a trace, no witnesses, nothing. A professional feel to them, yet no obvious similarities between the victims.'

'Did you check it out?'

'I called some New York cops I knew from the Academy programme and asked them to poke around their old files. Nobody's got back to me yet. But this woman . . .'

'You still remember her?'

'I've got a knack for faces. This girl was pretty and young, and she stuck in my mind. That detective's, too. She was his informant, now that I think about it. Will you bring me the cordless phone?'

I get him the phone, and he rings the field office, asking for Baxter. 'It's John,' he says. 'I think we caught a break . . . A big one . . .'

I'm LYING IN JOHN'S TUB, soaking in hot water up to my neck. Last night passed in a flurry of confusion. Prompted by John's recognition of the Argus photo, Daniel Baxter rousted the midnight homicide shifts at the NYPD. Using Argus-enhanced photos of the abstract Sleeping Women paintings, New York detectives managed to identify six of the eight unidentified victims in the NOKIDS case.

Once the women were identified, the story came together by itself. Between 1979 and 1984, a serial kidnap-murderer was operating in New York City area without anyone connecting the crimes. His victims were prostitutes and hitchhikers. The significance of this discovery was simple and devastating: the painter of The Sleeping Women had not begun his work two years ago in New Orleans, but more than twenty years ago in New York.

The ramifications were more complex. First, our youngest suspect, Frank Smith, had been only fifteen years old at the time. This alone did not exonerate him, but it shifted the focus of the investigation away from him. Second, not one Sleeping Woman had been sold at the time. Third, why would a serial killer murder eight women and then suddenly stop? In John's experience, only prison or death stopped serial murderers from pursuing their work. Had he been locked up for a decade and a half, only to emerge as hungry for victims as before?

John drank nonstop cups of coffee to fight the sedative effects of his painkillers, and sat on the sofa working out theory after theory in an attempt to fit the new parameters of the case. Too exhausted to be any use to him, I took another three Xanax, got into bed and slept.

Next thing I know, John's shaking me awake. 'A boat crew just fished the UNSUB's body out of the river, five miles downstream from where he went in. Baxter choppered a forensic team down to the site to fingerprint the corpse. Get dressed. We're about to meet the man who tried to kidnap you.'

BAXTER AND LENZ are standing in the main computer room with coffee cups in their hands when we arrive at the field office. 'Chopper got the UNSUB's fingerprints here five minutes ago,' Baxter says. 'If there's a match on the database, we'll have it any second.'

'Sir?' says a female technician, looking up at Baxter. 'We have a match. One hundred per cent.'

The technician flicks her trackball and clicks a button. A criminal record pops onto the screen. In the top right-hand corner is a photograph, the face in it a younger version of the man who shot Wendy.

'Conrad Frederick Hoffman,' reads the tech. 'Convicted felon. Born Newark, New Jersey, 1952.'

The three men tense around me.

'What was the crime?' asks Lenz.

'Murder.'

'Where did he serve his time?' asks John.

'Sing Sing, New York State,' says the tech. 'From 1984 to 1998.'

A more pregnant silence I've never heard. As if speaking with one voice, the three men say, 'Leon Gaines.'

John taps the shoulder of a male tech next to the female tech and says, 'Call up Leon Isaac Gaines. I need the exact years he was in Sing Sing.'

'Leon Isaac Gaines,' says the male tech. 'Two terms in Sing Sing, the first 1973 to 1978, the second 1985 to 1990.'

'Son of a bitch,' John breathes. 'That's a five-year intersect. They had to know each other.'

'Let's get back to the EOC,' says Baxter. 'We need the warden of Sing Sing and every convict we can get hold of who served during those years.'

John picks up a phone and dials the surveillance unit. 'John Kaiser here. Where's Leon Gaines right now? . . . Get a chopper in the air. I want zero chance of losing him when he comes out . . . OK.'

'Where's Gaines?' asks Baxter as he hangs up.

'At the Kenner Wal-Mart. Isn't it a little early for shopping?'

Baxter shrugs. 'He's a drunk and an addict, and he just woke up after sleeping twelve hours.'

11

Forty-five minutes later, we're grouped in SAC Bowles's office, and the mood is grim. After an hour of phone calls to Sing Sing no one has been able to establish a personal relationship between Conrad Hoffman and Leon Gaines.

'We have three options,' says Baxter. 'One, arrest Gaines now and interrogate him. Two, question him but don't arrest him. Three, wait until we have more information.'

'You can't wait!' I cry in disbelief. 'You've already wasted too much time. Thalia Laveau could be dying somewhere right now!'

'I think Laveau is dead already,' says Lenz, not even looking at me. 'Even if she's not, Gaines may not know where she is. If he's merely the painter in the conspiracy, I mean.'

'*You* think she's dead?' I ask, coming half out of my chair. 'And how many times have you been right in the past week? Once?'

The four men gape at me in amazement, but I can't hold in my anger any longer. 'Right now, Thalia is wherever all The Sleeping Women were painted. In the house where the courtyard is. The house *you can't find*. And if that painter is Leon Gaines, Thalia is waiting for an artist who won't ever show up, because he knows we're watching him. She could be dying while Gaines strolls around Wal-Mart, laughing at us!'

'That's true,' John says quietly. 'But Gaines can't help us with Thalia without admitting complicity in murder. The reality is that right now, we have no way to make Gaines talk. No legal way, anyhow.'

In the strange hush that follows this statement, I ask, 'What about the girlfriend? Linda Knapp? If you could send someone over to talk to her away from him, she might recant her support for his alibis. She did it once.'

Baxter is not convinced, but the others have no objection, so a female agent is dispatched to Gaines's house.

The phone on Bowles's desk rings. Bowles must recognise the caller's number because he activates the speakerphone before answering.

'Sir, this is Agent Liebe,' says a male voice. 'My agents inside Wal-Mart lost visual with the suspect a couple of minutes ago. We're in the store in force now, but it's full of people. I think maybe—'

'Shut it down!' Baxter orders. 'Nobody goes in or out.'

IN THE TWELVE MINUTES it takes us to get to Kenner Wal-Mart, two agents sifting through the trapped customers and four searching the aisles and lavatories have turned up no sign of Leon Gaines, though his car still sits in the parking lot.

In the security room at the back of the store, a bank of video monitor displays feeds from three dozen video cameras mounted at various locations in the ceiling of the store. 'He's been gone fifteen minutes, minimum,' says John. 'He must have used some sort of disguise to evade the surveillance. He could be anywhere.'

A muted ring sounds in the room. John pulls his cellphone from his jacket. 'Kaiser here . . . Just now? . . . Put him through.' He looks at Baxter. 'Roger Wheaton just called the office and asked them to page me. He said it was an emergency.'

'Hello?' John covers his open ear. 'Yes, sir, John Kaiser . . . Can you get out of the building? . . . I understand. Can you get them out? . . . Listen to me, Mr Wheaton. If you can't get them out, get yourself out. We're on the way.'

John whirls to face us. 'Gaines just sandbagged Roger Wheaton in his office at the Woldenberg Art Centre. Gaines claimed he's being framed by the FBI and that he needs money to leave the country.'

'Is he armed?' asks Baxter.

John nods. 'Wheaton told Gaines he would drive him to the bank and get him money, but that his wallet and keys were down in the gallery. Gaines told Wheaton if he wasn't back in two minutes, he'd take students hostage and start killing them. Wheaton ran down to another office and called us.'

Baxter takes out his cellphone and hits a speed-dial button. 'This is Baxter. Give me SAC Bowles, right now . . . Patrick? Leon Gaines is at the art centre at Tulane, and he probably has hostages. We need SWAT out there a.s.a.p. . . . How many choppers do you have in the air? . . . Send them both to the Kenner Wal-Mart parking lot . . . He did? I guess that's no surprise. OK . . . I'll keep you posted.' Baxter looks at John. 'The FBI agent that went to Gaines's house reported back. Gaines beat his girlfriend and left her for dead before he went shopping. Let's move.'

HURTLING OVER NEW ORLEANS at a hundred knots, John and Baxter ride the lead chopper, Dr Lenz and I the one behind. Below us, Audubon Park stretches north from the river to St Charles Avenue; north of St Charles begins the rectangular garden that is Tulane University.

Parked at the centre of one grassy quadrangle I see two police cars with their lights flashing, while beside them an olive-drab Huey helicopter sits like a harbinger of battle, its main rotor slowly turning. The FBI SWAT team has probably deployed from that chopper.

We dip forward and come to rest thirty yards from the lead chopper. John jumps out of his cockpit and runs towards us, while Baxter moves towards the waiting NOPD cops.

'It's not good!' John yells as I get out and run in a crouch beneath our rotor. 'Gaines has a male hostage in a second-floor office. He's come to the window to show he has a gun to the guy's head. SWAT has set up a command post under the trees in front of the building.'

Baxter runs over from the squad car. 'Let's get over there, John!'

'Who's the negotiator?' Dr Lenz asks, appearing suddenly.

'Ed Davis,' John replies. 'He's good.'

Baxter starts running towards a large building on the north edge of the quad that I now recognise as the Woldenberg Art Centre. John and I follow, with Lenz puffing after us. From this angle, the building appears as two three-storey brick boxes separated by a one-storey section fronted with arches. If I remember correctly, the classical boxes house classrooms, studios and offices, while the long section houses the art gallery, where Wheaton's painting awaits its first public showing. Gaines must be inside one of the two end sections.

The closer we get to the building, the harder it is to see. Massive spreading oaks line the road in front of it, obscuring most of the windows. Beneath one of the oaks, a knot of men in black body armour with 'FBI' stencilled in yellow crouch round what looks like a map. Baxter takes out his cellphone and dials a number. I edge in to listen to the SWAT leader briefing John, while Lenz hovers beside him.

'Gaines is still on the second floor,' says the SWAT leader, who has a patch on his flak vest that reads Burnette. 'He's keeping his gun to the hostage's head when we can see him, but most of the time our view is obscured by blinds. There's no high ground for snipers, so we're going to put a man up in the Huey and have the pilot hold a hover until we get some scaffolding out here. We've rescued about forty students and faculty so far, but there may be twenty or so still on the floor with Gaines. He's barricaded the main access door, and some of those kids could be completely ignorant of the danger.'

'Have you established contact with Gaines?' John asks.

'A secretary just gave Ed Davis the number of the office. He's talking now.'

As Burnette points across the lane, a man dressed in civilian clothes pockets a cellphone and runs towards us. 'He wants a plane to take him to Mexico. I tried opening a dialogue, but he hung up. The guy sounds like a hard case. This could take a while.'

Baxter steps up to Burnette and says, 'SAC Bowles just designated Dr Lenz the hostage negotiator for this event. He also put me in tactical command on the ground. I've got no problem if you want to verify that.'

The SWAT leader shakes his head. 'It's fine with me.' The negotiator looks like he wants to argue, but suddenly someone yells, 'There he is!'

Two floors above us, wedged in front of some venetian blinds, stands Roger Wheaton. His long face is pressed flat against the windowpane, and there's a large pistol pressed against his ear.

'Goddamn it,' John mutters. 'I told him to get out.'

'Dial that office and give me your phone,' Lenz tells the negotiator. Then he looks at Burnette. 'Tell your snipers to stand down.'

As the former negotiator makes his call, SWAT leader Burnette says, 'Mr Baxter, my sniper can shoot that pistol out of Gaines's hand. He can do it from here. I've seen him do it under pressure.'

Baxter shakes his head. 'That's not an option yet.'

'Yes, hello?' says Lenz. 'Leon? . . . This is Dr Arthur Lenz . . . I was at your house the other day . . . Yes. I'm here because I know you need to talk to someone who's not bound by the normal rules . . . That's right. Some cases fall outside the lines, and this is one of them.'

When I look back up at the window, Wheaton has gone.

Lenz lowers his voice. 'Your demands aren't out of the question, Leon. But everything has a price. You know that. You may *seem* to hold all the cards. But you're assuming you know what our priorities are. There are twelve families who care more about you getting a lethal injection than they do about a dying artist whose life you might shorten by a few months.'

A dull pop slowly registers in my brain.

'Gunshot!' yells a SWAT agent.

'Put a sniper up in the Huey,' orders Baxter. 'Get a thermal imaging scope up there with him. We need to see through those blinds.'

As Burnette runs to the next oak tree, a woman screams from the direction of the art centre. Then the front door of the studio wing crashes open and a dozen students pour through it. Behind them, running with an awkward lope, is Wheaton.

'Are you all right?' John asks as he takes Wheaton by the arm. The artist's mouth and nose are covered with blood. 'Were you hit?'

'No,' Wheaton coughs. 'We struggled, and Leon hit me with the gun. He could have shot me, but he didn't.'

'We heard a gunshot,' John says in a taut voice. 'Was anyone hit?'

'His gun went off during our struggle. He didn't shoot anybody.'

'Is he alone up there now?'

Wheaton shakes his head. 'He had two female students barricaded in an adjacent office.' Wheaton suddenly recognises me. 'Oh—hello.'

'I'm glad you're all right,' I tell him.

'*That's Sarah! Oh my God!*'

The sound of screaming college girls is more piercing than a siren. Looking up at the window, I see a petite brunette pressed to the pane, the gun barrel huge beside her head.

John sits Wheaton down beneath an oak tree. Baxter, the SWAT leader and I cluster round them.

'Did you see any other weapons besides the pistol?' John asks Wheaton.

'No. But he has a bag with him.'

A heavy, beating sound ricochets off the face of the art centre. The

Huey is climbing into a hover fifty yards from the window behind which Gaines holds his hostage. Execution will soon be an option.

John raises his voice above the rotor noise. 'Has Gaines said anything to you to indicate he's guilty of the abductions?'

Wheaton shakes his head. 'He claims you're framing him. He said, "Those assholes need a patsy, and I'm it." He wanted cash.'

'Did he know you called the FBI?'

'Probably.' Wheaton's gloved hands are shaking. 'But I had to go back up there. If I tried to get everyone out, he'd have heard me, and he might have panicked and done something crazy. The safest thing was to offer myself as a hostage.'

'That took guts,' John says, but the artist just shakes his head.

'Leon doesn't want to shoot anybody, Agent Kaiser. He's scared to death. If you give him a way out of this, he'll take it.'

John looks sceptical. 'Mr Wheaton, some time last night, Leon beat his girlfriend into a coma. Then he left her for dead.'

A look of sadness comes over the artist's face. 'Good God. I met that girl.' The sadness is quickly replaced by a look of concern. 'That's still no reason to shoot him.'

'I don't know about that,' I say. 'But Gaines may be the only one who knows where Thalia Laveau is, or my sister and the rest.'

John looks over his shoulder at Lenz, who is angrily punching numbers into the commandeered cellphone. 'Any luck?'

'He's not answering.'

'Could someone help me stand up, please?' Wheaton asks. 'I may have to be sick.'

Baxter pulls the artist to his feet. 'An ambulance is on the way.'

'I'm sorry,' Wheaton apologises, as he doubles over and vomits on the grass. 'I'm just going to walk a bit, clear my head.'

Dr Lenz appears and taps Baxter's arm. 'Gaines told me that if we don't land one of our helicopters on the roof of the art centre in five minutes, he'll kill that girl. He says he's got another one up there.'

John looks at Wheaton. 'You said there were two girls, didn't you?'

Wheaton nods, then wobbles on his feet.

'I've got him,' I tell John, as I lead Wheaton away. John nods, then turns to address a group of black-clad SWAT men. Wheaton walks aimlessly along the grass in front of the Woldenberg Centre.

'They're not going to listen to me. They're going to kill Leon.'

The sound of a loudhailer reverberates across the quad, and Dr Lenz begins addressing Gaines through the window glass.

'I don't want to see this,' Wheaton says. 'I'm going home.'

'You're in no shape to drive. I'll get a cop to drive you.'

'I'm fine. Really. But my keys are in the gallery with my bag, and I don't think that cop is going to let me get them.'

He points to an FBI agent standing beneath the entrance arch. Wheaton's keys are far from Leon Gaines. 'I'll talk to him,' I say. 'You stay here.'

'Thank you. They're on the floor in the centre of the room.'

I trot across the grass. 'I need to get some keys for one of the hostages,' I call to the agent. 'They're in the gallery.'

'Nobody goes in,' he says.

'You've got a radio. Call John Kaiser.'

The agent lifts his walkie-talkie and makes the call.

'Go in with her,' John tells the agent. 'But don't let Wheaton go home yet. I don't want anyone else kidnapped. No more surprises.'

'Copy,' says the agent. His face softens as he opens the door and holds it for me. 'I'm Agent Aldridge, by the way.'

'Through here,' I tell Aldridge, leading him towards the access panel in the canvas circle.

'Wow,' Aldridge says softly, once inside. 'This thing is massive.'

The lights are off in the gallery, but a flood of illumination pours through the skylights, bathing the masterpiece in a bluish glow.

'There's the bag,' I tell him, pointing to a leather tote lying in the middle of a huge dustsheet.

'Oh, shit,' says the agent, looking at his shoes. 'Look at this.'

The dustsheet around his shoes is stained with bright blue paint. '*Shit*. This is oil paint. It'll take—'

A shattering gunshot echoes through the building. Before the echo fades, Aldridge is moving towards me with his gun drawn.

'That was outside!' I tell him. 'A rifle. Give me your radio!'

He passes me his walkie-talkie with his free hand.

'This is Jordan Glass calling John Kaiser. John! It's Jordan!'

There's a crackle of static, then John's voice jitters from the radio as though he's talking while running. 'They had to shoot him, Jordan. We don't know if he's dead. We're going up now. Stay put for five minutes, then have the agent escort you to the command post.'

'OK. Be careful!'

'I wonder what happened,' says Aldridge. 'The guy probably panicked and got wild with his gun.'

I cannot reply. The knowledge that died with Gaines took part of me with it. My legs feel shaky. I fall to my knees.

'Are you OK?'

'Just give me a minute.'

'*Hey!*' Aldridge shouts, pointing his pistol at the access panel.

Roger Wheaton stands just inside the canvas circle, his face a mask of anguish. 'They killed him,' he says. 'I heard Leon yell through the window. A sniper shot him in the head.'

'Take it easy,' I tell Aldridge. 'It's his keys we came to get.'

The FBI agent lowers his gun.

'Gaines might still be alive,' I say without much conviction, but Wheaton just shakes his head.

I push myself to my feet with my hands and discover my palms are wet. Turning them over, I see red and yellow paint on my skin, bright primary shades like the blue on Aldridge's feet. This much paint couldn't be the result of spills. Wheaton must have been painting the forest floor too.

'Have I ruined anything?' I ask, holding up my palms.

Wheaton's face darkens as he realises I've smeared the paint.

'Hey, you shouldn't have sent us after the keys with it wet,' says Aldridge.

'Stay where you are,' says Wheaton. 'Both of you.'

The artist tiptoes across the dustsheet in a complicated path, like a military engineer walking through a minefield he just laid. As he passes Aldridge, he takes the agent's hand, then mine, and escorts us both to the edge of the floor. He smiles at me.

'You've discovered my surprise. I thought it would be dry by now.'

'May I look?'

'I suppose so.'

I reach down, lift the coarse material in my hands, and walk forward. Halfway across the room, I stop, my eyes transfixed by the images on the floor. They're bright, childlike human figures painted directly onto the hardwood in wide curves of red, yellow and blue.

'That looks like finger painting,' I say softly.

'It is. Think of what the critics will say!' Wheaton exults.

But I'm not thinking of the critics. I'm thinking that beside every figure is a large X, that all the figures have long hair, and that their mouths are open in huge wailing O's.

'That's freaky,' says Aldridge. 'You're the guy who painted this'— he points at a beautiful tree beside his shoulder, then back at the floor—'and you painted *that*?'

Wheaton touches Aldridge on the arm, and something crackles and flashes blue. The agent falls to the floor, jerking like a man having a fit. Then Wheaton turns to me, and the avuncular face is gone. A new intelligence stares out through his eyes: vulpine, knowing, cold, fearless. 'I'm *not* the man who painted that,' he says, pointing at The Clearing. 'The man who did is almost dead.'

With the slowness of nightmares, I scrabble at the right cuff of my jeans, reaching for the pistol John gave me, but as my hand closes on the butt of the .38, a vicious wasp stings my neck, and my arms begin jerking spastically. The room blurs and fades and for a moment I wonder if I'm dying.

CONSCIOUSNESS RETURNS before vision. I know I'm alive, because I'm cold. Shivering. I try to touch my face, but my arms won't move properly. My legs either. I focus all my energy on opening my eyes, but they don't open. Terror squirms in my chest like a rat trying to fight its way out of a bag.

Stop, says a voice in my mind, and I cling desperately to its echo. My father's voice. *Don't panic*, he says.

But I'm so afraid—

Without warning, my eyelids begin fluttering and my hands clench into fists. Something's happening to my muscles. A voice tells me to keep my eyes closed until I know more about my situation, but the hunger for light is too strong. Vision returns as swirling clouds, wisps of white on grey. Slowly, the clouds part to reveal an old-fashioned water heater. I'm in a bathtub, naked.

I try to turn my head, but my neck muscles refuse to obey my brain. I must be content with what I can see from this position. The wall opposite me is made of glass. The roof above is also glass, long shining triangles of it. Through the glass I see the sky, fading down to dusk. I'm in a conservatory. A conservatory with a bathtub in it. I'm almost convinced I'm dreaming when I hear the pad of feet.

'Welcome back,' says a familiar male voice.

With superhuman effort I turn my head to the left and find a scene so bizarre I am rendered speechless.

Roger Wheaton stands partly behind an artist's easel, a paintbrush in his white-gloved hand, working feverishly on a large canvas that I cannot see. He is naked but for a white cloth tied round his waist and between his legs, like those used by artists to cover the genitals of Jesus in Crucifixion paintings. Wheaton's body is surprisingly well muscled, but his torso is lined with bruises and haemorrhages.

My first attempt to speak is only a rasp. But then saliva comes, and I get the words out. 'Where am I?'

In one sense this is a rhetorical question. I'm in the place eleven other women occupied before me—twelve, including Thalia. I'm in the killing house. I am one of The Sleeping Women.

'Where do you think you are?' Wheaton's gaze moves from the canvas to me, then back again.

'The killing house,' I reply.

He seems not to hear.

'Where's Thalia?'

'She felt no pain,' he says, as though this mitigates the situation.

I shut my eyes, recalling Frank Smith's description of Wheaton's suicide plan: *Insulin is painless* . . . But I force myself to put Thalia out of my mind. 'What's wrong with my arms?'

Wheaton ignores me, flicking the brush over the canvas with remarkable speed. A belated impulse makes me turn over my own hand. The left one. It seems to take an eternity, but finally, on the outside of my wrist, I see a plastic tube running into one of my veins. The tube runs in a serpentine loop round the base of an aluminium stand and up to a bag hanging from an IV tree. I try to yank it out but haven't enough muscular control.

Wheaton admonishes me with an upraised finger. 'There is Valium in your bag. And a muscle relaxant. But that can easily change. So please, don't bother the equipment.'

Valium? My second-favourite drug . . .

'I expected you to be unconscious for at least another hour.'

Wheaton suddenly straightens, then turns as though looking at himself in a mirror. Which is exactly what he is doing. To my right, propped against the wall, is a huge mirror like the ones used in ballet studios. Wheaton is not only painting me—he's painting *himself.*

'What are you painting?'

'My masterpiece. I call it "Apotheosis".'

'I thought the circular painting was your masterpiece.'

He laughs softly. 'That was *his* masterpiece. Roger's. The weakling. *The fag.*'

My stomach turns a slow somersault. Dear God. Two FBI profilers and a psychiatrist sit brainstorming round a table, and the photographer turns out to be right.

MPD, Dr Lenz called it. Multiple-personality disorder. What else did Lenz say? *Always caused by extreme sexual or physical abuse* . . .

'If you're not Roger Wheaton,' I say carefully, 'who are you?'

'I have no name.'

'How did I get here?'

'You don't remember?' he asks, lifting his brush.

I do remember some things. Flashes of light, waves of vertigo. A grey sky, bubbles of glass, a bridge of white tubes, and a long fall. 'The roof. You took me out on the roof.'

Wheaton chuckles.

'But there were FBI agents up there.'

'Not after Leon was shot. They all wanted to see the trophy. There's a catwalk running from the art centre to the physical plant.'

'But how did you manage to carry me? You're ill.'

Wheaton's lips curl in disdain. 'That diagnosis is currently under review. Roger was weak. I am strong.'

What is he telling me? He's not sick any more? What did Lenz say about MPD? *There's a documented case of one personality needing heart medication to survive, and the other not . . .*

Wheaton keeps painting. 'I painted your sister,' he says suddenly, not looking up.

Oh God. 'I saw that painting,' I say aloud.

'You want to know if your sister is alive or dead, don't you?'

I close my eyes against tears, but they come anyway.

'Don't you already know?'

Through the tears I see Wheaton's eyes locked upon mine.

'Which is it?' he asks. 'Alive or dead?'

Trying to read him, I'm suddenly thrown back to the street in Sarajevo, to the instant the world blacked out and I felt a part of me die. Despite all my subsequent hopes, despite the phone call from Thailand, I knew then that Jane was dead. 'Dead,' I whisper.

Wheaton purses his lips and goes back to his painting.

'Am I right?'

'Yes,' Wheaton says. 'But you shouldn't be upset. She's far better off the way she is now.'

'*What?*'

'You've seen my paintings. The Sleeping Women. Surely you understand the purpose of the paintings?'

'No. I never have.'

Wheaton lowers his brush and stares at me with incredulity. 'The *release.* I've been painting the release.'

'The release?' I echo. 'From what?'

His face is like that of a monk trying to explain the Holy Trinity to a savage. 'The plight of being a woman.'

A moment ago I felt only grief. Now something harder quickens my blood. A desire to know, to understand.

'I don't understand what you're telling me.'

'Yes, you do. You've tried so hard to live as a man. You work relentlessly. You haven't married, you've no children. But that's no escape. And you're learning that, aren't you? Every month, the little seed inside you cries out to be fertilised. Your womb aches to be filled. You've let Kaiser use your body, haven't you? I read the signals the morning you came back with him, to the house on Audubon Place.'

So I'm not at Audubon Place. Of course I'm not. If I were, I would have heard the St Charles streetcar bell by now.

'Do you mean that killing women releases them from pain?'

'Of course. The life of woman is the life of a slave, broken by childbirth and marriage and housekeeping.'

'I do understand that,' I tell him. 'That's why I've lived the life I have. But the painting you're doing now must have a different theme.'

He nods, flicking his hand right, then left, his eye leading the strokes with lightning precision. 'It's my emergence,' he says. 'My freedom from the prison of duality.'

'From Roger, you mean?'

'Yes.' Again the strange smile. 'Roger's dead now.'

Roger's dead? 'How did he die?'

'I shed him, like a snake sheds its skin. It took a surprising amount of effort, but it had to be done. He was trying to kill me.'

'Roger went to Frank Smith for help, didn't he?'

Wheaton's eyes are on me now, trying to gauge the depth of my knowledge. 'That's right.'

'Why go to him? Why not to Conrad Hoffman? Your helper? Hoffman set up this place for you, didn't he?'

Wheaton looks at me like I'm three years old. 'Roger didn't know Conrad. Except from that first show, which he quickly forgot.'

I can't digest the information fast enough. 'Does—*did*—Roger, I mean—did he know about *you*?'

'Of course not.'

'But how do you hide all this work from him?'

'It's not difficult. Conrad and I set up this special place, and this is where I do my work.'

As Wheaton paints on, I ponder the chances of the FBI finding me here. They know what happened by now, of course. John and Baxter. Lenz. The NOPD. They know Gaines was not the killer. They've seen Wheaton's finger painting, found Agent Aldridge. But what could possibly lead John to this place? FBI planes shot total coverage of the French Quarter and the Garden District; dozens of agents are probably at the New Orleans courthouse right now, wading through the deeds to all those places with courtyards, searching for any connection to Roger Wheaton or Conrad Frederick Hoffman. Will they include houses with conservatories? Yes. John will be thorough.

I suddenly realise that I'm terribly hungry. 'I'm starving. Do you have any food?'

Wheaton sighs and looks up at the glass roof, checking the diminishing light. Then he walks to my left, out of my field of vision. Straining to turn my neck, I see him reach down into a brown grocery bag and bring out a flat narrow package about eight inches long. Beef jerky. Beside the grocery bag stands an Igloo ice chest. The standard three-foot-wide plastic model, big enough for two cases of beer. Or IV bags filled with saline and narcotics, I suppose.

Wheaton's gloved hands give him difficulty tearing open the plastic wrapper of the jerky, but he knows I can't manage it in my present state. At last he pulls it apart and walks over to the tub. With tremendous effort, I raise my hand and take the brown strip from him.

Ugh, I think as I slide the tacky stuff into my mouth. But when I grind the flat strip between my back teeth, my tongue savours the grease expressed from the meat like crème brûlée.

'How do you know Roger is dead?' I ask. If I have a potential ally in this room, his name is Roger Wheaton.

The artist laughs softly. 'You remember the finger painting on the floor at the gallery?'

'Yes.'

'That was his last gasp. His death throes. An infantile attempt at some sort of confession. Pathetic.'

'And now you don't need your—*his*—glasses any more?'

'You see me painting without them, don't you?'

'But you're still wearing your gloves.'

A tight smile. 'There's systemic damage. That will take time to heal.' He glances up at the darkening sky.

'There's one more thing I don't understand.'

He frowns, but I push on. 'You say you killed the women you painted to release them from their plight. Is that right?'

'Yes.'

'Yet each Sleeping Woman was raped before she died. How can you stand there and tell me you're sparing them pain, when you're putting them through the worst thing a woman can experience short of death?'

Wheaton has stopped painting. His eyes glower with anger and confusion. 'What are you talking about?'

'Conrad Hoffman. Before he died, he had a gun to my head. He told me he was going to rape me. And the last woman taken before Thalia—the one taken from Dorignac's—the pathologist found semen inside her.'

His head jerks as if avoiding a blow.

'Was it yours?' I ask softly.

Wheaton takes two steps towards me. 'You're lying.'

The prudent thing would be to stop, but my salvation may lie in the root of this paradox. 'The FBI is sure you killed the Dorignac's woman. They worked out the timing of Wingate's death, and they know when Hoffman flew back from New York. Hoffman couldn't have taken her.'

Wheaton is wheezing now, like a child with asthma. 'I took her, but—' He stands with his mouth open, unable to continue.

'Help me understand,' I plead. 'A man who saves a twelve-year-old girl from being raped in Vietnam turns round and helps some pervert rape the women he claims he's saving?'

Wheaton's chin is quivering.

'I guess it was Roger who saved that girl in Vietnam—'

'*No!*' A single, explosive syllable. '*I did that!*'

I say nothing. The fault line running through Wheaton's mind is torturing him more painfully than I possibly could. With a jerk of his head he looks up at the nearly dark sky. Then he walks to a table behind his easel, lifts a hypodermic syringe from it, and walks back towards me, his face devoid of emotion.

My new-found confidence vaporises, leaving pure terror in its wake, as Wheaton walks over to my IV tree and injects the contents of his syringe into my IV bag. My left arm begins to burn at the wrist, and tears of anger and helplessness flow from my eyes. I try to fight the unknown poison, but in a matter of seconds my eyelids fall as surely as shutters being pulled down by a man with a hook.

THIS TIME THE WORLD returns as stars in a black sky, blurred by glass, and the sound of a man sobbing. The anguished sobs seem to echo all the way from a distant planet. The planet of childhood, I suspect.

I'm shivering again, which is not such a bad thing. It's when you stop shivering that you're in trouble. I sense that Wheaton is lying on the floor somewhere, but I can't see him. As I try to make out objects in the room, an amazing new reality comes to me.

My muscles are under my control.

Leaning back, I look up at the silver line of my IV stand. The hanging bag is flat. Whatever was keeping my muscles in limbo has stopped flowing into me. After flexing my cramped limbs, I decide I can probably get out of the tub. The problem is Wheaton. I must know how close he is, and what he will do when he hears noise. Reaching out with my right hand, I turn the hot-water tap and wait.

For a few seconds the new water is cold. Then it begins to warm, and blissful heat flows around me, bringing blood to my bluish skin. The water continues to run, but Wheaton doesn't come to investigate. Gingerly, I stand on shaky legs and climb out of the tub.

My muscles still aren't quite my own, but they do function. The IV tube in my hand presents a problem, but the IV stand has wheels. With careful steps, I drag the stand over to the glass wall of the conservatory. What I find is discouraging. The first four feet of glass above the brick wall supporting the conservatory is encased in a diamond-shaped metal mesh. There's a glass door leading outside, but it too has mesh between its metal struts, and a heavy padlock ensures that the door remains closed.

The space my body displaced in the tub is filling quickly. What options do I have? Creep into the house proper and try to slip past Wheaton? But the sobs I heard came from close by, not far away. He may be lying on a sofa in the next room, my pistol in his hand.

Think, says my father. *What do you know that he doesn't? What's near to hand that can help you?*

What do I know? That I'm more than half addicted to Xanax, which is a cousin of Valium. It's probably a cross-tolerance between those drugs that's made it possible for me to wake and tiptoe around while Wheaton believes me to be asleep. What is near to hand that can help me? The table from which Wheaton took the hypodermic is bare. The room is empty. *Not quite empty,* I realise. On the floor behind my end of the tub sits the Igloo ice chest and the grocery bag.

I drag the IV stand towards them.

The bag is half filled with junk food. Pop-Tarts. Hostess Twinkies. Beef jerky. I stare at the boxes and bags, sensing important activity deep in my brain, but not quite understanding it. Slowly, the logic makes itself known to me. These aren't weapons. They are defences.

Reaching into the bag, I quietly open the boxes and remove three shining foil packs of Pop-Tarts and a handful of cellophane-wrapped Twinkies. These I stash between the tub and the mirror Wheaton uses to paint himself into his picture. Moving to the Igloo, I say a silent prayer, then pop open the white fastener and lift the lid. It's dark inside, so I blindly push my hands towards the bottom. They plunge into a rattling Arctic ocean of ice and water, with floating islands that feel like beer bottles. In seconds, pain radiates up my arms.

God bless you, you sick bastard, I say silently. My heart pounds with new hope, but I can't linger here. Warm water is lapping at my feet. The bathtub is overflowing, and not quietly. But this too is good. The spillover will wipe out the wet traces of my journey around the room, and perhaps convince Wheaton that I'm still in poor control of my faculties. I climb back into the near-scalding water, and am reaching for the tap when I hear a noise in the dark.

'*What are you doing?*' bellows a groggy voice.

Footsteps approach the tub, the tap squeaks, and the water stops running. Then I hear a clatter behind my head. My IV bag rattles in the stand. He's changing it.

'Soon,' he hisses. 'Tomorrow.'

As he walks away, my wrist begins to burn again. *Valium*, I tell myself, even as my eyes try to close. *Not insulin. Insulin doesn't burn.*

Pull out the tube, says my father.

I'm reaching for the IV catheter when my eyes go black.

12

I wake in full daylight, but I don't open my eyes. Wheaton will expect me to be unconscious longer. For an hour I lie with my eyes closed, reconstructing my environment from sound alone. Just as yesterday, Wheaton stands behind his easel, painting with sure, rapid strokes.

I have to slow him down. The longer I lie here alive, the more time John will have to find me. *Get him talking*, says my father.

When the sun shines noticeably brighter through my eyelids, I make a show of coming awake. 'How does it look?' I ask.

'As it should,' Wheaton answers in a clipped voice. He clearly doesn't recall last night's conversation with fondness. But then he continues, 'I saw a report on television this morning. If the local anchors aren't lying for the FBI, you told me the truth last night. About the rapes. I'd do anything to change that. I should have known, I suppose. Conrad always had poor impulse control. But if Conrad hadn't done it, someone else would have. In a different way, perhaps. The husband's way. But still, they're all better off now.'

'I understand about the plight. I understand The Sleeping Women. But I don't think you're telling me everything.'

His eyes flick to me. 'What do you mean?'

'Your feelings about women didn't just come to you out of the blue. They must have been shaped by a woman you knew.'

Wheaton's brush pauses in midair, then returns to the canvas.

'I know your mother disappeared when you were thirteen or fourteen.'

He stops painting altogether.

'I know what that's like. My father disappeared when I was twelve. In Cambodia. Everyone said he was dead, but I never believed it. I created all sorts of scenarios. He'd been wounded and had amnesia. He was crippled and couldn't get back. He was held prisoner. But as I got older, I realised that probably none of that was true.'

'You accepted that he was dead?'

'No. I came to believe something even more terrible. That he'd abandoned us. Maybe to be with another woman. Another family. Another little girl that he loved more than me.'

Wheaton is nodding.

'It almost killed me, thinking that.'

'It wasn't your fault. He was a man.'

'I know, but last night, I was thinking—dreaming—about you. And I saw a woman, your mother. She was holding a boy and trying to explain why she had to go. I asked her why she would leave you—'

Red blotches have appeared on Wheaton's face and neck. 'She never left me! I was the *only thing that kept her alive*.'

'What do you mean?'

His face goes through tortured contractions, as though he's reliving some horrible moment. Then he dips his brush in the paint and goes back to his canvas as if no conversation ever took place.

And then he begins talking.

'I was born during the war,' Wheaton says, painting with absolute assurance. 'In 1943. My father was in the Marine Corps, a hard, merciless man. He came home on leave after basic training, and that's when he fathered me. That's what he thought, anyway. When he was drafted, it was a liberation. Mother had to raise two sons of four and five on her own but at least she was free of the cutting voice, the brutal hand, the ruthless insistence of the nights when she protested in vain to the ceiling and the walls, begging God for some reprieve. God had finally answered her prayers. He had sent her the war.'

Wheaton smiles. 'A month after my father shipped out for the Pacific, a stranger came to the door asking for water. He had a limp, some disease had crippled him, and the army wouldn't take him. He worked on one of the government-funded artists' projects, as a painter. Mother fell in love with him. She worshipped art. Her prize possession was a book a dead aunt had bequeathed her. A big colour-plate thing called *Masterpieces of Western Art*. Anyway, the painter camped nearby for two weeks, and when he left, Mother was pregnant.

'I was born two weeks premature. It meant Mother could lie about my paternity and get away with it. At least for a while.

'Then my father came back from the war. He was just as brutal.

'My brothers worked the farm and helped my father trap when they weren't in school. My life was different. Mother treated me differently. Taught me things. Pinched pennies to buy me paint and canvas. She encouraged me to imitate the paintings in her book. My brothers made fun of me, but that was a small thing. In the summers, Mother and I spent our days in an old barn in the woods. We escaped.' A look of transcendence comes over Wheaton's face.

'It stood in a small clearing, with a stream flowing beside it. Part of the roof had fallen in, but we didn't mind. The sun fell through the hole in great yellow shafts, the way it does in Gothic cathedrals.'

'What did you paint there?' I ask, even as the answer comes to me. 'Did you paint your mother?'

'Who else could I paint? She would bring different clothes from the house, gauzy gowns, robes like those the women wore in classical paintings. Sometimes she would pose in the nude, like the nudes in her book. Hour after hour I would paint, and we would talk, and laugh, until the shafts of light began to fade, and we had to walk back to the dark little house of rage.'

'What happened? Did someone catch you with her in the nude?'

Wheaton closes his eyes. 'One afternoon, instead of trapping with my father, my brothers spied on us. They watched until Mother disrobed. Then they ran and got my father. When he burst into the barn and saw her naked, he went crazy. He told my brothers to hold me down, and he—he started to beat her. But instead of taking it, as she usually did, she fought back. She clawed his face, drew blood. When he saw that, he picked up an old scythe handle . . .'

Wheaton squints as though staring at a distant object. 'I can still hear the whistle it made. And the impact, like the sound of an eggshell. The way she fell. She was dead before she hit the floor.'

'Why isn't there any record of this?'

'There was no one around for miles. She had no family left.'

'What happened then? Did your father bury her?'

Wheaton looks at the floor, and his voice drops to a barely audible whisper. 'He came over to where my brothers were holding me down and told me to bury her. He said if I told anyone what had happened, he and my brothers would swear they'd caught me raping her in the barn, after she was dead. I'd be sent to a reform school in the city, where boys would beat me every day and sodomise me in the night. Then they left me with her.'

'I'm so sorry,' I murmur, but Wheaton doesn't hear me.

'I couldn't bury her.' His voice is almost a whine. 'I cried until my eyes were like sandpaper. Then I dragged her down to the stream and washed her from head to toe, cleaning away the blood and straightening her hair as best I could. I realised something then. Her agony was finally over. All her life was pain, and now it had ended. She was better off dead. Do you see?'

I do. I see how a shattered child made the mental journey to a state that allows him to kill women and believe he is doing a good thing.

'I went back to the barn and painted over what I'd been doing. Then, in the dying light, I painted Mother in her peace. It was the first time I'd seen her face completely relaxed. It was my birth as an artist. When I was finished, I took a shovel from the barn and buried her beside the stream.'

'What happened when you went home?'

My question seems to suck the humanity out of Wheaton's face. 'For four years, I lived like an animal. My father told the few people who asked that my mother had run away to New York. He became convinced that I was illegitimate. He couldn't prove it. He just *knew*. After that, they did things to Roger that you simply can't imagine. They starved him. Beat him. Worked him like a slave. The father used him sexually, to punish him.' Wheaton shakes his head dismissively. 'If it weren't for me, he'd never have survived.'

'How did you protect Roger?'

'I listened. I *watched*. My hearing grew frighteningly acute. I could hear them breathing in their sleep. If their breathing changed, I knew it. If they got out of bed, I knew Roger was in danger. I told him when to hide, when to run. When to hoard food. When to give in, and when to resist. That's how Roger survived.'

'Did you tell him to run away to New York?'

Wheaton resumes painting. 'Yes. But the city wasn't how I thought it would be. Roger tried to paint, but he couldn't make a go of it. People offered help, gave him food, a place to sleep, space to paint. But in exchange they wanted their pound of flesh. They wanted *him*. And he gave himself to them. What did it matter? For four years he moved among them—soft, greedy, grey old men—painting derivative work, doing anything they asked. Things had to change.'

A cruel smile touches Wheaton's lips. 'One day, walking down the street, I saw my opening. I darted into a recruiting office and joined the Marine Corps. The war in Vietnam was heating up, and before Roger knew what had happened, he was on his way there.

'That's where I came into my own. Vietnam. He couldn't make it without me. During the days he would poke along, joking and cursing, trying to fit in. But at night he made room for me. On patrol. On point. I could smell things he couldn't even *see*. I could hear bare feet bending grass at fifty yards. I kept him alive.'

'What about after?' I ask.

'I went back to New York, didn't I? I took my GI Bill money, went to NYU and painted. I did portraits to keep myself in groceries. I was searching for my destiny. And it found me. My surviving brother died in the merchant marine, and the farm went up for sale. I decided to buy it. Every day was a sweet revenge. Those rooms had witnessed all Mother's pain, and Roger filled them with colour and light. It was then that he began to paint The Clearing.'

'When did *you* start painting? The Sleeping Women?'

Wheaton purses his lips, like a man trying to recall the year he got married or joined the service. 'Seventy-eight, I think. I was driving out of New York, and I saw a girl hitchhiking. I asked where she was going, and she said, "Any place warm, man."'

'I drove her back to the farm. On the way, she got high. She had pills with her. Then she got sleepy. I asked if I could paint her, and she said yes. When I asked if I could paint her nude, she hesitated, but only a moment. I posed her in the tub and she dozed off.'

'But something happened,' I say hesitantly.

'Yes. Before I finished, she woke up. I was naked. I'm not sure how I got that way. I only know I was naked and painting, and I was aroused. The girl panicked. She fought. She gave me no choice. I pushed her under the water and held her there until she stopped fighting.'

'What did you do then?'

'I finished the painting.' Wheaton picks up his brush, dips it, and goes back to his work. 'She looked so peaceful. Much happier than she had when I picked her up. She was the first Sleeping Woman.'

'Tell me about Conrad Hoffman.'

'Roger had a one-man show in New York, and Conrad showed up for that. He saw something in The Clearing paintings that no one else did. He saw *me*. The germ of me. He was charismatic, young, dangerous. After the show we went for coffee. He didn't fawn over Roger, as some did. He sensed the power hidden in the paintings. The darkness. And I did something I never thought I would do.'

'You showed him your Sleeping Women.'

Wheaton nods cagily. 'There were only two then. He knew immediately that the women were dead, and revelled in it. When I saw that he understood, I felt some irresistible power well up within me. And I ravished him.'

'*What?*'

'I wasn't like Roger—face down and taking it in pain. *I* was the one in control. Conrad became a vessel for my power.' Seeing shock in my face, Wheaton says, 'Conrad was bisexual. He'd picked it up in jail.'

'And after that, he started helping you?'

Wheaton is painting with almost mechanical speed now. 'Conrad procured my subjects, mixed the drug cocktails, worked out what was best to keep them sedated while I worked. The insulin. He carried many burdens for me.'

'And he raped the women as a reward.'

Wheaton's brush hardly stutters. 'I suppose he did.'

'What made you stop? In New York, I mean?'

'Conrad killed someone in an argument. He was sentenced to fourteen years. When he was released he helped me begin my work again.'

'Why did you sell the paintings? Why take the risk? You already had money. Fame. Respect.'

'*Roger* had those things. But when collectors saw my Sleeping Women, they recognised an entirely different level of truth.'

'What do you plan to do with me?'

'I'm going to give you what you most want. I'm going to reunite you with your sister.'

'Is she buried here? Under this house?'

There's not even a hitch in Wheaton's brush stroke as he nods. It's almost more than I can bear.

'Your sister was a bit different from the others. I'm not sure how she managed it, but she made it out to the garden. Conrad caught her, but she fought, and he had to end it there. He buried her immediately. I finished painting her using only a photograph.'

For the first time in many hours, anger boils to the surface. Reaching out to the tap, I turn it—only this time I have turned on the cold tap. Wheaton doesn't seem to notice.

As I fight the tortured images summoned up by his words, he puts down his brush, and walks into the main house. There's a soft clatter followed by the low murmur of a voice. He's making a phone call.

I roll over, get to my knees, lean out and drag the Igloo cooler up to the tub. Praying the running water will cover the noise, I lift the cooler to the edge of the tub and dump the melting ice into it.

The icy shock sucks the breath right out of my lungs, but I haven't time to waste. Three bottles of Michelob have fallen into the tub. I put them back into the empty cooler, then slide it back to its place. A droning voice floats through the doorway to my left. I hear the word 'ticket' several times. Possibly the word 'departure'.

God, it's cold. I won't be able to stand much of this. My sluggish brain has already forgotten something critical. My insulin defence. Reaching down between the tub and mirror, I bring up a pack of Pop-Tarts and tear open the foil with stiff fingers. I break the hard pastries into pieces, shove them into my mouth and chew them just enough to get them down my throat.

Footsteps.

When Wheaton reappears, he walks to the easel and examines the canvas with a critical eye.

'Is the painting done?' I ask.

'What?' Wheaton says in a distant voice. 'Oh. Almost. I—'

The ringing telephone cuts him off. He looks confused. With a quick glance at me, he goes back into the house.

Turn on the hot water, says a voice in my head. *A little won't hurt—*

This time the footsteps return at a run. Wheaton rushes into the room, my Smith & Wesson featherweight .38 in his hands.

'What's the matter? What happened?'

'They hung up.' His voice is a ragged whisper. 'They listened for a few seconds before they hung up.'

I try to keep my eyes flat as hope blossoms in my chest. 'It was probably a kid. Or some pervert.'

Wheaton shakes his head. 'This place isn't safe any more.'

I feel a sudden urge to leap out of the freezing tub, but before I can act, Wheaton says, 'I know you can move.'

My heart stutters.

'Don't pretend you can't. I ran out of muscle relaxant. I have to get ready to leave. I'm going to put some more Valium into your IV.

Enough to knock you out for a while, but not enough to kill you.'

His face looks sincere, but I know who I'm talking to. 'You're lying.'

'Jordan. I could shoot you right now if I wanted to kill you. I shot a lot of people in Vietnam. That's not a problem.'

He crouches four feet from the tub and looks me in the eye. 'Why doesn't Valium work on you, Jordan? Do you have a little *habit*?'

'Maybe a little one.'

He laughs appreciatively. 'You're a sly one, aren't you?'

He stands and goes into the other room, then returns with a syringe. 'Stay right where you are. If you try anything, I'll have to shoot you.'

Wheaton walks out of my field of vision, and though I can't see him, I know what he's doing: injecting the contents of the syringe into my IV bag.

My wrist should start burning, but it doesn't. Wheaton reappears and crouches again, three feet away. 'How do you feel?' he says.

'Scared.'

'There's nothing to fear, Jordan. Don't fight it.'

'Fight what?'

'The Valium.'

'It's not Valium.' A wave of nausea rolls through me. 'Is it?'

'Why do you say that?'

'Because my wrist isn't burning.'

He sighs, then smiles with something like compassion. 'Trust a junkie to know her drugs. Soon you won't have a care in the world.'

The bathwater doesn't feel as cold as it did before, and for a second I'm thankful. Then I understand: the insulin is affecting my perception. The sugar that the Pop-Tarts flushed into my blood will give only limited immunity to the insulin, depending on the dose he gave me. If he comes no closer than he is now, I'll pass out before I can do anything to save myself. Near panic, I shake myself, then kick my legs up out of the tub, which sends me sliding down into the water. My head slips beneath the surface.

It takes a supreme act of will to hold my head under the water, but this is the only path to survival. I make a show of fighting to get my head above the water.

A shadow appears above the tub. Wheaton is looking down at me. With a macabre sense of dislocation, I watch my last moments on earth through his eyes. He wants to pull my head clear of the water; I can feel it. To give me a more humane death.

Starved of oxygen, my lungs burn to reach the surface. I can't wait for Wheaton to reach in. With a scream of desperation I explode out of the water, hands extended like claws. He tries to wheel backwards, but his feet haven't enough purchase on the wet floor to allow him to use his weight against me and I jerk his hands down into the icy tub.

His eyes go wide with the incomprehension of a child being tortured for reasons it cannot guess, and his feet go out from under him.

As I struggle to keep his hands pinned, one of his wrists jerks in my hand, and a muted explosion hammers my ears. He's firing the gun under the water. His wrist jerks again and again, and my ears ring like cymbals.

When silence returns, it shocks us both. Wheaton's face is bone white, and his arms have stopped struggling. The icy water has done its work. I let go of his wrists and scramble out of the tub. The IV stand crashes to the floor beside me, and the catheter pops out, sending a warm rush of blood down my hand.

Wheaton straightens slowly, and for a moment I think he's been shot. But he's not holding himself anywhere; he's struggling to remove the soaked gloves from his shaking hands. He looks like a burn victim trying to remove melted clothing. As I stare, his mouth forms an O and he roars in agony.

The scream snaps my trance. I turn towards the door of the main house, but when I try to run, my legs go watery. Panic balloons in my chest, cutting off my air. Is that the insulin too?

I need sugar. Rather than try to reach my stash by the tub, I fall backwards onto my bottom and scrabble around in the grocery bag. I rip open a Twinkie and stuff it into my mouth, swallowing it almost without chewing.

Wheaton is by the tub. He's trying to summon the courage to plunge his dying hands back into the ice to retrieve the gun.

I force myself to my feet as Wheaton plunges one arm in up to the elbow. He whirls to face me with the pistol rising when I charge him, arms outstretched. The gun bellows as my hands strike centre mass, driving him backwards over the tub.

Wheaton falls across the tub, straining to hold himself above the icy water. As I struggle to get off him, he jams the gun barrel into my throat and pulls the trigger.

There's a hollow click. Wild-eyed, he jerks back the gun to bludgeon me, but his flexing shoulder slips off the rim of the tub and sends him down into the water.

I stagger to the door behind the easel. Stumbling through it, I find myself in a wide hall much like the one in Jane's house. I start towards the front door, focusing on my balance, but two-thirds of the way there my legs give way and I fall headlong.

A pathetic end for a decently lived life. Naked. Alone. Lost in a white fog that blows with insidious silence, deadening the sound of my sobs, then the rasp of my breathing. Soon all will be whiteness.

As my ears chase the last hissing echo of my respiration, an inhuman screech splits my fading consciousness like an axe. There's a pounding of drums, then a shattering cacophony like a mirror breaking in the conservatory. Black insectile figures swarm over me, their metallic voices ringing against my eardrums. One is trying to ask me something, his goggle eyes wide and earnest, but I can't understand him. The goggle eyes vanish, and a human face appears in their place. John Kaiser's face.

He thinks I'm dead. I see it in his eyes. The fog has almost swallowed me. I have to tell him I'm alive. If I don't, he might bury me.

Two syllables fall from my lips with eerie clarity, and they trigger a burst of activity. The word I say is 'Sugar'. Then I slap my bloody IV hole like a monkey on amphetamines. '*Sugar, sugar, sugar . . .*'

A white-clad angel bends over me. 'I think she wants us to check her glucose level.'

Then the faces vanish.

'JORDAN? JORDAN? Wake up.'

A shadow floats over my eyes, and a face leans in.

John's face. It's creased with worry, and his eyes are red with fatigue. 'Do you know me?' he asks.

'Agent Kaiser. Right?'

'Thank God.'

'Wheaton?'

John shakes his head. 'He ran screaming into the hall when you were down. He had a gun. I shouted for SWAT not to fire, but by then someone had. He was killed instantly.'

'Where are we?'

'Charity Hospital. Your blood sugar's back to normal. The doctors say you're dehydrated, but their main worry was your brain.'

'That's always been my worry, too.' I pick at the bandage over the wrist where Wheaton's IV was. 'Thalia?'

John's eyes are sombre. He shakes his head. 'Once she evaded surveillance, there was nothing we could have done.'

I nod. 'Where was I?'

'Four blocks from Wheaton's house on Audubon Place. Five blocks from St Charles Avenue. One block from Tulane.'

'They had some nerve. What's happening there now?'

He gives me a hard look. 'They've taken two corpses from shallow graves under a crawl space.'

'Jane's?'

'No IDs yet.' He takes a deep breath, then lays his hand on my arm. 'Listen, there's something you're going to want to know.'

'What?' I ask, my throat tight with fear.

'We just got a message from Marcel de Becque. He wants to talk to you. In person. He says he'll send his jet if you need it.'

'Do I need it?'

'No. There are still serious questions in this case, and only de Becque can answer them now. Baxter says we can take the Bureau jet when you're strong enough.'

'Tell them to get the plane ready.'

John looks at me like a parent who knows his child will not take no for an answer. 'I guess we're taking a trip.'

OUR PILOT LANDS the FBI Lear at Grand Cayman's airport near Georgetown, but this time the governor of the islands has provided a black limousine to take us to de Becque's estate on North Bay.

The door is answered by Li, who leads us immediately to the great hall at the back of the mansion. Just as before, the tanned, silver-haired French expatriate stands at the window, staring out to sea.

'Mademoiselle Glass,' Li announces, and then she backs soundlessly down the hall.

De Becque turns and nods with courtly grace. 'I'm glad you came, *chérie*. I'm sorry to bring you so far, but alas, my legal situation does not allow me to travel to you. I have things to tell you that you must know.' He motions us deeper into the room. 'Come in. Please.'

John and I walk over to the sofa we sat on less than a week ago and sit side by side. De Becque remains standing, ill at ease.

'First, the matter of The Sleeping Women. I want to assure you that I never knew the identity of the painter, or of his associate. I did know Christopher Wingate, the art dealer, and it's him that what I have to say concerns. As you know, I bought the first five Sleeping Women he offered for sale. The sixth painting was also promised to me but Wingate "stiffed" me, as they say. He sold the painting to Hodai Takagi.'

'To open new markets,' John says. 'Right?'

'Quite so,' says de Becque. 'I was angry. I happened to know that Wingate was heavily invested in a development project in the Virgin

Islands. I made a few phone calls, and very shortly, Monsieur Wingate discovered he had made a very bad investment. His principal was wiped out. Wingate was infuriated by what I had done, and he sought revenge. Now, you should be aware that Wingate had visited my estate here. He learned a bit about my life. He saw many of my things, among them my collection of photographs.'

He walks over to the wall and takes down two black and white photos, then comes back to us. 'These were not hanging here during your last visit. Perhaps you'd like to see them?'

With a sense of foreboding, I take the frames from his hand. The first picture is of me, my standard publicity head shot. The second is of Jane, her graduation photo. My heart begins to pound.

'What are you doing with these?'

At last de Becque sits on the sofa opposite us. 'I knew your father much better than I led you to believe. He was a good friend to me, and I to him. But what you really want to know is this. Did your father die on the Cambodian border? Today I tell you—he did not.'

'Oh God.'

'He was shot there by the Khmer Rouge, yes. But he was found alive later by others. When I heard what had happened, I negotiated an exchange for him.'

'How badly was he hurt?'

'Very seriously. He had a head wound. There had been infection.' John takes my hand and squeezes tightly.

'He was not the same man he had been before the wound.'

'Did he know who he was?'

'He knew his name. He remembered certain things. Other things, no. His vision was impaired as well. Photography as a career was over for him. Though I don't think he much cared at that point. His frame of reference had been reduced to fundamental things. Food, shelter, wine . . . I had a plantation in Thailand, and he lived out his days there. He did simple work, he knew simple joys. He died in 1979.'

John squeezes my hand again, and I'm grateful for his presence. The emotions pouring through me now are too intense to bear alone. Amazement that my secret hope turned out to be true. Sadness that my father was not himself afterwards, that perhaps he did not remember me in any meaningful sense. But deeper than any of these wells a relief that even tears cannot express. My father did not abandon his family. He did not choose others over us. *My daddy didn't leave me.*

There is no sight quite like gentlemen in the presence of a lady reduced to tears. John blushes and reaches for a tissue he doesn't have, while de Becque pulls a silk handkerchief from his pocket.

'Take a moment, *ma chérie*,' he says in a soothing voice. 'Family matters . . . always difficult.'

'Thank you.' I wipe my eyes and blow my nose.

Before I can think of what to ask next, John speaks. 'Monsieur, your story began with the daughters, not the father. With the photographs. And a point about Christopher Wingate?'

De Becque nods. 'Wingate had cheated me, so I taught him a lesson about the consequences of breaking promises. Wingate was not content to learn this lesson. He wished to revenge himself upon me. To this end, he set about trying to hurt me as deeply as possible. This is not so easy as it might sound. I have no family in the ordinary sense. No hostages to fortune. Wingate had to look hard for a weakness.'

'I think I know where this is going,' John says. 'You're telling us Wingate chose Jane Lacour as a victim to hurt you. Right?'

'I believe it happened this way. Wingate never knew Roger Wheaton's identity, but I think he knew where the victims were coming from. I believe he had close ties with an associate of Wheaton's.'

'Conrad Hoffman,' says John.

'Perhaps,' says the Frenchman. 'In any case, by this time, I too had surmised that the girls in the paintings were being taken in New Orleans.'

'Jane was victim number five,' John says in a cold voice. 'You suspected all the way back then?'

De Becque suddenly looks very serious. 'I told you I *think* it happened this way. I had no proof. Wingate was casting about for a way to revenge himself upon me. One day, as he searched his memory, he remembered the story I'd told him of the famous Jonathan Glass, and of the lovely twin girls I watched from a distance: the world traveller, and the southern belle of St Charles Avenue.

'Once he'd hit upon the idea, the mechanics were simple. He sent a photograph and an address to Wheaton's associate, made a request, possibly promised a bounty, and the thing was done.'

John and I sit in stunned silence.

'So,' says de Becque. 'I believe Jane Lacour became the only Sleeping Woman chosen by someone other than Wheaton. And because I was watching New Orleans for other disappearances, I learned very quickly of Jane's disappearance. I owed my dead friend. I could not let this thing pass without taking steps.

'I sent an emissary to Wingate. He made clear that the death of Jane Lacour would mean not only the death of Christopher

Wingate, but the death of his women, children, parents—'

'Stop,' I plead. 'I don't think I want to know this.'

De Becque makes a gesture of apology. 'I merely wished you to be aware that I spared no effort.'

'But you didn't do much good, did you?' says John.

De Becque sighs. 'Some things, once set in motion, are difficult to stop, but I believe Wingate used all his influence to get Wheaton's associate to release Jane. The associate agreed to try.'

'He may have tried,' I tell them, recalling what Wheaton told me of Jane's death. 'Wheaton said Jane almost escaped. Hoffman only caught her in the yard, and he—he ended it there.'

De Becque reaches out and takes my hand. 'Prepare yourself, *chérie*. I have news for you. Your sister is alive.'

'Are you saying Hoffman didn't kill her?' asks John.

'*Oui*. Considering what Jordan just told me, I would guess this Hoffman released Jane, then lied to Wheaton to protect himself.'

'If Jane Lacour is alive,' says John, 'where has she been for the past thirteen months?'

'Thailand.' De Becque shrugs. 'I still have a plantation there. I found myself in a difficult position. Several women had been kidnapped. I knew more than I should about those events, in a legal sense. Normally, I would not have interfered. But this woman was special.'

'The phone call?' I say softly. 'The phone call from Thailand?'

'That was your sister. She was drinking at the time, a bit confused. She had learned the truth about your father, and it had upset her.'

'I want to go to Thailand,' I tell him. 'Right now.'

'There are other things you must know first.' The Frenchman stands and claps his hands twice. When Li appears in the far doorway de Becque nods, and she vanishes.

'Oh God,' I whisper. 'Don't tell me she's brain damaged or—'

'No, no. But she endured a traumatic experience at the hands of this Hoffman. He was a man of peculiar tastes.'

Now I understand my precognition of Jane's death in Sarajevo: perhaps she did not physically die; perhaps what I felt was the death of innocence that is every rape, the murder of part of the spirit.

'She has largely recovered now,' says de Becque, 'and naturally, she has desired to return home. I was unable to allow that. For legal reasons, and because I did not wish to stop the painter of The Sleeping Women. I make no apologies to anyone but you, Jordan. To you I apologise.'

'Please, take me to her!'

'You are on your way, *ma chérie.*'

'Don't let this guy get your hopes up,' John says. 'He's a—'

John comes out of his chair and stands with his mouth open.

In the doorway at the far end of the great room stands a mirror image of the woman he claims he loves.

'You son of a bitch,' John says softly to de Becque. 'How long would you have kept her?'

Jane is walking towards me, her cheeks red, her eyes glittering with tears. She is wearing a white robe like Li's and she looks more beautiful than she ever did, thinner perhaps, but with a self-awareness in her face and bearing that wasn't there before. When she is halfway across the room, I find the strength to take a step—and then to run. As I fly to her, a fleeting image passes through my mind: a tall man with a camera walks down a Mississippi road, a little girl on either side of him. That man is gone now, but not the little girls.

IT IS DUSK, and the lights glow warm and yellow through the windows of the house on St Charles Avenue.

Jane and I mount the steps together, hand in hand, unannounced. After much discussion, we agreed it would be best this way. Behind us, at the kerb, John waits in an FBI sedan. I look back at him, then raise my hand to knock on the door. 'Here we go,' I say.

After a moment, footsteps pad up the cavernous hallway and stop before the door. Then the knob turns and the great door opens, revealing Annabelle in her black and white uniform.

The old black woman starts to greet me, then freezes. Her hand flies halfway to her mouth, then stops. 'Is it . . .?'

'It's me, Annabelle,' Jane says in a quavering voice.

'Lord *Jesus.* Come here, missy.' She pulls Jane into her arms and squeezes tight.

Jane slowly disengages herself. 'Where are the children, Annabelle?'

'In the kitchen, waiting for me to fix supper.'

Annabelle takes Jane by the hand and leads her down the hall. At the kitchen door we pause, and Jane whispers something to Annabelle. The maid nods and goes in ahead of us. Henry's high-pitched voice asks her who was at the door, and Annabelle answers in a voice laced with excitement. 'You chil'ren close you eyes now. Your Aunt Jordan brought you a special present.'

'Aunt Jordan's here?' asks Lyn, in a voice that breaks my heart.

'You shut your eyes!' says Annabelle.

'They're shut!' cry the little voices.

As Jane takes my hand, I feel hers quivering. I look into her eyes, she nods, and we step through the door.

'You can look now,' I tell them.

When the hands slip down, the children's mouths drop, and their eyes flash with a light I haven't seen in twenty years of travelling.

'*Mama?*' Lyn asks in a hollow voice, her eyes on Jane.

Jane falls to her knees and Henry and Lyn rush to her breast. She enfolds them in a shuddering embrace, her eyes pouring tears. When the children find their voices, they begin jabbering questions, but Jane can only cradle their faces in her hands and shake her head.

'What's going on?' comes a deep voice from the hall. 'Annabelle?'

Marc Lacour looks from me to the back of the woman holding his children, his face clouded with confusion. Jane embraces the children once again, then stands and turns to face him.

'It's me,' Jane says. 'I'm home.'

Marc steps tentatively forward, then jerks her into his arms and hugs her tight enough to break her back.

'My God,' he whispers. 'My *God*, it's a miracle.'

'It is,' Jane says, reaching backwards with one hand.

I clasp that hand and squeeze it, and then I slip round them and through the kitchen door.

'Where are you going?' Jane asks.

I nod at the door. 'I need to talk to someone.'

She reaches out again. When I take her hand, she silently mouths two words. *Thank you.*

She lets my hand slip free, and then I'm walking down the long hall alone. For thirteen months Jane has lived in suspended animation, imprisoned by a man who saved her life, a desolate bird in a gilded cage. All that time, I trudged alone through a dark tunnel, burdened by guilt, haunted by loss, feeling hope die. But today . . .

Today I emerge into the light.

John is leaning against the passenger door of the FBI sedan, watching me for clues to what happened. I walk down the steps, take both his hands in mine, and kiss him lightly on the lips.

'Are we going in?' he asks.

'No. They need time alone.'

He takes me in his arms and squeezes me tight. 'We need time alone, too.'

'It's time to start living again, John.'

'That it is,' he says, reaching back to open the door. 'That it is.'

GREG ILES

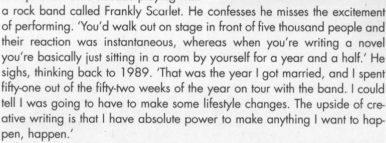

'I'm one of those people,' says Greg
Iles, 'who is lucky enough to have ability in several directions: drawing, painting, music and writing. But there was
never any doubt that my first talent was
the written word.'

Before he settled on a writing career,
Iles spent almost a decade playing with
a rock band called Frankly Scarlet. He confesses he misses the excitement
of performing. 'You'd walk out on stage in front of five thousand people and
their reaction was instantaneous, whereas when you're writing a novel
you're basically just sitting in a room by yourself for a year and a half.' He
sighs, thinking back to 1989. 'That was the year I got married, and I spent
fifty-one out of the fifty-two weeks of the year on tour with the band. I could
tell I was going to have to make some lifestyle changes. The upside of creative writing is that I have absolute power to make anything I want to happen, happen.'

Iles has lived all his life in Natchez, Mississippi, the 'jewel of the American
South'. The town lies on the Mississippi River some 200 kilometres north of
New Orleans, one of the settings for his seventh best seller, *Dead Sleep*.
Whenever he is at work on a new novel, he admits to becoming obsessive
about the task that lies ahead of him. 'I find it difficult to organise and plan
efficiently—I run purely on instinct, following whatever interests me that day
or that week. I think my family must find it hard that I tend to seek solitude
and to exclude myself from normal life in order to think and to work.'

Greg Iles's life has been particularly hectic of late. He has been putting
the finishing touches to a screenplay of *24 Hours*, his previous book, which
is being filmed in Vancouver with Kevin Bacon and Courtney Love in the star-
ring roles. He says of his first experience of Hollywood, 'If I hadn't been a
writer, I'd like to have been a film director. I'm just now breaking into film,
but as a writer of course, and the writer has very little power to affect the
film that is ultimately produced. In the film world, only the director has power
analogous to that which the novelist has over his universe.'

TANGO ONE. Original full-length edition © 2002 by Stephen Leather. British condensed edition © The Reader's Digest Association Limited, 2002.

BURIED AT SEA. Original full-length edition © 2002 by Paul Garrison. British condensed edition © The Reader's Digest Association Limited, 2002.

JULIE AND ROMEO. Original full-length edition © 2000 by Jeanne Ray. US condensed edition © The Reader's Digest Association Inc, 2000. British condensed edition © The Reader's Digest Association Limited, 2002.

DEAD SLEEP. Original full-length edition © 2001 by Greg Iles. British condensed edition © The Reader's Digest Association Limited, 2002.

The right to be identified as authors has been asserted by the following in accordance with sections 77 and 78 of the Copyright, Designs and Patents Act, 1988: Stephen Leather, Jeanne Ray and Greg Iles.

ACKNOWLEDGMENTS AND PICTURE CREDITS: *Tango One:* pages 6–8: Man's face: Digital Vision; photomontage: Rick Lecoat @ Shark Attack; *Buried at Sea:* pages 146–148: Illustration by Curtis Cozier; *Dead Sleep:* pages 394–396: Illustration by Les Edwards @ Arena.

DUSTJACKET CREDITS: Spine from top: Man's face: Digital Vision; photomontage: Rick Lecoat @ Shark Attack; Curtis Cozier; Les Edwards @ Arena.

Printed by Maury Imprimeur SA, Malesherbes, France
Bound by Reliures Brun SA, Malesherbes, France